The Shuttle

by

Frances Hodgson Burnett

The Echo Library 2007

Published by

The Echo Library

Echo Library
131 High St.
Teddington
Middlesex TW11 8HH

www.echo-library.com

Please report serious faults in the text to complaints@echo-library.com

ISBN 978-1-40684-496-2

CONTENTS

I.	THE WEAVING OF THE SHUTTLE
II.	A LACK OF PERCEPTION
III.	YOUNG LADY ANSTRUTHERS
IV.	A MISTAKE OF THE POSTBOY'S
V.	ON BOTH SIDES OF THE ATLANTIC
VI.	AN UNFAIR ENDOWMENT
VII.	ON BOARD THE "MERIDIANA"
VIII.	THE SECOND-CLASS PASSENGER
IX.	LADY JANE GREY
X.	"IS LADY ANSTRUTHERS AT HOME?"
XI.	"I THOUGHT YOU HAD ALL FORGOTTEN"
XII.	UGHTRED
XIII.	ONE OF THE NEW YORK DRESSES
XIV.	IN THE GARDENS
XV.	THE FIRST MAN
XVI.	THE PARTICULAR INCIDENT
XVII.	TOWNLINSON & SHEPPARD
XVIII.	THE FIFTEENTH EARL OF MOUNT DUNSTAN
XIX.	SPRING IN BOND STREET
XX.	THINGS OCCUR IN STORNHAM VILLAGE
XXI.	KEDGERS
XXII.	ONE OF MR. VANDERPOEL'S LETTERS
XXIII.	INTRODUCING G. SELDEN
XXIV.	THE POLITICAL ECONOMY OF STORNHAM
XXV.	"WE BEGAN TO MARRY THEM, MY GOOD FELLOW!"
XXVI.	"WHAT IT MUST BE TO BE YOU—JUST YOU!"
XXVII.	LIFE
XXVIII.	SETTING THEM THINKING
XXIX.	THE THREAD OF G. SELDEN
XXX.	A RETURN
XXXI.	NO, SHE WOULD NOT
XXXII.	A GREAT BALL
XXXIII.	FOR LADY JANE
XXXIV.	RED GODWYN
XXXV.	THE TIDAL WAVE
XXXVI.	BY THE ROADSIDE EVERYWHERE
XXXVII.	CLOSED CORRIDORS
XXXVIII.	AT SHANDY'S
XXXIX.	ON THE MARSHES
XL.	"DON'T GO ON WITH THIS"
XLI.	SHE WOULD DO SOMETHING
XLII.	IN THE BALLROOM
XLIII.	HIS CHANCE

4

XLIV.   A FOOTSTEP
XLV.   THE PASSING BELL
XLVI.   LISTENING
XLVII.   "I HAVE NO WORD OR LOOK TO REMEMBER"
XLVIII.   THE MOMENT
XLIX.   AT STORNHAM AND AT BROADMORLANDS
L.   THE PRIMEVAL THING

THE SHUTTLE

CHAPTER I

THE WEAVING OF THE SHUTTLE

No man knew when the Shuttle began its slow and heavy weaving from shore to shore, that it was held and guided by the great hand of Fate. Fate alone saw the meaning of the web it wove, the might of it, and its place in the making of a world's history. Men thought but little of either web or weaving, calling them by other names and lighter ones, for the time unconscious of the strength of the thread thrown across thousands of miles of leaping, heaving, grey or blue ocean.

Fate and Life planned the weaving, and it seemed mere circumstance which guided the Shuttle to and fro between two worlds divided by a gulf broader and deeper than the thousands of miles of salt, fierce sea—the gulf of a bitter quarrel deepened by hatred and the shedding of brothers' blood. Between the two worlds of East and West there was no will to draw nearer. Each held apart. Those who had rebelled against that which their souls called tyranny, having struggled madly and shed blood in tearing themselves free, turned stern backs upon their unconquered enemies, broke all cords that bound them to the past, flinging off ties of name, kinship and rank, beginning with fierce disdain a new life.

Those who, being rebelled against, found the rebels too passionate in their determination and too desperate in their defence of their strongholds to be less than unconquerable, sailed back haughtily to the world which seemed so far the greater power. Plunging into new battles, they added new conquests and splendour to their land, looking back with something of contempt to the half-savage West left to build its own civilisation without other aid than the strength of its own strong right hand and strong uncultured brain.

But while the two worlds held apart, the Shuttle, weaving slowly in the great hand of Fate, drew them closer and held them firm, each of them all unknowing for many a year, that what had at first been mere threads of gossamer, was forming a web whose strength in time none could compute, whose severance could be accomplished but by tragedy and convulsion.

The weaving was but in its early and slow-moving years when this story opens. Steamers crossed and recrossed the Atlantic, but they accomplished the journey at leisure and with heavy rollings and all such discomforts as small craft can afford. Their staterooms and decks were not crowded with people to whom the voyage was a mere incident—in many cases a yearly one. "A crossing" in those days was an event. It was planned seriously, long thought of, discussed and re-discussed, with and among the various members of the family to which the voyager belonged. A certain boldness, bordering on recklessness, was almost to be presupposed in the individual who, turning his back upon New York, Philadelphia, Boston, and like cities, turned his face towards "Europe." In those days when the Shuttle wove at leisure, a man did not lightly run over to London, or Paris, or Berlin, he gravely went to "Europe."

The journey being likely to be made once in a lifetime, the traveller's intention was to see as much as possible, to visit as many cities cathedrals, ruins, galleries, as his time and purse would allow. People who could speak with any degree of familiarity of Hyde Park, the Champs Elysees, the Pincio, had gained a certain dignity. The ability to touch with an intimate bearing upon such localities was a raison de plus for being asked out to tea or to dinner. To possess photographs and relics was to be of interest, to have seen European celebrities even at a distance, to have wandered about the outside of poets' gardens and philosophers' houses, was to be entitled to respect. The period was a far cry from the time when the Shuttle, having shot to and fro, faster and faster, week by week, month by month, weaving new threads into its web each year, has woven warp and woof until they bind far shore to shore.

It was in comparatively early days that the first thread we follow was woven into the web. Many such have been woven since and have added greater strength than any others, twining the cord of sex and home-building and race-founding. But this was a slight and weak one, being only the thread of the life of one of Reuben Vanderpoel's daughters—the pretty little simple one whose name was Rosalie.

They were—the Vanderpoels—of the Americans whose fortunes were a portion of the history of their country. The building of these fortunes had been a part of, or had created epochs and crises. Their millions could scarcely be regarded as private property. Newspapers bandied them about, so to speak, employing them as factors in argument, using them as figures of speech, incorporating them into methods of calculation. Literature touched upon them, moral systems considered them, stories for the young treated them gravely as illustrative.

The first Reuben Vanderpoel, who in early days of danger had traded with savages for the pelts of wild animals, was the lauded hero of stories of thrift and enterprise. Throughout his hard-working life he had been irresistibly impelled to action by an absolute genius of commerce, expressing itself at the outset by the exhibition of courage in mere exchange and barter. An alert power to perceive the potential value of things and the possible malleability of men and circumstances, had stood him in marvellous good stead. He had bought at low prices things which in the eyes of the less discerning were worthless, but, having obtained possession of such things, the less discerning had almost invariably awakened to the fact that, in his hands, values increased, and methods of remunerative disposition, being sought, were found. Nothing remained unutilisable. The practical, sordid, uneducated little man developed the power to create demand for his own supplies. If he was betrayed into an error, he quickly retrieved it. He could live upon nothing and consequently could travel anywhere in search of such things as he desired. He could barely read and write, and could not spell, but he was daring and astute. His untaught brain was that of a financier, his blood burned with the fever of but one desire—the desire to accumulate. Money expressed to his nature, not expenditure, but investment in such small or large properties as could be resold at profit in the near or far future. The future held fascinations for him. He bought nothing for his own pleasure or comfort, nothing which could not be sold or bartered again. He married a woman who was a trader's daughter and shared his passion for gain. She was of North of England blood, her father having been a hard-fisted small tradesman in an unimportant town, who had been daring enough to emigrate when emigration meant the facing of unknown dangers in a half-savage land. She had excited Reuben Vanderpoel's admiration by taking off her petticoat one bitter winter's day to sell it to a squaw in exchange for an ornament for which she chanced to know another squaw would pay with a skin of value. The first Mrs. Vanderpoel was as wonderful as her husband. They were both wonderful. They were the founders of the fortune which a century and a half later was the delight—in fact the piece de resistance—of New York society reporters, its enormity being restated in round figures when a blank space must be filled up. The method of statement lent itself to infinite variety and was always interesting to a particular class, some elements of which felt it encouraging to be assured that so much money could be a personal possession, some elements feeling the fact an additional argument to be used against the infamy of monopoly.

The first Reuben Vanderpoel transmitted to his son his accumulations and his fever for gain. He had but one child. The second Reuben built upon the foundations this afforded him, a fortune as much larger than the first as the rapid growth and increasing capabilities of the country gave him enlarging opportunities to acquire. It was no longer necessary to deal with savages: his powers were called upon to cope with those of white men who came to a new country to struggle for livelihood and fortune. Some were shrewd, some were desperate, some were dishonest. But shrewdness never outwitted, desperation never overcame, dishonesty never deceived the second Reuben Vanderpoel. Each characteristic ended by adapting itself to his own purposes and qualities, and as a result of each it was he who in any business transaction was the gainer. It was the common saying that the Vanderpoels were possessed of a money-making spell. Their spell lay in their entire mental and physical absorption in one idea. Their peculiarity was not so much that they wished to be rich as that Nature itself impelled them to collect wealth as the load-stone draws towards it iron. Having possessed nothing, they became rich, having become rich they became richer, having founded their fortunes on small schemes, they increased them by enormous ones. In time they attained that omnipotence of wealth which it would seem no circumstance can control or limit. The first Reuben Vanderpoel could not spell, the second could, the third was as well educated as a man could be whose sole profession is money-making. His children were taught all that expensive teachers and expensive opportunities could teach them. After the second generation the meagre and mercantile physical type of the Vanderpoels improved upon itself. Feminine good looks appeared and were made the most of. The Vanderpoel element invested even good looks to an advantage. The fourth Reuben Vanderpoel had no son and two daughters. They were brought up in a brown-stone mansion built upon a fashionable New York thoroughfare roaring with traffic. To the farthest point of the Rocky Mountains the number of dollars this "mansion" (it was always called so) had cost, was known. There may have existed Pueblo Indians who had heard rumours of the price of it. All the shop-keepers and farmers in the United States had read newspaper descriptions of its furnishings and knew the value of the brocade which hung in the bedrooms and boudoirs of the Misses Vanderpoel. It was a fact much cherished that Miss Rosalie's bath was of Carrara marble, and to good souls actively engaged in doing their own washing in small New England or Western towns, it was a distinct luxury to be aware that the water in the Carrara marble bath was perfumed with Florentine Iris. Circumstances such as these seemed to become personal possessions and even to lighten somewhat the burden of toil.

Rosalie Vanderpoel married an Englishman of title, and part of the story of her married life forms my prologue. Hers was of the early international marriages, and the republican mind had not yet adjusted itself to all that such alliances might imply. It was yet ingenuous, imaginative and confiding in such matters. A baronetcy and a manor house reigning over an old English village and over villagers in possible smock frocks, presented elements of picturesque dignity to people whose intimacy with such allurements had been limited by the novels of Mrs. Oliphant and other writers. The most ordinary little anecdotes in which vicarages, gamekeepers, and dowagers figured, were exciting in these early days. "Sir Nigel Anstruthers," when engraved upon a visiting card, wore an air of distinction almost startling. Sir Nigel himself was not as picturesque as his name, though he was not entirely without attraction, when for reasons of his own he chose to aim at agreeableness of bearing. He was a man with a good figure and a good voice, and but for a heaviness of feature the result of objectionable living, might have given the impression of being better looking than he really was. New York laid amused and at the same time, charmed stress upon the fact that he spoke with an "English accent." His enunciation was in fact clear cut and treated its vowels well. He was a man who observed with an air of accustomed punctiliousness such social rules and courtesies as he deemed it expedient to consider. An astute worldling had remarked that he was at once more ceremonious and more casual in his manner than men bred in America.

"If you invite him to dinner," the wording said, "or if you die, or marry, or meet with an accident, his notes of condolence or congratulation are prompt and civil, but the actual truth is that he cares nothing whatever about you or your relations, and if you don't please him he does not hesitate to sulk or be astonishingly rude, which last an American does not allow himself to be, as a rule."

By many people Sir Nigel was not analysed, but accepted. He was of the early English who came to New York, and was a novelty of interest, with his background of Manor House and village and old family name. He was very much talked of at vivacious ladies' luncheon parties, he was very much talked to at equally vivacious afternoon teas. At dinner parties he was furtively watched a good deal, but after dinner when he sat with the men over their wine, he was not popular. He was not perhaps exactly disliked, but men whose chief interest at that period lay in stocks and railroads, did not find conversation easy with a man whose sole occupation had been the shooting of birds and the hunting of foxes, when he was not absolutely loitering about London, with his time on his hands. The stories he told—and they were few—were chiefly anecdotes whose points gained their humour by the fact that a man was a comically bad shot or bad rider and either peppered a gamekeeper or was thrown into a ditch when his horse went over a hedge, and such relations did not increase in the poignancy of their interest by being filtered through brains accustomed to applying their powers to problems of speculation and commerce. He was not so dull but that he perceived this at an early stage of his visit to New York, which was probably the reason of the infrequency of his stories.

He on his side was naturally not quick to rise to the humour of a "big deal" or a big blunder made on Wall Street—or to the wit of jokes concerning them. Upon the whole he would have been glad to have understood such matters more clearly. His circumstances were such as had at last forced him to contemplate the world of money-makers with something of an annoyed respect. "These fellows" who had neither titles nor estates to keep up could make money. He, as he acknowledged disgustedly to himself, was much worse than a beggar. There was Stornham Court in a state of ruin—the estate going to the dogs, the farmhouses tumbling to pieces and he, so to speak, without a sixpence to bless himself with, and head over heels in debt. Englishmen of the rank which in bygone times had not associated itself with trade had begun at least to trifle with it—to consider its potentialities as factors possibly to be made useful by the aristocracy. Countesses had not yet spiritedly opened milliners' shops, nor belted Earls adorned the stage, but certain noblemen had dallied with beer and coquetted with stocks. One of the first commercial developments had been the discovery of America—particularly of New York—as a place where if one could make up one's mind to the plunge, one might marry one's sons profitably. At the outset it presented a field so promising as to lead to rashness and indiscretion on the part of persons not given to analysis of character and in consequence relying too serenely upon an ingenuousness which rather speedily revealed that it had its limits. Ingenuousness combining itself with remarkable alertness of perception on occasion, is rather American than English, and is, therefore, to the English mind, misleading.

At first younger sons, who "gave trouble" to their families, were sent out. Their names, their backgrounds of castles or manors, relatives of distinction, London seasons, fox hunting, Buckingham Palace and Goodwood Races, formed a picturesque allurement. That the castles and manors would belong to their elder brothers, that the relatives of distinction did not encourage intimacy with swarms of the younger branches of their families; that London seasons, hunting, and racing were for their elders and betters, were facts not realised in all their importance by the republican mind. In the course of time they were realised to the full, but in Rosalie Vanderpoel's nineteenth year they covered what was at that time almost unknown territory. One may rest assured Sir Nigel Anstruthers said nothing whatsoever in New York of an interview he had had before sailing with an intensely disagreeable great-aunt, who was the wife of a Bishop. She was a horrible old woman with a broad face, blunt features and a raucous voice, whose tones added acridity to her observations when she was indulging in her favourite pastime of interfering with the business of her acquaintances and relations.

"I do not know what you are going chasing off to America for, Nigel," she commented. "You can't afford it and it is perfectly ridiculous of you to take it upon yourself to travel for pleasure as if you were a man of means instead of being in such a state of pocket that Maria tells me you cannot pay your tailor. Neither the Bishop nor I can do anything for you and I hope you don't expect it. All I can hope is that you know yourself what you are going to America in search of, and that it is something more practical than buffaloes. You had better stop in New York. Those big shopkeepers' daughters are enormously rich, they say, and they are immensely pleased by attentions from men of your class. They say they'll marry anything if it has an aunt or a grandmother with a title. You can mention the Marchioness, you know. You need not refer to the fact that she thought your father a blackguard and your mother an interloper, and that you have never been invited to Broadmere since you were born. You can refer casually to me and to the Bishop and to the Palace, too. A Palace—even a Bishop's—ought to go a long way with Americans. They will think it is something royal." She ended her remarks with one of her most insulting snorts of laughter, and Sir Nigel became dark red and looked as if he would like to knock her down.

It was not, however, her sentiments which were particularly revolting to him. If she had expressed them in a manner more flattering to himself he would have felt that there was a good deal to be said for them. In fact, he had put the same thing to himself some time previously, and, in summing up the American matter, had reached certain thrifty decisions. The impulse to knock her down surged within him solely because he had a brutally bad temper when his vanity was insulted, and he was furious at her impudence in speaking to him as if he were a villager out of work whom she was at liberty to bully and lecture.

"For a woman who is supposed to have been born of gentle people," he said to his mother afterwards, "Aunt Marian is the most vulgar old beast I have ever beheld. She has the taste of a female costermonger." Which was entirely true, but it might be added that his own was no better and his points of view and morals wholly coincided with his taste.

Naturally Rosalie Vanderpoel knew nothing of this side of the matter. She had been a petted, butterfly child, who had been pretty and admired and indulged from her infancy; she had grown up into a petted, butterfly girl, pretty and admired and surrounded by inordinate luxury. Her world had been made up of good-natured, lavish friends and relations, who enjoyed themselves and felt a delight in her girlish toilettes and triumphs. She had spent her one season of belledom in being whirled from festivity to festivity, in dancing in rooms festooned with thousands of dollars' worth of flowers, in lunching or dining at tables loaded with roses and violets and orchids, from which ballrooms or feasts she had borne away wonderful "favours" and gifts, whose prices, being recorded in the newspapers, caused a thrill of delight or envy to pass over the land. She was a slim little creature, with quantities of light feathery hair like a French doll's. She had small hands and small feet and a small waist—a small brain also, it must be admitted, but she was an innocent, sweet-tempered girl with a childlike simpleness of mind. In fine, she was exactly the girl to find Sir Nigel's domineering temperament at once imposing and attractive, so long as it was cloaked by the ceremonies of external good breeding.

Her sister Bettina, who was still a child, was of a stronger and less susceptible nature. Betty—at eight—had long legs and a square but delicate small face. Her well-opened steel-blue eyes were noticeable for rather extravagant ink-black lashes and a straight young stare which seemed to accuse if not to condemn. She was being educated at a ruinously expensive school with a number of other inordinately rich little girls, who were all too wonderfully dressed and too lavishly supplied with pocket money. The school considered itself especially refined and select, but was in fact interestingly vulgar.

The inordinately rich little girls, who had most of them pretty and spiritual or pretty and piquant faces, ate a great many bon bons and chattered a great deal in high unmodulated voices about the parties their sisters and other relatives went to and the dresses they wore. Some of them were nice little souls, who in the future would emerge from their chrysalis state enchanting women, but they used colloquialisms freely, and had an ingenuous habit of referring to the prices of things. Bettina Vanderpoel, who was the richest and cleverest and most promisingly handsome among them, was colloquial to slanginess, but she had a deep, mellow, child voice and an amazing carriage.

She could not endure Sir Nigel Anstruthers, and, being an American child, did not hesitate to express herself with force, if with some crudeness. "He's a hateful thing," she said, "I loathe him. He's stuck up and he thinks you are afraid of him and he likes it."

Sir Nigel had known only English children, little girls who lived in that discreet corner of their parents' town or country houses known as "the schoolroom," apparently emerging only for daily walks with governesses; girls with long hair and boys in little high hats and with faces which seemed curiously made to match them. Both boys and girls were decently kept out of the way and not in the least dwelt on except when brought out for inspection during the holidays and taken to the pantomime.

Sir Nigel had not realised that an American child was an absolute factor to be counted with, and a "youngster" who entered the drawing-room when she chose and joined fearlessly in adult conversation was an element he considered annoying. It was quite true that Bettina talked too much and too readily at times, but it had not been explained to her that the opinions of eight years are not always of absorbing interest to the mature. It was also true that Sir Nigel was a great fool for interfering with what was clearly no affair of his in such a manner as would have made him an enemy even had not the child's instinct arrayed her against him at the outset.

"You American youngsters are too cheeky," he said on one of the occasions when Betty had talked too much. "If you were my sister and lived at Stornham Court, you would be learning lessons in the schoolroom and wearing a pinafore. Nobody ever saw my sister Emily when she was your age."

"Well, I'm not your sister Emily," retorted Betty, "and I guess I'm glad of it."

It was rather impudent of her, but it must be confessed that she was not infrequently rather impudent in a rude little-girl way, but she was serenely unconscious of the fact.

Sir Nigel flushed darkly and laughed a short, unpleasant laugh. If she had been his sister Emily she would have fared ill at the moment, for his villainous temper would have got the better of him.

"I 'guess' that I may be congratulated too," he sneered.

"If I was going to be anybody's sister Emily," said Betty, excited a little by the sense of the fray, "I shouldn't want to be yours."

"Now Betty, don't be hateful," interposed Rosalie, laughing, and her laugh was nervous. "There's Mina Thalberg coming up the front steps. Go and meet her."

Rosalie, poor girl, always found herself nervous when Sir Nigel and Betty were in the room together. She instinctively recognised their antagonism and was afraid Betty would do something an English baronet would think vulgar. Her simple brain could not have explained to her why it was that she knew Sir Nigel often thought New Yorkers vulgar. She was, however, quite aware of this but imperfectly concealed fact, and felt a timid desire to be explanatory.

When Bettina marched out of the room with her extraordinary carriage finely manifest, Rosy's little laugh was propitiatory.

"You mustn't mind her," she said. "She's a real splendid little thing, but she's got a quick temper. It's all over in a minute."

"They wouldn't stand that sort of thing in England," said Sir Nigel. "She's deucedly spoiled, you know."

He detested the child. He disliked all children, but this one awakened in him more than mere dislike. The fact was that though Betty herself was wholly unconscious of the subtle truth, the as yet undeveloped intellect which later made her a brilliant and captivating personality, vaguely saw him as he was, an unscrupulous, sordid brute, as remorseless an adventurer and swindler in his special line, as if he had been engaged in drawing false cheques and arranging huge jewel robberies, instead of planning to entrap into a disadvantageous marriage a girl whose gentleness and fortune could be used by a blackguard of reputable name. The man was cold-blooded enough to see that her gentle weakness was of value because it could be bullied, her money was to be counted on because it could be spent on himself and his degenerate vices and on his racked and ruined name and estate, which must be rebuilt and restocked at an early date by someone or other, lest they tumbled into ignominious collapse which could not be concealed. Bettina of the accusing eyes did not know that in the depth of her yet crude young being, instinct was summing up for her the potentialities of an unusually fine specimen of the British blackguard, but this was nevertheless the interesting truth. When later she was told that her sister had become engaged to Sir Nigel Anstruthers, a flame of colour flashed over her face, she stared silently a moment, then bit her lip and burst into tears.

"Well, Bett," exclaimed Rosalie, "you are the queerest thing I ever saw."

Bettina's tears were an outburst, not a flow. She swept them away passionately with her small handkerchief.

"He'll do something awful to you," she said. "He'll nearly kill you. I know he will. I'd rather be dead myself."

She dashed out of the room, and could never be induced to say a word further about the matter. She would indeed have found it impossible to express her intense antipathy and sense of impending calamity. She had not the phrases to make herself clear even to herself, and after all what controlling effort can one produce when one is only eight years old?

CHAPTER II

A LACK OF PERCEPTION

Mercantile as Americans were proclaimed to be, the opinion of Sir Nigel Anstruthers was that they were, on some points, singularly unbusinesslike. In the perfectly obvious and simple matter of the settlement of his daughter's fortune, he had felt that Reuben Vanderpoel was obtuse to the point of idiocy. He seemed to have none of the ordinary points of view. Naturally there was to Anstruthers' mind but one point of view to take. A man of birth and rank, he argued, does not career across the Atlantic to marry a New York millionaire's daughter unless he anticipates deriving some advantage from the alliance. Such a man—being of Anstruthers' type—would not have married a rich woman even in his own country with out making sure that advantages were to accrue to himself as a result of the union. "In England," to use his own words, "there was no nonsense about it." Women's fortunes as well as themselves belonged to their husbands, and a man who was master in his own house could make his wife do as he chose. He had seen girls with money managed very satisfactorily by fellows who held a tight rein, and were not moved by tears, and did not allow talking to relations. If he had been desirous of marrying and could have afforded to take a penniless wife, there were hundreds of portionless girls ready to thank God for a decent chance to settle themselves for life, and one need not stir out of one's native land to find them.

But Sir Nigel had not in the least desired to saddle himself with a domestic encumbrance, in fact nothing would have induced him to consider the step if he had not been driven hard by circumstances. His fortunes had reached a stage where money must be forthcoming somehow—from somewhere. He and his mother had been living from hand to mouth, so to speak, for years, and they had also been obliged to keep up appearances, which is sometimes embittering even to persons of amiable tempers. Lady Anstruthers, it is true, had lived in the country in as niggardly a manner as possible. She had narrowed her existence to absolute privation, presenting at the same time a stern, bold front to the persons who saw her, to the insufficient staff of servants, to the village to the vicar and his wife, and the few far-distant neighbours who perhaps once a year drove miles to call or leave a card. She was an old woman sufficiently unattractive to find no difficulty in the way of limiting her acquaintances. The unprepossessing wardrobe she had gathered in the passing years was remade again and again by the village dressmaker. She wore dingy old silk gowns and appalling bonnets, and mantles dripping with rusty fringes and bugle beads, but these mitigated not in the least the unflinching arrogance of her bearing, or the simple, intolerant rudeness which she considered proper and becoming in persons like herself. She did not of course allow that there existed many persons like herself.

That society rejoiced in this fact was but the stamp of its inferiority and folly. While she pinched herself and harried her few hirelings at Stornham it was necessary for Sir Nigel to show himself in town and present as decent an appearance as possible. His vanity was far too arrogant to allow of his permitting himself to drop out of the world to which he could not afford to belong. That he should have been forgotten or ignored would have been intolerable to him. For a few years he was invited to dine at good houses, and got shooting and hunting as part of the hospitality of his acquaintances. But a man who cannot afford to return hospitalities will find that he need not expect to avail himself of those of his acquaintances to the end of his career unless he is an extremely engaging person. Sir Nigel Anstruthers was not an engaging person. He never gave a thought to the comfort or interest of any other human being than himself. He was also dominated by the kind of nasty temper which so reveals itself when let loose that its owner cannot control it even when it would be distinctly to his advantage to do so.

Finding that he had nothing to give in return for what he took as if it were his right, society gradually began to cease to retain any lively recollection of his existence. The tradespeople he had borne himself loftily towards awakened to the fact that he was the kind of man it was at once safe and wise to dun, and therefore proceeded to make his life a burden to him. At his clubs he had never been a member surrounded and rejoiced over when he made his appearance. The time came when he began to fancy that he was rather edged away from, and he endeavoured to sustain his dignity by being sulky and making caustic speeches when he was approached. Driven occasionally down to Stornham by actual pressure of circumstances, he found the outlook there more embittering still.

Lady Anstruthers laid the bareness of the land before him without any effort to palliate unpleasantness. If he chose to stalk about and look glum, she could sit still and call his attention to revolting truths which he could not deny. She could point out to him that he had no money, and that tenants would not stay in houses which were tumbling to pieces, and work land which had been starved. She could tell him just how long a time had elapsed since wages had been paid and accounts cleared off. And she had an engaging, unbiassed way of seeming to drive these maddening details home by the mere manner of her statement.

"You make the whole thing as damned disagreeable as you can," Nigel would snarl.

"I merely state facts," she would reply with acrid serenity.

A man who cannot keep up his estate, pay his tailor or the rent of his lodgings in town, is in a strait which may drive him to desperation. Sir Nigel Anstruthers borrowed some money, went to New York and made his suit to nice little silly Rosalie Vanderpoel.

But the whole thing was unexpectedly disappointing and surrounded by irritating circumstances. He found himself face to face with a state of affairs such as he had not contemplated. In England when a man married, certain practical matters could be inquired into and arranged by solicitors, the amount of the prospective bride's fortune, the allowances and settlements to be made, the position of the bridegroom with regard to pecuniary matters. To put it simply, a man found out where he stood and what he was to gain. But, at first to his sardonic entertainment and later to his disgusted annoyance, Sir Nigel gradually discovered that in the matter of marriage, Americans had an ingenuous tendency to believe in the sentimental feelings of the parties concerned. The general impression seemed to be that a man married purely for love, and that delicacy would make it impossible for him to ask questions as to what his bride's parents were in a position to hand over to him as a sort of indemnity for the loss of his bachelor freedom. Anstruthers began to discover this fact before he had been many weeks in New York. He reached the realisation of its existence by processes of exclusion and inclusion, by hearing casual remarks people let drop, by asking roundabout and careful questions, by leading both men and women to the innocent expounding of certain points of view. Millionaires, it appeared, did not expect to make allowances to men who married their daughters; young women, it transpired, did not in the least realise that a man should be liberally endowed in payment for assuming the duties of a husband. If rich fathers made allowances, they made them to their daughters themselves, who disposed of them as they pleased. In this case, of course, Sir Nigel privately argued with fine acumen, it became the husband's business to see that what his wife pleased should be what most agreeably coincided with his own views and conveniences.

His most illuminating experience had been the hearing of some men, hard-headed, rich stockbrokers with a vulgar sense of humour, enjoying themselves quite uproariously one night at a club, over a story one of them was relating of an unsatisfactory German son-in-law who had demanded an income. He was a man of small title, who had married the narrator's daughter, and after some months spent in his father-in-law's house, had felt it but proper that his financial position should be put on a practical footing.

"He brought her back after the bridal tour to make us a visit," said the storyteller, a sharp-featured man with a quaint wry mouth, which seemed to express a perpetual, repressed appreciation of passing events. "I had nothing to say against that, because we were all glad to see her home and her mother had been missing her. But weeks passed and months passed and there was no mention made of them going over to settle in the Slosh we'd heard so much of, and in time it came out that the Slosh thing"—Anstruthers realised with gall in his soul that the "brute," as he called him, meant "Schloss," and that his mispronunciation was at once a matter of humour and derision—"wasn't his at all. It was his elder brother's. The whole lot of them were counts and not one of them seemed to own a dime. The Slosh count hadn't more than twenty-five cents and he wasn't the kind to deal any of it out to his family. So Lily's count would have to go clerking in a dry goods store, if he promised to support himself. But he didn't propose to do it. He thought he'd got on to a soft thing. Of course we're an easy-going lot and we should have stood him if he'd been a nice fellow. But he wasn't. Lily's mother used to find her crying in her bedroom and it came out by degrees that it was because Adolf had been quarrelling with her and saying sneering things about her family. When her mother talked to him he was insulting. Then bills began to come in and Lily was expected to get me to pay them. And they were not the kind of bills a decent fellow calls on another man to pay. But I did it five or six times to make it easy for her. I didn't tell her that they gave an older chap than himself sidelights on the situation. But that didn't work well. He thought I did it because I had to, and he began to feel free and easy about it, and didn't try to cover up his tracks so much when he sent in a new lot. He was always working Lily. He began to consider himself master of the house. He intimated that a private carriage ought to be kept for them. He said it was beggarly that he should have to consider the rest of the family when he wanted to go out. When I got on to the situation, I began to enjoy it. I let him spread himself for a while just to see what he would do. Good Lord! I couldn't have believed that any fellow could have thought any other fellow could be such a fool as he thought I was. He went perfectly crazy after a month or so and ordered me about and patronised me as if I was a bootblack he meant to teach something to. So at last I had a talk with Lily and told her I was going to put an end to it. Of course she cried and was half frightened to death, but by that time he had ill-used her so that she only wanted to get rid of him. So I sent for him and had a talk with him in my office. I led him on to saying all he had on his mind. He explained to me what a condescension it was for a man like himself to marry a girl like Lily. He made a dignified, touching picture of all the disadvantages of such an alliance and all the advantages they ought to bring in exchange to the man who bore up under them. I rubbed my head and looked worried every now and then and cleared my throat apologetically just to warm him up. I can tell you that fellow felt happy, downright happy when he saw how humbly I listened to him. He positively swelled up with hope and comfort. He thought I was going to turn out well, real well. I was going to pay up just as a vulgar New York father-in-law ought to do, and thank God for the blessed privilege. Why, he was real eloquent about his blood and his ancestors and the hoary-headed Slosh. So when he'd finished, I cleared my throat in a nervous, ingratiating kind of way again and I asked him kind of anxiously what he thought would be the proper thing for a base-born New York millionaire to do under the circumstances—what he would approve of himself."

Sir Nigel was disgusted to see the narrator twist his mouth into a sweet, shrewd, repressed grin even as he expectorated into the nearest receptacle. The grin was greeted by a shout of laughter from his companions.

"What did he say, Stebbins?" someone cried.

"He said," explained Mr. Stebbins deliberately, "he said that an allowance was the proper thing. He said that a man of his rank must have resources, and that it wasn't dignified for him to have to ask his wife or his wife's father for money when he wanted it. He said an allowance was what he felt he had a right to expect. And then he twisted his moustache and said, 'what proposition' did I make—what would I allow him?"

The storyteller's hearers evidently knew him well. Their laughter was louder than before.

"Let's hear the rest, Joe! Let's hear it!"

"Well," replied Mr. Stebbins almost thoughtfully, "I just got up and said, 'Well, it won't take long for me to answer that. I've always been fond of my children, and Lily is rather my pet. She's always had everything she wanted, and she always shall. She's a good girl and she deserves it. I'll allow you——" The significant deliberation of his drawl could scarcely be described. "I'll allow you just five minutes to get out of this room, before I kick you out, and if I kick you out of the room, I'll kick you down the stairs, and if I kick you down the stairs, I shall have got my blood comfortably warmed up and I'll kick you down the street and round the block and down to Hoboken, because you're going to take the steamer there and go back to the place you came from, to the Slosh thing or whatever you call it. We haven't a damned bit of use for you here.' And believe it or not, gentlemen——" looking round with the wry-mouthed smile, "he took that passage and back he went. And Lily's living with her mother and I mean to hold on to her."

Sir Nigel got up and left the club when the story was finished. He took a long walk down Broadway, gnawing his lip and holding his head in the air. He used blasphemous language at intervals in a low voice. Some of it was addressed to his fate and some of it to the vulgar mercantile coarseness and obtuseness of other people.

"They don't know what they are talking of," he said. "It is unheard of. What do they expect? I never thought of this. Damn it! I'm like a rat in a trap."

It was plain enough that he could not arrange his fortune as he had anticipated when he decided to begin to make love to little pink and white, doll-faced Rosy Vanderpoel. If he began to demand monetary advantages in his dealing with his future wife's people in their settlement of her fortune, he might arouse suspicion and inquiry. He did not want inquiry either in connection with his own means or his past manner of living. People who hated him would be sure to crop up with stories of things better left alone. There were always meddling fools ready to interfere.

His walk was long and full of savage thinking. Once or twice as he realised what the disinterestedness of his sentiments was supposed to be, a short laugh broke from him which was rather like the snort of the Bishopess.

"I am supposed to be moonstruck over a simpering American chit— moonstruck! Damn!" But when he returned to his hotel he had made up his mind and was beginning to look over the situation in evil cold blood. Matters must be settled without delay and he was shrewd enough to realise that with his temper and its varied resources a timid girl would not be difficult to manage. He had seen at an early stage of their acquaintance that Rosy was greatly impressed by the superiority of his bearing, that he could make her blush with embarrassment when he conveyed to her that she had made a mistake, that he could chill her miserably when he chose to assume a lofty stiffness. A man's domestic armoury was filled with weapons if he could make a woman feel gauche, inexperienced, in the wrong. When he was safely married, he could pave the way to what he felt was the only practical and feasible end.

If he had been marrying a woman with more brains, she would be more difficult to subdue, but with Rosalie Vanderpoel, processes were not necessary. If you shocked, bewildered or frightened her with accusations, sulks, or sneers, her light, innocent head was set in such a whirl that the rest was easy. It was possible, upon the whole, that the thing might not turn out so infernally ill after all. Supposing that it had been Bettina who had been the marriageable one! Appreciating to the full the many reasons for rejoicing that she had not been, he walked in gloomy reflection home.

CHAPTER III

YOUNG LADY ANSTRUTHERS

When the marriage took place the event was accompanied by an ingenuously elate flourish of trumpets. Miss Vanderpoel's frocks were multitudinous and wonderful, as also her jewels purchased at Tiffany's. She carried a thousand trunks—more or less—across the Atlantic. When the ship steamed away from the dock, the wharf was like a flower garden in the blaze of brilliant and delicate attire worn by the bevy of relatives and intimates who stood waving their handkerchiefs and laughingly calling out farewell good wishes.

Sir Nigel's mental attitude was not a sympathetic or admiring one as he stood by his bride's side looking back. If Rosy's half happy, half tearful excitement had left her the leisure to reflect on his expression, she would not have felt it encouraging.

"What a deuce of a row Americans make," he said even before they were out of hearing of the voices. "It will be a positive rest to be in a country where the women do not cackle and shriek with laughter."

He said it with that simple rudeness which at times professed to be almost impersonal, and which Rosalie had usually tried to believe was the outcome of a kind of cool British humour. But this time she started a little at his words.

"I suppose we do make more noise than English people," she admitted a second or so later. "I wonder why?" And without waiting for an answer— somewhat as if she had not expected or quite wanted one—she leaned a little farther over the side to look back, waving her small, fluttering handkerchief to the many still in tumult on the wharf. She was not perceptive or quick enough to take offence, to realise that the remark was significant and that Sir Nigel had already begun as he meant to go on. It was far from being his intention to play the part of an American husband, who was plainly a creature in whom no authority vested itself. Americans let their women say and do anything, and were capable of fetching and carrying for them. He had seen a man run upstairs for his wife's wrap, cheerfully, without the least apparent sense that the service was the part of a footman if there was one in the house, a parlour maid if there was not. Sir Nigel had been brought up in the good Early Victorian days when "a nice little woman to fetch your slippers for you" figured in certain circles as domestic bliss. Girls were educated to fetch slippers as retrievers were trained to go into the water after sticks, and terriers to bring back balls thrown for them.

The new Lady Anstruthers had, it supervened, several opportunities to obtain a new view of her bridegroom's character before their voyage across the Atlantic was over. At this period of the slower and more cumbrous weaving of the Shuttle, the world had not yet awakened even to the possibilities of the ocean greyhound. An Atlantic voyage at times was capable of offering to a bride and bridegroom days enough to begin to glance into their future with a premonition of the waning of the honeymoon, at least, and especially if they were not sea-proof, to wish wearily that the first half of it were over. Rosalie was not weary, but she began to be bewildered. As she had never been a clever girl or quick to perceive, and had spent her life among women-indulging American men, she was not prepared with any precedent which made her situation clear. The first time Sir Nigel showed his temper to her she simply stared at him, her eyes looking like those of a puzzled, questioning child. Then she broke into her nervous little laugh, because she did not know what else to do. At his second outbreak her stare was rather startled and she did not laugh.

Her first awakening was to an anxious wonderment concerning certain moods of gloom, or what seemed to be gloom, to which he seemed prone. As she lay in her steamer chair he would at times march stiffly up and down the deck, apparently aware of no other existence than his own, his features expressing a certain clouded resentment of whose very unexplainableness she secretly stood in awe. She was not astute enough, poor girl, to leave him alone, and when with innocent questionings she endeavoured to discover his trouble, the greatest mystification she encountered was that he had the power to make her feel that she was in some way taking a liberty, and showing her lack of tact and perspicuity.

"Is anything the matter, Nigel?" she asked at first, wondering if she were guilty of silliness in trying to slip her hand into his. She was sure she had been when he answered her.

"No," he said chillingly.

"I don't believe you are happy," she returned. "Somehow you seem so—so different."

"I have reasons for being depressed," he replied, and it was with a stiff finality which struck a note of warning to her, signifying that it would be better taste in her to put an end to her simple efforts.

She vaguely felt herself put in the wrong, and he preferred that it should be so. It was the best form of preparation for any mood he might see that it might pay him to show her in the future. He was, in fact, confronting disdainfully his position. He had her on his hands and he was returning to his relations with no definite advantage to exhibit as the result of having married her. She had been supplied with an income but he had no control over it. It would not have been so if he had not been in such straits that he had been afraid to risk his chance by making a stand. To have a wife with money, a silly, sweet temper and no will of her own, was of course better than to be penniless, head over heels in debt and hemmed in by difficulties on every side. He had seen women trained to give in to anything rather than be bullied in public, to accede in the end to any demand rather than endure the shame of a certain kind of scene made before servants, and a certain kind of insolence used to relatives and guests. The quality he found most maddeningly irritating in Rosalie was her obviously absolute unconsciousness of the fact that it was entirely natural and proper that her resources should be in her husband's hands. He had, indeed, even in these early days, made a tentative effort or so in the form of a suggestive speech; he had given her openings to give him an opening to put things on a practical basis, but she had never had the intelligence to see what he was aiming at, and he had found himself almost floundering ungracefully in his remarks, while she had looked at him without a sign of comprehension in her simple, anxious blue eyes. The creature was actually trying to understand him and could not. That was the worst of it, the blank wall of her unconsciousness, her childlike belief that he was far too grand a personage to require anything. These were the things he was thinking over when he walked up and down the deck in unamiable solitariness. Rosy awakened to the amazed consciousness of the fact that, instead of being pleased with the luxury and prettiness of her wardrobe and appointments, he seemed to dislike and disdain them.

"You American women change your clothes too much and think too much of them," was one of his first amiable criticisms. "You spend more than well-bred women should spend on mere dresses and bonnets. In New York it always strikes an Englishman that the women look endimanche at whatever time of day you come across them."

"Oh, Nigel!" cried Rosy woefully. She could not think of anything more to say than, "Oh, Nigel!"

"I am sorry to say it is true," he replied loftily. That she was an American and a New Yorker was being impressed upon poor little Lady Anstruthers in a new way—somehow as if the mere cold statement of the fact put a fine edge of sarcasm to any remark. She was of too innocent a loyalty to wish that she was neither the one nor the other, but she did wish that Nigel was not so prejudiced against the places and people she cared for so much.

She was sitting in her stateroom enfolded in a dressing gown covered with cascades of lace, tied with knots of embroidered ribbon, and her maid, Hannah, who admired her greatly, was brushing her fair long hair with a gold-backed brush, ornamented with a monogram of jewels.

If she had been a French duchess of a piquant type, or an English one with an aquiline nose, she would have been beyond criticism; if she had been a plump, over-fed woman, or an ugly, ill-natured, gross one, she would have looked vulgar, but she was a little, thin, fair New Yorker, and though she was not beyond criticism—if one demanded high distinction—she was pretty and nice to look at. But Nigel Anstruthers would not allow this to her. His own tailors' bills being far in arrears and his pocket disgustingly empty, the sight of her ingenuous sumptuousness and the gay, accustomed simpleness of outlook with which she accepted it as her natural right, irritated him and roused his venom. Bills would remain unpaid if she was permitted to spend her money on this sort of thing without any consideration for the requirements of other people.

He inhaled the air and made a gesture of distaste.

"This sachet business is rather overpowering," he said. "It is the sort of thing a woman should be particularly discreet about."

"Oh, Nigel!" cried the poor girl agitatedly. "Hannah, do go and call the steward to open the windows. Is it really strong?" she implored as Hannah went out. "How dreadful. It's only orris and I didn't know Hannah had put it in the trunks."

"My dear Rosalie," with a wave of the hand taking in both herself and her dressing case, "it is all too strong."

"All—wh—what?" gaspingly.

"The whole thing. All that lace and love knot arrangement, the gold-backed brushes and scent bottles with diamonds and rubies sticking in them."

"They—they were wedding presents. They came from Tiffany's. Everyone thought them lovely."

"They look as if they belonged to the dressing table of a French woman of the demi-monde. I feel as if I had actually walked into the apartment of some notorious Parisian soubrette."

Rosalie Vanderpoel was a clean-minded little person, her people were of the clean-minded type, therefore she did not understand all that this ironic speech implied, but she gathered enough of its significance to cause her to turn first red and then pale and then to burst into tears. She was crying and trying to conceal the fact when Hannah returned. She bent her head and touched her eyes furtively while her toilette was completed.

Sir Nigel had retired from the scene, but he had done so feeling that he had planted a seed and bestowed a practical lesson. He had, it is true, bestowed one, but again she had not understood its significance and was only left bewildered and unhappy. She began to be nervous and uncertain about herself and about his moods and points of view. She had never been made to feel so at home. Everyone had been kind to her and lenient to her lack of brilliancy. No one had expected her to be brilliant, and she had been quite sweet-temperedly resigned to the fact that she was not the kind of girl who shone either in society or elsewhere. She did not resent the fact that she knew people said of her, "She isn't in the least bit bright, Rosy Vanderpoel, but she's a nice, sweet little thing." She had tried to be nice and sweet and had aspired to nothing higher.

But now that seemed so much less than enough. Perhaps Nigel ought to have married one of the clever ones, someone who would have known how to understand him and who would have been more entertaining than she could be. Perhaps she was beginning to bore him, perhaps he was finding her out and beginning to get tired. At this point the always too ready tears would rise to her eyes and she would be overwhelmed by a sense of homesickness. Often she cried herself silently to sleep, longing for her mother—her nice, comfortable, ordinary mother, whom she had several times felt Nigel had some difficulty in being unreservedly polite to—though he had been polite on the surface.

By the time they landed she had been living under so much strain in her effort to seem quite unchanged, that she had lost her nerve. She did not feel well and was sometimes afraid that she might do something silly and hysterical in spite of herself, begin to cry for instance when there was really no explanation for her doing it. But when she reached London the novelty of everything so excited her that she thought she was going to be better, and then she said to herself it would be proved to her that all her fears had been nonsense. This return of hope made her quite light-spirited, and she was almost gay in her little outbursts of delight and admiration as she drove about the streets with her husband. She did not know that her ingenuous ignorance of things he had known all his life, her rapture over common monuments of history, led him to say to himself that he felt rather as if he were taking a housemaid to see a Lord Mayor's Show.

Before going to Stornham Court they spent a few days in town. There had been no intention of proclaiming their presence to the world, and they did not do so, but unluckily certain tradesmen discovered the fact that Sir Nigel Anstruthers had returned to England with the bride he had secured in New York. The conclusion to be deduced from this circumstance was that the particular moment was a good one at which to send in bills for "acct. rendered." The tradesmen quite shared Anstruthers' point of view. Their reasoning was delightfully simple and they were wholly unaware that it might have been called gross. A man over his head and ears in debt naturally expected his creditors would be paid by the young woman who had married him. America had in these days been so little explored by the thrifty impecunious well-born that its ingenuous sentimentality in certain matters was by no means comprehended.

By each post Sir Nigel received numerous bills. Sometimes letters accompanied them, and once or twice respectful but firm male persons brought them by hand and demanded interviews which irritated Sir Nigel extremely. Given time to arrange matters with Rosalie, to train her to some sense of her duty, he believed that the "acct. rendered" could be wiped off, but he saw he must have time. She was such a little fool. Again and again he was furious at the fate which had forced him to take her.

The truth was that Rosalie knew nothing whatever about unpaid bills. Reuben Vanderpoel's daughters had never encountered an indignant tradesman in their lives. When they went into "stores" they were received with unfeigned rapture. Everything was dragged forth to be displayed to them, attendants waited to leap forth to supply their smallest behest. They knew no other phase of existence than the one in which one could buy anything one wanted and pay any price demanded for it.

Consequently Rosalie did not recognise signs which would have been obviously recognisable by the initiated. If Sir Nigel Anstruthers had been a nice young fellow who had loved her, and he had been honest enough to make a clean breast of his difficulties, she would have thrown herself into his arms and implored him effusively to make use of all her available funds, and if the supply had been insufficient, would have immediately written to her father for further donations, knowing that her appeal would be responded to at once. But Sir Nigel Anstruthers cherished no sentiment for any other individual than himself, and he had no intention of explaining that his mere vanity had caused him to mislead her, that his rank and estate counted for nothing and that he was in fact a pauper loaded with dishonest debts. He wanted money, but he wanted it to be given to him as if he conferred a favour by receiving it. It must be transferred to him as though it were his by right. What did a man marry for? Therefore his wife's unconsciousness that she was inflicting outrage upon him by her mere mental attitude filled his being with slowly rising gall.

Poor Rosalie went joyfully forth shopping after the manner of all newly arrived Americans. She bought new toilettes and gewgaws and presents for her friends and relations in New York, and each package which was delivered at the hotel added to Sir Nigel's rage.

That the little blockhead should be allowed to do what she liked with her money and that he should not be able to forbid her! This he said to himself at intervals of five minutes through the day—which led to another small episode.

"You are spending a great deal of money," he said one morning in his condemnatory manner. Rosalie looked up from the lace flounce which had just been delivered and gave the little nervous laugh, which was becoming entirely uncertain of propitiating.

"Am I?" she answered. "They say all Americans spend a good deal."

"Your money ought to be in proper hands and properly managed," he went on with cold precision. "If you were an English woman, your husband would control it."

"Would he?" The simple, sweet-tempered obtuseness of her tone was an infuriating thing to him. There was the usual shade of troubled surprise in her eyes as they met his. "I don't think men in America ever do that. I don't believe the nice ones want to. You see they have such a pride about always giving things to women, and taking care of them. I believe a nice American man would break stones in the street rather than take money from a woman—even his wife. I mean while he could work. Of course if he was ill or had ill luck or anything like that, he wouldn't be so proud as not to take it from the person who loved him most and wanted to help him. You do sometimes hear of a man who won't work and lets his wife support him, but it's very seldom, and they are always the low kind that other men look down on."

"Wanted to help him." Sir Nigel selected the phrase and quoted it between puffs of the cigar he held in his fine, rather cruel-looking hands, and his voice expressed a not too subtle sneer. "A woman is not 'helping' her husband when she gives him control of her fortune. She is only doing her duty and accepting her proper position with regard to him. The law used to settle the thing definitely."

"Did-did it?" Rosy faltered weakly. She knew he was offended again and that she was once more somehow in the wrong. So many things about her seemed to displease him, and when he was displeased he always reminded her that she was stupidly, objectionably guilty of not being an English woman.

Whatsoever it happened to be, the fault she had committed out of her depth of ignorance, he did not forget it. It was no habit of his to endeavour to dismiss offences. He preferred to hold them in possession as if they were treasures and to turn them over and over, in the mental seclusion which nourishes the growth of injuries, since within its barriers there is no chance of their being palliated by the apologies or explanations of the offender.

During their journey to Stornham Court the next day he was in one of his black moods. Once in the railway carriage he paid small attention to his wife, but sat rigidly reading his Times, until about midway to their destination he descended at a station and paid a visit to the buffet in the small refreshment room, after which he settled himself to doze in an exceedingly unbecoming attitude, his travelling cap pulled down, his rather heavy face congested with the dark flush Rosalie had not yet learned was due to the fact that he had hastily tossed off two or three whiskies and sodas. Though he was never either thick of utterance or unsteady on his feet, whisky and soda formed an important factor in his existence. When he was annoyed or dull he at once took the necessary precautions against being overcome by these feelings, and the effect upon a constitutionally evil temper was to transform it into an infernal one. The night had been a bad one for Rosy. Such floods of homesick longing had overpowered her that she had not been able to sleep. She had risen feeling shaky and hysterical and her nervousness had been added to by her fear that Nigel might observe her and make comment. Of course she told herself it was natural that he should not wish her to appear at Stornham Court looking a pale, pink-nosed little fright. Her efforts to be cheerful had indeed been somewhat touching, but they had met with small encouragement.

She thought the green-clothed country lovely as the train sped through it, and a lump rose in her small throat because she knew she might have been so happy if she had not been so frightened and miserable. The thing which had been dawning upon her took clearer, more awful form. Incidents she had tried to explain and excuse to herself, upon all sorts of futile, simple grounds, began to loom up before her in something like their actual proportions. She had heard of men who had changed their manner towards girls after they had married them, but she did not know they had begun to change so soon. This was so early in the honeymoon to be sitting in a railway carriage, in a corner remote from that occupied by a bridegroom, who read his paper in what was obviously intentional, resentful solitude. Emily Soame's father, she remembered it against her will, had been obliged to get a divorce for Emily after her two years of wretched married life. But Alfred Soames had been quite nice for six months at least. It seemed as if all this must be a dream, one of those nightmare things, in which you suddenly find yourself married to someone you cannot bear, and you don't know how it happened, because you yourself have had nothing to do with the matter. She felt that presently she must waken with a start and find herself breathing fast, and panting out, half laughing, half crying, "Oh, I am so glad it's not true! I am so glad it's not true!"

But this was true, and there was Nigel. And she was in a new, unexplored world. Her little trembling hands clutched each other. The happy, light girlish days full of ease and friendliness and decency seemed gone forever. It was not Rosalie Vanderpoel who pressed her colourless face against the glass of the window, looking out at the flying trees; it was the wife of Nigel Anstruthers, and suddenly, by some hideous magic, she had been snatched from the world to which she belonged and was being dragged by a gaoler to a prison from which she did not know how to escape. Already Nigel had managed to convey to her that in England a woman who was married could do nothing to defend herself against her husband, and that to endeavour to do anything was the last impossible touch of vulgar ignominy.

The vivid realisation of the situation seized upon her like a possession as she glanced sideways at her bridegroom and hurriedly glanced away again with a little hysterical shudder. New York, good-tempered, lenient, free New York, was millions of miles away and Nigel was so loathly near and—and so ugly. She had never known before that he was so ugly, that his face was so heavy, his skin so thick and coarse and his expression so evilly ill-tempered. She was not sufficiently analytical to be conscious that she had with one bound leaped to the appalling point of feeling uncontrollable physical abhorrence of the creature to whom she was chained for life. She was terrified at finding herself forced to combat the realisation that there were certain expressions of his countenance which made her feel sick with repulsion. Her self-reproach also was as great as her terror. He was her husband—her husband—and she was a wicked girl. She repeated the words to herself again and again, but remotely she knew that when she said, "He is my husband," that was the worst thing of all.

This inward struggle was a bad preparation for any added misery, and when their railroad journey terminated at Stornham Station she was met by new bewilderment.

The station itself was a rustic place where wild roses climbed down a bank to meet the very train itself. The station master's cottage had roses and clusters of lilies waving in its tiny garden. The station master, a good-natured, red-faced man, came forward, baring his head, to open the railroad carriage door with his own hand. Rosy thought him delightful and bowed and smiled sweet-temperedly to him and to his wife and little girls, who were curtseying at the garden gate. She was sufficiently homesick to be actually grateful to them for their air of welcoming her. But as she smiled she glanced furtively at Nigel to see if she was doing exactly the right thing.

He himself was not smiling and did not unbend even when the station master, who had known him from his boyhood, felt at liberty to offer a deferential welcome.

"Happy to see you home with her ladyship, Sir Nigel," he said; "very happy, if I may say so."

Sir Nigel responded to the respectful amiability with a half-military lifting of his right hand, accompanied by a grunt.

"D'ye do, Wells," he said, and strode past him to speak to the footman who had come from Stornham Court with the carriage.

The new and nervous little Lady Anstruthers, who was left to trot after her husband, smiled again at the ruddy, kind-looking fellow, this time in conscious deprecation. In the simplicity of her republican sympathy with a well-meaning fellow creature who might feel himself snubbed, she could have shaken him by the hand. She had even parted her lips to venture a word of civility when she was startled by hearing Sir Nigel's voice raised in angry rating.

"Damned bad management not to bring something else," she heard. "Kind of thing you fellows are always doing."

She made her way to the carriage, flurried again by not knowing whether she was doing right or wrong. Sir Nigel had given her no instructions and she had not yet learned that when he was in a certain humour there was equal fault in obeying or disobeying such orders as he gave.

The carriage from the Court—not in the least a new or smart equipage— was drawn up before the entrance of the station and Sir Nigel was in a rage because the vehicle brought for the luggage was too small to carry it all.

"Very sorry, Sir Nigel," said the coachman, touching his hat two or three times in his agitation. "Very sorry. The omnibus was a little out of order—the springs, Sir Nigel—and I thought——"

"You thought!" was the heated interruption. "What right had you to think, damn it! You are not paid to think, you are paid to do your work properly. Here are a lot of damned boxes which ought to go with us and—where's your maid?" wheeling round upon his wife.

Rosalie turned towards the woman, who was approaching from the waiting room.

"Hannah," she said timorously.

"Drop those confounded bundles," ordered Sir Nigel, "and show James the boxes her ladyship is obliged to have this evening. Be quick about it and don't pick out half a dozen. The cart can't take them."

Hannah looked frightened. This sort of thing was new to her, too. She shuffled her packages on to a seat and followed the footman to the luggage. Sir Nigel continued rating the coachman. Any form of violent self-assertion was welcome to him at any time, and when he was irritated he found it a distinct luxury to kick a dog or throw a boot at a cat. The springs of the omnibus, he argued, had no right to be broken when it was known that he was coming home. His anger was only added to by the coachman's halting endeavours in his excuses to veil a fact he knew his master was aware of, that everything at Stornham was more or less out of order, and that dilapidations were the inevitable result of there being no money to pay for repairs. The man leaned forward on his box and spoke at last in a low tone.

"The bus has been broken some time," he said. "It's—it's an expensive job, Sir Nigel. Her ladyship thought it better to——" Sir Nigel turned white about the mouth.

"Hold your tongue," he commanded, and the coachman got red in the face, saluted, biting his lips, and sat very stiff and upright on his box.

The station master edged away uneasily and tried to look as if he were not listening. But Rosalie could see that he could not help hearing, nor could the country people who had been passengers by the train and who were collecting their belongings and getting into their traps.

Lady Anstruthers was ignored and remained standing while the scene went on. She could not help recalling the manner in which she had been invariably received in New York on her return from any journey, how she was met by comfortable, merry people and taken care of at once. This was so strange, it was so queer, so different.

"Oh, never mind, Nigel dear," she said at last, with innocent indiscretion. "It doesn't really matter, you know."

Sir Nigel turned upon her a blaze of haughty indignation.

"If you'll pardon my saying so, it does matter," he said. "It matters confoundedly. Be good enough to take your place in the carriage."

He moved to the carriage door, and not too civilly put her in. She gasped a little for breath as she sat down. He had spoken to her as if she had been an impertinent servant who had taken a liberty. The poor girl was bewildered to the verge of panic. When he had ended his tirade and took his place beside her he wore his most haughtily intolerant air.

"May I request that in future you will be good enough not to interfere when I am reproving my servants," he remarked.

"I didn't mean to interfere," she apologised tremulously.

"I don't know what you meant. I only know what you did," was his response. "You American women are too fond of cutting in. An Englishman can think for himself without his wife's assistance."

The tears rose to her eyes. The introduction of the international question overpowered her as always.

"Don't begin to be hysterical," was the ameliorating tenderness with which he observed the two hot salt drops which fell despite her. "I should scarcely wish to present you to my mother bathed in tears."

She wiped the salt drops hastily away and sat for a moment silent in the corner of the carriage. Being wholly primitive and unanalytical, she was ashamed and began to blame herself. He was right. She must not be silly because she was unused to things. She ought not to be disturbed by trifles. She must try to be nice and look cheerful. She made an effort and did no speak for a few minutes. When she had recovered herself she tried again.

"English country is so pretty," she said, when she thought she was quite sure that her voice would not tremble. "I do so like the hedges and the darling little red-roofed cottages."

It was an innocent tentative at saying something agreeable which might propitiate him. She was beginning to realise that she was continually making efforts to propitiate him. But one of the forms of unpleasantness most enjoyable to him was the snubbing of any gentle effort at palliating his mood. He condescended in this case no response whatever, but merely continued staring contemptuously before him.

"It is so picturesque, and so unlike America," was the pathetic little commonplace she ventured next. "Ain't it, Nigel?"

He turned his head slowly towards her, as if she had taken a new liberty in disturbing his meditations.

"Wha—at?" he drawled.

It was almost too much for her to sustain herself under. Her courage collapsed.

"I was only saying how pretty the cottages were," she faltered. "And that there's nothing like this in America."

"You ended your remark by adding, 'ain't it,'" her husband condescended. "There is nothing like that in England. I shall ask you to do me the favour of leaving Americanisms out of your conversation when you are in the society of English ladies and gentlemen. It won't do."

"I didn't know I said it," Rosy answered feebly.

"That is the difficulty," was his response. "You never know, but educated people do."

There was nothing more to be said, at least for a girl who had never known what it was to be bullied. This one felt like a beggar or a scullery maid, who, being rated by her master, had not the refuge of being able to "give warning." She could never give warning. The Atlantic Ocean was between her and those who had loved and protected her all her short life, and the carriage was bearing her onwards to the home in which she was to live alone as this man's companion to the end of her existence.

She made no further propitiatory efforts, but sat and stared in simple blankness at the country, which seemed to increase in loveliness at each new point of view. Sometimes she saw sweet wooded, rolling lands made lovelier by the homely farmhouses and cottages enclosed and sheltered by thick hedges and trees; once or twice they drove past a park enfolding a great house guarded by its huge sentinel oaks and beeches; once the carriage passed through an adorable little village, where children played on the green and a square-towered grey church seemed to watch over the steep-roofed cottages and creeper-covered vicarage. If she had been a happy American tourist travelling in company with impressionable friends, she would have broken into ecstatic little exclamations of admiration every five minutes, but it had been driven home to her that to her present companion, to whom nothing was new, her rapture would merely represent the crudeness which had existed in contentment in a brown-stone house on a noisy thoroughfare, through a life which had been passed tramping up and down numbered streets and avenues.

They approached at last a second village with a green, a grass-grown street and the irregular red-tiled cottages, which to the unaccustomed eye seemed rather to represent studies for sketches than absolute realities. The bells in the church tower broke forth into a chime and people appeared at the doors of the cottages. The men touched their foreheads as the carriage passed, and the children made bobbing curtsies. Sir Nigel condescended to straighten himself a trifle in his seat, and recognised the greetings with the stiff, half-military salute. The poor girl at his side felt that he put as little feeling as possible into the movement, and that if she herself had been a bowing villager she would almost have preferred to be wholly ignored. She looked at him questioningly.

"Are they—must I?" she began.

"Make some civil recognition," answered Sir Nigel, as if he were instructing an ignorant child. "It is customary."

So she bowed and tried to smile, and the joyous clamour of the bells brought the awful lump into her throat again. It reminded her of the ringing of the chimes at the New York church on that day of her marriage, which had been so full of gay, luxurious bustle, so crowded with wedding presents, and flowers, and warm-hearted, affectionate congratulations, and good wishes uttered in merry American voices.

The park at Stornham Court was large and beautiful and old. The trees were magnificent, and the broad sweep of sward and rich dip of ferny dell all that the imagination could desire. The Court itself was old, and many-gabled and mellow-red and fine. Rosalie had learned from no precedent as yet that houses of its kind may represent the apotheosis of discomfort and dilapidation within, and only become more beautiful without. Tumbled-down chimneys and broken tiles, being clambered over by tossing ivy, are pictures to delight the soul.

As she descended from the carriage the girl was tremulous and uncertain of herself and much overpowered by the unbending air of the man-servant who received her as if she were a parcel in which it was no part of his duty to take the smallest interest. As she mounted the stone steps she caught a glimpse of broad gloom within the threshold, a big, square, dingy hall where some other servants were drawn up in a row. She had read of something of the sort in English novels, and she was suddenly embarrassed afresh by her realisation of the fact that she did not know what to do and that if she made a mistake Nigel would never forgive her.

An elderly woman came out of a room opening into the hall. She was an ugly woman of a rigid carriage, which, with the obvious intention of being severely majestic, was only antagonistic. She had a flaccid chin, and was curiously like Nigel. She had also his expression when he intended to be disagreeable. She was the Dowager Lady Anstruthers, and being an entirely revolting old person at her best, she objected extremely to the transatlantic bride who had made her a dowager, though she was determinedly prepared to profit by any practical benefit likely to accrue.

"Well, Nigel," she said in a deep voice. "Here you are at last."

This was of course a statement not to be refuted. She held out a leathern cheek, and as Sir Nigel also presented his, their caress of greeting was a singular and not effusive one.

"Is this your wife?" she asked, giving Rosalie a bony hand. And as he did not indignantly deny this to be the fact, she added, "How do you do?"

Rosalie murmured a reply and tried to control herself by making another effort to swallow the lump in her throat. But she could not swallow it. She had been keeping a desperate hold on herself too long. The bewildered misery of her awakening, the awkwardness of the public row at the station, the sulks which had filled the carriage to repletion through all the long drive, and finally the jangling bells which had so recalled that last joyous day at home—at home—had brought her to a point where this meeting between mother and son—these two stony, unpleasant creatures exchanging a reluctant rub of uninviting cheeks—as two savages might have rubbed noses—proved the finishing impetus to hysteria. They were so hideous, these two, and so ghastly comic and fantastic in their unresponsive glumness, that the poor girl lost all hold upon herself and broke into a trembling shriek of laughter.

"Oh!" she gasped in terror at what she felt to be her indecent madness. "Oh! how—how———" And then seeing Nigel's furious start, his mother's glare and all the servants' alarmed stare at her, she rushed staggering to the only creature she felt she knew—her maid Hannah, clutched her and broke down into wild sobbing.

"Oh, take me away!" she cried. "Oh, do! Oh, do! Oh, Hannah! Oh, mother—mother!"

"Take your mistress to her room," commanded Sir Nigel. "Go downstairs," he called out to the servants. "Take her upstairs at once and throw water in her face," to the excited Hannah.

And as the new Lady Anstruthers was half led, half dragged, in humiliated hysteric disorder up the staircase, he took his mother by the elbow, marched her into the nearest room and shut the door. There they stood and stared at each other, breathing quick, enraged breaths and looking particularly alike with their heavy-featured, thick-skinned, infuriated faces.

It was the Dowager who spoke first, and her whole voice and manner expressed all she intended that they should, all the derision, dislike and scathing resignment to a grotesque fate.

"Well," said her ladyship. "So THIS is what you have brought home from America!"

CHAPTER IV

A MISTAKE OF THE POSTBOY'S

As the weeks passed at Stornham Court the Atlantic Ocean seemed to Rosalie Anstruthers to widen endlessly, and gay, happy, noisy New York to recede until it was as far away as some memory of heaven. The girl had been born in the midst of the rattling, rumbling bustle, and it had never struck her as assuming the character of noise; she had only thought of it as being the cheerful confusion inseparable from town. She had been secretly offended and hurt when strangers said that New York was noisy and dirty; when they called it vulgar, she never wholly forgave them. She was of the New Yorkers who adore their New York as Parisians adore Paris and who feel that only within its beloved boundaries can the breath of life be breathed. People were often too hot or too cold there, but there was usually plenty of bright glaring sun, and the extremes of the weather had at least something rather dramatic about them. There were dramatic incidents connected with them, at any rate. People fell dead of sunstroke or were frozen to death, and the newspapers were full of anecdotes during a "cold snap" or a "torrid wave," which all made for excitement and conversation.

But at Stornham the rain seemed to young Lady Anstruthers to descend ceaselessly. The season was a wet one, and when she rose in the morning and looked out over the huge stretch of trees and sward she thought she always saw the rain falling either in hopeless sheets or more hopeless drizzle. The occasions upon which this was a dreary truth blotted out or blurred the exceptions, when in liquid ultramarine deeps of sky, floated islands and mountains of snow-white fleece, of a beauty of which she had before had no conception.

In the English novels she had read, places such as Stornham Court were always filled with "house parties," made up of wonderful town wits and beauties, who provided endless entertainment for each other, who played games, who hunted and shot pheasants and shone in dazzling amateur theatricals. There were, however, no visitors at Stornham, and there were in fact, no accommodations for any. There were numberless bedrooms, but none really fit for guests to occupy. Carpets and curtains were ancient and ragged, furniture was dilapidated, chimneys would not draw, beds were falling to pieces. The Dowager Lady Anstruthers had never either attracted desired, or been able to afford company. Her son's wife suffered from the resulting boredom and unpopularity without being able to comprehend the significance of the situation.

As the weeks dragged by a few heavy carriages deposited at the Court a few callers. Some of the visitors bore imposing titles, which made Rosalie very nervous and caused her hastily to array herself to receive them in toilettes much too pretty and delicate for the occasion. Her innocent idea was that she must do her husband credit by appearing as "stylish" as possible.

As a result she was stared at, either with open disfavour, or with well-bred, furtive criticism, and was described afterwards as being either "very American" or "very over-dressed." When she had lived in huge rooms in Fifth Avenue, Rosalie had changed her attire as many times a day as she had changed her fancy; every hour had been filled with engagements and amusements; the Vanderpoel carriages had driven up to the door and driven away again and again through the mornings and afternoons and until midnight and later. Someone was always going out or coming in. There had been in the big handsome house not much more of an air of repose than one might expect to find at a railway station; but the flurry, the coming and going, the calling and chatting had all been cheery, amiable. At Stornham, Rosalie sat at breakfast before unchanging boiled eggs, unfailing toast and unalterable broiled bacon, morning after morning. Sir Nigel sat and munched over the newspapers, his mother, with an air of relentless disapproval from a lofty height of both her food and companions, disposed of her eggs and her rasher at Rosalie's right hand. She had transferred to her daughter-in-law her previously occupied seat at the head of the table. This had been done with a carefully prepared scene of intense though correct disagreeableness, in which she had managed to convey all the rancour of her dethroned spirit and her disapproval and disdain of international alliances.

"It is of course proper that you should sit at the head of your husband's table," she had said, among other agreeable things. "A woman having devoted her life to her son must relinquish her position to the person he chooses to marry. If you should have a son you will give up your position to his wife. Since Nigel has married you, he has, of course, a right to expect that you will at least make an effort to learn something of what is required of women of your position."

"Sit down, Rosalie," said Nigel. "Of course you take the head of the table, and naturally you must learn what is expected of my wife, but don't talk confounded rubbish, mother, about devoting your life to your son. We have seen about as little of each other as we could help. We never agreed." They were both bullies and each made occasional efforts at bullying the other without any particular result. But each could at least bully the other into intensified unpleasantness.

The vicar's wife having made her call of ceremony upon the new Lady Anstruthers, followed up the acquaintance, and found her quite exotically unlike her mother-in-law, whose charities one may be sure had neither been lavish nor dispensed by any hand less impressive than her own. The younger woman was of wholly malleable material. Her sympathies were easily awakened and her purse was well filled and readily opened. Small families or large ones, newly born infants or newly buried ones, old women with "bad legs" and old men who needed comforts, equally touched her heart. She innocently bestowed sovereigns where an Englishwoman would have known that half-crowns would have been sufficient. As the vicaress was her almoner that lady felt her importance rapidly on the increase. When she left a cottage saying, "I'll speak to young Lady Anstruthers about you," the good woman of the house curtsied low and her husband touched his forehead respectfully.

But this did not advance the fortunes of Sir Nigel, who personally required of her very different things. Two weeks after her arrival at Stornham, Rosalie began to see that somehow she was regarded as a person almost impudently in the wrong. It appeared that if she had been an English girl she would have been quite different, that she would have been an advantage instead of a detriment. As an American she was a detriment. That seemed to go without saying. She tried to do everything she was told, and learn something from each cold insinuation. She did not know that her very amenability and timidity were her undoing. Sir Nigel and his mother thoroughly enjoyed themselves at her expense. They knew they could say anything they chose, and that at the most she would only break down into crying and afterwards apologise for being so badly behaved. If some practical, strong-minded person had been near to defend her she might have been rescued promptly and her tyrants routed. But she was a young girl, tender of heart and weak of nature. She used to cry a great deal when she was alone, and when she wrote to her mother she was too frightened to tell the truth concerning her unhappiness.

"Oh, if I could just see some of them!" she would wail to herself. "If I could just see mother or father or anybody from New York! Oh, I know I shall never see New York again, or Broadway or Fifth Avenue or Central Park—I never—never—never shall!" And she would grovel among her pillows, burying her face and half stifling herself lest her sobs should be heard. Her feeling for her husband had become one of terror and repulsion. She was almost more afraid of his patronising, affectionate moments than she was of his temper.

His conjugal condescensions made her feel vaguely—without knowing why—as if she were some lower order of little animal.

American women, he said, had no conception of wifely duties and affection. He had a great deal to say on the subject of wifely duty. It was part of her duty as a wife to be entirely satisfied with his society, and to be completely happy in the pleasure it afforded her. It was her wifely duty not to talk about her own family and palpitatingly expect letters by every American mail. He objected intensely to this letter writing and receiving, and his mother shared his prejudices.

"You have married an Englishman," her ladyship said. "You have put it out of his power to marry an Englishwoman, and the least consideration you can show is to let New York and Nine-hundredth street remain upon the other side of the Atlantic and not insist on dragging them into Stornham Court."

The Dowager Lady Anstruthers was very fine in her picture of her mental condition, when she realised, as she seemed periodically to do, that it was no longer possible for her son to make a respectable marriage with a woman of his own nation. The unadorned fact was that both she and Sir Nigel were infuriated by the simplicity which made Rosalie slow in comprehending that it was proper that the money her father allowed her should be placed in her husband's hands, and left there with no indelicate questioning. If she had been an English girl matters would have been made plain to her from the first and arranged satisfactorily before her marriage. Sir Nigel's mother considered that he had played the fool, and would not believe that New York fathers were such touchy, sentimental idiots as not to know what was expected of them.

They wasted no time, however, in coming to the point, and in a measure it was the vicaress who aided them. Not she entirely, however.

Since her mother-in-law's first mention of a possible son whose wife would eventually thrust her from her seat at the head of the table, Rosalie had several times heard this son referred to. It struck her that in England such things seemed discussed with more freedom than in America. She had never heard a young woman's possible family arranged for and made the subject of conversation in the more crude atmosphere of New York. It made her feel rather awkward at first. Then she began to realise that the son was part of her wifely duty also; that she was expected to provide one, and that he was in some way expected to provide for the estate—to rehabilitate it—and that this was because her father, being a rich man, would provide for him. It had also struck her that in England there was a tendency to expectation that someone would "provide" for someone else, that relatives even by marriage were supposed to "make allowances" on which it was quite proper for other persons to live. Rosalie had been accustomed to a community in which even rich men worked, and in which young and able-bodied men would have felt rather indignant if aunts or uncles had thought it necessary to pension them off as if they had been impotent paupers. It was Rosalie's son who was to be "provided for" in this case, and who was to "provide for" his father.

"When you have a son," her mother-in-law had remarked severely, "I suppose something will be done for Nigel and the estate."

This had been said before she had been ten days in the house, and had set her not-too-quick brain working. She had already begun to see that life at Stornham Court was not the luxurious affair it was in the house in Fifth Avenue. Things were shabby and queer and not at all comfortable. Fires were not lighted because a day was chilly and gloomy. She had once asked for one in her bedroom and her mother-in-law had reproved her for indecent extravagance in a manner which took her breath away.

"I suppose in America you have your house at furnace heat in July," she said. "Mere wastefulness and self-indulgence! That is why Americans are old women at twenty. They are shrivelled and withered by the unhealthy lives they lead. Stuffing themselves with sweets and hot bread and never breathing the fresh air."

Rosalie could not at the moment recall any withered and shrivelled old women of twenty, but she blushed and stammered as usual.

"It is never cold enough for fires in July," she answered, "but we—we never think fires extravagant when we are not comfortable without them."

"Coal must be cheaper than it is in England," said her ladyship. "When you have a daughter, I hope you do not expect to bring her up as girls are brought up in New York."

This was the first time Rosalie had heard of her daughter, and she was not ready enough to reply. She naturally went into her room and cried again, wondering what her father and mother would say if they knew that bedroom fires were considered vulgarly extravagant by an impressive member of the British aristocracy.

She was not at all strong at the time and was given to feeling chilly and miserable on wet, windy days. She used to cry more than ever and was so desolate that there were days when she used to go to the vicarage for companionship. On such days the vicar's wife would entertain her with stories of the villagers' catastrophes, and she would empty her purse upon the tea table and feel a little consoled because she was the means of consoling someone else.

"I suppose it gratifies your vanity to play the Lady Bountiful," Sir Nigel sneered one evening, having heard in the village what she was doing.

"I—never thought of such a thing," she stammered feebly. "Mrs. Brent said they were so poor."

"You throw your money about as if you were a child," said her mother-in-law. "It is a pity it is not put in the hands of some person with discretion."

It had begun to dawn upon Rosalie that her ladyship was deeply convinced that either herself or her son would be admirably discreet custodians of the money referred to. And even the dawning of this idea had frightened the girl. She was so inexperienced and ignorant that she felt it might be possible that in England one's husband and one's mother-in-law could do what they liked. It might be that they could take possession of one's money as they seemed to take possession of one's self and one's very soul. She would have been very glad to give them money, and had indeed wondered frequently if she might dare to offer it to them, if they would be outraged and insulted and slay her in their wrath at her purse-proud daring. She had tried to invent ways in which she could approach the subject, but had not been able to screw up her courage to any sticking point. She was so overpowered by her consciousness that they seemed continually to intimate that Americans with money were ostentatious and always laying stress upon the amount of their possessions. She had no conception of the primeval simpleness of their attitude in such matters, and that no ceremonies were necessary save the process of transferring sufficiently large sums as though they were the mere right of the recipients. She was taught to understand this later. In the meantime, however, ready as she would have been to give large sums if she had known how, she was terrified by the thought that it might be possible that she could be deprived of her bank account and reduced to the condition of a sort of dependent upon the humours of her lately acquired relations. She thought over this a good deal, and would have found immense relief if she dared have consulted anyone. But she could not make up her mind to reveal her unhappiness to her people. She had been married so recently, everybody had thought her marriage so delightful, she could not bear that her father and mother should be distressed by knowing that she was wretched. She also reflected with misery that New York would talk the matter over excitedly and that finally the newspapers would get hold of the gossip. She could even imagine interviewers calling at the house in Fifth Avenue and endeavouring to obtain particulars of the situation. Her father would be angry and refuse to give them, but that would make no difference; the newspapers would give them and everybody would read what they said, whether it was true or not. She could not possibly write facts, she thought, so her poor little letters were restrained and unlike herself, and to the warm-hearted souls in New York, even appearing stiff and unaffectionate, as if her aristocratic surroundings had chilled her love for them. In fact, it became far from easy for her to write at all, since Sir Nigel so disapproved of her interest in the American mail. His objections had indeed taken the form of his feeling himself quite within his rights when he occasionally intercepted letters from her relations, with a view of finding out whether they contained criticisms of himself, which would betray that she had been guilty of indiscreet confidences. He discovered that she had not apparently been so guilty, but it was evident that there were moments when Mrs. Vanderpoel was uneasy and disposed to ask anxious questions. When this occurred he destroyed the letters, and as a result of this precaution on his part her motherly queries seemed to be ignored, and she several times shed tears in the belief that Rosy had grown so patrician that she was capable of snubbing her mother in her resentment at feeling her privacy intruded upon and an unrefined effusiveness shown.

"I just feel as if she was beginning not to care about us at all, Betty," she said. "I couldn't have believed it of Rosy. She was always such an affectionate girl."

"I don't believe it now," replied Betty sharply. "Rosy couldn't grow hateful and stuck up. It's that nasty Nigel I know it is."

Sir Nigel's intention was that there should be as little intercourse between Fifth Avenue and Stornham Court as was possible. Among other things, he did not intend that a lot of American relations should come tumbling in when they chose to cross the Atlantic. He would not have it, and took discreet steps to prevent any accident of the sort. He wrote to America occasionally himself, and knowing well how to make himself civilly repellent, so subtly chilled his parents-in-law as to discourage in them more than once their half-formed plan of paying a visit to their child in her new home. He opened, read and reclosed all epistles to and from New York, and while Mrs. Vanderpoel was much hurt to find that Rosalie never condescended to make any response to her tentatives concerning her possible visit, Rosalie herself was mystified by the fact that the journey "to Europe" was never spoken of.

"I don't see why they never seem to think of coming over," she said plaintively one day. "They used to talk so much about it."

"They?" ejaculated the Dowager Lady Anstruthers. "Whom may you mean?"

"Mother and father and Betty and some of the others."

Her mother-in-law put up her eye-glasses to stare at her.

"The whole family?" she inquired.

"There are not so many of them," Rosalie answered.

"A family is always too many to descend upon a young woman when she is married," observed her ladyship unmovedly. Nigel glanced over the top of his Times.

"I may as well tell you that it would not do at all," he put in.

"Why—why not?" exclaimed Rosalie, aghast.

"Americans don't do in English society," slightingly.

"But they are coming over so much. They like London so—all Americans like London."

"Do they?" with a drawl which made Rosalie blush until the tears started to her eyes. "I am afraid the sentiment is scarcely mutual."

Rosalie turned and fled from the room. She turned and fled because she realised that she should burst out crying if she waited to hear another word, and she realised that of late she seemed always to be bursting out crying before one or the other of those two. She could not help it. They always seemed to be implying something slighting or scathing. They were always putting her in the wrong and hurting her feelings.

The day was damp and chill, but she put on her hat and ran out into the park. She went down the avenue and turned into a coppice. There, among the wet bracken, she sank down on the mossy trunk of a fallen tree and huddled herself in a small heap, her head on her arms, actually wailing.

"Oh, mother! Oh, mother!" she cried hysterically. "Oh, I do wish you would come. I'm so cold, mother; I'm so ill! I can't bear it! It seems as if you'd forgotten all about me! You're all so happy in New York that perhaps you have forgotten—perhaps you have! Oh, don't, mother—don't!"

It was a month later that through the vicar's wife she reached a discovery and a climax. She had heard one morning from this lady of a misfortune which had befallen a small farmer. It was a misfortune which was an actual catastrophe to a man in his position. His house had caught fire during a gale of wind and the fire had spread to the outbuildings and rickyard and swept away all his belongings, his house, his furniture, his hayricks, and stored grain, and even his few cows and horses. He had been a poor, hard-working fellow, and his small insurance had lapsed the day before the fire. He was absolutely ruined, and with his wife and six children stood face to face with beggary and starvation.

Rosalie Anstruthers entered the vicarage to find the poor woman who was his companion in calamity sobbing in the hall. A child of a few weeks was in her arms, and two small creatures clung crying to her skirts.

"We've worked hard," she wept; "we have, ma'am. Father, he's always been steady, an' up early an' late. P'r'aps it's the Lord's 'and, as you say, ma'am, but we've been decent people an' never missed church when we could 'elp it—father didn't deserve it—that he didn't."

She was heartbroken in her downtrodden hopelessness. Rosalie literally quaked with sympathy. She poured forth her pity in such words as the poor woman had never heard spoken by a great lady to a humble creature like herself. The villagers found the new Lady Anstruthers' interviews with them curiously simple and suggestive of an equality they could not understand. Stornham was a conservative old village, where the distinction between the gentry and the peasants was clearly marked. The cottagers were puzzled by Sir Nigel's wife, but they decided that she was kind, if unusual.

As Rosalie talked to the farmer's wife she longed for her father's presence. She had remembered a time when a man in his employ had lost his all by fire, the small house he had just made his last payment upon having been burned to the ground. He had lost one of his children in the fire, and the details had been heartrending. The entire Vanderpoel household had wept on hearing them, and Mr. Vanderpoel had drawn a cheque which had seemed like a fortune to the sufferer. A new house had been bought, and Mrs. Vanderpoel and her daughters and friends had bestowed furniture and clothing enough to make the family comfortable to the verge of luxury.

"See, you poor thing," said Rosalie, glowing with memories of this incident, her homesick young soul comforted by the mere likeness in the two calamities. "I brought my cheque book with me because I meant to help you. A man worked for my father had his house burned, just as yours was, and my father made everything all right for him again. I'll make it all right for you; I'll make you a cheque for a hundred pounds now, and then when your husband begins to build I'll give him some more."

The woman gasped for breath and turned pale. She was frightened. It really seemed as if her ladyship must have lost her wits a little. She could not mean this. The vicaress turned pale also.

"Lady Anstruthers," she said, "Lady Anstruthers, it—it is too much. Sir Nigel——"

"Too much!" exclaimed Rosalie. "They have lost everything, you know; their hayricks and cattle as well as their house; I guess it won't be half enough."

Mrs. Brent dragged her into the vicar's study and talked to her. She tried to explain that in English villages such things were not done in a manner so casual, as if they were the mere result of unconsidered feeling, as if they were quite natural things, such as any human person might do. When Rosalie cried: "But why not—why not? They ought to be." Mrs. Brent could not seem to make herself quite clear. Rosalie only gathered in a bewildered way that there ought to be more ceremony, more deliberation, more holding off, before a person of rank indulged in such munificence. The recipient ought to be made to feel it more, to understand fully what a great thing was being done.

"They will think you will do anything for them."

"So I will," said young Lady Anstruthers, "if I have the money when they are in such awful trouble. Suppose we lost everything in the world and there were people who could easily help us and wouldn't?"

"You and Sir Nigel—that is quite different," said Mrs. Brent. "I am afraid that if you do not discuss the matter and ask advice from your husband and mother-in-law they will be very much offended."

"If I were doing it with their money they would have the right to be," replied Rosalie, with entire ingenuousness. "I wouldn't presume to do such a thing as that. That wouldn't be right, of course."

"They will be angry with me," said the vicaress awkwardly. This queer, silly girl, who seemed to see nothing in the right light, frequently made her feel awkward. Mrs. Brent told her husband that she appeared to have no sense of dignity or proper appreciation of her position.

The wife of the farmer, John Wilson, carried away the cheque, quite stunned. She was breathless with amazement and turned rather faint with excitement, bewilderment and her sense of relief. She had to sit down in the vicarage kitchen for a few minutes and drink a glass of the thin vicarage beer.

Rosalie promised that she would discuss the matter and ask advice when she returned to the Court. Just as she left the house Mrs. Brent suddenly remembered something she had forgotten.

"The Wilson trouble completely drove it out of my mind," she said. "It was a stupid mistake of the postboy's. He left a letter of yours among mine when he came this morning. It was most careless. I shall speak to his father about it. It might have been important that you should receive it early."

When she saw the letter Rosalie uttered an exclamation. It was addressed in her father's handwriting.

"Oh!" she cried. "It's from father! And the postmark is Havre. What does it mean?"

She was so excited that she almost forgot to express her thanks. Her heart leaped up in her throat. Could they have come over from America—could they? Why was it written from Havre? Could they be near her?

She walked along the road choked with ecstatic, laughing sobs. Her hand shook so that she could scarcely tear open the envelope; she tore a corner of the letter, and when the sheet was spread open her eyes were full of wild, delighted tears, which made it impossible for her to see for the moment. But she swept the tears away and read this:

DEAR DAUGHTER:

It seems as if we had had pretty bad luck in not seeing you. We had counted on it very much, and your mother feels it all the more because she is weak after her illness. We don't quite understand why you did not seem to know about her having had diphtheria in Paris. You did not answer Betty's letter. Perhaps it missed you in some way. Things do sometimes go wrong in the mail, and several times your mother has thought a letter has been lost. She thought so because you seemed to forget to refer to things. We came over to leave Betty at a French school and we had expected to visit you later. But your mother fell ill of diphtheria and not hearing from you seemed to make her homesick, so we decided to return to New York by the next steamer. I ran over to London, however, to make some inquiries about you, and on the first day I arrived I met your husband in Bond Street. He at once explained to me that you had gone to a house party at some castle in Scotland, and said you were well and enjoying yourself very much, and he was on his way to join you. I am sorry, daughter, that it has turned out that we could not see each other. It seems a long time since you left us. But I am very glad, however, that you are so well and really like English life. If we had time for it I am sure it would be delightful. Your mother sends her love and wants very much to hear of all you are doing and enjoying. Hoping that we may have better luck the next time we cross—

Your affectionate father,
REUBEN L. VANDERPOEL.

Rosalie found herself running breathlessly up the avenue. She was clutching the letter still in her hand, and staggering from side to side. Now and then she uttered horrible little short cries, like an animal's. She ran and ran, seeing nothing, and now and then with the clenched hand in which the letter was crushed striking a sharp blow at her breast.

She stumbled up the big stone steps she had mounted on the day she was brought home as a bride. Her dress caught her feet and she fell on her knees and scrambled up again, gasping; she dashed across the huge dark hall, and, hurling herself against the door of the morning room, appeared, dishevelled, haggard-eyed, and with scarlet patches on her wild, white face, before the Dowager, who started angrily to her feet:

"Where is Nigel? Where is Nigel?" she cried out frenziedly.

"What in heaven's name do you mean by such manners?" demanded her ladyship. "Apologise at once!"

"Where is Nigel? Nigel! Nigel!" the girl raved. "I will see him—I will—I will see him!"

She who had been the mildest of sweet-tempered creatures all her life had suddenly gone almost insane with heartbroken, hysteric grief and rage. She did not know what she was saying and doing; she only realised in an agony of despair that she was a thing caught in a trap; that these people had her in their power, and that they had tricked and lied to her and kept her apart from what her girl's heart so cried out to and longed for. Her father, her mother, her little sister; they had been near her and had been lied to and sent away.

"You are quite mad, you violent, uncontrolled creature!" cried the Dowager furiously. "You ought to be put in a straitjacket and drenched with cold water."

Then the door opened again and Nigel strode in. He was in riding dress and was breathless and livid with anger. He was in a nice mood to confront a wife on the verge of screaming hysterics. After a bad half hour with his steward, who had been talking of impending disasters, he had heard by chance of Wilson's conflagration and the hundred-pound cheque. He had galloped home at the top of his horse's speed.

"Here is your wife raving mad," cried out his mother.

Rosalie staggered across the room to him. She held up her hand clenching the letter and shook it at him.

"My mother and father have been here," she shrieked. My mother has been ill. They wanted to come to see me. You knew and you kept it from me. You told my father lies—lies—hideous lies! You said I was away in Scotland—enjoying myself—when I was here and dying with homesickness. You made them think I did not care for them—or for New York! You have killed me! Why did you do such a wicked thing!

He looked at her with glaring eyes. If a man born a gentleman is ever in the mood to kick his wife to death, as costermongers do, he was in that mood. He had lost control over himself as completely as she had, and while she was only a desperate, hysteric girl, he was a violent man.

"I did it because I did not mean to have them here," he said. "I did it because I won't have them here."

"They shall come," she quavered shrilly in her wildness. "They shall come to see me. They are my own father and mother, and I will have them."

He caught her arm in such a grip that she must have thought he would break it, if she could have thought or felt anything.

"No, you will not have them," he ground forth between his teeth. "You will do as I order you and learn to behave yourself as a decent married woman should. You will learn to obey your husband and respect his wishes and control your devilish American temper."

"They have gone—gone!" wailed Rosalie. "You sent them away! My father, my mother, my sister!"

"Stop your indecent ravings!" ordered Sir Nigel, shaking her. "I will not submit to be disgraced before the servants."

"Put your hand over her mouth, Nigel," cried his mother. "The very scullery maids will hear."

She was as infuriated as her son. And, indeed, to behold civilised human beings in the state of uncontrolled violence these three had reached was a sight to shudder at.

"I won't stop," cried the girl. "Why did you take me away from everything— I was quite happy. Everybody was kind to me. I loved people, I had everything. No one ever—ever—ever ill-used anyone——"

Sir Nigel clutched her arm more brutally still and shook her with absolute violence. Her hair broke loose and fell about her awful little distorted, sobbing face.

"I did not take you to give you an opportunity to display your vulgar ostentation by throwing away hundred-pound cheques to villagers," he said. "I didn't take you to give you the position of a lady and be made a fool of by you."

"You have ruined him," burst forth his mother. "You have put it out of his power to marry an Englishwoman who would have known it was her duty to give something in return for his name and protection."

Her ladyship had begun to rave also, and as mother and son were of equal violence when they had ceased to control themselves, Rosalie began to find herself enlightened unsparingly. She and her people were vulgar sharpers. They had trapped a gentleman into a low American marriage and had not the decency to pay for what they had got. If she had been an Englishwoman, well born, and of decent breeding, all her fortune would have been properly transferred to her husband and he would have had the dispensing of it. Her husband would have been in the position to control her expenditure and see that she did not make a fool of herself. As it was she was the derision of all decent people, of all people who had been properly brought up and knew what was in good taste and of good morality.

First it was the Dowager who poured forth, and then it was Sir Nigel. They broke in on each other, they interrupted one another with exclamations and interpolations. They had so far lost themselves that they did not know they became grotesque in the violence of their fury. Rosalie's brain whirled. Her hysteria mounted and mounted. She stared first at one and then at the other, gasping and sobbing by turns; she swayed on her feet and clutched at a chair.

"I did not know," she broke forth at last, trying to make her voice heard in the storm. "I never understood. I knew something made you hate me, but I didn't know you were angry about money." She laughed tremulously and wildly. "I would have given it to you—father would have given you some—if you had been good to me." The laugh became hysterical beyond her management. Peal after peal broke from her, she shook all over with her ghastly merriment, sobbing at one and the same time.

"Oh! oh! oh!" she shrieked. "You see, I thought you were so aristocratic. I wouldn't have dared to think of such a thing. I thought an English gentleman— an English gentleman—oh! oh! to think it was all because I did not give you money—just common dollars and cents that—that I daren't offer to a decent American who could work for himself."

Sir Nigel sprang at her. He struck her with his open hand upon the cheek, and as she reeled she held up her small, feverish, shaking hand, laughing more wildly than before.

"You ought not to strike me," she cried. "You oughtn't! You don't know how valuable I am. Perhaps——" with a little, crazy scream—"perhaps I might have a son."

She fell in a shuddering heap, and as she dropped she struck heavily against the protruding end of an oak chest and lay upon the floor, her arms flung out and limp, as if she were a dead thing.

CHAPTER V

ON BOTH SIDES OF THE ATLANTIC

In the course of twelve years the Shuttle had woven steadily and—its movements lubricated by time and custom—with increasing rapidity. Threads of commerce it caught up and shot to and fro, with threads of literature and art, threads of life drawn from one shore to the other and back again, until they were bound in the fabric of its weaving. Coldness there had been between both lands, broad divergence of taste and thought, argument across seas, sometimes resentment, but the web in Fate's hands broadened and strengthened and held fast. Coldness faintly warmed despite itself, taste and thought drawn into nearer contact, reflecting upon their divergences, grew into tolerance and the knowledge that the diverging, seen more clearly, was not so broad; argument coming within speaking distance reasoned itself to logical and practical conclusions. Problems which had stirred anger began to find solutions. Books, in the first place, did perhaps more than all else. Cheap, pirated editions of English works, much quarrelled over by authors and publishers, being scattered over the land, brought before American eyes soft, home-like pictures of places which were, after all was said and done, the homes of those who read of them, at least in the sense of having been the birthplaces of fathers or grandfathers. Some subtle, far-reaching power of nature caused a stirring of the blood, a vague, unexpressed yearning and lingering over pages which depicted sweet, green lanes, broad acres rich with centuries of nourishment and care; grey church towers, red roofs, and village children playing before cottage doors. None of these things were new to those who pondered over them, kinsmen had dwelt on memories of them in their fireside talk, and their children had seen them in fancy and in dreams. Old grievances having had time to fade away and take on less poignant colour, the stirring of the blood stirred also imaginations, and wakened something akin to homesickness, though no man called the feeling by its name. And this, perhaps, was the strongest cord the Shuttle wove and was the true meaning of its power. Being drawn by it, Americans in increasing numbers turned their faces towards the older land. Gradually it was discovered that it was the simplest affair in the world to drive down to the wharves and take a steamer which landed one, after a more or less interesting voyage, in Liverpool, or at some other convenient port. From there one went to London, or Paris, or Rome; in fact, whithersoever one's fancy guided, but first or last it always led the traveller to the treading of green, velvet English turf. And once standing on such velvet, both men and women, looking about them, felt, despite themselves, the strange old thrill which some of them half resented and some warmly loved.

In the course of twelve years, a length of time which will transform a little girl wearing a short frock into a young woman wearing a long one, the pace of life and the ordering of society may become so altered as to appear amazing when one finds time to reflect on the subject. But one does not often find time.

Changes occur so gradually that one scarcely observes them, or so swiftly that they take the form of a kind of amazed shock which one gets over as quickly as one experiences it and realises that its cause is already a fixed fact.

In the United States of America, which have not yet acquired the serene sense of conservative self-satisfaction and repose which centuries of age may bestow, the spirit of life itself is the aspiration for change. Ambition itself only means the insistence on change. Each day is to be better than yesterday fuller of plans, of briskness, of initiative. Each to-day demands of to-morrow new men, new minds, new work. A to-day which has not launched new ships, explored new countries, constructed new buildings, added stories to old ones, may consider itself a failure, unworthy even of being consigned to the limbo of respectable yesterdays. Such a country lives by leaps and bounds, and the ten years which followed the marriage of Reuben Vanderpoel's eldest daughter made many such bounds and leaps. They were years which initiated and established international social relations in a manner which caused them to incorporate themselves with the history of both countries. As America discovered Europe, that continent discovered America. American beauties began to appear in English drawing-rooms and Continental salons. They were presented at court and commented upon in the Row and the Bois. Their little transatlantic tricks of speech and their mots were repeated with gusto. It became understood that they were amusing and amazing. Americans "came in" as the heroes and heroines of novels and stories. Punch delighted in them vastly. Shopkeepers and hotel proprietors stocked, furnished, and provisioned for them. They spent money enormously and were singularly indifferent (at the outset) under imposition. They "came over" in a manner as epoch-making, though less war-like than that of William the Conqueror.

International marriages ceased to be a novelty. As Bettina Vanderpoel grew up, she grew up, so to speak, in the midst of them. She saw her country, its people, its newspapers, its literature, innocently rejoiced by the alliances its charming young women contracted with foreign rank. She saw it affectionately, gleefully, rubbing its hands over its duchesses, its countesses, its miladies. The American Eagle spread its wings and flapped them sometimes a trifle, over this new but so natural and inevitable triumph of its virgins. It was of course only "American" that such things should happen. America ruled the universe, and its women ruled America, bullying it a little, prettily, perhaps. What could be more a matter of course than that American women, being aided by adoring fathers, brothers and husbands, sumptuously to ship themselves to other lands, should begin to rule these lands also? Betty, in her growing up, heard all this intimated. At twelve years old, though she had detested Rosalie's marriage, she had rather liked to hear people talk of the picturesqueness of places like Stornham Court, and of the life led by women of rank in their houses in town and country. Such talk nearly always involved the description of things and people, whose colour and tone had only reached her through the medium of books, most frequently fiction.

She was, however, of an unusually observing mind, even as a child, and the time came when she realised that the national bird spread its wings less proudly when the subject of international matches was touched upon, and even at such times showed signs of restlessness. Now and then things had not turned out as they appeared to promise; two or three seemingly brilliant unions had resulted in disaster. She had not understood all the details the newspapers cheerfully provided, but it was clear to her that more than one previously envied young woman had had practical reasons for discovering that she had made an astonishingly bad bargain. This being the case, she used frequently to ponder over the case of Rosy—Rosy! who had been swept away from them and swallowed up, as it seemed, by that other and older world. She was in certain ways a silent child, and no one but herself knew how little she had forgotten Rosy, how often she pondered over her, how sometimes she had lain awake in the night and puzzled out lines of argument concerning her and things which might be true.

The one grief of poor Mrs. Vanderpoel's life had been the apparent estrangement of her eldest child. After her first six months in England Lady Anstruthers' letters had become fewer and farther between, and had given so little information connected with herself that affectionate curiosity became discouraged. Sir Nigel's brief and rare epistles revealed so little desire for any relationship with his wife's family that gradually Rosy's image seemed to fade into far distance and become fainter with the passing of each month. It seemed almost an incredible thing, when they allowed themselves to think of it, but no member of the family had ever been to Stornham Court. Two or three efforts to arrange a visit had been made, but on each occasion had failed through some apparently accidental cause. Once Lady Anstruthers had been away, once a letter had seemingly failed to reach her, once her children had had scarlet fever and the orders of the physicians in attendance had been stringent in regard to visitors, even relatives who did not fear contagion.

"If she had been living in New York and her children had been ill I should have been with her all the time," poor Mrs. Vanderpoel had said with tears. "Rosy's changed awfully, somehow. Her letters don't sound a bit like she used to be. It seems as if she just doesn't care to see her mother and father."

Betty had frowned a good deal and thought intensely in secret. She did not believe that Rosy was ashamed of her relations. She remembered, however, it is true, that Clara Newell (who had been a schoolmate) had become very super-fine and indifferent to her family after her marriage to an aristocratic and learned German. Hers had been one of the successful alliances, and after living a few years in Berlin she had quite looked down upon New Yorkers, and had made herself exceedingly unpopular during her one brief visit to her relatives. She seemed to think her father and mother undignified and uncultivated, and she disapproved entirely of her sisters dress and bearing. She said that they had no distinction of manner and that all their interests were frivolous and unenlightened.

"But Clara always was a conceited girl," thought Betty. "She was always patronising people, and Rosy was only pretty and sweet. She always said herself that she had no brains. But she had a heart."

After the lapse of a few years there had been no further discussion of plans for visiting Stornham. Rosalie had become so remote as to appear almost unreachable. She had been presented at Court, she had had three children, the Dowager Lady Anstruthers had died. Once she had written to her father to ask for a large sum of money, which he had sent to her, because she seemed to want it very much. She required it to pay off certain debts on the estate and spoke touchingly of her boy who would inherit.

"He is a delicate boy, father," she wrote, "and I don't want the estate to come to him burdened."

When she received the money she wrote gratefully of the generosity shown her, but she spoke very vaguely of the prospect of their seeing each other in the future. It was as if she felt her own remoteness even more than they felt it themselves.

In the meantime Bettina had been taken to France and placed at school there. The resulting experience was an enlightening one, far more illuminating to the quick-witted American child than it would have been to an English, French, or German one, who would not have had so much to learn, and probably would not have been so quick at the learning.

Betty Vanderpoel knew nothing which was not American, and only vaguely a few things which were not of New York. She had lived in Fifth Avenue, attended school in a numbered street near her own home, played in and been driven round Central Park. She had spent the hot months of the summer in places up the Hudson, or on Long Island, and such resorts of pleasure. She had believed implicitly in all she saw and knew. She had been surrounded by wealth and decent good nature throughout her existence, and had enjoyed her life far too much to admit of any doubt that America was the most perfect country in the world, Americans the cleverest and most amusing people, and that other nations were a little out of it, and consequently sufficiently scant of resource to render pity without condemnation a natural sentiment in connection with one's occasional thoughts of them.

But hers was a mentality by no means ordinary. Inheritance in her nature had combined with circumstances, as it has a habit of doing in all human beings. But in her case the combinations were unusual and produced a result somewhat remarkable. The quality of brains which, in the first Reuben Vanderpoel had expressed itself in the marvellously successful planning and carrying to their ends of commercial and financial schemes, the absolute genius of penetration and calculation of the sordid and uneducated little trader in skins and barterer of goods, having filtered through two generations of gradual education and refinement of existence, which was no longer that of the mere trader, had been transformed in the great-granddaughter into keen, clear sight, level-headed perceptiveness and a logical sense of values. As the first Reuben had known by instinct the values of pelts and lands, Bettina knew by instinct the values of qualities, of brains, of hearts, of circumstances, and the incidents which affect them. She was as unaware of the significance of her great possession as were those around her. Nevertheless it was an unerring thing. As a mere child, unformed and uneducated by life, she had not been one of the small creatures to be deceived or flattered.

"She's an awfully smart little thing, that Betty," her New York aunts and cousins often remarked. "She seems to see what people mean, it doesn't matter what they say. She likes people you would not expect her to like, and then again she sometimes doesn't care the least for people who are thought awfully attractive."

As has been already intimated, the child was crude enough and not particularly well bred, but her small brain had always been at work, and each day of her life recorded for her valuable impressions. The page of her young mind had ceased to be a blank much earlier than is usual.

The comparing of these impressions with such as she received when her life in the French school was new afforded her active mental exercise.

She began with natural, secret indignation and rebellion. There was no other American pupil in the establishment besides herself. But for the fact that the name of Vanderpoel represented wealth so enormous as to amount to a sort of rank in itself, Bettina would not have been received. The proprietress of the institution had gravely disquieting doubts of the propriety of America. Her pupils were not accustomed to freedom of opinions and customs. An American child might either consciously or unconsciously introduce them. As this must be guarded against, Betty's first few months at the school were not agreeable to her. She was supervised and expurgated, as it were. Special Sisters were told off to converse and walk with her, and she soon perceived that conversations were not only French lessons in disguise, but were lectures on ethics, morals, and good manners, imperfectly concealed by the mask and domino of amiable entertainment. She translated into English after the following manner the facts her swift young perceptions gathered. There were things it was so inelegant to say that only the most impossible persons said them; there were things it was so inexcusable to do that when done their inexcusability assumed the proportions of a crime. There were movements, expressions, points of view, which one must avoid as one would avoid the plague. And they were all things, acts, expressions, attitudes of mind which Bettina had been familiar with from her infancy, and which she was well aware were considered almost entirely harmless and unobjectionable in New York, in her beloved New York, which was the centre of the world, which was bigger, richer, gayer, more admirable than any other city known upon the earth.

If she had not so loved it, if she had ever dreamed of the existence of any other place as being absolutely necessary, she would not have felt the thing so bitterly. But it seemed to her that all these amiable diatribes in exquisite French were directed at her New York, and it must be admitted that she was humiliated and enraged. It was a personal, indeed, a family matter. Her father, her mother, her relatives, and friends were all in some degree exactly the kind of persons whose speech, habits, and opinions she must conscientiously avoid. But for the instinct of summing up values, circumstances, and intentions, it is probable that she would have lost her head, let loose her temper and her tongue, and have become insubordinate. But the quickness of perception which had revealed practical potentialities to old Reuben Vanderpoel, revealed to her the value of French which was perfectly fluent, a voice which was musical, movements which were grace, manners which had a still beauty, and comparing these things with others less charming she listened and restrained herself, learning, marking, and inwardly digesting with a cleverness most enviable.

Among her fellow pensionnaires she met with discomforting illuminations, which were fine discipline also, though if she herself had been a less intellectual creature they might have been embittering. Without doubt Betty, even at twelve years, was intellectual. Hers was the practical working intellect which begins duty at birth and does not lay down its tools because the sun sets. The little and big girls who wrote their exercises at her side did not deliberately enlighten her, but she learned from them in vague ways that it was not New York which was the centre of the earth, but Paris, or Berlin, Madrid, London, or Rome. Paris and London were perhaps more calmly positive of themselves than other capitals, and were a little inclined to smile at the lack of seriousness in other claims. But one strange fact was more predominant than any other, and this was that New York was not counted as a civilised centre at all; it had no particular existence. Nobody expressed this rudely; in fact, it did not acquire the form of actual statement at any time. It was merely revealed by amiable and ingenuous unconsciousness of the circumstance that such a part of the world expected to be regarded or referred to at all. Betty began early to realise that as her companions did not talk of Timbuctoo or Zanzibar, so they did not talk of New York. Stockholm or Amsterdam seemed, despite their smallness, to be considered. No one denied the presence of Zanzibar on the map, but as it conveyed nothing more than the impression of being a mere geographical fact, there was no reason why one should dwell on it in conversation. Remembering all she had left behind, the crowded streets, the brilliant shop windows, the buzz of individual people, there were moments when Betty ground her strong little teeth. She wanted to express all these things, to call out, to explain, and command recognition for them. But her cleverness showed to her that argument or protestation would be useless. She could not make such hearers understand. There were girls whose interest in America was founded on their impression that magnificent Indian chieftains in blankets and feathers stalked about the streets of the towns, and that Betty's own thick black hair had been handed down to her by some beautiful Minnehaha or Pocahontas. When first she was approached by timid, tentative questionings revealing this point of view, Betty felt hot and answered with unamiable curtness. No, there were no red Indians in New York. There had been no red Indians in her family. She had neither grandmothers nor aunts who were squaws, if they meant that.

She felt so scornfully, so disgustedly indignant at their benighted ignorance, that she knew she behaved very well in saying so little in reply. She could have said so much, but whatsoever she had said would have conveyed nothing to them, so she thought it all out alone. She went over the whole ground and little realised how much she was teaching herself as she turned and tossed in her narrow, spotlessly white bed at night, arguing, comparing, drawing deductions from what she knew and did not know of the two continents. Her childish anger, combining itself with the practical, alert brain of Reuben Vanderpoel the first, developed in her a logical reasoning power which led her to arrive at many an excellent and curiously mature conclusion. The result was finely educational. All the more so that in her fevered desire for justification of the things she loved, she began to read books such as little girls do not usually take interest in. She found some difficulty in obtaining them at first, but a letter or two written to her father obtained for her permission to read what she chose. The third Reuben Vanderpoel was deeply fond of his younger daughter, and felt in secret a profound admiration for her, which was saved from becoming too obvious by the ever present American sense of humour.

"Betty seems to be going in for politics," he said after reading the letter containing her request and her first list of books. "She's about as mad as she can be at the ignorance of the French girls about America and Americans. She wants to fill up on solid facts, so that she can come out strong in argument. She's got an understanding of the power of solid facts that would be a fortune to her if she were a man."

It was no doubt her understanding of the power of facts which led her to learn everything well and to develop in many directions. She began to dip into political and historical volumes because she was furious, and wished to be able to refute idiocy, but she found herself continuing to read because she was interested in a way she had not expected. She began to see things. Once she made a remark which was prophetic. She made it in answer to a guileless observation concerning the gold mines with which Boston was supposed to be enriched.

"You don't know anything about America, you others," she said. "But you WILL know!"

"Do you think it will become the fashion to travel in America?" asked a German girl.

"Perhaps," said Betty. "But—it isn't so much that you will go to America. I believe it will come to you. It's like that—America. It doesn't stand still. It goes and gets what it wants."

She laughed as she ended, and so did the other girls. But in ten years' time, when they were young women, some of them married, some of them court beauties, one of them recalled this speech to another, whom she encountered in an important house in St. Petersburg, the wife of the celebrated diplomat who was its owner being an American woman.

Bettina Vanderpoel's education was a rather fine thing. She herself had more to do with it than girls usually have to do with their own training. In a few months' time those in authority in the French school found that it was not necessary to supervise and expurgate her. She learned with an interested rapacity which was at once unusual and amazing. And she evidently did not learn from books alone. Her voice, as an organ, had been musical and full from babyhood. It began to modulate itself and to express things most voices are incapable of expressing. She had been so built by nature that the carriage of her head and limbs was good to behold. She acquired a harmony of movement which caused her to lose no shade of grace and spirit. Her eyes were full of thought, of speculation, and intentness.

"She thinks a great deal for one so young," was said of her frequently by one or the other of her teachers. One finally went further and added, "She has genius."

This was true. She had genius, but it was not specialised. It was not genius which expressed itself through any one art. It was a genius for life, for living herself, for aiding others to live, for vivifying mere existence. She herself was, however, aware only of an eagerness of temperament, a passion for seeing, doing, and gaining knowledge. Everything interested her, everybody was suggestive and more or less enlightening.

Her relatives thought her original in her fancies. They called them fancies because she was so young. Fortunately for her, there was no reason why she should not be gratified. Most girls preferred to spend their holidays on the Continent. She elected to return to America every alternate year. She enjoyed the voyage and she liked the entire change of atmosphere and people.

"It makes me like both places more," she said to her father when she was thirteen. "It makes me see things."

Her father discovered that she saw everything. She was the pleasure of his life. He was attracted greatly by the interest she exhibited in all orders of things. He saw her make bold, ingenuous plunges into all waters, without any apparent consciousness that the scraps of knowledge she brought to the surface were unusual possessions for a schoolgirl. She had young views on the politics and commerce of different countries, as she had views on their literature. When Reuben Vanderpoel swooped across the American continent on journeys of thousands of miles, taking her as a companion, he discovered that he actually placed a sort of confidence in her summing up of men and schemes. He took her to see mines and railroads and those who worked them, and he talked them over with her afterward, half with a sense of humour, half with a sense of finding comfort in her intelligent comprehension of all he said.

She enjoyed herself immensely and gained a strong picturesqueness of character. After an American holiday she used to return to France, Germany, or Italy, with a renewed zest of feeling for all things romantic and antique. After a few years in the French convent she asked that she might be sent to Germany.

"I am gradually changing into a French girl," she wrote to her father. "One morning I found I was thinking it would be nice to go into a convent, and another day I almost entirely agreed with one of the girls who was declaiming against her brother who had fallen in love with a Californian. You had better take me away and send me to Germany."

Reuben Vanderpoel laughed. He understood Betty much better than most of her relations did. He knew when seriousness underlay her jests and his respect for her seriousness was great. He sent her to school in Germany. During the early years of her schooldays Betty had observed that America appeared upon the whole to be regarded by her schoolfellows principally as a place to which the more unfortunate among the peasantry emigrated as steerage passengers when things could become no worse for them in their own country. The United States was not mentally detached from any other portion of the huge Western Continent. Quite well-educated persons spoke casually of individuals having "gone to America," as if there were no particular difference between Brazil and Massachusetts.

"I wonder if you ever saw my cousin Gaston," a French girl once asked her as they sat at their desks. "He became very poor through ill living. He was quite without money and he went to America."

"To New York?" inquired Bettina.

"I am not sure. The town is called Concepcion."

"That is not in the United States," Betty answered disdainfully. "It is in Chili."

She dragged her atlas towards her and found the place.

"See," she said. "It is thousands of miles from New York." Her companion was a near-sighted, rather slow girl. She peered at the map, drawing a line with her finger from New York to Concepcion.

"Yes, they are at a great distance from one another," she admitted, "but they are both in America."

"But not both in the United States," cried Betty. "French girls always seem to think that North and South America are the same, that they are both the United States."

"Yes," said the slow girl with deliberation. "We do make odd mistakes sometimes." To which she added with entire innocence of any ironic intention. "But you Americans, you seem to feel the United States, your New York, to be all America."

Betty started a little and flushed. During a few minutes of rapid reflection she sat bolt upright at her desk and looked straight before her. Her mentality was of the order which is capable of making discoveries concerning itself as well as concerning others. She had never thought of this view of the matter before, but it was quite true. To passionate young patriots such as herself at least, that portion of the map covered by the United States was America. She suddenly saw also that to her New York had been America. Fifth Avenue Broadway, Central Park, even Tiffany's had been "America." She laughed and reddened a shade as she put the atlas aside having recorded a new idea. She had found out that it was not only Europeans who were local, which was a discovery of some importance to her fervid youth.

Because she thought so often of Rosalie, her attention was, during the passing years, naturally attracted by the many things she heard of such marriages as were made by Americans with men of other countries than their own. She discovered that notwithstanding certain commercial views of matrimony, all foreigners who united themselves with American heiresses were not the entire brutes primitive prejudice might lead one to imagine. There were rather one-sided alliances which proved themselves far from happy. The Cousin Gaston, for instance, brought home a bride whose fortune rebuilt and refurnished his dilapidated chateau and who ended by making of him a well-behaved and cheery country gentleman not at all to be despised in his amiable, if light-minded good nature and good spirits. His wife, fortunately, was not a young woman who yearned for sentiment. She was a nice-tempered, practical American girl, who adored French country life and knew how to amuse and manage her husband. It was a genial sort of menage and yet though this was an undeniable fact, Bettina observed that when the union was spoken of it was always referred to with a certain tone which conveyed that though one did not exactly complain of its having been undesirable, it was not quite what Gaston might have expected. His wife had money and was good-natured, but there were limitations to one's appreciation of a marriage in which husband and wife were not on the same plane.

"She is an excellent person, and it has been good for Gaston," said Bettina's friend. "We like her, but she is not—she is not——" She paused there, evidently seeing that the remark was unlucky. Bettina, who was still in short frocks, took her up.

"What is she not?" she asked.

"Ah!—it is difficult to explain—to Americans. It is really not exactly a fault. But she is not of his world."

"But if he does not like that," said Bettina coolly, "why did he let her buy him and pay for him?"

It was young and brutal, but there were times when the business perspicuity of the first Reuben Vanderpoel, combining with the fiery, wounded spirit of his young descendant, rendered Bettina brutal. She saw certain unadorned facts with unsparing young eyes and wanted to state them. After her frocks were lengthened, she learned how to state them with more fineness of phrase, but even then she was sometimes still rather unsparing.

In this case her companion, who was not fiery of temperament, only coloured slightly.

"It was not quite that," she answered. "Gaston really is fond of her. She amuses him, and he says she is far cleverer than he is."

But there were unions less satisfactory, and Bettina had opportunities to reflect upon these also. The English and Continental papers did not give enthusiastic, detailed descriptions of the marriages New York journals dwelt upon with such delight. They were passed over with a paragraph. When Betty heard them spoken of in France, Germany or Italy, she observed that they were not, as a rule, spoken of respectfully. It seemed to her that the bridegrooms were, in conversation, treated by their equals with scant respect. It appeared that there had always been some extremely practical reason for the passion which had led them to the altar. One generally gathered that they or their estates were very much out at elbow, and frequently their characters were not considered admirable by their relatives and acquaintances. Some had been rather cold shouldered in certain capitals on account of embarrassing little, or big, stories. Some had spent their patrimonies in riotous living. Those who had merely begun by coming into impoverished estates, and had later attenuated their resources by comparatively decent follies, were of the more desirable order. By the time she was nineteen, Bettina had felt the blood surge in her veins more than once when she heard some comments on alliances over which she had seen her compatriots glow with affectionate delight.

"It was time Ludlow married some girl with money," she heard said of one such union. "He had been playing the fool ever since he came into the estate. Horses and a lot of stupid women. He had come some awful croppers during the last ten years. Good-enough looking girl, they tell me—the American he has married—tremendous lot of money. Couldn't have picked it up on this side. English young women of fortune are not looking for that kind of thing. Poor old Billy wasn't good enough."

Bettina told the story to her father when they next met. She had grown into a tall young creature by this time. Her low, full voice was like a bell and was capable of ringing forth some fine, mellow tones of irony.

"And in America we are pleased," she said, "and flatter ourselves that we are receiving the proper tribute of adoration of our American wit and beauty. We plume ourselves on our conquests."

"No, Betty," said her father, and his reflective deliberation had meaning. "There are a lot of us who don't plume ourselves particularly in these days. We are not as innocent as we were when this sort of thing began. We are not as innocent as we were when Rosy was married." And he sighed and rubbed his forehead with the handle of his pen. "Not as innocent as we were when Rosy was married," he repeated.

Bettina went to him and slid her fine young arm round his neck. It was a long, slim, round arm with a wonderful power to caress in its curves. She kissed Vanderpoel's lined cheek.

"Have you had time to think much about Rosy?" she said.

"I've not had time, but I've done it," he answered. "Anything that hurts your mother hurts me. Sometimes she begins to cry in her sleep, and when I wake her she tells me she has been dreaming that she has seen Rosy."

"I have had time to think of her," said Bettina. "I have heard so much of these things. I was at school in Germany when Annie Butterfield and Baron von Steindahl were married. I heard it talked about there, and then my mother sent me some American papers."

She laughed a little, and for a moment her laugh did not sound like a girl's.

"Well, it's turned out badly enough," her father commented. "The papers had plenty to say about it later. There wasn't much he was too good to do to his wife, apparently."

"There was nothing too bad for him to do before he had a wife," said Bettina. "He was black. It was an insolence that he should have dared to speak to Annie Butterfield. Somebody ought to have beaten him."

"He beat her instead."

"Yes, and I think his family thought it quite natural. They said that she was so vulgar and American that she exasperated Frederick beyond endurance. She was not geboren, that was it." She laughed her severe little laugh again. "Perhaps we shall get tired in time," she added. "I think we are learning. If it is made a matter of business quite open and aboveboard, it will be fair. You know, father, you always said that I was businesslike."

There was interested curiosity in Vanderpoel's steady look at her. There were times when he felt that Betty's summing up of things was well worth listening to. He saw that now she was in one of her moods when it would pay one to hear her out. She held her chin up a little, and her face took on a fine stillness at once sweet and unrelenting. She was very good to look at in such moments.

"Yes," he answered, "you have a particularly level head for a girl."

"Well," she went on. "What I see is that these things are not business, and they ought to be. If a man comes to a rich American girl and says, 'I and my title are for sale. Will you buy us?' If the girl is—is that kind of a girl and wants that kind of man, she can look them both over and say, 'Yes, I will buy you,' and it can be arranged. He will not return the money if he is unsatisfactory, but she cannot complain that she has been deceived. She can only complain of that when he pretends that he asks her to marry him because he wants her for his wife, because he would want her for his wife if she were as poor as himself. Let it be understood that he is property for sale, let her make sure that he is the kind of property she wants to buy. Then, if, when they are married, he is brutal or impudent, or his people are brutal or impudent, she can say, 'I will forfeit the purchase money, but I will not forfeit myself. I will not stay with you.'"

"They would not like to hear you say that, Betty," said her father, rubbing his chin reflectively.

"No," she answered. "Neither the girl nor the man would like it, and it is their business, not mine. But it is practical and would prevent silly mistakes. It would prevent the girls being laughed at. It is when they are flattered by the choice made of them that they are laughed at. No one can sneer at a man or woman for buying what they think they want, and throwing it aside if it turns out a bad bargain."

She had seated herself near her father. She rested her elbow slightly on the table and her chin in the hollow of her hand. She was a beautiful young creature. She had a soft curving mouth, and a soft curving cheek which was warm rose. Taken in conjunction with those young charms, her next words had an air of incongruity.

"You think I am hard," she said. "When I think of these things I am hard—as hard as nails. That is an Americanism, but it is a good expression. I am angry for America. If we are sordid and undignified, let us get what we pay for and make the others acknowledge that we have paid."

She did not smile, nor did her father. Mr. Vanderpoel, on the contrary, sighed. He had a dreary suspicion that Rosy, at least, had not received what she had paid for, and he knew she had not been in the least aware that she had paid or that she was expected to do so. Several times during the last few years he had thought that if he had not been so hard worked, if he had had time, he would have seriously investigated the case of Rosy. But who is not aware that the profession of multimillionaire does not allow of any swerving from duty or of any interests requiring leisure?

"I wonder, Betty," he said quite deliberately, "if you know how handsome you are?"

"Yes," answered Bettina. "I think so. And I am tall. It is the fashion to be tall now. It was Early Victorian to be little. The Queen brought in the 'dear little woman,' and now the type has gone out."

"They will come to look at you pretty soon," said Vanderpoel. "What shall you say then?"

"I?" said Bettina, and her voice sounded particularly low and mellow. "I have a little monomania, father. Some people have a monomania for one thing and some for another. Mine is for NOT taking a bargain from the ducal remnant counter."

CHAPTER VI

AN UNFAIR ENDOWMENT

To Bettina Vanderpoel had been given, to an extraordinary extent, the extraordinary thing which is called beauty—which is a thing entirely set apart from mere good looks or prettiness. This thing is extraordinary because, if statistics were taken, the result would probably be the discovery that not three human beings in a million really possess it. That it should be bestowed at all— since it is so rare—seems as unfair a thing as appears to the mere mortal mind the bestowal of unbounded wealth, since it quite as inevitably places the life of its owner upon an abnormal plane. There are millions of pretty women, and billions of personable men, but the man or woman of entire physical beauty may cross one's pathway only once in a lifetime—or not at all. In the latter case it is natural to doubt the absolute truth of the rumours that the thing exists. The abnormal creature seems a mere freak of nature and may chance to be angel, criminal, total insipidity, virago or enchanter, but let such an one enter a room or appear in the street, and heads must turn, eyes light and follow, souls yearn or envy, or sink under the discouragement of comparison. With the complete harmony and perfect balance of the singular thing, it would be folly for the rest of the world to compete. A human being who had lived in poverty for half a lifetime, might, if suddenly endowed with limitless fortune, retain, to a certain extent, balance of mind; but the same creature having lived the same number of years a wholly unlovely thing, suddenly awakening to the possession of entire physical beauty, might find the strain upon pure sanity greater and the balance less easy to preserve. The relief from the conscious or unconscious tension bred by the sense of imperfection, the calm surety of the fearlessness of meeting in any eye a look not lighted by pleasure, would be less normal than the knowledge that no wish need remain unfulfilled, no fancy ungratified. Even at sixteen Betty was a long-limbed young nymph whose small head, set high on a fine slim column of throat, might well have been crowned with the garland of some goddess of health and the joy of life. She was light and swift, and being a creature of long lines and tender curves, there was pleasure in the mere seeing her move. The cut of her spirited lip, and delicate nostril, made for a profile at which one turned to look more than once, despite one's self. Her hair was soft and black and repeated its colour in the extravagant lashes of her childhood, which made mysterious the changeful dense blue of her eyes. They were eyes with laughter in them and pride, and a suggestion of many deep things yet unstirred. She was rather unusually tall, and her body had the suppleness of a young bamboo. The deep corners of her red mouth curled generously, and the chin, melting into the fine line of the lovely throat, was at once strong and soft and lovely. She was a creature of harmony, warm richness of colour, and brilliantly alluring life.

When her school days were over she returned to New York and gave herself into her mother's hands. Her mother's kindness of heart and sweet-tempered lovingness were touching things to Bettina. In the midst of her millions Mrs. Vanderpoel was wholly unworldly. Bettina knew that she felt a perpetual homesickness when she allowed herself to think of the daughter who seemed lost to her, and the girl's realisation of this caused her to wish to be especially affectionate and amenable. She was glad that she was tall and beautiful, not merely because such physical gifts added to the colour and agreeableness of life, but because hers gave comfort and happiness to her mother. To Mrs. Vanderpoel, to introduce to the world the loveliest debutante of many years was to be launched into a new future. To concern one's self about her exquisite wardrobe was to have an enlivening occupation. To see her surrounded, to watch eyes as they followed her, to hear her praised, was to feel something of the happiness she had known in those younger days when New York had been less advanced in its news and methods, and slim little blonde Rosalie had come out in white tulle and waltzed like a fairy with a hundred partners.

"I wonder what Rosy looks like now," the poor woman said involuntarily one day. Bettina was not a fairy. When her mother uttered her exclamation Bettina was on the point of going out, and as she stood near her, wrapped in splendid furs, she had the air of a Russian princess.

"She could not have worn the things you do, Betty," said the affectionate maternal creature. "She was such a little, slight thing. But she was very pretty. I wonder if twelve years have changed her much?"

Betty turned towards her rather suddenly.

"Mother," she said, "sometime, before very long, I am going to see."

"To see!" exclaimed Mrs. Vanderpoel. "To see Rosy!"

"Yes," Betty answered. "I have a plan. I have never told you of it, but I have been thinking over it ever since I was fifteen years old."

She went to her mother and kissed her. She wore a becoming but resolute expression.

"We will not talk about it now," she said. "There are some things I must find out."

When she had left the room, which she did almost immediately, Mrs. Vanderpoel sat down and cried. She nearly always shed a few tears when anyone touched upon the subject of Rosy. On her desk were some photographs. One was of Rosy as a little girl with long hair, one was of Lady Anstruthers in her wedding dress, and one was of Sir Nigel.

"I never felt as if I quite liked him," she said, looking at this last, "but I suppose she does, or she would not be so happy that she could forget her mother and sister."

There was another picture she looked at. Rosalie had sent it with the letter she wrote to her father after he had forwarded the money she asked for. It was a little study in water colours of the head of her boy. It was nothing but a head, the shoulders being fancifully draped, but the face was a peculiar one. It was over-mature, and unlovely, but for a mouth at once pathetic and sweet.

"He is not a pretty child," sighed Mrs. Vanderpoel. "I should have thought Rosy would have had pretty babies. Ughtred is more like his father than his mother."

She spoke to her husband later, of what Betty had said.

"What do you think she has in her mind, Reuben?" she asked.

"What Betty has in her mind is usually good sense," was his response. "She will begin to talk to me about it presently. I shall not ask questions yet. She is probably thinking: things over."

She was, in truth, thinking things over, as she had been doing for some time. She had asked questions on several occasions of English people she had met abroad. But a schoolgirl cannot ask many questions, and though she had once met someone who knew Sir Nigel Anstruthers, it was a person who did not know him well, for the reason that she had not desired to increase her slight acquaintance. This lady was the aunt of one of Bettina's fellow pupils, and she was not aware of the girl's relationship to Sir Nigel. What Betty gathered was that her brother-in-law was regarded as a decidedly bad lot, that since his marriage to some American girl he had seemed to have money which he spent in riotous living, and that the wife, who was said to be a silly creature, was kept in the country, either because her husband did not want her in London, or because she preferred to stay at Stornham. About the wife no one appeared to know anything, in fact.

"She is rather a fool, I believe, and Sir Nigel Anstruthers is the kind of man a simpleton would be obliged to submit to," Bettina had heard the lady say.

Her own reflections upon these comments had led her through various paths of thought. She could recall Rosalie's girlhood, and what she herself, as an unconsciously observing child, had known of her character. She remembered the simple impressionability of her mind. She had been the most amenable little creature in the world. Her yielding amiability could always be counted upon as a factor by the calculating; sweet-tempered to weakness, she could be beguiled or distressed into any course the desires of others dictated. An ill-tempered or self-pitying person could alter any line of conduct she herself wished to pursue.

"She was neither clever nor strong-minded," Betty said to herself. "A man like Sir Nigel Anstruthers could make what he chose of her. I wonder what he has done to her?"

Of one thing she thought she was sure. This was that Rosalie's aloofness from her family was the result of his design.

She comprehended, in her maturer years, the dislike of her childhood. She remembered a certain look in his face which she had detested. She had not known then that it was the look of a rather clever brute, who was malignant, but she knew now.

"He used to hate us all," she said to herself. "He did not mean to know us when he had taken Rosalie away, and he did not intend that she should know us."

She had heard rumours of cases somewhat parallel, cases in which girls' lives had become swamped in those of their husbands, and their husbands' families.

And she had also heard unpleasant details of the means employed to reach the desired results. Annie Butterfield's husband had forbidden her to correspond with her American relatives. He had argued that such correspondence was disturbing to her mind, and to the domestic duties which should be every decent woman's religion. One of the occasions of his beating her had been in consequence of his finding her writing to her mother a letter blotted with tears. Husbands frequently objected to their wives' relatives, but there was a special order of European husband who opposed violently any intimacy with American relations on the practical ground that their views of a wife's position, with regard to her husband, were of a revolutionary nature.

Mrs. Vanderpoel had in her possession every letter Rosalie or her husband had ever written. Bettina asked to be allowed to read them, and one morning seated herself in her own room before a blazing fire, with the collection on a table at her side. She read them in order. Nigel's began as they went on. They were all in one tone, formal, uninteresting, and requiring no answers. There was not a suggestion of human feeling in one of them.

"He wrote them," said Betty, "so that we could not say that he had never written."

Rosalie's first epistles were affectionate, but timid. At the outset she was evidently trying to conceal the fact that she was homesick. Gradually she became briefer and more constrained. In one she said pathetically, "I am such a bad letter writer. I always feel as if I want to tear up what I have written, because I never say half that is in my heart." Mrs. Vanderpoel had kissed that letter many a time. She was sure that a mark on the paper near this particular sentence was where a tear had fallen. Bettina was sure of this, too, and sat and looked at the fire for some time.

That night she went to a ball, and when she returned home, she persuaded her mother to go to bed.

"I want to have a talk with father," she exclaimed. "I am going to ask him something."

She went to the great man's private room, where he sat at work, even after the hours when less seriously engaged people come home from balls. The room he sat in was one of the apartments newspapers had with much detail described. It was luxuriously comfortable, and its effect was sober and rich and fine.

When Bettina came in, Vanderpoel, looking up to smile at her in welcome, was struck by the fact that as a background to an entering figure of tall, splendid girlhood in a ball dress it was admirable, throwing up all its whiteness and grace and sweep of line. He was always glad to see Betty. The rich strength of the life radiating from her, the reality and glow of her were good for him and had the power of detaching him from work of which he was tired.

She smiled back at him, and, coming forward took her place in a big armchair close to him, her lace-frilled cloak slipping from her shoulders with a soft rustling sound which seemed to convey her intention to stay.

"Are you too busy to be interrupted?" she asked, her mellow voice caressing him. "I want to talk to you about something I am going to do." She put out her hand and laid it on his with a clinging firmness which meant strong feeling. "At least, I am going to do it if you will help me," she ended.

"What is it, Betty?" he inquired, his usual interest in her accentuated by her manner.

She laid her other hand on his and he clasped both with his own.

"When the Worthingtons sail for England next month," she explained, "I want to go with them. Mrs. Worthington is very kind and will be good enough to take care of me until I reach London."

Mr. Vanderpoel moved slightly in his chair. Then their eyes met comprehendingly. He saw what hers held.

"From there you are going to Stornham Court!" he exclaimed.

"To see Rosy," she answered, leaning a little forward. "To SEE her.

"You believe that what has happened has not been her fault?" he said. There was a look in her face which warmed his blood.

"I have always been sure that Nigel Anstruthers arranged it."

"Do you think he has been unkind to her?"

"I am going to see," she answered.

"Betty," he said, "tell me all about it."

He knew that this was no suddenly-formed plan, and he knew it would be well worth while to hear the details of its growth. It was so interestingly like her to have remained silent through the process of thinking a thing out, evolving her final idea without having disturbed him by bringing to him any chaotic uncertainties.

"It's a sort of confession," she answered. "Father, I have been thinking about it for years. I said nothing because for so long I knew I was only a child, and a child's judgment might be worth so little. But through all those years I was learning things and gathering evidence. When I was at school, first in one country and then another, I used to tell myself that I was growing up and preparing myself to do a particular thing—to go to rescue Rosy."

"I used to guess you thought of her in a way of your own," Vanderpoel said, "but I did not guess you were thinking that much. You were always a solid, loyal little thing, and there was business capacity in your keeping your scheme to yourself. Let us look the matter in the face. Suppose she does not need rescuing. Suppose, after all, she is a comfortable, fine lady and adores her husband. What then?"

"If I should find that to be true, I will behave myself very well—as if we had expected nothing else. I will make her a short visit and come away. Lady Cecilia Orme, whom I knew in Florence, has asked me to stay with her in London. I will go to her. She is a charming woman. But I must first see Rosy—SEE her."

Mr. Vanderpoel thought the matter over during a few moments of silence.

"You do not wish your mother to go with you?" he said presently.

"I believe it will be better that she should not," she answered. "If there are difficulties or disappointments she would be too unhappy."

"Yes," he said slowly, "and she could not control her feelings. She would give the whole thing away, poor girl."

He had been looking at the carpet reflectively, and now he looked at Bettina.

"What are you expecting to find, at the worst?" he asked her. "The kind of thing which will need management while it is being looked into?"

"I do not know what I am expecting to find," was her reply. "We know absolutely nothing; but that Rosy was fond of us, and that her marriage has seemed to make her cease to care. She was not like that; she was not like that! Was she, father?"

"No, she wasn't," he exclaimed. The memory of her in her short-frocked and early girlish days, a pretty, smiling, effusive thing, given to lavish caresses and affectionate little surprises for them all, came back to him vividly. "She was the most affectionate girl I ever knew," he said. "She was more affectionate than you, Betty," with a smile.

Bettina smiled in return and bent her head to put a kiss on his hand, a warm, lovely, comprehending kiss.

"If she had been different I should not have thought so much of the change," she said. "I believe that people are always more or less LIKE themselves as long as they live. What has seemed to happen has been so unlike Rosy that there must be some reason for it."

"You think that she has been prevented from seeing us?"

"I think it so possible that I am not going to announce my visit beforehand."

"You have a good head, Betty," her father said.

"If Sir Nigel has put obstacles in our way before, he will do it again. I shall try to find out, when I reach London, if Rosalie is at Stornham. When I am sure she is there, I shall go and present myself. If Sir Nigel meets me at the park gates and orders his gamekeepers to drive me off the premises, we shall at least know that he has some reason for not wishing to regard the usual social and domestic amenities. I feel rather like a detective. It entertains me and excites me a little."

The deep blue of her eyes shone under the shadow of the extravagant lashes as she laughed.

"Are you willing that I should go, father?" she said next.

"Yes," he answered. "I am willing to trust you, Betty, to do things I would not trust other girls to try at. If you were not my girl at all, if you were a man on Wall Street, I should know you would be pretty safe to come out a little more than even in any venture you made. You know how to keep cool."

Bettina picked up her fallen cloak and laid it over her arm. It was made of billowy frills of Malines lace, such as only Vanderpoels could buy. She looked down at the amazing thing and touched up the frills with her fingers as she whimsically smiled.

"There are a good many girls who can be trusted to do things in these days," she said. "Women have found out so much. Perhaps it is because the heroines of novels have informed them. Heroines and heroes always bring in the new fashions in character. I believe it is years since a heroine 'burst into a flood of tears.' It has been discovered, really, that nothing is to be gained by it. Whatsoever I find at Stornham Court, I shall neither weep nor be helpless. There is the Atlantic cable, you know. Perhaps that is one of the reasons why heroines have changed. When they could not escape from their persecutors except in a stage coach, and could not send telegrams, they were more or less in everyone's hands. It is different now. Thank you, father, you are very good to believe in me."

CHAPTER VII

ON BOARD THE "MERIDIANA"

A large transatlantic steamer lying at the wharf on a brilliant, sunny morning just before its departure is an interesting and suggestive object to those who are fond of following suggestion to its end. One sometimes wonders if it is possible that the excitement in the dock atmosphere could ever become a thing to which one was sufficiently accustomed to be able to regard it as among things commonplace. The rumbling and rattling of waggons and carts, the loading and unloading of boxes and bales, the people who are late, and the people who are early, the faces which are excited, and the faces which are sad, the trunks and bales, and cranes which creak and groan, the shouts and cries, the hurry and confusion of movement, notwithstanding that every day has seen them all for years, have a sort of perennial interest to the looker-on.

This is, perhaps, more especially the case when the looker-on is to be a passenger on the outgoing ship; and the exhilaration of his point of view may greatly depend upon the reason for his voyage and the class by which he travels. Gaiety and youth usually appear upon the promenade deck, having taken saloon passage. Dulness, commerce, and eld mingling with them, it is true, but with a discretion which does not seem to dominate. Second-class passengers wear a more practical aspect, and youth among them is rarer and more grave. People who must travel second and third class make voyages for utilitarian reasons. Their object is usually to better themselves in one way or another. When they are going from Liverpool to New York, it is usually to enter upon new efforts and new labours. When they are returning from New York to Liverpool, it is often because the new life has proved less to be depended upon than the old, and they are bearing back with them bitterness of soul and discouragement of spirit.

On the brilliant spring morning when the huge liner Meridiana was to sail for England a young man, who was a second-class passenger, leaned upon the ship's rail and watched the turmoil on the wharf with a detached and not at all buoyant air.

His air was detached because he had other things in his mind than those merely passing before him, and he was not buoyant because they were not cheerful or encouraging subjects for reflection. He was a big young man, well hung together, and carrying himself well; his face was square-jawed and rugged, and he had dark red hair restrained by its close cut from waving strongly on his forehead. His eyes were red brown, and a few dark freckles marked his clear skin. He was of the order of man one looks at twice, having looked at him once, though one does not in the least know why, unless one finally reaches some degree of intimacy.

He watched the vehicles, heavy and light, roll into the big shed-like building and deposit their freight; he heard the voices and caught the sentences of instruction and comment; he saw boxes and bales hauled from the dock side to the deck and swung below with the rattling of machinery and chains. But these formed merely a noisy background to his mood, which was self-centred and gloomy. He was one of those who go back to their native land knowing themselves conquered. He had left England two years before, feeling obstinately determined to accomplish a certain difficult thing, but forces of nature combining with the circumstances of previous education and living had beaten him. He had lost two years and all the money he had ventured. He was going back to the place he had come from, and he was carrying with him a sense of having been used hardly by fortune, and in a way he had not deserved.

He had gone out to the West with the intention of working hard and using his hands as well as his brains; he had not been squeamish; he had, in fact, laboured like a ploughman; and to be obliged to give in had been galling and bitter. There are human beings into whose consciousness of themselves the possibility of being beaten does not enter. This man was one of them.

The ship was of the huge and luxuriously-fitted class by which the rich and fortunate are transported from one continent to another. Passengers could indulge themselves in suites of rooms and live sumptuously. As the man leaning on the rail looked on, he saw messengers bearing baskets and boxes of fruit and flowers with cards and notes attached, hurrying up the gangway to deliver them to waiting stewards. These were the farewell offerings to be placed in staterooms, or to await their owners on the saloon tables. Salter—the second-class passenger's name was Salter—had seen a few such offerings before on the first crossing. But there had not been such lavishness at Liverpool. It was the New Yorkers who were sumptuous in such matters, as he had been told. He had also heard casually that the passenger list on this voyage was to record important names, the names of multi-millionaire people who were going over for the London season.

Two stewards talking near him, earlier in the morning, had been exulting over the probable largesse such a list would result in at the end of the passage.

"The Worthingtons and the Hirams and the John William Spayters," said one. "They travel all right. They know what they want and they want a good deal, and they're willing to pay for it."

"Yes. They're not school teachers going over to improve their minds and contriving to cross in a big ship by economising in everything else. Miss Vanderpoel's sailing with the Worthingtons. She's got the best suite all to herself. She'll bring back a duke or one of those prince fellows. How many millions has Vanderpoel?"

"How many millions. How many hundred millions!" said his companion, gloating cheerfully over the vastness of unknown possibilities. "I've crossed with Miss Vanderpoel often, two or three times when she was in short frocks. She's the kind of girl you read about. And she's got money enough to buy in half a dozen princes."

"There are New Yorkers who won't like it if she does," returned the other. "There's been too much money going out of the country. Her suite is crammed full of Jack roses, now, and there are boxes waiting outside."

Salter moved away and heard no more. He moved away, in fact, because he was conscious that to a man in his case, this dwelling upon millions, this plethora of wealth, was a little revolting. He had walked down Broadway and seen the price of Jacqueminot roses, and he was not soothed or allured at this particular moment by the picture of a girl whose half-dozen cabins were crowded with them.

"Oh, the devil!" he said. "It sounds vulgar." And he walked up and down fast, squaring his shoulders, with his hands in the pockets of his rough, well-worn coat. He had seen in England something of the American young woman with millionaire relatives. He had been scarcely more than a boy when the American flood first began to rise. He had been old enough, however, to hear people talk. As he had grown older, Salter had observed its advance. Englishmen had married American beauties. American fortunes had built up English houses, which otherwise threatened to fall into decay. Then the American faculty of adaptability came into play. Anglo-American wives became sometimes more English than their husbands. They proceeded to Anglicise their relations, their relations' clothes, even, in time, their speech. They carried or sent English conventions to the States, their brothers ordered their clothes from West End tailors, their sisters began to wear walking dresses, to play out-of-door games and take active exercise. Their mothers tentatively took houses in London or Paris, there came a period when their fathers or uncles, serious or anxious business men, the most unsporting of human beings, rented castles or manors with huge moors and covers attached and entertained large parties of shooters or fishers who could be lured to any quarter by the promise of the particular form of slaughter for which they burned.

"Sheer American business perspicacity, that," said Salter, as he marched up and down, thinking of a particular case of this order. "There's something admirable in the practical way they make for what they want. They want to amalgamate with English people, not for their own sake, but because their women like it, and so they offer the men thousands of acres full of things to kill. They can get them by paying for them, and they know how to pay." He laughed a little, lifting his square shoulders. "Balthamor's six thousand acres of grouse moor and Elsty's salmon fishing are rented by the Chicago man. He doesn't care twopence for them, and does not know a pheasant from a caper-cailzie, but his wife wants to know men who do."

It must be confessed that Salter was of the English who were not pleased with the American Invasion. In some of his views of the matter he was a little prehistoric and savage, but the modern side of his character was too intelligent to lack reason. He was by no means entirely modern, however; a large part of his nature belonged to the age in which men had fought fiercely for what they wanted to get or keep, and when the amenities of commerce had not become powerful factors in existence.

"They're not a bad lot," he was thinking at this moment. "They are rather fine in a way. They are clever and powerful and interesting—more so than they know themselves. But it is all commerce. They don't come and fight with us and get possession of us by force. They come and buy us. They buy our land and our homes, and our landowners, for that matter—when they don't buy them, they send their women to marry them, confound it!"

He took half a dozen more strides and lifted his shoulders again.

"Beggarly lot as I am," he said, "unlikely as it seems that I can marry at all, I'm hanged if I don't marry an Englishwoman, if I give my life to a woman at all."

But, in fact, he was of the opinion that he should never give his life to any woman, and this was because he was, at this period, also of the opinion that there was small prospect of its ever being worth the giving or taking. It had been one of those lives which begin untowardly and are ruled by unfair circumstances.

He had a particularly well-cut and expressive mouth, and, as he went back to the ship's side and leaned on his folded arms on the rail again, its curves concealed a good deal of strong feeling.

The wharf was busier than before. In less than half an hour the ship was to sail. The bustle and confusion had increased. There were people hurrying about looking for friends, and there were people scribbling off excited farewell messages at the telegraph office. The situation was working up to its climax. An observing looker-on might catch glimpses of emotional scenes. Many of the passengers were already on board, parties of them accompanied by their friends were making their way up the gangplank.

Salter had just been watching a luxuriously cared-for little invalid woman being carried on deck in a reclining chair, when his attention was attracted by the sound of trampling hoofs and rolling wheels. Two noticeably big and smart carriages had driven up to the stopping-place for vehicles. They were gorgeously of the latest mode, and their tall, satin-skinned horses jangled silver chains and stepped up to their noses.

"Here come the Worthingtons, whosoever they may be," thought Salter. "The fine up-standing young woman is, no doubt, the multi-millionairess."

The fine, up-standing young woman WAS the multi-millionairess. Bettina walked up the gangway in the sunshine, and the passengers upon the upper deck craned their necks to look at her. Her carriage of her head and shoulders invariably made people turn to look.

"My, ain't she fine-looking!" exclaimed an excited lady beholder above. "I guess that must be Miss Vanderpoel, the multi-millionaire's daughter. Jane told me she'd heard she was crossing this trip."

Bettina heard her. She sometimes wondered if she was ever pointed out, if her name was ever mentioned without the addition of the explanatory statement that she was the multi-millionaire's daughter. As a child she had thought it ridiculous and tiresome, as she had grown older she had felt that only a remarkable individuality could surmount a fact so ever present.

It was like a tremendous quality which overshadowed everything else.

"It wounds my vanity, I have no doubt," she had said to her father. "Nobody ever sees me, they only see you and your millions and millions of dollars."

Salter watched her pass up the gangway. The phase through which he was living was not of the order which leads a man to dwell upon the beautiful and inspiriting as expressed by the female image. Success and the hopefulness which engender warmth of soul and quickness of heart are required for the development of such allurements. He thought of the Vanderpoel millions as the lady on the deck had thought of them, and in his mind somehow the girl herself appeared to express them. The rich up-springing sweep of her abundant hair, her height, her colouring, the remarkable shade and length of her lashes, the full curve of her mouth, all, he told himself, looked expensive, as if even nature herself had been given carte blanche, and the best possible articles procured for the money.

"She moves," he thought sardonically, "as if she were perfectly aware that she could pay for anything. An unlimited income, no doubt, establishes in the owner the equivalent to a sense of rank."

He changed his position for one in which he could command a view of the promenade deck where the arriving passengers were gradually appearing. He did this from the idle and careless curiosity which, though it is not a matter of absolute interest, does not object to being entertained by passing objects. He saw the Worthington party reappear. It struck Salter that they looked not so much like persons coming on board a ship, as like people who were returning to a hotel to which they were accustomed, and which was also accustomed to them. He argued that they had probably crossed the Atlantic innumerable times in this particular steamer. The deck stewards knew them and made obeisance with empressement. Miss Vanderpoel nodded to the steward Salter had heard discussing her. She gave him a smile of recognition and paused a moment to speak to him. Salter saw her sweep the deck with her glance and then designate a sequestered corner, such as the experienced voyager would recognise as being desirably sheltered. She was evidently giving an order concerning the placing of her deck chair, which was presently brought. An elegantly neat and decorous person in black, who was evidently her maid, appeared later, followed by a steward who carried cushions and sumptuous fur rugs. These being arranged, a delightful corner was left alluringly prepared. Miss Vanderpoel, after her instructions to the deck steward, had joined her party and seemed to be awaiting some arrival anxiously.

"She knows how to do herself well," Salter commented, "and she realises that forethought is a practical factor. Millions have been productive of composure. It is not unnatural, either."

It was but a short time later that the warning bell was rung. Stewards passed through the crowds calling out, "All ashore, if you please—all ashore." Final embraces were in order on all sides. People shook hands with fervour and laughed a little nervously. Women kissed each other and poured forth hurried messages to be delivered on the other side of the Atlantic. Having kissed and parted, some of them rushed back and indulged in little clutches again. Notwithstanding that the tide of humanity surges across the Atlantic almost as regularly as the daily tide surges in on its shores, a wave of emotion sweeps through every ship at such partings.

Salter stood on deck and watched the crowd dispersing. Some of the people were laughing and some had red eyes. Groups collected on the wharf and tried to say still more last words to their friends crowding against the rail.

The Worthingtons kept their places and were still looking out, by this time disappointedly. It seemed that the friend or friends they expected were not coming. Salter saw that Miss Vanderpoel looked more disappointed than the rest. She leaned forward and strained her eyes to see. Just at the last moment there was the sound of trampling horses and rolling wheels again. From the arriving carriage descended hastily an elderly woman, who lifted out a little boy excited almost to tears. He was a dear, chubby little person in flapping sailor trousers, and he carried a splendidly-caparisoned toy donkey in his arms. Salter could not help feeling slightly excited himself as they rushed forward. He wondered if they were passengers who would be left behind.

They were not passengers, but the arrivals Miss Vanderpoel had been expecting so ardently. They had come to say good-bye to her and were too late for that, at least, as the gangway was just about to be withdrawn.

Miss Vanderpoel leaned forward with an amazingly fervid expression on her face.

"Tommy! Tommy!" she cried to the little boy. "Here I am, Tommy. We can say good-bye from here."

The little boy, looking up, broke into a wail of despair.

"Betty! Betty! Betty!" he cried. "I wanted to kiss you, Betty."

Betty held out her arms. She did it with entire forgetfulness of the existence of any lookers-on, and with such outreaching love on her face that it seemed as if the child must feel her touch. She made a beautiful, warm, consoling bud of her mouth.

"We'll kiss each other from here, Tommy," she said. "See, we can. Kiss me, and I will kiss you."

Tommy held out his arms and the magnificent donkey. "Betty," he cried, "I brought you my donkey. I wanted to give it to you for a present, because you liked it."

Miss Vanderpoel bent further forward and addressed the elderly woman.

"Matilda," she said, "please pack Master Tommy's present and send it to me! I want it very much."

Tender smiles irradiated the small face. The gangway was withdrawn, and, amid the familiar sounds of a big craft's first struggle, the ship began to move. Miss Vanderpoel still bent forward and held out her arms.

"I will soon come back, Tommy," she cried, "and we are always friends."

The child held out his short blue serge arms also, and Salter watching him could not but be touched for all his gloom of mind.

"I wanted to kiss you, Betty," he heard in farewell. "I did so want to kiss you."

And so they steamed away upon the blue.

CHAPTER VIII

THE SECOND-CLASS PASSENGER

Up to a certain point the voyage was like all other voyages. During the first two days there were passengers who did not appear on deck, but as the weather was fair for the season of the year, there were fewer absentees than is usual. Indeed, on the third day the deck chairs were all filled, people who were given to tramping during their voyages had begun to walk their customary quota of carefully-measured miles the day. There were a few pale faces dozing here and there, but the general aspect of things had begun to be sprightly. Shuffleboard players and quoit enthusiasts began to bestir themselves, the deck steward appeared regularly with light repasts of beef tea and biscuits, and the brilliant hues of red, blue, or yellow novels made frequent spots of colour upon the promenade. Persons of some initiative went to the length of making tentative observations to their next-chair neighbours. The second-cabin passengers were cheerful, and the steerage passengers, having tumbled up, formed friendly groups and began to joke with each other.

The Worthingtons had plainly the good fortune to be respectable sailors. They reappeared on the second day and established regular habits, after the manner of accustomed travellers. Miss Vanderpoel's habits were regular from the first, and when Salter saw her he was impressed even more at the outset with her air of being at home instead of on board ship. Her practically well-chosen corner was an agreeable place to look at. Her chair was built for ease of angle and width, her cushions were of dark rich colours, her travelling rugs were of black fox fur, and she owned an adjustable table for books and accompaniments. She appeared early in the morning and walked until the sea air crimsoned her cheeks, she sat and read with evident enjoyment, she talked to her companions and plainly entertained them.

Salter, being bored and in bad spirits, found himself watching her rather often, but he knew that but for the small, comic episode of Tommy, he would have definitely disliked her. The dislike would not have been fair, but it would have existed in spite of himself. It would not have been fair because it would have been founded simply upon the ignoble resentment of envy, upon the poor truth that he was not in the state of mind to avoid resenting the injustice of fate in bestowing multi-millions upon one person and his offspring. He resented his own resentment, but was obliged to acknowledge its existence in his humour. He himself, especially and peculiarly, had always known the bitterness of poverty, the humiliation of seeing where money could be well used, indeed, ought to be used, and at the same time having ground into him the fact that there was no money to lay one's hand on. He had hated it even as a boy, because in his case, and that of his people, the whole thing was undignified and unbecoming. It was humiliating to him now to bring home to himself the fact that the thing for which he was inclined to dislike this tall, up-standing girl was her unconscious (he realised the unconsciousness of it) air of having always lived in the atmosphere of millions, of never having known a reason why she should not have anything she had a desire for. Perhaps, upon the whole, he said to himself, it was his own ill luck and sense of defeat which made her corner, with its cushions and comforts, her properly attentive maid, and her cold weather sables expressive of a fortune too colossal to be decent.

The episode of the plump, despairing Tommy he had liked, however. There had been a fine naturalness about it and a fine practicalness in her prompt order to the elderly nurse that the richly-caparisoned donkey should be sent to her. This had at once made it clear to the donor that his gift was too valuable to be left behind.

"She did not care twopence for the lot of us," was his summing up. "She might have been nothing but the nicest possible warm-hearted nursemaid or a cottage woman who loved the child."

He was quite aware that though he had found himself more than once observing her, she herself had probably not recognised the trivial fact of his existing upon that other side of the barrier which separated the higher grade of passenger from the lower. There was, indeed, no reason why she should have singled him out for observation, and she was, in fact, too frequently absorbed in her own reflections to be in the frame of mind to remark her fellow passengers to the extent which was generally customary with her. During her crossings of the Atlantic she usually made mental observation of the people on board. This time, when she was not talking to the Worthingtons, or reading, she was thinking of the possibilities of her visit to Stornham. She used to walk about the deck thinking of them and, sitting in her chair, sum them up as her eyes rested on the rolling and breaking waves.

There were many things to be considered, and one of the first was the perfectly sane suggestion her father had made.

"Suppose she does not want to be rescued? Suppose you find her a comfortable fine lady who adores her husband."

Such a thing was possible, though Bettina did not think it probable. She intended, however, to prepare herself even for this. If she found Lady Anstruthers plump and roseate, pleased with herself and her position, she was quite equal to making her visit appear a casual and conventional affair.

"I ought to wish it to be so," she thought, "and, yet, how disappointingly I should feel she had changed. Still, even ethical reasons would not excuse one for wishing her to be miserable." She was a creature with a number of passionate ideals which warred frequently with the practical side of her mentality. Often she used to walk up and down the deck or lean upon the ship's side, her eyes stormy with emotions.

"I do not want to find Rosy a heartless woman, and I do not want to find her wretched. What do I want? Only the usual thing—that what cannot be undone had never been done. People are always wishing that."

She was standing near the second-cabin barrier thinking this, the first time she saw the passenger with the red hair. She had paused by mere chance, and while her eyes were stormy with her thought, she suddenly became conscious that she was looking directly into other eyes as darkling as her own. They were those of a man on the wrong side of the barrier. He had a troubled, brooding face, and, as their gaze met, each of them started slightly and turned away with the sense of having unconsciously intruded and having been intruded upon.

"That rough-looking man," she commented to herself, "is as anxious and disturbed as I am."

Salter did look rough, it was true. His well-worn clothes had suffered somewhat from the restrictions of a second-class cabin shared with two other men. But the aspect which had presented itself to her brief glance had been not so much roughness of clothing as of mood expressing itself in his countenance. He was thinking harshly and angrily of the life ahead of him.

These looks of theirs which had so inadvertently encountered each other were of that order which sometimes startles one when in passing a stranger one finds one's eyes entangled for a second in his or hers, as the case may be. At such times it seems for that instant difficult to disentangle one's gaze. But neither of these two thought of the other much, after hurrying away. Each was too fully mastered by personal mood.

There would, indeed, have been no reason for their encountering each other further but for "the accident," as it was called when spoken of afterwards, the accident which might so easily have been a catastrophe. It occurred that night. This was two nights before they were to land.

Everybody had begun to come under the influence of that cheerfulness of humour, the sense of relief bordering on gaiety, which generally elates people when a voyage is drawing to a close. If one has been dull, one begins to gather one's self together, rejoiced that the boredom is over. In any case, there are plans to be made, thought of, or discussed.

"You wish to go to Stornham at once?" Mrs. Worthington said to Bettina. "How pleased Lady Anstruthers and Sir Nigel must be at the idea of seeing you with them after so long."

"I can scarcely tell you how I am looking forward to it," Betty answered.

She sat in her corner among her cushions looking at the dark water which seemed to sweep past the ship, and listening to the throb of the engines. She was not gay. She was wondering how far the plans she had made would prove feasible. Mrs. Worthington was not aware that her visit to Stornham Court was to be unannounced. It had not been necessary to explain the matter. The whole affair was simple and decorous enough. Miss Vanderpoel was to bid good-bye to her friends and go at once to her sister, Lady Anstruthers, whose husband's country seat was but a short journey from London. Bettina and her father had arranged that the fact should be kept from the society paragraphist. This had required some adroit management, but had actually been accomplished.

As the waves swished past her, Bettina was saying to herself, "What will Rosy say when she sees me! What shall I say when I see Rosy? We are drawing nearer to each other with every wave that passes."

A fog which swept up suddenly sent them all below rather early. The Worthingtons laughed and talked a little in their staterooms, but presently became quiet and had evidently gone to bed. Bettina was restless and moved about her room alone after she had sent away her maid. She at last sat down and finished a letter she had been writing to her father.

"As I near the land," she wrote, "I feel a sort of excitement. Several times to-day I have recalled so distinctly the picture of Rosy as I saw her last, when we all stood crowded upon the wharf at New York to see her off. She and Nigel were leaning upon the rail of the upper deck. She looked such a delicate, airy little creature, quite like a pretty schoolgirl with tears in her eyes. She was laughing and crying at the same time, and kissing both her hands to us again and again. I was crying passionately myself, though I tried to conceal the fact, and I remember that each time I looked from Rosy to Nigel's heavy face the poignancy of my anguish made me break forth again. I wonder if it was because I was a child, that he looked such a contemptuous brute, even when he pretended to smile. It is twelve years since then. I wonder—how I wonder, what I shall find."

She stopped writing and sat a few moments, her chin upon her hand, thinking. Suddenly she sprang to her feet in alarm. The stillness of the night was broken by wild shouts, a running of feet outside, a tumult of mingled sounds and motion, a dash and rush of surging water, a strange thumping and straining of engines, and a moment later she was hurled from one side of her stateroom to the other by a crashing shock which seemed to heave the ship out of the sea, shuddering as if the end of all things had come.

It was so sudden and horrible a thing that, though she had only been flung upon a pile of rugs and cushions and was unhurt, she felt as if she had been struck on the head and plunged into wild delirium. Above the sound of the dashing and rocking waves, the straining and roaring of hacking engines and the pandemonium of voices rose from one end of the ship to the other, one wild, despairing, long-drawn shriek of women and children. Bettina turned sick at the mad terror in it—the insensate, awful horror.

"Something has run into us!" she gasped, getting up with her heart leaping in her throat.

She could hear the Worthingtons' tempest of terrified confusion through the partitions between them, and she remembered afterwards that in the space of two or three seconds, and in the midst of their clamour, a hundred incongruous thoughts leaped through her brain. Perhaps they were this moment going down. Now she knew what it was like! This thing she had read of in newspapers! Now she was going down in mid-ocean, she, Betty Vanderpoel! And, as she sprang to clutch her fur coat, there flashed before her mental vision a gruesome picture of the headlines in the newspapers and the inevitable reference to the millions she represented.

"I must keep calm," she heard herself say, as she fastened the long coat, clenching her teeth to keep them from chattering. "Poor Daddy—poor Daddy!"

Maddening new sounds were all about her, sounds of water dashing and churning, sounds of voices bellowing out commands, straining and leaping sounds of the engines. What was it—what was it? She must at least find out.

Everybody was going mad in the staterooms, the stewards were rushing about, trying to quiet people, their own voices shaking and breaking into cracked notes. If the worst had happened, everyone would be fighting for life in a few minutes. Out on deck she must get and find out for herself what the worst was.

She was the first woman outside, though the wails and shrieks swelled below, and half-dressed, ghastly creatures tumbled gasping up the companionway.

"What is it?" she heard. "My God! what's happened? Where's the Captain! Are we going down! The boats! The boats!"

It was useless to speak to the seamen rushing by. They did not see, much less hear! She caught sight of a man who could not be a sailor, since he was standing still. She made her way to him, thankful that she had managed to stop her teeth chattering.

"What has happened to us?" she said.

He turned and looked at her straitly. He was the second-cabin passenger with the red hair.

"A tramp steamer has run into us in the fog," he answered.

"How much harm is done?"

"They are trying to find out. I am standing here on the chance of hearing something. It is madness to ask any man questions."

They spoke to each other in short, sharp sentences, knowing there was no time to lose.

"Are you horribly frightened?" he asked.

She stamped her foot.

"I hate it—I hate it!" she said, flinging out her hand towards the black, heaving water. "The plunge—the choking! No one could hate it more. But I want to DO something!"

She was turning away when he caught her hand and held her.

"Wait a second," he said. "I hate it as much as you do, but I believe we two can keep our heads. Those who can do that may help, perhaps. Let us try to quiet the people. As soon as I find out anything I will come to your friends' stateroom. You are near the boats there. Then I shall go back to the second cabin. You work on your side and I'll work on mine. That's all."

"Thank you. Tell the Worthingtons. I'm going to the saloon deck." She was off as she spoke.

Upon the stairway she found herself in the midst of a struggling panic-stricken mob, tripping over each other on the steps, and clutching at any garment nearest, to drag themselves up as they fell, or were on the point of falling. Everyone was crying out in question and appeal.

Bettina stood still, a firm, tall obstacle, and clutched at the hysteric woman who was hurled against her.

"I've been on deck," she said. "A tramp steamer has run into us. No one has time to answer questions. The first thing to do is to put on warm clothes and secure the life belts in case you need them."

At once everyone turned upon her as if she was an authority. She replied with almost fierce determination to the torrent of words poured forth.

"I know nothing further—only that if one is not a fool one must make sure of clothes and belts."

"Quite right, Miss Vanderpoel," said one young man, touching his cap in nervous propitiation.

"Stop screaming," Betty said mercilessly to the woman. "It's idiotic—the more noise you make the less chance you have. How can men keep their wits among a mob of shrieking, mad women?"

That the remote Miss Vanderpoel should have emerged from her luxurious corner to frankly bully the lot of them was an excellent shock for the crowd. Men, who had been in danger of losing their heads and becoming as uncontrolled as the women, suddenly realised the fact and pulled themselves together. Bettina made her way at once to the Worthingtons' staterooms.

There she found frenzy reigning. Blanche and Marie Worthington were darting to and fro, dragging about first one thing and then another. They were silly with fright, and dashed at, and dropped alternately, life belts, shoes, jewel cases, and wraps, while they sobbed and cried out hysterically. "Oh, what shall we do with mother! What shall we do!"

The manners of Betty Vanderpoel's sharp schoolgirl days returned to her in full force. She seized Blanche by the shoulder and shook her.

"What a donkey you are!" she said. "Put on your clothes. There they are," pushing her to the place where they hung. "Marie—dress yourself this moment. We may be in no real danger at all."

"Do you think not! Oh, Betty!" they wailed in concert. "Oh, what shall we do with mother!"

"Where is your mother?"

"She fainted—Louise——"

Betty was in Mrs. Worthington's cabin before they had finished speaking. The poor woman had fainted, and struck her cheek against a chair. She lay on the floor in her nightgown, with blood trickling from a cut on her face. Her maid, Louise, was wringing her hands, and doing nothing whatever.

"If you don't bring the brandy this minute," said the beautiful Miss Vanderpoel, "I'll box your ears. Believe me, my girl." She looked so capable of doing it that the woman was startled and actually offended into a return of her senses. Miss Vanderpoel had usually the best possible manners in dealing with her inferiors.

Betty poured brandy down Mrs. Worthington's throat and applied strong smelling salts until she gasped back to consciousness. She had just burst into frightened sobs, when Betty heard confusion and exclamations in the adjoining room. Blanche and Marie had cried out, and a man's voice was speaking. Betty went to them. They were in various stages of undress, and the red-haired second-cabin passenger was standing at the door.

"I promised Miss Vanderpoel——" he was saying, when Betty came forward. He turned to her promptly.

"I come to tell you that it seems absolutely to be relied on that there is no immediate danger. The tramp is more injured than we are."

"Oh, are you sure? Are you sure?" panted Blanche, catching at his sleeve.

"Yes," he answered. "Can I do anything for you?" he said to Bettina, who was on the point of speaking.

"Will you be good enough to help me to assist Mrs. Worthington into her berth, and then try to find the doctor."

He went into the next room without speaking. To Mrs. Worthington he spoke briefly a few words of reassurance. He was a powerful man, and laid her on her berth without dragging her about uncomfortably, or making her feel that her weight was greater than even in her most desponding moments she had suspected. Even her helplessly hysteric mood was illuminated by a ray of grateful appreciation.

"Oh, thank you—thank you," she murmured. "And you are quite sure there is no actual danger, Mr.——?"

"Salter," he terminated for her. "You may feel safe. The damage is really only slight, after all."

"It is so good of you to come and tell us," said the poor lady, still tremulous. "The shock was awful. Our introduction has been an alarming one. I—I don't think we have met during the voyage."

"No," replied Salter. "I am in the second cabin."

"Oh! thank you. It's so good of you," she faltered amiably, for want of inspiration. As he went out of the stateroom, Salter spoke to Bettina.

"I will send the doctor, if I can find him," he said. "I think, perhaps, you had better take some brandy yourself. I shall."

"It's queer how little one seems to realise even that there are second-cabin passengers," commented Mrs. Worthington feebly. "That was a nice man, and perfectly respectable. He even had a kind of—of manner."

CHAPTER IX

LADY JANE GREY

It seemed upon the whole even absurd that after a shock so awful and a panic wild enough to cause people to expose their very souls—for there were, of course, endless anecdotes to be related afterwards, illustrative of grotesque terror, cowardice, and utter abandonment of all shadows of convention—that all should end in an anticlimax of trifling danger, upon which, in a day or two, jokes might be made. Even the tramp steamer had not been seriously injured, though its injuries were likely to be less easy of repair than those of the Meridiana.

"Still," as a passenger remarked, when she steamed into the dock at Liverpool, "we might all be at the bottom of the Atlantic Ocean this morning. Just think what columns there would have been in the newspapers. Imagine Miss Vanderpoel's being drowned."

"I was very rude to Louise, when I found her wringing her hands over you, and I was rude to Blanche," Bettina said to Mrs. Worthington. "In fact I believe I was rude to a number of people that night. I am rather ashamed."

"You called me a donkey," said Blanche, "but it was the best thing you could have done. You frightened me into putting on my shoes, instead of trying to comb my hair with them. It was startling to see you march into the stateroom, the only person who had not been turned into a gibbering idiot. I know I was gibbering, and I know Marie was."

"We both gibbered at the red-haired man when he came in," said Marie. "We clutched at him and gibbered together. Where is the red-haired man, Betty? Perhaps we made him ill. I've not seen him since that moment."

"He is in the second cabin, I suppose," Bettina answered, "but I have not seen him, either."

"We ought to get up a testimonial and give it to him, because he did not gibber," said Blanche. "He was as rude and as sensible as you were, Betty."

They did not see him again, in fact, at that time. He had reasons of his own for preferring to remain unseen. The truth was that the nearer his approach to his native shores, the nastier, he was perfectly conscious, his temper became, and he did not wish to expose himself by any incident which might cause him stupidly and obviously to lose it.

The maid, Louise, however, recognised him among her companions in the third-class carriage in which she travelled to town. To her mind, whose opinions were regulated by neatly arranged standards, he looked morose and shabbily dressed. Some of the other second-cabin passengers had made themselves quite smart in various, not too distinguished ways. He had not changed his dress at all, and the large valise upon the luggage rack was worn and battered as if with long and rough usage. The woman wondered a little if he would address her, and inquire after the health of her mistress. But, being an astute creature, she only wondered this for an instant, the next she realised that, for one reason or another, it was clear that he was not of the tribe of second-rate persons who pursue an accidental acquaintance with their superiors in fortune, through sociable interchange with their footmen or maids.

When the train slackened its speed at the platform of the station, he got up, reaching down his valise and leaving the carriage, strode to the nearest hansom cab, waving the porter aside.

"Charing Cross," he called out to the driver, jumped in, and was rattled away.

. . . . .

During the years which had passed since Rosalie Vanderpoel first came to London as Lady Anstruthers, numbers of huge luxurious hotels had grown up, principally, as it seemed, that Americans should swarm into them and live at an expense which reminded them of their native land. Such establishments would never have been built for English people, whose habit it is merely to "stop" at hotels, not to LIVE in them. The tendency of the American is to live in his hotel, even though his intention may be only to remain in it two days. He is accustomed to doing himself extremely well in proportion to his resources, whether they be great or small, and the comforts, as also the luxuries, he allows himself and his domestic appendages are in a proportion much higher in its relation to these resources than it would be were he English, French, German, or Italians. As a consequence, he expects, when he goes forth, whether holiday-making or on business, that his hostelry shall surround him, either with holiday luxuries and gaiety, or with such lavishness of comfort as shall alleviate the wear and tear of business cares and fatigues. The rich man demands something almost as good as he has left at home, the man of moderate means something much better. Certain persons given to regarding public wants and desires as foundations for the fortune of business schemes having discovered this, the enormous and sumptuous hotel evolved itself from their astute knowledge of common facts. At the entrances of these hotels, omnibuses and cabs, laden with trunks and packages frequently bearing labels marked with red letters "S. S. So-and-So, Stateroom—Hold—Baggage-room," drew up and deposited their contents and burdens at regular intervals. Then men with keen, and often humorous faces or almost painfully anxious ones, their exceedingly well-dressed wives, and more or less attractive and vivacious-looking daughters, their eager little girls, and un-English-looking little boys, passed through the corridors in flocks and took possession of suites of rooms, sometimes for twenty-four hours, sometimes for six weeks.

The Worthingtons took possession of such a suite in such a hotel. Bettina Vanderpoel's apartments faced the Embankment. From her windows she could look out at the broad splendid, muddy Thames, slowly rolling in its grave, stately way beneath its bridges, bearing with it heavy lumbering barges, excited tooting little penny steamers and craft of various shapes and sizes, the errand or burden of each meaning a different story.

It had been to Bettina one of her pleasures of the finest epicurean flavour to reflect that she had never had any brief and superficial knowledge of England, as she had never been to the country at all in those earlier years, when her knowledge of places must necessarily have been always the incomplete one of either a schoolgirl traveller or a schoolgirl resident, whose views were limited by the walls of restriction built around her.

If relations of the usual ease and friendliness had existed between Lady Anstruthers and her family, Bettina would, doubtless, have known her sister's adopted country well. It would have been a thing so natural as to be almost inevitable, that she would have crossed the Channel to spend her holidays at Stornham. As matters had stood, however, the child herself, in the days when she had been a child, had had most definite private views on the subject of visits to England. She had made up her young mind absolutely that she would not, if it were decently possible to avoid it, set her foot upon English soil until she was old enough and strong enough to carry out what had been at first her passionately romantic plans for discovering and facing the truth of the reason for the apparent change in Rosy. When she went to England, she would go to Rosy. As she had grown older, having in the course of education and travel seen most Continental countries, she had liked to think that she had saved, put aside for less hasty consumption and more delicate appreciation of flavours, as it were, the country she was conscious she cared for most.

"It is England we love, we Americans," she had said to her father. "What could be more natural? We belong to it—it belongs to us. I could never be convinced that the old tie of blood does not count. All nationalities have come to us since we became a nation, but most of us in the beginning came from England. We are touching about it, too. We trifle with France and labour with Germany, we sentimentalise over Italy and ecstacise over Spain—but England we love. How it moves us when we go to it, how we gush if we are simple and effusive, how we are stirred imaginatively if we are of the perceptive class. I have heard the commonest little half-educated woman say the prettiest, clumsy, emotional things about what she has seen there. A New England schoolma'am, who has made a Cook's tour, will almost have tears in her voice as she wanders on with her commonplaces about hawthorn hedges and thatched cottages and white or red farms. Why are we not unconsciously pathetic about German cottages and Italian villas? Because we have not, in centuries past, had the habit of being born in them. It is only an English cottage and an English lane, whether white with hawthorn blossoms or bare with winter, that wakes in us that little yearning, grovelling tenderness that is so sweet. It is only nature calling us home."

Mrs. Worthington came in during the course of the morning to find her standing before her window looking out at the Thames, the Embankment, the hansom cabs themselves, with an absolutely serious absorption. This changed to a smile as she turned to greet her.

"I am delighted," she said. "I could scarcely tell you how much. The impression is all new and I am excited a little by everything. I am so intensely glad that I have saved it so long and that I have known it only as part of literature. I am even charmed that it rains, and that the cabmen's mackintoshes are shining and wet." She drew forward a chair, and Mrs. Worthington sat down, looking at her with involuntary admiration.

"You look as if you were delighted," she said. "Your eyes—you have amazing eyes, Betty! I am trying to picture to myself what Lady Anstruthers will feel when she sees you. What were you like when she married?"

Bettina sat down, smiling and looking, indeed, quite incredibly lovely. She was capable of a warmth and a sweetness which were as embracing as other qualities she possessed were powerful.

"I was eight years old," she said. "I was a rude little girl, with long legs and a high, determined voice. I know I was rude. I remember answering back."

"I seem to have heard that you did not like your brother-in-law, and that you were opposed to the marriage."

"Imagine the undisciplined audacity of a child of eight 'opposing' the marriage of her grown-up sister. I was quite capable of it. You see in those days we had not been trained at all (one had only been allowed tremendous liberty), and interfered conversationally with one's elders and betters at any moment. I was an American little girl, and American little girls were really—they really were!" with a laugh, whose musical sound was after all wholly non-committal.

"You did not treat Sir Nigel Anstruthers as one of your betters."

"He was one of my elders, at all events, and becomingness of bearing should have taught me to hold my little tongue. I am giving some thought now to the kind of thing I must invent as a suitable apology when I find him a really delightful person, full of virtues and accomplishments. Perhaps he has a horror of me."

"I should like to be present at your first meeting," Mrs. Worthington reflected. "You are going down to Stornham to-morrow?"

"That is my plan. When I write to you on my arrival, I will tell you if I encountered the horror." Then, with a swift change of subject and a lifting of her slender, velvet line of eyebrow, "I am only deploring that I have not time to visit the Tower."

Mrs. Worthington was betrayed into a momentary glance of uncertainty, almost verging in its significance on a gasp.

"The Tower? Of London? Dear Betty!"

Bettina's laugh was mellow with revelation.

"Ah!" she said. "You don't know my point of view; it's plain enough. You see, when I delight in these things, I think I delight most in my delight in them. It means that I am almost having the kind of feeling the fresh American souls had who landed here thirty years ago and revelled in the resemblance to Dickens's characters they met with in the streets, and were historically thrilled by the places where people's heads were chopped off. Imagine their reflections on Charles I., when they stood in Whitehall gazing on the very spot where that poor last word was uttered—'Remember.' And think of their joy when each crossing sweeper they gave disproportionate largess to, seemed Joe All Alones in the slightest disguise."

"You don't mean to say——" Mrs. Worthington was vaguely awakening to the situation.

"That the charm of my visit, to myself, is that I realise that I am rather like that. I have positively preserved something because I have kept away. You have been here so often and know things so well, and you were even so sophisticated when you began, that you have never really had the flavours and emotions. I am sophisticated, too, sophisticated enough to have cherished my flavours as a gourmet tries to save the bouquet of old wine. You think that the Tower is the pleasure of housemaids on a Bank Holiday. But it quite makes me quiver to think of it," laughing again. "That I laugh, is the sign that I am not as beautifully, freshly capable of enjoyment as those genuine first Americans were, and in a way I am sorry for it."

Mrs. Worthington laughed also, and with an enjoyment.

"You are very clever, Betty," she said.

"No, no," answered Bettina, "or, if I am, almost everybody is clever in these days. We are nearly all of us comparatively intelligent."

"You are very interesting at all events, and the Anstruthers will exult in you. If they are dull in the country, you will save them."

"I am very interested, at all events," said Bettina, "and interest like mine is quite passe. A clever American who lives in England, and is the pet of duchesses, once said to me (he always speaks of Americans as if they were a distant and recently discovered species), 'When they first came over they were a novelty. Their enthusiasm amused people, but now, you see, it has become vieux jeu. Young women, whose specialty was to be excited by the Tower of London and Westminster Abbey, are not novelties any longer. In fact, it's been done, and it's done FOR as a specialty.' And I am excited about the Tower of London. I may be able to restrain my feelings at the sight of the Beef Eaters, but they will upset me a little, and I must brace myself, I must indeed."

"Truly, Betty?" said Mrs. Worthington, regarding her with curiosity, arising from a faint doubt of her entire seriousness, mingled with a fainter doubt of her entire levity.

Betty flung out her hands in a slight, but very involuntary-looking, gesture, and shook her head.

"Ah!" she said, "it was all TRUE, you know. They were all horribly real—the things that were shuddered over and sentimentalised about. Sophistication, combined with imagination, makes them materialise again, to me, at least, now I am here. The gulf between a historical figure and a man or woman who could bleed and cry out in human words was broad when one was at school. Lady Jane Grey, for instance, how nebulous she was and how little one cared. She seemed invented merely to add a detail to one's lesson in English history. But, as we drove across Waterloo Bridge, I caught a glimpse of the Tower, and what do you suppose I began to think of? It was monstrous. I saw a door in the Tower and the stone steps, and the square space, and in the chill clear, early morning a little slender, helpless girl led out, a little, fair, real thing like Rosy, all alone—everyone she belonged to far away, not a man near who dared utter a word of pity when she turned her awful, meek, young, desperate eyes upon him. She was a pious child, and, no doubt, she lifted her eyes to the sky. I wonder if it was blue and its blueness broke her heart, because it looked as if it might have pitied such a young, patient girl thing led out in the fair morning to walk to the hacked block and give her trembling pardon to the black-visored man with the axe, and then 'commending her soul to God' to stretch her sweet slim neck out upon it."

"Oh, Betty, dear!" Mrs. Worthington expostulated.

Bettina sprang to her and took her hand in pretty appeal.

"I beg pardon! I beg pardon, I really do," she exclaimed. "I did not intend deliberately to be painful. But that—beneath the sophistication—is something of what I bring to England."

CHAPTER X

"IS LADY ANSTRUTHERS AT HOME?"

All that she had brought with her to England, combined with what she had called "sophistication," but which was rather her exquisite appreciation of values and effects, she took with her when she went the next day to Charing Cross Station and arranged herself at her ease in the railway carriage, while her maid bought their tickets for Stornham.

What the people in the station saw, the guards and porters, the men in the book stalls, the travellers hurrying past, was a striking-looking girl, whose colouring and carriage made one turn to glance after her, and who, having bought some periodicals and papers, took her place in a first-class compartment and watched the passersby interestedly through the open window. Having been looked at and remarked on during her whole life, Bettina did not find it disturbing that more than one corduroy-clothed porter and fresh-coloured, elderly gentleman, or freshly attired young one, having caught a glimpse of her through her window, made it convenient to saunter past or hover round. She looked at them much more frankly than they looked at her. To her they were all specimens of the types she was at present interested in. For practical reasons she was summing up English character with more deliberate intention than she had felt in the years when she had gradually learned to know Continental types and differentiate such peculiarities as were significant of their ranks and nations. As the first Reuben Vanderpoel had studied the countenances and indicative methods of the inhabitants of the new parts of the country in which it was his intention to do business, so the modernity of his descendant applied itself to observation for reasons parallel in nature though not in actual kind. As he had brought beads and firewater to bear as agents upon savages who would barter for them skins and products which might be turned into money, so she brought her nineteenth-century beauty, steadfastness of purpose and alertness of brain to bear upon the matter the practical dealing with which was the end she held in view. To bear herself in this matter with as practical a control of situations as that with which her great-grandfather would have borne himself in making a trade with a previously unknown tribe of Indians was quite her intention, though it had not occurred to her to put it to herself in any such form. Still, whether she was aware of the fact or not, her point of view was exactly what the first Reuben Vanderpoel's had been on many very different occasions. She had before her the task of dealing with facts and factors of which at present she knew but little. Astuteness of perception, self-command, and adaptability were her chief resources. She was ready, either for calm, bold approach, or equally calm and wholly non-committal retreat.

The perceptions she had brought with her filled her journey into Kent with delicious things, delicious recognition of beauties she had before known the existence of only through the reading of books, and the dwelling upon their charms as reproduced, more or less perfectly, on canvas. She saw roll by her, with the passing of the train, the loveliness of land and picturesqueness of living which she had saved for herself with epicurean intention for years. Her fancy, when detached from her thoughts of her sister, had been epicurean, and she had been quite aware that it was so. When she had left the suburbs and those villages already touched with suburbanity behind, she felt herself settle into a glow of luxurious enjoyment in the freshness of her pleasure in the familiar, and yet unfamiliar, objects in the thick-hedged fields, whose broad-branched, thick-foliaged oaks and beeches were more embowering in their shade, and sweeter in their green than anything she remembered that other countries had offered her, even at their best. Within the fields the hawthorn hedges beautifully enclosed were groups of resigned mother sheep with their young lambs about them. The curious pointed tops of the red hopkilns, piercing the trees near the farmhouses, wore an almost intentional air of adding picturesque detail. There were clusters of old buildings and dots of cottages and cottage gardens which made her now and then utter exclamations of delight. Little inarticulate Rosy had seen and felt it all twelve years before on her hopeless bridal home-coming when Nigel had sat huddled unbecomingly in the corner of the railway carriage. Her power of expression had been limited to little joyful gasps and obvious laudatory adjectives, smothered in their birth by her first glance at her bridegroom. Betty, in seeing it, knew all the exquisiteness of her own pleasure, and all the meanings of it.

Yes, it was England—England. It was the England of Constable and Morland, of Miss Mitford and Miss Austen, the Brontes and George Eliot. The land which softly rolled and clothed itself in the rich verdure of many trees, sometimes in lovely clusters, sometimes in covering copse, was Constable's; the ripe young woman with the fat-legged children and the farmyard beasts about her, as she fed the hens from the wooden piggin under her arm, was Morland's own. The village street might be Miss Mitford's, the well-to-do house Jane Austen's own fancy, in its warm brick and comfortable decorum. She laughed a little as she thought it.

"That is American," she said, "the habit of comparing every stick and stone and breathing thing to some literary parallel. We almost invariably say that things remind us of pictures or books—most usually books. It seems a little crude, but perhaps it means that we are an intensely literary and artistic people."

She continued to find comparisons revealing to her their appositeness, until her journey had ended by the train's slackening speed and coming to a standstill before the rural-looking little station which had presented its quaint aspect to Lady Anstruthers on her home-coming of years before.

It had not, during the years which certainly had given time for change, altered in the least. The station master had grown stouter and more rosy, and came forward with his respectful, hospitable air, to attend to the unusual-looking young lady, who was the only first-class passenger. He thought she must be a visitor expected at some country house, but none of the carriages, whose coachmen were his familiar acquaintances, were in waiting. That such a fine young lady should be paying a visit at any house whose owners did not send an equipage to attend her coming, struck him as unusual. The brougham from the "Crown," though a decent country town vehicle, seemed inadequate. Yet, there it stood drawn up outside the station, and she went to it with the manner of a young lady who had ordered its attendance and knew it would be there.

Wells felt a good deal of interest. Among the many young ladies who descended from the first-class compartments and passed through the little waiting-room on their way to the carriages of the gentry they were going to visit, he did not know when a young lady had "caught his eye," so to speak, as this one did. She was not exactly the kind of young lady one would immediately class mentally as "a foreigner," but the blue of her eyes was so deep, and her hair and eyelashes so dark, that these things, combining themselves with a certain "way" she had, made him feel her to be of a type unfamiliar to the region, at least.

He was struck, also, by the fact that the young lady had no maid with her. The truth was that Bettina had purposely left her maid in town. If awkward things occurred, the presence of an attendant would be a sort of complication. It was better, on the first approach, to be wholly unencumbered.

"How far are we from Stornham Court?" she inquired.

"Five miles, my lady," he answered, touching his cap. She expressed something which to the rural and ingenuous, whose standards were defined, demanded a recognition of probable rank.

"I'd like to know," was his comment to his wife when he went home to dinner, "who has gone to Stornham Court to-day. There's few enough visitors go there, and none such as her, for certain. She don't live anywhere on the line above here, either, for I've never seen her face before. She was a tall, handsome one—she was, but it isn't just that made you look after her. She was a clever one with a spirit, I'll be bound. I was wondering what her ladyship would have to say to her."

"Perhaps she was one of HIS fine ladies?" suggestively.

"That she wasn't, either. And, as for that, I wonder what he'd have to say to such as she is."

There was complexity of element enough in the thing she was on her way to do, Bettina was thinking, as she was driven over the white ribbon of country road that unrolled over rise and hollow, between the sheep-dotted greenness of fields and the scented hedges. The soft beauty enclosing her was a little shut out from her by her mental attitude. She brought forward for her own decisions upon suitable action a number of possible situations she might find herself called upon to confront. The one thing necessary was that she should be prepared for anything whatever, even for Rosy's not being pleased to see her, or for finding Sir Nigel a thoroughly reformed and amiable character.

"It is the thing which seemingly CANNOT happen which one is most likely to find one's self face to face with. It will be a little awkward to arrange, if he has developed every domestic virtue, and is delighted to see me."

Under such rather confusing conditions her plan would be to present to them, as an affectionate surprise, the unheralded visit, which might appear a trifle uncalled for. She felt happily sure of herself under any circumstances not partaking of the nature of collisions at sea. Yet she had not behaved absolutely ill at the time of the threatened catastrophe in the Meridiana. Her remembrance, an oddly sudden one, of the definite manner of the red-haired second-class passenger, assured her of that. He had certainly had all his senses about him, and he had spoken to her as a person to be counted on.

Her pulse beat a little more hurriedly as the brougham entered Stornham village. It was picturesque, but struck her as looking neglected. Many of the cottages had an air of dilapidation. There were many broken windows and unmended garden palings. A suggested lack of whitewash in several cases was not cheerful.

"I know nothing of the duties of English landlords," she said, looking through her carriage window, "but I should do it myself, if I were Rosy."

She saw, as she was taken through the park gateway, that that structure was out of order, and that damaged diamond panes peered out from under the thickness of the ivy massing itself over the lodge.

"Ah!" was her thought, "it does not promise as it should. Happy people do not let things fall to pieces."

Even winding avenue, and spreading sward, and gorse, and broom, and bracken, enfolding all the earth beneath huge trees, were not fair enough to remove a sudden remote fear which arose in her rapidly reasoning mind. It suggested to her a point of view so new that, while she was amazed at herself for not having contemplated it before, she found herself wishing that the coachman would drive rather more slowly, actually that she might have more time to reflect.

They were nearing a dip in the park, where there was a lonely looking pool. The bracken was thick and high there, and the sun, which had just broken through a cloud, had pierced the trees with a golden gleam.

A little withdrawn from this shaft of brightness stood two figures, a dowdy little woman and a hunchbacked boy. The woman held some ferns in her hand, and the boy was sitting down and resting his chin on his hands, which were folded on the top of a stick.

"Stop here for a moment," Bettina said to the coachman. "I want to ask that woman a question."

She had thought that she might discover if her sister was at the Court. She realised that to know would be a point of advantage. She leaned forward and spoke.

"I beg your pardon," she said, "I wonder if you can tell me——"

The woman came forward a little. She had a listless step and a faded, listless face.

"What did you ask?" she said.

Betty leaned still further forward.

"Can you tell me——" she began and stopped. A sense of stricture in the throat stopped her, as her eyes took in the washed-out colour of the thin face, the washed-out colour of the thin hair—thin drab hair, dragged in straight, hard unbecomingness from the forehead and cheeks.

Was it true that her heart was thumping, as she had heard it said that agitation made hearts thump?

She began again.

"Can you—tell me if—Lady Anstruthers is at home?" she inquired. As she said it she felt the blood surge up from the furious heart, and the hand she had laid on the handle of the door of the brougham clutched it involuntarily.

The dowdy little woman answered her indifferently, staring at her a little.

"I am Lady Anstruthers," she said.

Bettina opened the carriage door and stood upon the ground.

"Go on to the house," she gave order to the coachman, and, with a somewhat startled look, he drove away.

"Rosy!" Bettina's voice was a hushed, almost awed, thing. "YOU are Rosy?"

The faded little wreck of a creature began to look frightened.

"Rosy!" she repeated, with a small, wry, painful smile.

She was the next moment held in the folding of strong, young arms, against a quickly beating heart. She was being wildly kissed, and the very air seemed rich with warmth and life.

"I am Betty," she heard. "Look at me, Rosy! I am Betty. Look at me and remember!"

Lady Anstruthers gasped, and broke into a faint, hysteric laugh. She suddenly clutched at Bettina's arm. For a minute her gaze was wild as she looked up.

"Betty," she cried out. "No! No! No! I can't believe it! I can't! I can't!"

That just this thing could have taken place in her, Bettina had never thought. As she had reflected on her way from the station, the impossible is what one finds one's self face to face with. Twelve years should not have changed a pretty blonde thing of nineteen to a worn, unintelligent-looking dowdy of the order of dowdiness which seems to have lived beyond age and sex. She looked even stupid, or at least stupefied. At this moment she was a silly, middle-aged woman, who did not know what to do. For a few seconds Bettina wondered if she was glad to see her, or only felt awkward and unequal to the situation.

"I can't believe you," she cried out again, and began to shiver. "Betty! Little Betty? No! No! it isn't!"

She turned to the boy, who had lifted his chin from his stick, and was staring.

"Ughtred! Ughtred!" she called to him. "Come! She says—she says——"

She sat down upon a clump of heather and began to cry. She hid her face in her spare hands and broke into sobbing.

"Oh, Betty! No!" she gasped. "It's so long ago—it's so far away. You never came—no one—no one—came!"

The hunchbacked boy drew near. He had limped up on his stick. He spoke like an elderly, affectionate gnome, not like a child.

"Don't do that, mother," he said. "Don't let it upset you so, whatever it is."

"It's so long ago; it's so far away!" she wept, with catches in her breath and voice. "You never came!"

Betty knelt down and enfolded her again. Her bell-like voice was firm and clear.

"I have come now," she said. "And it is not far away. A cable will reach father in two hours."

Pursuing a certain vivid thought in her mind, she looked at her watch.

"If you spoke to mother by cable this moment," she added, with accustomed coolness, and she felt her sister actually start as she spoke, "she could answer you by five o'clock."

Lady Anstruther's start ended in a laugh and gasp more hysteric than her first. There was even a kind of wan awakening in her face, as she lifted it to look at the wonderful newcomer. She caught her hand and held it, trembling, as she weakly laughed.

"It must be Betty," she cried. "That little stern way! It is so like her. Betty—Betty—dear!" She fell into a sobbing, shaken heap upon the heather. The harrowing thought passed through Betty's mind that she looked almost like a limp bundle of shabby clothes. She was so helpless in her pathetic, apologetic hysteria.

"I shall—be better," she gasped. "It's nothing. Ughtred, tell her."

"She's very weak, really," said the boy Ughtred, in his mature way. "She can't help it sometimes. I'll get some water from the pool."

"Let me go," said Betty, and she darted down to the water. She was back in a moment. The boy was rubbing and patting his mother's hands tenderly.

"At any rate," he remarked, as one consoled by a reflection, "father is not at home."

CHAPTER XI

"I THOUGHT YOU HAD ALL FORGOTTEN."

As, after a singular half hour spent among the bracken under the trees, they began their return to the house, Bettina felt that her sense of adventure had altered its character. She was still in the midst of a remarkable sort of exploit, which might end anywhere or in anything, but it had become at once more prosaic in detail and more intense in its significance. What its significance might prove likely to be when she faced it, she had not known, it is true. But this was different from—from anything. As they walked up the sun-dappled avenue she kept glancing aside at Rosy, and endeavouring to draw useful conclusions. The poor girl's air of being a plain, insignificant frump, long past youth, struck an extraordinary and, for the time, unexplainable note. Her ill-cut, out-of-date dress, the cheap suit of the hunchbacked boy, who limped patiently along, helped by his crutch, suggested possible explanations which were without doubt connected with the thought which had risen in Bettina's mind, as she had been driven through the broken-hinged entrance gate. What extraordinary disposal was being made of Rosy's money? But her each glance at her sister also suggested complication upon complication.

The singular half hour under the trees by the pool, spent, after the first hysteric moments were over, in vague exclaimings and questions, which seemed half frightened and all at sea, had gradually shown her that she was talking to a creature wholly other than the Rosalie who had so well known and loved them all, and whom they had so well loved and known. They did not know this one, and she did not know them, she was even a little afraid of the stir and movement of their life and being. The Rosy they had known seemed to be imprisoned within the wall the years of her separated life had built about her. At each breath she drew Bettina saw how long the years had been to her, and how far her home had seemed to lie away, so far that it could not touch her, and was only a sort of dream, the recalling of which made her suddenly begin to cry again every few minutes. To Bettina's sensitively alert mind it was plain that it would not do in the least to drag her suddenly out of her prison, or cloister, whichsoever it might be. To do so would be like forcing a creature accustomed only to darkness, to stare at the blazing sun. To have burst upon her with the old impetuous, candid fondness would have been to frighten and shock her as if with something bordering on indecency. She could not have stood it; perhaps such fondness was so remote from her in these days that she had even ceased to be able to understand it.

"Where are your little girls?" Bettina asked, remembering that there had been notice given of the advent of two girl babies.

"They died," Lady Anstruthers answered unemotionally. "They both died before they were a year old. There is only Ughtred."

Betty glanced at the boy and saw a small flame of red creep up on his cheek. Instinctively she knew what it meant, and she put out her hand and lightly touched his shoulder.

"I hope you'll like me, Ughtred," she said.

He almost started at the sound of her voice, but when he turned his face towards her he only grew redder, and looked awkward without answering. His manner was that of a boy who was unused to the amenities of polite society, and who was only made shy by them.

Without warning, a moment or so later, Bettina stopped in the middle of the avenue, and looked up at the arching giant branches of the trees which had reached out from one side to the other, as if to clasp hands or encompass an interlacing embrace. As far as the eye reached, they did this, and the beholder stood as in a high stately pergola, with breaks of deep azure sky between. Several mellow, cawing rooks were floating solemnly beneath or above the branches, now wand then settling in some highest one or disappearing in the thick greenness.

Lady Anstruthers stopped when her sister did so, and glanced at her in vague inquiry. It was plain that she had outlived even her sense of the beauty surrounding her.

"What are you looking at, Betty?" she asked.

"At all of it," Betty answered. "It is so wonderful."

"She likes it," said Ughtred, and then rather slunk a step behind his mother, as if he were ashamed of himself.

"The house is just beyond those trees," said Lady Anstruthers.

They came in full view of it three minutes later. When she saw it, Betty uttered an exclamation and stopped again to enjoy effects.

"She likes that, too," said Ughtred, and, although he said it sheepishly, there was imperfectly concealed beneath the awkwardness a pleasure in the fact.

"Do you?" asked Rosalie, with her small, painful smile.

Betty laughed.

"It is too picturesque, in its special way, to be quite credible," she said.

"I thought that when I first saw it," said Rosy.

"Don't you think so, now?"

"Well," was the rather uncertain reply, "as Nigel says, there's not much good in a place that is falling to pieces."

"Why let it fall to pieces?" Betty put it to her with impartial promptness.

"We haven't money enough to hold it together," resignedly.

As they climbed the low, broad, lichen-blotched steps, whose broken stone balustrades were almost hidden in clutching, untrimmed ivy, Betty felt them to be almost incredible, too. The uneven stones of the terrace the steps mounted to were lichen-blotched and broken also. Tufts of green growths had forced themselves between the flags, and added an untidy beauty. The ivy tossed in branches over the red roof and walls of the house. It had been left unclipped, until it was rather an endlessly clambering tree than a creeper. The hall they entered had the beauty of spacious form and good, old oaken panelling. There were deep window seats and an ancient high-backed settle or so, and a massive table by the fireless hearth. But there were no pictures in places where pictures had evidently once hung, and the only coverings on the stone floor were the faded remnants of a central rug and a worn tiger skin, the head almost bald and a glass eye knocked out.

Bettina took in the unpromising details without a quiver of the extravagant lashes. These, indeed, and the eyes pertaining to them, seemed rather to sweep the fine roof, and a certain minstrel's gallery and staircase, than which nothing could have been much finer, with the look of an appreciative admirer of architectural features and old oak. She had not journeyed to Stornham Court with the intention of disturbing Rosy, or of being herself obviously disturbed. She had come to observe situations and rearrange them with that intelligence of which unconsidered emotion or exclamation form no part.

"It is the first old English house I have seen," she said, with a sigh of pleasure. "I am so glad, Rosy—I am so glad that it is yours."

She put a hand on each of Rosy's thin shoulders—she felt sharply defined bones as she did so—and bent to kiss her. It was the natural affectionate expression of her feeling, but tears started to Rosy's eyes, and the boy Ughtred, who had sat down in a window seat, turned red again, and shifted in his place.

"Oh, Betty!" was Rosy's faint nervous exclamation, "you seem so beautiful and—so—so strange—that you frighten me."

Betty laughed with the softest possible cheerfulness, shaking her a little.

"I shall not seem strange long," she said, "after I have stayed with you a few weeks, if you will let me stay with you."

"Let you! Let you!" in a sort of gasp.

Poor little Lady Anstruthers sank on to a settle and began to cry again. It was plain that she always cried when things occurred. Ughtred's speech from his window seat testified at once to that.

"Don't cry, mother," he said. "You know how we've talked that over together. It's her nerves," he explained to Bettina. "We know it only makes things worse, but she can't stop it."

Bettina sat on the settle, too. She herself was not then aware of the wonderful feeling the poor little spare figure experienced, as her softly strong young arms curved about it. She was only aware that she herself felt that this was a heart-breaking thing, and that she must not—MUST not let it be seen how much she recognised its woefulness. This was pretty, fair Rosy, who had never done a harm in her happy life—this forlorn thing was her Rosy.

"Never mind," she said, half laughing again. "I rather want to cry myself, and I am stronger than she is. I am immensely strong."

"Yes! Yes!" said Lady Anstruthers, wiping her eyes, and making a tremendous effort at self-respecting composure. "You are strong. I have grown so weak in—well, in every way. Betty, I'm afraid this is a poor welcome. You see—I'm afraid you'll find it all so different from—from New York."

"I wanted to find it different," said Betty.

"But—but—I mean—you know———" Lady Anstruthers turned helplessly to the boy. Bettina was struck with the painful truth that she looked even silly as she turned to him. "Ughtred—tell her," she ended, and hung her head.

Ughtred had got down at once from his seat and limped forward. His unprepossessing face looked as if he pulled his childishness together with an unchildish effort.

"She means," he said, in his awkward way, "that she doesn't know how to make you comfortable. The rooms are all so shabby—everything is so shabby. Perhaps you won't stay when you see."

Bettina perceptibly increased the firmness of her hold on her sister's body. It was as if she drew it nearer to her side in a kind of taking possession. She knew that the moment had come when she might go this far, at least, without expressing alarming things.

"You cannot show me anything that will frighten me," was the answer she made. "I have come to stay, Rosy. We can make things right if they require it. Why not?"

Lady Anstruthers started a little, and stared at her. She knew ten thousand reasons why things had not been made right, and the casual inference that such reasons could be lightly swept away as if by the mere wave of a hand, implied a power appertaining to a time seeming so lost forever that it was too much for her.

"Oh, Betty, Betty!" she cried, "you talk as if—you are so———!"

The fact, so simple to the members of the abnormal class to which she of a truth belonged, the class which heaped up its millions, the absolute knowledge that there was a great deal of money in the world and that she was of those who were among its chief owners, had ceased to seem a fact, and had vanished into the region of fairy stories.

That she could not believe it a reality revealed itself to Bettina, as by a flash, which was also a revelation of many things. There would be unpleasing truths to be learned, and she had not made her pilgrimage for nothing. But—in any event—there were advantages without doubt in the circumstance which subjected one to being perpetually pointed out as a daughter of a multi-millionaire. As this argued itself out for her with rapid lucidity, she bent and kissed Rosy once more. She even tried to do it lightly, and not to allow the rush of love and pity in her soul to betray her.

"I talk as if—as if I were Betty," she said. "You have forgotten. I have not. I have been looking forward to this for years. I have been planning to come to you since I was eleven years old. And here we sit."

"You didn't forget? You didn't?" faltered the poor wreck of Rosy. "Oh! Oh! I thought you had all forgotten me—quite—quite!"

And her face went down in her spare, small hands, and she began to cry again.

CHAPTER XII

UGHTRED

Bettina stood alone in her bedroom a couple of hours later. Lady Anstruthers had taken her to it, preparing her for its limitations by explaining that she would find it quite different from her room in New York. She had been pathetically nervous and flushed about it, and Bettina had also been aware that the apartment itself had been hastily, and with much moving of objects from one chamber to another, made ready for her.

The room was large and square and low. It was panelled in small squares of white wood. The panels were old enough to be cracked here and there, and the paint was stained and yellow with time, where it was not knocked or worn off. There was a small paned, leaded window which filled a large part of one side of the room, and its deep seat was an agreeable feature. Sitting in it, one looked out over several red-walled gardens, and through breaks in the trees of the park to a fair beyond. Bettina stood before this window for a few moments, and then took a seat in the embrasure, that she might gaze out and reflect at leisure.

Her genius, as has before been mentioned, was the genius for living, for being vital. Many people merely exist, are kept alive by others, or continue to vegetate because the persistent action of normal functions will allow of their doing no less. Bettina Vanderpoel had lived vividly, and in the midst of a self-created atmosphere of action from her first hour. It was not possible for her to be one of the horde of mere spectators. Wheresoever she moved there was some occult stirring of the mental, and even physical, air. Her pulses beat too strongly, her blood ran too fast to allow of inaction of mind or body. When, in passing through the village, she had seen the broken windows and the hanging palings of the cottages, it had been inevitable that, at once, she should, in thought, repair them, set them straight. Disorder filled her with a sort of impatience which was akin to physical distress. If she had been born a poor woman she would have worked hard for her living, and found an interest, almost an exhilaration, in her labour. Such gifts as she had would have been applied to the tasks she undertook. It had frequently given her pleasure to imagine herself earning her livelihood as a seamstress, a housemaid, a nurse. She knew what she could have put into her service, and how she could have found it absorbing. Imagination and initiative could make any service absorbing. The actual truth was that if she had been a housemaid, the room she set in order would have taken a character under her touch; if she had been a seamstress, her work would have been swiftly done, her imagination would have invented for her combinations of form and colour; if she had been a nursemaid, the children under her care would never have been sufficiently bored to become tiresome or intractable, and they also would have gained character to which would have been added an undeniable vividness of outlook. She could not have left them alone, so to speak. In obeying the mere laws of her being, she would have stimulated them. Unconsciously she had stimulated her fellow pupils at school; when she was his companion, her father had always felt himself stirred to interest and enterprise.

"You ought to have been a man, Betty," he used to say to her sometimes.

But Betty had not agreed with him.

"You say that," she once replied to him, "because you see I am inclined to do things, to change them, if they need changing. Well, one is either born like that, or one is not. Sometimes I think that perhaps the people who must ACT are of a distinct race. A kind of vigorous restlessness drives them. I remember that when I was a child I could not see a pin lying upon the ground without picking it up, or pass a drawer which needed closing, without giving it a push. But there has always been as much for women to do as for men."

There was much to be done here of one sort of thing and another. That was certain. As she gazed through the small panes of her large windows, she found herself overlooking part of a wilderness of garden, which revealed itself through an arch in an overgrown laurel hedge. She had glimpses of unkempt grass paths and unclipped topiary work which had lost its original form. Among a tangle of weeds rose the heads of clumps of daffodils, stirred by a passing wind of spring. In the park beyond a cuckoo was calling.

She was conscious both of the forlorn beauty and significance of the neglected garden, and of the clear quaintness of the cuckoo call, as she thought of other things.

"Her spirit and her health are broken," was her summing up. "Her prettiness has faded to a rag. She is as nervous as an ill-treated child. She has lost her wits. I do not know where to begin with her. I must let her tell me things as gradually as she chooses. Until I see Nigel I shall not know what his method with her has been. She looks as if she had ceased to care for things, even for herself. What shall I write to mother?"

She knew what she should write to her father. With him she could be explicit. She could record what she had found and what it suggested to her. She could also make clear her reason for hesitance and deliberation. His discretion and affection would comprehend the thing which she herself felt and which affection not combined with discretion might not take in. He would understand, when she told him that one of the first things which had struck her, had been that Rosy herself, her helplessness and timidity, might, for a period at least, form obstacles in their path of action. He not only loved Rosy, but realised how slight a sweet thing she had always been, and he would know how far a slight creature's gentleness might be overpowered and beaten down.

There was so much that her mother must be spared, there was indeed so little that it would be wise to tell her, that Bettina sat gently rubbing her forehead as she thought of it. The truth was that she must tell her nothing, until all was over, accomplished, decided. Whatsoever there was to be "over," whatsoever the action finally taken, must be a matter lying as far as possible between her father and herself. Mrs. Vanderpoel's trouble would be too keen, her anxiety too great to keep to herself, even if she were not overwhelmed by them. She must be told of the beauties and dimensions of Stornham, all relatable details of Rosy's life must be generously dwelt on. Above all Rosy must be made to write letters, and with an air of freedom however specious.

A knock on the door broke the thread of her reflection. It was a low-sounding knock, and she answered the summons herself, because she thought it might be Rosy's.

It was not Lady Anstruthers who stood outside, but Ughtred, who balanced himself on his crutches, and lifted his small, too mature, face.

"May I come in?" he asked.

Here was the unexpected again, but she did not allow him to see her surprise.

"Yes," she said. "Certainly you may."

He swung in and then turned to speak to her.

"Please shut the door and lock it," he said.

There was sudden illumination in this, but of an order almost whimsical. That modern people in modern days should feel bolts and bars a necessity of ordinary intercourse was suggestive. She was plainly about to receive enlightenment. She turned the key and followed the halting figure across the room.

"What are you afraid of?" she asked.

"When mother and I talk things over," he said, "we always do it where no one can see or hear. It's the only way to be safe."

"Safe from what?"

His eyes fixed themselves on her as he answered her almost sullenly.

"Safe from people who might listen and go and tell that we had been talking."

In his thwarted-looking, odd child-face there was a shade of appeal not wholly hidden by his evident wish not to be boylike. Betty felt a desire to kneel down suddenly and embrace him, but she knew he was not prepared for such a demonstration. He looked like a creature who had lived continually at bay, and had learned to adjust himself to any situation with caution and restraint.

"Sit down, Ughtred," she said, and when he did so she herself sat down, but not too near him.

Resting his chin on the handle of a crutch, he gazed at her almost protestingly.

"I always have to do these things," he said, "and I am not clever enough, or old enough. I am only eleven."

The mention of the number of his years was plainly not apologetic, but was a mere statement of his limitations. There the fact was, and he must make the best of it he could.

"What things do you mean?"

"Trying to make things easier—explaining things when she cannot think of excuses. To-day it is telling you what she is too frightened to tell you herself. I said to her that you must be told. It made her nervous and miserable, but I knew you must."

"Yes, I must," Betty answered. "I am glad she has you to depend on, Ughtred."

His crutch grated on the floor and his boy eyes forbade her to believe that their sudden lustre was in any way connected with restrained emotion.

"I know I seem queer and like a little old man," he said. "Mother cries about it sometimes. But it can't be helped. It is because she has never had anyone but me to help her. When I was very little, I found out how frightened and miserable she was. After his rages," he used no name, "she used to run into my nursery and snatch me up in her arms and hide her face in my pinafore. Sometimes she stuffed it into her mouth and bit it to keep herself from screaming. Once— before I was seven—I ran into their room and shouted out, and tried to fight for her. He was going out, and had his riding whip in his hand, and he caught hold of me and struck me with it—until he was tired."

Betty stood upright.

"What! What! What!" she cried out.

He merely nodded his head shortly. She saw what the thing had been by the way his face lost colour.

"Of course he said it was because I was impudent, and needed punishment," he said. "He said she had encouraged me in American impudence. It was worse for her than for me. She kneeled down and screamed out as if she was crazy, that she would give him what he wanted if he would stop."

"Wait," said Betty, drawing in her breath sharply. "'He,' is Sir Nigel? And he wanted something."

He nodded again.

"Tell me," she demanded, "has he ever struck her?"

"Once," he answered slowly, "before I was born—he struck her and she fell against something. That is why I am like this." And he touched his shoulder.

The feeling which surged through Betty Vanderpoel's being forced her to go and stand with her face turned towards the windows, her hands holding each other tightly behind her back.

"I must keep still," she said. "I must make myself keep still."

She spoke unconsciously half aloud, and Ughtred heard her and replied hurriedly.

"Yes," he said, "you must make yourself keep still. That is what we have to do whatever happens. That is one of the things mother wanted you to know. She is afraid. She daren't let you——"

She turned from the window, standing at her full height and looking very tall for a girl.

"She is afraid? She daren't? See—that will come to an end now. There are things which can be done."

He flushed nervously.

"That is what she was afraid you would say," he spoke fast and his hands trembled. "She is nearly wild about it, because she knows he will try to do something that will make you feel as if she does not want you."

"She is afraid of that?" Betty exclaimed.

"He'd do it! He'd do it—if you did not know beforehand."

"Oh!" said Betty, with unflinching clearness. "He is a liar, is he?"

The helpless rage in the unchildish eyes, the shaking voice, as he cried out in answer, were a shock. It was as if he wildly rejoiced that she had spoken the word.

"Yes, he's a liar—a liar!" he shrilled. "He's a liar and a bully and a coward. He'd—he'd be a murderer if he dared—but he daren't." And his face dropped on his arms folded on his crutch, and he broke into a passion of crying. Then Betty knew she might go to him. She went and knelt down and put her arm round him.

"Ughtred," she said, "cry, if you like, I should do it, if I were you. But I tell you it can all be altered—and it shall be."

He seemed quite like a little boy when he put out his hand to hers and spoke sobbingly:

"She—she says—that because you have only just come from America—and in America people—can do things—you will think you can do things here—and you don't know. He will tell lies about you lies you can't bear. She sat wringing her hands when she thought of it. She won't let you be hurt because you want to help her." He stopped abruptly and clutched her shoulder.

"Aunt Betty! Aunt Betty—whatever happens—whatever he makes her seem like—you are to know that it is not true. Now you have come—now she has seen you it would KILL her if you were driven away and thought she wanted you to go."

"I shall not think that," she answered, slowly, because she realised that it was well that she had been warned in time. "Ughtred, are you trying to tell me that above all things I must not let him think that I came here to help you, because if he is angry he will make us all suffer—and your mother most of all?"

"He'll find a way. We always know he will. He would either be so rude that you would not stay here—or he would make mother seem rude—or he would write lies to grandfather. Aunt Betty, she scarcely believes you are real yet. If she won't tell you things at first, please don't mind." He looked quite like a child again in his appeal to her, to try to understand a state of affairs so complicated. "Could you—could you wait until you have let her get—get used to you?"

"Used to thinking that there may be someone in the world to help her?" slowly. "Yes, I will. Has anyone ever tried to help her?"

"Once or twice people found out and were sorry at first, but it only made it worse, because he made them believe things."

"I shall not TRY, Ughtred," said Betty, a remote spark kindling in the deeps of the pupils of her steel-blue eyes. "I shall not TRY. Now I am going to ask you some questions."

Before he left her she had asked many questions which were pertinent and searching, and she had learned things she realised she could have learned in no other way and from no other person. But for his uncanny sense of the responsibility he clearly had assumed in the days when he wore pinafores, and which had brought him to her room to prepare her mind for what she would find herself confronted with in the way of apparently unexplainable obstacles, there was a strong likelihood that at the outset she might have found herself more than once dangerously at a loss. Yes, she would have been at a loss, puzzled, perhaps greatly discouraged. She was face to face with a complication so extraordinary.

That one man, through mere persistent steadiness in evil temper and domestic tyranny, should have so broken the creatures of his household into abject submission and hopelessness, seemed too incredible. Such a power appeared as remote from civilised existence in London and New York as did that which had inflicted tortures in the dungeons of castles of old. Prisoners in such dungeons could utter no cry which could reach the outside world; the prisoners at Stornham Court, not four hours from Hyde Park Corner, could utter none the world could hear, or comprehend if it heard it. Sheer lack of power to resist bound them hand and foot. And she, Betty Vanderpoel, was here upon the spot, and, as far as she could understand, was being implored to take no steps, to do nothing. The atmosphere in which she had spent her life, the world she had been born into, had not made for fearfulness that one would be at any time defenceless against circumstances and be obliged to submit to outrage. To be a Vanderpoel was, it was true, to be a shining mark for envy as for admiration, but the fact removed obstacles as a rule, and to find one's self standing before a situation with one's hands, figuratively speaking, tied, was new enough to arouse unusual sensations. She recalled, with an ironic sense of bewilderment, as a sort of material evidence of her own reality, the fact that not a week ago she had stepped on to English soil from the gangway of a solid Atlantic liner. It aided her to resist the feeling that she had been swept back into the Middle Ages.

"When he is angry," was one of the first questions she put to Ughtred, "what does he give as his reason? He must profess to have a reason."

"When he gets in a rage he says it is because mother is silly and common, and I am badly brought up. But we always know he wants money, and it makes him furious. He could kill us with rage."

"Oh!" said Betty. "I see."

"It began that time when he struck her. He said then that it was not decent that a woman who was married should keep her own money. He made her give him almost everything she had, but she wants to keep some for me. He tries to make her get more from grandfather, but she will not write begging letters, and she won't give him what she is saving for me."

It was a simple and sordid enough explanation in one sense, and it was one of which Bettina had known, not one parallel, but several. Having married to ensure himself power over unquestioned resources, the man had felt himself disgustingly taken in, and avenged himself accordingly. In him had been born the makings of a domestic tyrant who, even had he been favoured by fortune, would have wreaked his humours upon the defenceless things made his property by ties of blood and marriage, and who, being unfavoured, would do worse. Betty could see what the years had held for Rosy, and how her weakness and timidity had been considered as positive assets. A woman who will cry when she is bullied, may be counted upon to submit after she has cried. Rosy had submitted up to a certain point and then, with the stubbornness of a weak creature, had stood at timid bay for her young.

What Betty gathered was that, after the long and terrible illness which had followed Ughtred's birth, she had risen from what had been so nearly her deathbed, prostrated in both mind and body. Ughtred did not know all that he revealed when he touched upon the time which he said his mother could not quite remember—when she had sat for months staring vacantly out of her window, trying to recall something terrible which had happened, and which she wanted to tell her mother, if the day ever came when she could write to her again. She had never remembered clearly the details of the thing she had wanted to tell, and Nigel had insisted that her fancy was part of her past delirium. He had said that at the beginning of her delirium she had attacked and insulted his mother and himself but they had excused her because they realised afterwards what the cause of her excitement had been. For a long time she had been too brokenly weak to question or disbelieve, but, later she had vaguely known that he had been lying to her, though she could not refute what he said. She recalled, in course of time, a horrible scene in which all three of them had raved at each other, and she herself had shrieked and laughed and hurled wild words at Nigel, and he had struck her. That she knew and never forgot. She had been ill a year, her hair had fallen out, her skin had faded and she had begun to feel like a nervous, tired old woman instead of a girl. Girlhood, with all the past, had become unreal and too far away to be more than a dream. Nothing had remained real but Stornham and Nigel and the little hunchbacked baby. She was glad when the Dowager died and when Nigel spent his time in London or on the Continent and left her with Ughtred. When he said that he must spend her money on the estate, she had acquiesced without comment, because that insured his going away. She saw that no improvement or repairs were made, but she could do nothing and was too listless to make the attempt. She only wanted to be left alone with Ughtred, and she exhibited willpower only in defence of her child and in her obstinacy with regard to asking money of her father.

"She thought, somehow, that grandfather and grandmother did not care for her any more—that they had forgotten her and only cared for you," Ughtred explained. "She used to talk to me about you. She said you must be so clever and so handsome that no one could remember her. Sometimes she cried and said she did not want any of you to see her again, because she was only a hideous, little, thin, yellow old woman. When I was very little she told me stories about New York and Fifth Avenue. I thought they were not real places—I though they were places in fairyland."

Betty patted his shoulder and looked away for a moment when he said this. In her remote and helpless loneliness, to Rosy's homesick, yearning soul, noisy, rattling New York, Fifth Avenue with its traffic and people, its brown-stone houses and ricketty stages, had seemed like THAT—so splendid and bright and heart-filling, that she had painted them in colours which could belong only to fairyland. It said so much.

The thing she had suspected as she had talked to her sister was, before the interview ended, made curiously clear. The first obstacle in her pathway would be the shrinking of a creature who had been so long under dominion that the mere thought of seeing any steps taken towards her rescue filled her with alarm. One might be prepared for her almost praying to be let alone, because she felt that the process of her salvation would bring about such shocks and torments as she could not endure the facing of.

"She will have to get used to you," Ughtred kept saying. "She will have to get used to thinking things."

"I will be careful," Bettina answered. "She shall not be troubled. I did not come to trouble her."

CHAPTER XIII

ONE OF THE NEW YORK DRESSES

As she went down the staircase later, on her way to dinner, Miss Vanderpoel saw on all sides signs of the extent of the nakedness of the land. She was in a fine old house, stripped of most of its saleable belongings, uncared for, deteriorating year by year, gradually going to ruin. One need not possess particular keenness of sight to observe this, and she had chanced to see old houses in like condition in other countries than England. A man-servant, in a shabby livery, opened the drawing-room door for her. He was not a picturesque servitor of fallen fortunes, but an awkward person who was not accustomed to his duties. Betty wondered if he had been called in from the gardens to meet the necessities of the moment. His furtive glance at the tall young woman who passed him, took in with sudden embarrassment the fact that she plainly did not belong to the dispirited world bounded by Stornham Court. Without sparkling gems or trailing richness in her wake, she was suggestively splendid. He did not know whether it was her hair or the build of her neck and shoulders that did it, but it was revealed to him that tiaras and collars of stones which blazed belonged without doubt to her equipment. He recalled that there was a legend to the effect that the present Lady Anstruthers, who looked like a rag doll, had been the daughter of a rich American, and that better things might have been expected of her if she had not been such a poor-spirited creature. If this was her sister, she perhaps was a young woman of fortune, and that she was not of poor spirit was plain.

The large drawing-room presented but another aspect of the bareness of the rest of the house. In times probably long past, possibly in the Dowager Lady Anstruthers' early years of marriage, the walls had been hung with white and gold paper of a pattern which dominated the scene, and had been furnished with gilded chairs, tables, and ottomans. Some of these last had evidently been removed as they became too much out of repair for use or ornament. Such as remained, tarnished as to gilding and worn in the matter of upholstery, stood sparsely scattered on a desert of carpet, whose huge, flowered medallions had faded almost from view.

Lady Anstruthers, looking shy and awkward as she fingered an ornament on a small table, seemed singularly a part of her background. Her evening dress, slipping off her thin shoulders, was as faded and out of date as her carpet. It had once been delicately blue and gauzy, but its gauziness hung in crushed folds and its blue was almost grey. It was also the dress of a girl, not that of a colourless, worn woman, and her consciousness of its unfitness showed in her small-featured face as she came forward.

"Do you—recognise it, Betty?" she asked hesitatingly. "It was one of my New York dresses. I put it on because—because——" and her stammering ended helplessly.

"Because you wanted to remind me," Betty said. If she felt it easier to begin with an excuse she should be provided with one.

Perhaps but for this readiness to fall into any tone she chose to adopt Rosy might have endeavoured to carry her poor farce on, but as it was she suddenly gave it up.

"I put it on because I have no other," she said. "We never have visitors and I haven't dressed for dinner for so long that I seem to have nothing left that is fit to wear. I dragged this out because it was better than anything else. It was pretty once——" she gave a little laugh, "twelve years ago. How long years seem! Was I—was I pretty, Betty—twelve years ago?"

"Twelve years is not such a long time." Betty took her hand and drew her to a sofa. "Let us sit down and talk about it."

"There is nothing much to talk about. This is it——" taking in the room with a wave of her hand. "I am it. Ughtred is it."

"Then let us talk about England," was Bettina's light skim over the thin ice.

A red spot grew on each of Lady Anstruthers' cheek bones and made her faded eyes look intense.

"Let us talk about America," her little birdclaw of a hand clinging feverishly. "Is New York still—still——"

"It is still there," Betty answered with one of the adorable smiles which showed a deep dimple near her lip. "But it is much nearer England than it used to be."

"Nearer!" The hand tightened as Rosy caught her breath.

Betty bent rather suddenly and kissed her. It was the easiest way of hiding the look she knew had risen to her eyes. She began to talk gaily, half laughingly.

"It is quite near," she said. "Don't you realise it? Americans swoop over here by thousands every year. They come for business, they come for pleasure, they come for rest. They cannot keep away. They come to buy and sell—pictures and books and luxuries and lands. They come to give and take. They are building a bridge from shore to shore of their work, and their thoughts, and their plannings, out of the lives and souls of them. It will be a great bridge and great things will pass over it." She kissed the faded cheek again. She wanted to sweep Rosy away from the dreariness of "it." Lady Anstruthers looked at her with faintly smiling eyes. She did not follow all this quite readily, but she felt pleased and vaguely comforted.

"I know how they come here and marry," she said. "The new Duchess of Downes is an American. She had a fortune of two million pounds."

"If she chooses to rebuild a great house and a great name," said Betty, lifting her shoulders lightly, "why not—if it is an honest bargain? I suppose it is part of the building of the bridge."

Little Lady Anstruthers, trying to pull up the sleeves of the gauzy bodice slipping off her small, sharp bones, stared at her half in wondering adoration, half in alarm.

"Betty—you—you are so handsome—and so clever and strange," she fluttered. "Oh, Betty, stand up so that I can see how tall and handsome you are!"

Betty did as she was told, and upon her feet she was a young woman of long lines, and fine curves so inspiring to behold that Lady Anstruthers clasped her hands together on her knees in an excited gesture.

"Oh, yes! Oh, yes!" she cried. "You are just as wonderful as you looked when I turned and saw you under the trees. You almost make me afraid."

"Because I am wonderful?" said Betty. "Then I will not be wonderful any more."

"It is not because I think you wonderful, but because other people will. Would you rebuild a great house?" hesitatingly.

The fine line of Betty's black brows drew itself slightly together.

"No," she said.

"Wouldn't you?"

"How could the man who owned it persuade me that he was in earnest if he said he loved me? How could I persuade him that I was worth caring for and not a mere ambitious fool? There would be too much against us."

"Against you?" repeated Lady Anstruthers.

"I don't say I am fair," said Betty. "People who are proud are often not fair. But we should both of us have seen and known too much."

"You have seen me now," said Lady Anstruthers in her listless voice, and at the same moment dinner was announced and she got up from the sofa, so that, luckily, there was no time for the impersonal answer it would have been difficult to invent at a moment's notice. As they went into the dining-room Betty was thinking restlessly. She remembered all the material she had collected during her education in France and Germany, and there was added to it the fact that she HAD seen Rosy, and having her before her eyes she felt that there was small prospect of her contemplating the rebuilding of any great house requiring reconstruction.

There was fine panelling in the dining-room and a great fireplace and a few family portraits. The service upon the table was shabby and the dinner was not a bounteous meal. Lady Anstruthers in her girlish, gauzy dress and looking too small for her big, high-backed chair tried to talk rapidly, and every few minutes forgot herself and sank into silence, with her eyes unconsciously fixed upon her sister's face. Ughtred watched Betty also, and with a hungry questioning. The man-servant in the worn livery was not a sufficiently well-trained and experienced domestic to make any effort to keep his eyes from her. He was young enough to be excited by an innovation so unusual as the presence of a young and beautiful person surrounded by an unmistakable atmosphere of ease and fearlessness. He had been talking of her below stairs and felt that he had failed in describing her. He had found himself barely supported by the suggestion of a housemaid that sometimes these dresses that looked plain had been made in Paris at expensive places and had cost "a lot." He furtively examined the dress which looked plain, and while he admitted that for some mysterious reason it might represent expensiveness, it was not the dress which was the secret of the effect, but a something, not altogether mere good looks, expressed by the wearer. It was, in fact, the thing which the second-class passenger, Salter, had been at once attracted and stirred to rebellion by when Miss Vanderpoel came on board the Meridiana.

Betty did not look too small for her high-backed chair, and she did not forget herself when she talked. In spite of all she had found, her imagination was stirred by the surroundings. Her sense of the fine spaces and possibilities of dignity in the barren house, her knowledge that outside the windows there lay stretched broad views of the park and its heavy-branched trees, and that outside the gates stood the neglected picturesqueness of the village and all the rural and—to her—interesting life it slowly lived—this pleased and attracted her.

If she had been as helpless and discouraged as Rosalie she could see that it would all have meant a totally different and depressing thing, but, strong and spirited, and with the power of full hands, she was remotely rejoicing in what might be done with it all. As she talked she was gradually learning detail. Sir Nigel was on the Continent. Apparently he often went there; also it revealed itself that no one knew at what moment he might return, for what reason he would return, or if he would return at all during the summer. It was evident that no one had been at any time encouraged to ask questions as to his intentions, or to feel that they had a right to do so.

This she knew, and a number of other things, before they left the table. When they did so they went out to stroll upon the moss-grown stone terrace and listened to the nightingales throwing 'm into the air silver fountains of trilling song. When Bettina paused, leaning against the balustrade of the terrace that she might hear all the beauty of it, and feel all the beauty of the warm spring night, Rosy went on making her effort to talk.

"It is not much of a neighbourhood, Betty," she said. "You are too accustomed to livelier places to like it."

"That is my reason for feeling that I shall like it. I don't think I could be called a lively person, and I rather hate lively places."

"But you are accustomed—accustomed——" Rosy harked back uncertainly.

"I have been accustomed to wishing that I could come to you," said Betty. "And now I am here."

Lady Anstruthers laid a hand on her dress.

"I can't believe it! I can't believe it!" she breathed.

"You will believe it," said Betty, drawing the hand around her waist and enclosing in her own arm the narrow shoulders. "Tell me about the neighbourhood."

"There isn't any, really," said Lady Anstruthers. "The houses are so far away from each other. The nearest is six miles from here, and it is one that doesn't count.

"Why?"

"There is no family, and the man who owns it is so poor. It is a big place, but it is falling to pieces as this is."

"What is it called?"

"Mount Dunstan. The present earl only succeeded about three years ago. Nigel doesn't know him. He is queer and not liked. He has been away."

"Where?"

"No one knows. To Australia or somewhere. He has odd ideas. The Mount Dunstans have been awful people for two generations. This man's father was almost mad with wickedness. So was the elder son. This is a second son, and he came into nothing but debt. Perhaps he feels the disgrace and it makes him rude and ill-tempered. His father and elder brother had been in such scandals that people did not invite them.

"Do they invite this man?"

"No. He probably would not go to their houses if they did. And he went away soon after he came into the title."

"Is the place beautiful?"

"There is a fine deer park, and the gardens were wonderful a long time ago. The house is worth looking at—outside."

"I will go and look at it," said Betty.

"The carriage is out of order. There is only Ughtred's cart."

"I am a good walker," said Betty.

"Are you? It would be twelve miles—there and back. When I was in New York people didn't walk much, particularly girls."

"They do now," Betty answered. "They have learned to do it in England. They live out of doors and play games. They have grown athletic and tall."

As they talked the nightingales sang, sometimes near, sometimes in the distance, and scents of dewy grass and leaves and earth were wafted towards them. Sometimes they strolled up and down the terrace, sometimes they paused and leaned against the stone balustrade. Betty allowed Rosy to talk as she chose. She herself asked no obviously leading questions and passed over trying moments with lightness. Her desire was to place herself in a position where she might hear the things which would aid her to draw conclusions. Lady Anstruthers gradually grew less nervous and afraid of her subjects. In the wonder of the luxury of talking to someone who listened with sympathy, she once or twice almost forgot herself and made revelations she had not intended to make. She had often the manner of a person who was afraid of being overheard; sometimes, even when she was making speeches quite simple in themselves, her voice dropped and she glanced furtively aside as if there were chances that something she dreaded might step out of the shadow.

When they went upstairs together and parted for the night, the clinging of Rosy's embrace was for a moment almost convulsive. But she tried to laugh off its suggestion of intensity.

"I held you tight so that I could feel sure that you were real and would not melt away," she said. "I hope you will be here in the morning."

"I shall never really go quite away again, now I have come," Betty answered. "It is not only your house I have come into. I have come back into your life."

After she had entered her room and locked the door she sat down and wrote a letter to her father. It was a long letter, but a clear one. She painted a definite and detailed picture and made distinct her chief point.

"She is afraid of me," she wrote. "That is the first and worst obstacle. She is actually afraid that I will do something which will only add to her trouble. She has lived under dominion so long that she has forgotten that there are people who have no reason for fear. Her old life seems nothing but a dream. The first thing I must teach her is that I am to be trusted not to do futile things, and that she need neither be afraid of nor for me."

After writing these sentences she found herself leaving her desk and walking up and down the room to relieve herself. She could not sit still, because suddenly the blood ran fast and hot through her veins. She put her hands against her cheeks and laughed a little, low laugh.

"I feel violent," she said. "I feel violent and I must get over it. This is rage. Rage is worth nothing."

It was rage—the rage of splendid hot blood which surged in answer to leaping hot thoughts. There would have been a sort of luxury in giving way to the sway of it. But the self-indulgence would have been no aid to future action. Rage was worth nothing. She said it as the first Reuben Vanderpoel might have said of a useless but glittering weapon. "This gun is worth nothing," and cast it aside.

CHAPTER XIV

IN THE GARDENS

She came out upon the stone terrace again rather early in the morning. She wanted to wander about in the first freshness of the day, which was always an uplifting thing to her. She wanted to see the dew on the grass and on the ragged flower borders and to hear the tender, broken fluting of birds in the trees. One cuckoo was calling to another in the park, and she stopped and listened intently. Until yesterday she had never heard a cuckoo call, and its hollow mellowness gave her delight. It meant the spring in England, and nowhere else.

There was space enough to ramble about in the gardens. Paths and beds were alike overgrown with weeds, but some strong, early-blooming things were fighting for life, refusing to be strangled. Against the beautiful old red walls, over which age had stolen with a wonderful grey bloom, venerable fruit trees were spread and nailed, and here and there showed bloom, clumps of low-growing things sturdily advanced their yellowness or whiteness, as if defying neglect. In one place a wall slanted and threatened to fall, bearing its nectarine trees with it; in another there was a gap so evidently not of to-day that the heap of its masonry upon the border bed was already covered with greenery, and the roots of the fruit tree it had supported had sent up strong, insistent shoots.

She passed down broad paths and narrow ones, sometimes walking under trees, sometimes pushing her way between encroaching shrubs; she descended delightful mossy and broken steps and came upon dilapidated urns, in which weeds grew instead of flowers, and over which rampant but lovely, savage little creepers clambered and clung.

In one of the walled kitchen gardens she came upon an elderly gardener at work. At the sound of her approaching steps he glanced round and then stood up, touching his forelock in respectful but startled salute. He was so plainly amazed at the sight of her that she explained herself.

"Good-morning," she said. "I am her ladyship's sister, Miss Vanderpoel. I came yesterday evening. I am looking over your gardens."

He touched his forehead again and looked round him. His manner was not cheerful. He cast a troubled eye about him.

"They're not much to see, miss," he said. "They'd ought to be, but they're not. Growing things has to be fed and took care of. A man and a boy can't do it—nor yet four or five of 'em."

"How many ought there to be?" Betty inquired, with business-like directness. It was not only the dew on the grass she had come out to see.

"If there was eight or ten of us we might put it in order and keep it that way. It's a big place, miss."

Betty looked about her as he had done, but with a less discouraged eye.

"It is a beautiful place, as well as a large one," she said. "I can see that there ought to be more workers."

"There's no one," said the gardener, "as has as many enemies as a gardener, an' as many things to fight. There's grubs an' there's greenfly, an' there's drout', an' wet an' cold, an' mildew, an' there's what the soil wants and starves without, an' if you haven't got it nor yet hands an' feet an' tools enough, how's things to feed, an' fight an' live—let alone bloom an' bear?"

"I don't know much about gardens," said Miss Vanderpoel, "but I can understand that."

The scent of fresh bedewed things was in the air. It was true that she had not known much about gardens, but here standing in the midst of one she began to awaken to a new, practical interest. A creature of initiative could not let such a place as this alone. It was beauty being slowly slain. One could not pass it by and do nothing.

"What is your name?" she asked.

"Kedgers, miss. I've only been here about a twelve-month. I was took on because I'm getting on in years an' can't ask much wage."

"Can you spare time to take me through the gardens and show me things?"

Yes, he could do it. In truth, he privately welcomed an opportunity offering a prospect of excitement so novel. He had shown more flourishing gardens to other young ladies in his past years of service, but young ladies did not come to Stornham, and that one having, with such extraordinary unexpectedness arrived, should want to look over the desolation of these, was curious enough to rouse anyone to a sense of a break in accustomed monotony. The young lady herself mystified him by her difference from such others as he had seen. What the man in the shabby livery had felt, he felt also, and added to this was a sense of the practicalness of the questions she asked and the interest she showed and a way she had of seeming singularly to suggest by the look in her eyes and the tone of her voice that nothing was necessarily without remedy. When her ladyship walked through the place and looked at things, a pale resignation expressed itself in the very droop of her figure. When this one walked through the tumbled-down grape-houses, potting-sheds and conservatories, she saw where glass was broken, where benches had fallen and where roofs sagged and leaked. She inquired about the heating apparatus and asked that she might see it. She asked about the village and its resources, about labourers and their wages.

"As if," commented Kedgers mentally, "she was what Sir Nigel is—leastways what he'd ought to be an' ain't."

She led the way back to the fallen wall and stood and looked at it.

"It's a beautiful old wall," she said. "It should be rebuilt with the old brick. New would spoil it."

"Some of this is broken and crumbled away," said Kedgers, picking up a piece to show it to her.

"Perhaps old brick could be bought somewhere," replied the young lady speculatively. "One ought to be able to buy old brick in England, if one is willing to pay for it."

Kedgers scratched his head and gazed at her in respectful wonder which was almost trouble. Who was going to pay for things, and who was going to look for things which were not on the spot? Enterprise like this was not to be explained.

When she left him he stood and watched her upright figure disappear through the ivy-grown door of the kitchen gardens with a disturbed but elated expression on his countenance. He did not know why he felt elated, but he was conscious of elation. Something new had walked into the place. He stopped his work and grinned and scratched his head several times after he went back to his pottering among the cabbage plants.

"My word," he muttered. "She's a fine, straight young woman. If she was her ladyship things 'ud be different. Sir Nigel 'ud be different, too—or there'd be some fine upsets."

There was a huge stable yard, and Betty passed through that on her way back. The door of the carriage house was open and she saw two or three tumbled-down vehicles. One was a landau with a wheel off, one was a shabby, old-fashioned, low phaeton. She caught sight of a patently venerable cob in one of the stables. The stalls near him were empty.

"I suppose that is all they have to depend upon," she thought. "And the stables are like the gardens."

She found Lady Anstruthers and Ughtred waiting for her upon the terrace, each of them regarding her with an expression suggestive of repressed curiosity as she approached. Lady Anstruthers flushed a little and went to meet her with an eager kiss.

"You look like—I don't know quite what you look like, Betty!" she exclaimed.

The girl's dimple deepened and her eyes said smiling things.

"It is the morning—and your gardens," she answered. "I have been round your gardens."

"They were beautiful once, I suppose," said Rosy deprecatingly.

"They are beautiful now. There is nothing like them in America at least."

"I don't remember any gardens in America," Lady Anstruthers owned reluctantly, "but everything seemed so cheerful and well cared for and—and new. Don't laugh, Betty. I have begun to like new things. You would if you had watched old ones tumbling to pieces for twelve years."

"They ought not to be allowed to tumble to pieces," said Betty. She added her next words with simple directness. She could only discover how any advancing steps would be taken by taking them. "Why do you allow them to do it?"

Lady Anstruthers looked away, but as she looked her eyes passed Ughtred's.

"I!" she said. "There are so many other things to do. It would cost so much—such an enormity to keep it all in order."

"But it ought to be done—for Ughtred's sake."

"I know that," faltered Rosy, "but I can't help it."

"You can," answered Betty, and she put her arm round her as they turned to enter the house. "When you have become more used to me and my driving American ways I will show you how."

The lightness with which she said it had an odd effect on Lady Anstruthers. Such casual readiness was so full of the suggestion of unheard of possibilities that it was a kind of shock.

"I have been twelve years in getting un-used to you—I feel as if it would take twelve years more to get used again," she said.

"It won't take twelve weeks," said Betty.

CHAPTER XV

THE FIRST MAN

The mystery of the apparently occult methods of communication among the natives of India, between whom, it is said, news flies by means too strange and subtle to be humanly explainable, is no more difficult a problem to solve than that of the lightning rapidity with which a knowledge of the transpiring of any new local event darts through the slowest, and, as far as outward signs go, the least communicative English village slumbering drowsily among its pastures and trees.

That which the Hall or Manor House believed last night, known only to the four walls of its drawing-room, is discussed over the cottage breakfast tables as though presented in detail through the columns of the Morning Post. The vicarage, the smithy, the post office, the little provision shop, are instantaneously informed as by magic of such incidents of interest as occur, and are prepared to assist vicariously at any future developments. Through what agency information is given no one can tell, and, indeed, the agency is of small moment. Facts of interest are perhaps like flights of swallows and dart chattering from one red roof to another, proclaiming themselves aloud. Nothing is so true as that in such villages they are the property and innocent playthings of man, woman, and child, providing conversation and drama otherwise likely to be lacked.

When Miss Vanderpoel walked through Stornham village street she became aware that she was an exciting object of interest. Faces appeared at cottage windows, women sauntered to doors, men in the taproom of the Clock Inn left beer mugs to cast an eye on her; children pushed open gates and stared as they bobbed their curtsies; the young woman who kept the shop left her counter and came out upon her door step to pick up her straying baby and glance over its shoulder at the face with the red mouth, and the mass of black hair rolled upward under a rough blue straw hat. Everyone knew who this exotic-looking young lady was. She had arrived yesterday from London, and a week ago by means of a ship from far-away America, from the country in connection with which the rural mind curiously mixed up large wages, great fortunes and Indians. "Gaarge" Lunsden, having spent five years of his youth labouring heavily for sixteen shillings a week, had gone to "Meriker" and had earned there eight shillings a day. This was a well-known and much-talked over fact, and had elevated the western continent to a position of trust and importance it had seriously lacked before the emigration of Lunsden. A place where a man could earn eight shillings a day inspired interest as well as confidence. When Sir Nigel's wife had arrived twelve years ago as the new Lady Anstruthers, the story that she herself "had money" had been verified by her fine clothes and her way of handing out sovereigns in cases where the rest of the gentry, if they gave at all, would have bestowed tea and flannel or shillings. There had been for a few months a period of unheard of well-being in Stornham village; everyone remembered the hundred pounds the bride had given to poor Wilson when his place had burned down, but the village had of course learned, by its occult means, that Sir Nigel and the Dowager had been angry and that there had been a quarrel. Afterwards her ladyship had been dangerously ill, the baby had been born a hunchback, and a year had passed before its mother had been seen again. Since then she had been a changed creature; she had lost her looks and seemed to care for nothing but the child. Stornham village saw next to nothing of her, and it certainly was not she who had the dispensing of her fortune. Rumour said Sir Nigel lived high in London and foreign parts, but there was no high living at the Court. Her ladyship's family had never been near her, and belief in them and their wealth almost ceased to exist. If they were rich, Stornham felt that it was their business to mend roofs and windows and not allow chimneys and kitchen boilers to fall into ruin, the simple, leading article of faith being that even American money belonged properly to England.

As Miss Vanderpoel walked at a light, swinging pace through the one village street the gazers felt with Kedgers that something new was passing and stirring the atmosphere. She looked straight, and with a friendliness somehow dominating, at the curious women; her handsome eyes met those of the men in a human questioning; she smiled and nodded to the bobbing children. One of these, young enough to be uncertain on its feet, in running to join some others stumbled and fell on the path before her. Opening its mouth in the inevitable resultant roar, it was shocked almost into silence by the tall young lady stooping at once, picking it up, and cheerfully dusting its pinafore.

"Don't cry," she said; "you are not hurt, you know."

The deep dimple near her mouth showed itself, and the laugh in her eyes was so reassuring that the penny she put into the grubby hand was less productive of effect than her mere self. She walked on, leaving the group staring after her breathless, because of a sense of having met with a wonderful adventure. The grand young lady with the black hair and the blue hat and tall, straight body was the adventure. She left the same sense of event with the village itself. They talked of her all day over their garden palings, on their doorsteps, in the street; of her looks, of her height, of the black rim of lashes round her eyes, of the chance that she might be rich and ready to give half-crowns and sovereigns, of the "Meriker" she had come from, and above all of the reason for her coming.

Betty swung with the light, firm step of a good walker out on to the highway. To walk upon the fine, smooth old Roman road was a pleasure in itself, but she soon struck away from it and went through lanes and by-ways, following sign-posts because she knew where she was going. Her walk was to take her to Mount Dunstan and home again by another road. In walking, an objective point forms an interest, and what she had heard of the estate from Rosalie was a vague reason for her caring to see it. It was another place like Stornham, once dignified and nobly representative of fine things, now losing their meanings and values. Values and meanings, other than mere signs of wealth and power, there had been. Centuries ago strong creatures had planned and built it for such reasons as strength has for its planning and building. In

Bettina Vanderpoel's imagination the First Man held powerful and moving sway. It was he whom she always saw. In history, as a child at school, she had understood and drawn close to him. There was always a First Man behind all that one saw or was told, one who was the fighter, the human thing who snatched weapons and tools from stones and trees and wielded them in the carrying out of the thought which was his possession and his strength. He was the God made human; others waited, without knowledge of their waiting, for the signal he gave. A man like others—with man's body, hands, and limbs, and eyes—the moving of a whole world was subtly altered by his birth. One could not always trace him, but with stone axe and spear point he had won savage lands in savage ways, and so ruled them that, leaving them to other hands, their march towards less savage life could not stay itself, but must sweep on; others of his kind, striking rude harps, had so sung that the loud clearness of their wild songs had rung through the ages, and echo still in strains which are theirs, though voices of to-day repeat the note of them. The First Man, a Briton stained with woad and hung with skins, had tilled the luscious greenness of the lands richly rolling now within hedge boundaries. The square church towers rose, holding their slender corner spires above the trees, as a result of the First Man, Norman William. The thought which held its place, the work which did not pass away, had paid its First Man wages; but beauties crumbling, homes falling to waste, were bitter things. The First Man, who, having won his splendid acres, had built his home upon them and reared his young and passed his possession on with a proud heart, seemed but ill treated. Through centuries the home had enriched itself, its acres had borne harvests, its trees had grown and spread huge branches, full lives had been lived within the embrace of the massive walls, there had been loves and lives and marriages and births, the breathings of them made warm and full the very air. To Betty it seemed that the land itself would have worn another face if it had not been trodden by so many springing feet, if so many harvests had not waved above it, if so many eyes had not looked upon and loved it.

She passed through variations of the rural loveliness she had seen on her way from the station to the Court, and felt them grow in beauty as she saw them again. She came at last to a village somewhat larger than Stornham and marked by the signs of the lack of money-spending care which Stornham showed. Just beyond its limits a big park gate opened on to an avenue of massive trees. She stopped and looked down it, but could see nothing but its curves and, under the branches, glimpses of a spacious sweep of park with other trees standing in groups or alone in the sward. The avenue was unswept and untended, and here and there boughs broken off by wind.

Storms lay upon it. She turned to the road again and followed it, because it enclosed the park and she wanted to see more of its evident beauty. It was very beautiful. As she walked on she saw it rolled into woods and deeps filled with bracken; she saw stretches of hillocky, fine-grassed rabbit warren, and hollows holding shadowy pools; she caught the gleam of a lake with swans sailing slowly upon it with curved necks; there were wonderful lights and wonderful shadows, and brooding stillness, which made her footfall upon the road a too material thing.

Suddenly she heard a stirring in the bracken a yard or two away from her. Something was moving slowly among the waving masses of huge fronds and caused them to sway to and fro. It was an antlered stag who rose from his bed in the midst of them, and with majestic deliberation got upon his feet and stood gazing at her with a calmness of pose so splendid, and a liquid darkness and lustre of eye so stilly and fearlessly beautiful, that she caught her breath. He simply gazed as her as a great king might gaze at an intruder, scarcely deigning wonder.

As she had passed on her way, Betty had seen that the enclosing park palings were decaying, covered with lichen and falling at intervals. It had even passed through her mind that here was one of the demands for expenditure on a large estate, which limited resources could not confront with composure. The deer fence itself, a thing of wire ten feet high, to form an obstacle to leaps, she had marked to be in such condition as to threaten to become shortly a useless thing. Until this moment she had seen no deer, but looking beyond the stag and across the sward she now saw groups near each other, stags cropping or looking towards her with lifted heads, does at a respectful but affectionate distance from them, some caring for their fawns. The stag who had risen near her had merely walked through a gap in the boundary and now stood free to go where he would.

"He will get away," said Betty, knitting her black brows. Ah! what a shame!

Even with the best intentions one could not give chase to a stag. She looked up and down the road, but no one was within sight. Her brows continued to knit themselves and her eyes ranged over the park itself in the hope that some labourer on the estate, some woodman or game-keeper, might be about.

"It is no affair of mine," she said, "but it would be too bad to let him get away, though what happens to stray stags one doesn't exactly know."

As she said it she caught sight of someone, a man in leggings and shabby clothes and with a gun over his shoulder, evidently an under keeper. He was a big, rather rough-looking fellow, but as he lurched out into the open from a wood Betty saw that she could reach him if she passed through a narrow gate a few yards away and walked quickly.

He was slouching along, his head drooping and his broad shoulders expressing the definite antipodes of good spirits. Betty studied his back as she strode after him, her conclusion being that he was perhaps not a good-humoured man to approach at any time, and that this was by ill luck one of his less fortunate hours.

"Wait a moment, if you please," her clear, mellow voice flung out after him when she was within hearing distance. "I want to speak to you, keeper."

He turned with an air of far from pleased surprise. The afternoon sun was in his eyes and made him scowl. For a moment he did not see distinctly who was approaching him, but he had at once recognised a certain cool tone of command in the voice whose suddenness had roused him from a black mood. A few steps brought them to close quarters, and when he found himself looking into the eyes of his pursuer he made a movement as if to lift his cap, then checking himself, touched it, keeper fashion.

"Oh!" he said shortly. "Miss Vanderpoel! Beg pardon."

Bettina stood still a second. She had her surprise also. Here was the unexpected again. The under keeper was the red-haired second-class passenger of the Meridiana.

He did not look pleased to see her, and the suddenness of his appearance excluded the possibility of her realising that upon the whole she was at least not displeased to see him.

"How do you do?" she said, feeling the remark fantastically conventional, but not being inspired by any alternative. "I came to tell you that one of the stags has got through a gap in the fence."

"Damn!" she heard him say under his breath. Aloud he said, "Thank you."

"He is a splendid creature," she said. "I did not know what to do. I was glad to see a keeper coming."

"Thank you," he said again, and strode towards the place where the stag still stood gazing up the road, as if reflecting as to whether it allured him or not.

Betty walked back more slowly, watching him with interest. She wondered what he would find it necessary to do. She heard him begin a low, flute-like whistling, and then saw the antlered head turn towards him. The woodland creature moved, but it was in his direction. It had without doubt answered his call before and knew its meaning to be friendly. It went towards him, stretching out a tender sniffing nose, and he put his hand in the pocket of his rough coat and gave it something to eat. Afterwards he went to the gap in the fence and drew the wires together, fastening them with other wire, which he also took out of the coat pocket.

"He is not afraid of making himself useful," thought Betty. "And the animals know him. He is not as bad as he looks."

She lingered a moment watching him, and then walked towards the gate through which she had entered. He glanced up as she neared him.

"I don't see your carriage," he said. "Your man is probably round the trees."

"I walked," answered Betty. "I had heard of this place and wanted to see it."

He stood up, putting his wire back into his pocket.

"There is not much to be seen from the road," he said. "Would you like to see more of it?"

His manner was civil enough, but not the correct one for a servant. He did not say "miss" or touch his cap in making the suggestion. Betty hesitated a moment.

"Is the family at home?" she inquired.

"There is no family but—his lordship. He is off the place."

"Does he object to trespassers?"

"Not if they are respectable and take no liberties."

"I am respectable, and I shall not take liberties," said Miss Vanderpoel, with a touch of hauteur. The truth was that she had spent a sufficient number of years on the Continent to have become familiar with conventions which led her not to approve wholly of his bearing. Perhaps he had lived long enough in America to forget such conventions and to lack something which centuries of custom had decided should belong to his class. A certain suggestion of rough force in the man rather attracted her, and her slight distaste for his manner arose from the realisation that a gentleman's servant who did not address his superiors as was required by custom was not doing his work in a finished way. In his place she knew her own demeanour would have been finished.

"If you are sure that Lord Mount Dunstan would not object to my walking about, I should like very much to see the gardens and the house," she said. "If you show them to me, shall I be interfering with your duties?"

"No," he answered, and then for the first time rather glumly added, "miss."

"I am interested," she said, as they crossed the grass together, "because places like this are quite new to me. I have never been in England before."

"There are not many places like this," he answered, "not many as old and fine, and not many as nearly gone to ruin. Even Stornham is not quite as far gone."

"It is far gone," said Miss Vanderpoel. "I am staying there—with my sister, Lady Anstruthers."

"Beg pardon—miss," he said. This time he touched his cap in apology.

Enormous as the gulf between their positions was, he knew that he had offered to take her over the place because he was in a sense glad to see her again. Why he was glad he did not profess to know or even to ask himself. Coarsely speaking, it might be because she was one of the handsomest young women he had ever chanced to meet with, and while her youth was apparent in the rich red of her mouth, the mass of her thick, soft hair and the splendid blue of her eyes, there spoke in every line of face and pose something intensely more interesting and compelling than girlhood. Also, since the night they had come together on the ship's deck for an appalling moment, he had liked her better and rebelled less against the unnatural wealth she represented. He led her first to the wood from which she had seen him emerge.

"I will show you this first," he explained. "Keep your eyes on the ground until I tell you to raise them."

Odd as this was, she obeyed, and her lowered glance showed her that she was being guided along a narrow path between trees. The light was mellow golden-green, and birds were singing in the boughs above her. In a few minutes he stopped.

"Now look up," he said.

She uttered an exclamation when she did so. She was in a fairy dell thick with ferns, and at beautiful distances from each other incredibly splendid oaks spread and almost trailed their lovely giant branches. The glow shining through and between them, the shadows beneath them, their great boles and moss-covered roots, and the stately, mellow distances revealed under their branches, the ancient wildness and richness, which meant, after all, centuries of cultivation, made a picture in this exact, perfect moment of ripening afternoon sun of an almost unbelievable beauty.

"There is nothing lovelier," he said in a low voice, "in all England."

Bettina turned to look at him, because his tone was a curious one for a man like himself. He was standing resting on his gun and taking in the loveliness with a strange look in his rugged face.

"You—you love it!" she said.

"Yes," but with a suggestion of stubborn reluctance in the admission.

She was rather moved.

"Have you been keeper here long?" she asked.

"No—only a few years. But I have known the place all my life."

"Does Lord Mount Dunstan love it?"

"In his way—yes."

He was plainly not disposed to talk of his master. He was perhaps not on particularly good terms with him. He led her away and volunteered no further information. He was, upon the whole, uncommunicative. He did not once refer to the circumstance of their having met before. It was plain that he had no intention of presuming upon the fact that he, as a second-class passenger on a ship, had once been forced by accident across the barriers between himself and the saloon deck. He was stubbornly resolved to keep his place; so stubbornly that Bettina felt that to broach the subject herself would verge upon offence.

But the golden ways through which he led her made the afternoon one she knew she should never forget. They wandered through moss walks and alleys, through tangled shrubberies bursting into bloom, beneath avenues of blossoming horse-chestnuts and scented limes, between thickets of budding red and white may, and jungles of neglected rhododendrons; through sunken gardens and walled ones, past terraces with broken balustrades of stone, and fallen Floras and Dianas, past moss-grown fountains splashing in lovely corners. Arches, overgrown with yet unblooming roses, crumbled in their time stained beauty. Stillness brooded over it all, and they met no one. They scarcely broke the silence themselves. The man led the way as one who knew it by heart, and Bettina followed, not caring for speech herself, because the stillness seemed to add a spell of enchantment. What could one say, to a stranger, of such beauty so lost and given over to ruin and decay.

"But, oh!" she murmured once, standing still, with indrawn breath, "if it were mine!—if it were mine!" And she said the thing forgetting that her guide was a living creature and stood near.

Afterwards her memories of it all seemed to her like the memories of a dream. The lack of speech between herself and the man who led her, his often averted face, her own sense of the desertedness of each beauteous spot she passed through, the mossy paths which gave back no sound of footfalls as they walked, suggested, one and all, unreality. When at last they passed through a door half hidden in an ivied wall, and crossing a grassed bowling green, mounted a short flight of broken steps which led them to a point through which they saw the house through a break in the trees, this last was the final touch of all. It was a great place, stately in its masses of grey stone to which thick ivy clung. To Bettina it seemed that a hundred windows stared at her with closed, blind eyes. All were shuttered but two or three on the lower floors. Not one showed signs of life. The silent stone thing stood sightless among all of which it was dead master—rolling acres, great trees, lost gardens and deserted groves.

"Oh!" she sighed, "Oh!"

Her companion stood still and leaned upon his gun again, looking as he had looked before.

"Some of it," he said, "was here before the Conquest. It belonged to Mount Dunstans then."

"And only one of them is left," she cried, "and it is like this!"

"They have been a bad lot, the last hundred years," was the surly liberty of speech he took, "a bad lot."

It was not his place to speak in such manner of those of his master's house, and it was not the part of Miss Vanderpoel to encourage him by response. She remained silent, standing perhaps a trifle more lightly erect as she gazed at the rows of blind windows in silence.

Neither of them uttered a word for some time, but at length Bettina roused herself. She had a six-mile walk before her and must go.

"I am very much obliged to you," she began, and then paused a second. A curious hesitance came upon her, though she knew that under ordinary circumstances such hesitation would have been totally out of place. She had occupied the man's time for an hour or more, he was of the working class, and one must not be guilty of the error of imagining that a man who has work to do can justly spend his time in one's service for the mere pleasure of it. She knew what custom demanded. Why should she hesitate before this man, with his not too courteous, surly face. She felt slightly irritated by her own unpractical embarrassment as she put her hand into the small, latched bag at her belt.

"I am very much obliged, keeper," she said. "You have given me a great deal of your time. You know the place so well that it has been a pleasure to be taken about by you. I have never seen anything so beautiful—and so sad. Thank you—thank you." And she put a goldpiece in his palm.

His fingers closed over it quietly. Why it was to her great relief she did not know—because something in the simple act annoyed her, even while she congratulated herself that her hesitance had been absurd. The next moment she wondered if it could be possible that he had expected a larger fee. He opened his hand and looked at the money with a grim steadiness.

"Thank you, miss," he said, and touched his cap in the proper manner.

He did not look gracious or grateful, but he began to put it in a small pocket in the breast of his worn corduroy shooting jacket. Suddenly he stopped, as if with abrupt resolve. He handed the coin back without any change of his glum look.

"Hang it all," he said, "I can't take this, you know. I suppose I ought to have told you. It would have been less awkward for us both. I am that unfortunate beggar, Mount Dunstan, myself."

A pause was inevitable. It was a rather long one. After it, Betty took back her half-sovereign and returned it to her bag, but she pleased a certain perversity in him by looking more annoyed than confused.

"Yes," she said. "You ought to have told me, Lord Mount Dunstan."

He slightly shrugged his big shoulders.

"Why shouldn't you take me for a keeper? You crossed the Atlantic with a fourth-rate looking fellow separated from you by barriers of wood and iron. You came upon him tramping over a nobleman's estate in shabby corduroys and gaiters, with a gun over his shoulder and a scowl on his ugly face. Why should you leap to the conclusion that he is the belted Earl himself? There is no cause for embarrassment."

"I am not embarrassed," said Bettina.

"That is what I like," gruffly.

"I am pleased," in her mellowest velvet voice, "that you like it."

Their eyes met with a singular directness of gaze. Between them a spark passed which was not afterwards to be extinguished, though neither of them knew the moment of its kindling, and Mount Dunstan slightly frowned.

"I beg pardon," he said. "You are quite right. It had a deucedly patronising sound."

As he stood before her Betty was given her opportunity to see him as she had not seen him before, to confront the sum total of his physique. His red-brown eyes looked out from rather fine heavy brows, his features were strong and clear, though ruggedly cut, his build showed weight of bone, not of flesh, and his limbs were big and long. He would have wielded a battle-axe with power in centuries in which men hewed their way with them. Also it occurred to her he would have looked well in a coat of mail. He did not look ill in his corduroys and gaiters.

"I am a self-absorbed beggar," he went on. "I had been slouching about the place, almost driven mad by my thoughts, and when I saw you took me for a servant my fancy was for letting the thing go on. If I had been a rich man instead of a pauper I would have kept your half-sovereign."

"I should not have enjoyed that when I found out the truth," said Miss Vanderpoel.

"No, I suppose you wouldn't. But I should not have cared."

He was looking at her straightly and summing her up as she had summed him up. A man and young, he did not miss a line or a tint of her chin or cheek, shoulder, or brow, or dense, lifted hair. He had already, even in his guise of keeper, noticed one thing, which was that while at times her eyes were the blue of steel, sometimes they melted to the colour of bluebells under water. They had been of this last hue when she had stood in the sunken garden, forgetting him and crying low:

"Oh, if it were mine! If it were mine!"

He did not like American women with millions, but while he would not have said that he liked her, he did not wish her yet to move away. And she, too, did not wish, just yet, to move away. There was something dramatic and absorbing in the situation. She looked over the softly stirring grass and saw the sunshine was deepening its gold and the shadows were growing long. It was not a habit of hers to ask questions, but she asked one.

"Did you not like America?" was what she said.

"Hated it! Hated it! I went there lured by a belief that a man like myself, with muscle and will, even without experience, could make a fortune out of small capital on a sheep ranch. Wind and weather and disease played the devil with me. I lost the little I had and came back to begin over again—on nothing—here!" And he waved his hand over the park with its sward and coppice and bracken and the deer cropping in the late afternoon gold.

"To begin what again?" said Betty. It was an extraordinary enough thing, seen in the light of conventions, that they should stand and talk like this. But the spark had kindled between eye and eye, and because of it they suddenly had forgotten that they were strangers.

"You are an American, so it may not seem as mad to you as it would to others. To begin to build up again, in one man's life, what has taken centuries to grow—and fall into this."

"It would be a splendid thing to do," she said slowly, and as she said it her eyes took on their colour of bluebells, because what she had seen had moved her. She had not looked at him, but at the cropping deer as she spoke, but at her next sentence she turned to him again.

"Where should you begin?" she asked, and in saying it thought of Stornham.

He laughed shortly.

"That is American enough," he said. "Your people have not finished their beginnings yet and live in the spirit of them. I tell you of a wild fancy, and you accept it as a possibility and turn on me with, 'Where should you begin?'"

"That is one way of beginning," said Bettina. "In fact, it is the only way."

He did not tell her that he liked that, but he knew that he did like it and that her mere words touched him like a spur. It was, of course, her lifelong breathing of the atmosphere of millions which made for this fashion of moving at once in the direction of obstacles presenting to the rest of the world barriers seemingly insurmountable. And yet there was something else in it, some quality of nature which did not alone suggest the omnipotence of wealth, but another thing which might be even stronger and therefore carried conviction. He who had raged and clenched his hands in the face of his knowledge of the aspect his dream would have presented if he had revealed it to the ordinary practical mind, felt that a point of view like this was good for him. There was in it stimulus for a fleeting moment at least.

"That is a good idea," he answered. "Where should you begin?"

She replied quite seriously, though he could have imagined some girls rather simpering over the question as a casual joke.

"One would begin at the fences," she said. "Don't you think so?"

"That is practical."

"That is where I shall begin at Stornham," reflectively.

"You are going to begin at Stornham?"

"How could one help it? It is not as large or as splendid as this has been, but it is like it in a way. And it will belong to my sister's son. No, I could not help it."

"I suppose you could not." There was a hint of wholly unconscious resentment in his tone. He was thinking that the effect produced by their boundless wealth was to make these people feel as a race of giants might—even their women unknowingly revealed it.

"No, I could not," was her reply. "I suppose I am on the whole a sort of commercial working person. I have no doubt it is commercial, that instinct which makes one resent seeing things lose their value."

"Shall you begin it for that reason?"

"Partly for that one—partly for another." She held out her hand to him. "Look at the length of the shadows. I must go. Thank you, Lord Mount Dunstan, for showing me the place, and thank you for undeceiving me."

He held the side gate open for her and lifted his cap as she passed through. He admitted to himself, with some reluctance, that he was not content that she should go even yet, but, of course, she must go. There passed through his mind a remote wonder why he had suddenly unbosomed himself to her in a way so extraordinarily unlike himself. It was, he thought next, because as he had taken her about from one place to another he had known that she had seen in things what he had seen in them so long—the melancholy loneliness, the significance of it, the lost hopes that lay behind it, the touching pain of the stateliness wrecked. She had shown it in the way in which she tenderly looked from side to side, in the very lightness of her footfall, in the bluebell softening of her eyes. Oh, yes, she had understood and cared, American as she was! She had felt it all, even with her hideous background of Fifth Avenue behind her.

When he had spoken it had been in involuntary response to an emotion in herself.

So he stood, thinking, as he for some time watched her walking up the sunset-glowing road.

CHAPTER XVI

THE PARTICULAR INCIDENT

Betty Vanderpoel's walk back to Stornham did not, long though it was, give her time to follow to its end the thread of her thoughts. Mentally she walked again with her uncommunicative guide, through woodpaths and gardens, and stood gazing at the great blind-faced house. She had not given the man more than an occasional glance until he had told her his name. She had been too much absorbed, too much moved, by what she had been seeing. She wondered, if she had been more aware of him, whether his face would have revealed a great deal. She believed it would not. He had made himself outwardly stolid. But the thing must have been bitter. To him the whole story of the splendid past was familiar even if through his own life he had looked on only at gradual decay. There must be stories enough of men and women who had lived in the place, of what they had done, of how they had loved, of what they had counted for in their country's wars and peacemakings, great functions and law-building. To be able to look back through centuries and know of one's blood that sometimes it had been shed in the doing of great deeds, must be a thing to remember. To realise that the courage and honour had been lost in ignoble modern vices, which no sense of dignity and reverence for race and name had restrained— must be bitter—bitter! And in the role of a servant to lead a stranger about among the ruins of what had been—that must have been bitter, too. For a moment Betty felt the bitterness of it herself and her red mouth took upon itself a grim line. The worst of it for him was that he was not of that strain of his race who had been the "bad lot." The "bad lot" had been the weak lot, the vicious, the self-degrading. Scandals which had shut men out from their class and kind were usually of an ugly type. This man had a strong jaw, a powerful, healthy body, and clean, though perhaps hard, eyes. The First Man of them, who hewed his way to the front, who stood fierce in the face of things, who won the first lands and laid the first stones, might have been like him in build and look.

"It's a disgusting thing," she said to herself, "to think of the corrupt weaklings the strong ones dwindled down to. I hate them. So does he."

There had been many such of late years, she knew. She had seen them in Paris, in Rome, even in New York. Things with thin or over-thick bodies and receding chins and foreheads; things haunting places of amusement and finding inordinate entertainment in strange jokes and horseplay. She herself had hot blood and a fierce strength of rebellion, and she was wondering how, if the father and elder brother had been the "bad lot," he had managed to stand still, looking on, and keeping his hands off them.

The last gold of the sun was mellowing the grey stone of the terrace and enriching the green of the weeds thrusting themselves into life between the uneven flags when she reached Stornham, and passing through the house found Lady Anstruthers sitting there. In sustenance of her effort to keep up appearances, she had put on a weird little muslin dress and had elaborated the dressing of her thin hair. It was no longer dragged back straight from her face, and she looked a trifle less abject, even a shade prettier. Bettina sat upon the edge of the balustrade and touched the hair with light fingers, ruffling it a little becomingly.

"If you had worn it like this yesterday," she said, "I should have known you."

"Should you, Betty? I never look into a mirror if I can help it, but when I do I never know myself. The thing that stares back at me with its pale eyes is not Rosy. But, of course, everyone grows old."

"Not now! People are just discovering how to grow young instead."

Lady Anstruthers looked into the clear courage of her laughing eyes.

"Somehow," she said, "you say strange things in such a way that one feels as if they must be true, however—however unlike anything else they are."

"They are not as new as they seem," said Betty. "Ancient philosophers said things like them centuries ago, but people did not believe them. We are just beginning to drag them out of the dust and furbish them up and pretend they are ours, just as people rub up and adorn themselves with jewels dug out of excavations."

"In America people think so many new things," said poor little Lady Anstruthers with yearning humbleness.

"The whole civilised world is thinking what you call new things," said Betty. "The old ones won't do. They have been tried, and though they have helped us to the place we have reached, they cannot help us any farther. We must begin again."

"It is such a long time since I began," said Rosy, "such a long time."

"Then there must be another beginning for you, too. The hour has struck."

Lady Anstruthers rose with as involuntary a movement as if a strong hand had drawn her to her feet. She stood facing Betty, a pathetic little figure in her washed-out muslin frock and with her washed-out face and eyes and being, though on her faded cheeks a flush was rising.

"Oh, Betty!" she said, "I don't know what there is about you, but there is something which makes one feel as if you believed everything and could do everything, and as if one believes YOU. Whatever you were to say, you would make it seem TRUE. If you said the wildest thing in the world I should BELIEVE you."

Betty got up, too, and there was an extraordinary steadiness in her eyes.

"You may," she answered. "I shall never say one thing to you which is not a truth, not one single thing."

"I believe that," said Rosy Anstruthers, with a quivering mouth. "I do believe it so."

"I walked to Mount Dunstan," Betty said later.

"Really?" said Rosy. "There and back?"

"Yes, and all round the park and the gardens."

Rosy looked rather uncertain.

"Weren't you a little afraid of meeting someone?"

"I did meet someone. At first I took him for a gamekeeper. But he turned out to be Lord Mount Dunstan."

Lady Anstruthers gasped.

"What did he do?" she exclaimed. "Did he look angry at seeing a stranger? They say he is so ill-tempered and rude."

"I should feel ill-tempered if I were in his place," said Betty. "He has enough to rouse his evil passions and make him savage. What a fate for a man with any sense and decency of feeling! What fools and criminals the last generation of his house must have produced! I wonder how such things evolve themselves. But he is different—different. One can see it. If he had a chance—just half a chance—he would build it all up again. And I don't mean merely the place, but all that one means when one says 'his house.'"

"He would need a great deal of money," sighed Lady Anstruthers.

Betty nodded slowly as she looked out, reflecting, into the park.

"Yes, it would require money," was her admission.

"And he has none," Lady Anstruthers added. "None whatever."

"He will get some," said Betty, still reflecting. "He will make it, or dig it up, or someone will leave it to him. There is a great deal of money in the world, and when a strong creature ought to have some of it he gets it."

"Oh, Betty!" said Rosy. "Oh, Betty!"

"Watch that man," said Betty; "you will see. It will come."

Lady Anstruthers' mind, working at no time on complex lines, presented her with a simple modern solution.

"Perhaps he will marry an American," she said, and saying it, sighed again.

"He will not do it on purpose." Bettina answered slowly and with such an air of absence of mind that Rosy laughed a little.

"Will he do it accidentally, or against his will?" she said.

Betty herself smiled.

"Perhaps he will," she said. "There are Englishmen who rather dislike Americans. I think he is one of them."

It apparently became necessary for Lady Anstruthers, a moment later, to lean upon the stone balustrade and pick off a young leaf or so, for no reason whatever, unless that in doing so she averted her look from her sister as she made her next remark.

"Are you—when are you going to write to father and mother?"

"I have written," with unembarrassed evenness of tone. "Mother will be counting the days."

"Mother!" Rosy breathed, with a soft little gasp. "Mother!" and turned her face farther away. "What did you tell her?"

Betty moved over to her and stood close at her side. The power of her personality enveloped the tremulous creature as if it had been a sense of warmth.

"I told her how beautiful the place was, and how Ughtred adored you—and how you loved us all, and longed to see New York again."

The relief in the poor little face was so immense that Betty's heart shook before it. Lady Anstruthers looked up at her with adoring eyes.

"I might have known," she said; "I might have known that—that you would only say the right thing. You couldn't say the wrong thing, Betty."

Betty bent over her and spoke almost yearningly.

"Whatever happens," she said, "we will take care that mother is not hurt. She's too kind—she's too good—she's too tender."

"That is what I have remembered," said Lady Anstruthers brokenly. "She used to hold me on her lap when I was quite grown up. Oh! her soft, warm arms—her warm shoulder! I have so wanted her."

"She has wanted you," Betty answered. "She thinks of you just as she did when she held you on her lap."

"But if she saw me now—looking like this! If she saw me! Sometimes I have even been glad to think she never would."

"She will." Betty's tone was cool and clear. "But before she does I shall have made you look like yourself."

Lady Anstruthers' thin hand closed on her plucked leaves convulsively, and then opening let them drop upon the stone of the terrace.

"We shall never see each other. It wouldn't be possible," she said. "And there is no magic in the world now, Betty. You can't bring back——"

"Yes, you can," said Bettina. "And what used to be called magic is only the controlled working of the law and order of things in these days. We must talk it all over."

Lady Anstruthers became a little pale.

"What?" she asked, low and nervously, and Betty saw her glance sideways at the windows of the room which opened on to the terrace.

Betty took her hand and drew her down into a chair. She sat near her and looked her straight in the face.

"Don't be frightened," she said. "I tell you there is no need to be frightened. We are not living in the Middle Ages. There is a policeman even in Stornham village, and we are within four hours of London, where there are thousands."

Lady Anstruthers tried to laugh, but did not succeed very well, and her forehead flushed.

"I don't quite know why I seem so nervous," she said. "It's very silly of me."

She was still timid enough to cling to some rag of pretence, but Betty knew that it would fall away. She did the wisest possible thing, which was to make an apparently impersonal remark.

"I want you to go over the place with me and show me everything. Walls and fences and greenhouses and outbuildings must not be allowed to crumble away."

"What?" cried Rosy. "Have you seen all that already?" She actually stared at her. "How practical and—and American!"

"To see that a wall has fallen when you find yourself obliged to walk round a pile of grass-grown brickwork?" said Betty.

Lady Anstruthers still softly stared.

"What—what are you thinking of?" she asked.

"Thinking that it is all too beautiful——" Betty's look swept the loveliness spread about her, "too beautiful and too valuable to be allowed to lose its value and its beauty." She turned her eyes back to Rosy and the deep dimple near her mouth showed itself delightfully. "It is a throwing away of capital," she added.

"Oh!" cried Lady Anstruthers, "how clever you are! And you look so different, Betty."

"Do I look stupid?" the dimple deepening. "I must try to alter that."

"Don't try to alter your looks," said Rosy. "It is your looks that make you so—so wonderful. But usually women—girls——" Rosy paused.

"Oh, I have been trained," laughed Betty. "I am the spoiled daughter of a business man of genius. His business is an art and a science. I have had advantages. He has let me hear him talk. I even know some trifling things about stocks. Not enough to do me vital injury—but something. What I know best of all,"—her laugh ended and her eyes changed their look,—"is that it is a blunder to think that beauty is not capital—that happiness is not—and that both are not the greatest assets in the scheme. This," with a wave of her hand, taking in all they saw, "is beauty, and it ought to be happiness, and it must be taken care of. It is your home and Ughtred's——"

"It is Nigel's," put in Rosy.

"It is entailed, isn't it?" turning quickly. "He cannot sell it?"

"If he could we should not be sitting here," ruefully.

"Then he cannot object to its being rescued from ruin."

"He will object to—to money being spent on things he does not care for." Lady Anstruthers' voice lowered itself, as it always did when she spoke of her husband, and she indulged in the involuntary hasty glance about her.

"I am going to my room to take off my hat," Betty said. "Will you come with me?"

She went into the house, talking quietly of ordinary things, and in this way they mounted the stairway together and passed along the gallery which led to her room. When they entered it she closed the door, locked it, and, taking off her hat, laid it aside. After doing which she sat.

"No one can hear and no one can come in," she said. "And if they could, you are afraid of things you need not be afraid of now. Tell me what happened when you were so ill after Ughtred was born."

"You guessed that it happened then," gasped Lady Anstruthers.

"It was a good time to make anything happen," replied Bettina. "You were prostrated, you were a child, and felt yourself cast off hopelessly from the people who loved you."

"Forever! Forever!" Lady Anstruthers' voice was a sharp little moan. "That was what I felt—that nothing could ever help me. I dared not write things. He told me he would not have it—that he would stop any hysterical complaints— that his mother could testify that he behaved perfectly to me. She was the only person in the room with us when—when——"

"When?" said Betty.

Lady Anstruthers shuddered. She leaned forward and caught Betty's hand between her own shaking ones.

"He struck me! He struck me! He said it never happened—but it did—it did! Betty, it did! That was the one thing that came back to me clearest. He said that I was in delirious hysterics, and that I had struggled with his mother and himself, because they tried to keep me quiet, and prevent the servants hearing. One awful day he brought Lady Anstruthers into the room, and they stood over me, as I lay in bed, and she fixed her eyes on me and said that she—being an Englishwoman, and a person whose word would be believed, could tell people the truth—my father and mother, if necessary, that my spoiled, hysterical American tempers had created unhappiness for me—merely because I was bored by life in the country and wanted excitement. I tried to answer, but they would not let me, and when I began to shake all over, they said that I was throwing myself into hysterics again. And they told the doctor so, and he believed it."

The possibilities of the situation were plainly to be seen. Fate, in the form of temperament itself, had been against her. It was clear enough to Betty as she patted and stroked the thin hands. "I understand. Tell me the rest," she said.

Lady Anstruthers' head dropped.

"When I was loneliest, and dying of homesickness, and so weak that I could not speak without sobbing, he came to me—it was one morning after I had been lying awake all night—and he began to seem kinder. He had not been near me for two days, and I had thought I was going to be left to die alone—and mother would never know. He said he had been reflecting and that he was afraid that we had misunderstood each other—because we belonged to different countries, and had been brought up in different ways——" she paused.

"And that if you understood his position and considered it, you might both be quite happy," Betty gave in quiet termination.

Lady Anstruthers started.

"Oh, you know it all!" she exclaimed.

"Only because I have heard it before. It is an old trick. And because he seemed kind and relenting, you tried to understand—and signed something."

"I WANTED to understand. I WANTED to believe. What did it matter which of us had the money, if we liked each other and were happy? He told me things about the estate, and about the enormous cost of it, and his bad luck, and debts he could not help. And I said that I would do anything if—if we could only be like mother and father. And he kissed me and I signed the paper."

"And then?"

"He went to London the next day, and then to Paris. He said he was obliged to go on business. He was away a month. And after a week had passed, Lady Anstruthers began to be restless and angry, and once she flew into a rage, and told me I was a fool, and that if I had been an Englishwoman, I should have had some decent control over my husband, because he would have respected me. In time I found out what I had done. It did not take long."

"The paper you signed," said Betty, "gave him control over your money?"

A forlorn nod was the answer.

"And since then he has done as he chose, and he has not chosen to care for Stornham. And once he made you write to father, to ask for more money?"

"I did it once. I never would do it again. He has tried to make me. He always says it is to save Stornham for Ughtred."

"Nothing can take Stornham from Ughtred. It may come to him a ruin, but it will come to him."

"He says there are legal points I cannot understand. And he says he is spending money on it."

"Where?"

"He—doesn't go into that. If I were to ask questions, he would make me know that I had better stop. He says I know nothing about things. And he is right. He has never allowed me to know and—and I am not like you, Betty."

"When you signed the paper, you did not realise that you were doing something you could never undo and that you would be forced to submit to the consequences?"

"I—I didn't realise anything but that it would kill me to live as I had been living—feeling as if they hated me. And I was so glad and thankful that he seemed kinder. It was as if I had been on the rack, and he turned the screws back, and I was ready to do anything—anything—if I might be taken off. Oh, Betty! you know, don't you, that—that if he would only have been a little kind— just a little—I would have obeyed him always, and given him everything."

Betty sat and looked at her, with deeply pondering eyes. She was confronting the fact that it seemed possible that one must build a new soul for her as well as a new body. In these days of science and growing sanity of thought, one did not stand helpless before the problem of physical rebuilding, and—and perhaps, if one could pour life into a creature, the soul of it would respond, and wake again, and grow.

"You do not know where he is?" she said aloud. "You absolutely do not know?"

"I never know exactly," Lady Anstruthers answered. "He was here for a few days the week before you came. He said he was going abroad. He might appear to-morrow, I might not hear of him for six months. I can't help hoping now that it will be the six months."

"Why particularly now?" inquired Betty.

Lady Anstruthers flushed and looked shy and awkward.

"Because of—you. I don't know what he would say. I don't know what he would do."

"To me?" said Betty.

"It would be sure to be something unreasonable and wicked," said Lady Anstruthers. "It would, Betty."

"I wonder what it would be?" Betty said musingly.

"He has told lies for years to keep you all from me. If he came now, he would know that he had been found out. He would say that I had told you things. He would be furious because you have seen what there is to see. He would know that you could not help but realise that the money he made me ask for had not been spent on the estate. He,—Betty, he would try to force you to go away."

"I wonder what he would do?" Betty said again musingly. She felt interested, not afraid.

"It would be something cunning," Rosy protested. "It would be something no one could expect. He might be so rude that you could not remain in the room with him, or he might be quite polite, and pretend he was rather glad to see you. If he was only frightfully rude we should be safer, because that would not be an unexpected thing, but if he was polite, it would be because he was arranging something hideous, which you could not defend yourself against."

"Can you tell me," said Betty quite slowly, because, as she looked down at the carpet, she was thinking very hard, "the kind of unexpected thing he has done to you?" Lifting her eyes, she saw that a troubled flush was creeping over Lady Anstruthers' face.

"There—have been—so many queer things," she faltered. Then Betty knew there was some special thing she was afraid to talk about, and that if she desired to obtain illuminating information it would be well to go into the matter.

"Try," she said, "to remember some particular incident."

Lady Anstruthers looked nervous.

"Rosy," in the level voice, "there has been a particular incident—and I would rather hear of it from you than from him."

Rosy's lap held little shaking hands.

"He has held it over me for years," she said breathlessly. "He said he would write about it to father and mother. He says he could use it against me as evidence in—in the divorce court. He says that divorce courts in America are for women, but in England they are for men, and—he could defend himself against me."

The incongruity of the picture of the small, faded creature arraigned in a divorce court on charges of misbehaviour would have made Betty smile if she had been in smiling mood.

"What did he accuse you of?"

"That was the—the unexpected thing," miserably.

Betty took the unsteady hands firmly in her own.

"Don't be afraid to tell me," she said. "He knew you so well that he understood what would terrify you the most. I know you so well that I understand how he does it. Did he do this unexpected thing just before you wrote to father for the money?" As she quite suddenly presented the question, Rosy exclaimed aloud.

"How did you know?" she said. "You—you are like a lawyer. How could you know?"

How simple she was! How obviously an easy prey! She had been unconsciously giving evidence with every word.

"I have been thinking him over," Betty said. "He interests me. I have begun to guess that he always wants something when he professes that he has a grievance."

Then with drooping head, Rosy told the story.

"Yes, it happened before he made me write to father for so much money. The vicar was ill and was obliged to go away for six months. The clergyman who came to take his place was a young man. He was kind and gentle, and wanted to help people. His mother was with him and she was like him. They loved each other, and they were quite poor. His name was Ffolliott. I liked to hear him preach. He said things that comforted me. Nigel found out that he comforted me, and—when he called here, he was more polite to him than he had ever been to Mr. Brent. He seemed almost as if he liked him. He actually asked him to dinner two or three times. After dinner, he would go out of the room and leave us together. Oh, Betty!" clinging to her hands, "I was so wretched then, that sometimes I thought I was going out of my mind. I think I looked wild. I used to kneel down and try to pray, and I could not."

"Yes, yes," said Betty.

"I used to feel that if I could only have one friend, just one, I could bear it better. Once I said something like that to Nigel. He only shrugged his shoulders and sneered when I said it. But afterwards I knew he had remembered. One evening, when he had asked Mr. Ffolliott to dinner, he led him to talk about religion. Oh, Betty! It made my blood turn cold when he began. I knew he was doing it for some wicked reason. I knew the look in his eyes and the awful, agreeable smile on his mouth. When he said at last, 'If you could help my poor wife to find comfort in such things,' I began to see. I could not explain to anyone how he did it, but with just a sentence, dropped here and there, he seemed to tell the whole story of a silly, selfish, American girl, thwarted in her vulgar little ambitions, and posing as a martyr, because she could not have her own way in everything. He said once, quite casually, 'I'm afraid American women are rather spoiled.' And then he said, in the same tolerant way—'A poor man is a disappointment to an American girl. America does not believe in rank combined with lack of fortune.' I dared not defend myself. I am not clever enough to think of the right things to say. He meant Mr. Ffolliott to understand that I had married him because I thought he was grand and rich, and that I was a disappointed little spiteful shrew. I tried to act as if he was not hurting me, but my hands trembled, and a lump kept rising in my throat. When we returned to the drawing-room, and at last he left us together, I was praying and praying that I might be able to keep from breaking down."

She stopped and swallowed hard. Betty held her hands firmly until she went on.

"For a few minutes, I sat still, and tried to think of some new subject— something about the church or the village. But I could not begin to speak because of the lump in my throat. And then, suddenly, but quietly, Mr. Ffolliott got up. And though I dared not lift my eyes, I knew he was standing before the fire, quite near me. And, oh! what do you think he said, as low and gently as if his voice was a woman's. I did not know that people ever said such things now, or even thought them. But never, never shall I forget that strange minute. He said just this:

"'God will help you. He will. He will.'

"As if it was true, Betty! As if there was a God—and—He had not forgotten me. I did not know what I was doing, but I put out my hand and caught at his sleeve, and when I looked up into his face, I saw in his kind, good eyes, that he knew—that somehow—God knows how—he understood and that I need not utter a word to explain to him that he had been listening to lies."

"Did you talk to him?" Betty asked quietly.

"He talked to me. We did not even speak of Nigel. He talked to me as I had never heard anyone talk before. Somehow he filled the room with something real, which was hope and comfort and like warmth, which kept my soul from shivering. The tears poured from my eyes at first, but the lump in my throat went away, and when Nigel came back I actually did not feel frightened, though he looked at me and sneered quietly."

"Did he say anything afterwards?"

"He laughed a little cold laugh and said, 'I see you have been seeking the consolation of religion. Neurotic women like confessors. I do not object to your confessing, if you confess your own backslidings and not mine.'"

"That was the beginning," said Betty speculatively. "The unexpected thing was the end. Tell me the rest?"

"No one could have dreamed of it," Rosy broke forth. "For weeks he was almost like other people. He stayed at Stornham and spent his days in shooting. He professed that he was rather enjoying himself in a dull way. He encouraged me to go to the vicarage, he invited the Ffolliotts here. He said Mrs. Ffolliott was a gentlewoman and good for me. He said it was proper that I should interest myself in parish work. Once or twice he even brought some little message to me from Mr. Ffolliott."

It was a pitiably simple story. Betty saw, through its relation, the unconsciousness of the easily allured victim, the adroit leading on from step to step, the ordinary, natural, seeming method which arranged opportunities. The two had been thrown together at the Court, at the vicarage, the church and in the village, and the hawk had looked on and bided his time. For the first time in her years of exile, Rosy had begun to feel that she might be allowed a friend—though she lived in secret tremor lest the normal liberty permitted her should suddenly be snatched away.

"We never talked of Nigel," she said, twisting her hands. "But he made me begin to live again. He talked to me of Something that watched and would not leave me—would never leave me. I was learning to believe it. Sometimes when I walked through the wood to the village, I used to stop among the trees and look up at the bits of sky between the branches, and listen to the sound in the leaves—the sound that never stops—and it seemed as if it was saying something to me. And I would clasp my hands and whisper, 'Yes, yes,' 'I will,' 'I will.' I used to see Nigel looking at me at table with a queer smile in his eyes and once he said to me—'You are growing young and lovely, my dear. Your colour is improving. The counsels of our friend are of a salutary nature.' It would have made me nervous, but he said it almost good-naturedly, and I was silly enough even to wonder if it could be possible that he was pleased to see me looking less ill. It was true, Betty, that I was growing stronger. But it did not last long."

"I was afraid not," said Betty.

"An old woman in the lane near Bartyon Wood was ill. Mr. Ffolliott had asked me to go to see her, and I used to go. She suffered a great deal and clung to us both. He comforted her, as he comforted me. Sometimes when he was called away he would send a note to me, asking me to go to her. One day he wrote hastily, saying that she was dying, and asked if I would go with him to her cottage at once. I knew it would save time if I met him in the path which was a short cut. So I wrote a few words and gave them to the messenger. I said, 'Do not come to the house. I will meet you in Bartyon Wood.'"

Betty made a slight movement, and in her face there was a dawning of mingled amazement and incredulity. The thought which had come to her seemed—as Ughtred's locking of the door had seemed—too wild for modern days.

Lady Anstruthers saw her expression and understood it. She made a hopeless gesture with her small, bony hand.

"Yes," she said, "it is just like that. No one would believe it. The worst cleverness of the things he does, is that when one tells of them, they sound like lies. I have a bewildered feeling that I should not believe them myself if I had not seen them. He met the boy in the park and took the note from him. He came back to the house and up to my room, where I was dressing quickly to go to Mr. Ffolliott."

She stopped for quite a minute, rather as if to recover breath.

"He closed the door behind him and came towards me with the note in his hand. And I saw in a second the look that always terrifies me, in his face. He had opened the note and he smoothed out the paper quietly and said, 'What is this. I could not help it—I turned cold and began to shiver. I could not imagine what was coming."

"'Is it my note to Mr. Ffolliott?' I asked.

"'Yes, it is your note to Mr. Ffolliott,' and he read it aloud. "Do not come to the house. I will meet you in Bartyon Wood." That is a nice note for a man's wife to have written, to be picked up and read by a stranger, if your confessor is not cautious in the matter of letters from women——'

"When he begins a thing in that way, you may always know that he has planned everything—that you can do nothing—I always know. I knew then, and I knew I was quite white when I answered him:

"'I wrote it in a great hurry, Mrs. Farne is worse. We are going together to her. I said I would meet him—to save time.'

"He laughed, his awful little laugh, and touched the paper.

"'I have no doubt. And I have no doubt that if other persons saw this, they would believe it. It is very likely.

"'But you believe it,' I said. 'You know it is true. No one would be so silly—so silly and wicked as to——' Then I broke down and cried out. 'What do you mean? What could anyone think it meant?' I was so wild that I felt as if I was going crazy. He clenched my wrist and shook me.

"'Don't think you can play the fool with me,' he said. 'I have been watching this thing from the first. The first time I leave you alone with the fellow, I come back to find you have been giving him an emotional scene. Do you suppose your simpering good spirits and your imbecile pink cheeks told me nothing? They told me exactly this. I have waited to come upon it, and here it is. "Do not come to the house—I will meet you in the wood."'

"That was the unexpected thing. It was no use to argue and try to explain. I knew he did not believe what he was saying, but he worked himself into a rage, he accused me of awful things, and called me awful names in a loud voice, so that he could be heard, until I was dumb and staggering. All the time, I knew there was a reason, but I could not tell then what it was. He said at last, that he was going to Mr. Ffolliott. He said, 'I will meet him in the wood and I will take your note with me.'

"Betty, it was so shameful that I fell down on my knees. 'Oh, don't—don't—do that,' I said. 'I beg of you, Nigel. He is a gentleman and a clergyman. I beg and beg of you. If you will not, I will do anything—anything.' And at that minute I remembered how he had tried to make me write to father for money. And I cried out—catching at his coat, and holding him back. 'I will write to father as you asked me. I will do anything. I can't bear it.'"

"That was the whole meaning of the whole thing," said Betty with eyes ablaze. "That was the beginning, the middle and the end. What did he say?"

"He pretended to be made more angry. He said, 'Don't insult me by trying to bribe me with your vulgar money. Don't insult me.' But he gradually grew sulky instead of raging, and though he put the note in his pocket, he did not go to Mr. Ffolliott. And—I wrote to father."

"I remember that," Betty answered. "Did you ever speak to Mr. Ffolliott again?"

"He guessed—he knew—I saw it in his kind, brown eyes when he passed me without speaking, in the village. I daresay the villagers were told about the awful thing by some servant, who heard Nigel's voice. Villagers always know what is happening. He went away a few weeks later. The day before he went, I had walked through the wood, and just outside it, I met him. He stopped for one minute—just one—he lifted his hat and said, just as he had spoken them that first night—just the same words, 'God will help you. He will. He will.'"

A strange, almost unearthly joy suddenly flashed across her face.

"It must be true," she said. "It must be true. He has sent you, Betty. It has been a long time—it has been so long that sometimes I have forgotten his words. But you have come!"

"Yes, I have come," Betty answered. And she bent forward and kissed her gently, as if she had been soothing a child.

There were other questions to ask. She was obliged to ask them. "The unexpected thing" had been used as an instrument for years. It was always efficacious. Over the yearningly homesick creature had hung the threat that her father and mother, those she ached and longed for, could be told the story in such a manner as would brand her as a woman with a shameful secret. How could she explain herself? There were the awful, written words. He was her husband. He was remorseless, plausible. She dared not write freely. She had no witnesses to call upon. She had discovered that he had planned with composed steadiness that misleading impressions should be given to servants and village people. When the Brents returned to the vicarage, she had observed, with terror, that for some reason they stiffened, and looked askance when the Ffolliotts were mentioned.

"I am afraid, Lady Anstruthers, that Mr. Ffolliott was a great mistake," Mrs. Brent said once.

Lady Anstruthers had not dared to ask any questions. She had felt the awkward colour rising in her face and had known that she looked guilty. But if she had protested against the injustice of the remark, Sir Nigel would have heard of her words before the day had passed, and she shuddered to think of the result. He had by that time reached the point of referring to Ffolliott with sneering lightness, as "Your lover."

"Do you defend your lover to me," he had said on one occasion, when she had entered a timid protest. And her white face and wild helpless eyes had been such evidence as to the effect the word had produced, that he had seen the expediency of making a point of using it.

The blood beat in Betty Vanderpoel's veins.

"Rosy," she said, looking steadily in the faded face, "tell me this. Did you never think of getting away from him, of going somewhere, and trying to reach father, by cable, or letter, by some means?"

Lady Anstruthers' weary and wrinkled little smile was a pitiably illuminating thing.

"My dear" she said, "if you are strong and beautiful and rich and well dressed, so that people care to look at you, and listen to what you say, you can do things. But who, in England, will listen to a shabby, dowdy, frightened woman, when she runs away from her husband, if he follows her and tells people she is hysterical or mad or bad? It is the shabby, dowdy woman who is in the wrong. At first, I thought of nothing else but trying to get away. And once I went to Stornham station. I walked all the way, on a hot day. And just as I was getting into a third-class carriage, Nigel marched in and caught my arm, and held me back. I fainted and when I came to myself I was in the carriage, being driven back to the Court, and he was sitting opposite to me. He said, 'You fool! It would take a cleverer woman than you to carry that out.' And I knew it was the awful truth."

"It is not the awful truth now," said Betty, and she rose to her feet and stood looking before her, but with a look which did not rest on chairs and tables. She remained so, standing for a few moments of dead silence.

"What a fool he was!" she said at last. "And what a villain! But a villain is always a fool."

She bent, and taking Rosy's face between her hands, kissed it with a kiss which seemed like a seal. "That will do," she said. "Now I know. One must know what is in one's hands and what is not. Then one need not waste time in talking of miserable things. One can save one's strength for doing what can be done."

"I believe you would always think about DOING things," said Lady Anstruthers. "That is American, too."

"It is a quality Americans inherited from England," lightly; "one of the results of it is that England covers a rather large share of the map of the world. It is a practical quality. You and I might spend hours in talking to each other of what Nigel has done and what you have done, of what he has said, and of what you have said. We might give some hours, I daresay, to what the Dowager did and said. But wiser people than we are have found out that thinking of black things past is living them again, and it is like poisoning one's blood. It is deterioration of property."

She said the last words as if she had ended with a jest. But she knew what she was doing.

"You were tricked into giving up what was yours, to a person who could not be trusted. What has been done with it, scarcely matters. It is not yours, but Sir Nigel's. But we are not helpless, because we have in our hands the most powerful material agent in the world.

"Come, Rosy, and let us walk over the house. We will begin with that."

CHAPTER XVII

TOWNLINSON & SHEPPARD

During the whole course of her interesting life—and she had always found life interesting—Betty Vanderpoel decided that she had known no experience more absorbing than this morning spent in going over the long-closed and deserted portions of the neglected house. She had never seen anything like the place, or as full of suggestion. The greater part of it had simply been shut up and left to time and weather, both of which had had their effects. The fine old red roof, having lost tiles, had fallen into leaks that let in rain, which had stained and rotted walls, plaster, and woodwork; wind and storm had beaten through broken window panes and done their worst with such furniture and hangings as they found to whip and toss and leave damp and spotted with mould. They passed through corridors, and up and down short or long stairways, with stained or faded walls, and sometimes with cracked or fallen plastering and wainscotting. Here and there the oak flooring itself was uncertain. The rooms, whether large or small, all presented a like aspect of potential beauty and comfort, utterly uncared for and forlorn. There were many rooms, but none more than scantily furnished, and a number of them were stripped bare. Betty found herself wondering how long a time it had taken the belongings of the big place to dwindle and melt away into such bareness.

"There was a time, I suppose, when it was all furnished," she said.

"All these rooms were shut up when I came here," Rosy answered. "I suppose things worth selling have been sold. When pieces of furniture were broken in one part of the house, they were replaced by things brought from another. No one cared. Nigel hates it all. He calls it a rathole. He detests the country everywhere, but particularly this part of it. After the first year I had learned better than to speak to him of spending money on repairs."

"A good deal of money should be spent on repairs," reflected Betty, looking about her.

She was standing in the middle of a room whose walls were hung with the remains of what had been chintz, covered with a pattern of loose clusters of moss rosebuds. The dampness had rotted it until, in some places, it had fallen away in strips from its fastenings. A quaint, embroidered couch stood in one corner, and as Betty looked at it, a mouse crept from under the tattered valance, stared at her in alarm and suddenly darted back again, in terror of intrusion so unusual. A casement window swung open, on a broken hinge, and a strong branch of ivy, having forced its way inside, had thrown a covering of leaves over the deep ledge, and was beginning to climb the inner woodwork. Through the casement was to be seen a heavenly spread of country, whose rolling lands were clad softly in green pastures and thick-branched trees.

"This is the Rosebud Boudoir," said Lady Anstruthers, smiling faintly. "All the rooms have names. I thought them so delightful, when I first heard them.

The Damask Room—the Tapestry Room—the White Wainscot Room—My Lady's Chamber. It almost broke my heart when I saw what they looked like."

"It would be very interesting," Betty commented slowly, "to make them look as they ought to look."

A remote fear rose to the surface of the expression in Lady Anstruthers' eyes. She could not detach herself from certain recollections of Nigel—of his opinions of her family—of his determination not to allow it to enter as a factor in either his life or hers. And Betty had come to Stornham—Betty whom he had detested as a child—and in the course of two days, she had seemed to become a new part of the atmosphere, and to make the dead despair of the place begin to stir with life. What other thing than this was happening as she spoke of making such rooms as the Rosebud Boudoir "look as they ought to look," and said the words not as if they were part of a fantastic vision, but as if they expressed a perfectly possible thing?

Betty saw the doubt in her eyes, and in a measure, guessed at its meaning. The time to pause for argument had, however not arrived. There was too much to be investigated, too much to be seen. She swept her on her way. They wandered on through some forty rooms, more or less; they opened doors and closed them; they unbarred shutters and let the sun stream in on dust and dampness and cobwebs. The comprehension of the situation which Betty gained was as valuable as it was enlightening.

The descent into the lower part of the house was a new experience. Betty had not before seen huge, flagged kitchens, vaulted servants' halls, stone passages, butteries and dairies. The substantial masonry of the walls and arched ceilings, the stone stairway, and the seemingly endless offices, were interestingly remote in idea from such domestic modernities as chance views of up-to-date American household workings had provided her.

In the huge kitchen itself, an elderly woman, rolling pastry, paused to curtsy to them, with stolid curiosity in her heavy-featured face. In her character as "single-handed" cook, Mrs. Noakes had sent up uninviting meals to Lady Anstruthers for several years, but she had not seen her ladyship below stairs before. And this was the unexpected arrival—the young lady there had been "talk of" from the moment of her appearance. Mrs. Noakes admitted with the grudgingness of a person of uncheerful temperament, that looks like that always would make talk. A certain degree of vague mental illumination led her to agree with Robert, the footman, that the stranger's effectiveness was, perhaps, also, not altogether a matter of good looks, and certainly it was not an affair of clothes. Her brightish blue dress, of rough cloth, was nothing particular, notwithstanding the fit of it. There was "something else about her." She looked round the place, not with the casual indifference of a fine young lady, carelessly curious to see what she had not seen before, but with an alert, questioning interest.

"What a big place," she said to her ladyship. "What substantial walls! What huge joints must have been roasted before such a fireplace."

She drew near to the enormous, antiquated cooking place.

"People were not very practical when this was built," she said. "It looks as if it must waste a great deal of coal. Is it——?" she looked at Mrs. Noakes. "Do you like it?"

There was a practical directness in the question for which Mrs. Noakes was not prepared. Until this moment, it had apparently mattered little whether she liked things or not. The condition of her implements of trade was one of her grievances—the ancient fireplace and ovens the bitterest.

"It's out of order, miss," she answered. "And they don't use 'em like this in these days."

"I thought not," said Miss Vanderpoel.

She made other inquiries as direct and significant of the observing eye, and her passage through the lower part of the establishment left Mrs. Noakes and her companions in a strange but not unpleasurable state of ferment.

"Think of a young lady that's never had nothing to do with kitchens, going straight to that shameful old fireplace, and seeing what it meant to the woman that's got to use it. 'Do you like it?' she says. If she'd been a cook herself, she couldn't have put it straighter. She's got eyes."

"She's been using them all over the place," said Robert. "Her and her ladyship's been into rooms that's not been opened for years."

"More shame to them that should have opened 'em," remarked Mrs. Noakes. "Her ladyship's a poor, listless thing—but her spirit was broken long ago.

"This one will mend it for her, perhaps," said the man servant. "I wonder what's going to happen."

"Well, she's got a look with her—the new one—as if where she was things would be likely to happen. You look out. The place won't seem so dead and alive if we've got something to think of and expect."

"Who are the solicitors Sir Nigel employs?" Betty had asked her sister, when their pilgrimage through the house had been completed.

Messrs. Townlinson & Sheppard, a firm which for several generations had transacted the legal business of much more important estates than Stornham, held its affairs in hand. Lady Anstruthers knew nothing of them, but that they evidently did not approve of the conduct of their client. Nigel was frequently angry when he spoke of them. It could be gathered that they had refused to allow him to do things he wished to do—sell things, or borrow money on them.

"I think we must go to London and see them," Betty suggested.

Rosy was agitated. Why should one see them? What was there to be spoken of? Their going, Betty explained would be a sort of visit of ceremony—in a measure a precaution. Since Sir Nigel was apparently not to be reached, having given no clue as to where he intended to go, it might be discreet to consult Messrs. Townlinson & Sheppard with regard to the things it might be well to do—the repairs it appeared necessary to make at once. If Messrs. Townlinson & Sheppard approved of the doing of such work, Sir Nigel could not resent their action, and say that in his absence liberties had been taken. Such a course seemed businesslike and dignified.

It was what Betty felt that her father would do. Nothing could be complained of, which was done with the knowledge and under the sanction of the family solicitors.

"Then there are other things we must do. We must go to shops and theatres. It will be good for you to go to shops and theatres, Rosy."

"I have nothing but rags to wear," answered Lady Anstruthers, reddening.

"Then before we go we will have things sent down. People can be sent from the shops to arrange what we want."

The magic of the name, standing for great wealth, could, it was true, bring to them, not only the contents of shops, but the people who showed them, and were ready to carry out any orders. The name of Vanderpoel already stood, in London, for inexhaustible resource. Yes, it was simple enough to send for politely subservient saleswomen to bring what one wanted.

The being reminded in every-day matters of the still real existence of the power of this magic was the first step in the rebuilding of Lady Anstruthers. To realise that the wonderful and yet simple necromancy was gradually encircling her again, had its parallel in the taking of a tonic, whose effect was cumulative. She herself did not realise the working of it. But Betty regarded it with interest. She saw it was good for her, merely to look on at the unpacking of the New York boxes, which the maid, sent for from London, brought down with her.

As the woman removed, from tray after tray, the tissue-paper-enfolded layers of garments, Lady Anstruthers sat and watched her with normal, simply feminine interest growing in her eyes. The things were made with the absence of any limit in expenditure, the freedom with delicate stuffs and priceless laces which belonged only to her faint memories of a lost past.

Nothing had limited the time spent in the embroidering of this apparently simple linen frock and coat; nothing had restrained the hand holding the scissors which had cut into the lace which adorned in appliques and filmy frills this exquisitely charming ball dress.

"It is looking back so far," she said, waving her hand towards them with an odd gesture. "To think that it was once all like—like that."

She got up and went to the things, turning them over, and touching them with a softness, almost expressing a caress. The names of the makers stamped on bands and collars, the names of the streets in which their shops stood, moved her. She heard again the once familiar rattle of wheels, and the rush and roar of New York traffic.

Betty carried on the whole matter with lightness. She talked easily and casually, giving local colour to what she said. She described the abnormally rapid growth of the places her sister had known in her teens, the new buildings, new theatres, new shops, new people, the later mode of living, much of it learned from England, through the unceasing weaving of the Shuttle.

"Changing—changing—changing. That is what it is always doing—America. We have not reached repose yet. One wonders how long it will be before we shall. Now we are always hurrying breathlessly after the next thing—the new one—which we always think will be the better one. Other countries built themselves slowly. In the days of their building, the pace of life was a march. When America was born, the march had already begun to hasten, and as a nation we began, in our first hour, at the quickening speed. Now the pace is a race. New York is a kaleidoscope. I myself can remember it a wholly different thing. One passes down a street one day, and the next there is a great gap where some building is being torn down—a few days later, a tall structure of some sort is touching the sky. It is wonderful, but it does not tend to calm the mind. That is why we cross the Atlantic so much. The sober, quiet-loving blood our forbears brought from older countries goes in search of rest. Mixed with other things, I feel in my own being a resentment against newness and disorder, and an insistence on the atmosphere of long-established things."

But for years Lady Anstruthers had been living in the atmosphere of long-established things, and felt no insistence upon it. She yearned to hear of the great, changing Western world—of the great, changing city. Betty must tell her what the changes were. What were the differences in the streets—where had the new buildings been placed? How had Fifth Avenue and Madison Avenue and Broadway altered? Were not Gramercy Park and Madison Square still green with grass and trees? Was it all different? Would she not know the old places herself? Though it seemed a lifetime since she had seen them, the years which had passed were really not so many.

It was good for her to talk and be talked to in this manner Betty saw. Still handling her subject lightly, she presented picture after picture. Some of them were of the wonderful, feverish city itself—the place quite passionately loved by some, as passionately disliked by others. She herself had fallen into the habit, as she left childhood behind her, of looking at it with interested wonder—at its riot of life and power, of huge schemes, and almost superhuman labours, of fortunes so colossal that they seemed monstrosities in their relation to the world. People who in Rosalie's girlhood had lived in big ugly brownstone fronts, had built for themselves or for their children, houses such as, in other countries, would have belonged to nobles and princes, spending fortunes upon their building, filling them with treasures brought from foreign lands, from palaces, from art galleries, from collectors. Sometimes strange people built such houses and lived strange lavish, ostentatious lives in them, forming an overstrained, abnormal, pleasure-chasing world of their own. The passing of even ten years in New York counted itself almost as a generation; the fashions, customs, belongings of twenty years ago wore an air of almost picturesque antiquity.

"It does not take long to make an 'old New Yorker,'" she said. "Each day brings so many new ones."

There were, indeed, many new ones, Lady Anstruthers found. People who had been poor had become hugely rich, a few who had been rich had become poor, possessions which had been large had swelled to unnatural proportions. Out of the West had risen fortunes more monstrous than all others. As she told one story after another, Bettina realised, as she had done often before, that it was impossible to enter into description of the life and movements of the place,

without its curiously involving some connection with the huge wealth of it—
with its influence, its rise, its swelling, or waning.

"Somehow one cannot free one's self from it. This is the age of wealth and
invention—but of wealth before all else. Sometimes one is tired—tired of it."

"You would not be tired of it if—well, if you were I, said Lady Anstruthers
rather pathetically.

"Perhaps not," Betty answered. "Perhaps not."

She herself had seen people who were not tired of it in the sense in which
she was—the men and women, with worn or intently anxious faces, hastening
with the crowds upon the pavements, all hastening somewhere, in chase of that
small portion of the wealth which they earned by their labour as their daily share;
the same men and women surging towards elevated railroad stations, to seize on
places in the homeward-bound trains; or standing in tired-looking groups,
waiting for the approach of an already overfull street car, in which they must be
packed together, and swing to the hanging straps, to keep upon their feet. Their
way of being weary of it would be different from hers, they would be weary only
of hearing of the mountains of it which rolled themselves up, as it seemed, in
obedience to some irresistible, occult force.

On the day after Stornham village had learned that her ladyship and Miss
Vanderpoel had actually gone to London, the dignified firm of Townlinson &
Sheppard received a visit which created some slight sensation in their
establishment, though it had not been entirely unexpected. It had, indeed, been
heralded by a note from Miss Vanderpoel herself, who had asked that the
appointment be made. Men of Messrs. Townlinson & Sheppard's indubitable
rank in their profession could not fail to know the significance of the
Vanderpoel name. They knew and understood its weight perfectly well. When
their client had married one of Reuben Vanderpoel's daughters, they had felt
that extraordinary good fortune had befallen him and his estate. Their private
opinion had been that Mr. Vanderpoel's knowledge of his son-in-law must have
been limited, or that he had curiously lax American views of paternal duty. The
firm was highly reputable, long established strictly conservative, and somewhat
insular in its point of view. It did not understand, or seek to understand,
America. It had excellent reasons for thoroughly understanding Sir Nigel
Anstruthers. Its opinions of him it reserved to itself. If Messrs. Townlinson &
Sheppard had been asked to give a daughter into their client's keeping, they
would have flatly refused to accept the honour proposed. Mr. Townlinson had,
indeed, at the time of the marriage, admitted in strict confidence to his partner
that for his part he would have somewhat preferred to follow a daughter of his
own to her tomb. After the marriage the firm had found the situation confusing
and un-English. There had been trouble with Sir Nigel, who had plainly been
disappointed. At first it had appeared that the American magnate had shown
astuteness in refraining from leaving his son-in-law a free hand. Lady
Anstruthers' fortune was her own and not her husband's. Mr. Townlinson,
paying a visit to Stornham and finding the bride a gentle, childish-looking girl,
whose most marked expression was one of growing timorousness, had returned

with a grave face. He foresaw the result, if her family did not stand by her with firmness, which he also foresaw her husband would prevent if possible. It became apparent that the family did not stand by her—or were cleverly kept at a distance. There was a long illness, which seemed to end in the seclusion from the world, brought about by broken health. Then it was certain that what Mr. Townlinson had foreseen had occurred. The inexperienced girl had been bullied into submission. Sir Nigel had gained the free hand, whatever the means he had chosen to employ. Most improper—most improper, the whole affair. He had a great deal of money, but none of it was used for the benefit of the estate—his deformed boy's estate. Advice, dignified remonstrance, resulted only in most disagreeable scenes. Messrs. Townlinson & Sheppard could not exceed certain limits. The manner in which the money was spent was discreditable. There were avenues a respectable firm knew only by rumour, there were insane gambling speculations, which could only end in disaster, there were things one could not decently concern one's self with. Lady Anstruthers' family had doubtless become indignant and disgusted, and had dropped the whole affair. Sad for the poor woman, but not unnatural.

And now appears a Miss Vanderpoel, who wishes to appoint an interview with Messrs. Townlinson & Sheppard. What does she wish to say? The family is apparently taking the matter up. Is this lady an elder or a younger sister of Lady Anstruthers? Is she an older woman of that strong and rather trying American type one hears of, or is she younger than her ladyship, a pretty, indignant, totally unpractical girl, outraged by the state of affairs she has discovered, foolishly coming to demand of Messrs. Townlinson & Sheppard an explanation of things they are not responsible for? Will she, perhaps, lose her temper, and accuse and reproach, or even—most unpleasant to contemplate—shed hysterical tears?

It fell to Mr. Townlinson to receive her in the absence of Mr. Sheppard, who had been called to Northamptonshire to attend to great affairs. He was a stout, grave man with a heavy, well-cut face, and, when Bettina entered his room, his courteous reception of her reserved his view of the situation entirely.

She was not of the mature and rather alarming American type he had imagined possible, he felt some relief in marking at once. She was also not the pretty, fashionable young lady who might have come to scold him, and ask silly, irrational questions.

His ordinarily rather unillumined countenance changed somewhat in expression when she sat down and began to speak. Mr. Townlinson was impressed by the fact that it was at once unmistakably evident that whatsoever her reason for coming, she had not presented herself to ask irrelevant or unreasonable questions. Lady Anstruthers, she explained without superfluous phrase, had no definite knowledge of her husband's whereabouts, and it had seemed possible that Messrs. Townlinson & Sheppard might have received some information more recent that her own. The impersonal framing of this inquiry struck Mr. Townlinson as being in remarkably good taste, since it conveyed no condemnation of Sir Nigel, and no desire to involve Mr. Townlinson in expressing any. It refrained even from implying that the situation was an unusual one, which might be open to criticism. Excellent reserve and great cleverness, Mr. Townlinson commented inwardly. There were certainly few young ladies who would have clearly realised that a solicitor cannot be called upon to commit himself, until he has had time to weigh matters and decide upon them. His long and varied experience had included interviews in which charming, emotional women had expected him at once to "take sides." Miss Vanderpoel exhibited no signs of expecting anything of this kind, even when she went on with what she had come to say. Stornham Court and its surroundings were depreciating seriously in value through need of radical repairs etc. Her sister's comfort was naturally involved, and, as Mr. Townlinson would fully understand, her nephew's future. The sooner the process of dilapidation was arrested, the better and with the less difficulty. The present time was without doubt better than an indefinite future. Miss Vanderpoel, having fortunately been able to come to Stornham, was greatly interested, and naturally desirous of seeing the work begun. Her father also would be interested. Since it was not possible to consult Sir Nigel, it had seemed proper to consult his solicitors in whose hands the estate had been for so long a time. She was aware, it seemed, that not only Mr. Townlinson, but Mr. Townlinson's father, and also his grandfather, had legally represented the Anstruthers, as well as many other families. As there seemed no necessity for any structural changes, and the work done was such as could only rescue and increase the value of the estate, could there be any objection to its being begun without delay?

Certainly an unusual young lady. It would be interesting to discover how well she knew Sir Nigel, since it seemed that only a knowledge of him—his temper, his bitter, irritable vanity, could have revealed to her the necessity of the precaution she was taking without even intimating that it was a precaution. Extraordinarily clever girl.

Mr. Townlinson wore an air of quiet, business-like reflection.

"You are aware, Miss Vanderpoel, that the present income from the estate is not such as would justify anything approaching the required expenditure?"

"Yes, I am aware of that. The expense would be provided for by my father."

"Most generous on Mr. Vanderpoel's part," Mr. Townlinson commented. "The estate would, of course, increase greatly in value."

Circumstances had prevented her father from visiting Stornham, Miss Vanderpoel explained, and this had led to his being ignorant of a condition of things which he might have remedied. She did not explain what the particular circumstances which had separated the families had been, but Mr. Townlinson thought he understood. The condition existing could be remedied now, if Messrs. Townlinson & Sheppard saw no obstacles other than scarcity of money.

Mr. Townlinson's summing up of the matter expressed in effect that he saw none. The estate had been a fine one in its day. During the last sixty years it had become much impoverished. With conservative decorum of manner, he admitted that there had not been, since Sir Nigel's marriage, sufficient reason for the neglect of dilapidations. The firm had strongly represented to Sir Nigel that certain resources should not be diverted from the proper object of restoring the property, which was entailed upon his son. The son's future should beyond all have been considered in the dispensing of his mother's fortune.

He, by this time, comprehended fully that he need restrain no dignified expression of opinion in his speech with this young lady. She had come to consult with him with as clear a view of the proprieties and discretions demanded by his position as he had himself. And yet each, before the close of the interview, understood the point of view of the other. What he recognised was that, though she had not seen Sir Nigel since her childhood, she had in some astonishing way obtained an extraordinary insight into his character, and it was this which had led her to take her present step. She might not realise all she might have to contend with, but her conservative and formal action had surrounded her and her sister with a certain barrier of conventional protection, at once self-controlled, dignified, and astutely intelligent.

"Since, as you say, no structural changes are proposed, such as an owner might resent, and as Lady Anstruthers is the mother of the heir, and as Lady Anstruthers' father undertakes to defray all expenditure, no sane man could object to the restoration of the property. To do so would be to cause public opinion to express itself strongly against him. Such action would place him grossly in the wrong." Then he added with deliberation, realising that he was committing himself, and feeling firmly willing to do so for reasons of his own, "Sir Nigel is a man who objects strongly to putting himself—publicly—in the wrong."

"Thank you," said Miss Vanderpoel.

He had said this of intention for her enlightenment, and she was aware that he had done so.

"This will not be the first time that American fortunes have restored English estates," Mr. Townlinson continued amiably. "There have been many notable cases of late years. We shall be happy to place ourselves at your disposal at all times, Miss Vanderpoel. We are obliged to you for your consideration in the matter."

"Thank you," said Miss Vanderpoel again. "I wished to be sure that I should not be infringing any English rule I had no knowledge of."

"You will be infringing none. You have been most correct and courteous."

Before she went away Mr. Townlinson felt that he had been greatly enlightened as to what a young lady might know and be. She gave him singularly clear details as to what was proposed. There was so much to be done that he found himself opening his eyes slightly once or twice. But, of course, if Mr. Vanderpoel was prepared to spend money in a lavish manner, it was all to the good so far as the estate was concerned. They were stupendous, these people, and after all the heir was his grandson. And how striking it was that with all this power and readiness to use it, was evidently combined, even in this beautiful young person, the clearest business sense of the situation. What was done would be for the comfort of Lady Anstruthers and the future of her son. Sir Nigel, being unable to sell either house or lands, could not undo it.

When Mr. Townlinson accompanied his visitor to her carriage with dignified politeness he felt somewhat like an elderly solicitor who had found himself drawn into the atmosphere of a sort of intensely modern fairy tale. He saw two of his under clerks, with the impropriety of middle-class youth, looking out of an office window at the dark blue brougham and the tall young lady, whose beauty bloomed in the sunshine. He did not, on the whole, wonder at, though he deplored, the conduct of the young men. But they, of course, saw only what they colloquially described to each other as a "rippin' handsome girl." They knew nothing of the interesting interview.

He himself returned to his private room in a musing mood and thought it all over, his mind dwelling on various features of the international situation, and more than once he said aloud:

"Most remarkable. Very remarkable, indeed."

CHAPTER XVIII

THE FIFTEENTH EARL OF MOUNT DUNSTAN

James Hubert John Fergus Saltyre—fifteenth Earl of Mount Dunstan, "Jem Salter," as his neighbours on the Western ranches had called him, the red-haired, second-class passenger of the Meridiana, sat in the great library of his desolate great house, and stared fixedly through the open window at the lovely land spread out before him. From this particular window was to be seen one of the greatest views in England. From the upper nurseries he had lived in as a child he had seen it every day from morning until night, and it had seemed to his young fancy to cover all the plains of the earth. Surely the rest of the world, he had thought, could be but small—though somewhere he knew there was London where the Queen lived, and in London were Buckingham Palace and St. James Palace and Kensington and the Tower, where heads had been chopped off; and the Horse Guards, where splendid, plumed soldiers rode forth glittering, with thrilling trumpets sounding as they moved. These last he always remembered, because he had seen them, and once when he had walked in the park with his nurse there had been an excited stir in the Row, and people had crowded about a certain gate, through which an escorted carriage had been driven, and he had been made at once to take off his hat and stand bareheaded until it passed, because it was the Queen. Somehow from that afternoon he dated the first presentation of certain vaguely miserable ideas. Inquiries made of his attendant, when the cortege had swept by, had elicited the fact that the Royal Lady herself had children—little boys who were princes and little girls who were princesses. What curious and persistent child cross-examination on his part had drawn forth the fact that almost all the people who drove about and looked so happy and brilliant, were the fathers or mothers of little boys like, yet—in some mysterious way—unlike himself? And in what manner had he gathered that he was different from them? His nurse, it is true, was not a pleasant person, and had an injured and resentful bearing. In later years he realised that it had been the bearing of an irregularly paid menial, who rebelled against the fact that her place was not among people who were of distinction and high repute, and whose households bestowed a certain social status upon their servitors. She was a tall woman with a sour face and a bearing which conveyed a glum endurance of a position beneath her. Yes, it had been from her—Brough her name was—that he had mysteriously gathered that he was not a desirable charge, as regarded from the point of the servants' hall—or, in fact, from any other point. His people were not the people whose patronage was sought with anxious eagerness. For some reason their town house was objectionable, and Mount Dunstan was without attractions. Other big houses were, in some marked way, different. The town house he objected to himself as being gloomy and ugly, and possessing only a bare and battered nursery, from whose windows one could not even obtain a satisfactory view of the Mews, where at least, there were horses and grooms who hissed cheerfully while they curried and brushed them. He hated the town house and was, in fact, very glad that he was scarcely ever taken to it. People, it seemed, did not care to come either to the town house or to Mount Dunstan. That was why he did not know other little boys. Again—for the mysterious reason—people did not care that their children should associate with him. How did he discover this? He never knew exactly. He realised, however, that without distinct statements, he seemed to have gathered it through various disconnected talks with Brough. She had not remained with him long, having "bettered herself" greatly and gone away in glum satisfaction, but she had stayed long enough to convey to him things which became part of his existence, and smouldered in his little soul until they became part of himself. The ancestors who had hewn their way through their enemies with battle-axes, who had been fierce and cruel and unconquerable in their savage pride, had handed down to him a burning and unsubmissive soul. At six years old, walking with Brough in Kensington Gardens, and seeing other children playing under the care of nurses, who, he learned, were not inclined to make advances to his attendant, he dragged Brough away with a fierce little hand and stood apart with her, scowling haughtily, his head in the air, pretending that he disdained all childish gambols, and would have declined to join in them, even if he had been besought to so far unbend. Bitterness had been planted in him then, though he had not understood, and the sourness of Brough had been connected with no intelligence which might have caused her to suspect his feelings, and no one had noticed, and if anyone had noticed, no one would have cared in the very least.

When Brough had gone away to her far superior place, and she had been succeeded by one variety of objectionable or incompetent person after another, he had still continued to learn. In different ways he silently collected information, and all of it was unpleasant, and, as he grew older, it took for some years one form. Lack of resources, which should of right belong to persons of rank, was the radical objection to his people. At the town house there was no money, at Mount Dunstan there was no money. There had been so little money even in his grandfather's time that his father had inherited comparative beggary. The fourteenth Earl of Mount Dunstan did not call it "comparative" beggary, he called it beggary pure and simple, and cursed his progenitors with engaging frankness. He never referred to the fact that in his personable youth he had married a wife whose fortune, if it had not been squandered, might have restored his own. The fortune had been squandered in the course of a few years of riotous living, the wife had died when her third son was born, which event took place ten years after the birth of her second, whom she had lost through scarlet fever. James Hubert John Fergus Saltyre never heard much of her, and barely knew of her past existence because in the picture gallery he had seen a portrait of a tall, thin, fretful-looking young lady, with light ringlets, and pearls round her neck. She had not attracted him as a child, and the fact that he gathered that she had been his mother left him entirely unmoved. She was not a loveable-looking person, and, indeed, had been at once empty-headed, irritable, and worldly. He would probably have been no less lonely if she had lived. Lonely he was. His father was engaged in a career much too lively and interesting to himself to admit of his allowing himself to be bored by an unwanted and entirely superfluous child. The elder son, who was Lord Tenham, had reached a premature and degenerate maturity by the time the younger one made his belated appearance, and regarded him with unconcealed dislike. The worst thing which could have befallen the younger boy would have been intimate association with this degenerate youth.

As Saltyre left nursery days behind, he learned by degrees that the objection to himself and his people, which had at first endeavoured to explain itself as being the result of an unseemly lack of money, combined with that unpleasant feature, an uglier one—namely, lack of decent reputation. Angry duns, beggarliness of income, scarcity of the necessaries and luxuries which dignity of rank demanded, the indifference and slights of one's equals, and the ignoring of one's existence by exalted persons, were all hideous enough to Lord Mount Dunstan and his elder son—but they were not so hideous as was, to his younger son, the childish, shamed frenzy of awakening to the truth that he was one of a bad lot—a disgraceful lot, from whom nothing was expected but shifty ways, low vices, and scandals, which in the end could not even be kept out of the newspapers. The day came, in fact, when the worst of these was seized upon by them and filled their sheets with matter which for a whole season decent London avoided reading, and the fast and indecent element laughed, derided, or gloated over.

The memory of the fever of the monstrous weeks which had passed at this time was not one it was wise for a man to recall. But it was not to be forgotten—the hasty midnight arrival at Mount Dunstan of father and son, their haggard, nervous faces, their terrified discussions, and argumentative raging when they were shut up together behind locked doors, the appearance of legal advisers who looked as anxious as themselves, but failed to conceal the disgust with which they were battling, the knowledge that tongues were clacking almost hysterically in the village, and that curious faces hurried to the windows when even a menial from the great house passed, the atmosphere of below-stairs whispers, and jogged elbows, and winks, and giggles; the final desperate, excited preparations for flight, which might be ignominiously stopped at any moment by the intervention of the law, the huddling away at night time, the hot-throated fear that the shameful, self-branding move might be too late—the burning humiliation of knowing the inevitable result of public contempt or laughter when the world next day heard that the fugitives had put the English Channel between themselves and their country's laws.

Lord Tenham had died a few years later at Port Said, after descending into all the hells of degenerate debauch. His father had lived longer—long enough to make of himself something horribly near an imbecile, before he died suddenly in Paris. The Mount Dunstan who succeeded him, having spent his childhood and boyhood under the shadow of the "bad lot," had the character of being a big, surly, unattractive young fellow, whose eccentricity presented itself to those who knew his stock, as being of a kind which might develop at any time into any objectionable tendency. His bearing was not such as allured, and his fortune was not of the order which placed a man in the view of the world. He had no money to expend, no hospitalities to offer and apparently no disposition to connect himself with society. His wild-goose chase to America had, when it had been considered worth while discussing at all, been regarded as being very much the kind of thing a Mount Dunstan might do with some secret and disreputable end in view. No one had heard the exact truth, and no one would have been inclined to believe if they had heard it. That he had lived as plain Jem Salter, and laboured as any hind might have done, in desperate effort and mad hope, would not have been regarded as a fact to be credited. He had gone away, he had squandered money, he had returned, he was at Mount Dunstan again, living the life of an objectionable recluse—objectionable, because the owner of a place like Mount Dunstan should be a power and an influence in the county, should be counted upon as a dispenser of hospitalities, as a supporter of charities, as a dignitary of weight. He was none of these—living no one knew how, slouching about with his gun, riding or walking sullenly over the roads and marshland.

Just one man knew him intimately, and this one had been from his fifteenth year the sole friend of his life. He had come, then—the Reverend Lewis Penzance—a poor and unhealthy scholar, to be vicar of the parish of Dunstan. Only a poor and book-absorbed man would have accepted the position. What this man wanted was no more than quiet, pure country air to fill frail lungs, a roof over his head, and a place to pore over books and manuscripts. He was a born monk and celibate—in by-gone centuries he would have lived peacefully in some monastery, spending his years in the reading and writing of black letter and the illuminating of missals. At the vicarage he could lead an existence which was almost the same thing.

At Mount Dunstan there remained still the large remnant of a great library. A huge room whose neglected and half emptied shelves contained some strange things and wonderful ones, though all were in disorder, and given up to dust and natural dilapidation. Inevitably the Reverend Lewis Penzance had found his way there, inevitably he had gained indifferently bestowed permission to entertain himself by endeavouring to reduce to order and to make an attempt at cataloguing. Inevitably, also, the hours he spent in the place became the chief sustenance of his being.

There, one day, he had come upon an uncouth-looking boy with deep eyes and a shaggy crop of red hair. The boy was poring over an old volume, and was plainly not disposed to leave it. He rose, not too graciously, and replied to the elder man's greeting, and the friendly questions which followed. Yes, he was the youngest son of the house. He had nothing to do, and he liked the library. He often came there and sat and read things. There were some queer old books and a lot of stupid ones. The book he was reading now? Oh, that (with a slight reddening of his skin and a little awkwardness at the admission) was one of those he liked best. It was one of the queer ones, but interesting for all that. It was about their own people—the generations of Mount Dunstans who had lived in the centuries past. He supposed he liked it because there were a lot of odd stories and exciting things in it. Plenty of fighting and adventure. There had been some splendid fellows among them. (He was beginning to forget himself a little by this time.) They were afraid of nothing. They were rather like savages in the earliest days, but at that time all the rest of the world was savage. But they were brave, and it was odd how decent they were very often. What he meant was— what he liked was, that they were men—even when they were barbarians. You couldn't be ashamed of them. Things they did then could not be done now, because the world was different, but if—well, the kind of men they were might do England a lot of good if they were alive to-day. They would be different themselves, of course, in one way—but they must be the same men in others. Perhaps Mr. Penzance (reddening again) understood what he meant. He knew himself very well, because he had thought it all out, he was always thinking about it, but he was no good at explaining.

Mr. Penzance was interested. His outlook on the past and the present had always been that of a bookworm, but he understood enough to see that he had come upon a temperament novel enough to awaken curiosity. The apparently entirely neglected boy, of a type singularly unlike that of his father and elder brother, living his life virtually alone in the big place, and finding food to his taste in stories of those of his blood whose dust had mingled with the earth centuries ago, provided him with a new subject for reflection.

That had been the beginning of an unusual friendship. Gradually Penzance had reached a clear understanding of all the building of the young life, of its rankling humiliation, and the qualities of mind and body which made for rebellion. It sometimes thrilled him to see in the big frame and powerful muscles, in the strong nature and unconquerable spirit, a revival of what had burned and stirred through lives lived in a dim, almost mythical, past. There were legends of men with big bodies, fierce faces, and red hair, who had done big deeds, and conquered in dark and barbarous days, even Fate's self, as it had seemed. None could overthrow them, none could stand before their determination to attain that which they chose to claim. Students of heredity knew that there were curious instances of revival of type. There had been a certain Red Godwyn who had ruled his piece of England before the Conqueror came, and who had defied the interloper with such splendid arrogance and superhuman lack of fear that he had won in the end, strangely enough, the admiration and friendship of the royal savage himself, who saw, in his, a kindred savagery, a power to be well ranged, through love, if not through fear, upon his own side. This Godwyn had a deep attraction for his descendant, who knew the whole story of his fierce life—as told in one yellow manuscript and another—by heart. Why might not one fancy—Penzance was drawn by the imagining—this strong thing reborn, even as the offspring of a poorer effete type. Red Godwyn springing into being again, had been stronger than all else, and had swept weakness before him as he had done in other and far-off days.

In the old library it fell out in time that Penzance and the boy spent the greater part of their days. The man was a bookworm and a scholar, young Saltyre had a passion for knowledge. Among the old books and manuscripts he gained a singular education. Without a guide he could not have gathered and assimilated all he did gather and assimilate. Together the two rummaged forgotten shelves and chests, and found forgotten things. That which had drawn the boy from the first always drew and absorbed him—the annals of his own people. Many a long winter evening the pair turned over the pages of volumes and of parchment, and followed with eager interest and curiosity the records of wild lives—stories of warriors and abbots and bards, of feudal lords at ruthless war with each other, of besiegings and battles and captives and torments. Legends there were of small kingdoms torn asunder, of the slaughter of their kings, the mad fightings of their barons, and the faith or unfaith of their serfs. Here and there the eternal power revealed itself in some story of lawful or unlawful love—for dame or damsel, royal lady, abbess, or high-born nun— ending in the welding of two lives or in rapine, violence, and death. There were annals of early England, and of marauders, monks, and Danes. And, through all these, some thing, some man or woman, place, or strife linked by some tie with Mount Dunstan blood. In past generations, it seemed plain, there had been certain of the line who had had pride in these records, and had sought and collected them; then had been born others who had not cared. Sometimes the relations were inadequate, sometimes they wore an unauthentic air, but most of them seemed, even after the passing of centuries, human documents, and together built a marvellous great drama of life and power, wickedness and passion and daring deeds.

When the shameful scandal burst forth young Saltyre was seen by neither his father nor his brother. Neither of them had any desire to see him; in fact, each detested the idea of confronting by any chance his hot, intolerant eyes. "The Brat," his father had called him in his childhood, "The Lout," when he had grown big-limbed and clumsy. Both he and Tenham were sick enough, without being called upon to contemplate "The Lout," whose opinion, in any case, they preferred not to hear.

Saltyre, during the hideous days, shut himself up in the library. He did not leave the house, even for exercise, until after the pair had fled. His exercise he took in walking up and down from one end of the long room to another. Devils were let loose in him. When Penzance came to him, he saw their fury in his eyes, and heard it in the savagery of his laugh.

He kicked an ancient volume out of his way as he strode to and fro.

"There has been plenty of the blood of the beast in us in bygone times," he said, "but it was not like this. Savagery in savage days had its excuse. This is the beast sunk into the gibbering, degenerate ape."

Penzance came and spent hours of each day with him. Part of his rage was the rage of a man, but he was a boy still, and the boyishness of his bitterly hurt youth was a thing to move to pity. With young blood, and young pride, and young expectancy rising within him, he was at an hour when he should have felt himself standing upon the threshold of the world, gazing out at the splendid joys and promises and powerful deeds of it—waiting only the fit moment to step forth and win his place.

"But we are done for," he shouted once. "We are done for. And I am as much done for as they are. Decent people won't touch us. That is where the last Mount Dunstan stands." And Penzance heard in his voice an absolute break. He stopped and marched to the window at the end of the long room, and stood in dead stillness, staring out at the down-sweeping lines of heavy rain.

The older man thought many things, as he looked at his big back and body. He stood with his legs astride, and Penzance noted that his right hand was clenched on his hip, as a man's might be as he clenched the hilt of his sword— his one mate who might avenge him even when, standing at bay, he knew that the end had come, and he must fall. Primeval Force—the thin-faced, narrow-chested, slightly bald clergyman of the Church of England was thinking—never loses its way, or fails to sweep a path before it. The sun rises and sets, the seasons come and go, Primeval Force is of them, and as unchangeable. Much of it stood before him embodied in this strongly sentient thing. In this way the Reverend Lewis found his thoughts leading him, and he—being moved to the depths of a fine soul—felt them profoundly interesting, and even sustaining.

He sat in a high-backed chair, holding its arms with long thin hands, and looking for some time at James Hubert John Fergus Saltyre. He said, at last, in a sane level voice:

"Lord Tenham is not the last Mount Dunstan."

After which the stillness remained unbroken again for some minutes. Saltyre did not move or make any response, and, when he left his place at the window, he took up a book, and they spoke of other things.

When the fourteenth Earl died in Paris, and his younger son succeeded, there came a time when the two companions sat together in the library again. It was the evening of a long day spent in discouraging hard work. In the morning they had ridden side by side over the estate, in the afternoon they had sat and pored over accounts, leases, maps, plans. By nightfall both were fagged and neither in sanguine mood.

Mount Dunstan had sat silent for some time. The pair often sat silent. This pause was ended by the young man's rising and standing up, stretching his limbs.

"It was a queer thing you said to me in this room a few years ago," he said. "It has just come back to me."

Singularly enough—or perhaps naturally enough—it had also just arisen again from the depths of Penzance's subconsciousness.

"Yes," he answered, "I remember. To-night it suggests premonition. Your brother was not the last Mount Dunstan."

"In one sense he never was Mount Dunstan at all," answered the other man. Then he suddenly threw out his arms in a gesture whose whole significance it would have been difficult to describe. There was a kind of passion in it. "I am the last Mount Dunstan," he harshly laughed. "Moi qui vous parle! The last."

Penzance's eyes resting on him took upon themselves the far-seeing look of a man who watches the world of life without living in it. He presently shook his head.

"No," he said. "I don't see that. No—not the last. Believe me."

And singularly, in truth, Mount Dunstan stood still and gazed at him without speaking. The eyes of each rested in the eyes of the other. And, as had happened before, they followed the subject no further. From that moment it dropped.

Only Penzance had known of his reasons for going to America. Even the family solicitors, gravely holding interviews with him and restraining expression of their absolute disapproval of such employment of his inadequate resources, knew no more than that this Mount Dunstan, instead of wasting his beggarly income at Cairo, or Monte Carlo, or in Paris as the last one had done, prefers to waste it in newer places. The head of the firm, when he bids him good-morning and leaves him alone, merely shrugs his shoulders and returns to his letter writing with the corners of his elderly mouth hard set.

Penzance saw him off—and met him upon his return. In the library they sat and talked it over, and, having done so, closed the book of the episode.

He sat at the table, his eyes upon the wide-spread loveliness of the landscape, but his thought elsewhere. It wandered over the years already lived through, wandering backwards even to the days when existence, opening before the child eyes, was a baffling and vaguely unhappy thing.

When the door opened and Penzance was ushered in by a servant, his face wore the look his friend would have been rejoiced to see swept away to return no more.

Then let us take our old accustomed seat and begin some casual talk, which will draw him out of the shadows, and make him forget such things as it is not good to remember. That is what we have done many times in the past, and may find it well to do many a time again.

He begins with talk of the village and the country-side. Village stories are often quaint, and stories of the countryside are sometimes—not always—interesting. Tom Benson's wife has presented him with triplets, and there is great excitement in the village, as to the steps to be taken to secure the three guineas given by the Queen as a reward for this feat. Old Benny Bates has announced his intention of taking a fifth wife at the age of ninety, and is indignant that it has been suggested that the parochial authorities in charge of the "Union," in which he must inevitably shortly take refuge, may interfere with his rights as a citizen. The Reverend Lewis has been to talk seriously with him, and finds him at once irate and obdurate.

"Vicar," says old Benny, "he can't refuse to marry no man. Law won't let him." Such refusal, he intimates, might drive him to wild and riotous living. Remembering his last view of old Benny tottering down the village street in his white smock, his nut-cracker face like a withered rosy apple, his gnarled hand grasping the knotted staff his bent body leaned on, Mount Dunstan grinned a little. He did not smile when Penzance passed to the restoration of the ancient church at Mellowdene. "Restoration" usually meant the tearing away of ancient oaken, high-backed pews, and the instalment of smug new benches, suggesting suburban Dissenting chapels, such as the feudal soul revolts at. Neither did he smile at a reference to the gathering at Dunholm Castle, which was twelve miles away. Dunholm was the possession of a man who stood for all that was first and highest in the land, dignity, learning, exalted character, generosity, honour. He and the late Lord Mount Dunstan had been born in the same year, and had succeeded to their titles almost at the same time. There had arrived a period when they had ceased to know each other. All that the one man intrinsically was, the other man was not. All that the one estate, its castle, its village, its tenantry, represented, was the antipodes of that which the other stood for. The one possession held its place a silent, and perhaps, unconscious reproach to the other. Among the guests, forming the large house party which London social news had already recorded in its columns, were great and honourable persons, and interesting ones, men and women who counted as factors in all good and dignified things accomplished. Even in the present Mount Dunstan's childhood, people of their world had ceased to cross his father's threshold. As one or two of the most noticeable names were mentioned, mentally he recalled this, and Penzance, quick to see the thought in his eyes, changed the subject.

"At Stornham village an unexpected thing has happened," he said. "One of the relatives of Lady Anstruthers has suddenly appeared—a sister. You may remember that the poor woman was said to be the daughter of some rich American, and it seemed unexplainable that none of her family ever appeared, and things were allowed to go from bad to worse. As it was understood that there was so much money people were mystified by the condition of things."

"Anstruthers has had money to squander," said Mount Dunstan. "Tenham and he were intimates. The money he spends is no doubt his wife's. As her family deserted her she has no one to defend her."

"Certainly her family has seemed to neglect her for years. Perhaps they were disappointed in his position. Many Americans are extremely ambitious. These international marriages are often singular things. Now—apparently without having been expected—the sister appears. Vanderpoel is the name—Miss Vanderpoel."

"I crossed the Atlantic with her in the Meridiana," said Mount Dunstan.

"Indeed! That is interesting. You did not, of course, know that she was coming here."

"I knew nothing of her but that she was a saloon passenger with a suite of staterooms, and I was in the second cabin. Nothing? That is not quite true, perhaps. Stewards and passengers gossip, and one cannot close one's ears. Of course one heard constant reiteration of the number of millions her father possessed, and the number of cabins she managed to occupy. During the confusion and alarm of the collision, we spoke to each other."

He did not mention the other occasion on which he had seen her. There seemed, on the whole, no special reason why he should.

"Then you would recognise her, if you saw her. I heard to-day that she seems an unusual young woman, and has beauty."

"Her eyes and lashes are remarkable. She is tall. The Americans are setting up a new type."

"Yes, they used to send over slender, fragile little women. Lady Anstruthers was the type. I confess to an interest in the sister."

"Why?"

"She has made a curious impression. She has begun to do things. Stornham village has lost its breath." He laughed a little. "She has been going over the place and discussing repairs."

Mount Dunstan laughed also. He remembered what she had said. And she had actually begun.

"That is practical," he commented.

"It is really interesting. Why should a young woman turn her attention to repairs? If it had been her father—the omnipotent Mr. Vanderpoel—who had appeared, one would not have wondered at such practical activity. But a young lady—with remarkable eyelashes!"

His elbows were on the arm of his chair, and he had placed the tips of his fingers together, wearing an expression of such absorbed contemplation that Mount Dunstan laughed again.

"You look quite dreamy over it," he said.

"It allures me. Unknown quantities in character always allure me. I should like to know her. A community like this is made up of the absolutely known quantity—of types repeating themselves through centuries. A new one is almost a startling thing. Gossip over teacups is not usually entertaining to me, but I found myself listening to little Miss Laura Brunel this afternoon with rather marked attention. I confess to having gone so far as to make an inquiry or so. Sir Nigel Anstruthers is not often at Stornham. He is away now. It is plainly not he who is interested in repairs."

"He is on the Riviera, in retreat, in a place he is fond of," Mount Dunstan said drily. "He took a companion with him. A new infatuation. He will not return soon."

CHAPTER XIX

SPRING IN BOND STREET

The visit to London was part of an evolution of both body and mind to Rosalie Anstruthers. In one of the wonderful modern hotels a suite of rooms was engaged for them. The luxury which surrounded them was not of the order Rosalie had vaguely connected with hotels. Hotel-keepers had apparently learned many things during the years of her seclusion.

Vanderpoels, at least, could so establish themselves as not to greatly feel the hotel atmosphere. Carefully chosen colours textures, and appointments formed the background of their days, the food they ate was a thing produced by art, the servants who attended them were completely-trained mechanisms. To sit by a window and watch the kaleidoscopic human tide passing by on its way to its pleasure, to reach its work, to spend its money in unending shops, to show itself and its equipage in the park, was a wonderful thing to Lady Anstruthers. It all seemed to be a part of the life and quality of Betty, little Betty, whom she had remembered only as a child, and who had come to her a tall, strong young beauty, who had—it was resplendently clear—never known a fear in her life, and whose mere personality had the effect of making fears seem unreal.

She was taken out in a luxurious little brougham to shops whose varied allurements were placed eagerly at her disposal. Respectful persons, obedient to her most faintly-expressed desire, displayed garments as wonderful as those the New York trunks had revealed. She was besought to consider the fitness of articles whose exquisiteness she was almost afraid to look at. Her thin little body was wonderfully fitted, managed, encouraged to make the most of its long-ignored outlines.

"Her ladyship's slenderness is a great advantage," said the wisely inciting ones. "There is no such advantage as delicacy of line."

Summing up the character of their customer with the saleswoman's eye, they realised the discretion of turning to Miss Vanderpoel for encouragement, though she was the younger of the two, and bore no title. They were aware of the existence of persons of rank who were not lavish patrons, but the name of Vanderpoel held most promising suggestions. To an English shopkeeper the American has, of late years, represented the spender—the type which, whatsoever its rank and resources, has, mysteriously, always money to hand over counters in exchange for things it chances to desire to possess. Each year surges across the Atlantic a horde of these fortunate persons, who, to the sober, commercial British mind, appear to be free to devote their existences to travel and expenditure. This contingent appears shopping in the various shopping thoroughfares; it buys clothes, jewels, miscellaneous attractive things, making its purchases of articles useful or decorative with a freedom from anxiety in its enjoyment which does not mark the mood of the ordinary shopper. In the everyday purchaser one is accustomed to take for granted, as a factor in his expenditure, a certain deliberation and uncertainty; to the travelling American in

Europe, shopping appears to be part of the holiday which is being made the most of. Surely, all the neat, smart young persons who buy frocks and blouses, hats and coats, hosiery and chains, cannot be the possessors of large incomes; there must be, even in America, a middle class of middle-class resources, yet these young persons, male and female, and most frequently unaccompanied by older persons—seeing what they want, greet it with expressions of pleasure, waste no time in appropriating and paying for it, and go away as in relief and triumph—not as in that sober joy which is clouded by afterthought. The sales people are sometimes even vaguely cheered by their gay lack of any doubt as to the wisdom of their getting what they admire, and rejoicing in it. If America always buys in this holiday mood, it must be an enviable thing to be a shopkeeper in their New York or Boston or San Francisco. Who would not make a fortune among them? They want what they want, and not something which seems to them less desirable, but they open their purses and—frequently with some amused uncertainty as to the differences between sovereigns and half-sovereigns, florins and half-crowns—they pay their bills with something almost like glee. They are remarkably prompt about bills—which is an excellent thing, as they are nearly always just going somewhere else, to France or Germany or Italy or Scotland or Siberia. Those of us who are shopkeepers, or their salesmen, do not dream that some of them have incomes no larger than our own, that they work for their livings, that they are teachers journalists, small writers or illustrators of papers or magazines that they are unimportant soldiers of fortune, but, with their queer American insistence on exploration, and the ignoring of limitations, they have, somehow, managed to make this exultant dash for a few daring weeks or months of freedom and new experience. If we knew this, we should regard them from our conservative standpoint of provident decorum as improvident lunatics, being ourselves unable to calculate with their odd courage and their cheerful belief in themselves. What we do know is that they spend, and we are far from disdaining their patronage, though most of them have an odd little familiarity of address and are not stamped with that distinction which causes us to realise the enormous difference between the patron and the tradesman, and makes us feel the worm we remotely like to feel ourselves, though we would not for worlds acknowledge the fact. Mentally, and in our speech, both among our equals and our superiors, we condescend to and patronise them a little, though that, of course, is the fine old insular attitude it would be un-British to discourage. But, if we are not in the least definite concerning the position and resources of these spenders as a mass, we are quite sure of a select number. There is mention of them in the newspapers, of the town houses, the castles, moors, and salmon fishings they rent, of their yachts, their presentations actually at our own courts, of their presence at great balls, at Ascot and Goodwood, at the opera on gala nights. One staggers sometimes before the public summing-up of the amount of their fortunes. These people who have neither blood nor rank, these men who labour in their business offices, are richer than our great dukes, at the realising of whose wealth and possessions we have at times almost turned pale.

"Them!" chaffed a costermonger over his barrow. "Blimme, if some o' them blokes won't buy Buckin'am Pallis an' the 'ole R'yal Fambly some mornin' when they're out shoppin'."

The subservient attendants in more than one fashionable shop Betty and her sister visit, know that Miss Vanderpoel is of the circle, though her father has not as yet bought or hired any great estate, and his daughter has not been seen in London.

"Its queer we've never heard of her being presented," one shopgirl says to another. "Just you look at her."

She evidently knows what her ladyship ought to buy—what can be trusted not to overpower her faded fragility. The saleswomen, even if they had not been devoured by alert curiosity, could not have avoided seeing that her ladyship did not seem to know what should be bought, and that Miss Vanderpoel did, though she did not direct her sister's selection, but merely seemed to suggest with delicate restraint. Her taste was wonderfully perceptive. The things bought were exquisite, but a little colourless woman could wear them all with advantage to her restrictions of type.

As the brougham drove down Bond Street, Betty called Lady Anstruthers' attention to more than one passer-by.

"Look, Rosy," she said. "There is Mrs. Treat Hilyar in the second carriage to the right. You remember Josie Treat Hilyar married Lord Varick's son."

In the landau designated an elderly woman with wonderfully-dressed white hair sat smiling and bowing to friends who were walking. Lady Anstruthers, despite her eagerness, shrank back a little, hoping to escape being seen.

"Oh, it is the Lows she is speaking to—Tom and Alice—I did not know they had sailed yet."

The tall, well-groomed young man, with the nice, ugly face, was showing white teeth in a gay smile of recognition, and his pretty wife was lightly waving a slim hand in a grey suede glove.

"How cheerful and nice-tempered they look," said Rosy. "Tom was only twenty when I saw him last. Whom did he marry?"

"An English girl. Such a love. A Devonshire gentleman's daughter. In New York his friends called her Devonshire Cream and Roses. She is one of the pretty, flushy, pink ones."

"How nice Bond Street is on a spring morning like this," said Lady Anstruthers. "You may laugh at me for saying it, Betty, but somehow it seems to me more spring-like than the country."

"How clever of you!" laughed Betty. "There is so much truth in it." The people walking in the sunshine were all full of spring thoughts and plans. The colours they wore, the flowers in the women's hats and the men's buttonholes belonged to the season. The cheerful crowds of people and carriages had a sort of rushing stir of movement which suggested freshness. Later in the year everything looks more tired. Now things were beginning and everyone was rather inclined to believe that this year would be better than last. "Look at the shop windows," said Betty, "full of whites and pinks and yellows and blues—the colours of hyacinth and daffodil beds. It seems as if they insist that there never has been a winter and never will be one. They insist that there never was and never will be anything but spring."

"It's in the air." Lady Anstruthers' sigh was actually a happy one. "It is just what I used to feel in April when we drove down Fifth Avenue."

Among the crowds of freshly-dressed passers-by, women with flowery hats and light frocks and parasols, men with touches of flower-colour on the lapels of their coats, and the holiday look in their faces, she noted so many of a familiar type that she began to look for and try to pick them out with quite excited interest.

"I believe that woman is an American," she would say. "That girl looks as if she were a New Yorker," again. "That man's face looks as if it belonged to Broadway. Oh, Betty! do you think I am right? I should say those girls getting out of the hansom to go into Burnham & Staples' came from out West and are going to buy thousands of things. Don't they look like it?"

She began to lean forward and look on at things with an interest so unlike her Stornham listlessness that Betty's heart was moved.

Her face looked alive, and little waves of colour rose under her skin. Several times she laughed the natural little laugh of her girlhood which it had seemed almost too much to expect to hear again. The first of these laughs came when she counted her tenth American, a tall Westerner of the cartoon type, sauntering along with an expression of speculative enjoyment on his odd face, and evidently, though furtively, chewing tobacco.

"I absolutely love him, Betty," she cried. "You couldn't mistake him for anything else."

"No," answered Betty, feeling that she loved him herself, "not if you found him embalmed in the Pyramids."

They pleased themselves immensely, trying to guess what he would buy and take home to his wife and girls in his Western town—though Western towns were very grand and amazing in these days, Betty explained, and knew they could give points to New York. He would not buy the things he would have bought fifteen years ago. Perhaps, in fact, his wife and daughters had come with him to London and stayed at the Metropole or the Savoy, and were at this moment being fitted by tailors and modistes patronised by Royalty.

"Rosy, look! Do you see who that is? Do you recognise her? It is Mrs. Bellingham. She was little Mina Thalberg. She married Captain Bellingham. He was quite poor, but very well born—a nephew of Lord Dunholm's. He could not have married a poor girl—but they have been so happy together that Mina is growing fat, and spends her days in taking reducing treatments. She says she wouldn't care in the least, but Dicky fell in love with her waist and shoulder line."

The plump, pretty young woman getting out of her victoria before a fashionable hairdresser's looked radiant enough. She had not yet lost the waist and shoulder line, though her pink frock fitted her with discreet tightness. She paused a moment to pat and fuss prettily over the two blooming, curly children who were to remain under the care of the nurse, who sat on the back seat, holding the baby on her lap.

"I should not have known her," said Rosy. "She has grown pretty. She wasn't a pretty child."

"It's happiness—and the English climate—and Captain Dicky. They adore each other, and laugh at everything like a pair of children. They were immensely popular in New York last winter, when they visited Mina's people."

The effect of the morning upon Lady Anstruthers was what Betty had hoped it might be. The curious drawing near of the two nations began to dawn upon her as a truth. Immured in the country, not sufficiently interested in life to read newspapers, she had heard rumours of some of the more important marriages, but had known nothing of the thousand small details which made for the weaving of the web. Mrs. Treat Hilyar driving in a leisurely, accustomed fashion down Bond Street, and smiling casually at her compatriots, whose "sailing" was as much part of the natural order of their luxurious lives as their carriages, gave a definiteness to the situation. Mina Thalberg, pulling down the embroidered frocks over the round legs of her English-looking children, seemed to narrow the width of the Atlantic Ocean between Liverpool and the docks on the Hudson River.

She returned to the hotel with an appetite for lunch and a new expression in her eyes which made Ughtred stare at her.

"Mother," he said, "you look different. You look well. It isn't only your new dress and your hair."

The new style of her attire had certainly done much, and the maid who had been engaged to attend her was a woman who knew her duties. She had been called upon in her time to make the most of hair offering much less assistance to her skill than was supplied by the fine, fair colourlessness she had found dragged back from her new mistress's forehead. It was not dragged back now, but had really been done wonders with. Rosalie had smiled a little when she had looked at herself in the glass after the first time it was so dressed.

"You are trying to make me look as I did when mother saw me last, Betty," she said. "I wonder if you possibly could."

"Let us believe we can," laughed Betty. "And wait and see."

It seemed wise neither to make nor receive visits. The time for such things had evidently not yet come. Even the mention of the Worthingtons led to the revelation that Rosalie shrank from immediate contact with people. When she felt stronger, when she became more accustomed to the thought, she might feel differently, but just now, to be luxuriously one with the enviable part of London, to look on, to drink in, to drive here and there, doing the things she liked to do, ordering what was required at Stornham, was like the creating for her of a new heaven and a new earth.

When, one night, Betty took her with Ughtred to the theatre, it was to see a play written by an American, played by American actors, produced by an American manager. They had even engaged in theatrical enterprise, it seemed, their actors played before London audiences, London actors played in American theatres, vibrating almost yearly between the two continents and reaping rich harvests. Hearing rumours of this in the past, Lady Anstruthers had scarcely believed it entirely true. Now the practical reality was brought before her. The French, who were only separated from the English metropolis by a mere few miles of Channel, did not exchange their actors year after year in increasing numbers, making a mere friendly barter of each other's territory, as though each land was common ground and not divided by leagues of ocean travel.

"It seems so wonderful," Lady Anstruthers argued. "I have always felt as if they hated each other."

"They did once—but how could it last between those of the same blood—of the same tongue? If we were really aliens we might be a menace. But we are of their own." Betty leaned forward on the edge of the box, looking out over the crowded house, filled with almost as many Americans as English faces. She smiled, reflecting. "We were children put out to nurse and breathe new air in the country, and now we are coming home, vigorous, and full-grown."

She studied the audience for some minutes, and, as her glance wandered over the stalls, it took in more than one marked variety of type. Suddenly it fell on a face she delightedly recognised. It was that of the nice, speculative-eyed Westerner they had seen enjoying himself in Bond Street.

"Rosy," she said, "there is the Western man we love. Near the end of the fourth row."

Lady Anstruthers looked for him with eagerness.

"Oh, I see him! Next to the big one with the reddish hair."

Betty turned her attention to the man in question, whom she had not chanced to notice. She uttered an exclamation of surprise and interest.

"The big man with the red hair. How lovely that they should chance to sit side by side—the big one is Lord Mount Dunstan!"

The necessity of seeing his solicitors, who happened to be Messrs. Townlinson & Sheppard, had brought Lord Mount Dunstan to town. After a day devoted to business affairs, he had been attracted by the idea of going to the theatre to see again a play he had already seen in New York. It would interest him to observe its exact effect upon a London audience. While he had been in New York, he had gone with something of the same feeling to see a great English actor play to a crowded house. The great actor had been one who had returned to the country for a third or fourth time, and, in the enthusiasm he had felt in the atmosphere about him, Mount Dunstan had seen not only pleasure and appreciation of the man's perfect art, but—at certain tumultuous outbursts—an almost emotional welcome. The Americans, he had said to himself, were creatures of warmer blood than the English. The audience on that occasion had been, in mass, American. The audience he made one of now, was made up of both nationalities, and, in glancing over it, he realised how large was the number of Americans who came yearly to London. As Lady Anstruthers had done, he found himself selecting from the assemblage the types which were manifestly American, and those obviously English. In the seat next to himself sat a man of a type he felt he had learned by heart in the days of his life as Jem

Salter. At a short distance fluttered brilliantly an English professional beauty, with her male and female court about her. In the stage box, made sumptuous with flowers, was a royal party.

As this party had entered, "God save the Queen" had been played, and, in rising with the audience during the entry, he had recalled that the tune was identical with that of an American national air. How unconsciously inseparable—in spite of the lightness with which they regarded the curious tie between them—the two countries were. The people upon the stage were acting as if they knew their public, their bearing suggesting no sense of any barrier beyond the footlights. It was the unconsciousness and lightness of the mutual attitude which had struck him of late. Punch had long jested about "Fair Americans," who, in their first introduction to its pages, used exotic and cryptic language, beginning every sentence either with "I guess," or "Say, Stranger"; its male American had been of the Uncle Sam order and had invariably worn a "goatee." American witticisms had represented the Englishman in plaid trousers, opening his remarks with "Chawley, deah fellah," and unfailingly missing the point of any joke. Each country had cherished its type and good-naturedly derided it. In time this had modified itself and the joke had changed in kind. Many other things had changed, but the lightness of treatment still remained. And yet their blood was mingling itself with that of England's noblest and oldest of name, their wealth was making solid again towers and halls which had threatened to crumble. Ancient family jewels glittered on slender, young American necks, and above—sometimes somewhat careless—young American brows. And yet, so far, one was casual in one's thought of it all, still. On his own part he was obstinate Briton enough to rebel against and resent it. They were intruders. He resented them as he had resented in his boyhood the historical fact that, after all, an Englishman was a German—a savage who, five hundred years after the birth of Christ, had swooped upon Early Briton from his Engleland and Jutland, and ravaging with fire and sword, had conquered and made the land his possession, ravishing its very name from it and giving it his own. These people did not come with fire and sword, but with cable and telephone, and bribes of gold and fair women, but they were encroaching like the sea, which, in certain parts of the coast, gained a few inches or so each year. He shook his shoulders impatiently, and stiffened, feeling illogically antagonistic towards the good-natured, lantern-jawed man at his side.

The lantern-jawed man looked good-natured because he was smiling, and he was smiling because he saw something which pleased him in one of the boxes.

His expression of unqualified approval naturally directed Mount Dunstan's eye to the point in question, where it remained for some moments. This was because he found it resting upon Miss Vanderpoel, who sat before him in luminous white garments, and with a brilliant spark of ornament in the dense shadow of her hair. His sensation at the unexpected sight of her would, if it had expressed itself physically, have taken the form of a slight start. The luminous quality did not confine itself to the whiteness of her garments. He was aware of feeling that she looked luminous herself—her eyes, her cheek, the smile she bent upon the little woman who was her companion. She was a beautifully living thing.

Naturally, she was being looked at by others than himself. She was one of those towards whom glasses in a theatre turn themselves inevitably. The sweep and lift of her black hair would have drawn them, even if she had offered no other charm. Yes, he thought, here was another of them. To whom was she bringing her good looks and her millions? There were men enough who needed money, even if they must accept it under less alluring conditions. In the box next to the one occupied by the royal party was a man who was known to be waiting for the advent of some such opportunity. His was a case of dire, if outwardly stately, need. He was young, but a fool, and not noted for personal charms, yet he had, in one sense, great things to offer. There were, of course, many chances that he might offer them to her. If this happened, would she accept them? There was really no objection to him but his dulness, consequently there seemed many chances that she might. There was something akin to the pomp of royalty in the power her father's wealth implied. She could scarcely make an ordinary marriage. It would naturally be a sort of state affair. There were few men who had enough to offer in exchange for Vanderpoel millions, and of the few none had special attractions. The one in the box next to the royal party was a decent enough fellow. As young princesses were not infrequently called upon, by the mere exclusion of royal blood, to become united to young or mature princes without charm, so American young persons who were of royal possessions must find themselves limited. If you felt free to pick and choose from among young men in the Guards or young attaches in the Diplomatic Service with twopence a year, you might get beauty or wit or temperament or all three by good luck, but if you were of a royal house of New York or Chicago, you would probably feel you must draw lines and choose only such splendours as accorded with, even while differing from, your own.

Any possible connection of himself with such a case did not present itself to him. If it had done so, he would have counted himself, haughtily, as beyond the pale. It was for other men to do things of the sort; a remote antagonism of his whole being warred against the mere idea. It was bigoted prejudice, perhaps, but it was a strong thing.

A lovely shoulder and a brilliant head set on a long and slender neck have no nationality which can prevent a man's glance turning naturally towards them. His turned again during the last act of the play, and at a moment when he saw something rather like the thing he had seen when the Meridiana moved away from the dock and the exalted Miss Vanderpoel leaning upon the rail had held out her arms towards the child who had brought his toy to her as a farewell offering.

Sitting by her to-night was a boy with a crooked back—Mount Dunstan remembered hearing that the Anstruthers had a deformed son—and she was leaning towards him, her hand resting on his shoulder, explaining something he had not quite grasped in the action of the play. The absolute adoration in the boy's uplifted eyes was an interesting thing to take in, and the radiant warmth of her bright look was as unconscious of onlookers as it had been when he had seen it yearning towards the child on the wharf. Hers was the temperament which gave—which gave. He found himself restraining a smile because her look brought back to him the actual sound of the New York youngster's voice.

"I wanted to kiss you, Betty, oh, I did so want to kiss you!"

Anstruthers' boy—poor little beggar—looked as if he, too, in the face of actors and audience, and brilliance of light, wanted to kiss her.

CHAPTER XX

THINGS OCCUR IN STORNHAM VILLAGE

It would not have been possible for Miss Vanderpoel to remain long in social seclusion in London, and, before many days had passed, Stornham village was enlivened by the knowledge that her ladyship and her sister had returned to the Court. It was also evident that their visit to London had not been made to no purpose. The stagnation of the waters of village life threatened to become a whirlpool. A respectable person, who was to be her ladyship's maid, had come with them, and her ladyship had not been served by a personal attendant for years. Her ladyship had also appeared at the dinner-table in new garments, and with her hair done as other ladies wore theirs. She looked like a different woman, and actually had a bit of colour, and was beginning to lose her frightened way. Now it dawned upon even the dullest and least active mind that something had begun to stir.

It had been felt vaguely when the new young lady from "Meriker" had walked through the village street, and had drawn people to doors and windows by her mere passing. After the return from London the signs of activity were such as made the villagers catch their breaths in uttering uncertain exclamations, and caused the feminine element to catch up offspring or, dragging it by its hand, run into neighbours' cottages and stand talking the incredible thing over in lowered and rather breathless voices. Yet the incredible thing in question was— had it been seen from the standpoint of more prosperous villagers—anything but extraordinary. In entirely rural places the Castle, the Hall or the Manor, the Great House—in short—still retains somewhat of the old feudal power to bestow benefits or withhold them. Wealth and good will at the Manor supply work and resultant comfort in the village and its surrounding holdings. Patronised by the Great House the two or three small village shops bestir themselves and awaken to activity. The blacksmith swings his hammer with renewed spirit over the numerous jobs the gentry's stables, carriage houses, garden tools, and household repairs give to him. The carpenter mends and makes, the vicarage feels at ease, realising that its church and its charities do not stand unsupported. Small farmers and larger ones, under a rich and interested landlord, thrive and are able to hold their own even against the tricks of wind and weather. Farm labourers being, as a result, certain of steady and decent wage, trudge to and fro, with stolid cheerfulness, knowing that the pot boils and the children's feet are shod. Superannuated old men and women are sure of their broth and Sunday dinner, and their dread of the impending "Union" fades away. The squire or my lord or my lady can be depended upon to care for their old bones until they are laid under the sod in the green churchyard. With wealth and good will at the Great House, life warms and offers prospects. There are Christmas feasts and gifts and village treats, and the big carriage or the smaller ones stop at cottage doors and at once confer exciting distinction and carry good cheer.

But Stornham village had scarcely a remote memory of any period of such prosperity. It had not existed even in the older Sir Nigel's time, and certainly the present Sir Nigel's reign had been marked only by neglect, ill-temper, indifference, and a falling into disorder and decay. Farms were poorly worked, labourers were unemployed, there was no trade from the manor household, no carriages, no horses, no company, no spending of money. Cottages leaked, floors were damp, the church roof itself was falling to pieces, and the vicar had nothing to give. The helpless and old cottagers were carried to the "Union" and, dying there, were buried by the stinted parish in parish coffins.

Her ladyship had not visited the cottages since her child's birth. And now such inspiriting events as were everyday happenings in lucky places like Westerbridge and Wratcham and Yangford, showed signs of being about to occur in Stornham itself.

To begin with, even before the journey to London, Kedgers had made two or three visits to The Clock, and had been in a communicative mood. He had related the story of the morning when he had looked up from his work and had found the strange young lady standing before him, with the result that he had been "struck all of a heap." And then he had given a detailed account of their walk round the place, and of the way in which she had looked at things and asked questions, such as would have done credit to a man "with a 'ead on 'im."

"Nay! Nay!" commented Kedgers, shaking his own head doubtfully, even while with admiration. "I've never seen the like before—in young women— neither in lady young women nor in them that's otherwise."

Afterwards had transpired the story of Mrs. Noakes, and the kitchen grate, Mrs. Noakes having a friend in Miss Lupin, the village dressmaker.

"I'd not put it past her," was Mrs. Noakes' summing up, "to order a new one, I wouldn't."

The footman in the shabby livery had been a little wild in his statements, being rendered so by the admiring and excited state of his mind. He dwelt upon the matter of her "looks," and the way she lighted up the dingy dining-room, and so conversed that a man found himself listening and glancing when it was his business to be an unhearing, unseeing piece of mechanism.

Such simple records of servitors' impressions were quite enough for Stornham village, and produced in it a sense of being roused a little from sleep to listen to distant and uncomprehended, but not unagreeable, sounds.

One morning Buttle, the carpenter, looked up as Kedgers had done, and saw standing on the threshold of his shop the tall young woman, who was a sensation and an event in herself.

"You are the master of this shop?" she asked.

Buttle came forward, touching his brow in hasty salute.

"Yes, my lady," he answered. "Joseph Buttle, your ladyship."

"I am Miss Vanderpoel," dismissing the suddenly bestowed title with easy directness. "Are you busy? I want to talk to you."

No one had any reason to be "busy" at any time in Stornham village, no such luck; but Buttle did not smile as he replied that he was at liberty and placed himself at his visitor's disposal. The tall young lady came into the little shop, and took the chair respectfully offered to her. Buttle saw her eyes sweep the place as if taking in its resources.

"I want to talk to you about some work which must be done at the Court," she explained at once. "I want to know how much can be done by workmen of the village. How many men have you?"

"How many men had he?" Buttle wavered between gratification at its being supposed that he had "men" under him and grumpy depression because the illusion must be dispelled.

"There's me and Sim Soames, miss," he answered. "No more, an' no less."

"Where can you get more?" asked Miss Vanderpoel.

It could not be denied that Buttle received a mental shock which verged in its suddenness on being almost a physical one. The promptness and decision of such a query swept him off his feet. That Sim Soames and himself should be an insufficient force to combat with such repairs as the Court could afford was an idea presenting an aspect of unheard-of novelty, but that methods as coolly radical as those this questioning implied, should be resorted to, was staggering.

"Me and Sim has always done what work was done," he stammered. "It hasn't been much."

Miss Vanderpoel neither assented to nor dissented from this last palpable truth. She regarded Buttle with searching eyes. She was wondering if any practical ability concealed itself behind his dullness. If she gave him work, could he do it? If she gave the whole village work, was it too far gone in its unspurred stodginess to be roused to carrying it out?

"There is a great deal to be done now," she said. "All that can be done in the village should be done here. It seems to me that the villagers want work—new work. Do they?"

Work! New work! The spark of life in her steady eyes actually lighted a spark in the being of Joe Buttle. Young ladies in villages—gentry—usually visited the cottagers a bit if they were well-meaning young women—left good books and broth or jelly, pottered about and were seen at church, and playing croquet, and finally married and removed to other places, or gradually faded year by year into respectable spinsterhood. And this one comes in, and in two or three minutes shows that she knows things about the place and understands. A man might then take it for granted that she would understand the thing he daringly gathered courage to say.

"They want any work, miss—that they are sure of decent pay for—sure of it."

She did understand. And she did not treat his implication as an impertinence. She knew it was not intended as one, and, indeed, she saw in it a sort of earnest of a possible practical quality in Buttle. Such work as the Court had demanded had remained unpaid for with quiet persistence, until even bills had begun to lag and fall off. She could see exactly how it had been done, and comprehended quite clearly a lack of enthusiasm in the presence of orders from the Great House.

"All work will be paid for," she said. "Each week the workmen will receive their wages. They may be sure. I will be responsible."

"Thank you, miss," said Buttle, and he half unconsciously touched his forehead again.

"In a place like this," the young lady went on in her mellow voice, and with a reflective thoughtfulness in her handsome eyes, "on an estate like Stornham, no work that can be done by the villagers should be done by anyone else. The people of the land should be trained to do such work as the manor house, or cottages, or farms require to have done."

"How did she think that out?" was Buttle's reflection. In places such as Stornham, through generation after generation, the thing she had just said was accepted as law, clung to as a possession, any divergence from it being a grievance sullenly and bitterly grumbled over. And in places enough there was divergence in these days—the gentry sending to London for things, and having up workmen to do their best-paying jobs for them. The law had been so long a law that no village could see justice in outsiders being sent for, even to do work they could not do well themselves. It showed what she was, this handsome young woman—even though she did come from America—that she should know what was right.

She took a note-book out and opened it on the rough table before her.

"I have made some notes here," she said, "and a sketch or two. We must talk them over together."

If she had given Joe Buttle cause for surprise at the outset, she gave him further cause during the next half-hour. The work that was to be done was such as made him open his eyes, and draw in his breath. If he was to be allowed to do it—if he could do it—if it was to be paid for—it struck him that he would be a man set up for life. If her ladyship had come and ordered it to be done, he would have thought the poor thing had gone mad. But this one had it all jotted down in a clear hand, without the least feminine confusion of detail, and with here and there a little sharply-drawn sketch, such as a carpenter, if he could draw, which Buttle could not, might have made.

"There's not workmen enough in the village to do it in a year, miss," he said at last, with a gasp of disappointment.

She thought it over a minute, her pencil poised in her hand and her eyes on his face.

"Can you," she said, "undertake to get men from other villages, and superintend what they do? If you can do that, the work is still passing through your hands, and Stornham will reap the benefit of it. Your workmen will lodge at the cottages and spend part of their wages at the shops, and you who are a Stornham workman will earn the money to be made out of a rather large contract."

Joe Buttle became quite hot. If you have brought up a family for years on the proceeds of such jobs as driving a ten-penny nail in here or there, tinkering a hole in a cottage roof, knocking up a shelf in the vicarage kitchen, and mending a panel of fence, to be suddenly confronted with a proposal to engage workmen and undertake "contracts" is shortening to the breath and heating to the blood.

"Miss," he said, "we've never done big jobs, Sim Soames an' me. P'raps we're not up to it—but it'd be a fortune to us."

She was looking down at one of her papers and making pencil marks on it.

"You did some work last year on a little house at Tidhurst, didn't you?" she said.

To think of her knowing that! Yes, the unaccountable good luck had actually come to him that two Tidhurst carpenters, falling ill of the same typhoid at the same time, through living side by side in the same order of unsanitary cottage, he and Sim had been given their work to finish, and had done their best.

"Yes, miss," he answered.

"I heard that when I was inquiring about you. I drove over to Tidhurst to see the work, and it was very sound and well done. If you did that, I can at least trust you to do something at the Court which will prove to me what you are equal to. I want a Stornham man to undertake this."

"No Tidhurst man," said Joe Buttle, with sudden courage, "nor yet no Barnhurst, nor yet no Yangford, nor Wratcham shall do it, if I can look it in the face. It's Stornham work and Stornham had ought to have it. It gives me a brace-up to hear of it."

The tall young lady laughed beautifully and got up.

"Come to the Court to-morrow morning at ten, and we will look it over together," she said. "Good-morning, Buttle." And she went away.

In the taproom of The Clock, when Joe Buttle dropped in for his pot of beer, he found Fox, the saddler, and Tread, the blacksmith, and each of them fell upon the others with something of the same story to tell. The new young lady from the Court had been to see them, too, and had brought to each her definite little note-book. Harness was to be repaired and furbished up, the big carriage and the old phaeton were to be put in order, and Master Ughtred's cart was to be given new paint and springs.

"This is what she said," Fox's story ran, "and she said it so straightforward and business-like that the conceitedest man that lived couldn't be upset by it. 'I want to see what you can do,' she says. 'I am new to the place and I must find out what everyone can do, then I shall know what to do myself.' The way she sets them eyes on a man is a sight. It's the sense in them and the human nature that takes you."

"Yes, it's the sense," said Tread, "and her looking at you as if she expected you to have sense yourself, and understand that she's doing fair business. It's clear-headed like—her asking questions and finding out what Stornham men can do. She's having the old things done up so that she can find out, and so that she can prove that the Court work is going to be paid for. That's my belief."

"But what does it all mean?" said Joe Buttle, setting his pot of beer down on the taproom table, round which they sat in conclave. "Where's the money coming from? There's money somewhere."

Tread was the advanced thinker of the village. He had come—through reverses—from a bigger place. He read the newspapers.

"It'll come from where it's got a way of coming," he gave forth portentously. "It'll come from America. How they manage to get hold of so much of it there is past me. But they've got it, dang 'em, and they're ready to spend it for what they want, though they're a sharp lot. Twelve years ago there was a good bit of talk about her ladyship's father being one of them with the fullest pockets. She came here with plenty, but Sir Nigel got hold of it for his games, and they're the games that cost money. Her ladyship wasn't born with a backbone, poor thing, but this new one was, and her ladyship's father is her father, and you mark my words, there's money coming into Stornham, though it's not going to be played the fool with. Lord, yes! this new one has a backbone and good strong wrists and a good strong head, though I must say"—with a little masculine chuckle of admission— "it's a bit unnatural with them eyelashes and them eyes looking at you between 'em. Like blue water between rushes in the marsh."

Before the next twenty-four hours had passed a still more unlooked-for event had taken place. Long outstanding bills had been paid, and in as matter-of-fact manner as if they had not been sent in and ignored, in some cases for years. The settlement of Joe Buttle's account sent him to bed at the day's end almost light-headed. To become suddenly the possessor of thirty-seven pounds, fifteen and tenpence half-penny, of which all hope had been lost three years ago, was almost too much for any man. Six pounds, eight pounds, ten pounds, came into places as if sovereigns had been sixpences, and shillings farthings. More than one cottage woman, at the sight of the hoarded wealth in her staring goodman's hand, gulped and began to cry. If they had had it before, and in driblets, it would have been spent long since, now, in a lump, it meant shoes and petticoats and tea and sugar in temporary abundance, and the sense of this abundance was felt to be entirely due to American magic. America was, in fact, greatly lauded and discussed, the case of "Gaarge" Lumsden being much quoted.

CHAPTER XXI

KEDGERS

The work at Stornham Court went on steadily, though with no greater rapidity than is usually achieved by rural labourers. There was, however, without doubt, a certain stimulus in the occasional appearance of Miss Vanderpoel, who almost daily sauntered round the place to look on, and exchange a few words with the workmen. When they saw her coming, the men, hastily standing up to touch their foreheads, were conscious of a slight acceleration of being which was not quite the ordinary quickening produced by the presence of employers. It was, in fact, a sensation rather pleasing than anxious. Her interest in the work was, upon the whole, one which they found themselves beginning to share. The unusualness of the situation—a young woman, who evidently stood for many things and powers desirable, employing labourers and seeming to know what she intended them to do—was a thing not easy to get over, or be come accustomed to. But there she was, as easy and well mannered as you please—and with gentlefolks' ways, though, as an American, such finish could scarcely be expected from her. She knew each man's name, it was revealed gradually, and, what was more, knew what he stood for in the village, what cottage he lived in, how many children he had, and something about his wife. She remembered things and made inquiries which showed knowledge. Besides this, she represented, though perhaps they were scarcely yet fully awake to the fact, the promise their discouraged dulness had long lost sight of.

It actually became apparent that her ladyship, who walked with her, was altering day by day. Was it true that the bit of colour they had heard spoken of when she returned from town was deepening and fixing itself on her cheek? It sometimes looked like it. Was she a bit less stiff and shy-like and frightened in her way? Buttle mentioned to his friends at The Clock that he was sure of it. She had begun to look a man in the face when she talked, and more than once he had heard her laugh at things her sister said.

To one man more than to any other had come an almost unspeakable piece of luck through the new arrival—a thing which to himself, at least, was as the opening of the heavens. This man was the discouraged Kedgers. Miss Vanderpoel, coming with her ladyship to talk to him, found that the man was a person of more experience than might have been imagined. In his youth he had been an under gardener at a great place, and being fond of his work, had learned more than under gardeners often learn. He had been one of a small army of workers under the orders of an imposing head gardener, whose knowledge was a science. He had seen and taken part in what was done in orchid houses, orangeries, vineries, peach houses, conservatories full of wondrous tropical plants. But it was not easy for a man like himself, uneducated and lacking confidence of character, to advance as a bolder young man might have done. The all-ruling head gardener had inspired him with awe. He had watched him reverently, accumulating knowledge, but being given, as an underling, no opportunity to do more than obey orders. He had spent his life in obeying, and congratulated himself that obedience secured him his weekly wage.

"He was a great man—Mr. Timson—he was," he said, in talking to Miss Vanderpoel. "Ay, he was that. Knew everything that could happen to a flower or a s'rub or a vegetable. Knew it all. Had a lib'ery of books an' read 'em night an' day. Head gardener's cottage was good enough for gentry. The old Markis used to walk round the hothouses an' gardens talking to him by the hour. If you did what he told you EXACTLY like he told it to you, then you were all right, but if you didn't—well, you was off the place before you'd time to look round. Worked under him from twenty to forty. Then he died an' the new one that came in had new ways. He made a clean sweep of most of us. The men said he was jealous of Mr. Timson."

"That was bad for you, if you had a wife and children," Miss Vanderpoel said.

"Eight of us to feed," Kedgers answered. "A man with that on him can't wait, miss. I had to take the first place I could get. It wasn't a good one—poor parsonage with a big family an' not room on the place for the vegetables they wanted. Cabbages, an' potatoes, an' beans, an' broccoli. No time nor ground for flowers. Used to seem as if flowers got to be a kind of dream." Kedgers gave vent to a deprecatory half laugh. "Me—I was fond of flowers. I wouldn't have asked no better than to live among 'em. Mr. Timson gave me a book or two when his lordship sent him a lot of new ones. I've bought a few myself—though I suppose I couldn't afford it."

From the poor parsonage he had gone to a market gardener, and had evidently liked the work better, hard and unceasing as it had been, because he had been among flowers again. Sudden changes from forcing houses to chill outside dampness had resulted in rheumatism. After that things had gone badly. He began to be regarded as past his prime of strength. Lower wages and labour still as hard as ever, though it professed to be lighter, and therefore cheaper. At last the big neglected gardens of Stornham.

"What I'm seeing, miss, all the time, is what could be done with 'em. Wonderful it'd be. They might be the show of the county-if we had Mr. Timson here."

Miss Vanderpoel, standing in the sunshine on the broad weed-grown pathway, was conscious that he was remotely moving. His flowers—his flowers. They had been the centre of his rudimentary rural being. Each man or woman cared for some one thing, and the unfed longing for it left the life of the creature a thwarted passion. Kedgers, yearning to stir the earth about the roots of blooming things, and doomed to broccoli and cabbage, had spent his years unfed. No thing is a small thing. Kedgers, with the earth under his broad finger nails, and his half apologetic laugh, being the centre of his own world, was as large as Mount Dunstan, who stood thwarted in the centre of his. Chancing-for God knows what mystery of reason-to be born one of those having power, one might perhaps set in order a world like Kedgers'.

"In the course of twenty years' work under Timson," she said, "you must have learned a great deal from him."

"A good bit, miss—a good bit," admitted Kedgers. "If I hadn't ha' cared for the work, I might ha' gone on doing it with my eyes shut, but I didn't. Mr. Timson's heart was set on it as well as his head. An' mine got to be. But I wasn't even second or third under him—I was only one of a lot. He would have thought me fine an' impident if I'd told him I'd got to know a good deal of what he knew—and had some bits of ideas of my own."

"If you had men enough under you, and could order all you want," Miss Vanderpoel said tentatively, "you know what the place should be, no doubt."

"That I do, miss," answered Kedgers, turning red with feeling. "Why, if the soil was well treated, anything would grow here. There's situations for everything. There's shade for things that wants it, and south aspects for things that won't grow without the warmth of 'em. Well, I've gone about many a day when I was low down in my mind and worked myself up to being cheerful by just planning where I could put things and what they'd look like. Liliums, now, I could grow them in masses from June to October." He was becoming excited, like a war horse scenting battle from afar, and forgot himself. "The Lilium Giganteum—I don't know whether you've ever seen one, miss—but if you did, it'd almost take your breath away. A Lilium that grows twelve feet high and more, and has a flower like a great snow-white trumpet, and the scent pouring out of it so that it floats for yards. There's a place where I could grow them so that you'd come on them sudden, and you'd think they couldn't be true."

"Grow them, Kedgers, begin to grow them," said Miss Vanderpoel. "I have never seen them—I must see them."

Kedgers' low, deprecatory chuckle made itself heard again,

"Perhaps I'm going too fast," he said. "It would take a good bit of expense to do it, miss. A good bit."

Then Miss Vanderpoel made—and she made it in the simplest matter-of-fact manner, too—the startling remark which, three hours later, all Stornham village had heard of. The most astounding part of the remark was that it was uttered as if there was nothing in it which was not the absolutely natural outcome of the circumstances of the case.

"Expense which is proper and necessary need not be considered," she said. "Regular accounts will be kept and supervised, but you can have all that is required."

Then it appeared that Kedgers almost became pale. Being a foreigner, perhaps she did not know how much she was implying when she said such a thing to a man who had never held a place like Timson's.

"Miss," he hesitated, even shamefacedly, because to suggest to such a fine-mannered, calm young lady that she might be ignorant, seemed perilously near impertinence. "Miss, did you mean you wanted only the Lilium Giganteum, or—or other things, as well."

"I should like to see," she answered him, "all that you see. I should like to hear more of it all, when we have time to talk it over. I understand we should need time to discuss plans."

The quiet way she went on! Seeming to believe in him, almost as if he was Mr. Timson. The old feeling, born and fostered by the great head gardener's rule, reasserted itself.

"It means more to work—and someone over them, miss," he said. "If—if you had a man like Mr. Timson——"

"You have not forgotten what you learned. With men enough under you it can be put into practice."

"You mean you'd trust me, miss—same as if I was Mr. Timson?"

"Yes. If you ever feel the need of a man like Timson, no doubt we can find one. But you will not. You love the work too much."

Then still standing in the sunshine, on the weed-grown path, she continued to talk to him. It revealed itself that she understood a good deal. As he was to assume heavier responsibilities, he was to receive higher wages. It was his experience which was to be considered, not his years. This was a new point of view. The mere propeller of wheel-barrows and digger of the soil—particularly after having been attacked by rheumatism—depreciates in value after youth is past. Kedgers knew that a Mr. Timson, with a regiment of under gardeners, and daily increasing knowledge of his profession, could continue to direct, though years rolled by. But to such fortune he had not dared to aspire.

One of the lodges might be put in order for him to live in. He might have the hothouses to put in order, too; he might have implements, plants, shrubs, even some of the newer books to consult. Kedgers' brain reeled.

"You—think I am to be trusted, miss?" he said more than once. "You think it would be all right? I wasn't even second or third under Mr. Timson—but—if I say it as shouldn't—I never lost a chance of learning things. I was just mad about it. T'aint only Liliums—Lord, I know 'em all, as if they were my own children born an' bred—shrubs, coniferas, herbaceous borders that bloom in succession. My word! what you can do with just delphiniums an' campanula an' acquilegia an' poppies, everyday things like them, that'll grow in any cottage garden, an' bulbs an' annuals! Roses, miss—why, Mr. Timson had them in thickets—an' carpets—an' clambering over trees and tumbling over walls in sheets an' torrents—just know their ways an' what they want, an' they'll grow in a riot. But they want feeding—feeding. A rose is a gross feeder. Feed a Glory deejon, and watch over him, an' he'll cover a housetop an' give you two bloomings."

"I have never lived in an English garden. I should like to see this one at its best."

Leaving her with salutes of abject gratitude, Kedgers moved away bewildered. What man could believe it true? At three or four yards' distance he stopped and, turning, came back to touch his cap again.

"You understand, miss," he said. "I wasn't even second or third under Mr. Timson. I'm not deceiving you, am I, miss?"

"You are to be trusted," said Miss Vanderpoel, "first because you love the things—and next because of Timson."

CHAPTER XXII

ONE OF MR. VANDERPOEL'S LETTERS

Mr. Germen, the secretary of the great Mr. Vanderpoel, in arranging the neat stacks of letters preparatory to his chief's entrance to his private room each morning, knowing where each should be placed, understood that such as were addressed in Miss Vanderpoel's hand would be read before anything else. This had been the case even when she had just been placed in a French school, a tall, slim little girl, with immense demanding eyes, and a thick black plait of hair swinging between her straight, rather thin, shoulders. Between other financial potentates and their little girls, Mr. Germen knew that the oddly confidential relation which existed between these two was unusual. Her schoolgirl letters, it had been understood, should be given the first place on the stacks of envelopes each incoming ocean steamer brought in its mail bags. Since the beginning of her visit to her sister, Lady Anstruthers, the exact dates of mail steamers seemed to be of increased importance. Miss Vanderpoel evidently found much to write about. Each steamer brought a full-looking envelope to be placed in a prominent position.

On a hot morning in the early summer Mr. Germen found two or three— two of them of larger size and seeming to contain business papers. These he placed where they would be seen at once. Mr. Vanderpoel was a little later than usual in his arrival. At this season he came from his place in the country, and before leaving it this morning he had been talking to his wife, whom he found rather disturbed by a chance encounter with a young woman who had returned to visit her mother after a year spent in England with her English husband. This young woman, now Lady Bowen, once Milly Jones, had been one of the amusing marvels of New York. A girl neither rich nor so endowed by nature as to be able to press upon the world any special claim to consideration as a beauty, her enterprise, and the daring of her tactics, had been the delight of many a satiric onlooker. In her schooldays she had ingenuously mapped out her future career. Other American girls married men with titles, and she intended to do the same thing. The other little girls laughed, but they liked to hear her talk. All information regarding such unions as was to be found in the newspapers and magazines, she collected and studiously read—sometimes aloud to her companions.

Social paragraphs about royalties, dukes and duchesses, lords and ladies, court balls and glittering functions, she devoured and learned by heart. An abominably vulgar little person, she was an interestingly pertinacious creature, and wrought night and day at acquiring an air of fashionable elegance, at first naturally laying it on in such manner as suggested that it should be scraped off with a knife, but with experience gaining a certain specious knowledge of forms. How the over-mature child at school had assimilated her uncanny young worldliness, it would have been less difficult to decide, if possible sources had been less numerous. The air was full of it, the literature of the day, the chatter of afternoon teas, the gossip of the hour. Before she was fifteen she saw the indiscretion of her childish frankness, and realised that it might easily be detrimental to her ambitions. She said no more of her plans for her future, and even took the astute tone of carelessly treating as a joke her vulgar little past. But no titled foreigner appeared upon the horizon without setting her small, but business-like, brain at work. Her lack of wealth and assured position made her situation rather hopeless. She was not of the class of lucky young women whose parents' gorgeous establishments offered attractions to wandering persons of rank. She and her mother lived in a flat, and gave rather pathetic afternoon teas in return for such more brilliant hospitalities as careful and pertinacious calling and recalling obliged their acquaintances to feel they could not decently be left wholly out of. Milly and her anxious mother had worked hard. They lost no opportunity of writing a note, or sending a Christmas card, or an economical funeral wreath. By daily toil and the amicable ignoring of casualness of manner or slights, they managed to cling to the edge of the precipice of social oblivion, into whose depths a lesser degree of assiduity, or a greater sensitiveness, would have plunged them. Once—early in Milly's career, when her ever-ready chatter and her superficial brightness were a novelty, it had seemed for a short time that luck might be glancing towards her. A young man of foreign title and of Bohemian tastes met her at a studio dance, and, misled by the smartness of her dress and her always carefully carried air of careless prosperity, began to pay a delusive court to her. For a few weeks all her freshest frocks were worn assiduously and credit was strained to buy new ones. The flat was adorned with fresh flowers and several new yellow and pale blue cushions appeared at the little teas, which began to assume a more festive air. Desirable people, who went ordinarily to the teas at long intervals and through reluctant weakness, or sometimes rebellious amiability, were drummed up and brought firmly to the fore. Milly herself began to look pink and fluffy through mere hopeful good spirits. Her thin little laugh was heard incessantly, and people amusedly if they were good-tempered, derisively if they were spiteful, wondered if it really would come to something. But it did not. The young foreigner suddenly left New York, making his adieus with entire lightness. There was the end of it. He had heard something about lack of income and uncertainty of credit, which had suggested to him that discretion was the better part of valour. He married later a young lady in the West, whose father was a solid person.

Less astute young women, under the circumstances, would have allowed themselves a week or so of headache or influenza, but Milly did not. She made calls in the new frocks, and with such persistent spirit that she fished forth from the depths of indifferent hospitality two or three excellent invitations. She wore her freshest pink frock, and an amazingly clever little Parisian diamond crescent in her hair, at the huge Monson ball at Delmonico's, and it was recorded that it was on that glittering occasion that her "Uncle James" was first brought upon the scene. He was only mentioned lightly at first. It was to Milly's credit that he was not made too much of. He was casually touched upon as a very rich uncle, who lived in Dakota, and had actually lived there since his youth, letting his few relations know nothing of him. He had been rather a black sheep as a boy, but Milly's mother had liked him, and, when he had run away from New York, he had told her what he was going to do, and had kissed her when she cried, and had taken her daguerreotype with him. Now he had written, and it turned out that he was enormously rich, and was interested in Milly. From that time Uncle James formed an atmosphere. He did not appear in New York, but Milly spent the next season in London, and the Monsons, being at Hurlingham one day, had her pointed out to them as a new American girl, who was the idol of a millionaire uncle. She was not living in an ultra fashionable quarter, or with ultra fashionable people, but she was, on all occasions, they heard, beautifully dressed and beautifully—if a little heavily—hung with gauds and gems, her rings being said to be quite amazing and suggesting an impassioned lavishness on the part of Uncle James. London, having become inured to American marvels—Milly's bit of it—accepted and enjoyed Uncle James and all the sumptuous attributes of his Dakota.

English people would swallow anything sometimes, Mrs. Monson commented sagely, and yet sometimes they stared and evidently thought you were lying about the simplest things. Milly's corner of South Kensington had gulped down the Dakota uncle. Her managing in this way, if there was no uncle, was too clever and amusing. She had left her mother at home to scrimp and save, and by hook or by crook she had contrived to get a number of quite good things to wear. She wore them with such an air of accustomed resource that the jewels might easily—mixed with some relics of her mother's better days—be of the order of the clever little Parisian diamond crescent. It was Milly's never-laid-aside manner which did it. The announcement of her union with Sir Arthur Bowen was received in certain New York circles with little suppressed shrieks of glee. It had been so sharp of her to aim low and to realise so quickly that she could not aim high. The baronetcy was a recent one, and not unconnected with trade. Sir Arthur was not a rich man, and, had it leaked out, believed in Uncle James. If he did not find him all his fancy painted, Milly was clever enough to keep him quiet. She was, when all was said and done, one of the American women of title, her servants and the tradespeople addressed her as "my lady," and with her capacity for appropriating what was most useful, and her easy assumption of possessing all required, she was a very smart person indeed. She provided herself with an English accent, an English vocabulary, and an English manner, and in certain circles was felt to be most impressive.

At an afternoon function in the country Mrs. Vanderpoel had met Lady Bowen. She had been one of the few kindly ones, who in the past had given an occasional treat to Milly Jones for her girlhood's sake. Lady Bowen, having gathered a small group of hearers, was talking volubly to it, when the nice woman entered, and, catching sight of her, she swept across the room. It would not have been like Milly to fail to see and greet at once the wife of Reuben Vanderpoel. She would count anywhere, even in London sets it was not easy to connect one's self with. She had already discovered that there were almost as many difficulties to be surmounted in London by the wife of an unimportant baronet as there had been to be overcome in New York by a girl without money or place. It was well to have something in the way of information to offer in one's small talk with the lucky ones and Milly knew what subject lay nearest to Mrs. Vanderpoel's heart.

"Miss Vanderpoel has evidently been enjoying her visit to Stornham Court," she said, after her first few sentences. "I met Mrs. Worthington at the Embassy, and she said she had buried herself in the country. But I think she must have run up to town quietly for shopping. I saw her one day in Piccadilly, and I was almost sure Lady Anstruthers was with her in the carriage—almost sure."

Mrs. Vanderpoel's heart quickened its beat.

"You were so young when she married," she said. "I daresay you have forgotten her face."

"Oh, no!" Milly protested effusively. "I remember her quite well. She was so pretty and pink and happy-looking, and her hair curled naturally. I used to pray every night that when I grew up I might have hair and a complexion like hers."

Mrs. Vanderpoel's kind, maternal face fell.

"And you were not sure you recognised her? Well, I suppose twelve years does make a difference," her voice dragging a little.

Milly saw that she had made a blunder. The fact was she had not even guessed at Rosy's identity until long after the carriage had passed her.

"Oh, you see," she hesitated, "their carriage was not near me, and I was not expecting to see them. And perhaps she looked a little delicate. I heard she had been rather delicate."

She felt she was floundering, and bravely floundered away from the subject. She plunged into talk of Betty and people's anxiety to see her, and the fact that the society columns were already faintly heralding her. She would surely come soon to town. It was too late for the first Drawing-room this year. When did Mrs. Vanderpoel think she would be presented? Would Lady Anstruthers present her? Mrs. Vanderpoel could not bring her back to Rosy, and the nature of the change which had made it difficult to recognise her.

The result of this chance encounter was that she did not sleep very well, and the next morning talked anxiously to her husband.

"What I could see, Reuben, was that Milly Bowen had not known her at all, even when she saw her in the carriage with Betty. She couldn't have changed as much as that, if she had been taken care of, and happy."

Her affection and admiration for her husband were such as made the task of soothing her a comparatively simple thing. The instinct of tenderness for the mate his youth had chosen was an unchangeable one in Reuben Vanderpoel. He was not a primitive man, but in this he was as unquestioningly simple as if he had been a kindly New England farmer. He had outgrown his wife, but he had always loved and protected her gentle goodness. He had never failed her in her smallest difficulty, he could not bear to see her hurt. Betty had been his compeer and his companion almost since her childhood, but his wife was the tenderest care of his days. There was a strong sense of relief in his thought of Betty now.

It was good to remember the fineness of her perceptions, her clearness of judgment, and recall that they were qualities he might rely upon.

When he left his wife to take his train to town, he left her smiling again. She scarcely knew how her fears had been dispelled. His talk had all been kindly, practical, and reasonable. It was true Betty had said in her letter that Rosy had been rather delicate, and had not been taking very good care of herself, but that was to be remedied. Rosy had made a little joke or so about it herself.

"Betty says I am not fat enough for an English matron. I am drinking milk and breakfasting in bed, and am going to be massaged to please her. I believe we all used to obey Betty when she was a child, and now she is so tall and splendid, one would never dare to cross her. Oh, mother! I am so happy at having her with me!"

To reread just these simple things caused the suggestion of things not comfortably normal to melt away. Mrs. Vanderpoel sat down at a sunny window with her lap full of letters, and forgot Milly Bowen's floundering.

When Mr. Vanderpoel reached his office and glanced at his carefully arranged morning's mail, Mr. Germen saw him smile at the sight of the envelopes addressed in his daughter's hand. He sat down to read them at once, and, as he read, the smile of welcome became a shrewd and deeply interested one.

"She has undertaken a good-sized contract," he was saying to himself, "and she's to be trusted to see it through. It is rather fine, the way she manages to combine emotions and romance and sentiments with practical good business, without letting one interfere with the other. It's none of it bad business this, as the estate is entailed, and the boy is Rosy's. It's good business."

This was what Betty had written to her father in New York from Stornham Court.

"The things I am beginning to do, it would be impossible for me to resist doing, and it would certainly be impossible for you. The thing I am seeing I have never seen, at close hand, before, though I have taken in something almost its parallel as part of certain picturesqueness of scenes in other countries. But I am LIVING with this and also, through relationship to Rosy, I, in a measure, belong to it, and it belongs to me. You and I may have often seen in American villages crudeness, incompleteness, lack of comfort, and the composition of a picture, a rough ugliness the result of haste and unsettled life which stays nowhere long, but packs up its goods and chattels and wanders farther afield in search of something better or worse, in any case in search of change, but we have never seen ripe, gradual falling to ruin of what generations ago was beautiful. To me it is wonderful and tragic and touching. If you could see the Court, if you could see the village, if you could see the church, if you could see the people, all quietly disintegrating, and so dearly perfect in their way that if one knew absolutely that nothing could be done to save them, one could only stand still and catch one's breath and burst into tears. The church has stood since the Conquest, and, as it still stands, grey and fine, with its mass of square tower, and despite the state of its roof, is not yet given wholly to the winds and weather, it will, no doubt, stand a few centuries longer. The Court, however, cannot long remain a possible habitation, if it is not given a new lease of life. I do not mean that it will crumble to-morrow, or the day after, but we should not think it habitable now, even while we should admit that nothing could be more delightful to look at. The cottages in the village are already, many of them, amazing, when regarded as the dwellings of human beings. How long ago the cottagers gave up expecting that anything in particular would be done for them, I do not know. I am impressed by the fact that they are an unexpecting people. Their calm non-expectancy fills me with interest. Only centuries of waiting for their superiors in rank to do things for them, and the slow formation of the habit of realising that not to submit to disappointment was no use, could have produced the almost SERENITY of their attitude. It is all very well for newborn republican nations—meaning my native land—to sniff sternly and say that such a state of affairs is an insult to the spirit of the race. Perhaps it is now, but it was not apparently centuries ago, which was when it all began and when 'Man' and the 'Race' had not developed to the point of asking questions, to which they demand replies, about themselves and the things which happened to them. It began in the time of Egbert and Canute, and earlier, in the days of the Druids, when they used peacefully to allow themselves to be burned by the score, enclosed in wicker idols, as natural offerings to placate the gods. The modern acceptance of things is only a somewhat attenuated remnant of the ancient idea. And this is what I have to deal with and understand. When I begin to do the things I am going to do, with the aid of your practical advice, if I have your approval, the people will be at first rather afraid of me. They will privately suspect I am mad. It will, also, not seem at all unlikely that an American should be of unreasoningly extravagant and flighty mind. Stornham, having long slumbered in remote peace through lack of railroad convenience, still regards America as almost of the character of wild rumour. Rosy was their one American, and she disappeared from their view so soon that she had not time to make any lasting impression. I am asking myself how difficult, or how simple, it will be to quite understand these people, and to make them understand me. I greatly doubt its being simple. Layers and layers and layers of centuries must be far from easy to burrow through. They look simple, they do not know that they are not simple, but really they are not. Their point of view has been the point of view of the English peasant so many hundred years that an American point of view, which has had no more than a trifling century and a half to form itself in, may find its thews and sinews the less powerful of the two. When I walk down the village street, faces appear at windows, and figures, stolidly, at doors. What I see is that, vaguely and remotely, American though I am, the fact that I am of 'her ladyship's blood,' and that her ladyship—American though she is—has the claim on them of being the mother of the son of the owner of the land—stirs in them a feeling that I have a shadowy sort of relationship in the whole thing, and with regard to their bad roofs and bad chimneys, to their broken palings, and damp floors, to their comforts and discomforts, a sort of responsibility. That is the whole thing, and you—just you, father—will understand me when I say that

I actually like it. I might not like it if I were poor Rosy, but, being myself, I love it. There is something patriarchal in it which moves me.

"Is it an abounding and arrogant delight in power which makes it appeal to me, or is it something better? To feel that every man on the land, every woman, every child knew one, counted on one's honour and friendship, turned to one believingly in time of stress, to know that one could help and be a finely faithful thing, the very knowledge of it would give one vigour and warm blood in the veins. I wish I had been born to it, I wish the first sounds falling on my newborn ears had been the clanging of the peal from an old Norman church tower, calling out to me, 'Welcome; newcomer of our house, long life among us! Welcome!' Still, though the first sounds that greeted me were probably the rattling of a Fifth Avenue stage, I have brought them SOMETHING, and who knows whether I could have brought it from without the range of that prosaic, but cheerful, rattle."

The rest of the letter was detail of a business-like order. A large envelope contained the detail-notes of things to be done, notes concerning roofs, windows, flooring, park fences, gardens, greenhouses, tool houses, potting sheds, garden walls, gates, woodwork, masonry. Sharp little sketches, such as Buttle had seen, notes concerning Buttle, Fox, Tread, Kedgers, and less accomplished workmen; concerning wages of day labourers, hours, capabilities. Buttle, if he had chanced to see them, would have broken into a light perspiration at the idea of a young woman having compiled the documents. He had never heard of the first Reuben Vanderpoel.

Her father's reply to Betty was as long as her own to him, and gave her keen pleasure by its support, both of sympathetic interest and practical advice. He left none of her points unnoted, and dealt with each of them as she had most hoped and indeed had felt she knew he would. This was his final summing up:

"If you had been a boy, and I own I am glad you were not—a man wants a daughter—I should have been quite willing to allow you your flutter on Wall Street, or your try at anything you felt you would like to handle. It would have interested me to look on and see what you were made of, what you wanted, and how you set about trying to get it. It's a new kind of deal you have undertaken. It's more romantic than Wall Street, but I think I do see what you see in it. Even apart from Rosy and the boy, it would interest me to see what you would do with it. This is your 'flutter.' I like the way you face it. If you were a son instead of a daughter, I should see I might have confidence in you. I could not confide to Wall Street what I will tell you—which is that in the midst of the drive and swirl and tumult of my life here, I like what you see in the thing, I like your idea of the lord of the land, who should love the land and the souls born on it, and be the friend and strength of them and give the best and get it back in fair exchange. There's a steadiness in the thought of such a life among one's kind which has attractions for a man who has spent years in a maelstrom, snatching at what whirls among the eddies of it. Your notes and sketches and summing up of probable costs did us both credit—I say 'both' because your business education is the result of our long talks and journeyings together. You began to train for this when you began going to visit mines and railroads with me at twelve years old. I leave the whole thing in your hands, my girl, I leave Rosy in your hands, and in leaving Rosy to you, you know how I am trusting you with your mother. Your letters to her tell her only what is good for her. She is beginning to look happier and younger already, and is looking forward to the day when Rosy and the boy will come home to visit us, and when we shall go in state to Stornham Court. God bless her, she is made up of affection and simple trust, and that makes it easy to keep things from her. She has never been ill-treated, and she knows I love her, so when I tell her that things are coming right, she never doubts me.

"While you are rebuilding the place you will rebuild Rosy so that the sight of her may not be a pain when her mother sees her again, which is what she is living for."

CHAPTER XXIII

INTRODUCING G. SELDEN

A bird was perched upon a swaying branch of a slim young sapling near the fence-supported hedge which bounded the park, and Mount Dunstan had stopped to look at it and listen. A soft shower had fallen, and after its passing, the sun coming through the light clouds, there had broken forth again in the trees brief trills and calls and fluting of bird notes. The sward and ferns glittered fresh green under the raindrops; the young leaves on trees and hedge seemed visibly to uncurl, the uncovered earth looked richly dark and moist, and sent forth the fragrance from its deeps, which, rising to a man's nostrils, stirs and thrills him because it is the scent of life's self. The bird upon the sapling was a robin, the tiny round body perched upon his delicate legs, plump and bright plumaged for mating. He touched his warm red breast with his beak, fluffed out and shook his feathers, and, swelling his throat, poured forth his small, entranced song. It was a gay, brief, jaunty thing, but pure, joyous, gallant, liquid melody. There was dainty bravado in it, saucy demand and allurement. It was addressed to some invisible hearer of the tender sex, and wheresoever she might be hidden—whether in great branch or low thicket or hedge—there was hinted no doubt in her small wooer's note that she would hear it and in due time respond. Mount Dunstan, listening, even laughed at its confident music. The tiny thing uttering its Call of the World—jubilant in the surety of answer!

Having flung it forth, he paused a moment and waited, his small head turned sideways, his big, round, dew-bright black eye roguishly attentive. Then with more swelling of the throat he trilled and rippled gayly anew, undisturbed and undoubting, but with a trifle of insistence. Then he listened, tried again two or three times, with brave chirps and exultant little roulades. "Here am I, the bright-breasted, the liquid-eyed, the slender-legged, the joyous and conquering! Listen to me—listen to me. Listen and answer in the call of God's world." It was the joy and triumphant faith in the tiny note of the tiny thing—Life as he himself was, though Life whose mystery his man's hand could have crushed—which, while he laughed, set Mount Dunstan thinking. Spring warmth and spring scents and spring notes set a man's being in tune with infinite things.

The bright roulade began again, prolonged itself with renewed effort, rose to its height, and ended. From a bush in the thicket farther up the road a liquid answer came. And Mount Dunstan's laugh at the sound of it was echoed by another which came apparently from the bank rising from the road on the other side of the hedge, and accompanying the laugh was a good-natured nasal voice.

"She's caught on. There's no mistake about that. I guess it's time for you to hustle, Mr. Rob."

Mount Dunstan laughed again. Jem Salter had heard voices like it, and cheerful slang phrases of the same order in his ranch days. On the other side of his park fence there was evidently sitting, through some odd chance, an

American of the cheery, casual order, not sufficiently polished by travel to have lost his picturesque national characteristics.

Mount Dunstan put a hand on a broken panel of fence and leaped over into the road.

A bicycle was lying upon the roadside grass, and on the bank, looking as though he had been sheltering himself under the hedge from the rain, sat a young man in a cheap bicycling suit. His features were sharply cut and keen, his cap was pushed back from his forehead, and he had a pair of shrewdly careless boyish eyes.

Mount Dunstan liked the look of him, and seeing his natural start at the unheralded leap over the gap, which was quite close to him, he spoke.

"Good-morning," he said. "I am afraid I startled you."

"Good-morning," was the response. "It was a bit of a jolt seeing you jump almost over my shoulder. Where did you come from? You must have been just behind me."

"I was," explained Mount Dunstan. "Standing in the park listening to the robin."

The young fellow laughed outright.

"Say," he said, "that was pretty fine, wasn't it? Wasn't he getting it off his chest! He was an English robin, I guess. American robins are three or four times as big. I liked that little chap. He was a winner."

"You are an American?"

"Sure," nodding. "Good old Stars and Stripes for mine. First time I've been here. Came part for business and part for pleasure. Having the time of my life."

Mount Dunstan sat down beside him. He wanted to hear him talk. He had liked to hear the ranchmen talk. This one was of the city type, but his genial conversational wanderings would be full of quaint slang and good spirits. He was quite ready to converse, as was made manifest by his next speech.

"I'm biking through the country because I once had an old grandmother that was English, and she was always talking about English country, and how green things was, and how there was hedges instead of rail fences. She thought there was nothing like little old England. Well, as far as roads and hedges go, I'm with her. They're all right. I wanted a fellow I met crossing, to come with me, but he took a Cook's trip to Paris. He's a gay sort of boy. Said he didn't want any green lanes in his. He wanted Boolyvard." He laughed again and pushed his cap farther back on his forehead. "Said I wasn't much of a sport. I tell YOU, a chap that's got to earn his fifteen per, and live on it, can't be TOO much of a sport."

"Fifteen per?" Mount Dunstan repeated doubtfully.

His companion chuckled.

"I forgot I was talking to an Englishman. Fifteen dollars per week—that's what 'fifteen per' means. That's what he told me he gets at Lobenstien's brewery in New York. Fifteen per. Not much, is it?"

"How does he manage Continental travel on fifteen per?" Mount Dunstan inquired.

"He's a typewriter and stenographer, and he dug up some extra jobs to do at night. He's been working and saving two years to do this. We didn't come over on one of the big liners with the Four Hundred, you can bet. Took a cheap one, inside cabin, second class."

"By George!" said Mount Dunstan. "That was American."

The American eagle slightly flapped his wings. The young man pushed his cap a trifle sideways this time, and flushed a little.

"Well, when an American wants anything he generally reaches out for it."

"Wasn't it rather—rash, considering the fifteen per?" Mount Dunstan suggested. He was really beginning to enjoy himself.

"What's the use of making a dollar and sitting on it. I've not got fifteen per—steady—and here I am."

Mount Dunstan knew his man, and looked at him with inquiring interest. He was quite sure he would go on. This was a thing he had seen before—an utter freedom from the insular grudging reserve, a sort of occult perception of the presence of friendly sympathy, and an ingenuous readiness to meet it half way. The youngster, having missed his fellow-traveler, and probably feeling the lack of companionship in his country rides, was in the mood for self-revelation.

"I'm selling for a big concern," he said, "and I've got a first-class article to carry. Up to date, you know, and all that. It's the top notch of typewriting machines, the Delkoff. Ever seen it? Here's my card," taking a card from an inside pocket and handing it to him. It was inscribed:

J. BURRIDGE & SON,

DELKOFF TYPEWRITER CO.

BROADWAY, NEW YORK. G. SELDEN.

"That's my name," he said, pointing to the inscription in the corner. "I'm G. Selden, the junior assistant of Mr. Jones."

At the sight of the insignia of his trade, his holiday air dropped from him, and he hastily drew from another pocket an illustrated catalogue.

"If you use a typewriter," he broke forth, "I can assure you it would be to your interest to look at this." And as Mount Dunstan took the proffered pamphlet, and with amiable gravity opened it, he rapidly poured forth his salesman's patter, scarcely pausing to take his breath: "It's the most up-to-date machine on the market. It has all the latest improved mechanical appliances. You will see from the cut in the catalogue that the platen roller is easily removed without a long mechanical operation. All you do is to slip two pins back and off comes the roller. There is also another point worth mentioning—the ribbon switch. By using this ribbon switch you can write in either red or blue ink while you are using only one ribbon. By throwing the switch on this side, you can use thirteen yards on the upper edge of the ribbon, by reversing it, you use thirteen yards on the lower edge—thus getting practically twenty-six yards of good, serviceable ribbon out of one that is only thirteen yards long—making a saving of fifty per cent. in your ribbon expenditure alone, which you will see is quite an item to any enterprising firm."

He was obliged to pause here for a second or so, but as Mount Dunstan exhibited no signs of intending to use violence, and, on the contrary, continued to inspect the catalogue, he broke forth with renewed cheery volubility:

"Another advantage is the new basket shift. Also, the carriage on this machine is perfectly stationary and rigid. On all other machines it is fastened by a series of connecting bolts and links, which you will readily understand makes perfect alignment uncertain. Then our tabulator is a part and parcel of the instrument, costing you nothing more than the original price of the machine, which is one hundred dollars—without discount."

"It seems a good thing," said Mount Dunstan. "If I had much business to transact, I should buy one."

"If you bought one you'd HAVE business," responded Selden. "That's what's the matter. It's the up-to-date machines that set things humming. A slow, old-fashioned typewriter uses a firm's time, and time's money."

"I don't find it so," said Mount Dunstan. "I have more time than I can possibly use—and no money."

G. Selden looked at him with friendly interest. His experience, which was varied, had taught him to recognize symptoms. This nice, rough-looking chap, who, despite his rather shabby clothes, looked like a gentleman, wore an expression Jones's junior assistant had seen many a time before. He had seen it frequently on the countenances of other junior assistants who had tramped the streets and met more or less savage rebuffs through a day's length, without disposing of a single Delkoff, and thereby adding five dollars to the ten per. It was the kind of thing which wiped the youth out of a man's face and gave him a hard, worn look about the eyes. He had looked like that himself many an unfeeling day before he had learned to "know the ropes and not mind a bit of hot air." His buoyant, slangy soul was a friendly thing. He was a gregarious creature, and liked his fellow man. He felt, indeed, more at ease with him when he needed "jollying along." Reticence was not even etiquette in a case as usual as this.

"Say," he broke out, "perhaps I oughtn't to have worried you. Are you up against it? Down on your luck, I mean," in hasty translation.

Mount Dunstan grinned a little.

"That's a very good way of putting it," he answered. "I never heard 'up against it' before. It's good. Yes, I'm up against it.

"Out of a job?" with genial sympathy.

"Well, the job I had was too big for me. It needed capital." He grinned slightly again, recalling a phrase of his Western past. "I'm afraid I'm down and out."

"No, you're not," with cheerful scorn. "You're not dead, are you? S'long as a man's not been dead a month, there's always a chance that there's luck round the corner. How did you happen here? Are you piking it?"

Momentarily Mount Dunstan was baffled. G. Selden, recognising the fact, enlightened him. "That's New York again," he said, with a boyish touch of apology. "It means on the tramp. Travelling along the turnpike. You don't look as if you had come to that—though it's queer the sort of fellows you do meet piking sometimes. Theatrical companies that have gone to pieces on the road, you know. Perhaps—" with a sudden thought, "you're an actor. Are you?"

Mount Dunstan admitted to himself that he liked the junior assistant of Jones immensely. A more ingenuously common young man, a more innocent outsider, it had never been his blessed privilege to enter into close converse with, but his very commonness was a healthy, normal thing. It made no effort to wreathe itself with chaplets of elegance; it was beautifully unaware that such adornment was necessary. It enjoyed itself, youthfully; attacked the earning of its bread with genial pluck, and its good-natured humanness had touched him. He had enjoyed his talk; he wanted to hear more of it. He was not in the mood to let him go his way. To Penzance, who was to lunch with him to-day, he would present a study of absorbing interest.

"No," he answered. "I'm not an actor. My name is Mount Dunstan, and this place," with a nod over his shoulder, "is mine—but I'm up against it, nevertheless."

Selden looked a trifle disgusted. He began to pick up his bicycle. He had given a degree of natural sympathy, and this was an English chap's idea of a joke.

"I'm the Prince of Wales, myself," he remarked, "and my mother's expecting me to lunch at Windsor. So long, me lord," and he set his foot on the treadle.

Mount Dunstan rose, feeling rather awkward. The point seemed somewhat difficult to contend.

"It is not a joke," he said, conscious that he spoke rather stiffly.

"Little Willie's not quite as easy as he looks," was the cryptic remark of Mr. Selden.

Mount Dunstan lost his rather easily lost temper, which happened to be the best thing he could have done under the circumstances.

"Damn it," he burst out. "I'm not such a fool as I evidently look. A nice ass I should be to play an idiot joke like that. I'm speaking the truth. Go if you like— and be hanged."

Selden's attention was arrested. The fellow was in earnest. The place was his. He must be the earl chap he had heard spoken of at the wayside public house he had stopped at for a pot of beer. He dismounted from his bicycle, and came back, pushing it before him, good-natured relenting and awkwardness combining in his look.

"All right," he said. "I apologise—if it's cold fact. I'm not calling you a liar."

"Thank you," still a little stiffly, from Mount Dunstan.

The unabashed good cheer of G. Selden carried him lightly over a slightly difficult moment. He laughed, pushing his cap back, of course, and looking over the hedge at the sweep of park, with a group of deer cropping softly in the foreground.

"I guess I should get a bit hot myself," he volunteered handsomely, "if I was an earl, and owned a place like this, and a fool fellow came along and took me for a tramp. That was a pretty bad break, wasn't it? But I did say you didn't look

like it. Anyway you needn't mind me. I shouldn't get onto Pierpont Morgan or
W. K. Vanderbilt, if I met 'em in the street."

He spoke the two names as an Englishman of his class would have spoken
of the Dukes of Westminster or Marlborough. These were his nobles—the
heads of the great American houses, and entirely parallel, in his mind, with the
heads of any great house in England. They wielded the power of the world, and
could wield it for evil or good, as any prince or duke might. Mount Dunstan saw
the parallel.

"I apologise, all right," G. Selden ended genially.

"I am not offended," Mount Dunstan answered. "There was no reason why
you should know me from another man. I was taken for a gamekeeper a few
weeks since. I was savage a moment, because you refused to believe me—and
why should you believe me after all?"

G. Selden hesitated. He liked the fellow anyhow.

"You said you were up against it—that was it. And—and I've seen chaps
down on their luck often enough. Good Lord, the hard-luck stories I hear every
day of my life. And they get a sort of look about the eyes and mouth. I hate to
see it on any fellow. It makes me sort of sick to come across it even in a chap
that's only got his fool self to blame. I may be making another break, telling
you—but you looked sort of that way."

"Perhaps," stolidly, "I did." Then, his voice warming,

"It was jolly good-natured of you to think about it at all. Thank you."

"That's all right," in polite acknowledgment. Then with another look over
the hedge, "Say—what ought I to call you? Earl, or my Lord?"

"It's not necessary for you to call me anything in particular—as a rule. If you
were speaking of me, you might say Lord Mount Dunstan."

G. Selden looked relieved.

"I don't want to be too much off," he said. "And I'd like to ask you a favour.
I've only three weeks here, and I don't want to miss any chances."

"What chance would you like?"

"One of the things I'm biking over the country for, is to get a look at just
such a place as this. We haven't got 'em in America. My old grandmother was
always talking about them. Before her mother brought her to New York she'd
lived in a village near some park gates, and she chinned about it till she died.
When I was a little chap I liked to hear her. She wasn't much of an American.
Wore a black net cap with purple ribbons in it, and hadn't outlived her respect
for aristocracy. Gee!" chuckling, "if she'd heard what I said to you just now, I
reckon she'd have thrown a fit. Anyhow she made me feel I'd like to see the kind
of places she talked about. And I shall think myself in luck if you'll let me have a
look at yours—just a bike around the park, if you don't object—or I'll leave the
bike outside, if you'd rather."

"I don't object at all," said Mount Dunstan. "The fact is, I happened to be
on the point of asking you to come and have some lunch—when you got on
your bicycle."

Selden pushed his cap and cleared his throat.

"I wasn't expecting that," he said. "I'm pretty dusty," with a glance at his clothes. "I need a wash and brush up—particularly if there are ladies."

There were no ladies, and he could be made comfortable. This being explained to him, he was obviously rejoiced. With unembarrassed frankness, he expressed exultation. Such luck had not, at any time, presented itself to him as a possibility in his holiday scheme.

"By gee," he ejaculated, as they walked under the broad oaks of the avenue leading to the house. "Speaking of luck, this is the limit! I can't help thinking of what my grandmother would say if she saw me."

He was a new order of companion, but before they had reached the house, Mount Dunstan had begun to find him inspiring to the spirits. His jovial, if crude youth, his unaffected acknowledgment of unaccustomedness to grandeur, even when in dilapidation, his delight in the novelty of the particular forms of everything about him—trees and sward, ferns and moss, his open self-congratulation, were without doubt cheerful things.

His exclamation, when they came within sight of the house itself, was for a moment disturbing to Mount Dunstan's composure.

"Hully gee!" he said. "The old lady was right. All I've thought about 'em was 'way off. It's bigger than a museum." His approval was immense.

During the absence in which he was supplied with the "wash and brush up," Mount Dunstan found Mr. Penzance in the library. He explained to him what he had encountered, and how it had attracted him.

"You have liked to hear me describe my Western neighbours," he said. "This youngster is a New York development, and of a different type. But there is a likeness. I have invited to lunch with us, a young man whom—Tenham, for instance, if he were here—would call 'a bounder.' He is nothing of the sort. In his junior-assistant-salesman way, he is rather a fine thing. I never saw anything more decently human than his way of asking me—man to man, making friends by the roadside if I was 'up against it.' No other fellow I have known has ever exhibited the same healthy sympathy."

The Reverend Lewis was entranced. Already he was really quite flushed with interest. As Assyrian character, engraved upon sarcophogi, would have allured and thrilled him, so was he allured by the cryptic nature of the two or three American slang phrases Mount Dunstan had repeated to him. His was the student's simple ardour.

"Up against it," he echoed. "Really! Dear! Dear! And that signifies, you say——"

"Apparently it means that a man has come face to face with an obstacle difficult or impossible to overcome."

"But, upon my word, that is not bad. It is strong figure of speech. It brings up a picture. A man hurrying to an end—much desired—comes unexpectedly upon a stone wall. One can almost hear the impact. He is up against it. Most vivid. Excellent! Excellent!"

The nature of Selden's calling was such that he was not accustomed to being received with a hint of enthusiastic welcome. There was something almost akin to this in the vicar's courteously amiable, aquiline countenance when he rose to shake hands with the young man on his entrance. Mr. Penzance was indeed slightly disappointed that his greeting was not responded to by some characteristic phrasing. His American was that of Sam Slick and Artemus Ward, Punch and various English witticisms in anecdote. Life at the vicarage of Dunstan had not revealed to him that the model had become archaic.

The revelation dawned upon him during his intercourse with G. Selden. The young man in his cheap bicycling suit was a new development. He was markedly unlike an English youth of his class, as he was neither shy, nor laboriously at his ease. That he was at his ease to quite an amazing degree might perhaps have been remotely resented by the insular mind, accustomed to another order of bearing in its social inferiors, had it not been so obviously founded on entire unconsciousness of self, and so mingled with open appreciation of the unanticipated pleasures of the occasion. Nothing could have been farther from G. Selden than any desire to attempt to convey the impression that he had enjoyed the hospitality of persons of rank on previous occasions. He found indeed a gleeful point in the joke of the incongruousness of his own presence amid such surroundings.

"What Little Willie was expecting," he remarked once, to the keen joy of Mr. Penzance, "was a hunk of bread and cheese at a village saloon somewhere. I ought to have said 'pub,' oughtn't I? You don't call them saloons here."

He was encouraged to talk, and in his care-free fluency he opened up many vistas to the interested Mr. Penzance, who found himself, so to speak, whirled along Broadway, rushed up the steps of the elevated railroad and struggling to obtain a seat, or a strap to hang to on a Sixth Avenue train. The man was saturated with the atmosphere of the hot battle he lived in. From his childhood he had known nothing but the fever heat of his "little old New York," as he called it with affectionate slanginess, and any temperature lower than that he was accustomed to would have struck him as being below normal. Penzance was impressed by his feeling of affection for the amazing city of his birth. He admired, he adored it, he boasted joyously of its perfervid charm.

"Something doing," he said. "That's what my sort of a fellow likes— something doing. You feel it right there when you walk along the streets. Little old New York for mine. It's good enough for Little Willie. And it never stops. Why, Broadway at night——"

He forgot his chop, and leaned forward on the table to pour forth his description. The manservant, standing behind Mount Dunstan's chair, forgot himself also, thought he was a trained domestic whose duty it was to present dishes to the attention without any apparent mental processes. Certainly it was not his business to listen, and gaze fascinated. This he did, however, actually for the time unconscious of his breach of manners. The very crudity of the language used, the oddly sounding, sometimes not easily translatable slang phrases, used as if they were a necessary part of any conversation—the blunt, uneducated bareness of figure—seemed to Penzance to make more roughly vivid the picture dashed off. The broad thoroughfare almost as thronged by night as by day.

Crowds going to theatres, loaded electric cars, whizzing and clanging bells, the elevated railroad rushing and roaring past within hearing, theatre fronts flaming with electric light, announcements of names of theatrical stars and the plays they appeared in, electric light advertisements of brands of cigars, whiskies, breakfast foods, all blazing high in the night air in such number and with such strength of brilliancy that the whole thoroughfare was as bright with light as a ballroom or a theatre. The vicar felt himself standing in the midst of it all, blinded by the glare.

"Sit down on the sidewalk and read your newspaper, a book, a magazine—any old thing you like," with an exultant laugh.

The names of the dramatic stars blazing over entrances to the theatres were often English names, their plays English plays, their companies made up of English men and women. G. Selden was as familiar with them and commented upon their gifts as easily as if he had drawn his drama from the Strand instead of from Broadway. The novels piled up in the stations of what he called "the L" (which revealed itself as being a New-York-haste abbreviation of Elevated railroad), were in large proportion English novels, and he had his ingenuous estimate of English novelists, as well as of all else.

"Ruddy, now," he said; "I like him. He's all right, even though we haven't quite caught onto India yet."

The dazzle and brilliancy of Broadway so surrounded Penzance that he found it necessary to withdraw himself and return to his immediate surroundings, that he might recover from his sense of interested bewilderment. His eyes fell upon the stern lineaments of a Mount Dunstan in a costume of the time of Henry VIII. He was a burly gentleman, whose ruff-shortened thick neck and haughty fixedness of stare from the background of his portrait were such as seemed to eliminate him from the scheme of things, the clanging of electric cars, and the prevailing roar of the L. Confronted by his gaze, electric light advertisements of whiskies, cigars, and corsets seemed impossible.

"He's all right," continued G. Selden. "I'm ready to separate myself from one fifty any time I see a new book of his. He's got the goods with him."

The richness of colloquialism moved the vicar of Mount Dunstan to deep enjoyment.

"Would you mind—I trust you won't," he apologised courteously, "telling me exactly the significance of those two last sentences. In think I see their meaning, but——"

G. Selden looked good-naturedly apologetic himself.

"Well, it's slang—you see," he explained. "I guess I can't help it. You—" flushing a trifle, but without any touch of resentment in the boyish colour, "you know what sort of a chap I am. I'm not passing myself off as anything but an ordinary business hustler, am I—just under salesman to a typewriter concern? I shouldn't like to think I'd got in here on any bluff. I guess I sling in slang every half dozen words——."

"My dear boy," Penzance was absolutely moved and he spoke with warmth quite paternal, "Lord Mount Dunstan and I are genuinely interested—genuinely. He, because he knows New York a little, and I because I don't. I am an elderly man, and have spent my life buried in my books in drowsy villages. Pray go on. Your American slang has frequently a delightful meaning—a fantastic hilarity, or common sense, or philosophy, hidden in its origin. In that it generally differs from English slang, which—I regret to say—is usually founded on some silly catch word. Pray go on. When you see a new book by Mr. Kipling, you are ready to 'separate yourself from one fifty' because he 'has the goods with him.'"

G. Selden suppressed an involuntary young laugh.

"One dollar and fifty cents is usually the price of a book," he said. "You separate yourself from it when you take it out of your clothes—I mean out of your pocket—and pay it over the counter."

"There's a careless humour in it," said Mount Dunstan grimly. "The suggestion of parting is not half bad. On the whole, it is subtle."

"A great deal of it is subtle," said Penzance, "though it all professes to be obvious. The other sentence has a commercial sound."

"When a man goes about selling for a concern," said the junior assistant of Jones, "he can prove what he says, if he has the goods with him. I guess it came from that. I don't know. I only know that when a man is a straight sort of fellow, and can show up, we say he's got the goods with him."

They sat after lunch in the library, before an open window, looking into a lovely sunken garden. Blossoms were breaking out on every side, and robins, thrushes, and blackbirds chirped and trilled and whistled, as Mount Dunstan and Penzance led G. Selden on to paint further pictures for them.

Some of them were rather painful, Penzance thought. As connected with youth, they held a touch of pathos Selden was all unconscious of. He had had a hard life, made up, since his tenth year, of struggles to earn his living. He had sold newspapers, he had run errands, he had swept out a "candy store." He had had a few years at the public school, and a few months at a business college, to which he went at night, after work hours. He had been "up against it good and plenty," he told them. He seemed, however, to have had a knack of making friends and of giving them "a boost along" when such a chance was possible. Both of his listeners realised that a good many people had liked him, and the reason was apparent enough to them.

"When a chap gets sorry for himself," he remarked once, "he's down and out. That's a stone-cold fact. There's lots of hard-luck stories that you've got to hear anyhow. The fellow that can keep his to himself is the fellow that's likely to get there."

"Get there?" the vicar murmured reflectively, and Selden chuckled again.

"Get where he started out to go to—the White House, if you like. The fellows that have got there kept their hardluck stories quiet, I bet. Guess most of 'em had plenty during election, if they were the kind to lie awake sobbing on their pillows because their feelings were hurt."

He had never been sorry for himself, it was evident, though it must be admitted that there were moments when the elderly English clergyman, whose most serious encounters had been annoying interviews with cottagers of disrespectful manner, rather shuddered as he heard his simple recital of days when he had tramped street after street, carrying his catalogue with him, and trying to tell his story of the Delkoff to frantically busy men who were driven mad by the importunate sight of him, to worried, ill-tempered ones who broke into fury when they heard his voice, and to savage brutes who were only restrained by law from kicking him into the street.

"You've got to take it, if you don't want to lose your job. Some of them's as tired as you are. Sometimes, if you can give 'em a jolly and make 'em laugh, they'll listen, and you may unload a machine. But it's no merry jest just at first— particularly in bad weather. The first five weeks I was with the Delkoff I never made a sale. Had to live on my ten per, and that's pretty hard in New York. Three and a half for your hall bedroom, and the rest for your hash and shoes. But I held on, and gradually luck began to turn, and I began not to care so much when a man gave it to me hot."

The vicar of Mount Dunstan had never heard of the "hall bedroom" as an institution. A dozen unconscious sentences placed it before his mental vision. He thought it horribly touching. A narrow room at the back of a cheap lodging house, a bed, a strip of carpet, a washstand—this the sole refuge of a male human creature, in the flood tide of youth, no more than this to come back to nightly, footsore and resentful of soul, after a day's tramp spent in forcing himself and his wares on people who did not want him or them, and who found infinite variety in the forcefulness of their method of saying so.

"What you know, when you go into a place, is that nobody wants to see you, and no one will let you talk if they can help it. The only thing is to get in and rattle off your stunt before you can be fired out."

Sometimes at first he had gone back at night to the hall bedroom, and sat on the edge of the narrow bed, swinging his feet, and asking himself how long he could hold out. But he had held out, and evidently developed into a good salesman, being bold and of imperturbable good spirits and temper, and not troubled by hypersensitiveness. Hearing of the "hall bedroom," the coldness of it in winter, and the breathless heat in summer, the utter loneliness of it at all times and seasons, one could not have felt surprise if the grown-up lad doomed to its narrowness as home had been drawn into the electric-lighted gaiety of Broadway, and being caught in its maelstrom, had been sucked under to its lowest depths. But it was to be observed that G. Selden had a clear eye, and a healthy skin, and a healthy young laugh yet, which were all wonderfully to his credit, and added enormously to one's liking for him.

"Do you use a typewriter?" he said at last to Mr. Penzance. "It would cut out half your work with your sermons. If you do use one, I'd just like to call your attention to the Delkoff. It's the most up-to-date machine on the market to-day," drawing out the catalogue.

"I do not use one, and I am extremely sorry to say that I could not afford to buy one," said Mr. Penzance with considerate courtesy, "but do tell me about it. I am afraid I never saw a typewriter."

It was the most hospitable thing he could have done, and was of the tact of courts. He arranged his pince nez, and taking the catalogue, applied himself to it.

G. Selden's soul warmed within him. To be listened to like this. To be treated as a gentleman by a gentleman—by "a fine old swell like this—Hully gee!"

"This isn't what I'm used to," he said with genuine enjoyment. "It doesn't matter, your not being ready to buy now. You may be sometime, or you may run up against someone who is. Little Willie's always ready to say his piece."

He poured it forth with glee—the improved mechanical appliances, the cuts in the catalogue, the platen roller, the ribbon switch, the twenty-six yards of red or blue typing, the fifty per cent. saving in ribbon expenditure alone, the new basket shift, the stationary carriage, the tabulator, the superiority to all other typewriting machines—the price one hundred dollars without discount. And both Mount Dunstan and Mr. Penzance listened entranced, examined cuts in the catalogue, asked questions, and in fact ended by finding that they must repress an actual desire to possess the luxury. The joy their attitude bestowed upon Selden was the thing he would feel gave the finishing touch to the hours which he would recall to the end of his days as the "time of his life." Yes, by gee! he was having "the time of his life."

Later he found himself feeling—as Miss Vanderpoel had felt—rather as if the whole thing was a dream. This came upon him when, with Mount Dunstan and Penzance, he walked through the park and the curiously beautiful old gardens. The lovely, soundless quiet, broken into only by bird notes, or his companions' voices, had an extraordinary effect on him.

"It's so still you can hear it," he said once, stopping in a velvet, moss-covered path. "Seems like you've got quiet shut up here, and you've turned it on till the air's thick with it. Good Lord, think of little old Broadway keeping it up, and the L whizzing and thundering along every three minutes, just the same, while we're standing here! You can't believe it."

It would have gone hard with him to describe to them the value of his enjoyment. Again and again there came back to him the memory of the grandmother who wore the black net cap trimmed with purple ribbons. Apparently she had remained to the last almost contumaciously British. She had kept photographs of Queen Victoria and the Prince Consort on her bedroom mantelpiece, and had made caustic, international comparisons. But she had seen places like this, and her stories became realities to him now. But she had never thought of the possibility of any chance of his being shown about by the lord of the manor himself—lunching, by gee! and talking to them about typewriters. He vaguely knew that if the grandmother had not emigrated, and he had been born in Dunstan village, he would naturally have touched his forehead to Mount Dunstan and the vicar when they passed him in the road, and conversation between them would have been an unlikely thing. Somehow things had been changed by Destiny—perhaps for the whole of them, as years had passed.

What he felt when he stood in the picture gallery neither of his companions could at first guess. He ceased to talk, and wandered silently about. Secretly he found himself a trifle awed by being looked down upon by the unchanging eyes of men in strange, rich garments—in corslet, ruff, and doublet, velvet, powder, curled love locks, brocade and lace. The face of long-dead loveliness smiled out from its canvas, or withheld itself haughtily from his salesman's gaze. Wonderful bare white shoulders, and bosoms clasped with gems or flowers and lace, defied him to recall any treasures of Broadway to compare with them. Elderly dames, garbed in stiff splendour, held stiff, unsympathetic inquiry in their eyes, as they looked back upon him. What exactly was a thirty shilling bicycle suit doing there? In the Delkoff, plainly none were interested. A pretty, masquerading shepherdess, with a lamb and a crook, seemed to laugh at him from under her broad beribboned straw hat. After looking at her for a minute or so, he gave a half laugh himself—but it was an awkward one.

"She's a looker," he remarked. "They're a lot of them lookers—not all—but a fair show——"

"A looker," translated Mount Dunstan in a low voice to Penzance, "means, I believe, a young women with good looks—a beauty."

"Yes, she IS a looker, by gee," said G. Selden, "but—but—" the awkward half laugh, taking on a depressed touch of sheepishness, "she makes me feel 'way off—they all do."

That was it. Surrounded by them, he was fascinated but not cheered. They were all so smilingly, or disdainfully, or indifferently unconscious of the existence of the human thing of his class. His aspect, his life, and his desires were as remote as those of prehistoric man. His Broadway, his L railroad, his Delkoff—what were they where did they come into the scheme of the Universe? They silently gazed and lightly smiled or frowned THROUGH him as he stood. He was probably not in the least aware that he rather loudly sighed.

"Yes," he said, "they make me feel 'way off. I'm not in it. But she is a looker. Get onto that dimple in her cheek."

Mount Dunstan and Penzance spent the afternoon in doing their best for him. He was well worth it. Mr. Penzance was filled with delight, and saturated with the atmosphere of New York.

"I feel," he said, softly polishing his eyeglasses and almost affectionately smiling, "I really feel as if I had been walking down Broadway or Fifth Avenue. I believe that I might find my way to—well, suppose we say Weber & Field's," and G. Selden shouted with glee.

Never before, in fact, had he felt his heart so warmed by spontaneous affection as it was by this elderly, somewhat bald and thin-faced clergyman of the Church of England. This he had never seen before. Without the trained subtlety to have explained to himself the finely sweet and simply gracious deeps of it, he was moved and uplifted. He was glad he had "come across" it, he felt a vague regret at passing on his way, and leaving it behind. He would have liked to feel that perhaps he might come back. He would have liked to present him with a Delkoff, and teach him how to run it. He had delighted in Mount Dunstan, and rejoiced in him, but he had rather fallen in love with Penzance. Certain American doubts he had had of the solidity and permanency of England's position and power were somewhat modified. When fellows like these two stood at the first rank, little old England was a pretty safe proposition.

After they had given him tea among the scents and songs of the sunken garden outside the library window, they set him on his way. The shadows were lengthening and the sunlight falling in deepening gold when they walked up the avenue and shook hands with him at the big entrance gates.

"Well, gentlemen," he said, "you've treated me grand—as fine as silk, and it won't be like Little Willie to forget it. When I go back to New York it'll be all I can do to keep from getting the swell head and bragging about it. I've enjoyed myself down to the ground, every minute. I'm not the kind of fellow to be likely to be able to pay you back your kindness, but, hully gee! if I could I'd do it to beat the band. Good-bye, gentlemen—and thank you—thank you."

Across which one of their minds passed the thought that the sound of the hollow impact of a trotting horse's hoofs on the road, which each that moment became conscious of hearing was the sound of the advancing foot of Fate? It crossed no mind among the three. There was no reason why it should. And yet at that moment the meaning of the regular, stirring sound was a fateful thing.

"Someone on horseback," said Penzance.

He had scarcely spoken before round the curve of the road she came. A finely slender and spiritedly erect girl's figure, upon a satin-skinned bright chestnut with a thoroughbred gait, a smart groom riding behind her. She came towards them, was abreast them, looked at Mount Dunstan, a smiling dimple near her lip as she returned his quick salute.

"Miss Vanderpoel," he said low to the vicar, "Lady Anstruther's sister."

Mr. Penzance, replacing his own hat, looked after her with surprised pleasure.

"Really," he exclaimed, "Miss Vanderpoel! What a fine girl! How unusually handsome!"

Selden turned with a gasp of delighted, amazed recognition.

"Miss Vanderpoel," he burst forth, "Reuben Vanderpoel's daughter! The one that's over here visiting her sister. Is it that one—sure?"

"Yes," from Mount Dunstan without fervour. "Lady Anstruthers lives at Stornham, about six miles from here."

"Gee," with feverish regret. "If her father was there, and I could get next to him, my fortune would be made."

"Should you," ventured Penzance politely, "endeavour to sell him a typewriter?"

"A typewriter! Holy smoke! I'd try to sell him ten thousand. A fellow like that syndicates the world. If I could get next to him——" and he mounted his bicycle with a laugh.

"Get next," murmured Penzance.

"Get on the good side of him," Mount Dunstan murmured in reply.

"So long, gentlemen, good-bye, and thank you again," called G. Selden as he wheeled off, and was carried soundlessly down the golden road.

CHAPTER XXIV

THE POLITICAL ECONOMY OF STORNHAM

The satin-skinned chestnut was one of the new horses now standing in the Stornham stables. There were several of them—a pair for the landau, saddle horses, smart young cobs for phaeton or dog cart, a pony for Ughtred—the animals necessary at such a place at Stornham. The stables themselves had been quickly put in order, grooms and stable boys kept them as they had not been kept for years. The men learned in a week's time that their work could not be done too well. There were new carriages as well as horses. They had come from London after Lady Anstruthers and her sister returned from town. The horses had been brought down by their grooms—immensely looked after, blanketed, hooded, and altogether cared for as if they were visiting dukes and duchesses. They were all fine, handsome, carefully chosen creatures. When they danced and sidled through the village on their way to the Court, they created a sensation. Whosoever had chosen them had known his business. The older vehicles had been repaired in the village by Tread, and did him credit. Fox had also done his work well.

Plenty more of it had come into their work-shops. Tools to be used on the estate, garden implements, wheelbarrows, lawn rollers, things needed about the house, stables, and cottages, were to be attended to. The church roof was being repaired. Taking all these things and the "doing up" of the Court itself, there was more work than the village could manage, and carpenters, bricklayers, and decorators were necessarily brought from other places. Still Joe Buttle and Sim Soames were allowed to lead in all such things as lay within their capabilities. It was they who made such a splendid job of the entrance gates and the lodges. It was astonishing how much was done, and how the sense of life in the air—the work of resulting prosperity, made men begin to tread with less listless steps as they went to and from their labour. In the cottages things were being done which made downcast women bestir themselves and look less slatternly. Leaks mended here, windows there, the hopeless copper in the tiny washhouse replaced by a new one, chimneys cured of the habit of smoking, a clean, flowered paper put on a wall, a coat of whitewash—they were small matters, but produced great effect.

Betty had begun to drop into the cottages, and make the acquaintance of their owners. Her first visits, she observed, created great consternation. Women looked frightened or sullen, children stared and refused to speak, clinging to skirts and aprons. She found the atmosphere clear after her second visit. The women began to talk, and the children collected in groups and listened with cheerful grins. She could pick up little Jane's kitten, or give a pat to small Thomas' mongrel dog, in a manner which threw down barriers.

"Don't put out your pipe," she said to old Grandfather Doby, rising totteringly respectful from his chimney-side chair. "You have only just lighted it. You mustn't waste a whole pipeful of tobacco because I have come in."

The old man, grown childish with age, tittered and shuffled and giggled. Such a joke as the grand young lady was having with him. She saw he had only just lighted his pipe. The gentry joked a bit sometimes. But he was afraid of his grandson's wife, who was frowning and shaking her head.

Betty went to him, and put her hand on his arm.

"Sit down," she said, "and I will sit by you." And she sat down and showed him that she had brought a package of tobacco with her, and actually a wonder of a red and yellow jar to hold it, at the sight of which unheard-of joys his rapture was so great that his trembling hands could scarcely clasp his treasures.

"Tee-hee! Tee-hee-ee! Deary me! Thankee—thankee, my lady," he tittered, and he gazed and blinked at her beauty through heavenly tears.

"Nearly a hundred years old, and he has lived on sixteen shillings a week all his life, and earned it by working every hour between sunrise and sunset," Betty said to her sister, when she went home. "A man has one life, and his has passed like that. It is done now, and all the years and work have left nothing in his old hands but his pipe. That's all. I should not like to put it out for him. Who am I that I can buy him a new one, and keep it filled for him until the end? How did it happen? No," suddenly, "I must not lose time in asking myself that. I must get the new pipe."

She did it—a pipe of great magnificence—such as drew to the Doby cottage as many callers as the village could provide, each coming with fevered interest, to look at it—to be allowed to hold and examine it for a few moments, guessing at its probable enormous cost, and returning it reverently, to gaze at Doby with respect—the increase of which can be imagined when it was known that he was not only possessor of the pipe, but of an assurance that he would be supplied with as much tobacco as he could use, to the end of his days. From the time of the advent of the pipe, Grandfather Doby became a man of mark, and his life in the chimney corner a changed thing. A man who owns splendours and unlimited, excellent shag may like friends to drop in and crack jokes—and even smoke a pipe with him—a common pipe, which, however, is not amiss when excellent shag comes free.

"He lives in a wild whirl of gaiety—a social vortex," said Betty to Lady Anstruthers, after one of her visits. "He is actually rejuvenated. I must order some new white smocks for him to receive his visitors in. Someone brought him an old copy of the Illustrated London News last night. We will send him illustrated papers every week."

In the dull old brain, God knows what spark of life had been relighted. Young Mrs. Doby related with chuckles that granddad had begged that his chair might be dragged to the window, that he might sit and watch the village street. Sitting there, day after day, he smoked and looked at his pictures, and dozed and dreamed, his pipe and tobacco jar beside him on the window ledge. At any sound of wheels or footsteps his face lighted, and if, by chance, he caught a glimpse of Betty, he tottered to his feet, and stood hurriedly touching his bald forehead with a reverent, palsied hand.

"'Tis 'urr," he would say, enrapt. "I seen 'urr—I did." And young Mrs. Doby knew that this was his joy, and what he waited for as one waits for the coming of the sun.

"'Tis 'urr! 'Tis 'urr!"

The vicar's wife, Mrs. Brent, who since the affair of John Wilson's fire had dropped into the background and felt it indiscreet to present tales of distress at the Court, began to recover her courage. Her perfunctory visits assumed a new character. The vicarage had, of course, called promptly upon Miss Vanderpoel, after her arrival. Mrs. Brent admired Miss Vanderpoel hugely.

"You seem so unlike an American," she said once in her most tactful, ingratiating manner—which was very ingratiating indeed.

"Do I? What is one like when one is like an American? I am one, you know."

"I can scarcely believe it," with sweet ardour.

"Pray try," said Betty with simple brevity, and Mrs. Brent felt that perhaps Miss Vanderpoel was not really very easy to get on with.

"She meant to imply that I did not speak through my nose, and talk too much, and too vivaciously, in a shrill voice," Betty said afterwards, in talking the interview over with Rosy. "I like to convince myself that is not one's sole national characteristic. Also it was not exactly Mrs. Brent's place to kindly encourage me with the information that I do not seem to belong to my own country."

Lady Anstruthers laughed, and Betty looked at her inquiringly.

"You said that just like—just like an Englishwoman."

"Did I?" said Betty.

Mrs. Brent had come to talk to her because she did not wish to trouble dear Lady Anstruthers. Lady Anstruthers already looked much stronger, but she had been delicate so long that one hesitated to distress her with village matters. She did not add that she realised that she was coming to headquarters. The vicar and herself were much disturbed about a rather tiresome old woman—old Mrs. Welden—who lived in a tiny cottage in the village. She was eighty-three years old, and a respectable old person—a widow, who had reared ten children. The children had all grown up, and scattered, and old Mrs. Welden had nothing whatever to live on. No one knew how she lived, and really she would be better off in the workhouse. She could be sent to Brexley Union, and comfortably taken care of, but she had that singular, obstinate dislike to going, which it was so difficult to manage. She had asked for a shilling a week from the parish, but that could not be allowed her, as it would merely uphold her in her obstinate intention of remaining in her cottage, and taking care of herself—which she could not do. Betty gathered that the shilling a week would be a drain on the parish funds, and would so raise the old creature to affluence that she would feel she could defy fate. And the contumacity of old men and women should not be strengthened by the reckless bestowal of shillings.

Knowing that Miss Vanderpoel had already gained influence among the village people, Mrs. Brent said, she had come to ask her if she would see old

Mrs. Welden and argue with her in such a manner as would convince her that the workhouse was the best place for her. It was, of course, so much pleasanter if these old people could be induced to go to Brexley willingly.

"Shall I be undermining the whole Political Economy of Stornham if I take care of her myself?" suggested Betty.

"You—you will lead others to expect the same thing will be done for them."

"When one has resources to draw on," Miss Vanderpoel commented, "in the case of a woman who has lived eighty-three years and brought up ten children until they were old and strong enough to leave her to take care of herself, it is difficult for the weak of mind to apply the laws of Political Economics. I will go and see old Mrs. Welden."

If the Vanderpoels would provide for all the obstinate old men and women in the parish, the Political Economics of Stornham would proffer no marked objections. "A good many Americans," Mrs. Brent reflected, "seemed to have those odd, lavish ways," as witness Lady Anstruthers herself, on her first introduction to village life. Miss Vanderpoel was evidently a much stronger character, and extremely clever, and somehow the stream of the American fortune was at last being directed towards Stornham—which, of course, should have happened long ago. A good deal was "being done," and the whole situation looked more promising. So was the matter discussed and summed up, the same evening after dinner, at the vicarage.

Betty found old Mrs. Welden's cottage. It was in a green lane, turning from the village street—which was almost a green lane itself. A tiny hedged-in front garden was before the cottage door. A crazy-looking wicket gate was in the hedge, and a fuschia bush and a few old roses were in the few yards of garden. There were actually two or three geraniums in the window, showing cheerful scarlet between the short, white dimity curtains.

"A house this size and of this poverty in an American village," was Betty's thought, "would be a bare and straggling hideousness, with old tomato cans in the front yard. Here is one of the things we have to learn from them."

When she knocked at the door an old woman opened it. She was a well-preserved and markedly respectable old person, in a decent print frock and a cap. At the sight of her visitor she beamed and made a suggestion of curtsey.

"How do you do, Mrs. Welden?" said Betty. "I am Lady Anstruthers' sister, Miss Vanderpoel. I thought I would like to come and see you."

"Thank you, miss, I am obliged for the kindness, miss. Won't you come in and have a chair?"

There were no signs of decrepitude about her, and she had a cheery old eye. The tiny front room was neat, though there was scarcely space enough in it to contain the table covered with its blue-checked cotton cloth, the narrow sofa, and two or three chairs. There were a few small coloured prints, and a framed photograph or so on the walls, and on the table was a Bible, and a brown earthenware teapot, and a plate.

"Tom Wood's wife, that's neighbour next door to me," she said, "gave me a pinch o' tea—an' I've just been 'avin it. Tom Woods, miss, 'as just been took on by Muster Kedgers as one of the new under gardeners at the Court."

Betty found her delightful. She made no complaints, and was evidently pleased with the excitement of receiving a visitor. The truth was, that in common with every other old woman, she had secretly aspired to being visited some day by the amazing young lady from "Meriker." Betty had yet to learn of the heartburnings which may be occasioned by an unconscious favouritism. She was not aware that when she dropped in to talk to old Doby, his neighbour, old Megworth, peered from behind his curtains, with the dew of envy in his rheumy eyes.

"S'ems," he mumbled, "as if they wasn't nobody now in Stornham village but Gaarge Doby—s'ems not." They were very fierce in their jealousy of attention, and one must beware of rousing evil passions in the octogenarian breast.

The young lady from "Meriker" had not so far had time to make a call at any cottage in old Mrs. Welden's lane—and she had knocked just at old Mrs. Welden's door. This was enough to put in good spirits even a less cheery old person.

At first Betty wondered how she could with delicacy ask personal questions. A few minutes' conversation, however, showed her that the personal affairs of Sir Nigel's tenants were also the affairs of not only himself, but of such of his relatives as attended to their natural duty. Her presence in the cottage, and her interest in Mrs. Welden's ready flow of simple talk, were desirable and proper compliments to the old woman herself. She was a decent and self-respecting old person, but in her mind there was no faintest glimmer of resentment of questions concerning rent and food and the needs of her simple, hard-driven existence. She had answered such questions on many occasions, when they had not been asked in the manner in which her ladyship's sister asked them. Mrs. Brent had scolded her and "poked about" her cottage, going into her tiny "wash 'us," and up into her infinitesimal bedroom under the slanting roof, to see that they were kept clean. Miss Vanderpoel showed no disposition to "poke." She sat and listened, and made an inquiry here and there, in a nice voice and with a smile in her eyes. There was some pleasure in relating the whole history of your eighty-three years to a young lady who listened as if she wanted to hear it. So old Mrs. Welden prattled on. About her good days, when she was young, and was kitchenmaid at the parsonage in a village twenty miles away; about her marriage with a young farm labourer; about his "steady" habits, and the comfort they had together, in spite of the yearly arrival of a new baby, and the crowding of the bit of a cottage his master allowed them. Ten of 'em, and it had been "up before sunrise, and a good bit of hard work to keep them all fed and clean." But she had not minded that until Jack died quite sudden after a sunstroke. It was odd how much colour her rustic phraseology held. She made Betty see it all. The apparent natural inevitableness of their being turned out of the cottage, because another man must have it; the years during which she worked her way while the ten were growing up, having measles, and chicken pox, and scarlet fever, one dying here and there, dropping out quite in the natural order of things, and being buried by the parish in corners of the ancient church yard. Three of them "was took" by scarlet fever, then one of a "decline," then one or two by other illnesses. Only four reached man and womanhood. One had gone to Australia, but he never was one to write, and after a year or two, Betty gathered, he had seemed to melt away into the great distance. Two girls had married, and Mrs. Welden could not say they had been "comf'able." They could barely feed themselves and their swarms of children. The other son had never been steady like his father. He had at last gone to London, and London had swallowed him up. Betty was struck by the fact that she did not seem to feel that the mother of ten might have expected some return for her labours, at eighty-three.

Her unresentful acceptance of things was at once significant and moving. Betty found her amazing. What she lived on it was not easy to understand. She seemed rather like a cheerful old bird, getting up each unprovided-for morning, and picking up her sustenance where she found it.

"There's more in the sayin' 'the Lord pervides' than a good many thinks," she said with a small chuckle, marked more by a genial and comfortable sense of humour than by an air of meritoriously quoting the vicar. "He DO."

She paid one and threepence a week in rent for her cottage, and this was the most serious drain upon her resources. She apparently could live without food or fire, but the rent must be paid. "An' I do get a bit be'ind sometimes," she confessed apologetically, "an' then it's a trouble to get straight."

Her cottage was one of a short row, and she did odd jobs for the women who were her neighbours. There were always babies to be looked after, and "bits of 'elp" needed, sometimes there were "movings" from one cottage to another, and "confinements" were plainly at once exhilarating and enriching. Her temperamental good cheer, combined with her experience, made her a desirable companion and assistant. She was engagingly frank.

"When they're new to it, an' a bit frightened, I just give 'em a cup of 'ot tea, an' joke with 'em to cheer 'em up," she said. "I says to Charles Jenkins' wife, as lives next door, 'come now, me girl, it's been goin' on since Adam an' Eve, an' there's a good many of us left, isn't there?' An' a fine boy it was, too, miss, an' 'er up an' about before 'er month."

She was paid in sixpences and spare shillings, and in cups of tea, or a fresh-baked loaf, or screws of sugar, or even in a garment not yet worn beyond repair. And she was free to run in and out, and grow a flower or so in her garden, and talk with a neighbour over the low dividing hedge.

"They want me to go into the 'Ouse,'" reaching the dangerous subject at last. "They say I'll be took care of an' looked after. But I don't want to do it, miss. I want to keep my bit of a 'ome if I can, an' be free to come an' go. I'm eighty-three, an' it won't be long. I 'ad a shilling a week from the parish, but they stopped it because they said I ought to go into the 'Ouse.'"

She looked at Betty with a momentarily anxious smile.

"P'raps you don't quite understand, miss," she said. "It'll seem like nothin' to you—a place like this."

"It doesn't," Betty answered, smiling bravely back into the old eyes, though she felt a slight fulness of the throat. "I understand all about it."

It is possible that old Mrs. Welden was a little taken aback by an attitude which, satisfactory to her own prejudices though it might be, was, taken in connection with fixed customs, a trifle unnatural.

"You don't mind me not wantin' to go?" she said.

"No," was the answer, "not at all."

Betty began to ask questions. How much tea, sugar, soap, candles, bread, butter, bacon, could Mrs. Welden use in a week? It was not very easy to find out the exact quantities, as Mrs. Welden's estimates of such things had been based, during her entire existence, upon calculation as to how little, not how much she could use.

When Betty suggested a pound of tea, a half pound—the old woman smiled at the innocent ignorance the suggestion of such reckless profusion implied.

"Oh, no! Bless you, miss, no! I couldn't never do away with it. A quarter, miss—that'd be plenty—a quarter."

Mrs. Welden's idea of "the best," was that at two shillings a pound. Quarter of a pound would cost sixpence (twelve cents, thought Betty). A pound of sugar would be twopence, Mrs. Welden would use half a pound (the riotous extravagance of two cents). Half a pound of butter, "Good tub butter, miss," would be ten pence three farthings a pound. Soap, candles, bacon, bread, coal, wood, in the quantities required by Mrs. Welden, might, with the addition of rent, amount to the dizzying height of eight or ten shillings.

"With careful extravagance," Betty mentally summed up, "I might spend almost two dollars a week in surrounding her with a riot of luxury."

She made a list of the things, and added some extras as an idea of her own. Life had not afforded her this kind of thing before, she realised. She felt for the first time the joy of reckless extravagance, and thrilled with the excitement of it.

"You need not think of Brexley Union any more," she said, when she, having risen to go, stood at the cottage door with old Mrs. Welden. "The things I have written down here shall be sent to you every Saturday night. I will pay your rent."

"Miss—miss!" Mrs. Welden looked affrighted. "It's too much, miss. An' coals eighteen pence a hundred!"

"Never mind," said her ladyship's sister, and the old woman, looking up into her eyes, found there the colour Mount Dunstan had thought of as being that of bluebells under water. "I think we can manage it, Mrs. Welden. Keep yourself as warm as you like, and sometime I will come and have a cup of tea with you and see if the tea is good."

"Oh! Deary me!" said Mrs. Welden. "I can't think what to say, miss. It lifts everythin'—everythin'. It's not to be believed. It's like bein' left a fortune."

When the wicket gate swung to and the young lady went up the lane, the old woman stood staring after her. And here was a piece of news to run into Charley

Jenkins' cottage and tell—and what woman or man in the row would quite believe it?

CHAPTER XXV

"WE BEGAN TO MARRY THEM, MY GOOD FELLOW!"

Lord Dunholm and his eldest son, Lord Westholt, sauntered together smoking their after-dinner cigars on the broad-turfed terrace overlooking park and gardens which seemed to sweep without boundary line into the purplish land beyond. The grey mass of the castle stood clear-cut against the blue of a sky whose twilight was still almost daylight, though in the purity of its evening stillness a star already hung, here and there, and a young moon swung low. The great spaces about them held a silence whose exquisite entirety was marked at intervals by the distant bark of a shepherd dog driving his master's sheep to the fold, their soft, intermittent plaints—the mother ewes' mellow answering to the tender, fretful lambs—floated on the air, a lovely part of the ending day's repose. Where two who are friends stroll together at such hours, the great beauty makes for silence or for thoughtful talk. These two men—father and son—were friends and intimates, and had been so from Westholt's first memory of the time when his childish individuality began to detach itself from the background of misty and indistinct things. They had liked each other, and their liking and intimacy had increased with the onward moving and change of years. After sixty sane and decently spent active years of life, Lord Dunholm, in either country tweed or evening dress, was a well-built and handsome man; at thirty-three his son was still like him.

"Have you seen her?" he was saying.

"Only at a distance. She was driving Lady Anstruthers across the marshes in a cart. She drove well and——" he laughed as he flicked the ash from his cigar—"the back of her head and shoulders looked handsome."

"The American young woman is at present a factor which is without doubt to be counted with," Lord Dunholm put the matter without lightness. "Any young woman is a factor, but the American young woman just now—just now——" He paused a moment as though considering. "It did not seem at all necessary to count with them at first, when they began to appear among us. They were generally curiously exotic, funny little creatures with odd manners and voices. They were often most amusing, and one liked to hear them chatter and see the airy lightness with which they took superfluous, and sometimes unsuperfluous, conventions, as a hunter takes a five-barred gate. But it never occurred to us to marry them. We did not take them seriously enough. But we began to marry them—we began to marry them, my good fellow!"

The final words broke forth with such a suggestion of sudden anxiety that, in spite of himself, Westholt laughed involuntarily, and his father, turning to look at him, laughed also. But he recovered his seriousness.

"It was all rather a muddle at first," he went on. "Things were not fairly done, and certain bad lots looked on it as a paying scheme on the one side, while it was a matter of silly, little ambitions on the other. But that it is an extraordinary country there is no sane denying—huge, fabulously resourceful in every way—area, variety of climate, wealth of minerals, products of all sorts, soil to grow anything, and sun and rain enough to give each thing what it needs; last, or rather first, a people who, considered as a nation, are in the riot of youth, and who began by being English—which we Englishmen have an innocent belief is the one method of 'owning the earth.' That figure of speech is an Americanism I carefully committed to memory. Well, after all, look at the map—look at the map! There we are."

They had frequently discussed together the question of the development of international relations. Lord Dunholm, a man of far-reaching and clear logic, had realised that the oddly unaccentuated growth of intercourse between the two countries might be a subject to be reflected on without lightness.

"The habit we have of regarding America and Americans as rather a joke," he had once said, "has a sort of parallel in the condescendingly amiable amusement of a parent at the precocity or whimsicalness of a child. But the child is shooting up amazingly—amazingly. In a way which suggests divers possibilities."

The exchange of visits between Dunholm and Stornham had been rare and formal. From the call made upon the younger Lady Anstruthers on her marriage, the Dunholms had returned with a sense of puzzled pity for the little American bride, with her wonderful frock and her uneasy, childish eyes. For some years Lady Anstruthers had been too delicate to make or return calls. One heard painful accounts of her apparent wretched ill-health and of the condition of her husband's estate.

"As the relations between the two families have evidently been strained for years," Lord Dunholm said, "it is interesting to hear of the sudden advent of the sister. It seems to point to reconciliation. And you say the girl is an unusual person.

"From what one hears, she would be unusual if she were an English girl who had spent her life on an English estate. That an American who is making her first visit to England should seem to see at once the practical needs of a neglected place is a thing to wonder at. What can she know about it, one thinks. But she apparently does know. They say she has made no mistakes—even with the village people. She is managing, in one way or another, to give work to every man who wants it. Result, of course—unbounded rustic enthusiasm."

Lord Dunholm laughed between the soothing whiffs of his cigar.

"How clever of her! And what sensible good feeling! Yes—yes! She evidently has learned things somewhere. Perhaps New York has found it wise to begin to give young women professional training in the management of English estates. Who knows? Not a bad idea."

It was the rustic enthusiasm, Westholt explained, which had in a manner spread her fame. One heard enlightening and illustrative anecdotes of her. He related several well worth hearing. She had evidently a sense of humour and unexpected perceptions.

"One detail of the story of old Doby's meerschaum," Westholt said, "pleased me enormously. She managed to convey to him—without hurting his aged feelings or overwhelming him with embarrassment—that if he preferred a clean churchwarden or his old briarwood, he need not feel obliged to smoke the new pipe. He could regard it as a trophy. Now, how did she do that without filling him with fright and confusion, lest she might think him not sufficiently grateful for her present? But they tell me she did it, and that old Doby is rapturously happy and takes the meerschaum to bed with him, but only smokes it on Sundays—sitting at his window blowing great clouds when his neighbours are coming from church. It was a clever girl who knew that an old fellow might secretly like his old pipe best."

"It was a deliciously clever girl," said Lord Dunholm. "One wants to know and make friends with her. We must drive over and call. I confess, I rather congratulate myself that Anstruthers is not at home."

"So do I," Westholt answered. "One wonders a little how far he and his sister-in-law will 'foregather' when he returns. He's an unpleasant beggar."

A few days later Mrs. Brent, returning from a call on Mrs. Charley Jenkins, was passed by a carriage whose liveries she recognised half way up the village street. It was the carriage from Dunholm Castle. Lord and Lady Dunholm and Lord Westholt sat in it. They were, of course, going to call at the Court. Miss Vanderpoel was beginning to draw people. She naturally would. She would be likely to make quite a difference in the neighbourhood now that it had heard of her and Lady Anstruthers had been seen driving with her, evidently no longer an unvisitable invalid, but actually decently clothed and in her right mind. Mrs. Brent slackened her steps that she might have the pleasure of receiving and responding gracefully to salutations from the important personages in the landau. She felt that the Dunholms were important. There were earldoms AND earldoms, and that of Dunholm was dignified and of distinction.

A common-looking young man on a bicycle, who had wheeled into the village with the carriage, riding alongside it for a hundred yards or so, stopped before the Clock Inn and dismounted, just as Mrs. Brent neared him. He saw her looking after the equipage, and lifting his cap spoke to her civilly.

"This is Stornham village, ain't it, ma'am?" he inquired.

"Yes, my man." His costume and general aspect seemed to indicate that he was of the class one addressed as "my man," though there was something a little odd about him.

"Thank you. That wasn't Miss Vanderpoel's eldest sister in that carriage, was it?"

"Miss Vanderpoel's——" Mrs. Brent hesitated. "Do you mean Lady Anstruthers?"

"I'd forgotten her name. I know Miss Vanderpoel's eldest sister lives at Stornham—Reuben S. Vanderpoel's daughter."

"Lady Anstruthers' younger sister is a Miss Vanderpoel, and she is visiting at Stornham Court now." Mrs. Brent could not help adding, curiously, "Why do you ask?"

"I am going to see her. I'm an American."

Mrs. Brent coughed to cover a slight gasp. She had heard remarkable things of the democratic customs of America. It was painful not to be able to ask questions.

"The lady in the carriage was the Countess of Dunholm," she said rather grandly. "They are going to the Court to call on Miss Vanderpoel."

"Then Miss Vanderpoel's there yet. That's all right. Thank you, ma'am," and lifting his cap again he turned into the little public house.

The Dunholm party had been accustomed on their rare visits to Stornham to be received by the kind of man-servant in the kind of livery which is a manifest, though unwilling, confession. The men who threw open the doors were of regulation height, well dressed, and of trained bearing. The entrance hall had lost its hopeless shabbiness. It was a complete and picturesquely luxurious thing. The change suggested magic. The magic which had been used, Lord Dunholm reflected, was the simplest and most powerful on earth. Given surroundings, combined with a gift for knowing values of form and colour, if you have the power to spend thousands of guineas on tiger skins, Oriental rugs, and other beauties, barrenness is easily transformed.

The drawing-room wore a changed aspect, and at a first glance it was to be seen that in poor little Lady Anstruthers, as she had generally been called, there was to be noted alteration also. In her case the change, being in its first stages, could not perhaps be yet called transformation, but, aided by softly pretty arrangement of dress and hair, a light in her eyes, and a suggestion of pink under her skin, one recalled that she had once been a pretty little woman, and that after all she was only about thirty-two years old.

That her sister, Miss Vanderpoel, had beauty, it was not necessary to hesitate in deciding. Neither Lord Dunholm nor his wife nor their son did hesitate. A girl with long limbs an alluring profile, and extraordinary black lashes set round lovely Irish-blue eyes, possesses physical capital not to be argued about.

She was not one of the curious, exotic little creatures, whose thin, though sometimes rather sweet, and always gay, high-pitched young voices Lord Dunholm had been so especially struck by in the early days of the American invasion. Her voice had a tone one would be likely to remember with pleasure. How well she moved—how well her black head was set on her neck! Yes, she was of the new type—the later generation.

These amazing, oddly practical people had evolved it—planned it, perhaps, bought—figuratively speaking—the architects and material to design and build it—bought them in whatever country they found them, England, France, Italy Germany—pocketing them coolly and carrying them back home to develop, complete, and send forth into the world when their invention was a perfected thing. Struck by the humour of his fancy, Lord Dunholm found himself smiling into the Irish-blue eyes. They smiled back at him in a way which warmed his heart. There were no pauses in the conversation which followed. In times past, calls at Stornham had generally held painfully blank moments. Lady Dunholm was as pleased as her husband. A really charming girl was an enormous acquisition to the neighbourhood.

Westholt, his father saw, had found even more than the story of old Doby's pipe had prepared him to expect.

Country calls were not usually interesting or stimulating, and this one was. Lord Dunholm laid subtly brilliant plans to lead Miss Vanderpoel to talk of her native land and her views of it. He knew that she would say things worth hearing. Incidentally one gathered picturesque detail. To have vibrated between the two continents since her thirteenth year, to have spent a few years at school in one country, a few years in another, and yet a few years more in still another, as part of an arranged educational plan; to have crossed the Atlantic for the holidays, and to have journeyed thousands of miles with her father in his private car; to make the visits of a man of great schemes to his possessions of mines, railroads, and lands which were almost principalities—these things had been merely details of her life, adding interest and variety, it was true, but seeming the merely normal outcome of existence. They were normal to Vanderpoels and others of their class who were abnormalities in themselves when compared with the rest of the world.

Her own very lack of any abnormality reached, in Lord Dunholm's mind, the highest point of illustration of the phase of life she beautifully represented—for beautiful he felt its rare charms were.

When they strolled out to look at the gardens he found talk with her no less a stimulating thing. She told her story of Kedgers, and showed the chosen spot where thickets of lilies were to bloom, with the giants lifting white archangel trumpets above them in the centre.

"He can be trusted," she said. "I feel sure he can be trusted. He loves them. He could not love them so much and not be able to take care of them." And as she looked at him in frank appeal for sympathy, Lord Dunholm felt that for the moment she looked like a tall, queenly child.

But pleased as he was, he presently gave up his place at her side to Westholt. He must not be a selfish old fellow and monopolise her. He hoped they would see each other often, he said charmingly. He thought she would be sure to like Dunholm, which was really a thoroughly English old place, marked by all the features she seemed so much attracted by. There were some beautiful relics of the past there, and some rather shocking ones—certain dungeons, for instance, and a gallows mount, on which in good old times the family gallows had stood. This had apparently been a working adjunct to the domestic arrangements of every respectable family, and that irritating persons should dangle from it had been a simple domestic necessity, if one were to believe old stories.

"It was then that nobles were regarded with respect," he said, with his fine smile. "In the days when a man appeared with clang of arms and with javelins and spears before, and donjon keeps in the background, the attitude of bent knees and awful reverence were the inevitable results. When one could hang a servant on one's own private gallows, or chop off his hand for irreverence or disobedience—obedience and reverence were a rule. Now, a month's notice is the extremity of punishment, and the old pomp of armed servitors suggests comic opera. But we can show you relics of it at Dunholm."

He joined his wife and began at once to make himself so delightful to Rosy that she ceased to be afraid of him, and ended by talking almost gaily of her London visit.

Betty and Westholt walked together. The afternoon being lovely, they had all sauntered into the park to look at certain views, and the sun was shining between the trees. Betty thought the young man almost as charming as his father, which was saying much. She had fallen wholly in love with Lord Dunholm—with his handsome, elderly face, his voice, his erect bearing, his fine smile, his attraction of manner, his courteous ease and wit. He was one of the men who stood for the best of all they had been born to represent. Her own father, she felt, stood for the best of all such an American as himself should be. Lord Westholt would in time be what his father was. He had inherited from him good looks, good feeling, and a sense of humour. Yes, he had been given from the outset all that the other man had been denied. She was thinking of Mount Dunstan as "the other man," and spoke of him.

"You know Lord Mount Dunstan?" she said.

Westholt hesitated slightly.

"Yes—and no," he answered, after the hesitation. "No one knows him very well. You have not met him?" with a touch of surprise in his tone.

"He was a passenger on the Meridiana when I last crossed the Atlantic. There was a slight accident and we were thrown together for a few moments. Afterwards I met him by chance again. I did not know who he was."

Lord Westholt showed signs of hesitation anew. In fact, he was rather disturbed. She evidently did not know anything whatever of the Mount Dunstans. She would not be likely to hear the details of the scandal which had obliterated them, as it were, from the decent world.

The present man, though he had not openly been mixed up with the hideous thing, had borne the brand because he had not proved himself to possess any qualities likely to recommend him. It was generally understood that he was a bad lot also. To such a man the allurements such a young woman as Miss Vanderpoel would present would be extraordinary. It was unfortunate that she should have been thrown in his way. At the same time it was not possible to state the case clearly during one's first call on a beautiful stranger.

"His going to America was rather spirited," said the mellow voice beside him. "I thought only Americans took their fates in their hands in that way. For a man of his class to face a rancher's life means determination. It means the spirit——" with a low little laugh at the leap of her imagination—"of the men who were Mount Dunstans in early days and went forth to fight for what they meant to have. He went to fight. He ought to have won. He will win some day."

"I do not know about fighting," Lord Westholt answered. Had the fellow been telling her romantic stories? "The general impression was that he went to America to amuse himself."

"No, he did not do that," said Betty, with simple finality. "A sheep ranch is not amusing——" She stopped short and stood still for a moment. They had been walking down the avenue, and she stopped because her eyes had been caught by a figure half sitting, half lying in the middle of the road, a prostrate bicycle near it. It was the figure of a cheaply dressed young man, who, as she looked, seemed to make an ineffectual effort to rise.

"Is that man ill?" she exclaimed. "I think he must be." They went towards him at once, and when they reached him he lifted a dazed white face, down which a stream of blood was trickling from a cut on his forehead. He was, in fact, very white indeed, and did not seem to know what he was doing.

"I am afraid you are hurt," Betty said, and as she spoke the rest of the party joined them. The young man vacantly smiled, and making an unconscious-looking pass across his face with his hand, smeared the blood over his features painfully. Betty kneeled down, and drawing out her handkerchief, lightly wiped the gruesome smears away. Lord Westholt saw what had happened, having given a look at the bicycle.

"His chain broke as he was coming down the incline, and as he fell he got a nasty knock on this stone," touching with his foot a rather large one, which had evidently fallen from some cartload of building material.

The young man, still vacantly smiling, was fumbling at his breast pocket. He began to talk incoherently in good, nasal New York, at the mere sound of which Lady Anstruthers made a little yearning step forward.

"Superior any other," he muttered. "Tabulator spacer—marginal release key—call your 'tention—instantly—'justable—Delkoff—no equal on market." And having found what he had fumbled for, he handed a card to Miss Vanderpoel and sank unconscious on her breast.

"Let me support him, Miss Vanderpoel," said Westholt, starting forward.

"Never mind, thank you," said Betty. "If he has fainted I suppose he must be laid flat on the ground. Will you please to read the card."

It was the card Mount Dunstan had read the day before.

J. BURRIDGE & SON,

DELKOFF TYPEWRITER CO.

BROADWAY, NEW YORK. G. SELDEN.

"He is probably G. Selden," said Westholt. "Travelling in the interests of his firm, poor chap. The clue is not of much immediate use, however."

They were fortunately not far from the house, and Westholt went back quickly to summon servants and send for the village doctor. The Dunholms were kindly sympathetic, and each of the party lent a handkerchief to staunch the bleeding. Lord Dunholm helped Miss Vanderpoel to lay the young man down carefully.

"I am afraid," he said; "I am really afraid his leg is broken. It was twisted under him. What can be done with him?"

Miss Vanderpoel looked at her sister.

"Will you allow him to be carried to the house temporarily, Rosy?" she asked. "There is apparently nothing else to be done."

"Yes, yes," said Lady Anstruthers. "How could one send him away, poor fellow! Let him be carried to the house."

Miss Vanderpoel smiled into Lord Dunholm's much approving, elderly eyes.

"G. Selden is a compatriot," she said. "Perhaps he heard I was here and came to sell me a typewriter."

Lord Westholt returning with two footmen and a light mattress, G. Selden was carried with cautious care to the house. The afternoon sun, breaking through the branches of the ancestral oaks, kindly touched his keen-featured, white young face. Lord Dunholm and Lord Westholt each lent a friendly hand, and Miss Vanderpoel, keeping near, once or twice wiped away an insistent trickle of blood which showed itself from beneath the handkerchiefs. Lady Dunholm followed with Lady Anstruthers.

Afterwards, during his convalescence, G. Selden frequently felt with regret that by his unconsciousness of the dignity of his cortege at the moment he had missed feeling himself to be for once in a position he would have designated as "out of sight" in the novelty of its importance. To have beheld him, borne by nobles and liveried menials, accompanied by ladies of title, up the avenue of an English park on his way to be cared for in baronial halls, would, he knew, have added a joy to the final moments of his grandmother, which the consolations of religion could scarcely have met equally in competition. His own point of view, however, would not, it is true, have been that of the old woman in the black net cap and purple ribbons, but of a less reverent nature. His enjoyment, in fact, would have been based upon that transatlantic sense of humour, whose soul is glee at the incompatible, which would have been full fed by the incongruity of "Little Willie being yanked along by a bunch of earls, and Reuben S. Vanderpoel's daughters following the funeral." That he himself should have been unconscious of the situation seemed to him like "throwing away money."

The doctor arriving after he had been put to bed found slight concussion of the brain and a broken leg. With Lady Anstruthers' kind permission, it would certainly be best that he should remain for the present where he was. So, in a bedroom whose windows looked out upon spreading lawns and broad-branched trees, he was as comfortably established as was possible. G. Selden, through the capricious intervention of Fate, if he had not "got next" to Reuben S. Vanderpoel himself, had most undisputably "got next" to his favourite daughter.

As the Dunholm carriage rolled down the avenue there reigned for a few minutes a reflective silence. It was Lady Dunholm who broke it. "That," she said in her softly decided voice, "that is a nice girl."

Lord Dunholm's agreeable, humorous smile flickered into evidence.

"That is it," he said. "Thank you, Eleanor, for supplying me with a quite delightful early Victorian word. I believe I wanted it. She is a beauty and she is clever. She is a number of other things—but she is also a nice girl. If you will allow me to say so, I have fallen in love with her."

"If you will allow me to say so," put in Westholt, "so have I—quite fatally."

"That," said his father, with speculation in his eye, "is more serious."

CHAPTER XXVI

"WHAT IT MUST BE TO YOU—JUST YOU!"

G. Selden, awakening to consciousness two days later, lay and stared at the chintz covering of the top of his four-post bed through a few minutes of vacant amazement. It was a four-post bed he was lying on, wasn't it? And his leg was bandaged and felt unmovable. The last thing he remembered was going down an incline in a tree-bordered avenue. There was nothing more. He had been all right then. Was this a four-post bed or was it not? Yes, it was. And was it part of the furnishings of a swell bedroom—the kind of bedroom he had never been in before? Tip top, in fact? He stared and tried to recall things—but could not, and in his bewilderment exclaimed aloud.

"Well," he said, "if this ain't the limit! You may search ME!"

A respectable person in a white apron came to him from the other side of the room. It was Buttle's wife, who had been hastily called in.

"Sh—sh," she said soothingly. "Don't you worry. Nobody ain't goin' to search you. Nobody ain't. There! Sh, sh, sh," rather as if he were a baby. Beginning to be conscious of a curious sense of weakness, Selden lay and stared at her in a helplessness which might have been considered pathetic. Perhaps he had got "bats in his belfry," and there was no use in talking.

At that moment, however, the door opened and a young lady entered. She was "a looker," G. Selden's weakness did not interfere with his perceiving. "A looker, by gee!" She was dressed, as if for going out, in softly tinted, exquisite things, and a large, strange hydrangea blue flower under the brim of her hat rested on soft and full black hair. The black hair gave him a clue. It was hair like that he had seen as Reuben S. Vanderpoel's daughter rode by when he stood at the park gates at Mount Dunstan. "Bats in his belfry," of course.

"How is he?" she said to the nurse.

"He's been seeming comfortable all day, miss," the woman answered, "but he's light-headed yet. He opened his eyes quite sensible looking a bit ago, but he spoke queer. He said something was the limit, and that we might search him."

Betty approached the bedside to look at him, and meeting the disturbed inquiry in his uplifted eyes, laughed, because, seeing that he was not delirious, she thought she understood. She had not lived in New York without hearing its argot, and she realised that the exclamation which had appeared delirium to Mrs. Buttle had probably indicated that the unexplainableness of the situation in which G. Selden found himself struck him as reaching the limit of probability, and that the most extended search of his person would fail to reveal any clue to satisfactory explanation.

She bent over him, with her laugh still shining in her eyes.

"I hope you feel better. Can you tell me?" she said.

His voice was not strong, but his answer was that of a young man who knew what he was saying.

"If I'm not off my head, ma'am, I'm quite comfortable, thank you," he replied.

"I am glad to hear that," said Betty. "Don't be disturbed. Your mind is quite clear."

"All I want," said G. Selden impartially, "is just to know where I'm at, and how I blew in here. It would help me to rest better."

"You met with an accident," the "looker" explained, still smiling with both lips and eyes. "Your bicycle chain broke and you were thrown and hurt yourself. It happened in the avenue in the park. We found you and brought you in. You are at Stornham Court, which belongs to Sir Nigel Anstruthers. Lady Anstruthers is my sister. I am Miss Vanderpoel."

"Hully gee!" ejaculated G. Selden inevitably. "Hully GEE!" The splendour of the moment was such that his brain whirled. As it was not yet in the physical condition to whirl with any comfort, he found himself closing his eyes weakly.

"That's right," Miss Vanderpoel said. "Keep them closed. I must not talk to you until you are stronger. Lie still and try not to think. The doctor says you are getting on very well. I will come and see you again."

As the soft sweep of her dress reached the door he managed to open his eyes.

"Thank you, Miss Vanderpoel," he said. "Thank you, ma'am." And as his eyelids closed again he murmured in luxurious peace: "Well, if that's her—she can have ME—and welcome!"

She came to see him again each day—sometimes in a linen frock and garden hat, sometimes in her soft tints and lace and flowers before or after her drive in the afternoon, and two or three times in the evening, with lovely shoulders and wonderfully trailing draperies—looking like the women he had caught far-off glimpses of on the rare occasion of his having indulged himself in the highest and most remotely placed seat in the gallery at the opera, which inconvenience he had borne not through any ardent desire to hear the music, but because he wanted to see the show and get "a look-in" at the Four Hundred. He believed very implicitly in his Four Hundred, and privately—though perhaps almost unconsciously—cherished the distinction his share of them conferred upon him, as fondly as the English young man of his rudimentary type cherishes his dukes and duchesses. The English young man may revel in his coroneted beauties in photograph shops, the young American dwells fondly on flattering, or very unflattering, reproductions of his multi-millionaires' wives and daughters in the voluminous illustrated sheets of his Sunday paper, without which life would be a wretched and savourless thing.

Selden had never seen Miss Vanderpoel in his Sunday paper, and here he was lying in a room in the same house with her. And she coming in to see him and talk to him as if he was one of the Four Hundred himself! The comfort and luxury with which he found himself surrounded sank into insignificance when compared with such unearthly luck as this. Lady Anstruthers came in to see him also, and she several times brought with her a queer little lame fellow, who was spoken of as "Master Ughtred." "Master" was supposed by G. Selden to be a sort of title conferred upon the small sons of baronets and the like. The children he knew in New York and elsewhere answered to the names of Bob, or Jimmy, or Bill. No parallel to "Master" had been in vogue among them.

Lady Anstruthers was not like her sister. She was a little thing, and both she and Master Ughtred seemed fond of talking of New York. She had not been home for years, and the youngster had never seen it at all. He had some queer ideas about America, and seemed never to have seen anything but Stornham and the village. G. Selden liked him, and was vaguely sorry for a little chap to whom a description of the festivities attendant upon the Fourth of July and a Presidential election seemed like stories from the Arabian Nights.

"Tell me about the Tammany Tiger, if you please," he said once. "I want to know what kind of an animal it is."

From a point of view somewhat different from that of Mount Dunstan and Mr. Penzance, Betty Vanderpoel found talk with him interesting. To her he did not wear the aspect of a foreign product. She had not met and conversed with young men like him, but she knew of them. Stringent precautions were taken to protect her father from their ingenuous enterprises. They were not permitted to enter his offices; they were even discouraged from hovering about their neighbourhood when seen and suspected. The atmosphere, it was understood, was to be, if possible, disinfected of agents. This one, lying softly in the four-post bed, cheerfully grateful for the kindness shown him, and plainly filled with delight in his adventure, despite the physical discomforts attending it, gave her, as he began to recover, new views of the life he lived in common with his kind. It was like reading scenes from a realistic novel of New York life to listen to his frank, slangy conversation. To her, as well as to Mr. Penzance, sidelights were thrown upon existence in the "hall bedroom" and upon previously unknown phases of business life in Broadway and roaring "downtown" streets.

His determination, his sharp readiness, his control of temper under rebuff and superfluous harshness, his odd, impersonal summing up of men and things, and good-natured patience with the world in general, were, she knew, business assets. She was even moved—no less—by the remote connection of such a life with that of the first Reuben Vanderpoel who had laid the huge, solid foundations of their modern fortune. The first Reuben Vanderpoel must have seen and known the faces of men as G. Selden saw and knew them. Fighting his way step by step, knocking pertinaciously at every gateway which might give ingress to some passage leading to even the smallest gain, meeting with rebuff and indifference only to be overcome by steady and continued assault—if G. Selden was a nuisance, the first Vanderpoel had without doubt worn that aspect upon innumerable occasions. No one desires the presence of the man who while having nothing to give must persist in keeping himself in evidence, even if by strategy or force. From stories she was familiar with, she had gathered that the first Reuben Vanderpoel had certainly lacked a certain youth of soul she felt in this modern struggler for life. He had been the cleverer man of the two; G. Selden she secretly liked the better.

The curiosity of Mrs. Buttle, who was the nurse, had been awakened by a singular feature of her patient's feverish wanderings.

"He keeps muttering, miss, things I can't make out about Lord Mount Dunstan, and Mr. Penzance, and some child he calls Little Willie. He talks to them the same as if he knew them—same as if he was with them and they were talking to him quite friendly."

One morning Betty, coming to make her visit of inquiry found the patient looking thoughtful, and when she commented upon his air of pondering, his reply cast light upon the mystery.

"Well, Miss Vanderpoel," he explained, "I was lying here thinking of Lord Mount Dunstan and Mr. Penzance, and how well they treated me—I haven't told you about that, have I?

"That explains what Mrs. Buttle said," she answered. "When you were delirious you talked frequently to Lord Mount Dunstan and Mr. Penzance. We both wondered why."

Then he told her the whole story. Beginning with his sitting on the grassy bank outside the park, listening to the song of the robin, he ended with the adieux at the entrance gates when the sound of her horse's trotting hoofs had been heard by each of them.

"What I've been lying here thinking of," he said, "is how queer it was it happened just that way. If I hadn't stopped just that minute, and if you hadn't gone by, and if Lord Mount Dunstan hadn't known you and said who you were, Little Willie would have been in London by this time, hustling to get a cheap bunk back to New York in."

"Because?" inquired Miss Vanderpoel.

G. Selden laughed and hesitated a moment. Then he made a clean breast of it.

"Say, Miss Vanderpoel," he said, "I hope it won't make you mad if I own up. Ladies like you don't know anything about chaps like me. On the square and straight out, when I seen you and heard your name I couldn't help remembering whose daughter you was. Reuben S. Vanderpoel spells a big thing. Why, when I was in New York we fellows used to get together and talk about what it'd mean to the chap who could get next to Reuben S. Vanderpoel. We used to count up all the business he does, and all the clerks he's got under him pounding away on typewriters, and how they'd be bound to get worn out and need new ones. And we'd make calculations how many a man could unload, if he could get next. It was a kind of typewriting junior assistant fairy story, and we knew it couldn't happen really. But we used to chin about it just for the fun of the thing. One of the boys made up a thing about one of us saving Reuben S.'s life—dragging him from under a runaway auto and, when he says, 'What can I do to show my gratitude, young man?' him handing out his catalogue and saying, 'I should like to call your attention to the Delkoff, sir,' and getting him to promise he'd never use any other, as long as he lived!"

Reuben S. Vanderpoel's daughter laughed as spontaneously as any girl might have done. G. Selden laughed with her. At any rate, she hadn't got mad, so far.

"That was what did it," he went on. "When I rode away on my bike I got thinking about it and could not get it out of my head. The next day I just stopped on the road and got off my wheel, and I says to myself: 'Look here, business is business, if you ARE travelling in Europe and lunching at Buckingham Palace with the main squeeze. Get busy! What'll the boys say if they hear you've missed a chance like this? YOU hit the pike for Stornham Castle, or whatever it's called, and take your nerve with you! She can't do more than have you fired out, and you've been fired before and got your breath after it. So I turned round and made time. And that was how I happened on your avenue. And perhaps it was because I was feeling a bit rattled I lost my hold when the chain broke, and pitched over on my head. There, I've got it off my chest. I was thinking I should have to explain somehow."

Something akin to her feeling of affection for the nice, long-legged Westerner she had seen rambling in Bond Street touched Betty again. The Delkoff was the centre of G. Selden's world as the flowers were of Kedgers', as the "little 'ome" was of Mrs. Welden's.

"Were you going to try to sell ME a typewriter?" she asked.

"Well," G. Selden admitted, "I didn't know but what there might be use for one, writing business letters on a big place like this. Straight, I won't say I wasn't going to try pretty hard. It may look like gall, but you see a fellow has to rush things or he'll never get there. A chap like me HAS to get there, somehow."

She was silent a few moments and looked as if she was thinking something over. Her silence and this look on her face actually caused to dawn in the breast of Selden a gleam of daring hope. He looked round at her with a faint rising of colour.

"Say, Miss Vanderpoel—say——" he began, and then broke off.

"Yes?" said Betty, still thinking.

"C-COULD you use one—anywhere?" he said. "I don't want to rush things too much, but—COULD you?"

"Is it easy to learn to use it?"

"Easy!" his head lifted from his pillow. "It's as easy as falling off a log. A baby in a perambulator could learn to tick off orders for its bottle. And—on the square—there isn't its equal on the market, Miss Vanderpoel—there isn't." He fumbled beneath his pillow and actually brought forth his catalogue.

"I asked the nurse to put it there. I wanted to study it now and then and think up arguments. See—adjustable to hold with perfect ease an envelope, an index card, or a strip of paper no wider than a postage stamp. Unsurpassed paper feed, practical ribbon mechanism—perfect and permanent alignment."

As Mount Dunstan had taken the book, Betty Vanderpoel took it. Never had G. Selden beheld such smiling in eyes about to bend upon his catalogue.

"You will raise your temperature," she said, "if you excite yourself. You mustn't do that. I believe there are two or three people on the estate who might be taught to use a typewriter. I will buy three. Yes—we will say three."

She would buy three. He soared to heights. He did not know how to thank her, though he did his best. Dizzying visions of what he would have to tell "the boys" when he returned to New York flashed across his mind. The daughter of Reuben S. Vanderpoel had bought three Delkoffs, and he was the junior assistant who had sold them to her.

"You don't know what it means to me, Miss Vanderpoel," he said, "but if you were a junior salesman you'd know. It's not only the sale—though that's a rake-off of fifteen dollars to me—but it's because it's YOU that's bought them. Gee!" gazing at her with a frank awe whose obvious sincerity held a queer touch of pathos. "What it must be to be YOU—just YOU!"

She did not laugh. She felt as if a hand had lightly touched her on her naked heart. She had thought of it so often—had been bewildered restlessly by it as a mere child—this difference in human lot—this chance. Was it chance which had placed her entity in the centre of Bettina Vanderpoel's world instead of in that of some little cash girl with hair raked back from a sallow face, who stared at her as she passed in a shop—or in that of the young Frenchwoman whose life was spent in serving her, in caring for delicate dresses and keeping guard over ornaments whose price would have given to her own humbleness ease for the rest of existence? What did it mean? And what Law was laid upon her? What Law which could only work through her and such as she who had been born with almost unearthly power laid in their hands—the reins of monstrous wealth, which guided or drove the world? Sometimes fear touched her, as with this light touch an her heart, because she did not KNOW the Law and could only pray that her guessing at it might be right. And, even as she thought these things, G. Selden went on.

"You never can know," he said, "because you've always been in it. And the rest of the world can't know, because they've never been anywhere near it." He stopped and evidently fell to thinking.

"Tell me about the rest of the world," said Betty quietly.

He laughed again.

"Why, I was just thinking to myself you didn't know a thing about it. And it's queer. It's the rest of us that mounts up when you come to numbers. I guess it'd run into millions. I'm not thinking of beggars and starving people, I've been rushing the Delkoff too steady to get onto any swell charity organisation, so I don't know about them. I'm just thinking of the millions of fellows, and women, too, for the matter of that, that waken up every morning and know they've got to hustle for their ten per or their fifteen per—if they can stir it up as thick as that. If it's as much as fifty per, of course, seems like to me, they're on Easy Street. But sometimes those that's got to fifty per—or even more—have got more things to do with it—kids, you know, and more rent and clothes. They've got to get at it just as hard as we have. Why, Miss Vanderpoel, how many people do you suppose there are in a million that don't have to worry over their next month's grocery bills, and the rent of their flat? I bet there's not ten—and I don't know the ten."

He did not state his case uncheerfully. "The rest of the world" represented to him the normal condition of things.

"Most married men's a bit afraid to look an honest grocery bill in the face. And they WILL come in—as regular as spring hats. And I tell YOU, when a man's got to live on seventy-five a month, a thing that'll take all the strength and energy out of a twenty-dollar bill sorter gets him down on the mat."

Like old Mrs. Welden's, his roughly sketched picture was a graphic one.

"'Tain't the working that bothers most of us. We were born to that, and most of us would feel like deadbeats if we were doing nothing. It's the earning less than you can live on, and getting a sort of tired feeling over it. It's the having to make a dollar-bill look like two, and watching every other fellow try to do the same thing, and not often make the trip. There's millions of us—just millions— every one of us with his Delkoff to sell——" his figure of speech pleased him and he chuckled at his own cleverness—"and thinking of it, and talking about it, and—under his vest—half afraid that he can't make it. And what you say in the morning when you open your eyes and stretch yourself is, 'Hully gee! I've GOT to sell a Delkoff to-day, and suppose I shouldn't, and couldn't hold down my job!' I began it over my feeding bottle. So did all the people I know. That's what gave me a sort of a jolt just now when I looked at you and thought about you being YOU—and what it meant."

When their conversation ended she had a much more intimate knowledge of New York than she had ever had before, and she felt it a rich possession. She had heard of the "hall bedroom" previously, and she had seen from the outside the "quick lunch" counter, but G. Selden unconsciously escorted her inside and threw upon faces and lives the glare of a flashlight.

"There was a thing I've been thinking I'd ask you, Miss Vanderpoel," he said just before she left him. "I'd like you to tell me, if you please. It's like this. You see those two fellows treated me as fine as silk. I mean Lord Mount Dunstan and Mr. Penzance. I never expected it. I never saw a lord before, much less spoke to one, but I can tell you that one's just about all right—Mount Dunstan. And the other one—the old vicar—I've never taken to anyone since I was born like I took to him. The way he puts on his eye-glasses and looks at you, sorter kind and curious about you at the same time! And his voice and his way of saying his words—well, they just GOT me—sure. And they both of 'em did say they'd like to see me again. Now do you think, Miss Vanderpoel, it would look too fresh—if I was to write a polite note and ask if either of them could make it convenient to come and take a look at me, if it wouldn't be too much trouble. I don't WANT to be too fresh—and perhaps they wouldn't come anyhow—and if it is, please won't you tell me, Miss Vanderpoel?"

Betty thought of Mount Dunstan as he had stood and talked to her in the deepening afternoon sun. She did not know much of him, but she thought— having heard G. Selden's story of the lunch—that he would come. She had never seen Mr. Penzance, but she knew she should like to see him.

"I think you might write the note," she said. "I believe they would come to see you."

"Do you?" with eager pleasure. "Then I'll do it. I'd give a good deal to see them again. I tell you, they are just It—both of them."

CHAPTER XXVII

LIFE

Mount Dunstan, walking through the park next morning on his way to the vicarage, just after post time, met Mr. Penzance himself coming to make an equally early call at the Mount. Each of them had a letter in his hand, and each met the other's glance with a smile.

"G. Selden," Mount Dunstan said. "And yours?"

"G. Selden also," answered the vicar. "Poor young fellow, what ill-luck. And yet—is it ill-luck? He says not."

"He tells me it is not," said Mount Dunstan. "And I agree with him."

Mr. Penzance read his letter aloud.

"DEAR SIR:

"This is to notify you that owing to my bike going back on me when going down hill, I met with an accident in Stornham Park. Was cut about the head and leg broken. Little Willie being far from home and mother, you can see what sort of fix he'd been in if it hadn't been for the kindness of Reuben S. Vanderpoel's daughters—Miss Bettina and her sister Lady Anstruthers. The way they've had me taken care of has been great. I've been under a nurse and doctor same as if I was Albert Edward with appendycytus (I apologise if that's not spelt right). Dear Sir, this is to say that I asked Miss Vanderpoel if I should be butting in too much if I dropped a line to ask if you could spare the time to call and see me. It would be considered a favour and appreciated by

"G. SELDEN,

"Delkoff Typewriter Co. Broadway.

"P. S. Have already sold three Delkoffs to Miss Vanderpoel."

"Upon my word," Mr. Penzance commented, and his amiable fervour quite glowed, "I like that queer young fellow—I like him. He does not wish to 'butt in too much.' Now, there is rudimentary delicacy in that. And what a humorous, forceful figure of speech! Some butting animal—a goat, I seem to see, preferably—forcing its way into a group or closed circle of persons."

His gleeful analysis of the phrase had such evident charm for him that Mount Dunstan broke into a shout of laughter, even as G. Selden had done at the adroit mention of Weber & Fields.

"Shall we ride over together to see him this morning? An hour with G. Selden, surrounded by the atmosphere of Reuben S. Vanderpoel, would be a cheering thing," he said.

"It would," Mr. Penzance answered. "Let us go by all means. We should not, I suppose," with keen delight, "be 'butting in' upon Lady Anstruthers too early?" He was quite enraptured with his own aptness. "Like G. Selden, I should not like to 'butt in,'" he added.

The scent and warmth and glow of a glorious morning filled the hour. Combining themselves with a certain normal human gaiety which surrounded the mere thought of G. Selden, they were good things for Mount Dunstan. Life was strong and young in him, and he had laughed a big young laugh, which had, perhaps tended to the waking in him of the feeling he was suddenly conscious of—that a six-mile ride over a white, tree-dappled, sunlit road would be pleasant enough, and, after all, if at the end of the gallop one came again upon that other in whom life was strong and young, and bloomed on rose-cheek and was the far fire in the blue deeps of lovely eyes, and the slim straightness of the fair body, why would it not be, in a way, all to the good? He had thought of her on more than one day, and felt that he wanted to see her again.

"Let us go," he answered Penzance. "One can call on an invalid at any time. Lady Anstruthers will forgive us."

In less than an hour's time they were on their way. They laughed and talked as they rode, their horses' hoofs striking out a cheerful ringing accompaniment to their voices. There is nothing more exhilarating than the hollow, regular ring and click-clack of good hoofs going well over a fine old Roman road in the morning sunlight. They talked of the junior assistant salesman and of Miss Vanderpoel. Penzance was much pleased by the prospect of seeing "this delightful and unusual girl." He had heard stories of her, as had Lord Westholt. He knew of old Doby's pipe, and of Mrs. Welden's respite from the Union, and though such incidents would seem mere trifles to the dweller in great towns, he had himself lived and done his work long enough in villages to know the village mind and the scale of proportions by which its gladness and sadness were measured. He knew more of all this than Mount Dunstan could, since Mount Dunstan's existence had isolated itself, from rather gloomy choice. But as he rode, Mount Dunstan knew that he liked to hear these things. There was the suggestion of new life and new thought in them, and such suggestion was good for any man—or woman, either—who had fallen into living in a dull, narrow groove.

"It is the new life in her which strikes me," he said. "She has brought wealth with her, and wealth is power to do the good or evil that grows in a man's soul; but she has brought something more. She might have come here and brought all the sumptuousness of a fashionable young beauty, who drove through the village and drew people to their windows, and made clodhoppers scratch their heads and pull their forelocks, and children bob curtsies and stare. She might have come and gone and left a mind-dazzling memory and nothing else. A few sovereigns tossed here and there would have earned her a reputation—but, by gee! to quote Selden—she has begun LIVING with them, as if her ancestors had done it for six hundred years. And what I see is that if she had come without a penny in her pocket she would have done the same thing." He paused a pondering moment, and then drew a sharp breath which was an exclamation in itself. "She's Life!" he said. "She's Life itself! Good God! what a thing it is for a man or woman to be Life—instead of a mass of tissue and muscle and nerve, dragged about by the mere mechanism of living!"

Penzance had listened seriously.

"What you say is very suggestive," he commented. "It strikes me as true, too. You have seen something of her also, at least more than I have."

"I did not think these things when I saw her—though I suppose I felt them unconsciously. I have reached this way of summing her up by processes of exclusion and inclusion. One hears of her, as you know yourself, and one thinks her over."

"You have thought her over?"

"A lot," rather grumpily. "A beautiful female creature inevitably gives an unbeautiful male creature something to think of—if he is not otherwise actively employed. I am not. She has become a sort of dawning relief to my hopeless humours. Being a low and unworthy beast, I am sometimes resentful enough of the unfairness of things. She has too much."

When they rode through Stornham village they saw signs of work already done and work still in hand. There were no broken windows or palings or hanging wicket gates; cottage gardens had been put in order, and there were evidences of such cheering touches as new bits of window curtain and strong-looking young plants blooming between them. So many small, but necessary, things had been done that the whole village wore the aspect of a place which had taken heart, and was facing existence in a hopeful spirit. A year ago Mount Dunstan and his vicar riding through it had been struck by its neglected and dispirited look.

As they entered the hall of the Court Miss Vanderpoel was descending the staircase. She was laughing a little to herself, and she looked pleased when she saw them.

"It is good of you to come," she said, as they crossed the hall to the drawing-room. "But I told him I really thought you would. I have just been talking to him, and he was a little uncertain as to whether he had assumed too much."

"As to whether he had 'butted in,'" said Mr. Penzance. "I think he must have said that."

"He did. He also was afraid that he might have been 'too fresh.'" answered Betty.

"On our part," said Mr. Penzance, with gentle glee, "we hesitated a moment in fear lest we also might appear to be 'butting in.'"

Then they all laughed together. They were laughing when Lady Anstruthers entered, and she herself joined them. But to Mount Dunstan, who felt her to be somehow a touching little person, there was manifest a tenderness in her feeling for G. Selden. For that matter, however, there was something already beginning to be rather affectionate in the attitude of each of them. They went upstairs to find him lying in state upon a big sofa placed near a window, and his joy at the sight of them was a genuine, human thing. In fact, he had pondered a good deal in secret on the possibility of these swell people thinking he had "more than his share of gall" to expect them to remember him after he passed on his junior assistant salesman's way. Reuben S. Vanderpoel's daughters were of the highest of his Four Hundred, but they were Americans, and Americans were not as a rule so "stuck on themselves" as the English. And here these two swells came as friendly as you please. And that nice old chap that was a vicar, smiling and giving him "the glad hand"!

Betty and Mount Dunstan left Mr. Penzance talking to the convalescent after a short time. Mount Dunstan had asked to be shown the gardens. He wanted to see the wonderful things he had heard had been already done to them.

They went down the stairs together and passed through the drawing-room into the pleasure grounds. The once neglected lawns had already been mown and rolled, clipped and trimmed, until they spread before the eye huge measures of green velvet; even the beds girdling and adorning them were brilliant with flowers.

"Kedgers!" said Betty, waving her hand. "In my ignorance I thought we must wait for blossoms until next year; but it appears that wonders can be brought all ready to bloom for one from nursery gardens, and can be made to grow with care—and daring—and passionate affection. I have seen Kedgers turn pale with anguish as he hung over a bed of transplanted things which seemed to droop too long. They droop just at first, you know, and then they slowly lift their heads, slowly, as if to listen to a Voice calling—calling. Once I sat for quite a long time before a rose, watching it. When I saw it BEGIN to listen, I felt a little trembling pass over my body. I seemed to be so strangely near to such a strange thing. It was Life—Life coming back—in answer to what we cannot hear."

She had begun lightly, and then her voice had changed. It was very quiet at the end of her speaking. Mount Dunstan simply repeated her last words.

"To what we cannot hear."

"One feels it so much in a garden," she said. "I have never lived in a garden of my own. This is not mine, but I have been living in it—with Kedgers. One is so close to Life in it—the stirring in the brown earth, the piercing through of green spears, that breaking of buds and pouring forth of scent! Why shouldn't one tremble, if one thinks? I have stood in a potting shed and watched Kedgers fill a shallow box with damp rich mould and scatter over it a thin layer of infinitesimal seeds; then he moistens them and carries them reverently to his altars in a greenhouse. The ledges in Kedgers' green-houses are altars. I think he offers prayers before them. Why not? I should. And when one comes to see them, the moist seeds are swelled to fulness, and when one comes again they are bursting. And the next time, tiny green things are curling outward. And, at last, there is a fairy forest of tiniest pale green stems and leaves. And one is standing close to the Secret of the World! And why should not one prostrate one's self, breathing softly—and touching one's awed forehead to the earth?"

Mount Dunstan turned and looked at her—a pause in his step—they were walking down a turfed path, and over their heads meeting branches of new leaves hung. Something in his movement made her turn and pause also. They both paused—and quite unknowingly.

"Do you know," he said, in a low and rather unusual voice, "that as we were on our way here, I said of you to Penzance, that you were Life—YOU!"

For a few seconds, as they stood so, his look held her—their eyes involuntarily and strangely held each other. Something softly glowing in the sunlight falling on them both, something raining down in the song of a rising skylark trilling in the blue a field away, something in the warmed incense of blossoms near them, was calling—calling in the Voice, though they did not know they heard. Strangely, a splendid blush rose in a fair flood under her skin. She was conscious of it, and felt a second's amazed impatience that she should colour like a schoolgirl suspecting a compliment. He did not look at her as a man looks who has made a pretty speech. His eyes met hers straight and thoughtfully, and he repeated his last words as he had before repeated hers.

"That YOU were Life—you!"

The bluebells under water were for the moment incredibly lovely. Her feeling about the blush melted away as the blush itself had done.

"I am glad you said that!" she answered. "It was a beautiful thing to say. I have often thought that I should like it to be true."

"It is true," he said.

Then the skylark, showering golden rain, swept down to earth and its nest in the meadow, and they walked on.

She learned from him, as they walked together, and he also learned from her, in a manner which built for them as they went from point to point, a certain degree of delicate intimacy, gradually, during their ramble, tending to make discussion and question possible. Her intelligent and broad interest in the work on the estate, her frank desire to acquire such practical information as she lacked, aroused in himself an interest he had previously seen no reason that he should feel. He realised that his outlook upon the unusual situation was being illuminated by an intelligence at once brilliant and fine, while it was also full of nice shading. The situation, of course, WAS unusual. A beautiful young sister-in-law appearing upon the dark horizon of a shamefully ill-used estate, and restoring, with touches of a wand of gold, what a fellow who was a blackguard should have set in order years ago. That Lady Anstruthers' money should have rescued her boy's inheritance instead of being spent upon lavish viciousness went without saying. What Mount Dunstan was most struck by was the perfect clearness, and its combination with a certain judicial good breeding, in Miss Vanderpoel's view of the matter. She made no confidences, beautifully candid as her manner was, but he saw that she clearly understood the thing she was doing, and that if her sister had had no son she would not have done this, but something totally different. He had an idea that Lady Anstruthers would have been swiftly and lightly swept back to New York, and Sir Nigel left to his own devices, in which case Stornham Court and its village would gradually have crumbled to decay. It was for Sir Ughtred Anstruthers the place was being restored. She was quite clear on the matter of entail. He wondered at first—not unnaturally—how a girl had learned certain things she had an obviously clear knowledge of. As they continued to converse he learned. Reuben S. Vanderpoel was without doubt a man remarkable not only in the matter of being the owner of vast wealth. The rising flood of his millions had borne him upon its strange surface a thinking, not an unthinking being—in fact, a strong and fine intelligence. His thousands of miles of yearly journeying in his sumptuous private car had been the means of his accumulating not merely added gains, but ideas, points of view, emotions, a human outlook worth counting as an asset. His daughter, when she had travelled with him, had seen and talked with him of all he himself had seen. When she had not been his companion she had heard from him afterwards all best worth hearing. She had become—without any special process—familiar with the technicalities of huge business schemes, with law and commerce and political situations. Even her childish interest in the world of enterprise and labour had been passionate. So she had acquired—inevitably, while almost unconsciously—a remarkable education.

"If he had not been HIMSELF he might easily have grown tired of a little girl constantly wanting to hear things—constantly asking questions," she said. "But he did not get tired. We invented a special knock on the door of his private room. It said, 'May I come in, father?' If he was busy he answered with one knock on his desk, and I went away. If he had time to talk he called out, 'Come, Betty,' and I went to him. I used to sit upon the floor and lean against his knee. He had a beautiful way of stroking my hair or my hand as he talked. He trusted me. He told me of great things even before he had talked of them to men. He knew I would never speak of what was said between us in his room. That was part of his trust. He said once that it was a part of the evolution of race, that men had begun to expect of women what in past ages they really only expected of each other."

Mount Dunstan hesitated before speaking.

"You mean—absolute faith—apart from affection?"

"Yes. The power to be quite silent, even when one is tempted to speak—if to speak might betray what it is wiser to keep to one's self because it is another man's affair. The kind of thing which is good faith among business men. It applies to small things as much as to large, and to other things than business."

Mount Dunstan, recalling his own childhood and his own father, felt again the pressure of the remote mental suggestion that she had had too much, a childhood and girlhood like this, the affection and companionship of a man of large and ordered intelligence, of clear and judicial outlook upon an immense area of life and experience. There was no cause for wonder that her young womanhood was all it presented to himself, as well as to others. Recognising the shadow of resentment in his thought, he swept it away, an inward sense making it clear to him that if their positions had been reversed, she would have been more generous than himself.

He pulled himself together with an unconscious movement of his shoulders. Here was the day of early June, the gold of the sun in its morning, the green shadows, the turf they walked on together, the skylark rising again from the meadow and showering down its song. Why think of anything else. What a line that was which swept from her chin down her long slim throat to its hollow! The colour between the velvet of her close-set lashes—the remembrance of her curious splendid blush—made the man's lost and unlived youth come back to him. What did it matter whether she was American or English—what did it matter whether she was insolently rich or beggarly poor? He would let himself go and forget all but the pleasure of the sight and hearing of her.

So as they went they found themselves laughing together and talking without restraint. They went through the flower and kitchen gardens; they saw the once fallen wall rebuilt now with the old brick; they visited the greenhouses and came upon Kedgers entranced with business, but enraptured at being called upon to show his treasures. His eyes, turning magnetised upon Betty, revealed the story of his soul. Mount Dunstan remarked that when he spoke to her of his flowers it was as if there existed between them the sympathy which might be engendered between two who had sat up together night after night with delicate children.

"He's stronger to-day, miss," he said, as they paused before a new wonderful bloom. "What he's getting now is good for him. I had to change his food, miss, but this seems all right. His colour's better."

Betty herself bent over the flower as she might have bent over a child. Her eyes softened, she touched a leaf with a slim finger, as delicately as if it had been a new-born baby's cheek. As Mount Dunstan watched her he drew a step nearer to her side. For the first time in his life he felt the glow of a normal and simple pleasure untouched by any bitterness.

CHAPTER XXVIII

SETTING THEM THINKING

Old Doby, sitting at his open window, with his pipe and illustrated papers on the table by his side, began to find life a series of thrills. The advantage of a window giving upon the village street unspeakably increased. For many years he had preferred the chimney corner greatly, and had rejoiced at the drawing in of winter days when a fire must be well kept up, and a man might bend over it, and rub his hands slowly gazing into the red coals or little pointed flames which seemed the only things alive and worthy the watching. The flames were blue at the base and yellow at the top, and jumped looking merry, and caught at bits of black coal, and set them crackling and throwing off splinters till they were ablaze and as much alive as the rest. A man could get comfort and entertainment therefrom. There was naught else so good to live with. Nothing happened in the street, and every dull face that passed was an old story, and told an old tale of stupefying hard labour and hard days.

But now the window was a better place to sit near. Carts went by with men whistling as they walked by the horses heads. Loads of things wanted for work at the Court. New faces passed faces of workmen—sometimes grinning, "impident youngsters," who larked with the young women, and called out to them as they passed their cottages, if a good-looking one was loitering about her garden gate. Old Doby chuckled at their love-making chaff, remembering dimly that seventy years ago he had been just as proper a young chap, and had made love in the same way. Lord, Lord, yes! He had been a bold young chap as ever winked an eye. Then, too, there were the vans, heavy-loaded and closed, and coming along slowly. Every few days, at first, there had come a van from "Lunnon." Going to the Court, of course. And to sit there, and hear the women talk about what might be in them, and to try to guess one's self, that was a rare pastime. Fine things going to the Court these days—furniture and grandeur filling up the shabby or empty old rooms, and making them look like other big houses—same as Westerbridge even, so the women said. The women were always talking and getting bits of news somehow, and were beginning to be worth listening to, because they had something more interesting to talk about than children's worn-out shoes, and whooping cough.

Doby heard everything first from them. "Dang the women, they always knowed things fust." It was them as knowed about the smart carriages as began to roll through the one village street. They were gentry's carriages, with fine, stamping horses, and jingling silver harness, and big coachmen, and tall footmen, and such like had long ago dropped off showing themselves at Stornham.

"But now the gentry has heard about Miss Vanderpoel, and what's being done at the Court, and they know what it means," said young Mrs. Doby. "And they want to see her, and find out what she's like. It's her brings them."

Old Doby chuckled and rubbed his hands. He knew what she was like. That straight, slim back of hers, and the thick twist of black hair, and the way she had of laughing at you, as cheery as if a bell was ringing. Aye, he knew all about that.

"When they see her once, they'll come agen, for sure," he quavered shrilly, and day by day he watched for the grand carriages with vivid eagerness. If a day or two passed without his seeing one, he grew fretful, and was injured, feeling that his beauty was being neglected! "None to-day, nor yet yest'day," he would cackle. "What be they folk a-doin'?"

Old Mrs. Welden, having heard of the pipe, and come to see it, had struck up an acquaintance with him, and dropped in almost every day to talk and sit at his window. She was a young thing, by comparison, and could bring him lively news, and, indeed, so stir him up with her gossip that he was in danger of becoming a young thing himself. Her groceries and his tobacco were subjects whose interest was undying.

A great curiosity had been awakened in the county, and visitors came from distances greater than such as ordinarily include usual calls. Naturally, one was curious about the daughter of the Vanderpoel who was a sort of national institution in his own country. His name had not been so much heard of in England when Lady Anstruthers had arrived but there had, at first, been felt an interest in her. But she had been a failure—a childish-looking girl—whose thin, fair, prettiness had no distinction, and who was obviously overwhelmed by her surroundings. She had evidently had no influence over Sir Nigel, and had not been able to prevent his making ducks and drakes of her money, which of course ought to have been spent on the estate. Besides which a married woman represented fewer potentialities than a handsome unmarried girl entitled to expectations from huge American wealth.

So the carriages came and came again, and, stately or unstately far-off neighbours sat at tea upon the lawn under the trees, and it was observed that the methods and appointments of the Court had entirely changed. Nothing looked new and American. The silently moving men-servants could not have been improved upon, there was plainly an excellent chef somewhere, and the massive silver was old and wonderful. Upon everybody's word, the change was such as it was worth a long drive merely to see!

The most wonderful thing, however, was Lady Anstruthers herself. She had begun to grow delicately plump, her once drawn and haggard face had rounded out, her skin had smoothed, and was actually becoming pink and fair, a nimbus of pale fine hair puffed airily over her forehead, and she wore the most charming little clothes, all of which made her look fifteen years younger than she had seemed when, on the grounds of ill-health, she had retired into seclusion. The renewed relations with her family, the atmosphere by which she was surrounded, had evidently given her a fresh lease of life, and awakened in her a new courage.

When the summer epidemic of garden parties broke forth, old Doby gleefully beheld, day after day, the Court carriage drive by bearing her ladyship and her sister attired in fairest shades and tints "same as if they was flowers."

Their delicate vaporousness, and rare colours, were sweet delights to the old man, and he and Mrs. Welden spent happy evenings discussing them as personal possessions. To these two Betty WAS a personal possession, bestowing upon them a marked distinction. They were hers and she was theirs. No one else so owned her. Heaven had given her to them that their last years might be lighted with splendour.

On her way to one of the garden parties she stopped the carriage before old Doby's cottage, and went in to him to speak a few words. She was of pale convolvulus blue that afternoon, and Doby, standing up touching his forelock and Mrs. Welden curtsying, gazed at her with prayer in their eyes. She had a few flowers in her hand, and a book of coloured photographs of Venice.

"These are pictures of the city I told you about—the city built in the sea— where the streets are water. You and Mrs. Welden can look at them together," she said, as she laid flowers and book down. "I am going to Dunholm Castle to a garden party this afternoon. Some day I will come and tell you about it."

The two were at the window staring spellbound, as she swept back to the carriage between the sweet-williams and Canterbury bells bordering the narrow garden path.

"Do you know I really went in to let them see my dress," she said, when she rejoined Lady Anstruthers. "Old Doby's granddaughter told me that he and Mrs. Welden have little quarrels about the colours I wear. It seems that they find my wardrobe an absorbing interest. When I put the book on the table, I felt Doby touch my sleeve with his trembling old hand. He thought I did not know."

"What will they do with Venice?" asked Rosy.

"They will believe the water is as blue as the photographs make it—and the palaces as pink. It will seem like a chapter out of Revelations, which they can believe is true and not merely 'Scriptur,'—because *I* have been there. I wish I had been to the City of the Gates of Pearl, and could tell them about that."

On the lawns at the garden parties she was much gazed at and commented upon. Her height and her long slender neck held her head above those of other girls, the dense black of her hair made a rich note of shadow amid the prevailing English blondness. Her mere colouring set her apart. Rosy used to watch her with tender wonder, recalling her memory of nine-year-old Betty, with the long slim legs and the demanding and accusing child-eyes. She had always been this creature even in those far-off days. At the garden party at Dunholm Castle it became evident that she was, after a manner, unusually the central figure of the occasion. It was not at all surprising, people said to each other. Nothing could have been more desirable for Lord Westholt. He combined rank with fortune, and the Vanderpoel wealth almost constituted rank in itself. Both Lord and Lady Dunholm seemed pleased with the girl. Lord Dunholm showed her great attention. When she took part in the dancing on the lawn, he looked on delightedly. He walked about the gardens with her, and it was plain to see that their conversation was not the ordinary polite effort to accord, usually marking the talk between a mature man and a merely pretty girl. Lord Dunholm sometimes laughed with unfeigned delight, and sometimes the two seemed to talk of grave things.

"Such occasions as these are a sort of yearly taking of the social census of the county," Lord Dunholm explained. "One invites ALL one's neighbours and is invited again. It is a friendly duty one owes."

"I do not see Lord Mount Dunstan," Betty answered. "Is he here?"

She had never denied to herself her interest in Mount Dunstan, and she had looked for him. Lord Dunholm hesitated a second, as his son had done at Miss Vanderpoel's mention of the tabooed name. But, being an older man, he felt more at liberty to speak, and gave her a rather long kind look.

"My dear young lady," he said, "did you expect to see him here?"

"Yes, I think I did," Betty replied, with slow softness. "I believe I rather hoped I should."

"Indeed! You are interested in him?"

"I know him very little. But I am interested. I will tell you why."

She paused by a seat beneath a tree, and they sat down together. She gave, with a few swift vivid touches, a sketch of the red-haired second-class passenger on the Meridiana, of whom she had only thought that he was an unhappy, rough-looking young man, until the brief moment in which they had stood face to face, each comprehending that the other was to be relied on if the worst should come to the worst. She had understood his prompt disappearance from the scene, and had liked it. When she related the incident of her meeting with him when she thought him a mere keeper on his own lands, Lord Dunholm listened with a changed and thoughtful expression. The effect produced upon her imagination by what she had seen, her silent wandering through the sad beauty of the wronged place, led by the man who tried stiffly to bear himself as a servant, his unintended self-revelations, her clear, well-argued point of view charmed him. She had seen the thing set apart from its county scandal, and so had read possibilities others had been blind to. He was immensely touched by certain things she said about the First Man.

"He is one of them," she said. "They find their way in the end—they find their way. But just now he thinks there is none. He is standing in the dark— where the roads meet."

"You think he will find his way?" Lord Dunholm said. "Why do you think so?"

"Because I KNOW he will," she answered. "But I cannot tell you WHY I know."

"What you have said has been interesting to me, because of the light your own thought threw upon what you saw. It has not been Mount Dunstan I have been caring for, but for the light you saw him in. You met him without prejudice, and you carried the light in your hand. You always carry a light, my impression is," very quietly. "Some women do."

"The prejudice you speak of must be a bitter thing for a proud man to bear. Is it a just prejudice? What has he done?"

Lord Dunholm was gravely silent for a few moments.

"It is an extraordinary thing to reflect,"—his words came slowly—"that it may NOT be a just prejudice. *I* do not know that he has done anything—but seem rather sulky, and be the son of his father, and the brother of his brother."

"And go to America," said Betty. "He could have avoided doing that—but he cannot be called to account for his relations. If that is all—the prejudice is NOT just."

"No, it is not," said Lord Dunholm, "and one feels rather awkward at having shared it. You have set me thinking again, Miss Vanderpoel."

CHAPTER XXIX

THE THREAD OF G. SELDEN

The Shuttle having in its weaving caught up the thread of G. Selden's rudimentary existence and drawn it, with the young man himself, across the sea, used curiously the thread in question, in the forming of the design of its huge web. As wool and coarse linen are sometimes interwoven with rich silk for decorative or utilitarian purposes, so perhaps was this previously unvalued material employed.

It was, indeed, an interesting truth that the young man, during his convalescence, without his own knowledge, acted as a species of magnet which drew together persons who might not easily otherwise have met. Mr. Penzance and Mount Dunstan rode over to see him every few days, and their visits naturally established relations with Stornham Court much more intimate than could have formed themselves in the same length of time under any of the ordinary circumstances of country life. Conventionalities lost their prominence in friendly intercourse with Selden. It was not, however, that he himself desired to dispense with convention. His intense wish to "do the right thing," and avoid giving offence was the most ingenuous and touching feature of his broad cosmopolitan good nature.

"If I ever make a break, sir," he had once said, with almost passionate fervour, in talking to Mr. Penzance, "please tell me, and set me on the right track. No fellow likes to look like a hoosier, but I don't mind that half as much as—as seeming not to APPRECIATE."

He used the word "appreciate" frequently. It expressed for him many degrees of thanks.

"I tell you that's fine," he said to Ughtred, who brought him a flower from the garden. "I appreciate that."

To Betty he said more than once:

"You know how I appreciate all this, Miss Vanderpoel. You DO know I appreciate it, don't you?"

He had an immense admiration for Mount Dunstan, and talked to him a great deal about America, often about the sheep ranch, and what it might have done and ought to have done. But his admiration for Mr. Penzance became affection. To him he talked oftener about England, and listened to the vicar's scholarly stories of its history, its past glories and its present ones, as he might have listened at fourteen to stories from the Arabian Nights.

These two being frequently absorbed in conversation, Mount Dunstan was rather thrown upon Betty's hands. When they strolled together about the place or sat under the deep shade of green trees, they talked not only of England and America, but of divers things which increased their knowledge of each other. It is points of view which reveal qualities, tendencies, and innate differences, or accordances of thought, and the points of view of each interested the other.

"Mr. Selden is asking Mr. Penzance questions about English history," Betty said, on one of the afternoons in which they sat in the shade. "I need not ask you questions. You ARE English history."

"And you are American history," Mount Dunstan answered.

"I suppose I am."

At one of their chance meetings Miss Vanderpoel had told Lord Dunholm and Lord Westholt something of the story of G. Selden. The novelty of it had delighted and amused them. Lord Dunholm had, at points, been touched as Penzance had been. Westholt had felt that he must ride over to Stornham to see the convalescent. He wanted to learn some New York slang.

He would take lessons from Selden, and he would also buy a Delkoff—two Delkoffs, if that would be better. He knew a hard-working fellow who ought to have a typewriter.

"Heath ought to have one," he had said to his father. Heath was the house-steward. "Think of the letters the poor chap has to write to trades-people to order things, and unorder them, and blackguard the shopkeepers when they are not satisfactory. Invest in one for Heath, father."

"It is by no means a bad idea," Lord Dunholm reflected. "Time would be saved by the use of it, I have no doubt."

"It saves time in any department where it can be used," Betty had answered. "Three are now in use at Stornham, and I am going to present one to Kedgers. This is a testimonial I am offering. Three weeks ago I began to use the Delkoff. Since then I have used no other. If YOU use them you will introduce them to the county."

She understood the feeling of the junior assistant, when he found himself in the presence of possible purchasers. Her blood tingled slightly. She wished she had brought a catalogue.

"We will come to Stornham to see the catalogue," Lord Dunholm promised.

"Perhaps you will read it aloud to us," Westholt suggested gleefully.

"G. Selden knows it by heart, and will repeat it to you with running comments. Do you know I shall be very glad if you decide to buy one—or two—or three," with an uplift of the Irish blue eyes to Lord Dunholm. "The blood of the first Reuben Vanderpoel stirs in my veins—also I have begun to be fond of G. Selden."

Therefore it occurred that on the afternoon referred to Lady Anstruthers appeared crossing the sward with two male visitors in her wake.

"Lord Dunholm and Lord Westholt," said Betty, rising.

For this meeting between the men Selden was, without doubt, responsible. While his father talked to Mount Dunstan, Westholt explained that they had come athirst for the catalogue. Presently Betty took him to the sheltered corner of the lawn, where the convalescent sat with Mr. Penzance.

But, for a short time, Lord Dunholm remained to converse with Mount Dunstan. In a way the situation was delicate. To encounter by chance a neighbour whom one—for reasons—has not seen since his childhood, and to be equal to passing over and gracefully obliterating the intervening years, makes demand even upon finished tact. Lord Dunholm's world had been a large one, and he had acquired experience tending to the development of the most perfect methods. If G. Selden had chanced to be the magnet which had decided his course this special afternoon, Miss Vanderpoel it was who had stirred in him sufficient interest in Mount Dunstan to cause him to use the best of these methods when he found himself face to face with him.

He beautifully eliminated the years, he eliminated all but the facts that the young man's father and himself had been acquaintances in youth, that he remembered Mount Dunstan himself as a child, that he had heard with interest of his visit to America. Whatsoever the young man felt, he made no sign which presented obstacles. He accepted the eliminations with outward composure. He was a powerful-looking fellow, with a fine way of carrying his shoulders, and an eye which might be able to light savagely, but just now, at least, he showed nothing of the sulkiness he was accused of.

Lord Dunholm progressed admirably with him. He soon found that he need not be upon any strain with regard to the eliminations. The man himself could eliminate, which was an assistance.

They talked together when they turned to follow the others to the retreat of G. Selden.

"Have you bought a Delkoff?" Lord Dunholm inquired.

"If I could have afforded it, I should have bought one."

"I think that we have come here with the intention of buying three. We did not know we required them until Miss Vanderpoel recited half a page of the catalogue to us."

"Three will mean a 'rake off' of fifteen dollars to G. Selden," said Mount Dunstan. It was, he saw, necessary that he should explain the meaning of a "rake off," and he did so to his companion's entertainment.

The afternoon was a satisfactory one. They were all kind to G. Selden, and he on his part was an aid to them. In his innocence he steered three of them, at least, through narrow places into an open sea of easy intercourse. This was a good beginning. The junior assistant was recovering rapidly, and looked remarkably well. The doctor had told him that he might try to use his leg. The inside cabin of the cheap Liner and "little old New York" were looming up before him. But what luck he had had, and what a holiday! It had been enough to set a fellow up for ten years' work. It would set up the boys merely to be told about it. He didn't know what HE had ever done to deserve such luck as had happened to him. For the rest of his life he would he waving the Union Jack alongside of the Stars and Stripes.

Mr. Penzance it was who suggested that he should try the strength of the leg now.

"Yes," Mount Dunstan said. "Let me help you."

As he rose to go to him, Westholt good-naturedly got up also. They took their places at either side of his invalid chair and assisted him to rise and stand on his feet.

"It's all right, gentlemen. It's all right," he called out with a delighted flush, when he found himself upright. "I believe I could stand alone. Thank you. Thank you."

He was able, leaning on Mount Dunstan's arm, to take a few steps. Evidently, in a short time, he would find himself no longer disabled.

Mr. Penzance had invited him to spend a week at the vicarage. He was to do this as soon as he could comfortably drive from the one place to the other. After receiving the invitation he had sent secretly to London for one of the Delkoffs he had brought with him from America as a specimen. He cherished in private a plan of gently entertaining his host by teaching him to use the machine. The vicar would thus be prepared for that future in which surely a Delkoff must in some way fall into his hands. Indeed, Fortune having at length cast an eye on himself, might chance to favour him further, and in time he might be able to send a "high-class machine" as a grateful gift to the vicarage. Perhaps Mr. Penzance would accept it because he would understand what it meant of feeling and appreciation.

During the afternoon Lord Dunholm managed to talk a good deal with Mount Dunstan. There was no air of intention in his manner, nevertheless intention was concealed beneath its courteous amiability. He wanted to get at the man. Before they parted he felt he had, perhaps, learned things opening up new points of view.

. . . . .

In the smoking-room at Dunholm that night he and his son talked of their chance encounter. It seemed possible that mistakes had been made about Mount Dunstan. One did not form a definite idea of a man's character in the course of an afternoon, but he himself had been impressed by a conviction that there had been mistakes.

"We are rather a stiff-necked lot—in the country—when we allow ourselves to be taken possession of by an idea," Westholt commented.

"I am not at all proud of the way in which we have taken things for granted," was his father's summing up. "It is, perhaps, worth observing," taking his cigar from his mouth and smiling at the end of it, as he removed the ash, "that, but for Miss Vanderpoel and G. Selden, we might never have had an opportunity of facing the fact that we may not have been giving fair play. And one has prided one's self on one's fair play."

CHAPTER XXX

A RETURN

At the close of a long, warm afternoon Betty Vanderpoel came out upon the square stone terrace overlooking the gardens, and that part of the park which, enclosing them, caused them, as they melted into its greenness, to lose all limitations and appear to be only a more blooming bit of the landscape.

Upon the garden Betty's eyes dwelt, as she stood still for some minutes taking in their effect thoughtfully.

Kedgers had certainly accomplished much. His close-trimmed lawns did him credit, his flower beds were flushed and azured, purpled and snowed with bloom. Sweet tall spires, hung with blue or white or rosy flower bells, lifted their heads above the colour of lower growths. Only the fervent affection, the fasting and prayer of a Kedgers could have done such wonders with new things and old. The old ones he had cherished and allured into a renewal of existence—the new ones he had so coaxed out of their earthen pots into the soil, luxuriously prepared for their reception, and had afterwards so nourished and bedewed with soft waterings, so supported, watched over and adored that they had been almost unconscious of their transplanting. Without assistants he could have done nothing, but he had been given a sufficient number of under gardeners, and had even managed to inspire them with something of his own ambition and solicitude. The result was before Betty's eyes in an aspect which, to such as knew the gardens well,—the Dunholms, for instance,—was astonishing in its success.

"I've had privileges, miss, and so have the flowers," Kedgers had said warmly, when Miss Vanderpoel had reported to him, for his encouragement, Dunholm Castle's praise. "Not one of 'em has ever had to wait for his food and drink, nor to complain of his bed not being what he was accustomed to. They've not had to wait for rain, for we've given it to 'em from watering cans, and, thank goodness, the season's been kind to 'em."

Betty, descending the terrace steps, wandered down the paths between the flower beds, glancing about her as she went. The air of neglect and desolation had been swept away. Buttle and Tim Soames had been given as many privileges as Kedgers. The chief points impressed upon them had been that the work must be done, not only thoroughly, but quickly. As many additional workmen as they required, as much solid material as they needed, but there must be a despatch which at first it staggered them to contemplate. They had not known such methods before. They had been accustomed to work under money limitation throughout their lives, and, when work must be done with insufficient aid, it must be done slowly. Economy had been the chief factor in all calculations, speed had not entered into them, so leisureliness had become a fixed habit. But it seemed American to sweep leisureliness away into space with a free gesture.

"It must be done QUICKLY," Miss Vanderpoel had said. "If ten men cannot do it quickly enough, you must have twenty—or as many more as are needed. It is time which must be saved just now."

Time more than money, it appeared. Buttle's experience had been that you might take time, if you did not charge for it. When time began to mean money, that was a different matter. If you did work by the job, you might drive in a few nails, loiter, and return without haste; if you worked by the hour, your absence would be inquired into. In the present case no one could loiter. That was realised early. The tall girl, with the deep straight look at you, made you realise that without spoken words. She expected energy something like her own. She was a new force and spurred them. No man knew how it was done, but, when she appeared among them—even in the afternoon—"lookin' that womany," holding up her thin dress over lace petticoats, the like of which had not been seen before, she looked on with just the same straight, expecting eyes. They did not seem to doubt in the least that she would find that great advance had been made.

So advance had been made, and work accomplished. As Betty walked from one place to another she saw the signs of it with gratification. The place was not the one she had come to a few months ago. Hothouses, outbuildings, stables were in repair. Work was still being done in different places. In the house itself carpenters or decorators were enclosed in some rooms, and at their business, but exterior order prevailed. In the courtyard stablemen were at work, and her own groom came forward touching his forehead. She paid a visit to the horses. They were fine creatures, and, when she entered their stalls, made room for her and whinnied gently, in well-founded expectation of sugar and bread which were kept in a cupboard awaiting her visits. She smoothed velvet noses and patted satin sides, talking to Mason a little before she went her way.

Then she strolled into the park. The park was always a pleasure. She was in a thoughtful mood, and the soft green shadowed silence lured her. The summer wind hus-s-shed the branches as it lightly waved them, the brown earth of the avenue was sun-dappled, there were bird notes and calls to be heard here and there and everywhere, if one only arrested one's attention a moment to listen. And she was in a listening and dreaming mood—one of the moods in which bird, leaf, and wind, sun, shade, and scent of growing things have part.

And yet her thoughts were of mundane things.

It was on this avenue that G. Selden had met with his accident. He was still at Dunstan vicarage, and yesterday Mount Dunstan, in calling, had told them that Mr. Penzance was applying himself with delighted interest to a study of the manipulation of the Delkoff.

The thought of Mount Dunstan brought with it the thought of her father. This was because there was frequently in her mind a connection between the two. How would the man of schemes, of wealth, and power almost unbounded, regard the man born with a load about his neck—chained to earth by it, standing in the midst of his hungering and thirsting possessions, his hands empty of what would feed them and restore their strength? Would he see any solution of the problem? She could imagine his looking at the situation through his gaze at the man, and considering both in his summing up.

"Circumstances and the man," she had heard him say. "But always the man first."

Being no visionary, he did not underestimate the power of circumstance. This Betty had learned from him. And what could practically be done with circumstance such as this? The question had begun to recur to her. What could she herself have done in the care of Rosy and Stornham, if chance had not placed in her hand the strongest lever? What she had accomplished had been easy—easy. All that had been required had been the qualities which control of the lever might itself tend to create in one. Given—by mere chance again—imagination and initiative, the moving of the lever did the rest. If chance had not been on one's side, what then? And where was this man's chance? She had said to Rosy, in speaking of the wealth of America, "Sometimes one is tired of it." And Rosy had reminded her that there were those who were not tired of it, who could bear some of the burden of it, if it might be laid on their own shoulders. The great beautiful, blind-faced house, awaiting its slow doom in the midst of its lonely unfed lands—what could save it, and all it represented of race and name, and the stately history of men, but the power one professed to call base and sordid—mere money? She felt a sudden impatience at herself for having said she was tired of it. That was a folly which took upon itself the aspect of an affectation.

And, if a man could not earn money—or go forth to rob richer neighbours of it as in the good old marauding days—or accept it if it were offered to him as a gift—what could he do? Nothing. If he had been born a village labourer, he could have earned by the work of his hands enough to keep his cottage roof over him, and have held up his head among his fellows. But for such as himself there was no mere labour which would avail. He had not that rough honest resource. Only the decent living and orderly management of the generations behind him would have left to him fairly his own chance to hold with dignity the place in the world into which Fate had thrust him at the outset—a blind, newborn thing of whom no permission had been asked.

"If I broke stones upon the highway for twelve hours a day, I might earn two shillings," he had said to Betty, on the previous day. "I could break stones well," holding out a big arm, "but fourteen shillings a week will do no more than buy bread and bacon for a stonebreaker."

He was ordinarily rather silent and stiff in his conversational attitude towards his own affairs. Betty sometimes wondered how she herself knew so much about them—how it happened that her thoughts so often dwelt upon them. The explanation she had once made to herself had been half irony, half serious reflection.

"It is a result of the first Reuben Vanderpoel. It is because I am of the fighting commercial stock, and, when I see a business problem, I cannot leave it alone, even when it is no affair of mine."

As an exposition of the type of the commercial fighting-stock she presented, as she paused beneath overshadowing trees, an aspect beautifully suggesting a far different thing.

She stood—all white from slim shoe to tilted parasol,—and either the result of her inspection of the work done by her order, or a combination of her summer-day mood with her feeling for the problem, had given her a special radiance. It glowed on lip and cheek, and shone in her Irish eyes.

She had paused to look at a man approaching down the avenue. He was not a labourer, and she did not know him. Men who were not labourers usually rode or drove, and this one was walking. He was neither young nor old, and, though at a distance his aspect was not attracting, she found that she regarded him curiously, and waited for him to draw nearer.

The man himself was glancing about him with a puzzled look and knitted forehead. When he had passed through the village he had seen things he had not expected to see; when he had reached the entrance gate, and—for reasons of his own—dismissed his station trap, he had looked at the lodge scrutinisingly, because he was not prepared for its picturesque trimness. The avenue was free from weeds and in order, the two gates beyond him were new and substantial. As he went on his way and reached the first, he saw at about a hundred yards distance a tall girl in white standing watching him. Things which were not easily explainable always irritated him. That this place—which was his own affair—should present an air of mystery, did not improve his humour, which was bad to begin with. He had lately been passing through unpleasant things, which had left him feeling himself tricked and made ridiculous—as only women can trick a man and make him ridiculous, he had said to himself. And there had been an acrid consolation in looking forward to the relief of venting one's self on a woman who dare not resent.

"What has happened, confound it!" he muttered, when he caught sight of the girl. "Have we set up a house party?" And then, as he saw more distinctly, "Damn! What a figure!"

By this time Betty herself had begun to see more clearly. Surely this was a face she remembered—though the passing of years and ugly living had thickened and blurred, somewhat, its always heavy features. Suddenly she knew it, and the look in its eyes—the look she had, as a child, unreasoningly hated.

Nigel Anstruthers had returned from his private holiday.

As she took a few quiet steps forward to meet him, their eyes rested on each other. After a night or two in town his were slightly bloodshot, and the light in them was not agreeable.

It was he who spoke first, and it is possible that he did not quite intend to use the expletive which broke from him. But he was remembering things also. Here were eyes he, too, had seen before—twelve years ago in the face of an objectionable, long-legged child in New York. And his own hatred of them had been founded in his own opinion on the best of reasons. And here they gazed at him from the face of a young beauty—for a beauty she was.

"Damn it!" he exclaimed; "it is Betty."

"Yes," she answered, with a faint, but entirely courteous, smile. "It is. I hope you are very well."

She held out her hand. "A delicious hand," was what he said to himself, as he took it. And what eyes for a girl to have in her head were those which looked out at him between shadows. Was there a hint of the devil in them? He thought so—he hoped so, since she had descended on the place in this way. But WHAT the devil was the meaning of her being on the spot at all? He was, however, far beyond the lack of astuteness which might have permitted him to express this last thought at this particular juncture. He was only betrayed into stupid mistakes, afterwards to be regretted, when rage caused him utterly to lose control of his wits. And, though he was startled and not exactly pleased, he was not in a rage now. The eyelashes and the figure gave an agreeable fillip to his humour. Howsoever she had come, she was worth looking at.

"How could one expect such a delightful thing as this?" he said, with a touch of ironic amiability. "It is more than one deserves."

"It is very polite of you to say that," answered Betty.

He was thinking rapidly as he stood and gazed at her. There were, in truth, many things to think of under circumstances so unexpected.

"May I ask you to excuse my staring at you?" he inquired with what Rosy had called his "awful, agreeable smile." "When I saw you last you were a fierce nine-year-old American child. I use the word 'fierce' because—if you'll pardon my saying so—there was a certain ferocity about you."

"I have learned at various educational institutions to conceal it," smiled Betty.

"May I ask when you arrived?"

"A short time after you went abroad."

"Rosalie did not inform me of your arrival."

"She did not know your address. You had forgotten to leave it."

He had made a mistake and realised it. But she presented to him no air of having observed his slip. He paused a few seconds, still regarding her and still thinking rapidly. He recalled the mended windows and roofs and palings in the village, the park gates and entrance. Who the devil had done all that? How could a mere handsome girl be concerned in it? And yet—here she was.

"When I drove through the village," he said next, "I saw that some remarkable changes had taken place on my property. I feel as if you can explain them to me."

"I hope they are changes which meet with your approval."

"Quite—quite," a little curtly. "Though I confess they mystify me. Though I am the son-in-law of an American multimillionaire, I could not afford to make such repairs myself."

A certain small spitefulness which was his most frequent undoing made it impossible for him to resist adding the innuendo in his last sentence. And again he saw it was a folly. The impersonal tone of her reply simply left him where he had placed himself.

"We were sorry not to be able to reach you. As it seemed well to begin the work at once, we consulted Messrs. Townlinson & Sheppard."

"We?" he repeated. "Am I to have the pleasure," with a slight wryness of the mouth, "of finding Mr. Vanderpoel also at Stornham?"

"No—not yet. As I was on the spot, I saw your solicitors and asked their advice and approval—for my father. If he had known how necessary the work was, it would have been done before, for Ughtred's sake."

Her voice was that of a person who, in stating obvious facts, provides no approach to enlightening comment upon them. And there was in her manner the merest gracious impersonality.

"Do I understand that Mr. Vanderpoel employed someone to visit the place and direct the work?"

"It was really not difficult to direct. It was merely a matter of engaging labour and competent foremen."

An odd expression rose in his eyes.

"You suggest a novel idea, upon my word," he said. "Is it possible—you see I know something of America—is it possible I must thank YOU for the working of this magic?"

"You need not thank me," she said, rather slowly, because it was necessary that she also should think of many things at once. "I could not have helped doing it."

She wished to make all clear to him before he met Rosy. She knew it was not unnatural that the unexpectedness of his appearance might deprive Lady Anstruthers of presence of mind. Instinct told her that what was needed in intercourse with him was, above all things, presence of mind.

"I will tell you about it," she said. "We will walk slowly up and down here, if you do not object."

He did not object. He wanted to hear the story as he could not hear it from his nervous little fool of a wife, who would be frightened into forgetting things and their sequence. What he meant to discover was where he stood in the matter—where his father-in-law stood, and, rather specially, to have a chance to sum up the weaknesses and strengths of the new arrival. That would be to his interest. In talking this thing over she would unconsciously reveal how much vanity or emotion or inexperience he might count upon as factors safe to use in one's dealings with her in the future.

As he listened he was supported by the fact that he did not lose consciousness of the eyes and the figure. But for these it is probable that he would have gone blind with fury at certain points which forced themselves upon him. The first was that there had been an absurd and immense expenditure which would simply benefit his son and not himself. He could not sell or borrow money on what had been given. Apparently the place had been re-established on a footing such as it had not rested upon during his own generation, or his father's. As he loathed life in the country, it was not he who would enjoy its luxury, but his wife and her child. The second point was that these people—this girl—had somehow had the sharpness to put themselves in the right, and to place him in a position at which he could not complain without putting himself in the wrong. Public opinion would say that benefits had been heaped upon him, that the correct thing had been done correctly with the knowledge and approval of the legal advisers of his family. It had been a masterly thing, that visit to Townlinson & Sheppard. He was obliged to aid his self-control by a glance at the eyelashes. She was a new sort of girl, this Betty, whose childhood he had loathed, and, to his jaded taste, novelty appealed enormously. Her attraction for him was also added to by the fact that he was not at all sure that there was not combined with it a pungent spice of the old detestation. He was repelled as well as allured. She represented things which he hated. First, the mere material power, which no man can bully, whatsoever his humour. It was the power he most longed for and, as he could not hope to possess it, most sneered at and raged against. Also, as she talked, it was plain that her habit of self-control and her sense of resource would be difficult to deal with. He was a survival of the type of man whose simple creed was that women should not possess resources, as when they possessed them they could rarely be made to behave themselves.

But while he thought these things, he walked by her side and both listened and talked smiling the agreeable smile.

"You will pardon my dull bewilderment," he said. "It is not unnatural, is it—in a mere outsider?"

And Betty, with the beautiful impersonal smile, said:

"We felt it so unfortunate that even your solicitors did not know your address."

When, at length, they turned and strolled towards the house, a carriage was drawing up before the door, and at the sight of it, Betty saw her companion slightly lift his eyebrows. Lady Anstruthers had been out and was returning. The groom got down from the box, and two men-servants appeared upon the steps. Lady Anstruthers descended, laughing a little as she talked to Ughtred, who had been with her. She was dressed in clear, pale grey, and the soft rose lining of her parasol warmed the colour of her skin.

Sir Nigel paused a second and put up his glass.

"Is that my wife?" he said. "Really! She quite recalls New York."

The agreeable smile was on his lips as he hastened forward. He always more or less enjoyed coming upon Rosalie suddenly. The obvious result was a pleasing tribute to his power.

Betty, following him, saw what occurred.

Ughtred saw him first, and spoke quick and low.

"Mother!" he said.

The tone of his voice was evidently enough. Lady Anstruthers turned with an unmistakable start. The rose lining of her parasol ceased to warm her colour. In fact, the parasol itself stepped aside, and she stood with a blank, stiff, white face.

"My dear Rosalie," said Sir Nigel, going towards her. "You don't look very glad to see me."

He bent and kissed her quite with the air of a devoted husband. Knowing what the caress meant, and seeing Rosy's face as she submitted to it, Betty felt rather cold. After the conjugal greeting he turned to Ughtred.

"You look remarkably well," he said.

Betty came forward.

"We met in the park, Rosy," she explained. "We have been talking to each other for half an hour."

The atmosphere which had surrounded her during the last three months had done much for Lady Anstruthers' nerves. She had the power to recover herself. Sir Nigel himself saw this when she spoke.

"I was startled because I was not expecting to see you," she said. "I thought you were still on the Riviera. I hope you had a pleasant journey home."

"I had an extraordinarily pleasant surprise in finding your sister here," he answered. And they went into the house.

In descending the staircase on his way to the drawing-room before dinner, Sir Nigel glanced about him with interested curiosity. If the village had been put in order, something more had been done here. Remembering the worn rugs and the bald-headed tiger, he lifted his brows. To leave one's house in a state of resigned dilapidation and return to find it filled with all such things as comfort combined with excellent taste might demand, was an enlivening experience—or would have been so under some circumstances. As matters stood, perhaps, he might have felt better pleased if things had been less well done. But they were very well done. They had managed to put themselves in the right in this also. The rich sobriety of colour and form left no opening for supercilious comment—which was a neat weapon it was annoying to be robbed of.

The drawing-room was fresh, brightly charming, and full of flowers. Betty was standing before an open window with her sister. His wife's shoulders, he observed at once, had absolutely begun to suggest contours. At all events, her bones no longer stuck out. But one did not look at one's wife's shoulders when one could turn from them to a fairness of velvet and ivory. "You know," he said, approaching them, "I find all this very amazing. I have been looking out of my window on to the gardens."

"It is Betty who has done it all," said Rosy.

"I did not suspect you of doing it, my dear Rosalie," smiling. "When I saw Betty standing in the avenue, I knew at once that it was she who had mended the chimney-pots in the village and rehung the gates."

For the present, at least, it was evident that he meant to be sufficiently amiable. At the dinner table he was conversational and asked many questions, professing a natural interest in what had been done. It was not difficult to talk to a girl whose eyes and shoulders combined themselves with a quick wit and a power to attract which he reluctantly owned he had never seen equalled. His reluctance arose from the fact that such a power complicated matters. He must be on the defensive until he knew what she was going to do, what he must do himself, and what results were probable or possible. He had spent his life in intrigue of one order or another. He enjoyed outwitting people and rather preferred to attain an end by devious paths. He began every acquaintance on the defensive. His argument was that you never knew how things would turn out, consequently, it was as well to conduct one's self at the outset with the discreet forethought of a man in the presence of an enemy. He did not know how things would turn out in Betty's case, and it was a little confusing to find one's self watching her with a sense of excitement. He would have preferred to be cool—to be cold—and he realised that he could not keep his eyes off her.

"I remember, with regret," he said to her later in the evening, "that when you were a child we were enemies."

"I am afraid we were," was Betty's impartial answer.

"I am sure it was my fault," he said. "Pray forget it. Since you have accomplished such wonders, will you not, in the morning, take me about the place and explain to me how it has been done?"

When Betty went to her room she dismissed her maid as soon as possible, and sat for some time alone and waiting. She had had no opportunity to speak to Rosy in private, and she was sure she would come to her. In the course of half an hour she heard a knock at the door.

Yes, it was Rosy, and her newly-born colour had fled and left her looking dragged again. She came forward and dropped into a low chair near Betty, letting her face fall into her hands.

"I'm very sorry, Betty," she half whispered, "but it is no use."

"What is no use?" Betty asked.

"Nothing is any use. All these years have made me such a coward. I suppose I always was a coward, but in the old days there never was anything to be afraid of."

"What are you most afraid of now?"

"I don't know. That is the worst. I am afraid of HIM—just of himself—of the look in his eyes—of what he may be planning quietly. My strength dies away when he comes near me."

"What has he said to you?" she asked.

"He came into my dressing-room and sat and talked. He looked about from one thing to another and pretended to admire it all and congratulated me. But though he did not sneer at what he saw, his eyes were sneering at me. He talked about you. He said that you were a very clever woman. I don't know how he manages to imply that a very clever woman is something cunning and debased—but it means that when he says it. It seems to insinuate things which make one grow hot all over."

She put out a hand and caught one of Betty's.

"Betty, Betty," she implored. "Don't make him angry. Don't."

"I am not going to begin by making him angry," Betty said. "And I do not think he will try to make me angry—at first."

"No, he will not," cried Rosalie. "And—and you remember what I told you when first we talked about him?"

"And do you remember," was Betty's answer, "what I said to you when I first met you in the park? If we were to cable to New York this moment, we could receive an answer in a few hours."

"He would not let us do it," said Rosy. "He would stop us in some way—as he stopped my letters to mother—as he stopped me when I tried to run away. Oh, Betty, I know him and you do not."

"I shall know him better every day. That is what I must do. I must learn to know him. He said something more to you than you have told me, Rosy. What was it?"

"He waited until Detcham left me," Lady Anstruthers confessed, more than half reluctantly. "And then he got up to go away, and stood with his hands resting on the chairback, and spoke to me in a low, queer voice. He said, 'Don't try to play any tricks on me, my good girl—and don't let your sister try to play any. You would both have reason to regret it.'"

She was a half-hypnotised thing, and Betty, watching her with curious but tender eyes, recognised the abnormality.

"Ah, if I am a clever woman," she said, "he is a clever man. He is beginning to see that his power is slipping away. That was what G. Selden would call 'bluff.'"

CHAPTER XXXI

NO, SHE WOULD NOT

Sir Nigel did not invite Rosalie to accompany them, when the next morning, after breakfast, he reminded Betty of his suggestion of the night before, that she should walk over the place with him, and show him what had been done. He preferred to make his study of his sister-in-law undisturbed.

There was no detail whose significance he missed as they went about together. He had keen eyes and was a quite sufficiently practical person on such matters as concerned his own interests. In this case it was to his interest to make up his mind as to what he might gain or lose by the appearance of his wife's family. He did not mean to lose—if it could be helped—anything either of personal importance or material benefit. And it could only be helped by his comprehending clearly what he had to deal with. Betty was, at present, the chief factor in the situation, and he was sufficiently astute to see that she might not be easy to read. His personal theories concerning women presented to him two or three effective ways of managing them. You made love to them, you flattered them either subtly or grossly, you roughly or smoothly bullied them, or you harrowed them with haughty indifference—if your love-making had produced its proper effect—when it was necessary to lure or drive or trick them into submission. Women should be made useful in one way or another. Little fool as she was, Rosalie had been useful. He had, after all was said and done, had some comparatively easy years as the result of her existence. But she had not been useful enough, and there had even been moments when he had wondered if he had made a mistake in separating her entirely from her family. There might have been more to be gained if he had allowed them to visit her and had played the part of a devoted husband in their presence. A great bore, of course, but they could not have spent their entire lives at Stornham. Twelve years ago, however, he had known very little of Americans, and he had lost his temper. He was really very fond of his temper, and rather enjoyed referring to it with tolerant regret as being a bad one and beyond his control—with a manner which suggested that the attribute was the inevitable result of strength of character and masculine spirit. The luxury of giving way to it was a great one, and it was exasperating as he walked about with this handsome girl to find himself beginning to suspect that, where she was concerned, some self-control might be necessary. He was led to this thought because the things he took in on all sides could only have been achieved by a person whose mind was a steadily-balanced thing. In one's treatment of such a creature, methods must be well chosen. The crudest had sufficed to overwhelm Rosalie. He tried two or three little things as experiments during their walk.

The first was to touch with dignified pathos on the subject of Ughtred. Betty, he intimated gently, could imagine what a man's grief and disappointment might be on finding his son and heir deformed in such a manner. The delicate reserve with which he managed to convey his fear that Rosalie's own uncontrolled hysteric attacks had been the cause of the misfortune was very well done. She had, of course, been very young and much spoiled, and had not learned self-restraint, poor girl.

It was at this point that Betty first realised a certain hideous thing. She must actually remain silent—there would be at the outset many times when she could only protect her sister by refraining from either denial or argument. If she turned upon him now with refutation, it was Rosy who would be called upon to bear the consequences. He would go at once to Rosy, and she herself would have done what she had said she would not do—she would have brought trouble upon the poor girl before she was strong enough to bear it. She suspected also that his intention was to discover how much she had heard, and if she might be goaded into betraying her attitude in the matter.

But she was not to be so goaded. He watched her closely and her very colour itself seemed to be under her own control. He had expected—if she had heard hysteric, garbled stories from his wife—to see a flame of scarlet leap up on the cheek he was admiring. There was no such leap, which was baffling in itself. Could it be that experience had taught Rosalie the discretion of keeping her mouth shut?

"I am very fond of Ughtred," was the sole comment he was granted. "We made friends from the first. As he grows older and stronger, his misfortune may be less apparent. He will be a very clever man."

"He will be a very clever man if he is at all like——" He checked himself with a slight movement of his shoulders. "I was going to say a thing utterly banal. I beg your pardon. I forgot for the moment that I was not talking to an English girl."

It was so stupid that she turned and looked at him, smiling faintly. But her answer was quite mild and soft.

"Do not deprive me of compliments because I am a mere American," she said. "I am very fond of them, and respond at once."

"You are very daring," he said, looking straight into her eyes—"deliciously so. American women always are, I think."

"The young devil," he was saying internally. "The beautiful young devil! She throws one off the track."

He found himself more and more attracted and exasperated as they made their rounds. It was his sense of being attracted which was the cause of his exasperation. A girl who could stir one like this would be a dangerous enemy. Even as a friend she would not be safe, because one faced the absurd peril of losing one's head a little and forgetting the precautions one should never lose sight of where a woman was concerned—the precautions which provided for one's holding a good taut rein in one's own hands.

They went from gardens to greenhouses, from greenhouses to stables, and he was on the watch for the moment when she would reveal some little feminine pose or vanity, but, this morning, at least, she laid none bare. She did not strike him as a being of angelic perfections, but she was very modern and not likely to show easily any openings in her armour.

"Of course, I continue to be amazed," he commented, "though one ought not to be amazed at anything which evolves from your extraordinary country. In spite of your impersonal air, I shall persist in regarding you as my benefactor. But, to be frank, I always told Rosalie that if she would write to your father he would certainly put things in order."

"She did write once, you will remember," answered Betty.

"Did she?" with courteous vagueness. "Really, I am afraid I did not hear of it. My poor wife has her own little ideas about the disposal of her income."

And Betty knew that she was expected to believe that Rosy had hoarded the money sent to restore the place, and from sheer weak miserliness had allowed her son's heritage to fall to ruin. And but for Rosy's sake, she might have stopped upon the path and, looking at him squarely, have said, "You are lying to me. And I know the truth."

He continued to converse amiably.

"Of course, it is you one must thank, not only for rousing in the poor girl some interest in her personal appearance, but also some interest in her neighbours. Some women, after they marry and pass girlhood, seem to release their hold on all desire to attract or retain friends. For years Rosalie has given herself up to a chronic semi-invalidism. When the mistress of a house is always depressed and languid and does not return visits, neighbours become discouraged and drop off, as it were."

If his wife had told stories to gain her sympathy his companion would be sure to lose her temper and show her hand. If he could make her openly lose her temper, he would have made an advance.

"One can quite understand that," she said. "It is a great happiness to me to see Rosy gaining ground every day. She has taken me out with her a good many times, and people are beginning to realise that she likes to see them at Stornham."

"You are very delightful," he said, "with your 'She has taken me out.' When I glanced at the magnificent array of cards on the salver in the hall, I realised a number of things, and quite vulgarly lost my breath. The Dunholms have been very amiable in recalling our existence. But charming Americans—of your order—arouse amiable emotions."

"I am very amiable myself," said Betty.

It was he who flushed now. He was losing patience at feeling himself held with such lightness at arm's length, and at being, in spite of himself, somehow compelled to continue to assume a jocular courtesy.

"No, you are not," he answered.

"Not?" repeated Betty, with an incredulous lifting of her brows.

"You are charming and clever, but I rather suspect you of being a vixen. At all events you are a spirited young woman and quick-witted enough to understand the attraction you must have for the sordid herd."

And then he became aware—if not of an opening in her armour—at least of a joint in it. For he saw, near her ear, a deepening warmth. That was it. She was quick-witted, and she hid somewhere a hot pride.

"I confess, however," he proceeded cheerfully, "that notwithstanding my own experience of the habits of the sordid herd, I saw one card I was surprised to find, though really"—shrugging his shoulders—"I ought to have been less surprised to find it than to find any other. But it was bold. I suppose the fellow is desperate."

"You are speaking of——?" suggested Betty.

"Of Mount Dunstan. Hang it all, it WAS bold!" As if in half-amused disgust.

As she had walked through the garden paths, Betty had at intervals bent and gathered a flower, until she held in one hand a loose, fair sheaf. At this moment she stooped to break off a spire of pale blue campanula. And she was—as with a shock—struck with a consciousness that she bent because she must—because to do so was a refuge—a concealment of something she must hide. It had come upon her without a second's warning. Sir Nigel was right. She was a vixen—a virago. She was in such a rage that her heart sprang up and down and her cheek and eyes were on fire. Her long-trained control of herself was gone. And her shock was a lightning-swift awakening to the fact that she felt all this—she must hide her face—because it was this one man—just this one and no other—who was being dragged into this thing with insult.

It was an awakening, and she broke off, rather slowly, one—two—three—even four campanula stems before she stood upright again.

As for Nigel Anstruthers—he went on talking in his low-pitched, disgusted voice.

"Surely he might count himself out of the running. There will be a good deal of running, my dear Betty. You fair Americans have learned that by this time. But that a man who has not even a decent name to offer—who is blackballed by his county—should coolly present himself as a pretendant is an insolence he should be kicked for."

Betty arranged her campanulas carefully. There was no exterior reason why she should draw sword in Lord Mount Dunstan's defence. He had certainly not seemed to expect anything intimately interested from her. His manner she had generally felt to be rather restrained. But one could, in a measure, express one's self.

"Whatsoever the 'running,'" she remarked, "no pretendant has complimented me by presenting himself, so far—and Lord Mount Dunstan is physically an unusually strong man."

"You mean it would be difficult to kick him? Is this partisanship? I hope not. Am I to understand," he added with deliberation, "that Rosalie has received him here?"

"Yes."

"And that you have received him, also—as you have received Lord Westholt?"

"Quite."

"Then I must discuss the matter with Rosalie. It is not to be discussed with you."

"You mean that you will exercise your authority in the matter?"

"In England, my dear girl, the master of a house is still sometimes guilty of exercising authority in matters which concern the reputation of his female relatives. In the absence of your father, I shall not allow you, while you are under my roof, to endanger your name in any degree. I am, at least, your brother by marriage. I intend to protect you."

"Thank you," said Betty.

"You are young and extremely handsome, you will have an enormous fortune, and you have evidently had your own way all your life. A girl, such as you are, may either make a magnificent marriage or a ridiculous and humiliating one. Neither American young women, nor English young men, are as disinterested as they were some years ago. Each has begun to learn what the other has to give."

"I think that is true," commented Betty.

"In some cases there is a good deal to be exchanged on both sides. You have a great deal to give, and should get exchange worth accepting. A beggared estate and a tainted title are not good enough."

"That is businesslike," Betty made comment again.

Sir Nigel laughed quietly.

"The fact is—I hope you won't misunderstand my saying it—you do not strike me as being UN-businesslike, yourself."

"I am not," answered Betty.

"I thought not," rather narrowing his eyes as he watched her, because he believed that she must involuntarily show her hand if he irritated her sufficiently. "You do not impress me as being one of the girls who make unsuccessful marriages. You are a modern New York beauty—not an early Victorian sentimentalist." He did not despair of results from his process of irritation. To gently but steadily convey to a beautiful and spirited young creature that no man could approach her without ulterior motive was rather a good idea. If one could make it clear—with a casual air of sensibly taking it for granted—that the natural power of youth, wit, and beauty were rendered impotent by a greatness of fortune whose proportions obliterated all else; if one simply argued from the premise that young love was no affair of hers, since she must always be regarded as a gilded chattel, whose cost was writ large in plain figures, what girl, with blood in her veins, could endure it long without wincing? This girl had undue, and, as he regarded such matters, unseemly control over her temper and her nerves, but she had blood enough in her veins, and presently she would say or do something which would give him a lead.

"When you marry——" he began.

She lifted her head delicately, but ended the sentence for him with eyes which were actually not unsmiling.

"When I marry, I shall ask something in exchange for what I have to give."

"If the exchange is to be equal, you must ask a great deal," he answered. "That is why you must be protected from such fellows as Mount Dunstan."

"If it becomes necessary, perhaps I shall be able to protect myself," she said.

"Ah!" regretfully, "I am afraid I have annoyed you—and that you need protection more than you suspect." If she were flesh and blood, she could scarcely resist resenting the implication contained in this. But resist it she did, and with a cool little smile which stirred him to sudden, if irritated, admiration.

She paused a second, and used the touch of gentle regret herself.

"You have wounded my vanity by intimating that my admirers do not love me for myself alone."

He paused, also, and, narrowing his eyes again, looked straight between her lashes.

"They ought to love you for yourself alone," he said, in a low voice. "You are a deucedly attractive girl."

"Oh, Betty," Rosy had pleaded, "don't make him angry—don't make him angry."

So Betty lifted her shoulders slightly without comment.

"Shall we go back to the house now?" she said. "Rosalie will naturally be anxious to hear that what has been done in your absence has met with your approval."

In what manner his approval was expressed to Rosalie, Betty did not hear this morning, at least. Externally cool though she had appeared, the process had not been without its results, and she felt that she would prefer to be alone.

"I must write some letters to catch the next steamer," she said, as she went upstairs.

When she entered her room, she went to her writing table and sat down, with pen and paper before her. She drew the paper towards her and took up the pen, but the next moment she laid it down and gave a slight push to the paper. As she did so she realised that her hand trembled.

"I must not let myself form the habit of falling into rages—or I shall not be able to keep still some day, when I ought to do it," she whispered. "I am in a fury—a fury." And for a moment she covered her face.

She was a strong girl, but a girl, notwithstanding her powers. What she suddenly saw was that, as if by one movement of some powerful unseen hand, Rosy, who had been the centre of all things, had been swept out of her thought. Her anger at the injustice done to Rosy had been as nothing before the fire which had flamed in her at the insult flung at the other. And all that was undue and unbalanced. One might as well look the thing straightly in the face. Her old child hatred of Nigel Anstruthers had sprung up again in ten-fold strength. There was, it was true, something abominable about him, something which made his words more abominable than they would have been if another man had uttered them—but, though it was inevitable that his method should rouse one, where those of one's own blood were concerned, it was not enough to fill one with raging flame when his malignity was dealing with those who were almost strangers. Mount Dunstan was almost a stranger—she had met Lord Westholt oftener. Would she have felt the same hot beat of the blood, if Lord Westholt had been concerned? No, she answered herself frankly, she would not.

CHAPTER XXXII

A GREAT BALL

A certain great ball, given yearly at Dunholm Castle, was one of the most notable social features of the county. It took place when the house was full of its most interestingly distinguished guests, and, though other balls might be given at other times, this one was marked by a degree of greater state. On several occasions the chief guests had been great personages indeed, and to be bidden to meet them implied a selection flattering in itself. One's invitation must convey by inference that one was either brilliant, beautiful, or admirable, if not important.

Nigel Anstruthers had never appeared at what the uninvited were wont, with derisive smiles, to call The Great Panjandrum Function—which was an ironic designation not employed by such persons as received cards bidding them to the festivity. Stornham Court was not popular in the county; no one had yearned for the society of the Dowager Lady Anstruthers, even in her youth; and a not too well-favoured young man with an ill-favoured temper, noticeably on the lookout for grievances, is not an addition to one's circle. At nineteen Nigel had discovered the older Lord Mount Dunstan and his son Tenham to be congenial acquaintances, and had been so often absent from home that his neighbours would have found social intercourse with him difficult, even if desirable. Accordingly, when the county paper recorded the splendours of The Great Panjandrum Function—which it by no means mentioned by that name—the list of "Among those present" had not so far contained the name of Sir Nigel Anstruthers.

So, on a morning a few days after his return, the master of Stornham turned over a card of invitation and read it several times before speaking.

"I suppose you know what this means," he said at last to Rosalie, who was alone with him.

"It means that we are invited to Dunholm Castle for the ball, doesn't it?"

Her husband tossed the card aside on the table.

"It means that Betty will be invited to every house where there is a son who must be disposed of profitably.

"She is invited because she is beautiful and clever. She would be invited if she had no money at all," said Rosy daringly. She was actually growing daring, she thought sometimes. It would not have been possible to say anything like this a few months ago.

"Don't make silly mistakes," said Nigel. "There are a good many handsome girls who receive comparatively little attention. But the hounds of war are let loose, when one of your swollen American fortunes appears. The obviousness of it 'virtuously' makes me sick. It's as vulgar—as New York."

What befel next brought to Sir Nigel a shock of curious enlightenment, but no one was more amazed than Rosy herself. She felt, when she heard her own voice, as if she must be rather mad.

"I would rather," she said quite distinctly, "that you did not speak to me of New York in that way."

"What!" said Anstruthers, staring at her with contempt which was derision.

"It is my home," she answered. "It is not proper that I should hear it spoken of slightingly."

"Your home! It has not taken the slightest notice of you for twelve years. Your people dropped you as if you were a hot potato."

"They have taken me up again." Still in amazement at her own boldness, but somehow learning something as she went on.

He walked over to her side, and stood before her.

"Look here, Rosalie," he said. "You have been taking lessons from your sister. She is a beauty and young and you are not. People will stand things from her they will not take from you. I would stand some things myself, because it rather amuses a man to see a fine girl peacocking. It's merely ridiculous in you, and I won't stand it—not a bit of it."

It was not specially fortunate for him that the door opened as he was speaking, and Betty came in with her own invitation in her hand. He was quick enough, however, to turn to greet her with a shrug of his shoulders.

"I am being favoured with a little scene by my wife," he explained. "She is capable of getting up excellent little scenes, but I daresay she does not show you that side of her temper."

Betty took a comfortable chintz-covered, easy chair. Her expression was evasively speculative.

"Was it a scene I interrupted?" she said. "Then I must not go away and leave you to finish it. You were saying that you would not 'stand' something. What does a man do when he will not 'stand' a thing? It always sounds so final and appalling—as if he were threatening horrible things such as, perhaps, were a resource in feudal times. What IS the resource in these dull days of law and order—and policemen?"

"Is this American chaff?" he was disagreeably conscious that he was not wholly successful in his effort to be lofty.

The frankness of Betty's smile was quite without prejudice.

"Dear me, no," she said. "It is only the unpicturesque result of an unfeminine knowledge of the law. And I was thinking how one is limited—and yet how things are simplified after all."

"Simplified!" disgustedly.

"Yes, really. You see, if Rosy were violent she could not beat you—even if she were strong enough—because you could ring the bell and give her into custody. And you could not beat her because the same unpleasant thing would happen to you. Policemen do rob things of colour, don't they? And besides, when one remembers that mere vulgar law insists that no one can be forced to live with another person who is brutal or loathsome, that's simple, isn't it? You could go away from Rosy," with sweet clearness, "at any moment you wished—as far away as you liked."

"You seem to forget," still feeling that convincing loftiness was not easy, "that when a man leaves his wife, or she deserts him, it is she who is likely to be called upon to bear the onus of public opinion."

"Would she be called upon to bear it under all circumstances?"

"Damned clever woman as you are, you know that she would, as well as I know it." He made an abrupt gesture with his hand. "You know that what I say is true. Women who take to their heels are deucedly unpopular in England."

"I have not been long in England, but I have been struck by the prevalence of a sort of constitutional British sense of fair play among the people who really count. The Dunholms, for instance, have it markedly. In America it is the men who force women to take to their heels who are deucedly unpopular. The Americans' sense of fair play is their most English quality. It was brought over in ships by the first colonists—like the pieces of fine solid old furniture, one even now sees, here and there, in houses in Virginia."

"But the fact remains," said Nigel, with an unpleasant laugh, "the fact remains, my dear girl."

"The fact that does remain," said Betty, not unpleasantly at all, and still with her gentle air of mere unprejudiced speculation, "is that, if a man or woman is properly ill-treated—PROPERLY—not in any amateurish way—they reach the point of not caring in the least—nothing matters, but that they must get away from the horror of the unbearable thing —never to see or hear of it again is heaven enough to make anything else a thing to smile at. But one could settle the other point by experimenting. Suppose you run away from Rosy, and then we can see if she is cut by the county."

His laugh was unpleasant again.

"So long as you are with her, she will not be cut. There are a number of penniless young men of family in this, as well as the adjoining, counties. Do you think Mount Dunstan would cut her?"

She looked down at the carpet thoughtfully a moment, and then lifted her eyes.

"I do not think so," she answered. "But I will ask him."

He was startled by a sudden feeling that she might be capable of it.

"Oh, come now," he said, "that goes beyond a joke. You will not do any such absurd thing. One does not want one's domestic difficulties discussed by one's neighbours."

Betty opened coolly surprised eyes.

"I did not understand it was a personal matter," she remarked. "Where do the domestic difficulties come in?"

He stared at her a few seconds with the look she did not like, which was less likeable at the moment, because it combined itself with other things.

"Hang it," he muttered. "I wish I could keep my temper as you can keep yours," and he turned on his heel and left the room.

Rosy had not spoken. She had sat with her hands in her lap, looking out of the window. She had at first had a moment of terror. She had, indeed, once uttered in her soul the abject cry: "Don't make him angry, Betty—oh, don't, don't!" And suddenly it had been stilled, and she had listened. This was because she realised that Nigel himself was listening. That made her see what she had not dared to allow herself to see before. These trite things were true. There were laws to protect one. If Betty had not been dealing with mere truths, Nigel would have stopped her. He had been supercilious, but he could not contradict her.

"Betty," she said, when her sister came to her, "you said that to show ME things, as well as to show them to him. I knew you did, and listened to every word. It was good for me to hear you."

"Clear-cut, unadorned facts are like bullets," said Betty. "They reach home, if one's aim is good. The shiftiest people cannot evade them."

. . . . .

A certain thing became evident to Betty during the time which elapsed between the arrival of the invitations and the great ball. Despite an obvious intention to assume an amiable pose for the time being, Sir Nigel could not conceal a not quite unexplainable antipathy to one individual. This individual was Mount Dunstan, whom it did not seem easy for him to leave alone. He seemed to recur to him as a subject, without any special reason, and this somewhat puzzled Betty until she heard from Rosalie of his intimacy with Lord Tenham, which, in a measure, explained it. The whole truth was that "The Lout," as he had been called, had indulged in frank speech in his rare intercourse with his brother and his friends, and had once interfered with hot young fury in a matter in which the pair had specially wished to avoid all interference. His open scorn of their methods of entertaining themselves they had felt to be disgusting impudence, which would have been deservedly punished with a horsewhip, if the youngster had not been a big-muscled, clumsy oaf, with a dangerous eye. Upon this footing their acquaintance had stood in past years, and to decide—as Sir Nigel had decided—that the oaf in question had begun to make his bid for splendid fortune under the roof of Stornham Court itself was a thing not to be regarded calmly. It was more than he could stand, and the folly of temper, which was forever his undoing, betrayed him into mistakes more than once. This girl, with her beauty and her wealth, he chose to regard as a sort of property rightfully his own. She was his sister-in-law, at least; she was living under his roof; he had more or less the power to encourage or discourage such aspirants as appeared. Upon the whole there was something soothing to one's vanity in appearing before the world as the person at present responsible for her. It gave a man a certain dignity of position, and his chief girding at fate had always risen from the fact that he had not had dignity of position. He would not be held cheap in this matter, at least. But sometimes, as he looked at the girl he turned hot and sick, as it was driven home to him that he was no longer young, that he had never been good-looking, and that he had cut the ground from under his feet twelve years ago, when he had married Rosalie! If he could have waited—if he could have done several other things—perhaps the clever acting of a part, and his power of domination might have given him a chance. Even that blackguard of a Mount Dunstan had a better one now. He was young, at least, and free—and a big strong beast. He was forced, with bitter reluctance, to admit that he himself was not even particularly strong—of late he had felt it hideously.

So he detested Mount Dunstan the more for increasing reasons, as he thought the matter over. It would seem, perhaps, but a subtle pleasure to the normal mind, but to him there was pleasure—support—aggrandisement—in referring to the ill case of the Mount Dunstan estate, in relating illustrative anecdotes, in dwelling upon the hopelessness of the outlook, and the notable unpopularity of the man himself. A confiding young lady from the States was required, he said on one occasion, but it would be necessary that she should be a young person of much simplicity, who would not be alarmed or chilled by the obvious. No one would realise this more clearly than Mount Dunstan himself. He said it coldly and casually, as if it were the simplest matter of fact. If the fellow had been making himself agreeable to Betty, it was as well that certain points should be—as it were inadvertently—brought before her.

Miss Vanderpoel was really rather fine, people said to each other afterwards, when she entered the ballroom at Dunholm Castle with her brother-in-law. She bore herself as composedly as if she had been escorted by the most admirable and dignified of conservative relatives, instead of by a man who was more definitely disliked and disapproved of than any other man in the county whom decent people were likely to meet. Yet, she was far too clever a girl not to realise the situation clearly, they said to each other. She had arrived in England to find her sister a neglected wreck, her fortune squandered, and her existence stripped bare of even such things as one felt to be the mere decencies. There was but one thing to be deduced from the facts which had stared her in the face. But of her deductions she had said nothing whatever, which was, of course, remarkable in a young person. It may be mentioned that, perhaps, there had been those who would not have been reluctant to hear what she must have had to say, and who had even possibly given her a delicate lead. But the lead had never been taken. One lady had even remarked that, on her part, she felt that a too great reserve verged upon secretiveness, which was not a desirable girlish quality.

Of course the situation had been so much discussed that people were naturally on the lookout for the arrival of the Stornham party, as it was known that Sir Nigel had returned home, and would be likely to present himself with his wife and sister-in-law. There was not a dowager present who did not know how and where he had reprehensibly spent the last months. It served him quite right that the Spanish dancing person had coolly left him in the lurch for a younger and more attractive, as well as a richer man. If it were not for Miss Vanderpoel, one need not pretend that one knew nothing about the affair—in fact, if it had not been for Miss Vanderpoel, he would not have received an invitation—and poor Lady Anstruthers would be sitting at home, still the forlorn little frump and invalid she had so wonderfully ceased to be since her sister had taken her in hand. She was absolutely growing even pretty and young, and her clothes were really beautiful. The whole thing was amazing.

Betty, as well as Rosalie and Nigel—knew that many people turned undisguisedly to look at them—even to watch them as they came into the splendid ballroom. It was a splendid ballroom and a stately one, and Lord Dunholm and Lord Westholt shared a certain thought when they met her, which was that hers was distinctly the proud young brilliance of presence which figured most perfectly against its background. Much as people wanted to look at Sir Nigel, their eyes were drawn from him to Miss Vanderpoel. After all it was she who made him an object of interest. One wanted to know what she would do with him—how she would "carry him off." How much did she know of the distaste people felt for him, since she would not talk or encourage talk? The Dunholms could not have invited her and her sister, and have ignored him; but did she not guess that they would have ignored him, if they could? and was there not natural embarrassment in feeling forced to appear in pomp, as it were, under his escort?

But no embarrassment was perceptible. Her manner committed her to no recognition of a shadow of a flaw in the character of her companion. It even carried a certain conviction with it, and the lookers-on felt the impossibility of suggesting any such flaw by their own manner. For this evening, at least, the man must actually be treated as if he were an entirely unobjectionable person. It appeared as if that was what the girl wanted, and intended should happen.

This was what Nigel himself had begun to perceive, but he did not put it pleasantly. Deucedly clever girl as she was, he said to himself, she saw that it would be more agreeable to have no nonsense talked, and no ruffling of tempers. He had always been able to convey to people that the ruffling of his temper was a thing to be avoided, and perhaps she had already been sharp enough to realise this was a fact to be counted with. She was sharp enough, he said to himself, to see anything.

The function was a superb one. The house was superb, the rooms of entertainment were in every proportion perfect, and were quite renowned for the beauty of the space they offered; the people themselves were, through centuries of dignified living, so placed that intercourse with their kind was an easy and delightful thing. They need never doubt either their own effect, or the effect of their hospitalities. Sir Nigel saw about him all the people who held enviable place in the county. Some of them he had never known, some of them had long ceased to recall his existence. There were those among them who lifted lorgnettes or stuck monocles into their eyes as he passed, asking each other in politely subdued tones who the man was who seemed to be in attendance on Miss Vanderpoel. Nigel knew this and girded at it internally, while he made the most of his suave smile.

The distinguished personage who was the chief guest was to be seen at the upper end of the room talking to a tall man with broad shoulders, who was plainly interesting him for the moment. As the Stornham party passed on, this person, making his bow, retired, and, as he turned towards them, Sir Nigel recognising him, the agreeable smile was for the moment lost.

"How in the name of Heaven did Mount Dunstan come here?" broke from him with involuntary heat.

"Would it be rash to conclude," said Betty, as she returned the bow of a very grand old lady in black velvet and an imposing tiara, "that he came in response to invitation?"

The very grand old lady seemed pleased to see her, and, with a royal little sign, called her to her side. As Betty Vanderpoel was a great success with the Mrs. Weldens and old Dobys of village life, she was also a success among grand old ladies. When she stood before them there was a delicate submission in her air which was suggestive of obedience to the dignity of their years and state. Strongly conservative and rather feudal old persons were much pleased by this. In the present irreverent iconoclasm of modern times, it was most agreeable to talk to a handsome creature who was as beautifully attentive as if she had been a specially perfect young lady-in-waiting.

This one even patted Betty's hand a little, when she took it. She was a great county potentate, who was known as Lady Alanby of Dole—her house being one of the most ancient and interesting in England.

"I am glad to see you here to-night," she said. "You are looking very nice. But you cannot help that."

Betty asked permission to present her sister and brother-in-law. Lady Alanby was polite to both of them, but she gave Nigel a rather sharp glance through her gold pince-nez as she greeted him.

"Janey and Mary," she said to the two girls nearest her, "I daresay you will kindly change your chairs and let Lady Anstruthers and Miss Vanderpoel sit next to me."

The Ladies Jane and Mary Lithcom, who had been ordered about by her from their infancy, obeyed with polite smiles. They were not particularly pretty girls, and were of the indigent noble. Jane, who had almost overlarge blue eyes, sighed as she reseated herself a few chairs lower down.

"It does seem beastly unfair," she said in a low voice to her sister, "that a girl such as that should be so awfully good-looking. She ought to have a turned-up nose."

"Thank you," said Mary, "I have a turned-up nose myself, and I've got nothing to balance it."

"Oh, I didn't mean a nice turned-up nose like yours," said Jane; "I meant an ugly one. Of course Lady Alanby wants her for Tommy." And her manner was not resigned.

"What she, or anyone else for that matter," disdainfully, "could want with Tommy, I don't know," replied Mary.

"I do," answered Jane obstinately. "I played cricket with him when I was eight, and I've liked him ever since. It is AWFUL," in a smothered outburst, "what girls like us have to suffer."

Lady Mary turned to look at her curiously.

"Jane," she said, "are you SUFFERING about Tommy?"

"Yes, I am. Oh, what a question to ask in a ballroom! Do you want me to burst out crying?"

"No," sharply, "look at the Prince. Stare at that fat woman curtsying to him. Stare and then wink your eyes."

Lady Alanby was talking about Mount Dunstan.

"Lord Dunholm has given us a lead. He is an old friend of mine, and he has been talking to me about it. It appears that he has been looking into things seriously. Modern as he is, he rather tilts at injustices, in a quiet way. He has satisfactorily convinced himself that Lord Mount Dunstan has been suffering for the sins of the fathers—which must be annoying."

"Is Lord Dunholm quite sure of that?" put in Sir Nigel, with a suggestively civil air.

Old Lady Alanby gave him an unencouraging look.

"Quite," she said. "He would be likely to be before he took any steps."

"Ah," remarked Nigel. "I knew Lord Tenham, you see."

Lady Alanby's look was more unencouraging still. She quietly and openly put up her glass and stared. There were times when she had not the remotest objection to being rude to certain people.

"I am sorry to hear that," she observed. "There never was any room for mistake about Tenham. He is not usually mentioned."

"I do not think this man would be usually mentioned, if everything were known," said Nigel.

Then an appalling thing happened. Lady Alanby gazed at him a few seconds, and made no reply whatever. She dropped her glass, and turned again to talk to Betty. It was as if she had turned her back on him, and Sir Nigel, still wearing an amiable exterior, used internally some bad language.

"But I was a fool to speak of Tenham," he thought. "A great fool."

A little later Miss Vanderpoel made her curtsy to the exalted guest, and was commented upon again by those who looked on. It was not at all unnatural that one should find ones eyes following a girl who, representing a sort of royal power, should have the good fortune of possessing such looks and bearing.

Remembering his child bete noir of the long legs and square, audacious little face, Nigel Anstruthers found himself restraining a slight grin as he looked on at her dancing. Partners flocked about her like bees, and Lady Alanby of Dole, and other very grand old or middle-aged ladies all found the evening more interesting because they could watch her.

"She is full of spirit," said Lady Alanby, "and she enjoys herself as a girl should. It is a pleasure to look at her. I like a girl who gets a magnificent colour and stars in her eyes when she dances. It looks healthy and young."

It was Tommy Miss Vanderpoel was dancing with when her ladyship said this. Tommy was her grandson and a young man of greater rank than fortune. He was a nice, frank, heavy youth, who loved a simple county life spent in tramping about with guns, and in friendly hobnobbing with the neighbours, and eating great afternoon teas with people whose jokes were easy to understand, and who were ready to laugh if you tried a joke yourself. He liked girls, and especially he liked Jane Lithcom, but that was a weakness his grandmother did not at all encourage, and, as he danced with Betty Vanderpoel, he looked over her shoulder more than once at a pair of big, unhappy blue eyes, whose owner sat against the wall.

Betty Vanderpoel herself was not thinking of Tommy. In fact, during this brilliant evening she faced still further developments of her own strange case. Certain new things were happening to her. When she had entered the ballroom she had known at once who the man was who stood before the royal guest—she had known before he bowed low and withdrew. And her recognition had brought with it a shock of joy. For a few moments her throat felt hot and pulsing. It was true—the things which concerned him concerned her. All that happened to him suddenly became her affair, as if in some way they were of the same blood. Nigel's slighting of him had infuriated her; that Lord Dunholm had offered him friendship and hospitality was a thing which seemed done to herself, and filled her with gratitude and affection; that he should be at this place, on this special occasion, swept away dark things from his path. It was as if it were stated without words that a conservative man of the world, who knew things as they were, having means of reaching truths, vouched for him and placed his dignity and firmness at his side.

And there was the gladness at the sight of him. It was an overpoweringly strong thing. She had never known anything like it. She had not seen him since Nigel's return, and here he was, and she knew that her life quickened in her because they were together in the same room. He had come to them and said a few courteous words, but he had soon gone away. At first she wondered if it was because of Nigel, who at the time was making himself rather ostentatiously amiable to her. Afterwards she saw him dancing, talking, being presented to people, being, with a tactful easiness, taken care of by his host and hostess, and Lord Westholt. She was struck by the graceful magic with which this tactful ease surrounded him without any obviousness. The Dunholms had given a lead, as Lady Alanby had said, and the rest were following it and ignoring intervals with reposeful readiness. It was wonderfully well done. Apparently there had been no past at all. All began with this large young man, who, despite his Viking type, really looked particularly well in evening dress. Lady Alanby held him by her chair for some time, openly enjoying her talk with him, and calling up Tommy, that they might make friends.

After a while, Betty said to herself, he would come and ask for a dance. But he did not come, and she danced with one man after another. Westholt came to her several times and had more dances than one. Why did the other not come? Several times they whirled past each other, and when it occurred they looked—both feeling it an accident—into each other's eyes.

The strong and strange thing—that which moves on its way as do birth and death, and the rising and setting of the sun—had begun to move in them. It was no new and rare thing, but an ancient and common one—as common and ancient as death and birth themselves; and part of the law as they are. As it comes to royal persons to whom one makes obeisance at their mere passing by, as it comes to scullery maids in royal kitchens, and grooms in royal stables, as it comes to ladies-in-waiting and the women who serve them, so it had come to these two who had been drawn near to each other from the opposite sides of the earth, and each started at the touch of it, and withdrew a pace in bewilderment, and some fear.

"I wish," Mount Dunstan was feeling throughout the evening, "that her eyes had some fault in their expression—that they drew one less—that they drew ME less. I am losing my head."

"It would be better," Betty thought, "if I did not wish so much that he would come and ask me to dance with him—that he would not keep away so. He is keeping away for a reason. Why is he doing it?"

The music swung on in lovely measures, and the dancers swung with it. Sir Nigel walked dutifully through the Lancers once with his wife, and once with his beautiful sister-in-law. Lady Anstruthers, in her new bloom, had not lacked partners, who discovered that she was a childishly light creature who danced extremely well. Everyone was kind to her, and the very grand old ladies, who admired Betty, were absolutely benign in their manner. Betty's partners paid ingenuous court to her, and Sir Nigel found he had not been mistaken in his estimate of the dignity his position of escort and male relation gave to him.

Rosy, standing for a moment looking out on the brilliancy and state about her, meeting Betty's eyes, laughed quiveringly.

"I am in a dream," she said.

"You have awakened from a dream," Betty answered.

From the opposite side of the room someone was coming towards them, and, seeing him, Rosy smiled in welcome.

"I am sure Lord Mount Dunstan is coming to ask you to dance with him," she said. "Why have you not danced with him before, Betty?"

"He has not asked me," Betty answered. "That is the only reason."

"Lord Dunholm and Lord Westholt called at the Mount a few days after they met him at Stornham," Rosalie explained in an undertone. "They wanted to know him. Then it seems they found they liked each other. Lady Dunholm has been telling me about it. She says Lord Dunholm thanks you, because you said something illuminating. That was the word she used—'illuminating.' I believe you are always illuminating, Betty."

Mount Dunstan was certainly coming to them. How broad his shoulders looked in his close-fitting black coat, how well built his whole strong body was, and how steadily he held his eyes! Here and there one sees a man or woman who is, through some trick of fate, by nature a compelling thing unconsciously demanding that one should submit to some domineering attraction. One does not call it domineering, but it is so. This special creature is charged unfairly with more than his or her single share of force. Betty Vanderpoel thought this out as this "other one" came to her. He did not use the ballroom formula when he spoke to her. He said in rather a low voice:

"Will you dance with me?"

"Yes," she answered.

Lord Dunholm and his wife agreed afterwards that so noticeable a pair had never before danced together in their ballroom. Certainly no pair had ever been watched with quite the same interested curiosity. Some onlookers thought it singular that they should dance together at all, some pleased themselves by reflecting on the fact that no other two could have represented with such picturesqueness the opposite poles of fate and circumstance. No one attempted to deny that they were an extraordinarily striking-looking couple, and that one's eyes followed them in spite of one's self.

"Taken together they produce an effect that is somehow rather amazing," old Lady Alanby commented. "He is a magnificently built man, you know, and she is a magnificently built girl. Everybody should look like that. My impression would be that Adam and Eve did, but for the fact that neither of them had any particular character. That affair of the apple was so silly. Eve has always struck me as being the kind of woman who, if she lived to-day, would run up stupid bills at her dressmakers and be afraid to tell her husband. That wonderful black head of Miss Vanderpoel's looks very nice poised near Mount Dunstan's dark red one."

"I am glad to be dancing with him," Betty was thinking. "I am glad to be near him."

"Will you dance this with me to the very end," asked Mount Dunstan—"to the very late note?"

"Yes," answered Betty.

He had spoken in a low but level voice—the kind of voice whose tone places a man and woman alone together, and wholly apart from all others by whomsoever they are surrounded. There had been no preliminary speech and no explanation of the request followed. The music was a perfect thing, the brilliant, lofty ballroom, the beauty of colour and sound about them, the jewels and fair faces, the warm breath of flowers in the air, the very sense of royal presence and its accompanying state and ceremony, seemed merely a naturally arranged background for the strange consciousness each held close and silently—knowing nothing of the mind of the other.

This was what was passing through the man's mind.

"This is the thing which most men experience several times during their lives. It would be reason enough for all the great deeds and all the crimes one hears of. It is an enormous kind of anguish and a fearful kind of joy. It is scarcely to be borne, and yet, at this moment, I could kill myself and her, at the thought of losing it. If I had begun earlier, would it have been easier? No, it would not. With me it is bound to go hard. At twenty I should probably not have been able to keep myself from shouting it aloud, and I should not have known that it was only the working of the Law. 'Only!' Good God, what a fool I am! It is because it is only the Law that I cannot escape, and must go on to the end, grinding my teeth together because I cannot speak. Oh, her smooth young cheek! Oh, the deep shadows of her lashes! And while we sway round and round together, I hold her slim strong body in the hollow of my arm."

It was, quite possibly, as he thought this that Nigel Anstruthers, following him with his eyes as he passed, began to frown. He had been watching the pair as others had, he had seen what others saw, and now he had an idea that he saw something more, and it was something which did not please him. The instinct of the male bestirred itself—the curious instinct of resentment against another man—any other man. And, in this case, Mount Dunstan was not any other man, but one for whom his antipathy was personal.

"I won't have that," he said to himself. "I won't have it."

. . . . .

The music rose and swelled, and then sank into soft breathing, as they moved in harmony together, gliding and swirling as they threaded their way among other couples who swirled and glided also, some of them light and smiling, some exchanging low-toned speech—perhaps saying words which, unheard by others, touched on deep things. The exalted guest fell into momentary silence as he looked on, being a man much attracted by physical fineness and temperamental power and charm. A girl like that would bring a great deal to a man and to the country he belonged to. A great race might be founded on such superbness of physique and health and beauty. Combined with abnormal resources, certainly no more could be asked. He expressed something of the kind to Lord Dunholm, who stood near him in attendance.

To herself Betty was saying: "That was a strange thing he asked me. It is curious that we say so little. I should never know much about him. I have no intelligence where he is concerned—only a strong, stupid feeling, which is not like a feeling of my own. I am no longer Betty Vanderpoel—and I wish to go on dancing with him—on and on—to the last note, as he said."

She felt a little hot wave run over her cheek uncomfortably, and the next instant the big arm tightened its clasp of her—for just one second—not more than one. She did not know that he, himself, had seen the sudden ripple of red colour, and that the equally sudden contraction of the arm had been as unexpected to him and as involuntary as the quick wave itself. It had horrified and made him angry. He looked the next instant entirely stiff and cold.

"He did not know it happened," Betty resolved.

"The music is going to stop," said Mount Dunstan. "I know the waltz. We can get once round the room again before the final chord. It was to be the last note—the very last," but he said it quite rigidly, and Betty laughed.

"Quite the last," she answered.

The music hastened a little, and their gliding whirl became more rapid—a little faster—a little faster still—a running sweep of notes, a big, terminating harmony, and the thing was over.

"Thank you," said Mount Dunstan. "One will have it to remember." And his tone was slightly sardonic.

"Yes," Betty acquiesced politely.

"Oh, not you. Only I. I have never waltzed before."

Betty turned to look at him curiously.

"Under circumstances such as these," he explained. "I learned to dance at a particularly hideous boys' school in France. I abhorred it. And the trend of my life has made it quite easy for me to keep my twelve-year-old vow that I would never dance after I left the place, unless I WANTED to do it, and that, especially, nothing should make me waltz until certain agreeable conditions were fulfilled. Waltzing I approved of—out of hideous schools. I was a pig-headed, objectionable child. I detested myself even, then."

Betty's composure returned to her.

"I am trusting," she remarked, "that I may secretly regard myself as one of the agreeable conditions to be fulfilled. Do not dispel my hopes roughly."

"I will not," he answered. "You are, in fact, several of them."

"One breathes with much greater freedom," she responded.

This sort of cool nonsense was safe. It dispelled feelings of tenseness, and carried them to the place where Sir Nigel and Lady Anstruthers awaited them. A slight stir was beginning to be felt throughout the ballroom. The royal guest was retiring, and soon the rest began to melt away. The Anstruthers, who had a long return drive before them, were among those who went first.

When Lady Anstruthers and her sister returned from the cloak room, they found Sir Nigel standing near Mount Dunstan, who was going also, and talking to him in an amiably detached manner. Mount Dunstan, himself, did not look amiable, or seem to be saying much, but Sir Nigel showed no signs of being disturbed.

"Now that you have ceased to forswear the world," he said as his wife approached, "I hope we shall see you at Stornham. Your visits must not cease because we cannot offer you G. Selden any longer."

He had his own reasons for giving the invitation—several of them. And there was a satisfaction in letting the fellow know, casually, that he was not in the ridiculous position of being unaware of what had occurred during his absence—that there had been visits—and also the objectionable episode of the American bounder. That the episode had been objectionable, he knew he had adroitly conveyed by mere tone and manner.

Mount Dunstan thanked him in the usual formula, and then spoke to Betty.

"G. Selden left us tremulous and fevered with ecstatic anticipation. He carried your kind letter to Mr. Vanderpoel, next to his heart. His brain seemed to whirl at the thought of what 'the boys' would say, when he arrived with it in New York. You have materialised the dream of his life!"

"I have interested my father," Betty answered, with a brilliant smile. "He liked the romance of the Reuben S. Vanderpoel who rewarded the saver of his life by unbounded orders for the Delkoff."

. . . . .

As their carriage drove away, Sir Nigel bent forward to look out of the window, and having done it, laughed a little.

"Mount Dunstan does not play the game well," he remarked.

It was annoying that neither Betty nor his wife inquired what the game in question might be, and that his temperament forced him into explaining without encouragement.

"He should have 'stood motionless with folded arms,' or something of the sort, and 'watched her equipage until it was out of sight.'"

"And he did not?" said Betty.

"He turned on his heel as soon as the door was shut."

"People ought not to do such things," was her simple comment. To which it seemed useless to reply.

CHAPTER XXXIII

FOR LADY JANE

There is no one thing on earth of such interest as the study of the laws of temperament, which impel, support, or entrap into folly and danger the being they rule. As a child, not old enough to give a definite name to the thing she watched and pondered on, in child fashion, Bettina Vanderpoel had thought much on this subject. As she had grown older, she had never been ignorant of the workings of her own temperament, and she had looked on for years at the laws which had wrought in her father's being—the laws of strength, executive capacity, and that pleasure in great schemes, which is roused less by a desire for gain than for a strongly-felt necessity for action, resulting in success. She mentally followed other people on their way, sometimes asking herself how far the individual was to be praised or blamed for his treading of the path he seemed to choose. And now there was given her the opportunity to study the workings of the nature of Nigel Anstruthers, which was a curious thing.

He was not an individual to be envied. Never was man more tormented by lack of power to control his special devil, at the right moment of time, and therefore, never was there one so inevitably his own frustration. This Betty saw after the passing of but a few days, and wondered how far he was conscious or unconscious of the thing. At times it appeared to her that he was in a state of unrest—that he was as a man wavering between lines of action, swayed at one moment by one thought, at another by an idea quite different, and that he was harried because he could not hold his own with himself.

This was true. The ball at Dunholm Castle had been enlightening, and had wrought some changes in his points of view. Also other factors had influenced him. In the first place, the changed atmosphere of Stornham, the fitness and luxury of his surroundings, the new dignity given to his position by the altered aspect of things, rendered external amiability more easy. To ride about the country on a good horse, or drive in a smart phaeton, or suitable carriage, and to find that people who a year ago had passed him with the merest recognition, saluted him with polite intention, was, to a certain degree, stimulating to a vanity which had been long ill-fed. The power which produced these results should, of course, have been in his own hands—his money-making father-in-law should have seen that it was his affair to provide for that—but since he had not done so, it was rather entertaining that it should be, for the present, in the hands of this extraordinarily good-looking girl.

He had begun by merely thinking of her in this manner—as "this extraordinarily good-looking girl," and had not, for a moment, hesitated before the edifying idea of its not being impossible to arrange a lively flirtation with her. She was at an age when, in his opinion, girlhood was poised for flight with adventure, and his tastes had not led him in the direction of youth which was fastidious. His Riviera episode had left his vanity blistered and requiring some soothing application. His life had worked evil with him, and he had fallen ill on the hands of a woman who had treated him as a shattered, useless thing whose day was done and with whom strength and bloom could not be burdened. He had kept his illness a hidden secret, on his return to Stornham, his one desire having been to forget—even to disbelieve in it, but dreams of its suggestion sometimes awakened him at night with shudders and cold sweat. He was hideously afraid of death and pain, and he had had monstrous pain—and while he had lain battling with it, upon his bed in the villa on the Mediterranean, he had been able to hear, in the garden outside, the low voices and laughter of the Spanish dancer and the healthy, strong young fool who was her new adorer.

When he had found himself face to face with Betty in the avenue, after the first leap of annoyance, which had suddenly died down into perversely interested curiosity, he could have laughed outright at the novelty and odd unexpectedness of the situation. The ill-mannered, impudently-staring, little New York beast had developed into THIS! Hang it! No man could guess what the embryo female creature might result in. His mere shakiness of physical condition added strength to her attraction. She was like a young goddess of health and life and fire; the very spring of her firm foot upon the moss beneath it was a stimulating thing to a man whose nerves sprung secret fears upon him. There were sparks between the sweep of her lashes, but she managed to carry herself with the air of being as cool as a cucumber, which gave spice to the effort to "upset" her. If she did not prove suitably amenable, there would be piquancy in getting the better of her— in stirring up unpleasant little things, which would make it easier for her to go away than remain on the spot—if one should end by choosing to get rid of her. But, for the moment, he had no desire to get rid of her. He wanted to see what she intended to do—to see the thing out, in fact. It amused him to hear that Mount Dunstan was on her track. There exists for persons of a certain type a pleasure full-fed by the mere sense of having "got even" with an opponent. Throughout his life he had made a point of "getting even" with those who had irritatingly crossed his path, or much disliked him. The working out of small or large plans to achieve this end had formed one of his most agreeable recreations. He had long owed Mount Dunstan a debt, which he had always meant to pay. He had not intended to forget the episode of the nice little village girl with whom Tenham and himself had been getting along so enormously well, when the raging young ass had found them out, and made an absurdly exaggerated scene, even going so far as threatening to smash the pair of them, marching off to the father and mother, and setting the vicar on, and then scratching together—God knows how—money enough to pack the lot off to America, where they had since done well. Why should a man forgive another who had made him look like a schoolboy and a fool? So, to find Mount Dunstan rushing down a steep hill into this thing, was edifying. You cannot take much out of a man if you never encounter him. If you meet him, you are provided by Heaven with opportunities. You can find out what he feels most sharply, and what he will suffer most by being deprived of. His impression was that there was a good deal to be got out of Mount Dunstan. He was an obstinate, haughty devil, and just the fellow to conceal with a fury of pride a score of tender places in his hide.

At the ball he had seen that the girl's effect had been of a kind which even money and good looks uncombined with another thing might not have produced. And she had the other thing—whatsoever it might be. He observed the way in which the Dunholms met and greeted her, he marked the glance of the royal personage, and his manner, when after her presentation he conversed with and detained her, he saw the turning of heads and exchange of remarks as she moved through the rooms. Most especially, he took in the bearing of the very grand old ladies, led by Lady Alanby of Dole. Barriers had thrown themselves down, these portentous, rigorous old pussycats admired her, even liked her.

"Upon my word," he said to himself. "She has a way with her, you know. She is a combination of Ethel Newcome and Becky Sharp. But she is more level-headed than either of them, There's a touch of Trix Esmond, too."

The sense of the success which followed her, and the gradually-growing excitement of looking on at her light whirls of dance, the carnation of her cheek, and the laughter and pleasure she drew about her, had affected him in a way by which he was secretly a little exhilarated. He was conscious of a rash desire to force his way through these laughing, vaunting young idiots, juggle or snatch their dances away from them, and seize on the girl himself. He had not for so long a time been impelled by such agreeable folly that he had sometimes felt the stab of the thought that he was past it. That it should rise in him again made him feel young. There was nothing which so irritated him against Mount Dunstan as his own rebelling recognition of the man's youth, the strength of his fine body, his high-held head and clear eye.

These things and others it was which swayed him, as was plain to Betty in the time which followed, to many changes of mood.

"Are you sorry for a man who is ill and depressed," he asked one day, "or do you despise him?"

"I am sorry."

"Then be sorry for me."

He had come out of the house to her as she sat on the lawn, under a broad, level-branched tree, and had thrown himself upon a rug with his hands clasped behind his head.

"Are you ill?"

"When I was on the Riviera I had a fall." He lied simply. "I strained some muscle or other, and it has left me rather lame. Sometimes I have a good deal of pain."

"I am very sorry," said Betty. "Very."

A woman who can be made sorry it is rarely impossible to manage. To dwell with pathetic patience on your grievances, if she is weak and unintelligent, to deplore, with honest regret, your faults and blunders, if she is strong, are not bad ideas.

He looked at her reflectively.

"Yes, you are capable of being sorry," he decided. For a few moments of silence his eyes rested upon the view spread before him. To give the expression of dignified reflection was not a bad idea either.

"Do you know," he said at length, "that you produce an extraordinary effect upon me, Betty?"

She was occupying herself by adding a few stitches to one of Rosy's ancient strips of embroidery, and as she answered, she laid it flat upon her knee to consider its effect.

"Good or bad?" she inquired, with delicate abstraction.

He turned his face towards her again—this time quickly.

"Both," he answered. "Both."

His tone held the flash of a heat which he felt should have startled her slightly. But apparently it did not.

"I do not like 'both,'" with composed lightness. "If you had said that you felt yourself develop angelic qualities when you were near me, I should feel flattered, and swell with pride. But 'both' leaves me unsatisfied. It interferes with the happy little conceit that one is an all-pervading, beneficent power. One likes to contemplate a large picture of one's self—not plain, but coloured—as a wholesale reformer."

"I see. Thank you," stiffly and flushing. "You do not believe me."

Her effect upon him was such that, for the moment, he found himself choosing to believe that he was in earnest. His desire to impress her with his mood had actually led to this result. She ought to have been rather moved—a little fluttered, perhaps, at hearing that she disturbed his equilibrium.

"You set yourself against me, as a child, Betty," he said. "And you set yourself against me now. You will not give me fair play. You might give me fair play." He dropped his voice at the last sentence, and knew it was well done. A touch of hopelessness is not often lost on a woman.

"What would you consider fair play?" she inquired.

"It would be fair to listen to me without prejudice—to let me explain how it has happened that I have appeared to you a—a blackguard—I have no doubt you would call it—and a fool." He threw out his hand in an impatient gesture—impatient of himself—his fate—the tricks of bad fortune which it implied had made of him a more erring mortal than he would have been if left to himself, and treated decently.

"Do not put it so strongly," with conservative politeness.

"I don't refuse to admit that I am handicapped by a devil of a temperament. That is an inherited thing."

"Ah!" said Betty. "One of the temperaments one reads about—for which no one is to be blamed but one's deceased relatives. After all, that is comparatively easy to deal with. One can just go on doing what one wants to do—and then condemn one's grandparents severely."

A repellent quality in her—which had also the trick of transforming itself into an exasperating attraction—was that she deprived him of the luxury he had been most tenacious of throughout his existence. If the injustice of fate has failed to bestow upon a man fortune, good looks or brilliance, his exercise of the power to disturb, to enrage those who dare not resent, to wound and take the nonsense out of those about him, will, at all events, preclude the possibility of his being passed over as a factor not to be considered. If to charm and bestow gives the sense of power, to thwart and humiliate may be found not wholly unsatisfying.

But in her case the inadequacy of the usual methods had forced itself upon him. It was as if the dart being aimed at her, she caught it in her hand in its flight, broke off its point and threw it lightly aside without comment. Most women cannot resist the temptation to answer a speech containing a sting or a reproach. It was part of her abnormality that she could let such things go by in a detached silence, which did not express even the germ of comment or opinion upon them. This, he said, was the result of her beastly sense of security, which, in its turn, was the result of the atmosphere of wealth she had breathed since her birth. There had been no obstacle which could not be removed for her, no law of limitation had laid its rein on her neck. She had not been taught by her existence the importance of propitiating opinion. Under such conditions, how was fear to be learned? She had not learned it. But for the devil in the blue between her lashes, he realised that he should have broken loose long ago.

"I suppose I deserved that for making a stupid appeal to sympathy," he remarked. "I will not do it again."

If she had been the woman who can be gently goaded into reply, she would have made answer to this. But she allowed the observation to pass, giving it free flight into space, where it lost itself after the annoying manner of its kind.

"Have you any objection to telling me why you decided to come to England this year?" he inquired, with a casual air, after the pause which she did not fill in.

The bluntness of the question did not seem to disturb her. She was not sorry, in fact, that he had asked it. She let her work lie upon her knee, and leaned back in her low garden chair, her hands resting upon its wicker arms. She turned on him a clear unprejudiced gaze.

"I came to see Rosy. I have always been very fond of her. I did not believe that she had forgotten how much we had loved her, or how much she had loved us. I knew that if I could see her again I should understand why she had seemed to forget us."

"And when you saw her, you, of course, decided that I had behaved, to quote my own words—like a blackguard and a fool."

"It is, of course, very rude to say you have behaved like a fool, but—if you'll excuse my saying so—that is what has impressed me very much. Don't you know," with a moderation, which singularly drove itself home, "that if you had been kind to her, and had made her happy, you could have had anything you wished for—without trouble?"

This was one of the unadorned facts which are like bullets. Disgustedly, he found himself veering towards an outlook which forced him to admit that there was probably truth in what she said, and he knew he heard more truth as she went on.

"She would have wanted only what you wanted, and she would not have asked much in return. She would not have asked as much as I should. What you did was not businesslike." She paused a moment to give thought to it. "You paid too high a price for the luxury of indulging the inherited temperament. Your luxury was not to control it. But it was a bad investment."

"The figure of speech is rather commercial," coldly.

"It is curious that most things are, as a rule. There is always the parallel of profit and loss whether one sees it or not. The profits are happiness and friendship—enjoyment of life and approbation. If the inherited temperament supplies one with all one wants of such things, it cannot be called a loss, of course."

"You think, however, that mine has not brought me much?"

"I do not know. It is you who know."

"Well," viciously, "there HAS been a sort of luxury in it in lashing out with one's heels, and smashing things—and in knowing that people prefer to keep clear."

She lifted her shoulders a little.

"Then perhaps it has paid."

"No," suddenly and fiercely, "damn it, it has not!"

And she actually made no reply to that.

"What do you mean to do?" he questioned as bluntly as before. He knew she would understand what he meant.

"Not much. To see that Rosy is not unhappy any more. We can prevent that. She was out of repair—as the house was. She is being rebuilt and decorated. She knows that she will be taken care of."

"I know her better than you do," with a laugh. "She will not go away. She is too frightened of the row it would make—of what I should say. I should have plenty to say. I can make her shake in her shoes."

Betty let her eyes rest full upon him, and he saw that she was softly summing him up—quite without prejudice, merely in interested speculation upon the workings of type.

"You are letting the inherited temperament run away with you at this moment," she reflected aloud—her quiet scrutiny almost abstracted. "It was foolish to say that."

He had known it was foolish two seconds after the words had left his lips. But a temper which has been allowed to leap hedges, unchecked throughout life, is in peril of forming a habit of taking them even at such times as a leap may land its owner in a ditch. This last was what her interested eyes were obviously saying. It suited him best at the moment to try to laugh.

"Don't look at me like that," he threw off. "As if you were calculating that two and two make four."

"No prejudice of mine can induce them to make five or six—or three and a half," she said. "No prejudice of mine—or of yours."

The two and two she was calculating with were the likelihoods and unlikelihoods of the inherited temperament, and the practical powers she could absolutely count on if difficulty arose with regard to Rosy.

He guessed at this, and began to make calculations himself.

But there was no further conversation for them, as they were obliged to rise to their feet to receive visitors. Lady Alanby of Dole and Sir Thomas, her grandson, were being brought out of the house to them by Rosalie.

He went forward to meet them—his manner that of the graceful host. Lady Alanby, having been welcomed by him, and led to the most comfortable, tree-shaded chair, found his bearing so elegantly chastened that she gazed at him with private curiosity. To her far-seeing and highly experienced old mind it seemed the bearing of a man who was "up to something." What special thing did he chance to be "up to"? His glance certainly lurked after Miss Vanderpoel oddly. Was he falling in unholy love with the girl, under his stupid little wife's very nose?

She could not, however, give her undivided attention to him, as she wished to keep her eye on her grandson and—outrageously enough fit happened that just as tea was brought out and Tommy was beginning to cheer up and quite come out a little under the spur of the activities of handing bread and butter and cress sandwiches, who should appear but the two Lithcom girls, escorted by their aunt, Mrs. Manners, with whom they lived. As they were orphans without money, if the Manners, who were rather well off, had not taken them in, they would have had to go to the workhouse, or into genteel amateur shops, as they were not clever enough for governesses.

Mary, with her turned-up nose, looked just about as usual, but Jane had a new frock on which was exactly the colour of the big, appealing eyes, with their trick of following people about. She looked a little pale and pathetic, which somehow gave her a specious air of being pretty, which she really was not at all. The swaying young thinness of those very slight girls whose soft summer muslins make them look like delicate bags tied in the middle with fluttering ribbons, has almost invariably a foolish attraction for burly young men whose characters are chiefly marked by lack of forethought, and Lady Alanby saw Tommy's robust young body give a sort of jerk as the party of three was brought across the grass. After it he pulled himself together hastily, and looked stiff and pink, shaking hands as if his elbow joint was out of order, being at once too loose and too rigid. He began to be clumsy with the bread and butter, and, ceasing his talk with Miss Vanderpoel, fell into silence. Why should he go on talking? he thought. Miss Vanderpoel was a cracking handsome girl, but she was too clever for him, and he had to think of all sorts of new things to say when he talked to her. And—well, a fellow could never imagine himself stretched out on the grass, puffing happily away at a pipe, with a girl like that sitting near him, smiling—the hot turf smelling almost like hay, the hot blue sky curving overhead, and both the girl and himself perfectly happy—chock full of joy— though neither of them were saying anything at all. You could imagine it with some girls—you DID imagine it when you wakened early on a summer morning, and lay in luxurious stillness listening to the birds singing like mad.

Lady Jane was a nicely-behaved girl, and she tried to keep her following blue eyes fixed on the grass, or on Lady Anstruthers, or Miss Vanderpoel, but there was something like a string, which sometimes pulled them in another direction, and once when this had happened—quite against her will—she was terrified to find Lady Alanby's glass lifted and fixed upon her.

As Lady Alanby's opinion of Mrs. Manners was but a poor one, and as Mrs. Manners was stricken dumb by her combined dislike and awe of Lady Alanby, a slight stiffness might have settled upon the gathering if Betty had not made an effort. She applied herself to Lady Alanby and Mrs. Manners at once, and ended by making them talk to each other. When they left the tea table under the trees to look at the gardens, she walked between them, playing upon the primeval horticultural passions which dominate the existence of all respectable and normal country ladies, until the gulf between them was temporarily bridged. This being achieved, she adroitly passed them over to Lady Anstruthers, who, Nigel observed with some curiosity, accepted the casual responsibility without manifest discomfiture.

To the aching Tommy the manner in which, a few minutes later, he found himself standing alone with Jane Lithcom in a path of clipped laurels was almost bewilderingly simple. At the end of the laurel walk was a pretty peep of the country, and Miss Vanderpoel had brought him to see it. Nigel Anstruthers had been loitering behind with Jane and Mary. As Miss Vanderpoel turned with him into the path, she stooped and picked a blossom from a clump of speedwell growing at the foot of a bit of wall.

"Lady Jane's eyes are just the colour of this flower," she said.

"Yes, they are," he answered, glancing down at the lovely little blue thing as she held it in her hand. And then, with a thump of the heart, "Most people do not think she is pretty, but I—" quite desperately—"I DO." His mood had become rash.

"So do I," Betty Vanderpoel answered.

Then the others joined them, and Miss Vanderpoel paused to talk a little— and when they went on she was with Mary and Nigel Anstruthers, and he was with Jane, walking slowly, and somehow the others melted away, turning in a perfectly natural manner into a side path. Their own slow pace became slower. In fact, in a few moments, they were standing quite still between the green walls. Jane turned a little aside, and picked off some small leaves, nervously. He saw the muslin on her chest lift quiveringly.

"Oh, little Jane!" he said in a big, shaky whisper. The following eyes incontinently brimmed over. Some shining drops fell on the softness of the blue muslin.

"Oh, Tommy," giving up, "it's no use—talking at all."

"You mustn't think—you mustn't think—ANYTHING," he falteringly commanded, drawing nearer, because it was impossible not to do it.

What he really meant, though he did not know how decorously to say it, was that she must not think that he could be moved by any tall beauty, towards the splendour of whose possessions his revered grandmother might be driving him.

"I am not thinking anything," cried Jane in answer. "But she is everything, and I am nothing. Just look at her—and then look at me, Tommy."

"I'll look at you as long as you'll let me," gulped Tommy, and he was boy enough and man enough to put a hand on each of her shoulders, and drown his longing in her brimming eyes.

. . . . .

Mary and Miss Vanderpoel were talking with a curious intimacy, in another part of the garden, where they were together alone, Sir Nigel having been reattached to Lady Alanby.

"You have known Sir Thomas a long time?" Betty had just said.

"Since we were children. Jane reminded me at the Dunholms' ball that she had played cricket with him when she was eight."

"They have always liked each other?" Miss Vanderpoel suggested.

Mary looked up at her, and the meeting of their eyes was frank to revelation. But for the clear girlish liking for herself she saw in Betty Vanderpoel's, Mary would have known her next speech to be of imbecile bluntness. She had heard that Americans often had a queer, delightful understanding of unconventional things. This splendid girl was understanding her.

"Oh! You SEE!" she broke out. "You left them together on purpose!"

"Yes, I did." And there was a comprehension so deep in her look that Mary knew it was deeper than her own, and somehow founded on some subtler feeling than her own. "When two people want so much—care so much to be together," Miss Vanderpoel added quite slowly—even as if the words rather forced themselves from her, "it seems as if the whole world ought to help them—everything in the world—the very wind, and rain, and sun, and stars—oh, things have no RIGHT to keep them apart."

Mary stared at her, moved and fascinated. She scarcely knew that she caught at her hand.

"I have never been in the state that Jane is," she poured forth. "And I can't understand how she can be such a fool, but—but we care about each other more than most girls do—perhaps because we have had no people. And it's the kind of thing there is no use talking against, it seems. It's killing the youngness in her. If it ends miserably, it will be as if she had had an illness, and got up from it a faded, done-for spinster with a stretch of hideous years to live. Her blue eyes will look like boiled gooseberries, because she will have cried all the colour out of them. Oh! You UNDERSTAND! I see you do."

Before she had finished both Miss Vanderpoel's hands were holding hers.

"I do! I do," she said. And she did, as a year ago she had not known she could. "Is it Lady Alanby?" she ventured.

"Yes. Tommy will be helplessly poor if she does not leave him her money. And she won't if he makes her angry. She is very determined. She will leave it to an awful cousin if she gets in a rage. And Tommy is not clever. He could never earn his living. Neither could Jane. They could NEVER marry. You CAN'T defy relatives, and marry on nothing, unless you are a character in a book."

"Has she liked Lady Jane in the past?" Miss Vanderpoel asked, as if she was, mentally, rapidly going over the ground, that she might quite comprehend everything.

"Yes. She used to make rather a pet of her. She didn't like me. She was taken by Jane's meek, attentive, obedient ways. Jane was born a sweet little affectionate worm. Lady Alanby can't hate her, even now. She just pushes her out of her path."

"Because?" said Betty Vanderpoel.

Mary prefaced her answer with a brief, half-embarrassed laugh.

"Because of YOU."

"Because she thinks———?"

"I don't see how she can believe he has much of a chance. I don't think she does—but she will never forgive him if he doesn't make a try at finding out whether he has one or not."

"It is very businesslike," Betty made observation.

Mary laughed.

"We talk of American business outlook," she said, "but very few of us English people are dreamy idealists. We are of a coolness and a daring—when we are dealing with questions of this sort. I don't think you can know the thing you have brought here. You descend on a dull country place, with your money and your looks, and you simply STAY and amuse yourself by doing extraordinary things, as if there was no London waiting for you. Everyone knows this won't last. Next season you will be presented, and have a huge success. You will be whirled about in a vortex, and people will sit on the edge, and cast big strong lines, baited with the most glittering things they can get together. You won't be able to get away. Lady Alanby knows there would be no chance for Tommy then. It would be too idiotic to expect it. He must make his try now."

Their eyes met again, and Miss Vanderpoel looked neither shocked nor angry, but an odd small shadow swept across her face. Mary, of course, did not know that she was thinking of the thing she had realised so often—that it was not easy to detach one's self from the fact that one was Reuben S. Vanderpoel's daughter. As a result of it here one was indecently and unwillingly disturbing the lives of innocent, unassuming lovers.

"And so long as Sir Thomas has not tried—and found out—Lady Jane will be made unhappy?"

"If he were to let you escape without trying, he would not be forgiven. His grandmother has had her own way all her life."

"But suppose after I went away someone else came?"

Mary shook her head.

"People like you don't HAPPEN in one neighbourhood twice in a lifetime. I am twenty-six and you are the first I have seen."

"And he will only be safe if?"

Mary Lithcom nodded.

"Yes—IF," she answered. "It's silly—and frightful—but it is true."

Miss Vanderpoel looked down on the grass a few moments, and then seemed to arrive at a decision.

"He likes you? You can make him understand things?" she inquired.

"Yes."

"Then go and tell him that if he will come here and ask me a direct question, I will give him a direct answer—which will satisfy Lady Alanby."

Lady Mary caught her breath.

"Do you know, you are the most wonderful girl I ever saw!" she exclaimed. "But if you only knew what I feel about Janie!" And tears rushed into her eyes.

"I feel just the same thing about my sister," said Miss Vanderpoel. "I think Rosy and Lady Jane are rather alike."

. . . . .

When Tommy tramped across the grass towards her he was turning red and white by turns, and looking somewhat like a young man who was being marched up to a cannon's mouth. It struck him that it was an American kind of thing he was called upon to do, and he was not an American, but British from the top of his closely-cropped head to the rather thick soles of his boots. He was, in truth, overwhelmed by his sense of his inadequacy to the demands of the brilliantly conceived, but unheard-of situation. Joy and terror swept over his being in waves.

The tall, proud, wood-nymph look of her as she stood under a tree, waiting for him, would have struck his courage dead on the spot and caused him to turn and flee in anguish, if she had not made a little move towards him, with a heavenly, every-day humanness in her eyes. The way she managed it was an amazing thing. He could never have managed it at all himself.

She came forward and gave him her hand, and really it was HER hand which held his own comparatively steady.

"It is for Lady Jane," she said. "That prevents it from being ridiculous or improper. It is for Lady Jane. Her eyes," with a soft-touched laugh, "are the colour of the blue speedwell I showed you. It is the colour of babies' eyes. And hers look as theirs do—as if they asked everybody not to hurt them."

He actually fell upon his knee, and bending his head over her hand, kissed it half a dozen times with adoration. Good Lord, how she SAW and KNEW!

"If Jane were not Jane, and you were not YOU," the words rushed from him, "it would be the most outrageous—the most impudent thing a man ever had the cheek to do."

"But it is not." She did not draw her hand away, and oh, the girlish kindness of her smiling, supporting look. "You came to ask me if——"

"If you would marry me, Miss Vanderpoel," his head bending over her hand again. "I beg your pardon, I beg your pardon. Oh Lord, I do.'

"I thank you for the compliment you pay me," she answered. "I like you very much, Sir Thomas—and I like you just now more than ever—but I could not marry you. I should not make you happy, and I should not be happy myself. The truth is——" thinking a moment, "each of us really belongs to a different kind of person. And each of knows the fact."

"God bless you," he said. "I think you know everything in the world a woman can know—and remain an angel."

It was an outburst of eloquence, and she took it in the prettiest way—with the prettiest laugh, which had in it no touch of mockery or disbelief in him.

"What I have said is quite final—if Lady Alanby should inquire," she said—adding rather quickly, "Someone is coming."

It pleased her to see that he did not hurry to his feet clumsily, but even stood upright, with a shade of boyish dignity, and did not release her hand before he had bent his head low over it again.

Sir Nigel was bringing with him Lady Alanby, Mrs. Manners, and his wife, and when Betty met his eyes, she knew at once that he had not made his way to this particular garden without intention. He had discovered that she was with Tommy, and it had entertained him to break in upon them.

"I did not intend to interrupt Sir Thomas at his devotions," he remarked to her after dinner. "Accept my apologies."

"It did not matter in the least, thank you," said Betty.

. . . . .

"I am glad to be able to say, Thomas, that you did not look an entire fool when you got up from your knees, as we came into the rose garden." Thus Lady Alanby, as their carriage turned out of Stornham village.

"I'm glad myself," Tommy answered.

"What were you doing there? Even if you were asking her to marry you, it was not necessary to go that far. We are not in the seventeenth century."

Then Tommy flushed.

"I did not intend to do it. I could not help it. She was so—so nice about everything. That girl is an angel. I told her so."

"Very right and proper spirit to approach her in," answered the old woman, watching him keenly. "Was she angel enough to say she would marry you?"

Tommy, for some occult reason, had the courage to stare back into his grandmother's eyes, quite as if he were a man, and not a hobbledehoy, expecting to be bullied.

"She does not want me," he answered. "And I knew she wouldn't. Why should she? I did what you ordered me to do, and she answered me as I knew she would. She might have snubbed me, but she has such a way with her—such a way of saying things and understanding, that—that—well, I found myself on one knee, kissing her hand—as if I was being presented at court."

Old Lady Alanby looked out on the passing landscape.

"Well, you did your best," she summed the matter up at last, "if you went down on your knees involuntarily. If you had done it on purpose, it would have been unpardonable."

CHAPTER XXXIV

RED GODWYN

Stornham Court had taken its proper position in the county as a place which was equal to social exchange in the matter of entertainment. Sir Nigel and Lady Anstruthers had given a garden party, according to the decrees of the law obtaining in country neighbourhoods. The curiosity to behold Miss Vanderpoel, and the change which had been worked in the well-known desolation and disrepair, precluded the possibility of the refusal of any invitations sent, the recipient being in his or her right mind, and sound in wind and limb. That astonishing things had been accomplished, and that the party was a successful affair, could not but be accepted as truths. Garden parties had been heard of, were a trifle repetitional, and even dull, but at this one there was real music and real dancing, and clever entertainments were given at intervals in a green-embowered little theatre, erected for the occasion. These were agreeable additions to mere food and conversation, which were capable of palling.

To the garden party the Anstruthers did not confine themselves. There were dinner parties at Stornham, and they also were successful functions. The guests were of those who make for the success of such entertainments.

"I called upon Mount Dunstan this afternoon," Sir Nigel said one evening, before the first of these dinners. "He might expect it, as one is asking him to dine. I wish him to be asked. The Dunholms have taken him up so tremendously that no festivity seems complete without him."

He had been invited to the garden party, and had appeared, but Betty had seen little of him. It is easy to see little of a guest at an out-of-door festivity. In assisting Rosalie to attend to her visitors she had been much occupied, but she had known that she might have seen more of him, if he had intended that it should be so. He did not—for reasons of his own—intend that it should be so, and this she became aware of. So she walked, played in the bowling green, danced and talked with Westholt, Tommy Alanby and others.

"He does not want to talk to me. He will not, if he can avoid it," was what she said to herself.

She saw that he rather sought out Mary Lithcom, who was not accustomed to receiving special attention. The two walked together, danced together, and in adjoining chairs watched the performance in the embowered theatre. Lady Mary enjoyed her companion very much, but she wondered why he had attached himself to her.

Betty Vanderpoel asked herself what they talked to each other about, and did not suspect the truth, which was that they talked a good deal of herself.

"Have you seen much of Miss Vanderpoel?" Lady Mary had begun by asking.

"I have SEEN her a good deal, as no doubt you have."

Lady Mary's plain face expressed a somewhat touched reflectiveness.

"Do you know," she said, "that the garden parties have been a different thing this whole summer, just because one always knew one would see her at them?"

A short laugh from Mount Dunstan.

"Jane and I have gone to every garden party within twenty miles, ever since we left the schoolroom. And we are very tired of them. But this year we have quite cheered up. When we are dressing to go to something dull, we say to each other, 'Well, at any rate, Miss Vanderpoel will be there, and we shall see what she has on, and how her things are made,' and that's something—besides the fun of watching people make up to her, and hearing them talk about the men who want to marry her, and wonder which one she will take. She will not take anyone in this place," the nice turned-up nose slightly suggesting a derisive sniff. "Who is there who is suitable?"

Mount Dunstan laughed shortly again.

"How do you know I am not an aspirant myself?" he said. He had a mirthless sense of enjoyment in his own brazenness. Only he himself knew how brazen the speech was.

Lady Mary looked at him with entire composure.

"I am quite sure you are not an aspirant for anybody. And I happen to know that you dislike moneyed international marriages. You are so obviously British that, even if I had not been told that, I should know it was true. Miss Vanderpoel herself knows it is true."

"Does she?"

"Lady Alanby spoke of it to Sir Nigel, and I heard Sir Nigel tell her."

"Exactly the kind of unnecessary thing he would be likely to repeat." He cast the subject aside as if it were a worthless superfluity and went on: "When you say there is no one suitable, you surely forget Lord Westholt."

"Yes, it's true I forgot him for the moment. But—" with a laugh—"one rather feels as if she would require a royal duke or something of that sort."

"You think she expects that kind of thing?" rather indifferently.

"She? She doesn't think of the subject. She simply thinks of other things—of Lady Anstruthers and Ughtred, of the work at Stornham and the village life, which gives her new emotions and interest. She also thinks about being nice to people. She is nicer than any girl I know."

"You feel, however, she has a right to expect it?" still without more than a casual air of interest.

"Well, what do you feel yourself?" said Lady Mary. "Women who look like that—even when they are not millionairesses—usually marry whom they choose. I do not believe that the two beautiful Miss Gunnings rolled into one would have made anything as undeniable as she is. One has seen portraits of them. Look at her as she stands there talking to Tommy and Lord Dunholm!"

Internally Mount Dunstan was saying: "I am looking at her, thank you," and setting his teeth a little.

But Lady Mary was launched upon a subject which swept her along with it, and she—so to speak—ground the thing in.

"Look at the turn of her head! Look at her mouth and chin, and her eyes with the lashes sweeping over them when she looks down! You must have noticed the effect when she lifts them suddenly to look at you. It's so odd and lovely that it—it almost——"

"Almost makes you jump," ended Mount Dunstan drily.

She did not laugh and, in fact, her expression became rather sympathetically serious.

"Ah," she said, "I believe you feel a sort of rebellion against the unfairness of the way things are dealt out. It does seem unfair, of course. It would be perfectly disgraceful—if she were different. I had moments of almost hating her until one day not long ago she did something so bewitchingly kind and understanding of other people's feelings that I gave up. It was clever, too," with a laugh, "clever and daring. If she were a young man she would make a dashing soldier."

She did not give him the details of the story, but went on to say in effect what she had said to Betty herself of the inevitable incidentalness of her stay in the country. If she had not evidently come to Stornham this year with a purpose, she would have spent the season in London and done the usual thing. Americans were generally presented promptly, if they had any position—sometimes when they had not. Lady Alanby had heard that the fact that she was with her sister had awakened curiosity and people were talking about her.

"Lady Alanby said in that dry way of hers that the arrival of an unmarried American fortune in England was becoming rather like the visit of an unmarried royalty. People ask each other what it means and begin to arrange for it. So far, only the women have come, but Lady Alanby says that is because the men have had no time to do anything but stay at home and make the fortunes. She believes that in another generation there will be a male leisure class, and then it will swoop down too, and marry people. She was very sharp and amusing about it. She said it would help them to rid themselves of a plethora of wealth and keep them from bursting."

She was an amiable, if unsentimental person, Mary Lithcom—and was, quite without ill nature, expressing the consensus of public opinion. These young women came to the country with something practical to exchange in these days, and as there were men who had certain equivalents to offer, so also there were men who had none, and whom decency should cause to stand aside. Mount Dunstan knew that when she had said, "Who is there who is suitable?" any shadow of a thought of himself as being in the running had not crossed her mind. And this was not only for the reasons she had had the ready composure to name, but for one less conquerable.

Later, having left Mary Lithcom, he decided to take a turn by himself. He had done his duty as a masculine guest. He had conversed with young women and old ones, had danced, visited gardens and greenhouses, and taken his part in all things. Also he had, in fact, reached a point when a few minutes of solitude seemed a good thing. He found himself turning into the clipped laurel walk, where Tommy Alanby had stood with Jane Lithcom, and he went to the end of it and stood looking out on the view.

"Look at the turn of her head," Lady Mary had said. "Look at her mouth and chin." And he had been looking at them the whole afternoon, not because he had intended to do so, but because it was not possible to prevent himself from doing it.

This was one of the ironies of fate. Orthodox doctrine might suggest that it was to teach him that his past rebellion had been undue. Orthodox doctrine was ever ready with these soothing little explanations. He had raged and sulked at Destiny, and now he had been given something to rage for.

"No one knows anything about it until it takes him by the throat," he was thinking, "and until it happens to a man he has no right to complain. I was not starving before. I was not hungering and thirsting—in sight of food and water. I suppose one of the most awful things in the world is to feel this and know it is no use."

He was not in the condition to reason calmly enough to see that there might be one chance in a thousand that it was of use. At such times the most intelligent of men and women lose balance and mental perspicacity. A certain degree of unreasoning madness possesses them. They see too much and too little. There were, it was true, a thousand chances against him, but there was one for him—the chance that selection might be on his side. He had not that balance of thought left which might have suggested to him that he was a man young and powerful, and filled with an immense passion which might count for something. All he saw was that he was notably in the position of the men whom he had privately disdained when they helped themselves by marriage. Such marriages he had held were insults to the manhood of any man and the womanhood of any woman. In such unions neither party could respect himself or his companion. They must always in secret doubt each other, fret at themselves, feel distaste for the whole thing. Even if a man loved such a woman, and the feeling was mutual, to whom would it occur to believe it—to see that they were not gross and contemptible? To no one. Would it have occurred to himself that such an extenuating circumstance was possible? Certainly it would not. Pig-headed pride and obstinacy it might be, but he could not yet face even the mere thought of it—even if his whole position had not been grotesque. Because, after all, it was grotesque that he should even argue with himself. She—before his eyes and the eyes of all others—the most desirable of women; people dinning it in one's ears that she was surrounded by besiegers who waited for her to hold out her sceptre, and he—well, what was he! Not that his mental attitude was that of a meek and humble lover who felt himself unworthy and prostrated himself before her shrine with prayers—he was, on the contrary, a stout and obstinate Briton finding his stubbornly-held beliefs made as naught by a certain obsession—an intolerable longing which wakened with him in the morning, which sank into troubled sleep with him at night—the longing to see her, to speak to her, to stand near her, to breathe the air of her. And possessed by this—full of the overpowering strength of it—was a man likely to go to a woman and say, "Give your life and desirableness to me; and incidentally support me, feed me, clothe me, keep the roof over my head, as if I were an impotent beggar"?

"No, by God!" he said. "If she thinks of me at all it shall be as a man. No, by God, I will not sink to that!"

. . . . .

A moving touch of colour caught his eye. It was the rose of a parasol seen above the laurel hedge, as someone turned into the walk. He knew the colour of it and expected to see other parasols and hear voices. But there was no sound, and unaccompanied, the wonderful rose-thing moved towards him.

"The usual things are happening to me," was his thought as it advanced. "I am hot and cold, and just now my heart leaped like a rabbit. It would be wise to walk off, but I shall not do it. I shall stay here, because I am no longer a reasoning being. I suppose that a horse who refuses to back out of his stall when his stable is on fire feels something of the same thing."

When she saw him she made an involuntary-looking pause, and then recovering herself, came forward.

"I seem to have come in search of you," she said. "You ought to be showing someone the view really—and so ought I."

"Shall we show it to each other?" was his reply.

"Yes." And she sat down on the stone seat which had been placed for the comfort of view lovers. "I am a little tired—just enough to feel that to slink away for a moment alone would be agreeable. It IS slinking to leave Rosalie to battle with half the county. But I shall only stay a few minutes."

She sat still and gazed at the beautiful lands spread before her, but there was no stillness in her mind, neither was there stillness in his. He did not look at the view, but at her, and he was asking himself what he should be saying to her if he were such a man as Westholt. Though he had boldness enough, he knew that no man—even though he is free to speak the best and most passionate thoughts of his soul—could be sure that he would gain what he desired. The good fortune of Westholt, or of any other, could but give him one man's fair chance.

But having that chance, he knew he should not relinquish it soon. There swept back into his mind the story of the marriage of his ancestor, Red Godwyn, and he laughed low in spite of himself.

Miss Vanderpoel looked up at him quickly.

"Please tell me about it, if it is very amusing," she said.

"I wonder if it will amuse you," was his answer. "Do you like savage romance?"

"Very much."

It might seem a propos de rien, but he did not care in the least. He wanted to hear what she would say.

"An ancestor of mine—a certain Red Godwyn—was a barbarian immensely to my taste. He became enamoured of rumours of the beauty of the daughter and heiress of his bitterest enemy. In his day, when one wanted a thing, one rode forth with axe and spear to fight for it."

"A simple and alluring method," commented Betty. "What was her name?"

She leaned in light ease against the stone back of her seat, the rose light cast by her parasol faintly flushed her. The silence of their retreat seemed accentuated by its background of music from the gardens. They smiled a second bravely into each other's eyes, then their glances became entangled, as they had done for a moment when they had stood together in Mount Dunstan park. For one moment each had been held prisoner then—now it was for longer.

"Alys of the Sea-Blue Eyes."

Betty tried to release herself, but could not.

"Sometimes the sea is grey," she said.

His own eyes were still in hers.

"Hers were the colour of the sea on a day when the sun shines on it, and there are large fleece-white clouds floating in the blue above. They sparkled and were often like bluebells under water."

"Bluebells under water sounds entrancing," said Betty.

He caught his breath slightly.

"They were—entrancing," he said. "That was evidently the devil of it— saving your presence."

"I have never objected to the devil," said Betty. "He is an energetic, hard-working creature and paints himself an honest black. Please tell me the rest."

"Red Godwyn went forth, and after a bloody fight took his enemy's castle. If we still lived in like simple, honest times, I should take Dunholm Castle in the same way. He also took Alys of the Eyes and bore her away captive."

"From such incidents developed the germs of the desire for female suffrage," Miss Vanderpoel observed gently.

"The interest of the story lies in the fact that apparently the savage was either epicure or sentimentalist, or both. He did not treat the lady ill. He shut her in a tower chamber overlooking his courtyard, and after allowing her three days to weep, he began his barbarian wooing. Arraying himself in splendour he ordered her to appear before him. He sat upon the dais in his banquet hall, his retainers gathered about him—a great feast spread. In archaic English we are told that the board groaned beneath the weight of golden trenchers and flagons. Minstrels played and sang, while he displayed all his splendour."

"They do it yet," said Miss Vanderpoel, "in London and New York and other places."

"The next day, attended by his followers, he took her with him to ride over his lands. When she returned to her tower chamber she had learned how powerful and great a chieftain he was. She 'laye softely' and was attended by many maidens, but she had no entertainment but to look out upon the great green court. There he arranged games and trials of strength and skill, and she saw him bigger, stronger, and more splendid than any other man. He did not even lift his eyes to her window. He also sent her daily a rich gift."

"How long did this go on?"

"Three months. At the end of that time he commanded her presence again in his banquet hall. He told her the gates were opened, the drawbridge down and an escort waiting to take her back to her father's lands, if she would."

"What did she do?"

"She looked at him long—and long. She turned proudly away—in the sea-blue eyes were heavy and stormy tears, which seeing——"

"Ah, he saw them?" from Miss Vanderpoel.

"Yes. And seizing her in his arms caught her to his breast, calling for a priest to make them one within the hour. I am quoting the chronicle. I was fifteen when I read it first."

"It is spirited," said Betty, "and Red Godwyn was almost modern in his methods."

While professing composure and lightness of mood, the spell which works between two creatures of opposite sex when in such case wrought in them and made them feel awkward and stiff. When each is held apart from the other by fate, or will, or circumstance, the spell is a stupefying thing, deadening even the clearness of sight and wit.

"I must slink back now," Betty said, rising. "Will you slink back with me to give me countenance? I have greatly liked Red Godwyn."

So it occurred that when Nigel Anstruthers saw them again it was as they crossed the lawn together, and people looked up from ices and cups of tea to follow their slow progress with questioning or approving eyes.

CHAPTER XXXV

THE TIDAL WAVE

There was only one man to speak to, and it being the nature of the beast—so he harshly put it to himself—to be absolutely impelled to speech at such times, Mount Dunstan laid bare his breast to him, tearing aside all the coverings pride would have folded about him. The man was, of course, Penzance, and the laying bare was done the evening after the story of Red Godwyn had been told in the laurel walk.

They had driven home together in a profound silence, the elder man as deep in thought as the younger one. Penzance was thinking that there was a calmness in having reached sixty and in knowing that the pain and hunger of earlier years would not tear one again. And yet, he himself was not untorn by that which shook the man for whom his affection had grown year by year. It was evidently very bad—very bad, indeed. He wondered if he would speak of it, and wished he would, not because he himself had much to say in answer, but because he knew that speech would be better than hard silence.

"Stay with me to-night," Mount Dunstan said, as they drove through the avenue to the house. "I want you to dine with me and sit and talk late. I am not sleeping well."

They often dined together, and the vicar not infrequently slept at the Mount for mere companionship's sake. Sometimes they read, sometimes went over accounts, planned economies, and balanced expenditures. A chamber still called the Chaplain's room was always kept in readiness. It had been used in long past days, when a household chaplain had sat below the salt and left his patron's table before the sweets were served. They dined together this night almost as silently as they had driven homeward, and after the meal they went and sat alone in the library.

The huge room was never more than dimly lighted, and the far-off corners seemed more darkling than usual in the insufficient illumination of the far from brilliant lamps. Mount Dunstan, after standing upon the hearth for a few minutes smoking a pipe, which would have compared ill with old Doby's Sunday splendour, left his coffee cup upon the mantel and began to tramp up and down—out of the dim light into the shadows, back out of the shadows into the poor light.

"You know," he said, "what I think about most things—you know what I feel."

"I think I do."

"You know what I feel about Englishmen who brand themselves as half men and marked merchandise by selling themselves and their houses and their blood to foreign women who can buy them. You know how savage I have been at the mere thought of it. And how I have sworn——"

"Yes, I know what you have sworn," said Mr. Penzance.

It struck him that Mount Dunstan shook and tossed his head rather like a bull about to charge an enemy.

"You know how I have felt myself perfectly within my rights when I blackguarded such men and sneered at such women—taking it for granted that each was merchandise of his or her kind and beneath contempt. I am not a foul-mouthed man, but I have used gross words and rough ones to describe them."

"I have heard you."

Mount Dunstan threw back his head with a big, harsh laugh. He came out of the shadow and stood still.

"Well," he said, "I am in love—as much in love as any lunatic ever was—with the daughter of Reuben S. Vanderpoel. There you are—and there *I* am!"

"It has seemed to me," Penzance answered, "that it was almost inevitable."

"My condition is such that it seems to ME that it would be inevitable in the case of any man. When I see another man look at her my blood races through my veins with an awful fear and a wicked heat. That will show you the point I have reached." He walked over to the mantelpiece and laid his pipe down with a hand Penzance saw was unsteady. "In turning over the pages of the volume of Life," he said, "I have come upon the Book of Revelations."

"That is true," Penzance said.

"Until one has come upon it one is an inchoate fool," Mount Dunstan went on. "And afterwards one is—for a time at least—a sort of madman raving to one's self, either in or out of a straitjacket—as the case may be. I am wearing the jacket—worse luck! Do you know anything of the state of a man who cannot utter the most ordinary words to a woman without being conscious that he is making mad love to her? This afternoon I found myself telling Miss Vanderpoel the story of Red Godwyn and Alys of the Sea-Blue Eyes. I did not make a single statement having any connection with myself, but throughout I was calling on her to think of herself and of me as of those two. I saw her in my own arms, with the tears of Alys on her lashes. I was making mad love, though she was unconscious of my doing it."

"How do you know she was unconscious?" remarked Mr. Penzance. "You are a very strong man."

Mount Dunstan's short laugh was even a little awful, because it meant so much. He let his forehead drop a moment on to his arms as they rested on the mantelpiece.

"Oh, my God!" he said. But the next instant his head lifted itself. "It is the mystery of the world—this thing. A tidal wave gathering itself mountain high and crashing down upon one's helplessness might be as easily defied. It is supposed to disperse, I believe. That has been said so often that there must be truth in it. In twenty or thirty or forty years one is told one will have got over it. But one must live through the years—one must LIVE through them—and the chief feature of one's madness is that one is convinced that they will last forever."

"Go on," said Mr. Penzance, because he had paused and stood biting his lip. "Say all that you feel inclined to say. It is the best thing you can do. I have never gone through this myself, but I have seen and known the amazingness of it for many years. I have seen it come and go."

"Can you imagine," Mount Dunstan said, "that the most damnable thought of all—when a man is passing through it—is the possibility of its GOING? Anything else rather than the knowledge that years could change or death could end it! Eternity seems only to offer space for it. One knows—but one does not believe. It does something to one's brain."

"No scientist, howsoever profound, has ever discovered what," the vicar mused aloud.

"The Book of Revelations has shown to me how—how MAGNIFICENT life might be!" Mount Dunstan clenched and unclenched his hands, his eyes flashing. "Magnificent—that is the word. To go to her on equal ground to take her hands and speak one's passion as one would—as her eyes answered. Oh, one would know! To bring her home to this place—having made it as it once was— to live with her here—to be WITH her as the sun rose and set and the seasons changed—with the joy of life filling each of them. SHE is the joy of Life—the very heart of it. You see where I am—you see!"

"Yes," Penzance answered. He saw, and bowed his head, and Mount Dunstan knew he wished him to continue.

"Sometimes—of late—it has been too much for me and I have given free rein to my fancy—knowing that there could never be more than fancy. I was doing it this afternoon as I watched her move about among the people. And Mary Lithcom began to talk about her." He smiled a grim smile. "Perhaps it was an intervention of the gods to drag me down from my impious heights. She was quite unconscious that she was driving home facts like nails—the facts that every man who wanted money wanted Reuben S. Vanderpoel's daughter—and that the young lady, not being dull, was not unaware of the obvious truth! And that men with prizes to offer were ready to offer them in a proper manner. Also that she was only a brilliant bird of passage, who, in a few months, would be caught in the dazzling net of the great world. And that even Lord Westholt and Dunholm Castle were not quite what she might expect. Lady Mary was sincerely interested. She drove it home in her ardour. She told me to LOOK at her—to LOOK at her mouth and chin and eyelashes—and to make note of what she stood for in a crowd of ordinary people. I could have laughed aloud with rage and self-mockery."

Mr. Penzance was resting his forehead on his hand, his elbow on his chair's arm.

"This is profound unhappiness," he said. "It is profound unhappiness."

Mount Dunstan answered by a brusque gesture.

"But it will pass away," went on Penzance, "and not as you fear it must," in answer to another gesture, fiercely impatient. "Not that way. Some day—or night—you will stand here together, and you will tell her all you have told me. I KNOW it will be so."

"What!" Mount Dunstan cried out. But the words had been spoken with such absolute conviction that he felt himself become pale.

It was with the same conviction that Penzance went on.

"I have spent my quiet life in thinking of the forces for which we find no explanation—of the causes of which we only see the effects. Long ago in looking at you in one of my pondering moments I said to myself that YOU were of the Primeval Force which cannot lose its way—which sweeps a clear pathway for itself as it moves—and which cannot be held back. I said to you just now that because you are a strong man you cannot be sure that a woman you are—even in spite of yourself—making mad love to, is unconscious that you are doing it. You do not know what your strength lies in. I do not, the woman does not, but we must all feel it, whether we comprehend it or no. You said of this fine creature, some time since, that she was Life, and you have just said again something of the same kind. It is quite true. She is Life, and the joy of it. You are two strong forces, and you are drawing together."

He rose from his chair, and going to Mount Dunstan put his hand on his shoulder, his fine old face singularly rapt and glowing.

"She is drawing you and you are drawing her, and each is too strong to release the other. I believe that to be true. Both bodies and souls do it. They are not separate things. They move on their way as the stars do—they move on their way."

As he spoke, Mount Dunstan's eyes looked into his fixedly. Then they turned aside and looked down upon the mantel against which he was leaning. He aimlessly picked up his pipe and laid it down again. He was paler than before, but he said no single word.

"You think your reasons for holding aloof from her are the reasons of a man." Mr. Penzance's voice sounded to him remote. "They are the reasons of a man's pride—but that is not the strongest thing in the world. It only imagines it is. You think that you cannot go to her as a luckier man could. You think nothing shall force you to speak. Ask yourself why. It is because you believe that to show your heart would be to place yourself in the humiliating position of a man who might seem to her and to the world to be a base fellow."

"An impudent, pushing, base fellow," thrust in Mount Dunstan fiercely. "One of a vulgar lot. A thing fancying even its beggary worth buying. What has a man—whose very name is hung with tattered ugliness—to offer?"

Penzance's hand was still on his shoulder and his look at him was long.

"His very pride," he said at last, "his very obstinacy and haughty, stubborn determination. Those broken because the other feeling is the stronger and overcomes him utterly."

A flush leaped to Mount Dunstan's forehead. He set both elbows on the mantel and let his forehead fall on his clenched fists. And the savage Briton rose in him.

"No!" he said passionately. "By God, no!"

"You say that," said the older man, "because you have not yet reached the end of your tether. Unhappy as you are, you are not unhappy enough. Of the two, you love yourself the more—your pride and your stubbornness."

"Yes," between his teeth. "I suppose I retain yet a sort of respect—and affection—for my pride. May God leave it to me!"

Penzance felt himself curiously exalted; he knew himself unreasoningly passing through an oddly unpractical, uplifted moment, in whose impelling he singularly believed.

"You are drawing her and she is drawing you," he said. "Perhaps you drew each other across seas. You will stand here together and you will tell her of this—on this very spot."

Mount Dunstan changed his position and laughed roughly, as if to rouse himself. He threw out his arm in a big, uneasy gesture, taking in the room.

"Oh, come," he said. "You talk like a seer. Look about you. Look! I am to bring her here!"

"If it is the primeval thing she will not care. Why should she?"

"She! Bring a life like hers to this! Or perhaps you mean that her own wealth might make her surroundings becoming—that a man would endure that?"

"If it is the primeval thing, YOU would not care. You would have forgotten that you two had ever lived an hour apart."

He spoke with a deep, moved gravity—almost as if he were speaking of the first Titan building of the earth. Mount Dunstan staring at his delicate, insistent, elderly face, tried to laugh again—and failed because the effort seemed actually irreverent. It was a singular hypnotic moment, indeed. He himself was hypnotised. A flashlight of new vision blazed before him and left him dumb. He took up his pipe hurriedly, and with still unsteady fingers began to refill it. When it was filled he lighted it, and then without a word of answer left the hearth and began to tramp up and down the room again—out of the dim light into the shadows, back out of the shadows and into the dim light again, his brow working and his teeth holding hard his amber mouthpiece.

The morning awakening of a normal healthy human creature should be a joyous thing. After the soul's long hours of release from the burden of the body, its long hours spent—one can only say in awe at the mystery of it, "away, away"—in flight, perhaps, on broad, tireless wings, beating softly in fair, far skies, breathing pure life, to be brought back to renew the strength of each dawning day; after these hours of quiescence of limb and nerve and brain, the morning life returning should unseal for the body clear eyes of peace at least. In time to come this will be so, when the soul's wings are stronger, the body more attuned to infinite law and the race a greater power—but as yet it often seems as though the winged thing came back a lagging and reluctant rebel against its fate and the chain which draws it back a prisoner to its toil.

It had seemed so often to Mount Dunstan—oftener than not. Youth should not know such awakening, he was well aware; but he had known it sometimes even when he had been a child, and since his return from his ill-starred struggle in America, the dull and reluctant facing of the day had become a habit. Yet on the morning after his talk with his friend—the curious, uplifted, unpractical talk which had seemed to hypnotise him—he knew when he opened his eyes to the light that he had awakened as a man should awake—with an unreasoning sense of pleasure in the life and health of his own body, as he stretched mighty limbs, strong after the night's rest, and feeling that there was work to be done. It was all unreasoning—there was no more to be done than on those other days which he had wakened to with bitterness, because they seemed useless and empty of any worth—but this morning the mere light of the sun was of use, the rustle of the small breeze in the leaves, the soft floating past of the white clouds, the mere fact that the great blind-faced, stately house was his own, that he could tramp far over lands which were his heritage, unfed though they might be, and that the very rustics who would pass him in the lanes were, so to speak, his own people: that he had name, life, even the common thing of hunger for his morning food—it was all of use.

An alluring picture—of a certain deep, clear bathing pool in the park rose before him. It had not called to him for many a day, and now he saw its dark blueness gleam between flags and green rushes in its encircling thickness of shrubs and trees.

He sprang from his bed, and in a few minutes was striding across the grass of the park, his towels over his arm, his head thrown back as he drank in the freshness of the morning-scented air. It was scented with dew and grass and the breath of waking trees and growing things; early twitters and thrills were to be heard here and there, insisting on morning joyfulness; rabbits frisked about among the fine-grassed hummocks of their warren and, as he passed, scuttled back into their holes, with a whisking of short white tails, at which he laughed with friendly amusement. Cropping stags lifted their antlered heads, and fawns with dappled sides and immense lustrous eyes gazed at him without actual fear, even while they sidled closer to their mothers. A skylark springing suddenly from the grass a few yards from his feet made him stop short once and stand looking upward and listening. Who could pass by a skylark at five o'clock on a summer's morning—the little, heavenly light-heart circling and wheeling, showering down diamonds, showering down pearls, from its tiny pulsating, trilling throat?

"Do you know why they sing like that? It is because all but the joy of things has been kept hidden from them. They knew nothing but life and flight and mating, and the gold of the sun. So they sing." That she had once said.

He listened until the jewelled rain seemed to have fallen into his soul. Then he went on his way smiling as he knew he had never smiled in his life before. He knew it because he realised that he had never before felt the same vigorous, light normality of spirit, the same sense of being as other men. It was as though something had swept a great clear space about him, and having room for air he breathed deep and was glad of the commonest gifts of being.

The bathing pool had been the greatest pleasure of his uncared-for boyhood. No one knew which long passed away Mount Dunstan had made it. The oldest villager had told him that it had "allus ben there," even in his father's time. Since he himself had known it he had seen that it was kept at its best.

Its dark blue depths reflected in their pellucid clearness the water plants growing at its edge and the enclosing shrubs and trees. The turf bordering it was velvet-thick and green, and a few flag-steps led down to the water. Birds came there to drink and bathe and preen and dress their feathers. He knew there were often nests in the bushes—sometimes the nests of nightingales who filled the soft darkness or moonlight of early June with the wonderfulness of nesting song. Sometimes a straying fawn poked in a tender nose, and after drinking delicately stole away, as if it knew itself a trespasser.

To undress and plunge headlong into the dark sapphire water was a rapturous thing. He swam swiftly and slowly by turns, he floated, looking upward at heaven's blue, listening to birds' song and inhaling all the fragrance of the early day. Strength grew in him and life pulsed as the water lapped his limbs. He found himself thinking with pleasure of a long walk he intended to take to see a farmer he must talk to about his hop gardens; he found himself thinking with pleasure of other things as simple and common to everyday life—such things as he ordinarily faced merely because he must, since he could not afford an experienced bailiff. He was his own bailiff, his own steward, merely, he had often thought, an unsuccessful farmer of half-starved lands. But this morning neither he nor they seemed so starved, and—for no reason—there was a future of some sort.

He emerged from his pool glowing, the turf feeling like velvet beneath his feet, a fine light in his eyes.

"Yes," he said, throwing out his arms in a lordly stretch of physical well-being, "it might be a magnificent thing—mere strong living. THIS is magnificent."

CHAPTER XXXVI

BY THE ROADSIDE EVERYWHERE

His breakfast and the talk over it with Penzance seemed good things. It suddenly had become worth while to discuss the approaching hop harvest and the yearly influx of the hop pickers from London. Yesterday the subject had appeared discouraging enough. The great hop gardens of the estate had been in times past its most prolific source of agricultural revenue and the boast and wonder of the hop-growing county. The neglect and scant food of the lean years had cost them their reputation. Each season they had needed smaller bands of "hoppers," and their standard had been lowered. It had been his habit to think of them gloomily, as of hopeless and irretrievable loss. Because this morning, for a remote reason, the pulse of life beat strong in him he was taking a new view. Might not study of the subject, constant attention and the application of all available resource to one end produce appreciable results? The idea presented itself in the form of a thing worth thinking of.

"It would provide an outlook and give one work to do," he put it to his companion. "To have a roof over one's head, a sound body, and work to do, is not so bad. Such things form the whole of G. Selden's cheerful aim. His spirit is alight within me. I will walk over and talk to Bolter."

Bolter was a farmer whose struggle to make ends meet was almost too much for him. Holdings whose owners, either through neglect or lack of money, have failed to do their duty as landlords in the matter of repairs of farmhouses, outbuildings, fences, and other things, gradually fall into poor hands. Resourceful and prosperous farmers do not care to hold lands under unprosperous landlords. There were farms lying vacant on the Mount Dunstan estate, there were others whose tenants were uncertain rent payers or slipshod workers or dishonest in small ways. Waste or sale of the fertiliser which should have been given to the soil as its due, neglect in the case of things whose decay meant depreciation of property and expense to the landlord, were dishonesties. But Mount Dunstan knew that if he turned out Thorn and Fittle, whom no watching could wholly frustrate in their tricks, Under Mount Farm and Oakfield Rise would stand empty for many a year. But for his poverty Bolter would have been a good tenant enough. He was in trouble now because, though his hops promised well, he faced difficulties in the matter of "pickers." Last year he had not been able to pay satisfactory prices in return for labour, and as a result the prospect of securing good workers was an unpromising one.

The hordes of men, women, and children who flock year after year to the hop-growing districts know each other. They learn also which may be called the good neighbourhoods and which the bad; the gardens whose holders are considered satisfactory as masters, and those who are undesirable. They know by experience or report where the best "huts" are provided, where tents are supplied, and where one must get along as one can.

Generally the regular flocks are under a "captain," who gathers his followers each season, manages them and looks after their interests and their employers'. In some cases the same captain brings his regiment to the same gardens year after year, and ends by counting himself as of the soil and almost of the family of his employer. Each hard, thick-fogged winter they fight through in their East End courts and streets, they look forward to the open-air weeks spent between long, narrow green groves of tall garlanded poles, whose wreathings hang thick with fresh and pungent-scented hop clusters. Children play "'oppin" in dingy rooms and alleys, and talk to each other of days when the sun shone hot and birds were singing and flowers smelling sweet in the hedgerows; of others when the rain streamed down and made mud of the soft earth, and yet there was pleasure in the gipsying life, and high cheer in the fire of sticks built in the field by some bold spirit, who hung over it a tin kettle to boil for tea. They never forgot the gentry they had caught sight of riding or driving by on the road, the parson who came to talk, and the occasional groups of ladies from the "great house" who came into the gardens to walk about and look at the bins and ask queer questions in their gentry-sounding voices. They never knew anything, and they always seemed to be entertained. Sometimes there were enterprising, laughing ones, who asked to be shown how to strip the hops into the bins, and after being shown played at the work for a little while, taking off their gloves and showing white fingers with rings on. They always looked as if they had just been washed, and as if all of their clothes were fresh from the tub, and when anyone stood near them it was observable that they smelt nice. Generally they gave pennies to the children before they left the garden, and sometimes shillings to the women. The hop picking was, in fact, a wonderful blend of work and holiday combined.

Mount Dunstan had liked the "hopping" from his first memories of it. He could recall his sensations of welcoming a renewal of interesting things when, season after season, he had begun to mark the early stragglers on the road. The stragglers were not of the class gathered under captains. They were derelicts— tramps who spent their summers on the highways and their winters in such workhouses as would take them in; tinkers, who differ from the tramps only because sometimes they owned a rickety cart full of strange household goods and drunken tenth-hand perambulators piled with dirty bundles and babies, these last propelled by robust or worn-out, slatternly women, who sat by the small roadside fire stirring the battered pot or tending the battered kettle, when resting time had come and food must be cooked. Gipsies there were who had cooking fires also, and hobbled horses cropping the grass. Now and then appeared a grand one, who was rumoured to be a Lee and therefore royal, and who came and lived regally in a gaily painted caravan. During the late summer weeks one began to see slouching figures tramping along the high road at intervals. These were men who were old, men who were middle-aged and some who were young, all of them more or less dust-grimed, weather-beaten, or ragged. Occasionally one was to be seen in heavy beery slumber under the hedgerow, or lying on the grass smoking lazily, or with painful thrift cobbling up a hole in a garment. Such as these were drifting in early that they might be on the ground when pickers were wanted. They were the forerunners of the regular army.

On his walk to West Ways, the farm Bolter lived on, Mount Dunstan passed two or three of these strays. They were the usual flotsam and jetsam, but on the roadside near a hop garden he came upon a group of an aspect so unusual that it attracted his attention. Its unusualness consisted in its air of exceeding bustling cheerfulness. It was a domestic group of the most luckless type, and ragged, dirty, and worn by an evidently long tramp, might well have been expected to look forlorn, discouraged, and out of spirits. A slouching father of five children, one plainly but a few weeks old, and slung in a dirty shawl at its mother's breast, an unhealthy looking slattern mother, two ancient perambulators, one piled with dingy bundles and cooking utensils, the seven-year-old eldest girl unpacking things and keeping an eye at the same time on the two youngest, who were neither of them old enough to be steady on their feet, the six-year-old gleefully aiding the slouching father to build the wayside fire. The mother sat upon the grass nursing her baby and staring about her with an expression at once stupefied and illuminated by some temporary bliss. Even the slouching father was grinning, as if good luck had befallen him, and the two youngest were tumbling about with squeals of good cheer. This was not the humour in which such a group usually dropped wearily on the grass at the wayside to eat its meagre and uninviting meal and rest its dragging limbs. As he drew near, Mount Dunstan saw that at the woman's side there stood a basket full of food and a can full of milk.

Ordinarily he would have passed on, but, perhaps because of the human glow the morning had brought him, he stopped and spoke.

"Have you come for the hopping?" he asked.

The man touched his forehead, apparently not conscious that the grin was yet on his face.

"Yes, sir," he answered.

"How far have you walked?"

"A good fifty miles since we started, sir. It took us a good bit. We was pretty done up when we stopped here. But we've 'ad a wonderful piece of good luck." And his grin broadened immensely.

"I am glad to hear that," said Mount Dunstan. The good luck was plainly of a nature to have excited them greatly. Chance good luck did not happen to people like themselves. They were in the state of mind which in their class can only be relieved by talk. The woman broke in, her weak mouth and chin quite unsteady.

"Seems like it can't be true, sir," she said. "I'd only just come out of the Union—after this one," signifying the new baby at her breast. "I wasn't fit to drag along day after day. We 'ad to stop 'ere 'cos I was near fainting away."

"She looked fair white when she sat down," put in the man. "Like she was goin' off."

"And that very minute," said the woman, "a young lady came by on 'orseback, an' the minute she sees me she stops her 'orse an' gets down."

"I never seen nothing like the quick way she done it," said the husband. "Sharp, like she was a soldier under order. Down an' give the bridle to the groom an' comes over."

"And kneels down," the woman took him up, "right by me an' says, 'What's the matter? What can I do?' an' finds out in two minutes an' sends to the farm for some brandy an' all this basketful of stuff," jerking her head towards the treasure at her side. "An' gives 'IM," with another jerk towards her mate, "money enough to 'elp us along till I'm fair on my feet. That quick it was—that quick," passing her hand over her forehead, "as if it wasn't for the basket," with a nervous, half-hysteric giggle, "I wouldn't believe but what it was a dream—I wouldn't."

"She was a very kind young lady," said Mount Dunstan, "and you were in luck."

He gave a few coppers to the children and strode on his way. The glow was hot in his heart, and he held his head high.

"She has gone by," he said. "She has gone by."

He knew he should find her at West Ways Farm, and he did so. Slim and straight as a young birch tree, and elate with her ride in the morning air, she stood silhouetted in her black habit against the ancient whitewashed brick porch as she talked to Bolter.

"I have been drinking a glass of milk and asking questions about hops," she said, giving him her hand bare of glove. "Until this year I have never seen a hop garden or a hop picker."

After the exchange of a few words Bolter respectfully melted away and left them together.

"It was such a wonderful day that I wanted to be out under the sky for a long time—to ride a long way," she explained. "I have been looking at hop gardens as I rode. I have watched them all the summer—from the time when there was only a little thing with two or three pale green leaves looking imploringly all the way up to the top of each immensely tall hop pole, from its place in the earth at the bottom of it—as if it was saying over and over again, under its breath, 'Can I get up there? Can I get up? Can I do it in time? Can I do it in time?' Yes, that was what they were saying, the little bold things. I have watched them ever since, putting out tendrils and taking hold of the poles and pulling and climbing like little acrobats. And curling round and unfolding leaves and more leaves, until at last they threw them out as if they were beginning to boast that they could climb up into the blue of the sky if the summer were long enough. And now, look at them!" her hand waved towards the great gardens. "Forests of them, cool green pathways and avenues with leaf canopies over them."

"You have seen it all," he said. "You do see things, don't you? A few hundred yards down the road I passed something you had seen. I knew it was you who had seen it, though the poor wretches had not heard your name."

She hesitated a moment, then stooped down and took up in her hand a bit of pebbled earth from the pathway. There was storm in the blue of her eyes as she held it out for him to look at as it lay on the bare rose-flesh of her palm.

"See," she said, "see, it is like that—what we give. It is like that." And she tossed the earth away.

"It does not seem like that to those others."

"No, thank God, it does not. But to one's self it is the mere luxury of self-indulgence, and the realisation of it sometimes tempts one to be even a trifle morbid. Don't you see," a sudden thrill in her voice startled him, "they are on the roadside everywhere all over the world."

"Yes. All over the world."

"Once when I was a child of ten I read a magazine article about the suffering millions and the monstrously rich, who were obviously to blame for every starved sob and cry. It almost drove me out of my childish senses. I went to my father and threw myself into his arms in a violent fit of crying. I clung to him and sobbed out, 'Let us give it all away; let us give it all away and be like other people!'"

"What did he say?"

"He said we could never be quite like other people. We had a certain load to carry along the highway. It was the thing the whole world wanted and which we ourselves wanted as much as the rest, and we could not sanely throw it away. It was my first lesson in political economy and I abhorred it. I was a passionate child and beat furiously against the stone walls enclosing present suffering. It was horrible to know that they could not be torn down. I cried out, 'When I see anyone who is miserable by the roadside I shall stop and give him everything he wants—everything!' I was ten years old, and thought it could be done."

"But you stop by the roadside even now."

"Yes. That one can do."

"You are two strong creatures and you draw each other," Penzance had said. "Perhaps you drew each other across seas. Who knows?"

Coming to West Ways on a chance errand he had, as it were, found her awaiting him on the threshold. On her part she had certainly not anticipated seeing him there, but—when one rides far afield in the sun there are roads towards which one turns as if answering a summoning call, and as her horse had obeyed a certain touch of the rein at a certain point her cheek had felt momentarily hot.

Until later, when the "picking" had fairly begun, the kilns would not be at work; but there was some interest even now in going over the ground for the first time.

"I have never been inside an oast house," she said; "Bolter is going to show me his, and explain technicalities."

"May I come with you?" he asked.

There was a change in him. Something had lighted in his eyes since the day before, when he had told her his story of Red Godwyn. She wondered what it was. They went together over the place, escorted by Bolter. They looked into the great circular ovens, on whose floors the hops would be laid for drying, they mounted ladder-like steps to the upper room where, when dried, the same hops would lie in soft, light piles, until pushed with wooden shovels into the long "pokes" to be pressed and packed into a solid marketable mass. Bolter was allowed to explain the technicalities, but it was plain that Mount Dunstan was familiar with all of them, and it was he who, with a sentence here and there, gave her the colour of things.

"When it is being done there is nearly always outside a touch of the sharp sweetness of early autumn," he said "The sun slanting through the little window falls on the pale yellow heaps, and there is a pungent scent of hops in the air which is rather intoxicating."

"I am coming later to see the entire process," she answered.

It was a mere matter of seeing common things together and exchanging common speech concerning them, but each was so strongly conscious of the other that no sentence could seem wholly impersonal. There are times when the whole world is personal to a mood whose intensity seems a reason for all things. Words are of small moment when the mere sound of a voice makes an unreasonable joy.

"There was that touch of sharp autumn sweetness in the air yesterday morning," she said. "And the chaplets of briony berries that look as if they had been thrown over the hedges are beginning to change to scarlet here and there. The wild rose-haws are reddening, and so are the clusters of berries on the thorn trees and bushes."

"There are millions of them," Mount Dunstan said, "and in a few weeks' time they will look like bunches of crimson coral. When the sun shines on them they will be wonderful to see."

What was there in such speeches as these to draw any two nearer and nearer to each other as they walked side by side—to fill the morning air with an intensity of life, to seem to cause the world to drop away and become as nothing? As they had been isolated during their waltz in the crowded ballroom at Dunholm Castle, so they were isolated now. When they stood in the narrow green groves of the hop garden, talking simply of the placing of the bins and the stripping and measuring of the vines, there might have been no human thing within a hundred miles—within a thousand. For the first time his height and strength conveyed to her an impression of physical beauty. His walk and bearing gave her pleasure. When he turned his red-brown eyes upon her suddenly she was conscious that she liked their colour, their shape, the power of the look in them. On his part, he—for the twentieth time—found himself newly moved by the dower nature had bestowed on her. Had the world ever held before a woman creature so much to be longed for?—abnormal wealth, New York and Fifth Avenue notwithstanding, a man could only think of folding arms round her and whispering in her lovely ear—follies, oaths, prayers, gratitude.

And yet as they went about together there was growing in Betty Vanderpoel's mind a certain realisation. It grew in spite of the recognition of the change in him—the new thing lighted in his eyes. Whatsoever he felt—if he felt anything—he would never allow himself speech. How could he? In his place she could not speak herself. Because he was the strong thing which drew her thoughts, he would not come to any woman only to cast at her feet a burden which, in the nature of things, she must take up. And suddenly she comprehended that the mere obstinate Briton in him—even apart from greater things—had an immense attraction for her. As she liked now the red-brown colour of his eyes and saw beauty in his rugged features, so she liked his British stubbornness and the pride which would not be beaten.

"It is the unconquerable thing, which leads them in their battles and makes them bear any horror rather than give in. They have taken half the world with it; they are like bulldogs and lions," she thought. "And—and I am glorying in it."

"Do you know," said Mount Dunstan, "that sometimes you suddenly fling out the most magnificent flag of colour—as if some splendid flame of thought had sent up a blaze?"

"I hope it is not a habit," she answered. "When one has a splendid flare of thought one should be modest about it."

What was there worth recording in the whole hour they spent together? Outwardly there had only been a chance meeting and a mere passing by. But each left something with the other and each learned something; and the record made was deep.

At last she was on her horse again, on the road outside the white gate.

"This morning has been so much to the good," he said. "I had thought that perhaps we might scarcely meet again this year. I shall become absorbed in hops and you will no doubt go away. You will make visits or go to the Riviera—or to New York for the winter?"

"I do not know yet. But at least I shall stay to watch the thorn trees load themselves with coral." To herself she was saying: "He means to keep away. I shall not see him."

As she rode off Mount Dunstan stood for a few moments, not moving from his place. At a short distance from the farmhouse gate a side lane opened upon the highway, and as she cantered in its direction a horseman turned in from it—a man who was young and well dressed and who sat well a spirited animal. He came out upon the road almost face to face with Miss Vanderpoel, and from where he stood Mount Dunstan could see his delighted smile as he lifted his hat in salute. It was Lord Westholt, and what more natural than that after an exchange of greetings the two should ride together on their way! For nearly three miles their homeward road would be the same.

But in a breath's space Mount Dunstan realised a certain truth—a simple, elemental thing. All the exaltation of the morning swooped and fell as a bird seems to swoop and fall through space. It was all over and done with, and he understood it. His normal awakening in the morning, the physical and mental elation of the first clear hours, the spring of his foot as he had trod the road, had all had but one meaning. In some occult way the hypnotic talk of the night before had formed itself into a reality, fantastic and unreasoning as it had been. Some insistent inner consciousness had seized upon and believed it in spite of him and had set all his waking being in tune to it. That was the explanation of his undue spirits and hope. If Penzance had spoken a truth he would have had a natural, sane right to feel all this and more. But the truth was that he, in his guise—was one of those who are "on the roadside everywhere—all over the world." Poetically figurative as the thing sounded, it was prosaic fact.

So, still hearing the distant sounds of the hoofs beating in cheerful diminuendo on the roadway, he turned about and went back to talk to Bolter.

CHAPTER XXXVII

CLOSED CORRIDORS

To spend one's days perforce in an enormous house alone is a thing likely to play unholy tricks with a man's mind and lead it to gloomy workings. To know the existence of a hundred or so of closed doors shut on the darkness of unoccupied rooms; to be conscious of flights of unmounted stairs, of stretches of untrodden corridors, of unending walls, from which the pictured eyes of long dead men and women stare, as if seeing things which human eyes behold not— is an eerie and unwholesome thing. Mount Dunstan slept in a large four-post bed in a chamber in which he might have died or been murdered a score of times without being able to communicate with the remote servants' quarters below stairs, where lay the one man and one woman who attended him. When he came late to his room and prepared for sleep by the light of two flickering candles the silence of the dead in tombs was about him; but it was only a more profound and insistent thing than the silence of the day, because it was the silence of the night, which is a presence. He used to tell himself with secret smiles at the fact that at certain times the fantasy was half believable—that there were things which walked about softly at night—things which did not want to be dead. He himself had picked them out from among the pictures in the gallery—pretty, light, petulant women; adventurous-eyed, full-blooded, eager men. His theory was that they hated their stone coffins, and fought their way back through the grey mists to try to talk and make love and to be seen of warm things which were alive. But it was not to be done, because they had no bodies and no voices, and when they beat upon closed doors they would not open. Still they came back—came back. And sometimes there was a rustle and a sweep through the air in a passage, or a creak, or a sense of waiting which was almost a sound.

"Perhaps some of them have gone when they have been as I am," he had said one black night, when he had sat in his room staring at the floor. "If a man was dragged out when he had not LIVED a day, he would come back I should come back if—God! A man COULD not be dragged away—like THIS!"

And to sit alone and think of it was an awful and a lonely thing—a lonely thing.

But loneliness was nothing new, only that in these months his had strangely intensified itself. This, though he was not aware of it, was because the soul and body which were the completing parts of him were within reach—and without it. When he went down to breakfast he sat singly at his table, round which twenty people might have laughed and talked. Between the dining-room and the library he spent his days when he was not out of doors. Since he could not afford servants, the many other rooms must be kept closed. It was a ghastly and melancholy thing to make, as he must sometimes, a sort of precautionary visit to the state apartments. He was the last Mount Dunstan, and he would never see them opened again for use, but so long as he lived under the roof he might by prevision check, in a measure, the too rapid encroachments of decay. To have a leak stopped here, a nail driven or a support put there, seemed decent things to do.

"Whom am I doing it for?" he said to Mr. Penzance. "I am doing it for myself—because I cannot help it. The place seems to me like some gorgeous old warrior come to the end of his days It has stood the war of things for century after century—the war of things. It is going now I am all that is left to it. It is all I have. So I patch it up when I can afford it, with a crutch or a splint and a bandage."

Late in the afternoon of the day on which Miss Vanderpoel rode away from West Ways with Lord Westholt, a stealthy and darkly purple cloud rose, lifting its ominous bulk against a chrysoprase and pink horizon. It was the kind of cloud which speaks of but one thing to those who watch clouds, or even casually consider them. So Lady Anstruthers felt some surprise when she saw Sir Nigel mount his horse before the stone steps and ride away, as it were, into the very heart of the coming storm.

"Nigel will be caught in the rain," she said to her sister. "I wonder why he goes out now. It would be better to wait until to-morrow."

But Sir Nigel did not think so. He had calculated matters with some nicety. He was not exactly on such terms with Mount Dunstan as would make a casual call seem an entirely natural thing, and he wished to drop in upon him for a casual call and in an unpremeditated manner. He meant to reach the Mount about the time the storm broke, under which circumstance nothing could bear more lightly an air of being unpremeditated than to take refuge in a chance passing.

Mount Dunstan was in the library. He had sat smoking his pipe while he watched the purple cloud roll up and spread itself, blotting out the chrysoprase and pink and blue, and when the branches of the trees began to toss about he had looked on with pleasure as the rush of big rain drops came down and pelted things. It was a fine storm, and there were some imposing claps of thunder and jagged flashes of lightning. As one splendid rattle shook the air he was surprised to hear a summons at the great hall door. Who on earth could be turning up at this time? His man Reeve announced the arrival a few moments later, and it was Sir Nigel Anstruthers. He had, he explained, been riding through the village when the deluge descended, and it had occurred to him to turn in at the park gates and ask a temporary shelter. Mount Dunstan received him with sufficient courtesy. His appearance was not a thing to rejoice over, but it could be endured. Whisky and soda and a smoke would serve to pass the hour, if the storm lasted so long.

Conversation was not the easiest thing in the world under the circumstances, but Sir Nigel led the way steadily after he had taken his seat and accepted the hospitalities offered. What a place it was—this! He had been struck for the hundredth time with the impressiveness of the mass of it, the sweep of the park and the splendid grouping of the timber, as he had ridden up the avenue. There was no other place like it in the county. Was there another like it in England?

"Not in its case, I hope," Mount Dunstan said.

There were a few seconds of silence. The rain poured down in splashing sheets and was swept in rattling gusts against the window panes.

"What the place needs is—an heiress," Anstruthers observed in the tone of a practical man. "I believe I have heard that your views of things are such that she should preferably NOT be an American."

Mount Dunstan did not smile, though he slightly showed his teeth.

"When I am driven to the wall," he answered, "I may not be fastidious as to nationality."

Nigel Anstruthers' manner was not a bad one. He chose that tone of casual openness which, while it does not wholly commit itself, may be regarded as suggestive of the amiable half confidence of speeches made as "man to man."

"My own opportunity of studying the genus American heiress within my own gates is a first-class one. I find that it knows what it wants and that its intention is to get it." A short laugh broke from him as he flicked the ash from his cigar on to the small bronze receptacle at his elbow. "It is not many years since it would have been difficult for a girl to be frank enough to say, 'When I marry I shall ask something in exchange for what I have to give.'"

"There are not many who have as much to give," said Mount Dunstan coolly.

"True," with a slight shrug. "You are thinking that men are glad enough to take a girl like that—even one who has not a shape like Diana's and eyes like the sea. Yes, by George," softly, and narrowing his lids, "she IS a handsome creature."

Mount Dunstan did not attempt to refute the statement, and Anstruthers laughed low again.

"It is an asset she knows the value of quite clearly. That is the interesting part of it. She has inherited the far-seeing commercial mind. She does not object to admitting it. She educated herself in delightful cold blood that she might be prepared for the largest prize appearing upon the horizon. She held things in view when she was a child at school, and obviously attacked her French, German, and Italian conjugations with a twelve-year-old eye on the future."

Mount Dunstan leaning back carelessly in his chair, laughed—as it seemed—with him. Internally he was saying that the man was a liar who might always be trusted to lie, but he knew with shamed fury that the lies were doing something to his soul—rolling dark vapours over it—stinging him, dragging away props, and making him feel they had been foolish things to lean on. This can always be done with a man in love who has slight foundation for hope. For some mysterious and occult reason civilisation has elected to treat the strange and great passion as if it were an unholy and indecent thing, whose dominion over him proper social training prevents any man from admitting openly. In passing through its cruelest phases he must bear himself as if he were immune, and this being the custom, he may be called upon to endure much without the relief of striking out with manly blows. An enemy guessing his case and possessing the infernal gift whose joy is to dishearten and do hurt with courteous despitefulness, may plant a poisoned arrow here and there with neatness and fine touch, while his bound victim can, with decency, neither start, nor utter brave howls, nor guard himself, but must sit still and listen, hospitably supplying smoke and drink and being careful not to make an ass of himself.

Therefore Mount Dunstan pushed the cigars nearer to his visitor and waved his hand hospitably towards the whisky and soda. There was no reason, in fact, why Anstruthers—or any one indeed, but Penzance, should suspect that he had become somewhat mad in secret. The man's talk was marked merely by the lightly disparaging malice which was rarely to be missed from any speech of his which touched on others. Yet it might have been a thing arranged beforehand, to suggest adroitly either lies or truth which would make a man see every sickeningly good reason for feeling that in this contest he did not count for a man at all.

"It has all been pretty obvious," said Sir Nigel. "There is a sort of cynicism in the openness of the siege. My impression is that almost every youngster who has met her has taken a shot. Tommy Alanby scrambling up from his knees in one of the rose-gardens was a satisfying sight. His much-talked-of-passion for Jane Lithcom was temporarily in abeyance."

The rain swirled in a torrent against the window, and casually glancing outside at the tossing gardens he went on.

"She is enjoying herself. Why not? She has the spirit of the huntress. I don't think she talks nonsense about friendship to the captives of her bow and spear. She knows she can always get what she wants. A girl like that MUST have an arrogance of mind. And she is not a young saint. She is one of the women born with THE LOOK in her eyes. I own I should not like to be in the place of any primeval poor brute who really went mad over her—and counted her millions as so much dirt."

Mount Dunstan answered with a shrug of his big shoulders:

"Apparently he would seem as remote from the reason of to-day as the men who lived on the land when Hengist and Horsa came—or when Caesar landed at Deal."

"He would seem as remote to her," with a shrug also. "I should not like to contend that his point of view would not interest her or that she would particularly discourage him. Her eyes would call him—without malice or intention, no doubt, but your early Briton ceorl or earl would be as well understood by her. Your New York beauty who has lived in the market place knows principally the prices of things."

He was not ill pleased with himself. He was putting it well and getting rather even with her. If this fellow with his shut mouth had a sore spot hidden anywhere he was giving him "to think." And he would find himself thinking, while, whatsoever he thought, he would be obliged to continue to keep his ugly mouth shut. The great idea was to say things WITHOUT saying them, to set your hearer's mind to saying them for you.

"What strikes one most is a sort of commercial brilliance in her," taking up his thread again after a smilingly reflective pause. "It quite exhilarates one by its novelty. There's spice in it. We English have not a look-in when we are dealing with Americans, and yet France calls us a nation of shopkeepers. My impression is that their women take little inventories of every house they enter, of every man they meet. I heard her once speaking to my wife about this place, as if she had lived in it. She spoke of the closed windows and the state of the gardens— of broken fountains and fallen arches. She evidently deplored the deterioration of things which represented capital. She has inventoried Dunholm, no doubt. That will give Westholt a chance. But she will do nothing until after her next year's season in London—that I'd swear. I look forward to next year. It will be worth watching. She has been training my wife. A sister who has married an Englishman and has at least spent some years of her life in England has a certain established air. When she is presented one knows she will be a sensation. After that——" he hesitated a moment, smiling not too pleasantly.

"After that," said Mount Dunstan, "the Deluge."

"Exactly. The Deluge which usually sweeps girls off their feet—but it will not sweep her off hers. She will stand quite firm in the flood and lose sight of nothing of importance which floats past."

Mount Dunstan took him up. He was sick of hearing the fellow's voice.

"There will be a good many things," he said; "there will be great personages and small ones, pomps and vanities, glittering things and heavy ones."

"When she sees what she wants," said Anstruthers, "she will hold out her hand, knowing it will come to her. The things which drown will not disturb her. I once made the blunder of suggesting that she might need protection against the importunate—as if she had been an English girl. It was an idiotic thing to do."

"Because?" Mount Dunstan for the moment had lost his head. Anstruthers had maddeningly paused.

"She answered that if it became necessary she might perhaps be able to protect herself. She was as cool and frank as a boy. No air pince about it— merely consciousness of being able to put things in their right places. Made a mere male relative feel like a fool."

"When ARE things in their right places?" To his credit be it spoken, Mount Dunstan managed to say it as if in the mere putting together of idle words. What man likes to be reminded of his right place! No man wants to be put in his right place. There is always another place which seems more desirable.

"She knows—if we others do not. I suppose my right place is at Stornham, conducting myself as the brother-in-law of a fair American should. I suppose yours is here—shut up among your closed corridors and locked doors. There must be a lot of them in a house like this. Don't you sometimes feel it too large for you?"

"Always," answered Mount Dunstan.

The fact that he added nothing else and met a rapid side glance with unmoving red-brown eyes gazing out from under rugged brows, perhaps irritated Anstruthers. He had been rather enjoying himself, but he had not enjoyed himself enough. There was no denying that his plaything had not openly flinched. Plainly he was not good at flinching. Anstruthers wondered how far a man might go. He tried again.

"She likes the place, though she has a natural disdain for its condition. That is practical American. Things which are going to pieces because money is not spent upon them—mere money, of which all the people who count for anything have so much—are inevitably rather disdained. They are 'out of it.' But she likes the estate." As he watched Mount Dunstan he felt sure he had got it at last—the right thing. "If you were a duke with fifty thousand a year," with a distinctly nasty, amicably humorous, faint laugh, "she would—by the Lord, I believe, she would take it over—and you with it."

Mount Dunstan got up. In his rough walking tweeds he looked over-big— and heavy—and perilous. For two seconds Nigel Anstruthers would not have been surprised if he had without warning slapped his face, or knocked him over, or whirled him out of his chair and kicked him. He would not have liked it, but—for two seconds—it would have been no surprise. In fact, he instinctively braced his not too firm muscles. But nothing of the sort occurred. During the two seconds—perhaps three—Mount Dunstan stood still and looked down at him. The brief space at an end, he walked over to the hearth and stood with his back to the big fireplace.

"You don't like her," he said, and his manner was that of a man dealing with a matter of fact. "Why do you talk about her?"

He had got away again—quite away.

An ugly flush shot over Anstruthers' face. There was one more thing to say—whether it was idiotic to say it or not. Things can always be denied afterwards, should denial appear necessary—and for the moment his special devil possessed him.

"I do not like her!" And his mouth twisted. "Do I not? I am not an old woman. I am a man—like others. I chance to like her—too much."

There was a short silence. Mount Dunstan broke it.

"Then," he remarked, "you had better emigrate to some country with a climate which suits you. I should say that England—for the present—does not."

"I shall stay where I am," answered Anstruthers, with a slight hoarseness of voice, which made it necessary for him to clear his throat. "I shall stay where she is. I will have that satisfaction, at least. She does not mind. I am only a racketty, middle-aged brother-in-law, and she can take care of herself. As I told you, she has the spirit of the huntress."

"Look here," said Mount Dunstan, quite without haste, and with an iron civility. "I am going to take the liberty of suggesting something. If this thing is true, it would be as well not to talk about it."

"As well for me—or for her?" and there was a serene significance in the query.

Mount Dunstan thought a few seconds.

"I confess," he said slowly, and he planted his fine blow between the eyes well and with directness. "I confess that it would not have occurred to me to ask you to do anything or refrain from doing it for her sake."

"Thank you. Perhaps you are right. One learns that one must protect one's self. I shall not talk—neither will you. I know that. I was a fool to let it out. The storm is over. I must ride home." He rose from his seat and stood smiling. "It would smash up things nicely if the new beauty's appearance in the great world were preceded by chatter of the unseemly affection of some adorer of ill repute. Unfairly enough it is always the woman who is hurt."

"Unless," said Mount Dunstan civilly, "there should arise the poor, primeval brute, in his neolithic wrath, to seize on the man to blame, and break every bone and sinew in his damned body."

"The newspapers would enjoy that more than she would," answered Sir Nigel. "She does not like the newspapers. They are too ready to disparage the multi-millionaire, and cackle about members of his family."

The unhidden hatred which still professed to hide itself in the depths of their pupils, as they regarded each other, had its birth in a passion as elemental as the quakings of the earth, or the rage of two lions in a desert, lashing their flanks in the blazing sun. It was well that at this moment they should part ways.

Sir Nigel's horse being brought, he went on the way which was his.

"It was a mistake to say what I did," he said before going. "I ought to have held my tongue. But I am under the same roof with her. At any rate, that is a privilege no other man shares with me."

He rode off smartly, his horse's hoofs splashing in the rain pools left in the avenue after the storm. He was not so sure after all that he had made a mistake, and for the moment he was not in the mood to care whether he had made one or not. His agreeable smile showed itself as he thought of the obstinate, proud brute he had left behind, sitting alone among his shut doors and closed corridors. They had not shaken hands either at meeting or parting. Queer thing it was—the kind of enmity a man could feel for another when he was upset by a woman. It was amusing enough that it should be she who was upsetting him after all these years—impudent little Betty, with the ferocious manner.

CHAPTER XXXVIII

AT SHANDY'S

On a late-summer evening in New York the atmosphere surrounding a certain corner table at Shandy's cheap restaurant in Fourteenth Street was stirred by a sense of excitement.

The corner table in question was the favourite meeting place of a group of young men of the G. Selden type, who usually took possession of it at dinner time—having decided that Shandy's supplied more decent food for fifty cents, or even for twenty-five, than was to be found at other places of its order. Shandy's was "about all right," they said to each other, and patronised it accordingly, three or four of them generally dining together, with a friendly and adroit manipulation of "portions" and "half portions" which enabled them to add variety to their bill of fare.

The street outside was lighted, the tide of passers-by was less full and more leisurely in its movements than it was during the seething, working hours of daylight, but the electric cars swung past each other with whiz and clang of bell almost unceasingly, their sound being swelled, at short intervals, by the roar and rumbling rattle of the trains dashing by on the elevated railroad. This, however, to the frequenters of Shandy's, was the usual accompaniment of every-day New York life and was regarded as a rather cheerful sort of thing.

This evening the four claimants of the favourite corner table had met together earlier than usual. Jem Belter, who "hammered" a typewriter at Schwab's Brewery, Tom Wetherbee, who was "in a downtown office," Bert Johnson, who was "out for the Delkoff," and Nick Baumgarten, who having for some time "beaten" certain streets as assistant salesman for the same illustrious machine, had been recently elevated to a "territory" of his own, and was therefore in high spirits.

"Say!" he said. "Let's give him a fine dinner. We can make it between us. Beefsteak and mushrooms, and potatoes hashed brown. He likes them. Good old G. S. I shall be right glad to see him. Hope foreign travel has not given him the swell head."

"Don't believe it's hurt him a bit. His letter didn't sound like it. Little Georgie ain't a fool," said Jem Belter.

Tom Wetherbee was looking over the letter referred to. It had been written to the four conjointly, towards the termination of Selden's visit to Mr. Penzance. The young man was not an ardent or fluent correspondent; but Tom Wetherbee was chuckling as he read the epistle.

"Say, boys," he said, "this big thing he's keeping back to tell us when he sees us is all right, but what takes me is old George paying a visit to a parson. He ain't no Young Men's Christian Association."

Bert Johnson leaned forward, and looked at the address on the letter paper.

"Mount Dunstan Vicarage," he read aloud. "That looks pretty swell, doesn't it?" with a laugh. "Say, fellows, you know Jepson at the office, the chap that prides himself on reading such a lot? He said it reminded him of the names of places in English novels. That Johnny's the biggest snob you ever set your tooth into. When I told him about the lord fellow that owns the castle, and that George seemed to have seen him, he nearly fell over himself. Never had any use for George before, but just you watch him make up to him when he sees him next."

People were dropping in and taking seats at the tables. They were all of one class. Young men who lived in hall bedrooms. Young women who worked in shops or offices, a couple here and there, who, living far uptown, had come to Shandy's to dinner, that they might go to cheap seats in some theatre afterwards. In the latter case, the girls wore their best hats, had bright eyes, and cheeks lightly flushed by their sense of festivity. Two or three were very pretty in their thin summer dresses and flowered or feathered head gear, tilted at picturesque angles over their thick hair. When each one entered the eyes of the young men at the corner table followed her with curiosity and interest, but the glances at her escort were always of a disparaging nature.

"There's a beaut!" said Nick Baumgarten. "Get onto that pink stuff on her hat, will you. She done it because it's just the colour of her cheeks."

They all looked, and the girl was aware of it, and began to laugh and talk coquettishly to the young man who was her companion.

"I wonder where she got Clarence?" said Jem Belter in sarcastic allusion to her escort. "The things those lookers have fastened on to them gets ME."

"If it was one of US, now," said Bert Johnson. Upon which they broke into simultaneous good-natured laughter.

"It's queer, isn't it," young Baumgarten put in, "how a fellow always feels sore when he sees another fellow with a peach like that? It's just straight human nature, I guess."

The door swung open to admit a newcomer, at the sight of whom Jem Belter exclaimed joyously: "Good old Georgie! Here he is, fellows! Get on to his glad rags."

"Glad rags" is supposed to buoyantly describe such attire as, by its freshness or elegance of style, is rendered a suitable adornment for festive occasions or loftier leisure moments. "Glad rags" may mean evening dress, when a young gentleman's wardrobe can aspire to splendour so marked, but it also applies to one's best and latest-purchased garb, in contradistinction to the less ornamental habiliments worn every day, and designated as "office clothes."

G. Selden's economies had not enabled him to give himself into the hands of a Bond Street tailor, but a careful study of cut and material, as spread before the eye in elegant coloured illustrations in the windows of respectable shops in less ambitious quarters, had resulted in the purchase of a well-made suit of smart English cut. He had a nice young figure, and looked extremely neat and tremendously new and clean, so much so, indeed, that several persons glanced at him a little admiringly as he was met half way to the corner table by his friends.

"Hello, old chap! Glad to see you. What sort of a voyage? How did you leave the royal family? Glad to get back?"

They all greeted him at once, shaking hands and slapping him on the back, as they hustled him gleefully back to the corner table and made him sit down.

"Say, garsong," said Nick Baumgarten to their favourite waiter, who came at once in answer to his summons, "let's have a porterhouse steak, half the size of this table, and with plenty of mushrooms and potatoes hashed brown. Here's Mr. Selden just returned from visiting at Windsor Castle, and if we don't treat him well, he'll look down on us."

G. Selden grinned. "How have you been getting on, Sam?" he said, nodding cheerfully to the man. They were old and tried friends. Sam knew all about the days when a fellow could not come into Shandy's at all, or must satisfy his strong young hunger with a bowl of soup, or coffee and a roll. Sam did his best for them in the matter of the size of portions, and they did their good-natured utmost for him in the affair of the pooled tip.

"Been getting on as well as can be expected," Sam grinned back. "Hope you had a fine time, Mr. Selden?"

"Fine! I should smile! Fine wasn't in it," answered Selden. "But I'm looking forward to a Shandy porterhouse steak, all the same."

"Did they give you a better one in the Strawnd?" asked Baumgarten, in what he believed to be a correct Cockney accent.

"You bet they didn't," said Selden. "Shandy's takes a lot of beating." That last is English.

The people at the other tables cast involuntary glances at them. Their eager, hearty young pleasure in the festivity of the occasion was a healthy thing to see. As they sat round the corner table, they produced the effect of gathering close about G. Selden. They concentrated their combined attention upon him, Belter and Johnson leaning forward on their folded arms, to watch him as he talked.

"Billy Page came back in August, looking pretty bum," Nick Baumgarten began. "He'd been painting gay Paree brick red, and he'd spent more money than he'd meant to, and that wasn't half enough. Landed dead broke. He said he'd had a great time, but he'd come home with rather a dark brown taste in his mouth, that he'd like to get rid of."

"He thought you were a fool to go off cycling into the country," put in Wetherbee, "but I told him I guessed that was where he was 'way off. I believed you'd had the best time of the two of you."

"Boys," said Selden, "I had the time of my life." He said it almost solemnly, and laid his hand on the table. "It was like one of those yarns Bert tells us. Half the time I didn't believe it, and half the time I was ashamed of myself to think it was all happening to me and none of your fellows were in it."

"Oh, well," said Jem Belter, "luck chases some fellows, anyhow. Look at Nick, there."

"Well," Selden summed the whole thing up, "I just FELL into it where it was so deep that I had to strike out all I knew how to keep from drowning."

"Tell us the whole thing," Nick Baumgarten put in; "from beginning to end. Your letter didn't give anything away."

"A letter would have spoiled it. I can't write letters anyhow. I wanted to wait till I got right here with you fellows round where I could answer questions. First off," with the deliberation befitting such an opening, "I've sold machines enough to pay my expenses, and leave some over."

"You have? Gee whiz! Say, give us your prescription. Glad I know you, Georgy!"

"And who do you suppose bought the first three?" At this point, it was he who leaned forward upon the table—his climax being a thing to concentrate upon. "Reuben S. Vanderpoel's daughter—Miss Bettina! And, boys, she gave me a letter to Reuben S., himself, and here it is."

He produced a flat leather pocketbook and took an envelope from an inner flap, laying it before them on the tablecloth. His knowledge that they would not have believed him if he had not brought his proof was founded on everyday facts. They would not have doubted his veracity, but the possibility of such delirious good fortune. What they would have believed would have been that he was playing a hilarious joke on them. Jokes of this kind, but not of this proportion, were common entertainments.

Their first impulse had been towards an outburst of laughter, but even before he produced his letter a certain truthful seriousness in his look had startled them. When he laid the envelope down each man caught his breath. It could not be denied that Jem Belter turned pale with emotion. Jem had never been one of the lucky ones.

"She let me read it," said G. Selden, taking the letter from its envelope with great care. "And I said to her: 'Miss Vanderpoel, would you let me just show that to the boys the first night I go to Shandy's?' I knew she'd tell me if it wasn't all right to do it. She'd know I'd want to be told. And she just laughed and said: 'I don't mind at all. I like "the boys." Here is a message to them. "Good luck to you all."'"

"She said that?" from Nick Baumgarten.

"Yes, she did, and she meant it. Look at this."

This was the letter. It was quite short, and written in a clear, definite hand.

"DEAR FATHER: This will be brought to you by Mr. G. Selden, of whom I have written to you. Please be good to him.

"Affectionately,

"BETTY."

Each young man read it in turn. None of them said anything just at first. A kind of awe had descended upon them—not in the least awe of Vanderpoel, who, with other multi-millionaires, were served up each week with cheerful neighbourly comment or equally neighbourly disrespect, in huge Sunday papers read throughout the land—but awe of the unearthly luck which had fallen without warning to good old G. S., who lived like the rest of them in a hall bedroom on ten per, earned by tramping the streets for the Delkoff.

"That girl," said G. Selden gravely, "that girl is a winner from Winnersville. I take off my hat to her. If it's the scheme that some people's got to have millions, and others have got to sell Delkoffs, that girl's one of those that's entitled to the millions. It's all right she should have 'em. There's no kick coming from me."

Nick Baumgarten was the first to resume wholly normal condition of mind.

"Well, I guess after you've told us about her there'll be no kick coming from any of us. Of course there's something about you that royal families cry for, and they won't be happy till they get. All of us boys knows that. But what we want to find out is how you worked it so that they saw the kind of pearl-studded hairpin you were."

"Worked it!" Selden answered. "I didn't work it. I've got a good bit of nerve, but I never should have had enough to invent what happened—just HAPPENED. I broke my leg falling off my bike, and fell right into a whole bunch of them—earls and countesses and viscounts and Vanderpoels. And it was Miss Vanderpoel who saw me first lying on the ground. And I was in Stornham Court where Lady Anstruthers lives—and she used to be Miss Rosalie Vanderpoel."

"Boys," said Bert Johnson, with friendly disgust, "he's been up to his neck in 'em."

"Cheer up. The worst is yet to come," chaffed Tom Wetherbee.

Never had such a dinner taken place at the corner table, or, in fact, at any other table at Shandy's. Sam brought beefsteaks, which were princely, mushrooms, and hashed brown potatoes in portions whose generosity reached the heart. Sam was on good terms with Shandy's carver, and had worked upon his nobler feelings. Steins of lager beer were ventured upon. There was hearty satisfying of fine hungers. Two of the party had eaten nothing but one "Quick Lunch" throughout the day, one of them because he was short of time, the other for economy's sake, because he was short of money. The meal was a splendid thing. The telling of the story could not be wholly checked by the eating of food. It advanced between mouthfuls, questions being asked and details given in answers. Shandy's became more crowded, as the hour advanced. People all over the room cast interested looks at the party at the corner table, enjoying itself so hugely. Groups sitting at the tables nearest to it found themselves excited by the things they heard.

"That young fellow in the new suit has just come back from Europe," said a man to his wife and daughter. "He seems to have had a good time."

"Papa," the daughter leaned forward, and spoke in a low voice, "I heard him say 'Lord Mount Dunstan said Lady Anstruthers and Miss Vanderpoel were at the garden party.' Who do you suppose he is?"

"Well, he's a nice young fellow, and he has English clothes on, but he doesn't look like one of the Four Hundred. Will you have pie or vanilla ice cream, Bessy?"

Bessy—who chose vanilla ice cream—lost all knowledge of its flavour in her absorption in the conversation at the next table, which she could not have avoided hearing, even if she had wished.

"She bent over the bed and laughed—just like any other nice girl—and she said, 'You are at Stornham Court, which belongs to Sir Nigel Anstruthers. Lady

Anstruthers is my sister. I am Miss Vanderpoel.' And, boys, she used to come and talk to me every day."

"George," said Nick Baumgarten, "you take about seventy-five bottles of Warner's Safe Cure, and rub yourself all over with St. Jacob's Oil. Luck like that ain't HEALTHY!"

. . . . .

Mr. Vanderpoel, sitting in his study, wore the interestedly grave look of a man thinking of absorbing things. He had just given orders that a young man who would call in the course of the evening should be brought to him at once, and he was incidentally considering this young man, as he reflected upon matters recalled to his mind by his impending arrival. They were matters he had thought of with gradually increasing seriousness for some months, and they had, at first, been the result of the letters from Stornham, which each "steamer day" brought. They had been of immense interest to him—these letters. He would have found them absorbing as a study, even if he had not deeply loved Betty. He read in them things she did not state in words, and they set him thinking.

He was not suspected by men like himself of concealing an imagination beneath the trained steadiness of his exterior, but he possessed more than the world knew, and it singularly combined itself with powers of logical deduction.

If he had been with his daughter, he would have seen, day by day, where her thoughts were leading her, and in what direction she was developing, but, at a distance of three thousand miles, he found himself asking questions, and endeavouring to reach conclusions. His affection for Betty was the central emotion of his existence. He had never told himself that he had outgrown the kind and pretty creature he had married in his early youth, and certainly his tender care for her and pleasure in her simple goodness had never wavered, but Betty had given him a companionship which had counted greatly in the sum of his happiness. Because imagination was not suspected in him, no one knew what she stood for in his life. He had no son; he stood at the head of a great house, so to speak—the American parallel of what a great house is in non-republican countries. The power of it counted for great things, not in America alone, but throughout the world. As international intimacies increased, the influence of such houses might end in aiding in the making of history. Enormous constantly increasing wealth and huge financial schemes could not confine their influence, but must reach far. The man whose hand held the lever controlling them was doing well when he thought of them gravely. Such a man had to do with more than his own mere life and living. This man had confronted many problems as the years had passed. He had seen men like himself die, leaving behind them the force they had controlled, and he had seen this force—controlled no longer—let loose upon the world, sometimes a power of evil, sometimes scattering itself aimlessly into nothingness and folly, which wrought harm. He was not an ambitious man, but—perhaps because he was not only a man of thought, but a Vanderpoel of the blood of the first Reuben—these were things he did not contemplate without restlessness. When Rosy had gone away and seemed lost to them, he had been glad when he had seen Betty growing, day by day, into a strong thing. Feminine though she was, she sometimes suggested to him the son who might have been his, but was not. As the closeness of their companionship increased with her years, his admiration for her grew with his love. Power left in her hands must work for the advancement of things, and would not be idly disseminated—if no antagonistic influence wrought against her. He had found himself reflecting that, after all was said, the marriage of such a girl had a sort of parallel in that of some young royal creature, whose union might make or mar things, which must be considered. The man who must inevitably strongly colour her whole being, and vitally mark her life, would, in a sense, lay his hand upon the lever also. If he brought sorrow and disorder with him, the lever would not move steadily. Fortunes such as his grow rapidly, and he was a richer man by millions than he had been when Rosalie had married Nigel Anstruthers. The memory of that marriage had been a painful thing to him, even before he had known the whole truth of its results. The man had been a common adventurer and scoundrel, despite the facts of good birth and the air of decent breeding. If a man who was as much a scoundrel, but cleverer—it would be necessary that he should be much cleverer—made the best of himself to Betty——! It was folly to think one could guess what a woman—or a man, either, for that matter—would love. He knew Betty, but no man knows the thing which comes, as it were, in the dark and claims its own—whether for good or evil. He had lived long enough to see beautiful, strong-spirited creatures do strange things, follow strange gods, swept away into seas of pain by strange waves.

"Even Betty," he had said to himself, now and then. "Even my Betty. Good God—who knows!"

Because of this, he had read each letter with keen eyes. They were long letters, full of detail and colour, because she knew he enjoyed them. She had a delightful touch. He sometimes felt as if they walked the English lanes together. His intimacy with her neighbours, and her neighbourhood, was one of his relaxations. He found himself thinking of old Doby and Mrs. Welden, as a sort of soporific measure, when he lay awake at night. She had sent photographs of Stornham, of Dunholm Castle, and of Dole, and had even found an old engraving of Lady Alanby in her youth. Her evident liking for the Dunholms had pleased him. They were people whose dignity and admirableness were part of general knowledge. Lord Westholt was plainly a young man of many attractions. If the two were drawn to each other—and what more natural—all would be well. He wondered if it would be Westholt. But his love quickened a sagacity which needed no stimulus. He said to himself in time that, though she liked and admired Westholt, she went no farther. That others paid court to her he could guess without being told. He had seen the effect she had produced when she had been at home, and also an unexpected letter to his wife from Milly Bowen had revealed many things. Milly, having noted Mrs. Vanderpoel's eager anxiety to hear direct news of Lady Anstruthers, was not the person to let fall from her hand a useful thread of connection. She had written quite at length, managing adroitly to convey all that she had seen, and all that she had heard. She had been making a visit within driving distance of Stornham, and had had the pleasure of meeting both Lady Anstruthers and Miss Vanderpoel at various parties. She was so sure that Mrs. Vanderpoel would like to hear how well Lady Anstruthers was looking, that she ventured to write. Betty's effect upon the county was made quite clear, as also was the interested expectation of her appearance in town next season. Mr. Vanderpoel, perhaps, gathered more from the letter than his wife did. In her mind, relieved happiness and consternation were mingled.

"Do you think, Reuben, that Betty will marry that Lord Westholt?" she rather faltered. "He seems very nice, but I would rather she married an American. I should feel as if I had no girls at all, if they both lived in England."

"Lady Bowen gives him a good character," her husband said, smiling. "But if anything untoward happens, Annie, you shall have a house of your own half way between Dunholm Castle and Stornham Court."

When he had begun to decide that Lord Westholt did not seem to be the man Fate was veering towards, he not unnaturally cast a mental eye over such other persons as the letters mentioned. At exactly what period his thought first dwelt a shade anxiously on Mount Dunstan he could not have told, but he at length became conscious that it so dwelt. He had begun by feeling an interest in his story, and had asked questions about him, because a situation such as his suggested query to a man of affairs. Thus, it had been natural that the letters should speak of him. What she had written had recalled to him certain rumours of the disgraceful old scandal. Yes, they had been a bad lot. He arranged to put a casual-sounding question or so to certain persons who knew English society well. What he gathered was not encouraging. The present Lord Mount Dunstan was considered rather a surly brute, and lived a mysterious sort of life which might cover many things. It was bad blood, and people were naturally shy of it. Of course, the man was a pauper, and his place a barrack falling to ruin. There had been something rather shady in his going to America or Australia a few years ago.

Good looking? Well, so few people had seen him. The lady, who was speaking, had heard that he was one of those big, rather lumpy men, and had an ill-tempered expression. She always gave a wide berth to a man who looked nasty-tempered. One or two other persons who had spoken of him had conveyed to Mr. Vanderpoel about the same amount of vaguely unpromising information. The episode of G. Selden had been interesting enough, with its suggestions of picturesque contrasts and combinations. Betty's touch had made the junior salesman attracting. It was a good type this, of a young fellow who, battling with the discouragements of a hard life, still did not lose his amazing good cheer and patience, and found healthy sleep and honest waking, even in the hall bedroom. He had consented to Betty's request that he would see him, partly because he was inclined to like what he had heard, and partly for a reason which Betty did not suspect. By extraordinary chance G. Selden had seen Mount Dunstan and his surroundings at close range. Mr. Vanderpoel had liked what he had gathered of Mount Dunstan's attitude towards a personality so singularly exotic to himself. Crude, uneducated, and slangy, the junior salesman was not in any degree a fool. To an American father with a daughter like Betty, the summing-up of a normal, nice-natured, common young denizen of the United States, fresh from contact with the effete, might be subtly instructive, and well worth hearing, if it was unconsciously expressed. Mr. Vanderpoel thought he knew how, after he had overcome his visitor's first awkwardness—if he chanced to be self-conscious—he could lead him to talk. What he hoped to do was to make him forget himself and begin to talk to him as he had talked to Betty, to ingenuously reveal impressions and points of view. Young men of his clean, rudimentary type were very definite about the things they liked and disliked, and could be trusted to reveal admiration, or lack of it, without absolute intention or actual statement. Being elemental and undismayed, they saw things cleared of the mists of social prejudice and modification. Yes, he felt he should be glad to hear of Lord Mount Dunstan and the Mount Dunstan estate from G. Selden in a happy moment of unawareness.

Why was it that it happened to be Mount Dunstan he was desirous to hear of? Well, the absolute reason for that he could not have explained, either. He had asked himself questions on the subject more than once. There was no well-founded reason, perhaps. If Betty's letters had spoken of Mount Dunstan and his home, they had also described Lord Westholt and Dunholm Castle. Of these two men she had certainly spoken more fully than of others. Of Mount Dunstan she had had more to relate through the incident of G. Selden. He smiled as he realised the importance of the figure of G. Selden. It was Selden and his broken leg the two men had ridden over from Mount Dunstan to visit. But for Selden, Betty might not have met Mount Dunstan again. He was reason enough for all she had said. And yet——! Perhaps, between Betty and himself there existed the thing which impresses and communicates without words. Perhaps, because their affection was unusual, they realised each other's emotions. The half-defined anxiety he felt now was not a new thing, but he confessed to himself that it had been spurred a little by the letter the last steamer had brought him. It was NOT Lord Westholt, it definitely appeared. He had asked her to be his wife, and she had declined his proposal.

"I could not have LIKED a man any more without being in love with him," she wrote. "I LIKE him more than I can say—so much, indeed, that I feel a little depressed by my certainty that I do not love him."

If she had loved him, the whole matter would have been simplified. If the other man had drawn her, the thing would not be simple. Her father foresaw all the complications—and he did not want complications for Betty. Yet emotions were perverse and irresistible things, and the stronger the creature swayed by them, the more enormous their power. But, as he sat in his easy chair and thought over it all, the one feeling predominant in his mind was that nothing mattered but Betty—nothing really mattered but Betty.

In the meantime G. Selden was walking up Fifth Avenue, at once touched and exhilarated by the stir about him and his sense of home-coming. It was pretty good to be in little old New York again. The hurried pace of the life about him stimulated his young blood. There were no street cars in Fifth Avenue, but there were carriages, waggons, carts, motors, all pantingly hurried, and fretting and struggling when the crowded state of the thoroughfare held them back. The beautifully dressed women in the carriages wore no light air of being at leisure. It was evident that they were going to keep engagements, to do things, to achieve objects.

"Something doing. Something doing," was his cheerful self-congratulatory thought. He had spent his life in the midst of it, he liked it, and it welcomed him back.

The appointment he was on his way to keep thrilled him into an uplifted mood. Once or twice a half-nervous chuckle broke from him as he tried to realise that he had been given the chance which a year ago had seemed so impossible that its mere incredibleness had made it a natural subject for jokes. He was going to call on Reuben S. Vanderpoel, and he was going because Reuben S. had made an appointment with him.

He wore his London suit of clothes and he felt that he looked pretty decent. He could only do his best in the matter of bearing. He always thought that, so long as a fellow didn't get "chesty" and kept his head from swelling, he was all right. Of course he had never been in one of these swell Fifth Avenue houses, and he felt a bit nervous—but Miss Vanderpoel would have told her father what sort of fellow he was, and her father was likely to be something like herself. The house, which had been built since Lady Anstruthers' marriage, was well "up-town," and was big and imposing. When a manservant opened the front door, the square hall looked very splendid to Selden. It was full of light, and of rich furniture, which was like the stuff he had seen in one or two special shop windows in Fifth Avenue—places where they sold magnificent gilded or carven coffers and vases, pieces of tapestry and marvellous embroideries, antiquities from foreign palaces. Though it was quite different, it was as swell in its way as the house at Mount Dunstan, and there were gleams of pictures on the walls that looked fine, and no mistake.

He was expected. The man led him across the hall to Mr. Vanderpoel's room. After he had announced his name he closed the door quietly and went away. Mr. Vanderpoel rose from an armchair to come forward to meet his visitor. He was tall and straight—Betty had inherited her slender height from him. His well-balanced face suggested the relationship between them. He had a steady mouth, and eyes which looked as if they saw much and far.

"I am glad to see you, Mr. Selden," he said, shaking hands with him. "You have seen my daughters, and can tell me how they are. Miss Vanderpoel has written to me of you several times."

He asked him to sit down, and as he took his chair Selden felt that he had been right in telling himself that Reuben S. Vanderpoel would be somehow like his girl. She was a girl, and he was an elderly man of business, but they were like each other. There was the same kind of straight way of doing things, and the same straight-seeing look in both of them.

It was queer how natural things seemed, when they really happened to a fellow. Here he was sitting in a big leather chair and opposite to him in its fellow sat Reuben S. Vanderpoel, looking at him with friendly eyes. And it seemed all right, too—not as if he had managed to "butt in," and would find himself politely fired out directly. He might have been one of the Four Hundred making a call. Reuben S. knew how to make a man feel easy, and no mistake. This G. Selden observed at once, though he had, in fact, no knowledge of the practical tact which dealt with him. He found himself answering questions about Lady Anstruthers and her sister, which led to the opening up of other subjects. He did not realise that he began to express ingenuous opinions and describe things. His listener's interest led him on, a question here, a rather pleased laugh there, were encouraging. He had enjoyed himself so much during his stay in England, and had felt his experiences so greatly to be rejoiced over, that they were easy to talk of at any time—in fact, it was even a trifle difficult not to talk of them—but, stimulated by the look which rested on him, by the deft word and ready smile, words flowed readily and without the restraint of self-consciousness.

"When you think that all of it sort of began with a robin, it's queer enough," he said. "But for that robin I shouldn't be here, sir," with a boyish laugh. "And he was an English robin—a little fellow not half the size of the kind that hops about Central Park."

"Let me hear about that," said Mr. Vanderpoel.

It was a good story, and he told it well, though in his own junior salesman phrasing. He began with his bicycle ride into the green country, his spin over the fine roads, his rest under the hedge during the shower, and then the song of the robin perched among the fresh wet leafage, his feathers puffed out, his red young satin-glossed breast pulsating and swelling. His words were colloquial enough, but they called up the picture.

"Everything sort of glittering with the sunshine on the wet drops, and things smelling good, like they do after rain—leaves, and grass, and good earth. I tell you it made a fellow feel as if the whole world was his brother. And when Mr. Rob. lit on that twig and swelled his red breast as if he knew the whole thing was his, and began to let them notes out, calling for his lady friend to come and go halves with him, I just had to laugh and speak to him, and that was when Lord Mount Dunstan heard me and jumped over the hedge. He'd been listening, too."

The expression Reuben S. Vanderpoel wore made it an agreeable thing to talk—to go on. He evidently cared to hear. So Selden did his best, and enjoyed himself in doing it. His style made for realism and brought things clearly before one. The big-built man in the rough and shabby shooting clothes, his way when he dropped into the grass to sit beside the stranger and talk, certain meanings in his words which conveyed to Vanderpoel what had not been conveyed to G. Selden. Yes, the man carried a heaviness about with him and hated the burden. Selden quite unconsciously brought him out strongly.

"I don't know whether I'm the kind of fellow who is always making breaks," he said, with his boy's laugh again, "but if I am, I never made a worse one than when I asked him straight if he was out of a job, and on the tramp. It showed what a nice fellow he was that he didn't get hot about it. Some fellows would.

He only laughed—sort of short—and said his job had been more than he could handle, and he was afraid he was down and out."

Mr. Vanderpoel was conscious that so far he was somewhat attracted by this central figure. G. Selden was also proving satisfactory in the matter of revealing his excellently simple views of persons and things.

"The only time he got mad was when I wouldn't believe him when he told me who he was. I was a bit hot in the collar myself. I'd felt sorry for him, because I thought he was a chap like myself, and he was up against it. I know what that is, and I'd wanted to jolly him along a bit. When he said his name was Mount Dunstan, and the place belonged to him, I guessed he thought he was making a joke. So I got on my wheel and started off, and then he got mad for keeps. He said he wasn't such a damned fool as he looked, and what he'd said was true, and I could go and be hanged."

Reuben S. Vanderpoel laughed. He liked that. It sounded like decent British hot temper, which he had often found accompanied honest British decencies.

He liked other things, as the story proceeded. The picture of the huge house with the shut windows, made him slightly restless. The concealed imagination, combined with the financier's resentment of dormant interests, disturbed him. That which had attracted Selden in the Reverend Lewis Penzance strongly attracted himself. Also, a man was a good deal to be judged by his friends. The man who lived alone in the midst of stately desolateness and held as his chief intimate a high-bred and gentle-minded scholar of ripe years, gave, in doing this, certain evidence which did not tell against him. The whole situation meant something a splendid, vivid-minded young creature might be moved by—might be allured by, even despite herself.

There was something fantastic in the odd linking of incidents—Selden's chance view of Betty as she rode by, his next day's sudden resolve to turn back and go to Stornham, his accident, all that followed seemed, if one were fanciful—part of a scheme prearranged

"When I came to myself," G. Selden said, "I felt like that fellow in the Shakespeare play that they dress up and put to bed in the palace when he's drunk. I thought I'd gone off my head. And then Miss Vanderpoel came." He paused a moment and looked down on the carpet, thinking. "Gee whiz! It WAS queer," he said.

Betty Vanderpoel's father could almost hear her voice as the rest was told. He knew how her laugh had sounded, and what her presence must have been to the young fellow. His delightful, human, always satisfying Betty!

Through this odd trick of fortune, Mount Dunstan had begun to see her. Since, through the unfair endowment of Nature—that it was not wholly fair he had often told himself—she was all the things that desire could yearn for, there were many chances that when a man saw her he must long to see her again, and there were the same chances that such an one as Mount Dunstan might long also, and, if Fate was against him, long with a bitter strength. Selden was not aware that he had spoken more fully of Mount Dunstan and his place than of other things. That this had been the case, had been because Mr. Vanderpoel had intended it should be so. He had subtly drawn out and encouraged a detailed account of the time spent at Mount Dunstan vicarage. It was easily encouraged. Selden's affectionate admiration for the vicar led him on to enthusiasm. The quiet house and garden, the old books, the afternoon tea under the copper beech, and the long talks of old things, which had been so new to the young New Yorker, had plainly made a mark upon his life, not likely to be erased even by the rush of after years.

"The way he knew history was what got me," he said. "And the way you got interested in it, when he talked. It wasn't just HISTORY, like you learn at school, and forget, and never see the use of, anyhow. It was things about men, just like yourself—hustling for a living in their way, just as we're hustling in Broadway. Most of it was fighting, and there are mounds scattered about that are the remains of their forts and camps. Roman camps, some of them. He took me to see them. He had a little old pony chaise we trundled about in, and he'd draw up and we'd sit and talk. 'There were men here on this very spot,' he'd say, 'looking out for attack, eating, drinking, cooking their food, polishing their weapons, laughing, and shouting—MEN—Selden, fifty-five years before Christ was born—and sometimes the New Testament times seem to us so far away that they are half a dream.' That was the kind of thing he'd say, and I'd sometimes feel as if I heard the Romans shouting. The country about there was full of queer places, and both he and Lord Dunstan knew more about them than I know about Twenty-third Street."

"You saw Lord Mount Dunstan often?" Mr. Vanderpoel suggested.

"Every day, sir. And the more I saw him, the more I got to like him. He's all right. But it's hard luck to be fixed as he is—that's stone-cold truth. What's a man to do? The money he ought to have to keep up his place was spent before he was born. His father and his eldest brother were a bum lot, and his grandfather and great-grandfather were fools. He can't sell the place, and he wouldn't if he could. Mr. Penzance was so fond of him that sometimes he'd say things. But," hastily, "perhaps I'm talking too much."

"You happen to be talking about questions I have been greatly interested in. I have thought a good deal at times of the position of the holders of large estates they cannot afford to keep up. This special instance is a case in point."

G. Selden felt himself in luck again. Reuben S., quite evidently, found his subject worthy of undivided attention. Selden had not heartily liked Lord Mount Dunstan, and lived in the atmosphere surrounding him, looking about him with sharp young New York eyes, without learning a good deal.

He had seen the practical hardship of the situation, and laid it bare.

"What Mr. Penzance says is that he's like the men that built things in the beginning—fought for them—fought Romans and Saxons and Normans—perhaps the whole lot at different times. I used to like to get Mr. Penzance to tell stories about the Mount Dunstans. They were splendid. It must be pretty fine to look back about a thousand years and know your folks have been something. All the same its pretty fierce to have to stand alone at the end of it, not able to help yourself, because some of your relations were crazy fools. I don't wonder he feels mad."

"Does he?" Mr. Vanderpoel inquired.

"He's straight," said G. Selden sympathetically. "He's all right. But only money can help him, and he's got none, so he has to stand and stare at things falling to pieces. And—well, I tell you, Mr. Vanderpoel, he LOVES that place— he's crazy about it. And he's proud—I don't mean he's got the swell-head, because he hasn't—but he's just proud. Now, for instance, he hasn't any use for men like himself that marry just for money. He's seen a lot of it, and it's made him sick. He's not that kind."

He had been asked and had answered a good many questions before he went away, but each had dropped into the talk so incidentally that he had not recognised them as queries. He did not know that Lord Mount Dunstan stood out a clearly defined figure in Mr. Vanderpoel's mind, a figure to be reflected upon, and one not without its attraction.

"Miss Vanderpoel tells me," Mr. Vanderpoel said, when the interview was drawing to a close, "that you are an agent for the Delkoff typewriter."

G. Selden flushed slightly.

"Yes, sir," he answered, "but I didn't——"

"I hear that three machines are in use on the Stornham estate, and that they have proved satisfactory."

"It's a good machine," said G. Selden, his flush a little deeper.

Mr. Vanderpoel smiled.

"You are a business-like young man," he said, "and I have no doubt you have a catalogue in your pocket."

G. Selden was a business-like young man. He gave Mr. Vanderpoel one serious look, and the catalogue was drawn forth.

"It wouldn't be business, sir, for me to be caught out without it," he said. "I shouldn't leave it behind if I went to a funeral. A man's got to run no risks."

"I should like to look at it."

The thing had happened. It was not a dream. Reuben S. Vanderpoel, clothed and in his right mind, had, without pressure being exerted upon him, expressed his desire to look at the catalogue—to examine it—to have it explained to him at length.

He listened attentively, while G. Selden did his best. He asked a question now and then, or made a comment. His manner was that of a thoroughly composed man of business, but he was remembering what Betty had told him of the "ten per," and a number of other things. He saw the flush come and go under the still boyish skin, he observed that G. Selden's hand was not wholly steady, though he was making an effort not to seem excited. But he was excited. This actually meant—this thing so unimportant to multi-millionaires—that he was having his "chance," and his young fortunes were, perhaps, in the balance.

"Yes," said Reuben S., when he had finished, "it seems a good, up-to-date machine."

"It's the best on the market," said G. Selden, "out and out, the best."

"I understand you are only junior salesman?"

"Yes, sir. Ten per and five dollars on every machine I sell. If I had a territory, I should get ten."

"Then," reflectively, "the first thing is to get a territory."

"Perhaps I shall get one in time, if I keep at it," said Selden courageously.

"It is a good machine. I like it," said Mr. Vanderpoel. "I can see a good many places where it could be used. Perhaps, if you make it known at your office that when you are given a good territory, I shall give preference to the Delkoff over other typewriting machines, it might—eh?"

A light broke out upon G. Selden's countenance—a light radiant and magnificent. He caught his breath. A desire to shout—to yell—to whoop, as when in the society of "the boys," was barely conquered in time.

"Mr. Vanderpoel," he said, standing up, "I—Mr. Vanderpoel—sir—I feel as if I was having a pipe dream. I'm not, am I?"

"No," answered Mr. Vanderpoel, "you are not. I like you, Mr. Selden. My daughter liked you. I do not mean to lose sight of you. We will begin, however, with the territory, and the Delkoff. I don't think there will be any difficulty about it."

. . . . .

Ten minutes later G. Selden was walking down Fifth Avenue, wondering if there was any chance of his being arrested by a policeman upon the charge that he was reeling, instead of walking steadily. He hoped he should get back to the hall bedroom safely. Nick Baumgarten and Jem Bolter both "roomed" in the house with him. He could tell them both. It was Jem who had made up the yarn about one of them saving Reuben S. Vanderpoel's life. There had been no life-saving, but the thing had come true.

"But, if it hadn't been for Lord Mount Dunstan," he said, thinking it over excitedly, "I should never have seen Miss Vanderpoel, and, if it hadn't been for Miss Vanderpoel, I should never have got next to Reuben S. in my life. Both sides of the Atlantic Ocean got busy to do a good turn to Little Willie. Hully gee!"

In his study Mr. Vanderpoel was rereading Betty's letters. He felt that he had gained a certain knowledge of Lord Mount Dunstan.

CHAPTER XXXIX

ON THE MARSHES

THE marshes stretched mellow in the autumn sun, sheep wandered about, nibbling contentedly, or lay down to rest in groups, the sky reflecting itself in the narrow dykes gave a blue colour to the water, a scent of the sea was in the air as one breathed it, flocks of plover rose, now and then, crying softly. Betty, walking with her dog, had passed a heron standing at the edge of a pool.

From her first discovery of them, she had been attracted by the marshes with their English suggestion of the Roman Campagna, their broad expanse of level land spread out to the sun and wind, the thousands of white sheep dotted or clustered as far as eye could reach, the hues of the marsh grass and the plants growing thick at the borders of the strips of water. Its beauty was all its own and curiously aloof from the softly-wooded, undulating world about it. Driving or walking along the high road—the road the Romans had built to London town long centuries ago—on either side of one were meadows, farms, scattered cottages, and hop gardens, but beyond and below stretched the marsh land, golden and grey, and always alluring one by its silence.

"I never pass it without wanting to go to it—to take solitary walks over it, to be one of the spots on it as the sheep are. It seems as if, lying there under the blue sky or the low grey clouds with all the world held at bay by mere space and stillness, they must feel something we know nothing of. I want to go and find out what it is."

This she had once said to Mount Dunstan.

So she had fallen into the habit of walking there with her dog at her side as her sole companion, for having need for time and space for thought, she had found them in the silence and aloofness.

Life had been a vivid and pleasurable thing to her, as far as she could look back upon it. She began to realise that she must have been very happy, because she had never found herself desiring existence other than such as had come to her day by day. Except for her passionate childish regret at Rosy's marriage, she had experienced no painful feeling. In fact, she had faced no hurt in her life, and certainly had been confronted by no limitations. Arguing that girls in their teens usually fall in love, her father had occasionally wondered that she passed through no little episodes of sentiment, but the fact was that her interests had been larger and more numerous than the interests of girls generally are, and her affectionate intimacy with himself had left no such small vacant spaces as are frequently filled by unimportant young emotions. Because she was a logical creature, and had watched life and those living it with clear and interested eyes, she had not been blind to the path which had marked itself before her during the summer's growth and waning. She had not, at first, perhaps, known exactly when things began to change for her—when the clarity of her mind began to be disturbed. She had thought in the beginning—as people have a habit of doing—that an instance—a problem—a situation had attracted her attention because it was absorbing enough to think over. Her view of the matter had been that as the same thing would have interested her father, it had interested herself. But from the morning when she had been conscious of the sudden fury roused in her by Nigel Anstruthers' ugly sneer at Mount Dunstan, she had better understood the thing which had come upon her. Day by day it had increased and gathered power, and she realised with a certain sense of impatience that she had not in any degree understood it when she had seen and wondered at its effect on other women. Each day had been like a wave encroaching farther upon the shore she stood upon. At the outset a certain ignoble pride—she knew it ignoble—filled her with rebellion. She had seen so much of this kind of situation, and had heard so much of the general comment. People had learned how to sneer because experience had taught them. If she gave them cause, why should they not sneer at her as at things? She recalled what she had herself thought of such things—the folly of them, the obviousness—the almost deserved disaster. She had arrogated to herself judgment of women—and men—who might, yes, who might have stood upon their strip of sand, as she stood, with the waves creeping in, each one higher, stronger, and more engulfing than the last. There might have been those among them who also had knowledge of that sudden deadly joy at the sight of one face, at the drop of one voice. When that wave submerged one's pulsing being, what had the world to do with one—how could one hear and think of what its speech might be? Its voice clamoured too far off.

As she walked across the marsh she was thinking this first phase over. She had reached a new one, and at first she looked back with a faint, even rather hard, smile. She walked straight ahead, her mastiff, Roland, padding along heavily close at her side. How still and wide and golden it was; how the cry of plover and lifting trill of skylark assured one that one was wholly encircled by solitude and space which were more enclosing than any walls! She was going to the mounds to which Mr. Penzance had trundled G. Selden in the pony chaise, when he had given him the marvellous hour which had brought Roman camp and Roman legions to life again. Up on the largest hillock one could sit enthroned, resting chin in hand and looking out under level lids at the unstirring, softly-living loveliness of the marsh-land world. So she was presently seated, with her heavy-limbed Roland at her feet. She had come here to try to put things clearly to herself, to plan with such reason as she could control. She had begun to be unhappy, she had begun—with some unfairness—to look back upon the Betty Vanderpoel of the past as an unwittingly self-sufficient young woman, to find herself suddenly entangled by things, even to know a touch of desperateness.

"Not to take a remnant from the ducal bargain counter," she was saying mentally. That was why her smile was a little hard. What if the remnant from the ducal bargain counter had prejudices of his own?

"If he were passionately—passionately in love with me," she said, with red staining her cheeks, "he would not come—he would not come—he would not come. And, because of that, he is more to me—MORE! And more he will become every day—and the more strongly he will hold me. And there we stand."

Roland lifted his fine head from his paws, and, holding it erect on a stiff, strong neck, stared at her in obvious inquiry. She put out her hand and tenderly patted him.

"He will have none of me," she said. "He will have none of me." And she faintly smiled, but the next instant shook her head a little haughtily, and, having done so, looked down with an altered expression upon the cloth of her skirt, because she had shaken upon it, from the extravagant lashes, two clear drops.

It was not the result of chance that she had seen nothing of him for weeks. She had not attempted to persuade herself of that. Twice he had declined an invitation to Stornham, and once he had ridden past her on the road when he might have stopped to exchange greetings, or have ridden on by her side. He did not mean to seem to desire, ever so lightly, to be counted as in the lists. Whether he was drawn by any liking for her or not, it was plain he had determined on this.

If she were to go away now, they would never meet again. Their ways in this world would part forever. She would not know how long it took to break him utterly—if such a man could be broken. If no magic change took place in his fortunes—and what change could come?—the decay about him would spread day by day. Stone walls last a long time, so the house would stand while every beauty and stateliness within it fell into ruin. Gardens would become wildernesses, terraces and fountains crumble and be overgrown, walls that were to-day leaning would fall with time. The years would pass, and his youth with them; he would gradually change into an old man while he watched the things he loved with passion die slowly and hard. How strange it was that lives should touch and pass on the ocean of Time, and nothing should result—nothing at all! When she went on her way, it would be as if a ship loaded with every aid of food and treasure had passed a boat in which a strong man tossed, starving to death, and had not even run up a flag.

"But one cannot run up a flag," she said, stroking Roland. "One cannot. There we stand."

To her recognition of this deadlock of Fate, there had been adding the growing disturbance caused by yet another thing which was increasingly troubling, increasingly difficult to face.

Gradually, and at first with wonderful naturalness of bearing, Nigel Anstruthers had managed to create for himself a singular place in her everyday life. It had begun with a certain personalness in his attitude, a personalness which was a thing to dislike, but almost impossible openly to resent. Certainly, as a self-invited guest in his house, she could scarcely protest against the amiability of his demeanour and his exterior courtesy and attentiveness of manner in his conduct towards her. She had tried to sweep away the objectionable quality in his bearing, by frankness, by indifference, by entire lack of response, but she had remained conscious of its increasing as a spider's web might increase as the spider spun it quietly over one, throwing out threads so impalpable that one could not brush them away because they were too slight to be seen. She was aware that in the first years of his married life he had alternately resented the scarcity of the invitations sent them and rudely refused such as were received. Since he had returned to find her at Stornham, he had insisted that no invitations should be declined, and had escorted his wife and herself wherever they went. What could have been conventionally more proper—what more improper than that he should have persistently have remained at home? And yet there came a time when, as they three drove together at night in the closed carriage, Betty was conscious that, as he sat opposite to her in the dark, when he spoke, when he touched her in arranging the robe over her, or opening or shutting the window, he subtly, but persistently, conveyed that the personalness of his voice, look, and physical nearness was a sort of hideous confidence between them which they were cleverly concealing from Rosalie and the outside world.

When she rode about the country, he had a way of appearing at some turning and making himself her companion, riding too closely at her side, and assuming a noticeable air of being engaged in meaningly confidential talk. Once, when he had been leaning towards her with an audaciously tender manner, they had been passed by the Dunholm carriage, and Lady Dunholm and the friend driving with her had evidently tried not to look surprised. Lady Alanby, meeting them in the same way at another time, had put up her glasses and stared in open disapproval. She might admire a strikingly handsome American girl, but her favour would not last through any such vulgar silliness as flirtations with disgraceful brothers-in-law. When Betty strolled about the park or the lanes, she much too often encountered Sir Nigel strolling also, and knew that he did not mean to allow her to rid herself of him. In public, he made a point of keeping observably close to her, of hovering in her vicinity and looking on at all she did with eyes she rebelled against finding fixed on her each time she was obliged to turn in his direction. He had a fashion of coming to her side and speaking in a dropped voice, which excluded others, as a favoured lover might. She had seen both men and women glance at her in half-embarrassment at their sudden sense of finding themselves slightly de trop. She had said aloud to him on one such occasion—and she had said it with smiling casualness for the benefit of Lady Alanby, to whom she had been talking:

"Don't alarm me by dropping your voice, Nigel. I am easily frightened—and Lady Alanby will think we are conspirators."

For an instant he was taken by surprise. He had been pleased to believe that there was no way in which she could defend herself, unless she would condescend to something stupidly like a scene. He flushed and drew himself up.

"I beg your pardon, my dear Betty," he said, and walked away with the manner of an offended adorer, leaving her to realise an odiously unpleasant truth—which is that there are incidents only made more inexplicable by an effort to explain. She saw also that he was quite aware of this, and that his offended departure was a brilliant inspiration, and had left her, as it were, in the lurch. To have said to Lady Alanby: "My brother-in-law, in whose house I am merely staying for my sister's sake, is trying to lead you to believe that I allow him to make love to me," would have suggested either folly or insanity on her own part. As it was—after a glance at Sir Nigel's stiffly retreating back—Lady Alanby merely looked away with a wholly uninviting expression.

When Betty spoke to him afterwards, haughtily and with determination, he laughed.

"My dearest girl," he said, "if I watch you with interest and drop my voice when I get a chance to speak to you, I only do what every other man does, and I do it because you are an alluring young woman—which no one is more perfectly aware of than yourself. Your pretence that you do not know you are alluring is the most captivating thing about you. And what do you think of doing if I continue to offend you? Do you propose to desert us—to leave poor Rosalie to sink back again into the bundle of old clothes she was when you came? For Heaven's sake, don't do that!"

All that his words suggested took form before her vividly. How well he understood what he was saying. But she answered him bravely.

"No. I do not mean to do that."

He watched her for a few seconds. There was curiosity in his eyes.

"Don't make the mistake of imagining that I will let my wife go with you to America," he said next. "She is as far off from that as she was when I brought her to Stornham. I have told her so. A man cannot tie his wife to the bedpost in these days, but he can make her efforts to leave him so decidedly unpleasant that decent women prefer to stay at home and take what is coming. I have seen that often enough 'to bank on it,' if I may quote your American friends."

"Do you remember my once saying," Betty remarked, "that when a woman has been PROPERLY ill-treated the time comes when nothing matters—nothing but release from the life she loathes?"

"Yes," he answered. "And to you nothing would matter but—excuse my saying it—your own damnable, headstrong pride. But Rosalie is different. Everything matters to her. And you will find it so, my dear girl."

And that this was at least half true was brought home to her by the fact that late the same night Rosy came to her white with crying.

"It is not your fault, Betty," she said. "Don't think that I think it is your fault, but he has been in my room in one of those humours when he seems like a devil. He thinks you will go back to America and try to take me with you. But, Betty, you must not think about me. It will be better for you to go. I have seen you again. I have had you for—for a time. You will be safer at home with father and mother."

Betty laid a hand on her shoulder and looked at her fixedly.

"What is it, Rosy?" she said. "What is it he does to you—that makes you like this?"

"I don't know—but that he makes me feel that there is nothing but evil and lies in the world and nothing can help one against them. Those things he says about everyone—men and women—things one can't repeat—make me sick. And when I try to deny them, he laughs."

"Does he say things about me?" Betty inquired, very quietly, and suddenly Rosalie threw her arms round her.

"Betty, darling," she cried, "go home—go home. You must not stay here."

"When I go, you will go with me," Betty answered. "I am not going back to mother without you."

She made a collection of many facts before their interview was at an end, and they parted for the night. Among the first was that Nigel had prepared for certain possibilities as wise holders of a fortress prepare for siege. A rather long sitting alone over whisky and soda had, without making him loquacious, heated his blood in such a manner as led him to be less subtle than usual. Drink did not make him drunk, but malignant, and when a man is in the malignant mood, he forgets his cleverness. So he revealed more than he absolutely intended. It was to be gathered that he did not mean to permit his wife to leave him, even for a visit; he would not allow himself to be made ridiculous by such a thing. A man who could not control his wife was a fool and deserved to be a laughing-stock. As Ughtred and his future inheritance seemed to have become of interest to his grandfather, and were to be well nursed and taken care of, his intention was that the boy should remain under his own supervision. He could amuse himself well enough at Stornham, now that it had been put in order, if it was kept up properly and he filled it with people who did not bore him. There were people who did not bore him—plenty of them. Rosalie would stay where she was and receive his guests. If she imagined that the little episode of Ffolliott had been entirely dormant, she was mistaken. He knew where the man was, and exactly how serious it would be to him if scandal was stirred up. He had been at some trouble to find out. The fellow had recently had the luck to fall into a very fine living. It had been bestowed on him by the old Duke of Broadmorlands, who was the most strait-laced old boy in England. He had become so in his disgust at the light behaviour of the wife he had divorced in his early manhood. Nigel cackled gently as he detailed that, by an agreeable coincidence, it happened that her Grace had suddenly become filled with pious fervour—roused thereto by a good-looking locum tenens—result, painful discoveries—the pair being now rumoured to be keeping a lodging-house together somewhere in Australia. A word to good old Broadmorlands would produce the effect of a lighted match on a barrel of gunpowder. It would be the end of Ffolliott. Neither would it be a good introduction to Betty's first season in London, neither would it be enjoyed by her mother, whom he remembered as a woman with primitive views of domestic rectitude. He smiled the awful smile as he took out of his pocket the envelope containing the words his wife had written to Mr. Ffolliott, "Do not come to the house. Meet me at Bartyon Wood." It did not take much to convince people, if one managed things with decent forethought. The Brents, for instance, were fond neither of her nor of Betty, and they had never forgotten the questionable conduct of their locum tenens. Then, suddenly, he had changed his manner and had sat down, laughing, and drawn Rosalie to his knee and kissed her—yes, he had kissed her and told her not to look like a little fool or act like one. Nothing unpleasant would happen if she behaved herself. Betty had improved her greatly, and she had grown young and pretty again. She looked quite like a child sometimes, now that her bones were covered and she dressed well. If she wanted to please him she could put her arms round his neck and kiss him, as he had kissed her.

"That is what has made you look white," said Betty.

"Yes. There is something about him that sometimes makes you feel as if the very blood in your veins turned white," answered Rosy—in a low voice, which the next moment rose. "Don't you see—don't you see," she broke out, "that to displease him would be like murdering Mr. Ffolliott—like murdering his mother and mine—and like murdering Ughtred, because he would be killed by the shame of things—and by being taken from me. We have loved each other so much—so much. Don't you see?"

"I see all that rises up before you," Betty said, "and I understand your feeling that you cannot save yourself by bringing ruin upon an innocent man who helped you. I realise that one must have time to think it over. But, Rosy," a sudden ring in her voice, "I tell you there is a way out—there is a way out! The end of the misery is coming—and it will not be what he thinks."

"You always believe——" began Rosy.

"I know," answered Betty. "I know there are some things so bad that they cannot go on. They kill themselves through their own evil. I KNOW! I KNOW! That is all."

CHAPTER LX

"DON'T GO ON WITH THIS"

Of these things, as of others, she had come to her solitude to think. She looked out over the marshes scarcely seeing the wandering or resting sheep, scarcely hearing the crying plover, because so much seemed to confront her, and she must look it all well in the face. She had fulfilled the promise she had made to herself as a child. She had come in search of Rosy, she had found her as simple and loving of heart as she had ever been. The most painful discoveries she had made had been concealed from her mother until their aspect was modified. Mrs. Vanderpoel need now feel no shock at the sight of the restored Rosy. Lady Anstruthers had been still young enough to respond both physically and mentally to love, companionship, agreeable luxuries, and stimulating interests. But for Nigel's antagonism there was now no reason why she should not be taken home for a visit to her family, and her long-yearned-for New York, no reason why her father and mother should not come to Stornham, and thus establish the customary social relations between their daughter's home and their own. That this seemed out of the question was owing to the fact that at the outset of his married life Sir Nigel had allowed himself to commit errors in tactics. A perverse egotism, not wholly normal in its rancour, had led him into deeds which he had begun to suspect of having cost him too much, even before Betty herself had pointed out to him their unbusinesslike indiscretion. He had done things he could not undo, and now, to his mind, his only resource was to treat them boldly as having been the proper results of decision founded on sound judgment, which he had no desire to excuse. A sufficiently arrogant loftiness of bearing would, he hoped, carry him through the matter. This Betty herself had guessed, but she had not realised that this loftiness of attitude was in danger of losing some of its effectiveness through his being increasingly stung and spurred by circumstances and feelings connected with herself, which were at once exasperating and at times almost overpowering. When, in his mingled dislike and admiration, he had begun to study his sister-in-law, and the half-amused weaving of the small plots which would make things sufficiently unpleasant to be used as factors in her removal from the scene, if necessary, he had not calculated, ever so remotely, on the chance of that madness besetting him which usually besets men only in their youth. He had imagined no other results to himself than a subtly-exciting private entertainment, such as would give spice to the dullness of virtuous life in the country. But, despite himself and his intentions, he had found the situation alter. His first uncertainty of himself had arisen at the Dunholm ball, when he had suddenly realised that he was detesting men who, being young and free, were at liberty to pay gallant court to the new beauty.

Perhaps the most disturbing thing to him had been his consciousness of his sudden leap of antagonism towards Mount Dunstan, who, despite his obvious lack of chance, somehow especially roused in him the rage of warring male instinct. There had been admissions he had been forced, at length, to make to himself. You could not, it appeared, live in the house with a splendid creature like this one—with her brilliant eyes, her beauty of line and movement before you every hour, her bloom, her proud fineness holding themselves wholly in their own keeping—without there being the devil to pay. Lately he had sometimes gone hot and cold in realising that, having once told himself that he might choose to decide to get rid of her, he now knew that the mere thought of her sailing away of her own choice was maddening to him. There WAS the devil to pay! It sometimes brought back to him that hideous shakiness of nerve which had been a feature of his illness when he had been on the Riviera with Teresita.

Of all this Betty only knew the outward signs which, taken at their exterior significance, were detestable enough, and drove her hard as she mentally dwelt on them in connection with other things. How easy, if she stood alone, to defy his evil insolence to do its worst, and leaving the place at an hour's notice, to sail away to protection, or, if she chose to remain in England, to surround herself with a bodyguard of the people in whose eyes his disrepute relegated a man such as Nigel Anstruthers to powerless nonentity. Alone, she could have smiled and turned her back upon him. But she was here to take care of Rosy. She occupied a position something like that of a woman who remains with a man and endures outrage because she cannot leave her child. That thought, in itself, brought Ughtred to her mind. There was Ughtred to be considered as well as his mother. Ughtred's love for and faith in her were deep and passionate things. He fed on her tenderness for him, and had grown stronger because he spent hours of each day talking, reading, and driving with her. The simple truth was that neither she nor Rosalie could desert Ughtred, and so long as Nigel managed cleverly enough, the law would give the boy to his father.

"You are obliged to prove things, you know, in a court of law," he had said, as if with casual amiability, on a certain occasion. "Proving things is the devil. People lose their tempers and rush into rows which end in lawsuits, and then find they can prove nothing. If I were a villain," slightly showing his teeth in an agreeable smile—"instead of a man of blameless life, I should go in only for that branch of my profession which could be exercised without leaving stupid evidence behind."

Since his return to Stornham the outward decorum of his own conduct had entertained him and he had kept it up with an increasing appreciation of its usefulness in the present situation. Whatsoever happened in the end, it was the part of discretion to present to the rural world about him an appearance of upright behaviour. He had even found it amusing to go to church and also to occasionally make amiable calls at the vicarage. It was not difficult, at such times, to refer delicately to his regret that domestic discomfort had led him into the error of remaining much away from Stornham. He knew that he had been even rather touching in his expression of interest in the future of his son, and the necessity of the boy's being protected from uncontrolled hysteric influences. And, in the years of Rosalie's unprotected wretchedness, he had taken excellent care that no "stupid evidence" should be exposed to view.

Of all this Betty was thinking and summing up definitely, point after point. Where was the wise and practical course of defence? The most unthinkable thing was that one could find one's self in a position in which action seemed inhibited. What could one do? To send for her father would surely end the matter—but at what cost to Rosy, to Ughtred, to Ffolliott, before whom the fair path to dignified security had so newly opened itself? What would be the effect of sudden confusion, anguish, and public humiliation upon Rosalie's carefully rebuilt health and strength—upon her mother's new hope and happiness? At moments it seemed as if almost all that had been done might be undone. She was beset by such a moment now, and felt for the time, at least, like a creature tied hand and foot while in full strength.

Certainly she was not prepared for the event which happened. Roland stiffened his ears, and, beginning a rumbling growl, ended it suddenly, realising it an unnecessary precaution.

He knew the man walking up the incline of the mound from the side behind them. So did Betty know him. It was Sir Nigel looking rather glowering and pale and walking slowly. He had discovered where she had meant to take refuge, and had probably ridden to some point where he could leave his horse and follow her at the expense of taking a short cut which saved walking.

As he climbed the mound to join her, Betty rose to her feet.

"My dear girl," he said, "don't get up as if you meant to go away. It has cost me some exertion to find you."

"It will not cost you any exertion to lose me," was her light answer. "I AM going away."

He had reached her, and stood still before her with scarcely a yard's distance between them. He was slightly out of breath and even a trifle livid. He leaned on his stick and his look at her combined leaping bad temper with something deeper.

"Look here!" he broke out, "why do you make such a point of treating me like the devil?"

Betty felt her heart give a hastened beat, not of fear, but of repulsion. This was the mood and manner which subjugated Rosalie. He had so raised his voice that two men in the distance, who might be either labourers or sportsmen, hearing its high tone, glanced curiously towards them.

"Why do you ask me a question which is totally absurd?" she said.

"It is not absurd," he answered. "I am speaking of facts, and I intend to come to some understanding about them."

For reply, after meeting his look a few seconds, she simply turned her back and began to walk away. He followed and overtook her.

"I shall go with you, and I shall say what I want to say," he persisted. "If you hasten your pace I shall hasten mine. I cannot exactly see you running away from me across the marsh, screaming. You wouldn't care to be rescued by those men over there who are watching us. I should explain myself to them in terms neither you nor Rosalie would enjoy. There! I knew Rosalie's name would pull you up. Good God! I wish I were a weak fool with a magnificent creature protecting me at all risks."

If she had not had blood and fire in her veins, she might have found it easy to answer calmly. But she had both, and both leaped and beat furiously for a few seconds. It was only human that it should be so. But she was more than a passionate girl of high and trenchant spirit, and she had learned, even in the days at the French school, what he had never been able to learn in his life—self-control. She held herself in as she would have held in a horse of too great fire and action. She was actually able to look—as the first Reuben Vanderpoel would have looked—at her capital of resource. But it meant taut holding of the reins.

"Will you tell me," she said, stopping, "what it is you want?"

"I want to talk to you. I want to tell you truths you would rather be told here than on the high road, where people are passing—or at Stornham, where the servants would overhear and Rosalie be thrown into hysterics. You will NOT run screaming across the marsh, because I should run screaming after you, and we should both look silly. Here is a rather scraggy tree. Will you sit on the mound near it—for Rosalie's sake?"

"I will not sit down," replied Betty, "but I will listen, because it is not a bad idea that I should understand you. But to begin with, I will tell you something." She stopped beneath the tree and stood with her back against its trunk. "I pick up things by noticing people closely, and I have realised that all your life you have counted upon getting your own way because you saw that people—especially women—have a horror of public scenes, and will submit to almost anything to avoid them. That is true very often, but not always."

Her eyes, which were well opened, were quite the blue of steel, and rested directly upon him. "I, for instance, would let you make a scene with me anywhere you chose—in Bond Street—in Piccadilly—on the steps of Buckingham Palace, as I was getting out of my carriage to attend a drawing-room—and you would gain nothing you wanted by it—nothing. You may place entire confidence in that statement."

He stared back at her, momentarily half-magnetised, and then broke forth into a harsh half-laugh.

"You are so damned handsome that nothing else matters. I'm hanged if it does!" and the words were an exclamation. He drew still nearer to her, speaking with a sort of savagery. "Cannot you see that you could do what you pleased with me? You are too magnificent a thing for a man to withstand. I have lost my head and gone to the devil through you. That is what I came to say."

In the few seconds of silence that followed, his breath came quickly again and he was even paler than before.

"You came to me to say THAT?" asked Betty.

"Yes—to say it before you drove me to other things."

Her gaze was for a moment even slightly wondering. He presented the curious picture of a cynical man of the world, for the time being ruled and impelled only by the most primitive instincts. To a clear-headed modern young woman of the most powerful class, he—her sister's husband—was making threatening love as if he were a savage chief and she a savage beauty of his tribe. All that concerned him was that he should speak and she should hear—that he should show her he was the stronger of the two.

"Are you QUITE mad?" she said.

"Not quite," he answered; "only three parts—but I am beyond my own control. That is the best proof of what has happened to me. You are an arrogant piece and you would defy me if you stood alone, but you don't, and, by the Lord! I have reached a point where I will make use of every lever I can lay my hand on—yourself, Rosalie, Ughtred, Ffolliott—the whole lot of you!"

The thing which was hardest upon her was her knowledge of her own strength—of what she might have allowed herself of flaming words and instant action—but for the memory of Rosy's ghastly little face, as it had looked when she cried out, "You must not think of me. Betty, go home—go home!" She held the white desperation of it before her mental vision and answered him even with a certain interested deliberateness.

"Do you know," she inquired, "that you are talking to me as though you were the villain in the melodrama?"

"There is an advantage in that," he answered, with an unholy smile. "If you repeat what I say, people will only think that you are indulging in hysterical exaggeration. They don't believe in the existence of melodrama in these days."

The cynical, absolute knowledge of this revealed so much that nerve was required to face it with steadiness.

"True," she commented. "Now I think I understand."

"No, you don't," he burst forth. "You have spent your life standing on a golden pedestal, being kowtowed to, and you imagine yourself immune from difficulties because you think you can pay your way out of anything. But you will find that you cannot pay your way out of this—or rather you cannot pay Rosalie's way out of it."

"I shall not try. Go on," said the girl. "What I do not understand, you must explain to me. Don't leave anything unsaid."

"Good God, what a woman you are!" he cried out bitterly. He had never seen such beauty in his life as he saw in her as she stood with her straight young body flat against the tree. It was not a matter of deep colour of eye, or high spirit of profile—but of something which burned him. Still as she was, she looked like a flame. She made him feel old and body-worn, and all the more senselessly furious.

"I believe you hate me," he raged. "And I may thank my wife for that." Then he lost himself entirely. "Why cannot you behave well to me? If you will behave well to me, Rosalie shall go her own way. If you even looked at me as you look at other men—but you do not. There is always something under your lashes which watches me as if I were a wild beast you were studying. Don't fancy yourself a dompteuse. I am not your man. I swear to you that you don't know what you are dealing with. I swear to you that if you play this game with me I will drag you two down if I drag myself with you. I have nothing much to lose. You and your sister have everything."

"Go on," Betty said briefly.

"Go on! Yes, I will go on. Rosalie and Ffolliott I hold in the hollow of my hand. As for you—do you know that people are beginning to discuss you? Gossip is easily stirred in the country, where people are so bored that they chatter in self-defence. I have been considered a bad lot. I have become curiously attached to my sister-in-law. I am seen hanging about her, hanging over her as we ride or walk alone together. An American young woman is not like an English girl—she is used to seeing the marriage ceremony juggled with. There's a trifle of prejudice against such young women when they are too rich and too handsome. Don't look at me like that!" he burst forth, with maddened sharpness, "I won't have it!"

The girl was regarding him with the expression he most resented—the reflection of a normal person watching an abnormal one, and studying his abnormality.

"Do you know that you are raving?" she said, with quiet curiosity—"raving?"

Suddenly he sat down on the low mound near him, and as he touched his forehead with his handkerchief, she saw that his hand actually shook.

"Yes," he answered, panting, "but 'ware my ravings! They mean what they say."

"You do yourself an injury when you give way to them"—steadily, even with a touch of slow significance—"a physical injury. I have noticed that more than once."

He sprang to his feet again. Every drop of blood left his face. For a second he looked as if he would strike her. His arm actually flung itself out—and fell.

"You devil!" he gasped. "You count on that? You she-devil!"

She left her tree and stood before him.

"Listen to me," she said. "You intimate that you have been laying melodramatic plots against me which will injure my good name. That is rubbish. Let us leave it at that. You threaten that you will break Rosy's heart and take her child from her, you say also that you will wound and hurt my mother to her death and do your worst to ruin an honest man——"

"And, by God, I will!" he raged. "And you cannot stop me, if——"

"I do not know whether I can stop you or not, though you may be sure I will try," she interrupted him, "but that is not what I was going to say." She drew a step nearer, and there was something in the intensity of her look which fascinated and held him for a moment. She was curiously grave. "Nigel, I believe in certain things you do not believe in. I believe black thoughts breed black ills to those who think them. It is not a new idea. There is an old Oriental proverb which says, 'Curses, like chickens, come home to roost.' I believe also that the worst—the very worst CANNOT be done to those who think steadily—steadily—only of the best. To you that is merely superstition to be laughed at. That is a matter of opinion. But—don't go on with this thing—DON'T GO ON WITH IT. Stop and think it over."

He stared at her furiously—tried to laugh outright, and failed because the look in her eyes was so odd in its strength and stillness.

"You think you can lay some weird spell upon me," he jeered sardonically.

"No, I don't," she answered. "I could not if I would. It is no affair of mine. It is your affair only—and there is nothing weird about it. Don't go on, I tell you. Think better of it."

She turned about without further speech, and walked away from him with light swiftness over the marsh. Oddly enough, he did not even attempt to follow her. He felt a little weak—perhaps because a certain thing she had said had brought back to him a familiar touch of the horrors. She had the eyes of a falcon under the odd, soft shade of the extraordinary lashes. She had seen what he thought no one but himself had realised. Having watched her retreating figure for a few seconds, he sat down—as suddenly as before—on the mound near the tree.

"Oh, damn her!" he said, his damp forehead on his hands. "Damn the whole universe!"

. . . . .

When Betty and Roland reached Stornham, the wicker-work pony chaise from the vicarage stood before the stone entrance steps. The drawing-room door was open, and Mrs. Brent was standing near it saying some last words to Lady Anstruthers before leaving the house, after a visit evidently made with an object. This Betty gathered from the solemnity of her manner.

"Betty," said Lady Anstruthers, catching sight of her, "do come in for a moment."

When Betty entered, both her sister and Mrs. Brent looked at her questioningly.

"You look a little pale and tired, Miss Vanderpoel," Mrs. Brent said, rather as if in haste to be the first to speak. "I hope you are not at all unwell. We need all our strength just now. I have brought the most painful news. Malignant typhoid fever has broken out among the hop pickers on the Mount Dunstan estate. Some poor creature was evidently sickening for it when he came from London. Three people died last night."

CHAPTER XLI

SHE WOULD DO SOMETHING

Sir Nigel's face was not a good thing to see when he appeared at the dinner table in the evening. As he took his seat the two footmen glanced quickly at each other, and the butler at the sideboard furtively thrust out his underlip. Not a man or woman in the household but had learned the signal denoting the moment when no service would please, no word or movement be unobjectionable. Lady Anstruthers' face unconsciously assumed its propitiatory expression, and she glanced at her sister more than once when Betty was unaware that she did so.

Until the soup had been removed, Sir Nigel scarcely spoke, merely making curt replies to any casual remark. This was one of his simple and most engaging methods of at once enjoying an ill-humour and making his wife feel that she was in some way to blame for it.

"Mount Dunstan is in a deucedly unpleasant position," he condescended at last. "I should not care to stand in his shoes."

He had not returned to the Court until late in the afternoon, but having heard in the village the rumour of the outbreak of fever, he had made inquiries and gathered detail.

"You are thinking of the outbreak of typhoid among the hop pickers?" said Lady Anstruthers. "Mrs. Brent thinks it threatens to be very serious."

"An epidemic, without a doubt," he answered. "In a wretched unsanitary place like Dunstan village, the wretches will die like flies."

"What will be done?" inquired Betty.

He gave her one of the unpleasant personal glances and laughed derisively.

"Done? The county authorities, who call themselves 'guardians,' will be frightened to death and will potter about and fuss like old women, and profess to examine and protect and lay restrictions, but everyone will manage to keep at a discreet distance, and the thing will run riot and do its worst. As far as one can see, there seems no reason why the whole place should not be swept away. No doubt Mount Dunstan has wisely taken to his heels already."

"I think that, on the contrary, there would be much doubt of that," Betty said. "He would stay and do what he could."

Sir Nigel shrugged his shoulders.

"Would he? I think you'll find he would not."

"Mrs. Brent tells me," Rosalie broke in somewhat hurriedly, "that the huts for the hoppers are in the worst possible condition. They are so dilapidated that the rain pours into them. There is no proper shelter for the people who are ill, and Lord Mount Dunstan cannot afford to take care of them."

"But he WILL—he WILL," broke forth Betty. Her head lifted itself and she spoke almost as if through her small, shut teeth. A wave of intense belief—high, proud, and obstinate, swept through her. It was a feeling so strong and vibrant that she felt as if Mount Dunstan himself must be reached and upborne by it—as if he himself must hear her.

Rosalie looked at her half-startled, and, for the moment held fascinated by the sudden force rising in her and by the splendid spark of light under her lids. She was reminded of the fierce little Betty of long ago, with her delicate, indomitable small face and the spirit which even at nine years old had somehow seemed so strong and straitly keen of sight that one had known it might always be trusted. Actually, in one way, she had not changed. She saw the truth of things. The next instant, however, inadvertently glancing towards her husband, she caught her breath quickly. Across his heavy-featured face had shot the sudden gleam of a new expression. It was as if he had at the moment recognised something which filled him with a rush of fury he himself was not prepared for. That he did not wish it to be seen she knew by his manner. There was a brief silence in which it passed away. He spoke after it, with disagreeable precision.

"He has had an enormous effect on you—that man," he said to Betty.

He spoke clearly so that she might have the pleasure of being certain that the menservants heard. They were close to the table, handing fruit—professing to be automatons, eyes down, faces expressing nothing, but as quick of hearing as it is said that blind men are. He knew that if he had been in her place and a thing as insultingly significant had been said to him, he should promptly have hurled the nearest object—plate, wineglass, or decanter—in the face of the speaker. He knew, too, that women cannot hurl projectiles without looking like viragos and fools. The weakly-feminine might burst into tears or into a silly rage and leave the table. There was a distinct breath's space of pause, and Betty, cutting a cluster from a bunch of hothouse grapes presented by the footman at her side, answered as clearly as he had spoken himself.

"He is strong enough to produce an effect on anyone," she said. "I think you feel that yourself. He is a man who will not be beaten in the end. Fortune will give him some good thing."

"He is a fellow who knows well enough on which hand of him good things lie," he said. "He will take all that offers itself."

"Why not?" Betty said impartially.

"There must be no riding or driving in the neighbourhood of the place," he said next. "I will have no risks run." He turned and addressed the butler. "Jennings, tell the servants that those are my orders."

He sat over his wine but a short time that evening, and when he joined his wife and sister-in-law in the drawing-room he went at once to Betty. In fact, he was in the condition when a man cannot keep away from a woman, but must invent some reason for reaching her whether it is fatuous or plausible.

"What I said to Jennings was an order to you as well as to the people below stairs. I know you are particularly fond of riding in the direction of Mount Dunstan. You are in my care so long as you are in my house."

"Orders are not necessary," Betty replied. "The day is past when one rushed to smooth pillows and give the wrong medicine when one's friends were ill. If one is not a properly-trained nurse, it is wiser not to risk being very much in the way."

He spoke over her shoulder, dropping his voice, though Lady Anstruthers sat apart, appearing to read.

"Don't think I am fool enough not to understand. You have yourself under magnificent control, but a woman passionately in love cannot keep a certain look out of her eyes."

He was standing on the hearth. Betty swung herself lightly round, facing him squarely. Her full look was splendid.

"If it is there—let it stay," she said. "I would not keep it out of my eyes if I could, and, you are right, I could not if I would—if it is there. If it is—let it stay."

The daring, throbbing, human truth of her made his brain whirl. To a man young and clean and fit to count as in the lists, to have heard her say the thing of a rival would have been hard enough, but base, degenerate, and of the world behind her day, to hear it while frenzied for her, was intolerable. And it was Mount Dunstan she bore herself so highly for. Whether melodrama is out of date or not there are, occasionally, some fine melodramatic touches in the enmities of to-day.

"You think you will reach him," he persisted. "You think you will help him in some way. You will not let the thing alone."

"Excuse my mentioning that whatsoever I take the liberty of doing will encroach on no right of yours," she said.

But, alone in her room, after she went upstairs, the face reflecting itself in the mirror was pale and its black brows were drawn together.

She sat down at the dressing-table, and, seeing the paled face, drew the black brows closer, confronting a complicating truth.

"If I were free to take Rosalie and Ughtred home to-morrow," she thought, "I could not bear to go. I should suffer too much."

She was suffering now. The strong longing in her heart was like a physical pain. No word or look of this one man had given her proof that his thoughts turned to her, and yet it was intolerable—intolerable—that in his hour of stress and need they were as wholly apart as if worlds rolled between them. At any dire moment it was mere nature that she should give herself in help and support. If, on the night at sea, when they had first spoken to each other, the ship had gone down, she knew that they two, strangers though they were, would have worked side by side among the frantic people, and have been among the last to take to the boats. How did she know? Only because, he being he, and she being she, it must have been so in accordance with the laws ruling entities. And now he stood facing a calamity almost as terrible—and she with full hands sat still.

She had seen the hop pickers' huts and had recognised their condition. Mere brick sheds in which the pickers slept upon bundles of hay or straw in their best days; in their decay they did not even provide shelter. In fine weather the hop gatherers slept well enough in them, cooking their food in gypsy-fashion in the open. When the rain descended, it must run down walls and drip through the holes in the roofs in streams which would soak clothes and bedding. The worst that Nigel and Mrs. Brent had implied was true. Illness of any order, under such circumstances, would have small chance of recovery, but malignant typhoid without shelter, without proper nourishment or nursing, had not one chance in a million. And he—this one man—stood alone in the midst of the tragedy—responsible and helpless. He would feel himself responsible as she herself would, if she were in his place. She was conscious that suddenly the event of the afternoon—the interview upon the marshes, had receded until it had become an almost unmeaning incident. What did the degenerate, melodramatic folly matter——!

She had restlessly left her chair before the dressing-table, and was walking to and fro. She paused and stood looking down at the carpet, though she scarcely saw it.

"Nothing matters but one thing—one person," she owned to herself aloud. "I suppose it is always like this. Rosy, Ughtred, even father and mother—everyone seems less near than they were. It is too strong—too strong. It is——" the words dropped slowly from her lips, "the strongest thing—in the world."

She lifted her face and threw out her hands, a lovely young half-sad smile curling the deep corners of her mouth. "Sometimes one feels so disdained," she said—"so disdained with all one's power. Perhaps I am an unwanted thing."

But even in this case there were aids one might make an effort to give. She went to her writing-table and sat thinking for some time. Afterwards she began to write letters. Three or four were addressed to London—one was to Mr. Penzance.

. . . . .

Mount Dunstan and his vicar were walking through the village to the vicarage. They had been to the hop pickers' huts to see the people who were ill of the fever. Both of them noticed that cottage doors and windows were shut, and that here and there alarmed faces looked out from behind latticed panes.

"They are in a panic of fear," Mount Dunstan said, "and by way of safeguard they shut out every breath of air and stifle indoors. Something must be done."

Catching the eye of a woman who was peering over her short white dimity blind, he beckoned to her authoritatively. She came to the door and hesitated there, curtsying nervously.

Mount Dunstan spoke to her across the hedge.

"You need not come out to me, Mrs. Binner. You may stay where you are," he said. "Are you obeying the orders given by the Guardians?"

"Yes, my lord. Yes, my lord," with more curtsys.

"Your health is very much in your own hands," he added.

"You must keep your cottage and your children cleaner than you have ever kept them before, and you must use the disinfectant I sent you. Keep away from the huts, and open your windows. If you don't open them, I shall come and do it for you. Bad air is infection itself. Do you understand?"

"Yes, my lord. Thank your lordship."

"Go in and open your windows now, and tell your neighbours to do the same. If anyone is ill let me know at once. The vicar and I will do our best for everyone."

By that time curiosity had overcome fear, and other cottage doors had opened. Mount Dunstan passed down the row and said a few words to each woman or man who looked out. Questions were asked anxiously and he answered them. That he was personally unafraid was comfortingly plain, and the mere sight of him was, on the whole, an unexplainable support.

"We heard said your lordship was going away," put in a stout mother with a heavy child on her arm, a slight testiness scarcely concealed by respectful good-manners. She was a matron with a temper, and that a Mount Dunstan should avoid responsibilities seemed highly credible.

"I shall stay where I am," Mount Dunstan answered. "My place is here."

They believed him, Mount Dunstan though he was. It could not be said that they were fond of him, but gradually it had been borne in upon them that his word was to be relied on, though his manner was unalluring and they knew he was too poor to do his duty by them or his estate. As he walked away with the vicar, windows were opened, and in one or two untidy cottages a sudden flourishing of mops and brooms began.

There was dark trouble in Mount Dunstan's face. In the huts they had left two men stiff on their straw, and two women and a child in a state of collapse. Added to these were others stricken helpless. A number of workers in the hop gardens, on realising the danger threatening them, had gathered together bundles and children, and, leaving the harvest behind, had gone on the tramp again. Those who remained were the weaker or less cautious, or were held by some tie to those who were already ill of the fever. The village doctor was an old man who had spent his blameless life in bringing little cottagers into the world, attending their measles and whooping coughs, and their father's and grandfather's rheumatics. He had never faced a village crisis in the course of his seventy-five years, and was aghast and flurried with fright. His methods remained those of his youth, and were marked chiefly by a readiness to prescribe calomel in any emergency. A younger and stronger man was needed, as well as a man of more modern training. But even the most brilliant practitioner of the hour could not have provided shelter and nourishment, and without them his skill would have counted as nothing. For three weeks there had been no rain, which was a condition of the barometer not likely to last. Already grey clouds were gathering and obscuring the blueness of the sky.

The vicar glanced upwards anxiously.

"When it comes," he said, "there will be a downpour, and a persistent one."

"Yes," Mount Dunstan answered.

He had lain awake thinking throughout the night. How was a man to sleep! It was as Betty Vanderpoel had known it would be. He, who—beggar though he might be—was the lord of the land, was the man to face the strait of these poor workers on the land, as his own. Some action must be taken. What action? As he walked by his friend's side from the huts where the dead men lay it revealed itself that he saw his way.

They were going to the vicarage to consult a medical book, but on the way there they passed a part of the park where, through a break in the timber the huge, white, blind-faced house stood on view. Mount Dunstan laid his hand on Mr. Penzance's shoulder and stopped him,

"Look there!" he said. "THERE are weather-tight rooms enough."

A startled expression showed itself on the vicar's face.

"For what?" he exclaimed.

"For a hospital," brusquely "I can give them one thing, at least—shelter."

"It is a very remarkable thing to think of doing," Mr. Penzance said.

"It is not so remarkable as that labourers on my land should die at my gate because I cannot give them decent roofs to cover them. There is a roof that will shield them from the weather. They shall be brought to the Mount."

The vicar was silent a moment, and a flush of sympathy warmed his face.

"You are quite right, Fergus," he said, "entirely right."

"Let us go to your study and plan how it shall be done," Mount Dunstan said.

As they walked towards the vicarage, he went on talking.

"When I lie awake at night, there is one thread which always winds itself through my thoughts whatsoever they are. I don't find that I can disentangle it. It connects itself with Reuben S. Vanderpoel's daughter. You would know that without my telling you. If you had ever struggled with an insane passion——"

"It is not insane, I repeat," put in Penzance unflinchingly.

"Thank you—whether you are right or wrong," answered Mount Dunstan, striding by his side. "When I am awake, she is as much a part of my existence as my breath itself. When I think things over, I find that I am asking myself if her thoughts would be like mine. She is a creature of action. Last night, as I lay awake, I said to myself, 'She would DO something. What would she do?' She would not be held back by fear of comment or convention. She would look about her for the utilisable, and she would find it somewhere and use it. I began to sum up the village resources and found nothing—until my thoughts led me to my own house. There it stood—empty and useless. If it were hers, and she stood in my place, she would make it useful. So I decided."

"You are quite right," Mr. Penzance said again.

They spent an hour in his library at the vicarage, arranging practical methods for transforming the great ballroom into a sort of hospital ward. It could be done by the removal of pieces of furniture from the many unused bedrooms. There was also the transportation of the patients from the huts to be provided for. But, when all this was planned out, each found himself looking at the other with an unspoken thought in his mind. Mount Dunstan first expressed it.

"As far as I can gather, the safety of typhoid fever patients depends almost entirely on scientific nursing, and the caution with which even liquid nourishment is given. The woman whose husband died this morning told me that he had seemed better in the night, and had asked for something to eat. She gave him a piece of bread and a slice of cold bacon, because he told her he fancied it. I could not explain to her, as she sat sobbing over him, that she had probably killed him. When we have patients in our ward, what shall we feed them on, and who will know how to nurse them? They do not know how to nurse each other, and the women in the village would not run the risk of undertaking to help us."

But, even before he had left the house, the problem was solved for them. The solving of it lay in the note Miss Vanderpoel had written the night before at Stornham.

When it was brought to him Mr. Penzance glanced up from certain calculations he was making upon a sheet of note-paper. The accumulating difficulties made him look worn and tired. He opened the note and read it gravely, and then as gravely, though with a change of expression, handed it to Mount Dunstan.

"Yes, she is a creature of action. She has heard and understood at once, and she has done something. It is immensely practical—it is fine—it—it is lovable."

"Do you mind my keeping it?" Mount Dunstan asked, after he had read it.

"Keep it by all means," the vicar answered. "It is worth keeping."

But it was quite brief. She had heard of the outbreak of fever among the hop pickers, and asked to be allowed to give help to the people who were suffering. They would need prompt aid. She chanced to know something of the requirements of such cases, and had written to London for certain supplies which would be sent to them at once. She had also written for nurses, who would be needed above all else. Might she ask Mr. Penzance to kindly call upon her for any further assistance required.

"Tell her we are deeply grateful," said Mount Dunstan, "and that she has given us greater help than she knows."

"Why not answer her note yourself?" Penzance suggested.

Mount Dunstan shook his head.

"No," he said shortly. "No."

CHAPTER XLII

IN THE BALLROOM

Though Dunstan village was cut off, by its misfortune, from its usual intercourse with its neighbours, in some mystic manner villages even at twenty miles' distance learned all it did and suffered, feared or hoped. It did not hope greatly, the rustic habit of mind tending towards a discouraged outlook, and cherishing the drama of impending calamity. As far as Yangford and Marling inmates of cottages and farmhouses were inclined to think it probable that Dunstan would be "swep away," and rumours of spreading death and disaster were popular. Tread, the advanced blacksmith at Stornham, having heard in his by-gone, better days of the Great Plague of London, was greatly in demand as a narrator of illuminating anecdotes at The Clock Inn.

Among the parties gathered at the large houses Mount Dunstan himself was much talked of. If he had been a popular man, he might have become a sort of hero; as he was not popular, he was merely a subject for discussion. The fever-stricken patients had been carried in carts to the Mount and given beds in the ballroom, which had been made into a temporary ward. Nurses and supplies had been sent for from London, and two energetic young doctors had taken the place of old Dr. Fenwick, who had been frightened and overworked into an attack of bronchitis which confined him to his bed. Where the money came from, which must be spent every day under such circumstances, it was difficult to say. To the simply conservative of mind, the idea of filling one's house with dirty East End hop pickers infected with typhoid seemed too radical. Surely he could have done something less extraordinary. Would everybody be expected to turn their houses into hospitals in case of village epidemics, now that he had established a precedent? But there were people who approved, and were warm in their sympathy with him. At the first dinner party where the matter was made the subject of argument, the beautiful Miss Vanderpoel, who was present, listened silently to the talk with such brilliant eyes that Lord Dunholm, who was in an elderly way her staunch admirer, spoke to her across the table:

"Tell us what YOU think of it, Miss Vanderpoel," he suggested.

She did not hesitate at all.

"I like it," she answered, in her clear, well-heard voice. "I like it better than anything I have ever heard."

"So do I," said old Lady Alanby shortly. "I should never have done it myself—but I like it just as you do."

"I knew you would, Lady Alanby," said the girl. "And you, too, Lord Dunholm."

"I like it so much that I shall write and ask if I cannot be of assistance," Lord Dunholm answered.

Betty was glad to hear this. Only quickness of thought prevented her from the error of saying, "Thank you," as if the matter were personal to herself. If

Mount Dunstan was restive under the obviousness of the fact that help was so sorely needed, he might feel less so if her offer was only one among others.

"It seems rather the duty of the neighbourhood to show some interest," put in Lady Alanby. "I shall write to him myself. He is evidently of a new order of Mount Dunstan. It's to be hoped he won't take the fever himself, and die of it He ought to marry some handsome, well-behaved girl, and re-found the family."

Nigel Anstruthers spoke from his side of the table, leaning slightly forward.

"He won't if he does not take better care of himself. He passed me on the road two days ago, riding like a lunatic. He looks frightfully ill—yellow and drawn and lined. He has not lived the life to prepare him for settling down to a fight with typhoid fever. He would be done for if he caught the infection."

"I beg your pardon," said Lord Dunholm, with quiet decision. "Unprejudiced inquiry proves that his life has been entirely respectable. As Lady Alanby says, he seems to be of a new order of Mount Dunstan."

"No doubt you are right," said Sir Nigel suavely. "He looked ill, notwithstanding."

"As to looking ill," remarked Lady Alanby to Lord Dunholm, who sat near her, "that man looks as if he was going to pieces pretty rapidly himself, and unprejudiced inquiry would not prove that his past had nothing to do with it."

Betty wondered if her brother-in-law were lying. It was generally safest to argue that he was. But the fever burned high at Mount Dunstan, and she knew by instinct what its owner was giving of the strength of his body and brain. A young, unmarried woman cannot go about, however, making anxious inquiries concerning the welfare of a man who has made no advance towards her. She must wait for the chance which brings news.

. . . . .

The fever, having ill-cared for and habitually ill fed bodies to work upon, wrought fiercely, despite the energy of the two young doctors and the trained nurses. There were many dark hours in the ballroom ward, hours filled with groans and wild ravings. The floating Terpsichorean goddesses upon the lofty ceiling gazed down with wondering eyes at haggard faces and plucking hands which sometimes, behind the screen drawn round their beds, ceased to look feverish, and grew paler and stiller, until they moved no more. But, at least, none had died through want of shelter and care. The supplies needed came from London each day. Lord Dunholm had sent a generous cheque to the aid of the sufferers, and so, also, had old Lady Alanby, but Miss Vanderpoel, consulting medical authorities and hospitals, learned exactly what was required, and necessities were forwarded daily in their most easily utilisable form.

"You generously told me to ask you for anything we found we required," Mr. Penzance wrote to her in his note of thanks. "My dear and kind young lady, you leave nothing to ask for. Our doctors, who are young and enthusiastic, are filled with delight in the completeness of the resources placed in their hands."

She had, in fact, gone to London to consult an eminent physician, who was an authority of world-wide reputation. Like the head of the legal firm of Townlinson & Sheppard, he had experienced a new sensation in the visit paid him by an indubitably modern young beauty, who wasted no word, and whose eyes, while he answered her amazingly clear questions, were as intelligently intent as those of an ardent and serious young medical student. What a surgical nurse she would have made! It seemed almost a pity that she evidently belonged to a class the members of which are rich enough to undertake the charge of entire epidemics, but who do not usually give themselves to such work, especially when they are young and astonishing in the matter of looks.

In addition to the work they did in the ballroom ward, Mount Dunstan and the vicar found much to do among the villagers. Ignorance and alarm combined to create dangers, even where they might not have been feared. Daily instruction and inspection of the cottages and their inmates was required. The knowledge that they were under control and supervision was a support to the frightened people and prevented their lapsing into careless habits. Also, there began to develop among them a secret dependence upon, and desire to please "his lordship," as the existing circumstances drew him nearer to them, and unconsciously they were attracted and dominated by his strength. The strong man carries his power with him, and, when Mount Dunstan entered a cottage and talked to its inmates, the anxious wife or surlily depressed husband was conscious of feeling a certain sense of security. It had been a queer enough thing, this he had done—bundling the infected hoppers out of their leaking huts and carrying them up to the Mount itself for shelter and care. At the most, gentlefolk generally gave soup or blankets or hospital tickets, and left the rest to luck, but, "gentry-way" or not, a man who did a thing like that would be likely to do other things, if they were needed, and gave folk a feeling of being safer than ordinary soup and blankets and hospital tickets could make them.

But "where did the money come from?" was asked during the first days. Beds and doctors, nurses and medicine, fine brandy and unlimited fowls for broth did not come up from London without being paid for. Pounds and pounds a day must be paid out to get the things that were delivered "regular" in hampers and boxes. The women talked to one another over their garden palings, the men argued together over their beer at the public house. Was he running into more debt? But even the village knew that Mount Dunstan credit had been exhausted long ago, and there had been no money at the Mount within the memory of man, so to speak.

One morning the matron with the sharp temper found out the truth, though the outburst of gratitude to Mount Dunstan which resulted in her enlightenment, was entirely spontaneous and without intention. Her doubt of his Mount Dunstan blood had grown into a sturdy liking even for his short speech and his often drawn-down brows.

"We've got more to thank your lordship for than common help," she said. "God Almighty knows where we'd all ha' been but for what you've done. Those poor souls you've nursed and fed——"

"I've not done it," he broke in promptly. "You're mistaken; I could not have done it. How could I?"

"Well," exclaimed the matron frankly, "we WAS wondering where things came from."

"You might well wonder. Have any of you seen Lady Anstruthers' sister, Miss Vanderpoel, ride through the village? She used sometimes to ride this way. If you saw her you will remember it.'

"The 'Merican young lady!" in ejaculatory delight. "My word, yes! A fine young woman with black hair? That rich, they say, as millions won't cover it."

"They won't," grimly. "Lord Dunholm and Lady Alanby of Dole kindly sent cheques to help us, but the American young lady was first on the field. She sent both doctors and nurses, and has supplied us with food and medicine every day. As you say, Mrs. Brown, God Almighty knows what would have become of us, but for what she has done."

Mrs. Brown had listened with rather open mouth. She caught her breath heartily, as a sort of approving exclamation.

"God bless her!" she broke out. "Girls isn't generally like that. Their heads is too full of finery. God bless her, 'Merican or no 'Merican! That's what I say."

Mount Dunstan's red-brown eyes looked as if she had pleased him.

"That's what I say, too," he answered. "God bless her!"

There was not a day which passed in which he did not involuntarily say the words to himself again and again. She had been wrong when she had said in her musings that they were as far apart as if worlds rolled between them. Something stronger than sight or speech drew them together. The thread which wove itself through his thoughts grew stronger and stronger. The first day her gifts arrived and he walked about the ballroom ward directing the placing of hospital cots and hospital aids and comforts, the spirit of her thought and intelligence, the individuality and cleverness of all her methods, brought her so vividly before him that it was almost as if she walked by his side, as if they spoke together, as if she said, "I have tried to think of everything. I want you to miss nothing. Have I helped you? Tell me if there is anything more." The thing which moved and stirred him was his knowledge that when he had thought of her she had also been thinking of him, or of what deeply concerned him. When he had said to himself, tossing on his pillow, "What would she DO?" she had been planning in such a way as answered his question. Each morning, when the day's supplies arrived, it was as if he had received a message from her.

As the people in the cottages felt the power of his temperament and depended upon him, so, also, did the patients in the ballroom ward. The feeling had existed from the outset and increased daily. The doctors and nurses told one another that his passing through the room was like the administering of a tonic. Patients who were weak and making no effort, were lifted upon the strong wave of his will and carried onward towards the shore of greater courage and strength.

Young Doctor Thwaite met him when he came in one morning, and spoke in a low voice:

"There is a young man behind the screen there who is very low," he said. "He had an internal haemorrhage towards morning, and has lost his pluck. He has a wife and three children. We have been doing our best for him with hot-water bottles and stimulants, but he has not the courage to help us. You have an extraordinary effect on them all, Lord Mount Dunstan. When they are depressed, they always ask when you are coming in, and this man—Patton, his name is—has asked for you several times. Upon my word, I believe you might set him going again."

Mount Dunstan walked to the bed, and, going behind the screen, stood looking down at the young fellow lying breathing pantingly. His eyes were closed as he laboured, and his pinched white nostrils drew themselves in and puffed out at each breath. A nurse on the other side of the cot had just surrounded him with fresh hot-water bottles.

Suddenly the sunken eyelids flew open, and the eyes met Mount Dunstan's in imploring anxiousness.

"Here I am, Patton," Mount Dunstan said. "You need not speak."

But he must speak. Here was the strength his sinking soul had longed for.

"Cruel bad—goin' fast—m' lord," he panted.

Mount Dunstan made a sign to the nurse, who gave him a chair. He sat down close to the bed, and took the bloodless hand in his own.

"No," he said, "you are not going. You'll stay here. I will see to that."

The poor fellow smiled wanly. Vague yearnings had led him sometimes, in the past, to wander into chapels or stop and listen to street preachers, and orthodox platitudes came back to him.

"God's—will," he trailed out.

"It's nothing of the sort. It's God's will that you pull yourself together. A man with a wife and three children has no right to slip out."

A yearning look flickered in the lad's eyes—he was scarcely more than a lad, having married at seventeen, and had a child each year.

"She's—a good—girl."

"Keep that in your mind while you fight this out," said Mount Dunstan. "Say it over to yourself each time you feel yourself letting go. Hold on to it. I am going to fight it out with you. I shall sit here and take care of you all day—all night, if necessary. The doctor and the nurse will tell me what to do. Your hand is warmer already. Shut your eyes."

He did not leave the bedside until the middle of the night.

By that time the worst was over. He had acted throughout the hours under the direction of nurse and doctor. No one but himself had touched the patient. When Patton's eyes were open, they rested on him with a weird growing belief. He begged his lordship to hold his hand, and was uneasy when he laid it down.

"Keeps—me—up," he whispered.

"He pours something into them—vigour—magnetic power—life. He's like a charged battery," Dr. Thwaite said to his co-workers. "He sat down by Patton just in time. It sets one to thinking."

Having saved Patton, he must save others. When a man or woman sank, or had increased fever, they believed that he alone could give them help. In delirium patients cried out for him. He found himself doing hard work, but he did not flinch from it. The adoration for him became a sort of passion. Haggard faces lighted up into life at the sound of his footstep, and heavy heads turned longingly on their pillows as he passed by. In the winter days to come there would be many an hour's talk in East End courts and alleys of the queer time when a score or more of them had lain in the great room with the dancing and floating goddesses looking down at them from the high, painted ceiling, and the swell, who was a lord, walking about among them, working for them as the nurses did, and sitting by some of them through awful hours, sometimes holding burning or slackening and chilling hands with a grip whose steadiness seemed to hold them back from the brink of the abyss they were slipping into. The mere ignorantly childish desire to do his prowess credit and to play him fair saved more than one man and woman from going out with the tide.

"It is the first time in my life that I have fairly counted among men. It's the first time I have known human affection, other than yours, Penzance. They want me, these people; they are better for the sight of me. It is a new experience, and it is good for a man's soul," he said.

CHAPTER XLIII

HIS CHANCE

Betty walked much alone upon the marshes with Roland at her side. At intervals she heard from Mr. Penzance, but his notes were necessarily brief, and at other times she could only rely upon report for news of what was occurring at Mount Dunstan. Lord Mount Dunstan's almost military supervision of and command over his villagers had certainly saved them from the horrors of an uncontrollable epidemic; his decision and energy had filled the alarmed Guardians with respect and this respect had begun to be shared by many other persons. A man as prompt in action, and as faithful to such responsibilities as many men might have found plausible reasons enough for shirking, inevitably assumed a certain dignity of aspect, when all was said and done. Lord Dunholm was most clear in his expressions of opinion concerning him. Lady Alanby of Dole made a practice of speaking of him in public frequently, always with admiring approval, and in that final manner of hers, to whose authority her neighbours had so long submitted. It began to be accepted as a fact that he was a new development of his race—as her ladyship had put it, "A new order of Mount Dunstan."

The story of his power over the stricken people, and of their passionate affection and admiration for him, was one likely to spread far, and be immensely popular. The drama of certain incidents appealed greatly to the rustic mind, and by cottage firesides he was represented with rapturous awe, as raising men, women, and children from the dead, by the mere miracle of touch. Mrs. Welden and old Doby revelled in thrilling, almost Biblical, versions of current anecdotes, when Betty paid her visits to them.

"It's like the Scripture, wot he done for that young man as the last breath had gone out of him, an' him lyin' stiffening fast. 'Young man, arise,' he says. 'The Lord Almighty calls. You've got a young wife an' three children to take care of. Take up your bed an' walk.' Not as he wanted him to carry his bed anywhere, but it was a manner of speaking. An' up the young man got. An' a sensible way," said old Mrs. Welden frankly, "for the Lord to look at it—for I must say, miss, if I was struck down for it, though I s'pose it's only my sinful ignorance—that there's times when the Lord seems to think no more of sweepin' away a steady eighteen-shillin' a week, and p'raps seven in family, an' one at the breast, an' another on the way—than if it was nothin'. But likely enough, eighteen shillin' a week an' confinements does seem paltry to the Maker of 'eaven an' earth."

But, to the girl walking over the marshland, the humanness of the things she heard gave to her the sense of nearness—of being almost within sight and sound—which Mount Dunstan himself had felt, when each day was filled with the result of her thought of the needs of the poor souls thrown by fate into his hands. In these days, after listening to old Mrs. Welden's anecdotes, through which she gathered the simpler truth of things, Betty was able to construct for herself a less Scriptural version of what she had heard. She was glad—glad in his sitting by a bedside and holding a hand which lay in his hot or cold, but always trusting to something which his strong body and strong soul gave without stint. There would be no restraint there. Yes, he was kind—kind—kind —with the kindness a woman loves, and which she, of all women, loved most. Sometimes she would sit upon some mound, and, while her eyes seemed to rest on the yellowing marsh and its birds and pools, they saw other things, and their colour grew deep and dark as the marsh water between the rushes.

The time was pressing when a change in her life must come. She frequently asked herself if what she saw in Nigel Anstruthers' face was the normal thinking of a sane man, which he himself could control. There had been moments when she had seriously doubted it. He was haggard, aging and restless. Sometimes he—always as if by chance—followed her as she went from one room to another, and would seat himself and fix his miserable eyes upon her for so long a time that it seemed he must be unconscious of what he was doing. Then he would appear suddenly to recollect himself and would start up with a muttered exclamation, and stalk out of the room. He spent long hours riding or driving alone about the country or wandering wretchedly through the Park and gardens. Once he went up to town, and, after a few days' absence, came back looking more haggard than before, and wearing a hunted look in his eyes. He had gone to see a physician, and, after having seen him, he had tried to lose himself in a plunge into deep and turbid enough waters; but he found that he had even lost the taste of high flavours, for which he had once had an epicurean palate. The effort had ended in his being overpowered again by his horrors—the horrors in which he found himself staring at that end of things when no pleasure had spice, no debauchery the sting of life, and men, such as he, stood upon the shore of time shuddering and naked souls, watching the great tide, bearing its treasures, recede forever, and leave them to the cold and hideous dark. During one day of his stay in town he had seen Teresita, who had at first stared half frightened by the change she saw in him, and then had told him truths he could have wrung her neck for putting into words.

"You look an old man," she said, with the foreign accent he had once found deliciously amusing, but which now seemed to add a sting. "And somesing is eating you op. You are mad in lofe with some beautiful one who will not look at you. I haf seen it in mans before. It is she who eats you op—your evil thinkings of her. It serve you right. Your eyes look mad."

He himself, at times, suspected that they did, and cursed himself because he could not keep cool. It was part of his horrors that he knew his internal furies were worse than folly, and yet he could not restrain them. The creeping suspicion that this was only the result of the simple fact that he had never tried to restrain any tendency of his own was maddening. His nervous system was a wreck. He drank a great deal of whisky to keep himself "straight" during the day, and he rose many times during his black waking hours in the night to drink more because he obstinately refused to give up the hope that, if he drank enough, it would make him sleep. As through the thoughts of Mount Dunstan, who was a clean and healthy human being, there ran one thread which would not disentangle itself, so there ran through his unwholesome thinking a thread which burned like fire. His secret ravings would not have been good to hear. His passion was more than half hatred, and a desire for vengeance, for the chance to re-assert his own power, to prove himself master, to get the better in one way or another of this arrogant young outsider and her high-handed pride. The condition of his mind was so far from normal that he failed to see that the things he said to himself, the plans he laid, were grotesque in their folly. The old cruel dominance of the man over the woman thing, which had seemed the mere natural working of the law among men of his race in centuries past, was awake in him, amid the limitations of modern days.

"My God," he said to himself more than once, "I would like to have had her in my hands a few hundred years ago. Women were kept in their places, then."

He was even frenzied enough to think over what he would have done, if such a thing had been—of her utter helplessness against that which raged in him—of the grey thickness of the walls where he might have held and wrought his will upon her—insult, torment, death. His alcohol-excited brain ran riot—but, when it did its foolish worst, he was baffled by one thing.

"Damn her!" he found himself crying out. "If I had hung her up and cut her into strips she would have died staring at me with her big eyes—without uttering a sound."

There was a long reach between his imaginings and the time he lived in. America had not been discovered in those decent days, and now a man could not beat even his own wife, or spend her money, without being meddled with by fools. He was thinking of a New York young woman of the nineteenth century who could actually do as she hanged pleased, and who pleased to be damned high and mighty. For that reason in itself it was incumbent upon a man to get even with her in one way or another. High and mightiness was not the hardest thing to reach. It offered a good aim.

His temper when he returned to Stornham was of the order which in past years had set Rosalie and her child shuddering and had sent the servants about the house with pale or sullen faces. Betty's presence had the odd effect of restraining him, and he even told her so with sneering resentment.

"There would be the devil to pay if you were not here," he said. "You keep me in order, by Jove! I can't work up steam properly when you watch me."

He himself knew that it was likely that some change would take place. She would not stay at Stornham and she would not leave his wife and child alone with him again. It would be like her to hold her tongue until she was ready with her infernal plans and could spring them on him. Her letters to her father had probably prepared him for such action as such a man would be likely to take. He could guess what it would be. They were free and easy enough in America in their dealings with the marriage tie. Their idea would doubtless be a divorce with custody of the child. He wondered a little that they had remained quiet so long. There had been American shrewdness in her coming boldly to Stornham to look over the ground herself and actually set the place in order. It did not present itself to his mind that what she had done had been no part of a scheme, but the mere result of her temperament and training. He told himself that it had been planned beforehand and carried out in hard-headed commercial American fashion as a matter of business. The thing which most enraged him was the implied cool, practical realisation of the fact that he, as inheritor of an entailed estate, was but owner in charge, and not young enough to be regarded as an insurmountable obstacle to their plans. He could not undo the greater part of what had been done, and they were calculating, he argued, that his would not be likely to be a long life, and if—if anything happened—Stornham would be Ughtred's and the whole vulgar lot of them would come over and take possession and swagger about the place as if they had been born on it. As to divorce or separation—if they took that line, he would at least give them a good run for their money. They would wish they had let sleeping dogs lie before the thing was over. The right kind of lawyer could bully Rosalie into saying anything he chose on the witness-stand. There was not much limit to the evidence a man could bring if he was experienced enough to be circumstantial, and knew whom he was dealing with. The very fact that the little fool could be made to appear to have been so sly and sanctimonious would stir the gall of any jury of men. His own condoning the matter for the sake of his sensitive boy, deformed by his mother's unrestrained and violent hysteria before his birth, would go a long way. Let them get their divorce, they would have paid for it, the whole lot of them, the beautiful Miss Vanderpoel and all. Such a story as the newspapers would revel in would not be a recommendation to Englishmen of unsmirched reputation. Then his exultation would suddenly drop as his mental excitement produced its effect of inevitable physical fatigue. Even if he made them pay for getting their own way, what would happen to himself afterwards? No morbid vanity of self-bolstering could make the outlook anything but unpromising. If he had not had such diabolical luck in his few investments he could have lived his own life. As it was, old Vanderpoel would possibly condescend to make him some insufficient allowance because Rosalie would wish that it might be done, and he would be expected to drag out to the end the kind of life a man pensioned by his wife's relatives inevitably does. If he attempted to live in the country he should blow out his brains. When his depression was at its worst, he saw himself aging and shabby, rambling about from one cheap Continental town to another, blackballed by good clubs, cold-shouldered even by the Teresitas, cut off from society by his limited means and the stories his wife's friends would spread. He ground his teeth when he thought of Betty. Her splendid vitality had done something to life for him—had given it savour. When he had come upon her in the avenue his blood had stirred, even though it had been maliciously, and there had been spice in his very resentment of her presence. And she would go away. He would not be likely to see her again if his wife broke with him; she would be swept out of his days. It was hideous to think of, and his rage would overpower him and his nerves go to pieces again.

"What are you going to do?" he broke forth suddenly one evening, when he found himself temporarily alone with her. "You are going to do something. I see it in your eyes."

He had been for some time watching her from behind his newspaper, while she, with an unread book upon her lap, had, in fact, been thinking deeply and putting to herself serious questions.

Her answer made him stir rather uncomfortably.

"I am going to write to my father to ask him to come to England."

So this was what she had been preparing to spring upon him. He laughed insolently.

"To ask him to come here?"

"With your permission."

"With mine? Does an American father-in-law wait for permission?"

"Is there any practical reason why you should prefer that he should NOT come?"

He left his seat and walked over to her.

"Yes. Your sending for him is a declaration of war."

"It need not be so. Why should it?"

"In this case I happen to be aware that it is. The choice is your own, I suppose," with ready bravado, "that you and he are prepared to face the consequences. But is Rosalie, and is your mother?"

"My father is a business man and will know what can be done. He will know what is worth doing," she answered, without noticing his question. "But," she added the words slowly, "I have been making up my mind—before I write to him—to say something to you—to ask you a question."

He made a mock sentimental gesture.

"To ask me to spare my wife, to 'remember that she is the mother of my child'?"

She passed over that also.

"To ask you if there is no possible way in which all this unhappiness can be ended decently."

"The only decent way of ending it would be that there should be no further interference. Let Rosalie supply the decency by showing me the consideration due from a wife to her husband. The place has been put in order. It was not for my benefit, and I have no money to keep it up. Let Rosalie be provided with means to do it."

As he spoke the words he realised that he had opened a way for embarrassing comment. He expected her to remind him that Rosalie had not come to him without money. But she said nothing about the matter. She never said the things he expected to hear.

"You do not want Rosalie for your wife," she went on "but you could treat her courteously without loving her. You could allow her the privileges other men's wives are allowed. You need not separate her from her family. You could allow her father and mother to come to her and leave her free to go to them sometimes. Will you not agree to that? Will you not let her live peaceably in her own simple way? She is very gentle and humble and would ask nothing more."

"She is a fool!" he exclaimed furiously. "A fool! She will stay where she is and do as I tell her."

"You knew what she was when you married her. She was simple and girlish and pretended to be nothing she was not. You chose to marry her and take her from the people who loved her. You broke her spirit and her heart. You would have killed her if I had not come in time to prevent it."

"I will kill her yet if you leave her," his folly made him say.

"You are talking like a feudal lord holding the power of life and death in his hands," she said. "Power like that is ancient history. You can hurt no one who has friends—without being punished."

It was the old story. She filled him with the desire to shake or disturb her at any cost, and he did his utmost. If she was proposing to make terms with him, he would show her whether he would accept them or not. He let her hear all he had said to himself in his worst moments—all that he had argued concerning what she and her people would do, and what his own actions would be—all his intention to make them pay the uttermost farthing in humiliation if he could not frustrate them. His methods would be definite enough. He had not watched his wife and Ffolliott for weeks to no end. He had known what he was dealing with. He had put other people upon the track and they would testify for him. He poured forth unspeakable statements and intimations, going, as usual, further than he had known he should go when he began. Under the spur of excitement his imagination served him well. At last he paused.

"Well," he put it to her, "what have you to say?"

"I?" with the remote intent curiosity growing in her eyes. "I have nothing to say. I am leaving you to say things."

"You will, of course, try to deny——" he insisted.

"No, I shall not. Why should I?"

"You may assume your air of magnificence, but I am dealing with uncomfortable factors." He stopped in spite of himself, and then burst forth in a new order of rage. "You are trying some confounded experiment on me. What is it?"

She rose from her chair to go out of the room, and stood a moment holding her book half open in her hand.

"Yes. I suppose it might be called an experiment," was her answer. "Perhaps it was a mistake. I wanted to make quite sure of something."

"Of what?"

"I did not want to leave anything undone. I did not want to believe that any man could exist who had not one touch of decent feeling to redeem him. It did not seem human."

White dints showed themselves about his nostrils.

"Well, you have found one," he cried. "You have a lashing tongue, by God, when you choose to let it go. But I could teach you a good many things, my girl. And before I have done you will have learned most of them."

But though he threw himself into a chair and laughed aloud as she left him, he knew that his arrogance and bullying were proving poor weapons, though they had done him good service all his life. And he knew, too, that it was mere simple truth that, as a result of the intellectual, ethical vagaries he scathingly derided—she had actually been giving him a sort of chance to retrieve himself, and that if he had been another sort of man he might have taken it.

CHAPTER XLIV

A FOOTSTEP

It was cold enough for fires in halls and bedrooms, and Lady Anstruthers often sat over hers and watched the glowing bed of coals with a fixed thoughtfulness of look. She was so sitting when her sister went to her room to talk to her, and she looked up questioningly when the door closed and Betty came towards her.

"You have come to tell me something," she said.

A slight shade of anxiousness showed itself in her eyes, and Betty sat down by her and took her hand. She had come because what she knew was that Rosalie must be prepared for any step taken, and the time had arrived when she must not be allowed to remain in ignorance even of things it would be unpleasant to put into words.

"Yes," she answered. "I want to talk to you about something I have decided to do. I think I must write to father and ask him to come to us."

Rosalie turned white, but though her lips parted as if she were going to speak, she said nothing.

"Do not be frightened," Betty said. "I believe it is the only thing to do."

"I know! I know!"

Betty went on, holding the hand a little closer. "When I came here you were too weak physically to be able to face even the thought of a struggle. I saw that. I was afraid it must come in the end, but I knew that at that time you could not bear it. It would have killed you and might have killed mother, if I had not waited; and until you were stronger, I knew I must wait and reason coolly about you—about everything."

"I used to guess—sometimes," said Lady Anstruthers.

"I can tell you about it now. You are not as you were then," Betty said. "I did not know Nigel at first, and I felt I ought to see more of him. I wanted to make sure that my child hatred of him did not make me unfair. I even tried to hope that when he came back and found the place in order and things going well, he might recognise the wisdom of behaving with decent kindness to you. If he had done that I knew father would have provided for you both, though he would not have left him the opportunity to do again what he did before. No business man would allow such a thing as that. But as time has gone by I have seen I was mistaken in hoping for a respectable compromise. Even if he were given a free hand he would not change. And now——" She hesitated, feeling it difficult to choose such words as would not be too unpleasant. How was she to tell Rosy of the ugly, morbid situation which made ordinary passiveness impossible. "Now there is a reason——" she began again.

To her surprise and relief it was Rosalie who ended for her. She spoke with the painful courage which strong affection gives a weak thing. Her face was pale no longer, but slightly reddened, and she lifted the hand which held hers and kissed it.

"You shall not say it," she interrupted her. "I will. There is a reason now why you cannot stay here—why you shall not stay here. That was why I begged you to go. You must go, even if I stay behind alone."

Never had the beautiful Miss Vanderpoel's eyes worn so fully their look of being bluebells under water. That this timid creature should so stand at bay to defend her was more moving than anything else could have been.

"Thank you, Rosy—thank you," she answered. "But you shall not be left alone. You must go, too. There is no other way. Difficulties will be made for us, but we must face them. Father will see the situation from a practical man's standpoint. Men know the things other men cannot do. Women don't. Generally they know nothing about the law and can be bullied into feeling that it is dangerous and compromising to inquire into it. Nigel has always seen that it was easy to manage women. A strong business man who has more exact legal information than he has himself will be a new factor to deal with. And he cannot make objectionable love to him. It is because he knows these things that he says that my sending for father will be a declaration of war."

"Did he say that?" a little breathlessly.

"Yes, and I told him that it need not be so. But he would not listen."

"And you are sure father will come?"

"I am sure. In a week or two he will be here."

Lady Anstruthers' lips shook, her eyes lifted themselves to Betty's in a touchingly distressed appeal. Had her momentary courage fled beyond recall? If so, that would be the worst coming to the worst, indeed. Yet it was not ordinary fear which expressed itself in her face, but a deeper piteousness, a sudden hopeless pain, baffling because it seemed a new emotion, or perhaps the upheaval of an old one long and carefully hidden.

"You will be brave?" Betty appealed to her. "You will not give way, Rosy?"

"Yes, I must be brave—I am not ill now. I must not fail you—I won't, Betty, but——"

She slipped upon the floor and dropped her face upon the girl's knee, sobbing.

Betty bent over her, putting her arms round the heaving shoulders, and pleading with her to speak. Was there something more to be told, something she did not know?

"Yes, yes. Oh, I ought to have told you long ago—but I have always been afraid and ashamed. It has made everything so much worse. I was afraid you would not understand and would think me wicked—wicked."

It was Betty who now lost a shade of colour. But she held the slim little body closer and kissed her sister's cheek.

"What have you been afraid and ashamed to tell me? Do not be ashamed any more. You must not hide anything, no matter what it is, Rosy. I shall understand."

"I know I must not hide anything, now that all is over and father is coming. It is—it is about Mr. Ffolliott."

"Mr. Ffolliott?" repeated Betty quite softly.

Lady Anstruthers' face, lifted with desperate effort, was like a weeping child's. So much so in its tear-wet simpleness and utter lack of any effort at concealment, that after one quick look at it Betty's hastened pulses ceased to beat at double-quick time.

"Tell me, dear," she almost whispered.

"Mr. Ffolliott himself does not know—and I could not help it. He was kind to me when I was dying of unkindness. You don't know what it was like to be drowning in loneliness and misery, and to see one good hand stretched out to help you. Before he went away—oh, Betty, I know it was awful because I was married!—I began to care for him very much, and I have cared for him ever since. I cannot stop myself caring, even though I am terrified."

Betty kissed her again with a passion of tender pity. Poor little, simple Rosy, too! The tide had crept around her also, and had swept her off her feet, tossing her upon its surf like a wisp of seaweed and bearing her each day farther from firm shore.

"Do not be terrified," she said. "You need only be afraid if—if you had told him."

"He will never know—never. Once in the middle of the night," there was anguish in the delicate face, pure anguish, "a strange loud cry wakened me, and it was I myself who had cried out—because in my sleep it had come home to me that the years would go on and on, and at last some day he would die and go out of the world—and I should die and go out of the world. And he would never know—even KNOW."

Betty's clasp of her loosened and she sat very still, looking straight before her into some unseen place.

"Yes," she said involuntarily. "Yes, *I* know—I know—I know."

Lady Anstruthers fell back a little to gaze at her.

"YOU know? YOU know?" she breathed. "Betty?"

But Betty at first did not speak. Her lovely eyes dwelt on the far-away place.

"Betty," whispered Rosy, "do you know what you have said?"

The lovely eyes turned slowly towards her, and the soft corners of Betty's mouth deepened in a curious unsteadiness.

"Yes. I did not intend to say it. But it is true. *I* know—I know—I know. Do not ask me how."

Rosalie flung her arms round her waist and for a moment hid her face.

"YOU! YOU!" she murmured, but stopped herself almost as she uttered the exclamation. "I will not ask you," she said when she spoke again. "But now I shall not be so ashamed. You are a beauty and wonderful, and I am not; but if you KNOW, that makes us almost the same. You will understand why I broke down. It was because I could not bear to think of what will happen. I shall be saved and taken home, but Nigel will wreak revenge on HIM. And I shall be the shame that is put upon him—only because he was kind—KIND. When father comes it will all begin." She wrung her hands, becoming almost hysterical.

"Hush," said Betty. "Hush! A man like that CANNOT be hurt, even by a man like Nigel. There is a way out—there IS. Oh, Rosy, we must BELIEVE it."

She soothed and caressed her and led her on to relieving her long locked-up misery by speech. It was easy to see the ways in which her feeling had made her life harder to bear. She was as inexperienced as a girl, and had accused herself cruelly. When Nigel had tormented her with evil, carefully chosen taunts, she had felt half guilty and had coloured scarlet or turned pale, afraid to meet his sneeringly smiling face. She had tried to forget the kind voice, the kindly, understanding eyes, and had blamed herself as a criminal because she could not.

"I had nothing else to remember—but unhappiness—and it seemed as if I could not help but remember HIM," she said as simply as the Rosy who had left New York at nineteen might have said it. "I was afraid to trust myself to speak his name. When Nigel made insulting speeches I could not answer him, and he used to say that women who had adventures should train their faces not to betray them every time they were looked at.

"Oh!" broke from Betty's lips, and she stood up on the hearth and threw out her hands. "I wish that for one day I might be a man—and your brother instead of your sister!"

"Why?"

Betty smiled strangely—a smile which was not amused—which was perhaps not a smile at all. Her voice as she answered was at once low and tense.

"Because, then I should know what to do. When a male creature cannot be reached through manhood or decency or shame, there is one way in which he can be punished. A man—a real man—should take him by his throat and lash him with a whip—while others look on—lash him until he howls aloud like a dog."

She had not expected to say it, but she had said it. Lady Anstruthers looked at her fascinated, and then she covered her face with her hands, huddling herself in a heap as she knelt on the rug, looking singularly small and frail.

"Betty," she said presently, in a new, awful little voice, "I—I will tell you something. I never thought I should dare to tell anyone alive. I have shuddered at it myself. There have been days—awful, helpless days, when I was sure there was no hope for me in all the world—when deep down in my soul I understood what women felt when they MURDERED people—crept to them in their wicked sleep and STRUCK them again—and again—and again. Like that!" She sat up suddenly, as if she did not know what she was doing, and uncovering her little ghastly face struck downward three fierce times at nothingness—but as if it were not nothingness, and as if she held something in her hand.

There was horror in it—Betty sprang at the hand and caught it.

"No! no!" she cried out. "Poor little Rosy! Darling little Rosy! No! no! no!"

That instant Lady Anstruthers looked up at her shocked and awake. She was Rosy again, and clung to her, holding to her dress, piteous and panting.

"No! no!" she said. "When it came to me in the night—it was always in the night—I used to get out of bed and pray that it might never, never come again, and that I might be forgiven—just forgiven. It was too horrible that I should even UNDERSTAND it so well." A woeful, wry little smile twisted her mouth. "I was not brave enough to have done it. I could never have DONE it, Betty;

but the thought was there—it was there! I used to think it had made a black mark on my soul."

. . . . .

The letter took long to write. It led a consecutive story up to the point where it culminated in a situation which presented itself as no longer to be dealt with by means at hand. Parts of the story previous letters had related, though some of them it had not seemed absolutely necessary to relate in detail. Now they must be made clear, and Betty made them so.

"Because you trusted me you made me trust myself," was one of the things she wrote. "For some time I felt that it was best to fight for my own hand without troubling you. I hoped perhaps I might be able to lead things to a decorous sort of issue. I saw that secretly Rosy hoped and prayed that it might be possible. She gave up expecting happiness before she was twenty, and mere decent peace would have seemed heaven to her, if she could have been allowed sometimes to see those she loved and longed for. Now that I must give up my hope—which was perhaps a rather foolish one—and now that I cannot remain at Stornham, she would have no defence at all if she were left alone. Her condition would be more hopeless than before, because Nigel would never forget that we had tried to rescue her and had failed. If I were a man, or if I were very much older, I need not be actually driven away, but as it is I think that you must come and take the matter into your own hands."

She had remained in her sister's room until long after midnight, and by the time the American letter was completed and sealed, a pale touch of dawning light was showing itself. She rose, and going to the window drew the blind up and looked out. The looking out made her open the window, and when she had done so she stood feeling the almost unearthly freshness of the morning about her. The mystery of the first faint light was almost unearthly, too. Trees and shrubs were beginning to take form and outline themselves against the still pallor of the dawn. Before long the waking of the birds would begin—a brief chirping note here and there breaking the silence and warning the world with faint insistence that it had begun to live again and must bestir itself. She had got out of her bed sometimes on a summer morning to watch the beauty of it, to see the flowers gradually reveal their colour to the eye, to hear the warmly nesting things begin their joyous day. There were fewer bird sounds now, and the garden beds were autumnal. But how beautiful it all was! How wonderful life in such a place might be if flowers and birds and sweep of sward, and mass of stately, broad-branched trees, were parts of the home one loved and which surely would in its own way love one in return. But soon all this phase of life would be over. Rosalie, once safe at home, would look back, remembering the place with a shudder. As Ughtred grew older the passing of years would dim miserable child memories, and when his inheritance fell to him he might return to see it with happier eyes. She began to picture to herself Rosy's voyage in the ship which would carry her across the Atlantic to her mother and the scenes connected in her mind only with a girl's happiness. Whatsoever happened before it took place, the voyage would be made in the end. And Rosalie would be like a creature in a dream—a heavenly, unbelievable dream. Betty could imagine how she would look wrapped up and sitting in her steamer chair, gazing out with rapturous eyes upon the racing waves.

"She will be happy," she thought. "But I shall not. No, I shall not."

She drew in the morning air and unconsciously turned towards the place where, across the rising and falling lands and behind the trees, she knew the great white house stood far away, with watchers' lights showing dimly behind the line of ballroom windows.

"I do not know how such a thing could be! I do not know how such a thing could be!" she said. "It COULD not." And she lifted a high head, not even asking herself what remote sense in her being so obstinately defied and threw down the glove to Fate.

Sounds gain a curious distinctness and meaning in the hour of the break of the dawn; in such an hour they seem even more significant than sounds heard in the dead of night. When she had gone to the window she had fancied that she heard something in the corridor outside her door, but when she had listened there had been only silence. Now there was sound again—that of a softly moved slippered foot. She went to the room's centre and waited. Yes, certainly something had stirred in the passage. She went to the door itself. The dragging step had hesitated—stopped. Could it be Rosalie who had come to her for something. For one second her impulse was to open the door herself; the next, she had changed her mind with a sense of shock. Someone had actually touched the handle and very delicately turned it. It was not pleasant to stand looking at it and see it turn. She heard a low, evidently unintentionally uttered exclamation, and she turned away, and with no attempt at softening the sound of her footsteps walked across the room, hot with passionate disgust. As well as if she had flung the door open, she knew who stood outside. It was Nigel Anstruthers, haggard and unseemly, with burned-out, sleepless eyes and bitten lip.

Bad and mad as she had at last seen the situation to be, it was uglier and more desperate than she could well know.

CHAPTER XLV

THE PASSING BELL

The following morning Sir Nigel did not appear at the breakfast table. He breakfasted in his own room, and it became known throughout the household that he had suddenly decided to go away, and his man was packing for the journey. What the journey or the reason for its being taken happened to be were things not explained to anyone but Lady Anstruthers, at the door of whose dressing room he appeared without warning, just as she was leaving it.

Rosalie started when she found herself confronting him. His eyes looked hot and hollow with feverish sleeplessness.

"You look ill," she exclaimed involuntarily. "You look as if you had not slept."

"Thank you. You always encourage a man. I am not in the habit of sleeping much," he answered. "I am going away for my health. It is as well you should know. I am going to look up old Broadmorlands. I want to know exactly where he is, in case it becomes necessary for me to see him. I also require some trifling data connected with Ffolliott. If your father is coming, it will be as well to be able to lay my hands on things. You can explain to Betty. Good-morning." He waited for no reply, but wheeled about and left her.

Betty herself wore a changed face when she came down. A cloud had passed over her blooming, as clouds pass over a morning sky and dim it. Rosalie asked herself if she had not noticed something like this before. She began to think she had. Yes, she was sure that at intervals there had been moments when she had glanced at the brilliant face with an uneasy and yet half-unrealising sense of looking at a glowing light temporarily waning. The feeling had been unrealisable, because it was not to be explained. Betty was never ill, she was never low-spirited, she was never out of humour or afraid of things—that was why it was so wonderful to live with her. But—yes, it was true—there had been days when the strong, fine light of her had waned. Lady Anstruthers' comprehension of it arose now from her memory of the look she had seen the night before in the eyes which suddenly had gazed straight before her, as into an unknown place.

"Yes, I know—I know—I know!" And the tone in the girl's voice had been one Rosy had not heard before.

Slight wonder—if you KNEW—at any outward change which showed itself, though in your own most desperate despite. It would be so even with Betty, who, in her sister's eyes, was unlike any other creature. But perhaps it would be better to make no comment. To make comment would be almost like asking the question she had been forbidden to ask.

While the servants were in the room during breakfast they talked of common things, resorting even to the weather and the news of the village. Afterwards they passed into the morning room together, and Betty put her arm around Rosalie and kissed her.

"Nigel has suddenly gone away, I hear," she said. "Do you know where he has gone?"

"He came to my dressing-room to tell me." Betty felt the whole slim body stiffen itself with a determination to seem calm. "He said he was going to find out where the old Duke of Broadmorlands was staying at present."

"There is some forethought in that," was Betty's answer. "He is not on such terms with the Duke that he can expect to be received as a casual visitor. It will require apt contrivance to arrange an interview. I wonder if he will be able to accomplish it?"

"Yes, he will," said Lady Anstruthers. "I think he can always contrive things like that." She hesitated a moment, and then added: "He said also that he wished to find out certain things about Mr. Ffolliott—'trifling data,' he called it—that he might be able to lay his hands on things if father came. He told me to explain to you."

"That was intended for a taunt—but it's a warning," Betty said, thinking the thing over. "We are rather like ladies left alone to defend a besieged castle. He wished us to feel that." She tightened her enclosing arm. "But we stand together—together. We shall not fail each other. We can face siege until father comes."

"You wrote to him last night?"

"A long letter, which I wish him to receive before he sails. He might decide to act upon it before leaving New York, to advise with some legal authority he knows and trusts, to prepare our mother in some way—to do some wise thing we cannot foresee the value of. He has known the outline of the story, but not exact details—particularly recent ones. I have held back nothing it was necessary he should know. I am going out to post the letter myself. I shall send a cable asking him to prepare to come to us after he has reflected on what I have written."

Rosalie was very quiet, but when, having left the room to prepare to go to the village, Betty came back to say a last word, her sister came to her and laid her hand on her arm.

"I have been so weak and trodden upon for years that it would not be natural for you to quite trust me," she said. "But I won't fail you, Betty—I won't."

The winter was drawing in, the last autumn days were short and often grey and dreary; the wind had swept the leaves from the trees and scattered them over park lands and lanes, where they lay a mellow-hued, rustling carpet, shifting with each chill breeze that blew. The berried briony garlands clung to the bared hedges, and here and there flared scarlet, still holding their red defiantly until hard frosts should come to shrivel and blacken them. The rare hours of sunshine were amber hours instead of golden.

As she passed through the park gate Betty was thinking of the first morning on which she had walked down the village street between the irregular rows of red-tiled cottages with the ragged little enclosing gardens. Then the air and sunshine had been of the just awakening spring, now the sky was brightly cold, and through the small-paned windows she caught glimpses of fireglow. A bent old man walking very slowly, leaning upon two sticks, had a red-brown woollen muffler wrapped round his neck. Seeing her, he stopped and shuffled the two sticks into one hand that he might leave the other free to touch his wrinkled forehead stiffly, his face stretching into a slow smile as she stopped to speak to him.

"Good-morning, Marlow," he said. "How is the rheumatism to-day?"

He was a deaf old man, whose conversation was carried on principally by guesswork, and it was easy for him to gather that when her ladyship's handsome young sister had given him greeting she had not forgotten to inquire respecting the "rheumatics," which formed the greater part of existence.

"Mornin', miss—mornin'," he answered in the high, cracked voice of rural ancientry. "Winter be nigh, an' they damp days be full of rheumatiz. 'T'int easy to get about on my old legs, but I be main thankful for they warm things you sent, miss. This 'ere," fumbling at his red-brown muffler proudly, "'tis a comfort on windy days, so 'tis, and warmth be a good thing to a man when he be goin' down hill in years."

"All of you who are not able to earn your own fires shall be warm this winter," her ladyship's handsome sister said, speaking closer to his ear. "You shall all be warm. Don't be afraid of the cold days coming."

He shuffled his sticks and touched his forehead again, looking up at her admiringly and chuckling.

"'T'will be a new tale for Stornham village," he cackled. "'T'will be a new tale. Thank ye, miss. Thank ye."

As she nodded smilingly and passed on, she heard him cackling still under his breath as he hobbled on his slow way, comforted and elate. How almost shamefully easy it was; a few loads of coal and faggots here and there, a few blankets and warm garments whose cost counted for so little when one's hands were full, could change a gruesome village winter into a season during which labour-stiffened and broken old things, closing their cottage doors, could draw their chairs round the hearth and hover luxuriously over the red glow, which in its comforting fashion of seeming to have understanding of the dull dreams in old eyes, was more to be loved than any human friend.

But she had not needed her passing speech with Marlow to stimulate realisation of how much she had learned to care for the mere living among these people, to whom she seemed to have begun to belong, and whose comfortably lighting faces when they met her showed that they knew her to be one who might be turned to in any hour of trouble or dismay. The centuries which had trained them to depend upon their "betters" had taught the slowest of them to judge with keen sight those who were to be trusted, not alone as power and wealth holders, but as creatures humanly upright and merciful with their kind.

"Workin' folk allus knows gentry," old Doby had once shrilled to her. "Gentry's gentry, an' us knows 'em wheresoever they be. Better'n they know theirselves. So us do!"

Yes, they knew. And though they accepted many things as being merely their natural rights, they gave an unsentimental affection and appreciation in return. The patriarchal note in the life was lovable to her. Each creature she passed was a sort of friend who seemed almost of her own blood. It had come to that. This particular existence was more satisfying to her than any other, more heart-filling and warmly complete.

"Though I am only an impostor," she thought; "I was born in Fifth Avenue; yet since I have known this I shall be quite happy in no other place than an English village, with a Norman church tower looking down upon it and rows of little gardens with spears of white and blue lupins and Canterbury bells standing guard before cottage doors."

And Rosalie—on the evening of that first strange day when she had come upon her piteous figure among the heather under the trees near the lake—Rosalie had held her arm with a hot little hand and had said feverishly:

"If I could hear the roar of Broadway again! Do the stages rattle as they used to, Betty? I can't help hoping that they do."

She carried her letter to the post and stopped to talk a few minutes with the postmaster, who transacted his official business in a small shop where sides of bacon and hams hung suspended from the ceiling, while groceries, flannels, dress prints, and glass bottles of sweet stuff filled the shelves. "Mr. Tewson's" was the central point of Stornham in a commercial sense. The establishment had also certain social qualifications.

Mr. Tewson knew the secrets of all hearts within the village radius, also the secrets of all constitutions. He knew by some occult means who had been "taken bad," or who had "taken a turn," and was aware at once when anyone was "sinkin' fast." With such differences of opinion as occasionally arose between the vicar and his churchwardens he was immediately familiar. The history of the fever among the hop pickers at Dunstan village he had been able to relate in detail from the moment of its outbreak. It was he who had first dramatically revealed the truth of the action Miss Vanderpoel had taken in the matter, which revelation had aroused such enthusiasm as had filled The Clock Inn to overflowing and given an impetus to the sale of beer. Tread, it was said, had even made a speech which he had ended with vague but excellent intentions by proposing the joint healths of her ladyship's sister and the "President of America." Mr. Tewson was always glad to see Miss Vanderpoel cross his threshold. This was not alone because she represented the custom of the Court, which since her arrival had meant large regular orders and large bills promptly paid, but that she brought with her an exotic atmosphere of interest and excitement.

He had mentioned to friends that somehow a talk with her made him feel "set up for the day." Betty was not at all sure that he did not prepare and hoard up choice remarks or bits of information as openings to conversation.

This morning he had thrilling news for her and began with it at once.

"Dr. Fenwick at Stornham is very low, miss," he said. "He's very low, you'll be sorry to hear. The worry about the fever upset him terrible and his bronchitis took him bad. He's an old man, you know."

Miss Vanderpoel was very sorry to hear it. It was quite in the natural order of things that she should ask other questions about Dunstan village and the Mount, and she asked several.

The fever was dying out and pale convalescents were sometimes seen in the village or strolling about the park. His lordship was taking care of the people and doing his best for them until they should be strong enough to return to their homes.

"But he's very strict about making it plain that it's you, miss, they have to thank for what he does."

"That is not quite just," said Miss Vanderpoel. "He and Mr. Penzance fought on the field. I only supplied some of the ammunition."

"The county doesn't think of him as it did even a year ago, miss," said Tewson rather smugly. "He was very ill thought of then among the gentry. It's wonderful the change that's come about. If he should fall ill there'll be a deal of sympathy."

"I hope there is no question of his falling ill," said Miss Vanderpoel.

Mr. Tewson lowered his voice confidentially. This was really his most valuable item of news.

"Well, miss," he admitted, "I have heard that he's been looking very bad for a good bit, and it was told me quite private, because the doctors and the vicar don't want the people to be upset by hearing it—that for a week he's not been well enough to make his rounds."

"Oh!" The exclamation was a faint one, but it was an exclamation. "I hope that means nothing really serious," Miss Vanderpoel added. "Everyone will hope so."

"Yes, miss," said Mr. Tewson, deftly twisting the string round the package he was tying up for her. "A sad reward it would be if he lost his life after doing all he has done. A sad reward! But there'd be a good deal of sympathy."

The small package contained trifles of sewing and knitting materials she was going to take to Mrs. Welden, and she held out her hand for it. She knew she did not smile quite naturally as she said her good-morning to Tewson. She went out into the pale amber sunshine and stood a few moments, glad to find herself bathed in it again. She suddenly needed air and light. "A sad reward!" Sometimes people were not rewarded. Brave men were shot dead on the battlefield when they were doing brave things; brave physicians and nurses died of the plagues they faithfully wrestled with. Here were dread and pain confronting her—Betty Vanderpoel—and while almost everyone else seemed to have faced them, she was wholly unused to their appalling clutch. What a life hers had been—that in looking back over it she should realise that she had never been touched by anything like this before! There came back to her the look of almost awed wonder in G. Selden's honest eyes when he said: "What it must be to be you— just YOU!" He had been thinking only of the millions and of the freedom from all everyday anxieties the millions gave. She smiled faintly as the thought crossed her brain. The millions! The rolling up of them year by year, because millions were breeders! The newspaper stories of them—the wonder at and belief in their power! It was all going on just as before, and yet here stood a Vanderpoel in an English village street, of no more worth as far as power to aid herself went than Joe Buttle's girl with the thick waist and round red cheeks. Jenny Buttle would have believed that her ladyship's rich American sister could do anything she chose, open any door, command any presence, sweep aside any obstacle with a wave of her hand. But of the two, Jenny Buttle's path would have laid straighter before her. If she had had "a young man" who had fallen ill she would have been free if his mother had cherished no objection to their "walking out"—to spend all her spare hours in his cottage, making gruel and poultices, crying until her nose and eyes were red, and pouring forth her hopes and fears to any neighbour who came in or out or hung over the dividing garden hedge. If the patient died, the deeper her mourning and the louder her sobs at his funeral the more respectable and deserving of sympathy and admiration would Jenny Buttle have been counted. Her ladyship's rich American sister had no "young man"; she had not at any time been asked to "walk out." Even in the dark days of the fever, each of which had carried thought and action of hers to the scene of trouble, there had reigned unbroken silence, except for the vicar's notes of warm and appreciative gratitude.

"You are very obstinate, Fergus," Mr. Penzance had said.

And Mount Dunstan had shaken his head fiercely and answered:

"Don't speak to me about it. Only obstinacy will save me from behaving like—other blackguards."

Mr. Penzance, carefully polishing his eyeglasses as he watched him, was not sparing in his comment.

"That is pure folly," he said, "pure bull-necked, stubborn folly, charging with its head down. Before it has done with you it will have made you suffer quite enough."

"Be sure of that," Mount Dunstan had said, setting his teeth, as he sat in his chair clasping his hands behind his head and glowering into space.

Mr. Penzance quietly, speculatively, looked him over, and reflected aloud—or, so it sounded.

"It is a big-boned and big-muscled characteristic, but there are things which are stronger. Some one minute will arrive—just one minute—which will be stronger. One of those moments when the mysteries of the universe are at work."

"Don't speak to me like that, I tell you!" Mount Dunstan broke out passionately. And he sprang up and marched out of the room like an angry man.

Miss Vanderpoel did not go to Mrs. Welden's cottage at once, but walked past its door down the lane, where there were no more cottages, but only hedges and fields on either side of her. "Not well enough to make his rounds" might mean much or little. It might mean a temporary breakdown from overfatigue or a sickening for deadly illness. She looked at a group of cropping sheep in a field and at a flock of rooks which had just alighted near it with cawing and flapping of wings. She kept her eyes on them merely to steady herself. The thoughts she had brought out with her had grown heavier and were horribly difficult to control. One must not allow one's self to believe the worst will come—one must not allow it.

She always held this rule before herself, and now she was not holding it steadily. There was nothing to do. She could write a mere note of inquiry to Mr. Penzance, but that was all. She could only walk up and down the lanes and think—whether he lay dying or not. She could do nothing, even if a day came when she knew that a pit had been dug in the clay and he had been lowered into it with creaking ropes, and the clods shovelled back upon him where he lay still—never having told her that he was glad that her being had turned to him and her heart cried aloud his name. She recalled with curious distinctness the effect of the steady toll of the church bell—the "passing bell."

She could hear it as she had heard it the first time it fell upon her ear, and she had inquired what it meant. Why did they call it the "passing bell"? All had passed before it began to toll—all had passed. If it tolled at Dunstan and the pit was dug in the churchyard before her father came, would he see, the moment they met, that something had befallen her—that the Betty he had known was changed—gone? Yes, he would see. Affection such as his always saw. Then he would sit alone with her in some quiet room and talk to her, and she would tell him the strange thing that had happened. He would understand—perhaps better than she.

She stopped abruptly in her walk and stood still. The hand holding her package was quite cold. This was what one must not allow one's self. But how the thoughts had raced through her brain! She turned and hastened her steps towards Mrs. Welden's cottage.

In Mrs. Welden's tiny back yard there stood a "coal lodge" suited to the size of the domicile and already stacked with a full winter's supply of coal. Therefore the well-polished and cleanly little grate in the living-room was bright with fire.

Old Doby, who had tottered round the corner to pay his fellow gossip a visit, was sitting by it, and old Mrs. Welden, clean as to cap and apron and small purple shoulder shawl, had evidently been allaying his natural anxiety as to the conduct of foreign sovereigns by reading in a loud voice the "print" under the pictures in an illustrated paper.

This occupation had, however, been interrupted a few moments before Miss Vanderpoel's arrival. Mrs. Bester, the neighbour in the next cottage, had stepped in with her youngest on her hip and was talking breathlessly. She paused to drop her curtsy as Betty entered, and old Doby stood up and made his salute with a trembling hand,

"She'll know," he said. "Gentry knows the ins an' outs of gentry fust. She'll know the rights."

"What has happened?"

Mrs. Bester unexpectedly burst into tears. There was an element in the female villagers' temperament which Betty had found was frequently unexpected in its breaking forth.

"He's down, miss," she said. "He's down with it crool bad. There'll be no savin' of him—none."

Betty laid her package of sewing cotton and knitting wool quietly on the blue and white checked tablecloth.

"Who—is he?" she asked.

"His lordship—and him just saved all Dunstan parish from death—to go like this!"

In Stornham village and in all others of the neighbourhood the feminine attitude towards Mount Dunstan had been one of strongly emotional admiration. The thwarted female longing for romance—the desire for drama and a hero had been fed by him. A fine, big young man, one that had been "spoke ill of" and regarded as an outcast, had suddenly turned the tables on fortune and made himself the central figure of the county, the talk of gentry in their grand houses, of cottage women on their doorsteps, and labourers stopping to speak to each other by the roadside. Magic stories had been told of him, beflowered with dramatic detail. No incident could have been related to his credit which would not have been believed and improved upon. Shut up in his village working among his people and unseen by outsiders, he had become a popular idol. Any scrap of news of him—any rumour, true or untrue, was seized upon and excitedly spread abroad. Therefore Mrs. Bester wept as she talked, and, if the truth must be told, enjoyed the situation. She was the first to tell the story to her ladyship's sister herself, as well as to Mrs. Welden and old Doby.

"It's Tom as brought it in," she said. "He's my brother, miss, an' he's one of the ringers. He heard it from Jem Wesgate, an' he heard it at Toomy's farm. They've been keepin' it hid at the Mount because the people that's ill hangs on his lordship so that the doctors daren't let them know the truth. They've been told he had to go to London an' may come back any day. What Tom was sayin', miss, was that we'd all know when it was over, for we'd hear the church bell toll here same as it'd toll at Dunstan, because they ringers have talked it over an' they're goin' to talk it over to-day with the other parishes—Yangford an' Meltham an' Dunholm an' them. Tom says Stornham ringers met just now at The Clock an' said that for a man that's stood by labouring folk like he has, toll they will, an' so ought the other parishes, same as if he was royalty, for he's made himself nearer. They'll toll the minute they hear it, miss. Lord help us!" with a fresh outburst of crying. "It don't seem like it's fair as it should be. When we hear the bell toll, miss——"

"Don't!" said her ladyship's handsome sister suddenly. "Please don't say it again."

She sat down by the table, and resting her elbows on the blue and white checked cloth, covered her face with her hands. She did not speak at all. In this tiny room, with these two old souls who loved her, she need not explain. She sat quite still, and Mrs. Welden after looking at her for a few seconds was prompted by some sublimely simple intuition, and gently sidled Mrs. Bester and her youngest into the little kitchen, where the copper was.

"Her helpin' him like she did, makes it come near," she whispered. "Dessay it seems as if he was a'most like a relation."

Old Doby sat and looked at his goddess. In his slowly moving old brain stirred far-off memories like long-dead things striving to come to life. He did not know what they were, but they wakened his dim eyes to a new seeing of the slim young shape leaning a little forward, the soft cloud of hair, the fair beauty of the cheek. He had not seen anything like it in his youth, but—it was Youth itself, and so was that which the ringers were so soon to toll for; and for some remote and unformed reason, to his scores of years they were pitiful and should be cheered. He bent forward himself and put out his ancient, veined and knotted, gnarled and trembling hand, to timorously touch the arm of her he worshipped and adored.

"God bless ye!" he said, his high, cracked voice even more shrill and thin than usual. "God bless ye!" And as she let her hands slip down, and, turning, gently looked at him, he nodded to her speakingly, because out of the dimness of his being, some part of Nature's working had strangely answered and understood.

CHAPTER XLVI

LISTENING

On her way back to the Court her eyes saw only the white road before her feet as she walked. She did not lift them until she found herself passing the lychgate at the entrance to the churchyard. Then suddenly she looked up at the square grey stone tower where the bells hung, and from which they called the village to church, or chimed for weddings—or gave slowly forth to the silent air one heavy, regular stroke after another. She looked and shuddered, and spoke aloud with a curious, passionate imploring, like a child's.

"Oh, don't toll! Don't toll! You must not! You cannot!" Terror had sprung upon her, and her heart was being torn in two in her breast. That was surely what it seemed like—this agonising ache of fear. Now from hour to hour she would be waiting and listening to each sound borne on the air. Her thought would be a possession she could not escape. When she spoke or was spoken to, she would be listening—when she was silent every echo would hold terror, when she slept—if sleep should come to her—her hearing would be awake, and she would be listening—listening even then. It was not Betty Vanderpoel who was walking along the white road, but another creature—a girl whose brain was full of abnormal thought, and whose whole being made passionate outcry against the thing which was being slowly forced upon her. If the bell tolled—suddenly, the whole world would be swept clean of life—empty and clean. If the bell tolled.

Before the entrance of the Court she saw, as she approached it, the vicarage pony carriage, standing as it had stood on the day she had returned from her walk on the marshes. She felt it quite natural that it should be there. Mrs. Brent always seized upon any fragment of news, and having seized on something now, she had not been able to resist the excitement of bringing it to Lady Anstruthers and her sister.

She was in the drawing-room with Rosalie, and was full of her subject and the emotion suitable to the occasion. She had even attained a certain modified dampness of handkerchief. Rosalie's handkerchief, however, was not damp. She had not even attempted to use it, but sat still, her eyes brimming with tears, which, when she saw Betty, brimmed over and slipped helplessly down her cheeks.

"Betty!" she exclaimed, and got up and went towards her, "I believe you have heard."

"In the village, I heard something—yes," Betty answered, and after giving greeting to Mrs. Brent, she led her sister back to her chair, and sat near her.

This—the thought leaped upon her—was the kind of situation she must be prepared to be equal to. In the presence of these who knew nothing, she must bear herself as if there was nothing to be known. No one but herself had the slightest knowledge of what the past months had brought to her—no one in the world. If the bell tolled, no one in the world but her father ever would know.

She had no excuse for emotion. None had been given to her. The kind of thing it was proper that she should say and do now, in the presence of Mrs. Brent, it would be proper and decent that she should say and do in all other cases. She must comport herself as Betty Vanderpoel would if she were moved only by ordinary human sympathy and regret.

"We must remember that we have only excited rumour to depend upon," she said. "Lord Mount Dunstan has kept his village under almost military law. He has put it into quarantine. No one is allowed to leave it, so there can be no direct source of information. One cannot be sure of the entire truth of what one hears. Often it is exaggerated cottage talk. The whole neighbourhood is wrought up to a fever heat of excited sympathy. And villagers like the drama of things."

Mrs. Brent looked at her admiringly, it being her fixed habit to admire Miss Vanderpoel, and all such as Providence had set above her.

"Oh, how wise you are, Miss Vanderpoel!" she exclaimed, even devoutly. "It is so nice of you to be calm and logical when everybody else is so upset. You are quite right about villagers enjoying the dramatic side of troubles. They always do. And perhaps things are not so bad as they say. I ought not to have let myself believe the worst. But I quite broke down under the ringers—I was so touched."

"The ringers?" faltered Lady Anstruthers.

"The leader came to the vicar to tell him they wanted permission to toll—if they heard tolling at Dunstan. Weaver's family lives within hearing of Dunstan church bells, and one of his boys is to run across the fields and bring the news to Stornham. And it was most touching, Miss Vanderpoel. They feel, in their rustic way, that Lord Mount Dunstan has not been treated fairly in the past. And now he seems to them a hero and a martyr—or like a great soldier who has died fighting."

"Who MAY die fighting," broke from Miss Vanderpoel sharply.

"Who—who may——" Mrs. Brent corrected herself, "though Heaven grant he will not. But it was the ringers who made me feel as if all really was over. Thank you, Miss Vanderpoel, thank you for being so practical and—and cool."

"It WAS touching," said Lady Anstruthers, her eyes brimming over again. "And what the villagers feel is true. It goes to one's heart," in a little outburst. "People have been unkind to him! And he has been lonely in that great empty place—he has been lonely. And if he is dying to-day, he is lonely even as he dies—even as he dies."

Betty drew a deep breath. For one moment there seemed to rise before her vision of a huge room, whose stately size made its bareness a more desolate thing. And Mr. Penzance bent low over the bed. She tore her thought away from it.

"No! No!" she cried out in low, passionate protest. "There will be love and yearning all about him everywhere. The villagers who are waiting—the poor things he has worked for—the very ringers themselves, are all pouring forth the same thoughts. He will feel even ours—ours too! His soul cannot be lonely."

A few minutes earlier, Mrs. Brent had been saying to herself inwardly: "She has not much heart after all, you know." Now she looked at her in amazement.

The blue bells were under water in truth—drenched and drowned. And yet as the girl stood up before her, she looked taller—more the magnificent Miss Vanderpoel than ever—though she expressed a new meaning.

"There is one thing the villagers can do for him," she said. "One thing we can all do. The bell has not tolled yet. There is a service for those who are—in peril. If the vicar will call the people to the church, we can all kneel down there—and ask to be heard. The vicar will do that I am sure—and the people will join him with all their hearts."

Mrs. Brent was overwhelmed.

"Dear, dear, Miss Vanderpoel!" she exclaimed. "THAT is touching, indeed it is! And so right and so proper. I will drive back to the village at once. The vicar's distress is as great as mine. You think of everything. The service for the sick and dying. How right—how right!"

With a sense of an increase of value in herself, the vicar, and the vicarage, she hastened back to the pony carriage, but in the hall she seized Betty's hand emotionally.

"I cannot tell you how much I am touched by this," she murmured. "I did not know you were—were a religious girl, my dear."

Betty answered with grave politeness.

"In times of great pain and terror," she said, "I think almost everybody is religious—a little. If that is the right word."

There was no ringing of the ordinary call to service. In less than an hour's time people began to come out of their cottages and wend their way towards the church. No one had put on his or her Sunday clothes. The women had hastily rolled down their sleeves, thrown off their aprons, and donned everyday bonnets and shawls. The men were in their corduroys, as they had come in from the fields, and the children wore their pinafores. As if by magic, the news had flown from house to house, and each one who had heard it had left his or her work without a moment's hesitation. They said but little as they made their way to the church. Betty, walking with her sister, was struck by the fact that there were more of them than formed the usual Sunday morning congregation. They were doing no perfunctory duty. The men's faces were heavily moved, most of the women wiped their eyes at intervals, and the children looked awed. There was a suggestion of hurried movement in the step of each—as if no time must be lost—as if they must begin their appeal at once. Betty saw old Doby tottering along stiffly, with his granddaughter and Mrs. Welden on either side of him. Marlow, on his two sticks, was to be seen moving slowly, but steadily.

Within the ancient stone walls, stiff old knees bent themselves with care, and faces were covered devoutly by work-hardened hands. As she passed through the churchyard Betty knew that eyes followed her affectionately, and that the touching of foreheads and dropping of curtsies expressed a special sympathy. In each mind she was connected with the man they came to pray for—with the work he had done—with the danger he was in. It was vaguely felt that if his life ended, a bereavement would have fallen upon her. This the girl knew.

The vicar lifted his bowed head and began his service. Every man, woman and child before him responded aloud and with a curious fervour—not in decorous fear of seeming to thrust themselves before the throne, making too much of their petitions, in the presence of the gentry. Here and there sobs were to be heard. Lady Anstruthers followed the service timorously and with tears. But Betty, kneeling at her side, by the round table in the centre of the great square Stornham pew, which was like a room, bowed her head upon her folded arms, and prayed her own intense, insistent prayer.

"God in Heaven!" was her inward cry. "God of all the worlds! Do not let him die. 'If ye ask anything in my name that I will do.' Christ said it. In the name of Jesus of Nazareth—do not let him die! All the worlds are yours—all the power—listen to us—listen to us. Lord, I believe—help thou my unbelief. If this terror robs me of faith, and I pray madly—forgive, forgive me. Do not count it against me as sin. You made him. He has suffered and been alone. It is not time—it is not time yet for him to go. He has known no joy and no bright thing. Do not let him go out of the warm world like a blind man. Do not let him die. Perhaps this is not prayer, but raging. Forgive—forgive! All power is gone from me. God of the worlds, and the great winds, and the myriad stars—do not let him die!"

She knew her thoughts were wild, but their torrent bore her with them into a strange, great silence. She did not hear the vicar's words, or the responses of the people. She was not within the grey stone walls. She had been drawn away as into the darkness and stillness of the night, and no soul but her own seemed near. Through the stillness and the dark her praying seemed to call and echo, clamouring again and again. It must reach Something—it must be heard, because she cried so loud, though to the human beings about her she seemed kneeling in silence. She went on and on, repeating her words, changing them, ending and beginning again, pouring forth a flood of appeal. She thought later that the flood must have been at its highest tide when, singularly, it was stemmed. Without warning, a wave of awe passed over her which strangely silenced her—and left her bowed and kneeling, but crying out no more. The darkness had become still, even as it had not been still before. Suddenly she cowered as she knelt and held her breath. Something had drawn a little near. No thoughts—no words—no cries were needed as the great stillness grew and spread, and folded her being within it. She waited—only waited. She did not know how long a time passed before she felt herself drawn back from the silent and shadowy places—awakening, as it were, to the sounds in the church.

"Our Father," she began to say, as simply as a child. "Our Father who art in Heaven—hallowed be thy name." There was a stirring among the congregation, and sounds of feet, as the people began to move down the aisle in reverent slowness. She caught again the occasional sound of a subdued sob. Rosalie gently touched her, and she rose, following her out of the big pew and passing down the aisle after the villagers.

Outside the entrance the people waited as if they wanted to see her again. Foreheads were touched as before, and eyes followed her. She was to the general mind the centre of the drama, and "the A'mighty" would do well to hear her. She had been doing his work for him "same as his lordship." They did not expect her to smile at such a time, when she returned their greetings, and she did not, but they said afterwards, in their cottages, that "trouble or not she was a wonder for looks, that she was—Miss Vanderpoel."

Rosalie slipped a hand through her arm, and they walked home together, very close to each other. Now and then there was a questioning in Rosy's look. But neither of them spoke once.

On an oak table in the hall a letter from Mr. Penzance was lying. It was brief, hurried, and anxious. The rumour that Mount Dunstan had been ailing was true, and that they had felt they must conceal the matter from the villagers was true also. For some baffling reason the fever had not absolutely declared itself, but the young doctors were beset by grave forebodings. In such cases the most serious symptoms might suddenly develop. One never knew. Mr. Penzance was evidently torn by fears which he desperately strove to suppress. But Betty could see the anguish on his fine old face, and between the lines she read dread and warning not put into words. She believed that, fearing the worst, he felt he must prepare her mind.

"He has lived under a great strain for months," he ended. "It began long before the outbreak of the fever. I am not strong under my sense of the cruelty of things—and I have never loved him as I love him to-day."

Betty took the letter to her room, and read it two or three times. Because she had asked intelligent questions of the medical authority she had consulted on her visit to London, she knew something of the fever and its habits. Even her unclerical knowledge was such as it was not well to reflect upon. She refolded the letter and laid it aside.

"I must not think. I must do something. It may prevent my listening," she said aloud to the silence of her room.

She cast her eyes about her as if in search. Upon her desk lay a notebook. She took it up and opened it. It contained lists of plants, of flower seeds, of bulbs, and shrubs. Each list was headed with an explanatory note.

"Yes, this will do," she said. "I will go and talk to Kedgers."

Kedgers and every man under him had been at the service, but they had returned to their respective duties. Kedgers, giving directions to some under gardeners who were clearing flower beds and preparing them for their winter rest, turned to meet her as she approached. To Kedgers the sight of her coming towards him on a garden path was a joyful thing. He had done wonders, it is true, but if she had not stood by his side with inspiration as well as confidence, he knew that things might have "come out different."

"You was born a gardener, miss—born one," he had said months ago.

It was the time when flower beds must be planned for the coming year. Her notebook was filled with memoranda of the things they must talk about.

It was good, normal, healthy work to do. The scent of the rich, damp, upturned mould was a good thing to inhale. They walked from one end to another, stood before clumps of shrubs, and studied bits of wall. Here a mass of blue might grow, here low things of white and pale yellow. A quickly-climbing rose would hang sheets of bloom over this dead tree. This sheltered wall would hold warmth for a Marechal Niel.

"You must take care of it all—even if I am not here next year," Miss Vanderpoel said.

Kedgers' absorbed face changed.

"Not here, miss," he exclaimed. "You not here! Things wouldn't grow, miss." He checked himself, his weather-toughened skin reddening because he was afraid he had perhaps taken a liberty. And then moving his hat uneasily on his head, he took another. "But it's true enough," looking down on the gravel walk, "we—we couldn't expect to keep you."

She did not look as if she had noticed the liberty, but she did not look quite like herself, Kedgers thought. If she had been another young lady, and but for his established feeling that she was somehow immune from all ills, he would have thought she had a headache, or was low in her mind.

She spent an hour or two with him, and together they planned for the changing seasons of the year to come. How she could keep her mind on a thing, and what a head she had for planning, and what an eye for colour! But yes— there was something a bit wrong somehow. Now and then she would stop and stand still for a moment, and suddenly it struck Kedgers that she looked as if she were listening.

"Did you think you heard something, miss?" he asked her once when she paused and wore this look.

"No," she answered, "no." And drew him on quickly—almost as if she did not want him to hear what she had seemed listening for.

When she left him and went back to the house, all the loveliness of spring, summer and autumn had been thought out and provided for. Kedgers stood on the path and looked after her until she passed through the terrace door. He chewed his lip uneasily. Then he remembered something and felt a bit relieved. It was the service he remembered.

"Ah! it's that that's upset her—and it's natural, seeing how she's helped him and Dunstan village. It's only natural." He chewed his lip again, and nodded his head in odd reflection. "Ay! Ay!" he summed her up. "She's a great lady that— she's a great lady—same as if she'd been born in a civilised land."

During the rest of the day the look of question in Rosalie's eyes changed in its nature. When her sister was near her she found herself glancing at her with a new feeling. It was a growing feeling, which gradually became—anxiousness. Betty presented to her the aspect of one withdrawn into some remote space. She was not living this day as her days were usually lived. She did not sit still or stroll about the gardens quietly. The consecutiveness of her action seemed broken. She did one thing after another, as if she must fill each moment. This was not her Betty. Lady Anstruthers watched and thought until, in the end, a new pained fear began to creep slowly into her mind, and make her feel as if she were slightly trembling though her hands did not shake. She did not dare to allow herself to think the thing she knew she was on the brink of thinking. She thrust it away from her, and tried not to think at all. Her Betty—her splendid Betty, whom nothing could hurt—who could not be touched by any awful thing—her dear Betty!

In the afternoon she saw her write notes steadily for an hour, then she went out into the stables and visited the horses, talked to the coachman and to her own groom. She was very kind to a village boy who had been recently taken on as an additional assistant in the stable, and who was rather frightened and shy. She knew his mother, who had a large family, and she had, indeed, given the boy his place that he might be trained under the great Mr. Buckham, who was coachman and head of the stables. She said encouraging things which quite cheered him, and she spoke privately to Mr. Buckham about him. Then she walked in the park a little, but not for long. When she came back Rosalie was waiting for her.

"I want to take a long drive," she said. "I feel restless. Will you come with me, Betty?" Yes, she would go with her, so Buckham brought the landau with its pair of big horses, and they rolled down the avenue, and into the smooth, white high road. He took them far—past the great marshes, between miles of bared hedges, past farms and scattered cottages. Sometimes he turned into lanes, where the hedges were closer to each other, and where, here and there, they caught sight of new points of view between trees. Betty was glad to feel Rosy's slim body near her side, and she was conscious that it gradually seemed to draw closer and closer. Then Rosy's hand slipped into hers and held it softly on her lap.

When they drove together in this way they were usually both of them rather silent and quiet, but now Rosalie spoke of many things—of Ughtred, of Nigel, of the Dunholms, of New York, and their father and mother.

"I want to talk because I'm nervous, I think," she said half apologetically. "I do not want to sit still and think too much—of father's coming. You don't mind my talking, do you, Betty?"

"No," Betty answered. "It is good for you and for me." And she met the pressure of Rosy's hand halfway.

But Rosy was talking, not because she did not want to sit still and think, but because she did not want Betty to do so. And all the time she was trying to thrust away the thought growing in her mind.

They spent the evening together in the library, and Betty read aloud. She read a long time—until quite late. She wished to tire herself as well as to force herself to stop listening.

When they said good-night to each other Rosy clung to her as desperately as she had clung on the night after her arrival. She kissed her again and again, and then hung her head and excused herself.

"Forgive me for being—nervous. I'm ashamed of myself," she said. "Perhaps in time I shall get over being a coward."

But she said nothing of the fact that she was not a coward for herself, but through a slowly formulating and struggled—against fear, which chilled her very heart, and which she could best cover by a pretence of being a poltroon.

She could not sleep when she went to bed. The night seemed crowded with strange, terrified thoughts. They were all of Betty, though sometimes she thought of her father's coming, of her mother in New York, and of Betty's steady working throughout the day. Sometimes she cried, twisting her hands together, and sometimes she dropped into a feverish sleep, and dreamed that she was watching Betty's face, yet was afraid to look at it.

She awakened suddenly from one of these dreams, and sat upright in bed to find the dawn breaking. She rose and threw on a dressing-gown, and went to her sister's room because she could not bear to stay away.

The door was not locked, and she pushed it open gently. One of the windows had its blind drawn up, and looked like a patch of dull grey. Betty was standing upright near it. She was in her night-gown, and a long black plait of hair hung over one shoulder heavily. She looked all black and white in strong contrast. The grey light set her forth as a tall ghost.

Lady Anstruthers slid forward, feeling a tightness in her chest.

"The dawn wakened me too," she said.

"I have been waiting to see it come," answered Betty. "It is going to be a dull, dreary day."

CHAPTER XLVII

"I HAVE NO WORD OR LOOK TO REMEMBER"

It was a dull and dreary day, as Betty had foreseen it would be. Heavy rain clouds hung and threatened, and the atmosphere was damp and chill. It was one of those days of the English autumn which speak only of the end of things, bereaving one of the power to remember next year's spring and summer, which, after all, must surely come. Sky is grey, trees are grey, dead leaves lie damp beneath the feet, sunlight and birds seem forgotten things. All that has been sad and to be regretted or feared hangs heavy in the air and sways all thought. In the passing of these hours there is no hope anywhere. Betty appeared at breakfast in short dress and close hat. She wore thick little boots, as if for walking.

"I am going to make visits in the village," she said. "I want a basket of good things to take with me. Stourton's children need feeding after their measles. They looked very thin when I saw them playing in the road yesterday."

"Yes, dear," Rosalie answered. "Mrs. Noakes shall prepare the basket. Good chicken broth, and jelly, and nourishing things. Jennings," to the butler, "you know the kind of basket Miss Vanderpoel wants. Speak to Mrs. Noakes, please."

"Yes, my lady," Jennings knew the kind of basket and so did Mrs. Noakes. Below stairs a strong sympathy with Miss Vanderpoel's movements had developed. No one resented the preparation of baskets. Somehow they were always managed, even if asked for at untimely hours.

Betty was sitting silent, looking out into the greyness of the autumn-smitten park.

"Are—are you listening for anything, Betty?" Lady Anstruthers asked rather falteringly. "You have a sort of listening look in your eyes."

Betty came back to the room, as it were.

"Have I," she said. "Yes, I think I was listening for—something."

And Rosalie did not ask her what she listened for. She was afraid she knew.

It was not only the Stourtons Betty visited this morning. She passed from one cottage to another—to see old women, and old men, as well as young ones, who for one reason or another needed help and encouragement. By one bedside she read aloud; by another she sat and told cheerful stories; she listened to talk in little kitchens, and in one house welcomed a newborn thing. As she walked steadily over grey road and down grey lanes damp mist rose and hung about her. And she did not walk alone. Fear walked with her, and anguish, a grey ghost by her side. Once she found herself standing quite still on a side path, covering her face with her hands. She filled every moment of the morning, and walked until she was tired. Before she went home she called at the post office, and Mr. Tewson greeted her with a solemn face. He did not wait to be questioned.

"There's been no news to-day, miss, so far," he said. "And that seems as if they might be so given up to hard work at a dreadful time that there's been no chance for anything to get out. When people's hanging over a man's bed at the end, it's as if everything stopped but that—that's stopping for all time."

After luncheon the rain began to fall softly, slowly, and with a suggestion of endlessness. It was a sort of mist itself, and became a damp shadow among the bare branches of trees which soon began to drip.

"You have been walking about all morning, and you are tired, dear," Lady Anstruthers said to her. "Won't you go to your room and rest, Betty?"

Yes, she would go to her room, she said. Some new books had arrived from London this morning, and she would look over them. She talked a little about her visits before she went, and when, as she talked, Ughtred came over to her and stood close to her side holding her hand and stroking it, she smiled at him sweetly—the smile he adored. He stroked the hand and softly patted it, watching her wistfully. Suddenly he lifted it to his lips, and kissed it again and again with a sort of passion.

"I love you so much, Aunt Betty," he cried. "We both love you so much. Something makes me love you to-day more than ever I did before. It almost makes me cry. I love you so."

She stooped swiftly and drew him into her arms and kissed him close and hard. He held his head back a little and looked into the blue under her lashes.

"I love your eyes," he said. "Anyone would love your eyes, Aunt Betty. But what is the matter with them? You are not crying at all, but—oh! what is the matter?"

"No, I am not crying at all," she said, and smiled—almost laughed.

But after she had kissed him again she took her books and went upstairs.

She did not lie down, and she did not read when she was alone in her room. She drew a long chair before the window and watched the slow falling of the rain. There is nothing like it—that slow weeping of the rain on an English autumn day. Soft and light though it was, the park began to look sodden. The bare trees held out their branches like imploring arms, the brown garden beds were neat and bare. The same rain was drip-dripping at Mount Dunstan—upon the desolate great house—upon the village—upon the mounds and ancient stone tombs in the churchyard, sinking into the earth—sinking deep, sucked in by the clay beneath—the cold damp clay. She shook herself shudderingly. Why should the thought come to her—the cold damp clay? She would not listen to it, she would think of New York, of its roaring streets and crash of sound, of the rush of fierce life there—of her father and mother. She tried to force herself to call up pictures of Broadway, swarming with crowds of black things, which, seen from the windows of its monstrous buildings, seemed like swarms of ants, burst out of ant-hills, out of a thousand ant-hills. She tried to remember shop windows, the things in them, the throngs going by, and the throngs passing in and out of great, swinging glass doors. She dragged up before her a vision of Rosalie, driving with her mother and herself, looking about her at the new buildings and changed streets, flushed and made radiant by the accelerated pace and excitement of her beloved New York. But, oh, the slow, penetrating rainfall, and—the cold damp clay!

She rose, making an involuntary sound which was half a moan. The long mirror set between two windows showed her momentarily an awful young figure, throwing up its arms. Was that Betty Vanderpoel—that?

"What does one do," she said, "when the world comes to an end? What does one do?"

All her days she had done things—there had always been something to do. Now there was nothing. She went suddenly to her bell and rang for her maid. The woman answered the summons at once.

"Send word to the stable that I want Childe Harold. I do not want Mason. I shall ride alone."

"Yes, miss," Ambleston answered, without any exterior sign of emotion. She was too well-trained a person to express any shade of her internal amazement. After she had transmitted the order to the proper manager she returned and changed her mistress's costume.

She had contemplated her task, and was standing behind Miss Vanderpoel's chair, putting the last touch to her veil, when she became conscious of a slight stiffening of the neck which held so well the handsome head, then the head slowly turned towards the window giving upon the front park. Miss Vanderpoel was listening to something, listening so intently that Ambleston felt that, for a few moments, she did not seem to breathe. The maid's hands fell from the veil, and she began to listen also. She had been at the service the day before. Miss Vanderpoel rose from her chair slowly—very slowly, and took a step forward. Then she stood still and listened again.

"Open that window, if you please," she commanded—"as if a stone image was speaking"—Ambleston said later. The window was thrown open, and for a few seconds they both stood still again. When Miss Vanderpoel spoke, it was as if she had forgotten where she was, or as if she were in a dream.

"It is the ringers," she said. "They are tolling the passing bell."

The serving woman was soft of heart, and had her feminine emotions. There had been much talk of this thing in the servant's hall. She turned upon Betty, and forgot all rules and training.

"Oh, miss!" she cried. "He's gone—he's gone! That good man—out of this hard world. Oh, miss, excuse me—do!" And as she burst into wild tears, she ran out of the room.

. . . . .

Rosalie had been sitting in the morning room. She also had striven to occupy herself with work. She had written to her mother, she had read, she had embroidered, and then read again. What was Betty doing—what was she thinking now? She laid her book down in her lap, and covering her face with her hands, breathed a desperate little prayer. That life should be pain and emptiness to herself, seemed somehow natural since she had married Nigel—but pain and emptiness for Betty—No! No! No! Not for Betty! Piteous sorrow poured upon her like a flood. She did not know how the time passed. She sat, huddled together in her chair, with hidden face. She could not bear to look at the rain and ghost mist out of doors. Oh, if her mother were only here, and she might speak to her! And as her loving tears broke forth afresh, she heard the door open.

"If you please, my lady—I beg your pardon, my lady," as she started and uncovered her face.

"What is it, Jennings?"

The figure at the door was that of the serious, elderly butler, and he wore a respectfully grave air.

"As your ladyship is sitting in this room, we thought it likely you would not hear, the windows being closed, and we felt sure, my lady, that you would wish to know——"

Lady Anstruthers' hands shook as they clung to the arms of her chair.

"To know——" she faltered. "Hear what?"

"The passing bell is tolling, my lady. It has just begun. It is for Lord Mount Dunstan. There's not a dry eye downstairs, your ladyship, not one."

He opened the windows, and she stood up. Jennings quietly left the room. The slow, heavy knell struck ponderously on the damp air, and she stood and shivered.

A moment or two later she turned, because it seemed as if she must.

Betty, in her riding habit, was standing motionless against the door, her wonderful eyes still as death, gazing at her, gazing in an awful, simple silence.

Oh, what was the use of being afraid to speak at such a time as this? In one moment Rosy was kneeling at her feet, clinging about her knees, kissing her hands, the very cloth of her habit, and sobbing aloud.

"Oh, my darling—my love—my own Betty! I don't know—and I won't ask—but speak to me—speak just a word—my dearest dear!"

Betty raised her up and drew her within the room, closing the door behind them.

"Kind little Rosy," she said. "I came to speak—because we two love each other. You need not ask, I will tell you. That bell is tolling for the man who taught me—to KNOW. He never spoke to me of love. I have not one word or look to remember. And now—— Oh, listen—listen! I have been listening since the morning of yesterday." It was an awful thing—her white face, with all the flame of life swept out of it.

"Don't listen—darling—darling!" Rosy cried out in anguish. "Shut your ears—shut your ears!" And she tried to throw her arms around the high black head, and stifle all sound with her embrace.

"I don't want to shut them," was the answer. "All the unkindness and misery are over for him, I ought to thank God—but I don't. I shall hear—O Rosy, listen!—I shall hear that to the end of my days."

Rosy held her tight, and rocked and sobbed.

"My Betty," she kept saying. "My Betty," and she could say no more. What more was there to say? At last Betty withdrew herself from her arms, and then Rosalie noticed for the first time that she wore the habit.

"Dearest," she whispered, "what are you going to do?"

"I was going to ride, and I am going to do it still. I must do something. I shall ride a long, long way—and ride hard. You won't try to keep me, Rosy. You will understand."

"Yes," biting her lip, and looking at her with large, awed eyes, as she patted her arm with a hand that trembled. "I would not hold you back, Betty, from anything in the world you chose to do."

And with another long, clinging clasp of her, she let her go.

Mason was standing by Childe Harold when she went down the broad steps. He also wore a look of repressed emotion, and stood with bared head bent, his eyes fixed on the gravel of the drive, listening to the heavy strokes of the bell in the church tower, rather as if he were taking part in some solemn ceremony.

He mounted her silently, and after he had given her the bridle, looked up, and spoke in a somewhat husky voice:

"The order was that you did not want me, miss? Was that correct?"

"Yes, I wish to ride alone."

"Yes, miss. Thank you, miss."

Childe Harold was in good spirits. He held up his head, and blew the breath through his delicate, dilated, red nostrils as he set out with his favourite sidling, dancing steps. Mason watched him down the avenue, saw the lodge keeper come out to open the gate, and curtsy as her ladyship's sister passed through it. After that he went slowly back to the stables, and sat in the harness-room a long time, staring at the floor, as the bell struck ponderously on his ear.

The woman who had opened the gate for her Betty saw had red eyes. She knew why.

"A year ago they all thought of him as an outcast. They would have believed any evil they had heard connected with his name. Now, in every cottage, there is weeping—weeping. And he lies deaf and dumb," was her thought.

She did not wish to pass through the village, and turned down a side road, which would lead her to where she could cross the marshes, and come upon lonely places. The more lonely, the better. Every few moments she caught her breath with a hard short gasp. The slow rain fell upon her, big round, crystal drops hung on the hedgerows, and dripped upon the grass banks below them; the trees, wreathed with mist, were like waiting ghosts as she passed them by; Childe Harold's hoof upon the road, made a hollow, lonely sound.

A thought began to fill her brain, and make insistent pressure upon it. She tried no more to thrust thought away. Those who lay deaf and dumb, those for whom people wept—where were they when the weeping seemed to sound through all the world? How far had they gone? Was it far? Could they hear and could they see? If one plead with them aloud, could they draw near to listen? Did they begin a long, long journey as soon as they had slipped away? The "wonder of the world," she had said, watching life swelling and bursting the seeds in Kedgers' hothouses! But this was a greater wonder still, because of its awesomeness. This man had been, and who dare say he was not—even now? The strength of his great body, the look in his red-brown eyes, the sound of his deep voice, the struggle, the meaning of him, where were they? She heard herself followed by the hollow echo of Childe Harold's hoofs, as she rode past copse and hedge, and wet spreading fields. She was this hour as he had been a month ago. If, with some strange suddenness, this which was Betty Vanderpoel, slipped from its body——She put her hand up to her forehead. It was unthinkable that there would be no more. Where was he now—where was he now?

This was the thought that filled her brain cells to the exclusion of all others. Over the road, down through by-lanes, out on the marshes. Where was he—where was he—WHERE? Childe Harold's hoofs began to beat it out as a refrain. She heard nothing else. She did not know where she was going and did not ask herself. She went down any road or lane which looked empty of life, she took strange turnings, without caring; she did not know how far she was afield.

Where was he now—this hour—this moment—where was he now? Did he know the rain, the greyness, the desolation of the world?

Once she stopped her horse on the loneliness of the marsh land, and looked up at the low clouds about her, at the creeping mist, the dank grass. It seemed a place in which a newly-released soul might wander because it did not yet know its way.

"If you should be near, and come to me, you will understand," her clear voice said gravely between the caught breaths, "what I gave you was nothing to you—but you took it with you. Perhaps you know without my telling you. I want you to know. When a man is dead, everything melts away. I loved you. I wish you had loved me."

CHAPTER XLVIII

THE MOMENT

In the unnatural unbearableness of her anguish, she lost sight of objects as she passed them, she lost all memory of what she did. She did not know how long she had been out, or how far she had ridden. When the thought of time or distance vaguely flitted across her mind, it seemed that she had been riding for hours, and might have crossed one county and entered another. She had long left familiar places behind. Riding through and inclosed by the mist, she, herself, might have been a wandering ghost, lost in unknown places. Where was he now—where was he now?

Afterwards she could not tell how or when it was that she found herself becoming conscious of the evidences that her horse had been ridden too long and hard, and that he was worn out with fatigue. She did not know that she had ridden round and round over the marshes, and had passed several times through the same lanes. Childe Harold, the sure of foot, actually stumbled, out of sheer weariness of limb. Perhaps it was this which brought her back to earth, and led her to look around her with eyes which saw material objects with comprehension. She had reached the lonely places, indeed and the evening was drawing on. She was at the edge of the marsh, and the land about her was strange to her and desolate. At the side of a steep lane, overgrown with grass, and seeming a mere cart-path, stood a deserted-looking, black and white, timbered cottage, which was half a ruin. Close to it was a dripping spinney, its trees forming a darkling background to the tumble-down house, whose thatch was rotting into holes, and its walls sagging forward perilously. The bit of garden about it was neglected and untidy, here and there windows were broken, and stuffed with pieces of ragged garments. Altogether a sinister and repellent place enough.

She looked at it with heavy eyes. (Where was he now—where was he now?—This repeating itself in the far chambers of her brain.) Her sight seemed dimmed, not only by the mist, but by a sinking faintness which possessed her. She did not remember how little food she had eaten during more than twenty-four hours. Her habit was heavy with moisture, and clung to her body; she was conscious of a hot tremor passing over her, and saw that her hands shook as they held the bridle on which they had lost their grip. She had never fainted in her life, and she was not going to faint now—women did not faint in these days—but she must reach the cottage and dismount, to rest under shelter for a short time. No smoke was rising from the chimney, but surely someone was living in the place, and could tell her where she was, and give her at least water for herself and her horse. Poor beast! how wickedly she must have been riding him, in her utter absorption in her thoughts. He was wet, not alone with rain, but with sweat. He snorted out hot, smoking breaths.

She spoke to him, and he moved forward at her command. He was trembling too. Not more than two hundred yards, and she turned him into the lane. But it was wet and slippery, and strewn with stones. His trembling and her uncertain hold on the bridle combined to produce disaster. He set his foot upon a stone which slid beneath it, he stumbled, and she could not help him to recover, so he fell, and only by Heaven's mercy not upon her, with his crushing, big-boned weight, and she was able to drag herself free of him before he began to kick, in his humiliated efforts to rise. But he could not rise, because he was hurt—and when she, herself, got up, she staggered, and caught at the broken gate, because in her wrenching leap for safety she had twisted her ankle, and for a moment was in cruel pain.

When she recovered from her shock sufficiently to be able to look at the cottage, she saw that it was more of a ruin than it had seemed, even at a short distance. Its door hung open on broken hinges, no smoke rose from the chimney, because there was no one within its walls to light a fire. It was quite empty. Everything about the place lay in dead and utter silence. In a normal mood she would have liked the mystery of the situation, and would have set about planning her way out of her difficulty. But now her mind made no effort, because normal interest in things had fallen away from her. She might be twenty miles from Stornham, but the possible fact did not, at the moment, seem to concern her. (Where is he now—where is he now?) Childe Harold was trying to rise, despite his hurt, and his evident determination touched her. He was too proud to lie in the mire. She limped to him, and tried to steady him by his bridle. He was not badly injured, though plainly in pain.

"Poor boy, it was my fault," she said to him as he at last struggled to his feet. "I did not know I was doing it. Poor boy!"

He turned a velvet dark eye upon her, and nosed her forgivingly with a warm velvet muzzle, but it was plain that, for the time, he was done for. They both moved haltingly to the broken gate, and Betty fastened him to a thorn tree near it, where he stood on three feet, his fine head drooping.

She pushed the gate open, and went into the house through the door which hung on its hinges. Once inside, she stood still and looked about her. If there was silence and desolateness outside, there was within the deserted place a stillness like the unresponse of death. It had been long since anyone had lived in the cottage, but tramps or gipsies had at times passed through it. Dead, blackened embers lay on the hearth, a bundle of dried grass which had been slept on was piled in the corner, an empty nail keg and a wooden box had been drawn before the big chimney place for some wanderer to sit on when the black embers had been hot and red.

Betty gave one glance around her and sat down upon the box standing on the bare hearth, her head sinking forward, her hands falling clasped between her knees, her eyes on the brick floor.

"Where is he now?" broke from her in a loud whisper, whose sound was mechanical and hollow. "Where is he now?"

And she sat there without moving, while the grey mist from the marshes crept close about the door and through it and stole about her feet.

So she sat long—long—in a heavy, far-off dream.

Along the road a man was riding with a lowering, fretted face. He had come across country on horseback, because to travel by train meant wearisome stops and changes and endlessly slow journeying, annoying beyond endurance to those who have not patience to spare. His ride would have been pleasant enough but for the slow mist-like rain. Also he had taken a wrong turning, because he did not know the roads he travelled. The last signpost he had passed, however, had given him his cue again, and he began to feel something of security. Confound the rain! The best road was slippery with it, and the haze of it made a man's mind feel befogged and lowered his spirits horribly—discouraged him—would worry him into an ill humour even if he had reason to be in a good one. As for him, he had no reason for cheerfulness—he never had for the matter of that, and just now——! What was the matter with his horse? He was lifting his head and sniffing the damp air restlessly, as if he scented or saw something. Beasts often seemed to have a sort of second sight—horses particularly.

What ailed him that he should prick up his ears and snort after his sniffing the mist! Did he hear anything? Yes, he did, it seemed. He gave forth suddenly a loud shrill whinny, turning his head towards a rough lane they were approaching, and immediately from the vicinity of a deserted-looking cottage behind a hedge came a sharp but mournful-sounding neigh in answer.

"What horse is that?" said Nigel Anstruthers, drawing in at the entrance to the lane and looking down it. "There is a fine brute with a side-saddle on," he added sharply. "He is waiting for someone. What is a woman doing there at this time? Is it a rendezvous? A good place——"

He broke off short and rode forward. "I'm hanged if it is not Childe Harold," he broke out, and he had no sooner assured himself of the fact than he threw himself from his saddle, tethered his horse and strode up the path to the broken-hinged door.

He stood on the threshold and stared. What a hole it was—what a hole! And there SHE sat—alone—eighteen or twenty miles from home—on a turned-up box near the black embers, her hands clasped loosely between her knees, her face rather awful, her eyes staring at the floor, as if she did not see it.

"Where is he now?" he heard her whisper to herself with soft weirdness. "Where is he now?"

Sir Nigel stepped into the place and stood before her. He had smiled with a wry unpleasantness when he had heard her evidently unconscious words.

"My good girl," he said, "I am sure I do not know where he is—but it is very evident that he ought to be here, since you have amiably put yourself to such trouble. It is fortunate for you perhaps that I am here before him. What does this mean?" the question breaking from him with savage authority.

He had dragged her back to earth. She sat upright and recognised him with a hideous sense of shock, but he did not give her time to speak. His instinct of male fury leaped within him.

"YOU!" he cried out. "It takes a woman like you to come and hide herself in a place of this sort, like a trolloping gipsy wench! It takes a New York millionairess or a Roman empress or one of Charles the Second's duchesses to plunge as deep as this. You, with your golden pedestal—you, with your ostentatious airs and graces—you, with your condescending to give a man a chance to repent his sins and turn over a new leaf! Damn it," rising to a sort of frenzy, "what are you doing waiting in a hole like this—in this weather—at this hour—you—you!"

The fool's flame leaped high enough to make him start forward, as if to seize her by the shoulder and shake her.

But she rose and stepped back to lean against the side of the chimney—to brace herself against it, so that she could stand in her lame foot's despite. Every drop of blood had been swept from her face, and her eyes looked immense. His coming was a good thing for her, though she did not know it. It brought her back from unearthly places. All her child hatred woke and blazed in her. Never had she hated a thing so, and it set her slow, cold blood running like something molten.

"Hold your tongue!" she said in a clear, awful young voice of warning. "And take care not to touch me. If you do—I have my whip here—I shall lash you across your mouth!"

He broke into ribald laughter. A certain sudden thought which had cut into him like a knife thrust into flesh drove him on.

"Do!" he cried. "I should like to carry your mark back to Stornham—and tell people why it was given. I know who you are here for. Only such fellows ask such things of women. But he was determined to be safe, if you hid in a ditch. You are here for Mount Dunstan—and he has failed you!"

But she only stood and stared at him, holding her whip behind her, knowing that at any moment he might snatch it from her hand. And she knew how poor a weapon it was. To strike out with it would only infuriate him and make him a wild beast. And it was becoming an agony to stand upon her foot. And even if it had not been so—if she had been strong enough to make a leap and dash past him, her horse stood outside disabled.

Nigel Anstruthers' eyes ran over her from head to foot, down the side of her mud-stained habit, while a curious light dawned in them.

"You have had a fall from your horse," he exclaimed. "You are lame!" Then quickly, "That was why Childe Harold was trembling and standing on three feet! By Jove!"

Then he sat down on the nail keg and began to laugh. He laughed for a full minute, but she saw he did not take his eyes from her.

"You are in as unpleasant a situation as a young woman can well be," he said, when he stopped. "You came to a dirty hole to be alone with a man who felt it safest not to keep his appointment. Your horse stumbled and disabled himself and you. You are twenty miles from home in a deserted cottage in a lane no one passes down even in good weather. You are frightened to death and you have given me even a better story to play with than your sister gave me. By Jove!"

His face was an unholy thing to look upon. The situation and her powerlessness were exciting him.

"No," she answered, keeping her eyes on his, as she might have kept them on some wild animal's, "I am not frightened to death."

His ugly dark flush rose.

"Well, if you are not," he said, "don't tell me so. That kind of defiance is not your best line just now. You have been disdaining me from magnificent New York heights for some time. Do you think that I am not enjoying this?"

"I cannot imagine anyone else who would enjoy it so much." And she knew the answer was daring, but would have made it if he had held a knife's point at her throat.

He got up, and walking to the door drew it back on its crazy hinges and managed to shut it close. There was a big wooden bolt inside and he forced it into its socket.

"Presently I shall go and put the horses into the cowshed," he said. "If I leave them standing outside they will attract attention. I do not intend to be disturbed by any gipsy tramp who wants shelter. I have never had you quite to myself before."

He sat down again and nursed his knee gracefully.

"And I have never seen you look as attractive," biting his under lip in cynical enjoyment. "To-day's adventure has roused your emotions and actually beautified you—which was not necessary. I daresay you have been furious and have cried. Your eyes do not look like mere eyes, but like splendid blue pools of tears. Perhaps *I* shall make you cry sometime, my dear Betty."

"No, you will not."

"Don't tempt me. Women always cry when men annoy them. They rage, but they cry as well."

"I shall not."

"It's true that most women would have begun to cry before this. That is what stimulates me. You will swagger to the end. You put the devil into me. Half an hour ago I was jogging along the road, languid and bored to extinction. And now——" He laughed outright in actual exultation. "By Jove!" he cried out. "Things like this don't happen to a man in these dull days! There's no such luck going about. We've gone back five hundred years, and we've taken New York with us." His laugh shut off in the middle, and he got up to thrust his heavy, congested face close to hers. "Here you are, as safe as if you were in a feudal castle, and here is your ancient enemy given his chance—given his chance. Do you think, by the Lord, he is going to give it up? No. To quote your own words, 'you may place entire confidence in that.'"

Exaggerated as it all was, somehow the melodrama dropped away from it and left bare, simple, hideous fact for her to confront. The evil in him had risen rampant and made him lose his head. He might see his senseless folly to-morrow and know he must pay for it, but he would not see it to-day. The place was not a feudal castle, but what he said was insurmountable truth. A ruined cottage on the edge of miles of marsh land, a seldom-trodden road, and night upon them! A wind was rising on the marshes now, and making low, steady moan. Horrible things had happened to women before, one heard of them with shudders when they were recorded in the newspapers. Only two days ago she had remembered that sometimes there seemed blunderings in the great Scheme of things. Was all this real, or was she dreaming that she stood here at bay, her back against the chimney-wall, and this degenerate exulting over her, while Rosy was waiting for her at Stornham—and at this very hour her father was planning his journey across the Atlantic?

"Why did you not behave yourself?" demanded Nigel Anstruthers, shaking her by the shoulder. "Why did you not realise that I should get even with you one day, as sure as you were woman and I was man?"

She did not shrink back, though the pupils of her eyes dilated. Was it the wildest thing in the world which happened to her—or was it not? Without warning—the sudden rush of a thought, immense and strange, swept over her body and soul and possessed her—so possessed her that it changed her pallor to white flame. It was actually Anstruthers who shrank back a shade because, for the moment, she looked so near unearthly.

"I am not afraid of you," she said, in a clear, unshaken voice. "I am not afraid. Something is near me which will stand between us—something which DIED to-day."

He almost gasped before the strangeness of it, but caught back his breath and recovered himself.

"Died to-day! That's recent enough," he jeered. "Let us hear about it. Who was it?"

"It was Mount Dunstan," she flung at him. "The church-bells were tolling for him when I rode away. I could not stay to hear them. It killed me—I loved him. You were right when you said it. I loved him, though he never knew. I shall always love him—though he never knew. He knows now. Those who died cannot go away when THAT is holding them. They must stay. Because I loved him, he may be in this place. I call on him——" raising her clear voice. "I call on him to stand between us."

He backed away from her, staring an evil, enraptured stare.

"What! There is that much temperament in you?" he said. "That was what I half-suspected when I saw you first. But you have hidden it well. Now it bursts forth in spite of you. Good Lord! What luck—what luck!"

He moved to the door and opened it.

"I am a very modern man, and I enjoy this to the utmost," he said. "What I like best is the melodrama of it—in connection with Fifth Avenue. I am perfectly aware that you will not discuss this incident in the future. You are a clever enough young woman to know that it will be more to your interest than to mine that it shall be kept exceedingly quiet."

The white fire had not died out of her and she stood straight.

"What I have called on will be near me, and will stand between us," she said.

Old though it was, the door was massive and heavy to lift. To open it cost him some muscular effort.

"I am going to the horses now," he explained before he dragged it back into its frame and shut her in. "It is safe enough to leave you here. You will stay where you are."

He felt himself secure in leaving her because he believed she could not move, and because his arrogance made it impossible for him to count on strength and endurance greater than his own. Of endurance he knew nothing and in his keen and cynical exultance his devil made a fool of him.

As she heard him walk down the path to the gate, Betty stood amazed at his lack of comprehension of her.

"He thinks I will stay here. He absolutely thinks I will wait until he comes back," she whispered to the emptiness of the bare room.

Before he had arrived she had loosened her boot, and now she stooped and touched her foot.

"If I were safe at home I should think I could not walk, but I can walk now—I can—I can—because I will bear the pain."

In such cottages there is always a door opening outside from the little bricked kitchen, where the copper stands. She would reach that, and, passing through, would close it behind her. After that SOMETHING would tell her what to do—something would lead her.

She put her lame foot upon the floor, and rested some of her weight upon it—not all. A jagged pain shot up from it through her whole side it seemed, and, for an instant, she swayed and ground her teeth.

"That is because it is the first step," she said. "But if I am to be killed, I will die in the open—I will die in the open."

The second and third steps brought cold sweat out upon her, but she told herself that the fourth was not quite so unbearable, and she stiffened her whole body, and muttered some words while she took a fifth and sixth which carried her into the tiny back kitchen.

"Father," she said. "Father, think of me now—think of me! Rosy, love me—love me and pray that I may come home. You—you who have died, stand very near!"

If her father ever held her safe in his arms again—if she ever awoke from this nightmare, it would be a thing never to let one's mind hark back to again—to shut out of memory with iron doors.

The pain had shot up and down, and her forehead was wet by the time she had reached the small back door. Was it locked or bolted—was it? She put her hand gently upon the latch and lifted it without making any sound. Thank God Almighty, it was neither bolted nor locked, the latch lifted, the door opened, and she slid through it into the shadow of the grey which was already almost the darkness of night. Thank God for that, too.

She flattened herself against the outside wall and listened. He was having difficulty in managing Childe Harold, who snorted and pulled back, offended and made rebellious by his savagely impatient hand. Good Childe Harold, good boy! She could see the massed outline of the trees of the spinney. If she could bear this long enough to get there—even if she crawled part of the way. Then it darted through her mind that he would guess that she would be sure to make for its cover, and that he would go there first to search.

"Father, think for me—you were so quick to think!" her brain cried out for her, as if she was speaking to one who could physically hear.

She almost feared she had spoken aloud, and the thought which flashed upon her like lightning seemed to be an answer given. He would be convinced that she would at once try to get away from the house. If she kept near it—somewhere—somewhere quite close, and let him search the spinney, she might get away to its cover after he gave up the search and came back. The jagged pain had settled in a sort of impossible anguish, and once or twice she felt sick. But she would die in the open—and she knew Rosalie was frightened by her absence, and was praying for her. Prayers counted and, yet, they had all prayed yesterday.

"If I were not very strong, I should faint," she thought. "But I have been strong all my life. That great French doctor—I have forgotten his name—said that I had the physique to endure anything."

She said these things that she might gain steadiness and convince herself that she was not merely living through a nightmare. Twice she moved her foot suddenly because she found herself in a momentary respite from pain, beginning to believe that the thing was a nightmare—that nothing mattered—because she would wake up presently—so she need not try to hide.

"But in a nightmare one has no pain. It is real and I must go somewhere," she said, after the foot was moved. Where could she go? She had not looked at the place as she rode up. She had only half-consciously seen the spinney. Nigel was swearing at the horses. Having got Childe Harold into the shed, there seemed to be nothing to fasten his bridle to. And he had yet to bring his own horse in and secure him. She must get away somewhere before the delay was over.

How dark it was growing! Thank God for that again! What was the rather high, dark object she could trace in the dimness near the hedge? It was sharply pointed, is if it were a narrow tent. Her heart began to beat like a drum as she recalled something. It was the shape of the sort of wigwam structure made of hop poles, after they were taken from the fields. If there was space between it and the hedge—even a narrow space—and she could crouch there? Nigel was furious because Childe Harold was backing, plunging, and snorting dangerously. She halted forward, shutting her teeth in her terrible pain. She could scarcely see, and did not recognise that near the wigwam was a pile of hop poles laid on top of each other horizontally. It was not quite as high as the hedge whose dark background prevented its being seen. Only a few steps more. No, she was awake—in a nightmare one felt only terror, not pain.

"YOU, WHO DIED TO-DAY," she murmured.

She saw the horizontal poles too late. One of them had rolled from its place and lay on the ground, and she trod on it, was thrown forward against the heap, and, in her blind effort to recover herself, slipped and fell into a narrow, grassed hollow behind it, clutching at the hedge. The great French doctor had not been quite right. For the first time in her life she felt herself sinking into bottomless darkness—which was what happened to people when they fainted.

When she opened her eyes she could see nothing, because on one side of her rose the low mass of the hop poles, and on the other was the long-untrimmed hedge, which had thrown out a thick, sheltering growth and curved above her like a penthouse. Was she awakening, after all? No, because the pain was awakening with her, and she could hear, what seemed at first to be quite loud sounds. She could not have been unconscious long, for she almost immediately recognised that they were the echo of a man's hurried footsteps upon the bare wooden stairway, leading to the bedrooms in the empty house. Having secured the horses, Nigel had returned to the cottage, and, finding her gone had rushed to the upper floor in search of her. He was calling her name angrily, his voice resounding in the emptiness of the rooms.

"Betty; don't play the fool with me!"

She cautiously drew herself further under cover, making sure that no end of her habit remained in sight. The overgrowth of the hedge was her salvation. If she had seen the spot by daylight, she would not have thought it a possible place of concealment.

Once she had read an account of a woman's frantic flight from a murderer who was hunting her to her death, while she slipped from one poor hiding place to another, sometimes crouching behind walls or bushes, sometimes lying flat in long grass, once wading waist-deep through a stream, and at last finding a miserable little fastness, where she hid shivering for hours, until her enemy gave up his search. One never felt the reality of such histories, but there was actually a sort of parallel in this. Mad and crude things were let loose, and the world of ordinary life seemed thousands of miles away.

She held her breath, for he was leaving the house by the front door. She heard his footsteps on the bricked path, and then in the lane. He went to the road, and the sound of his feet died away for a few moments. Then she heard them returning—he was back in the lane—on the brick path, and stood listening or, perhaps, reflecting. He muttered something exclamatory, and she heard a match struck, and shortly afterwards he moved across the garden patch towards the little spinney. He had thought of it, as she had believed he would. He would not think of this place, and in the end he might get tired or awakened to a sense of his lurid folly, and realise that it would be safer for him to go back to Stornham with some clever lie, trusting to his belief that there existed no girl but would shrink from telling such a story in connection with a man who would brazenly deny it with contemptuous dramatic detail. If he would but decide on this, she would be safe—and it would be so like him that she dared to hope. But, if he did not, she would lie close, even if she must wait until morning, when some labourer's cart would surely pass, and she would hear it jolting, and drag herself out, and call aloud in such a way that no man could be deaf. There was more room under her hedge than she had thought, and she found that she could sit up, by clasping her knees and bending her head, while she listened to every sound, even to the rustle of the grass in the wind sweeping across the marsh.

She moved very gradually and slowly, and had just settled into utter motionlessness when she realised that he was coming back through the garden—the straggling currant and gooseberry bushes were being trampled through.

"Betty, go home," Rosalie had pleaded. "Go home—go home." And she had refused, because she could not desert her.

She held her breath and pressed her hand against her side, because her heart beat, as it seemed to her, with an actual sound. He moved with unsteady steps from one point to another, more than once he stumbled, and his angry oath reached her; at last he was so near her hiding place that his short hard breathing was a distinct sound. A moment later he spoke, raising his voice, which fact brought to her a rush of relief, through its signifying that he had not even guessed her nearness.

"My dear Betty," he said, "you have the pluck of the devil, but circumstances are too much for you. You are not on the road, and I have been through the spinney. Mere logic convinces me that you cannot be far away. You may as well give the thing up. It will be better for you."

"You who died to-day—do not leave me," was Betty's inward cry, and she dropped her face on her knees.

"I am not a pleasant-tempered fellow, as you know, and I am losing my hold on myself. The wind is blowing the mist away, and there will be a moon. I shall find you, my good girl, in half an hour's time—and then we shall be jolly well even."

She had not dropped her whip, and she held it tight. If, when the moonlight revealed the pile of hop poles to him, he suspected and sprang at them to tear them away, she would be given strength to make one spring, even in her agony, and she would strike at his eyes—awfully, without one touch of compunction— she would strike—strike.

There was a brief silence, and then a match was struck again, and almost immediately she inhaled the fragrance of an excellent cigar.

"I am going to have a comfortable smoke and stroll about—always within sight and hearing. I daresay you are watching me, and wondering what will happen when I discover you, I can tell you what will happen. You are not a hysterical girl, but you will go into hysterics—and no one will hear you."

(All the power of her—body and soul—in one leap on him and then a lash that would cut to the bone. And it was not a nightmare—and Rosy was at Stornham, and her father looking over steamer lists and choosing his staterooms.)

He walked about slowly, the scent of his cigar floating behind him. She noticed, as she had done more than once before, that he seemed to slightly drag one foot, and she wondered why. The wind was blowing the mist away, and there was a faint growing of light. The moon was not full, but young, and yet it would make a difference. But the upper part of the hedge grew thick and close to the heap of wood, and, but for her fall, she would never have dreamed of the refuge.

She could only guess at his movements, but his footsteps gave some clue. He was examining the ground in as far as the darkness would allow. He went into the shed and round about it, he opened the door of the tiny coal lodge, and looked again into the small back kitchen. He came near—nearer—so near once that, bending sidewise, she could have put out a hand and touched him. He stood quite still, then made a step or so away, stood still again, and burst into a laugh once more.

"Oh, you are here, are you?" he said. "You are a fine big girl to be able to crowd yourself into a place like that!"

Hot and cold dew stood out on her forehead and made her hair damp as she held her whip hard.

"Come out, my dear!" alluringly. "It is not too soon. Or do you prefer that I should assist you?"

Her heart stood quite still—quite. He was standing by the wigwam of hop poles and thought she had hidden herself inside it. Her place under the hedge he had not even glanced at.

She knew he bent down and thrust his arm into the wigwam, for his fury at the result expressed itself plainly enough. That he had made a fool of himself was worse to him than all else. He actually wheeled about and strode away to the house.

Because minutes seemed hours, she thought he was gone long, but he was not away for twenty minutes. He had, in fact, gone into the bare front room again, and sitting upon the box near the hearth, let his head drop in his hands and remained in this position thinking. In the end he got up and went out to the shed where he had left the horses.

Betty was feeling that before long she might find herself making that strange swoop into the darkness of space again, and that it did not matter much, as one apparently lay quite still when one was unconscious—when she heard that one horse was being led out into the lane. What did that mean? Had he got tired of the chase—as the other man did—and was he going away because discomfort and fatigue had cooled and disgusted him—perhaps even made him feel that he was playing the part of a sensational idiot who was laying himself open to derision? That would be like him, too.

Presently she heard his footsteps once more, but he did not come as near her as before—in fact, he stood at some yards' distance when he stopped and spoke—in quite a new manner.

"Betty," his tone was even cynically cool, "I shall stalk you no more. The chase is at an end. I think I have taken all out of you I intended to. Perhaps it was a bad joke and was carried too far. I wanted to prove to you that there were circumstances which might be too much even for a young woman from New York. I have done it. Do you suppose I am such a fool as to bring myself within reach of the law? I am going away and will send assistance to you from the next house I pass. I have left some matches and a few broken sticks on the hearth in the cottage. Be a sensible girl. Limp in there and build yourself a fire as soon as you hear me gallop away. You must be chilled through. Now I am going."

He tramped across the bit of garden, down the brick path, mounted his horse and put it to a gallop at once. Clack, clack, clack—clacking fainter and fainter into the distance—and he was gone.

When she realised that the thing was true, the effect upon her of her sense of relief was that the growing likelihood of a second swoop into darkness died away, but one curious sob lifted her chest as she leaned back against the rough growth behind her. As she changed her position for a better one she felt the jagged pain again and knew that in the tenseness of her terror she had actually for some time felt next to nothing of her hurt. She had not even been cold, for the hedge behind and over her and the barricade before had protected her from both wind and rain. The grass beneath her was not damp for the same reason. The weary thought rose in her mind that she might even lie down and sleep. But she pulled herself together and told herself that this was like the temptation of believing in the nightmare. He was gone, and she had a respite—but was it to be anything more? She did not make any attempt to leave her place of concealment, remembering the strange things she had learned in watching him, and the strange terror in which Rosalie lived.

"One never knows what he will do next; I will not stir," she said through her teeth. "No, I will not stir from here."

And she did not, but sat still, while the pain came back to her body and the anguish to her heart—and sometimes such heaviness that her head dropped forward upon her knees again, and she fell into a stupefied half-doze.

From one such doze she awakened with a start, hearing a slight click of the gate. After it, there were several seconds of dead silence. It was the slightness of the click which was startling—if it had not been caused by the wind, it had been caused by someone's having cautiously moved it—and this someone wishing to make a soundless approach had immediately stood still and was waiting. There was only one person who would do that. By this time, the mist being blown away, the light of the moon began to make a growing clearness. She lifted her hand and delicately held aside a few twigs that she might look out.

She had been quite right in deciding not to move. Nigel Anstruthers had come back, and after his pause turned, and avoiding the brick path, stole over the grass to the cottage door. His going had merely been an inspiration to trap her, and the wood and matches had been intended to make a beacon light for him. That was like him, as well. His horse he had left down the road.

But the relief of his absence had been good for her, and she was able to check the shuddering fit which threatened her for a moment. The next, her ears awoke to a new sound. Something was stumbling heavily about the patch of garden—some animal. A cropping of grass, a snorting breath, and more stumbling hoofs, and she knew that Childe Harold had managed to loosen his bridle and limp out of the shed. The mere sense of his nearness seemed a sort of protection.

He had limped and stumbled to the front part of the garden before Nigel heard him. When he did hear, he came out of the house in the humour of a man the inflaming of whose mood has been cumulative; Childe Harold's temper also was not to be trifled with. He threw up his head, swinging the bridle out of reach; he snorted, and even reared with an ugly lashing of his forefeet.

"Good boy!" whispered Betty. "Do not let him take you—do not!"

If he remained where he was he would attract attention if anyone passed by. "Fight, Childe Harold, be as vicious as you choose—do not allow yourself to be dragged back."

And fight he did, with an ugliness of temper he had never shown before—with snortings and tossed head and lashed—out heels, as if he knew he was fighting to gain time and with a purpose.

But in the midst of the struggle Nigel Anstruthers stopped suddenly. He had stumbled again, and risen raging and stained with damp earth. Now he stood still, panting for breath—as still as he had stood after the click of the gate. Was he—listening? What was he listening to? Had she moved in her excitement, and was it possible he had caught the sound? No, he was listening to something else. Far up the road it echoed, but coming nearer every moment, and very fast. Another horse—a big one—galloping hard. Whosoever it was would pass this place; it could only be a man—God grant that he would not go by so quickly that his attention would not be arrested by a shriek! Cry out she must—and if he did not hear and went galloping on his way she would have betrayed herself and be lost.

She bit off a groan by biting her lip.

"You who died to-day—now—now!"

Nearer and nearer. No human creature could pass by a thing like this—it would not be possible. And Childe Harold, backing and fighting, scented the other horse and neighed fiercely and high. The rider was slackening his pace; he was near the lane. He had turned into it and stopped. Now for her one frantic cry—but before she could gather power to give it forth, the man who had stopped had flung himself from his saddle and was inside the garden speaking. A big voice and a clear one, with a ringing tone of authority.

"What are you doing here? And what is the matter with Miss Vanderpoel's horse?" it called out.

Now there was danger of the swoop into the darkness—great danger—though she clutched at the hedge that she might feel its thorns and hold herself to the earth.

"YOU!" Nigel Anstruthers cried out. "You!" and flung forth a shout of laughter.

"Where is she?" fiercely. "Lady Anstruthers is terrified. We have been searching for hours. Only just now I heard on the marsh that she had been seen to ride this way. Where is she, I say?"

A strong, angry, earthly voice—not part of the melodrama—not part of a dream, but a voice she knew, and whose sound caused her heart to leap to her throat, while she trembled from head to foot, and a light, cold dampness broke forth on her skin. Something had been a dream—her wild, desolate ride—the slew tolling; for the voice which commanded with such human fierceness was that of the man for whom the heavy bell had struck forth from the church tower.

Sir Nigel recovered himself brilliantly. Not that he did not recognise that he had been a fool again and was in a nasty place; but it was not for the first time in his life, and he had learned how to brazen himself out of nasty places.

"My dear Mount Dunstan," he answered with tolerant irritation, "I have been having a devil of a time with female hysterics. She heard the bell toll and ran away with the idea that it was for you, and paid you the compliment of losing her head. I came on her here when she had ridden her horse half to death and they had both come a cropper. Confound women's hysterics! I could do nothing with her. When I left her for a moment she ran away and hid herself. She is concealed somewhere on the place or has limped off on to the marsh. I wish some New York millionairess would work herself into hysteria on my humble account."

"Those are lies," Mount Dunstan answered—"every damned one of them!"

He wheeled around to look about him, attracted by a sound, and in the clearing moonlight saw a figure approaching which might have risen from the earth, so far as he could guess where it had come from. He strode over to it, and it was Betty Vanderpoel, holding her whip in a clenched hand and showing to his eagerness such hunted face and eyes as were barely human. He caught her unsteadiness to support it, and felt her fingers clutch at the tweed of his coatsleeve and move there as if the mere feeling of its rough texture brought heavenly comfort to her and gave her strength.

"Yes, they are lies, Lord Mount Dunstan," she panted. "He said that he meant to get what he called 'even' with me. He told me I could not get away from him and that no one would hear me if I cried out for help. I have hidden like some hunted animal." Her shaking voice broke, and she held the cloth of his sleeve tightly. "You are alive—alive!" with a sudden sweet wildness. "But it is true the bell tolled! While I was crouching in the dark I called to you—who died to-day—to stand between us!"

The man absolutely shuddered from head to foot.

"I was alive, and you see I heard you and came," he answered hoarsely.

He lifted her in his arms and carried her into the cottage. Her cheek felt the enrapturing roughness of his tweed shoulder as he did it. He laid her down on the couch of hay and turned away.

"Don't move," he said. "I will come back. You are safe."

If there had been more light she would have seen that his jaw was set like a bulldog's, and there was a red spark in his eyes—a fearsome one. But though she did not clearly see, she KNEW, and the nearness of the last hours swept away all relenting.

Nigel Anstruthers having discreetly waited until the two had passed into the house, and feeling that a man would be an idiot who did not remove himself from an atmosphere so highly charged, was making his way toward the lane and was, indeed, halfway through the gate when heavy feet were behind him and a grip of ugly strength wrenched him backward.

"Your horse is cropping the grass where you left him, but you are not going to him," said a singularly meaning voice. "You are coming with me."

Anstruthers endeavoured to convince himself that he did not at that moment turn deadly sick and that the brute would not make an ass of himself.

"Don't be a bally fool!" he cried out, trying to tear himself free.

The muscular hand on his shoulder being reinforced by another, which clutched his collar, dragged him back, stumbling ignominiously through the gooseberry bushes towards the cart-shed. Betty lying upon her bed of hay heard the scuffling, mingled with raging and gasping curses. Childe Harold, lifting his head from his cropping of the grass, looked after the violently jerking figures and snorted slightly, snuffing with dilated red nostrils. As a war horse scenting blood and battle, he was excited.

When Mount Dunstan got his captive into the shed the blood which had surged in Red Godwyn's veins was up and leaping. Anstruthers, his collar held by a hand with fingers of iron, writhed about and turned a livid, ghastly face upon his captor.

"You have twice my strength and half my age, you beast and devil!" he foamed in a half shriek, and poured forth frightful blasphemies.

"That counts between man and man, but not between vermin and executioner," gave back Mount Dunstan.

The heavy whip, flung upward, whistled down through the air, cutting through cloth and linen as though it would cut through flesh to bone.

"By God!" shrieked the writhing thing he held, leaping like a man who has been shot. "Don't do that again! DAMN you!" as the unswerving lash cut down again—again.

What followed would not be good to describe. Betty through the open door heard wild and awful things—and more than once a sound as if a dog were howling.

When the thing was over, one of the two—his clothes cut to ribbons, his torn white linen exposed, lay, a writhing, huddled worm, hiccoughing frenzied sobs upon the earth in a corner of the cart-shed. The other man stood over him, breathless and white, but singularly exalted.

"You won't want your horse to-night, because you can't use him," he said. "I shall put Miss Vanderpoel's saddle upon him and ride with her back to Stornham. You think you are cut to pieces, but you are not, and you'll get over it. I'll ask you to mark, however, that if you open your foul mouth to insinuate lies concerning either Lady Anstruthers or her sister I will do this thing again in public some day—on the steps of your club—and do it more thoroughly."

He walked into the cottage soon afterwards looking, to Betty Vanderpoel's eyes, pale and exceptionally big, and also more a man than it is often given even to the most virile male creature to look—and he walked to the side of her resting place and stood there looking down.

"I thought I heard a dog howl," she said.

"You did hear a dog howl," he answered. He said no other word, and she asked no further question. She knew what he had done, and he was well aware that she knew it.

There was a long, strangely tense silence. The light of the moon was growing. She made at first no effort to rise, but lay still and looked up at him from under splendid lifted lashes, while his own gaze fell into the depth of hers like a plummet into a deep pool. This continued for almost a full minute, when he turned quickly away and walked to the hearth, indrawing a heavy breath.

He could not endure that which beset him; it was unbearable, because her eyes had maddeningly seemed to ask him some wistful question. Why did she let her loveliness so call to him. She was not a trifler who could play with meanings. Perhaps she did not know what her power was. Sometimes he could believe that beautiful women did not.

In a few moments, almost before he could reach her, she was rising, and when she got up she supported herself against the open door, standing in the moonlight. If he was pale, she was pale also, and her large eyes would not move from his face, so drawing him that he could not keep away from her.

"Listen," he broke out suddenly. "Penzance told me—warned me—that some time a moment would come which would be stronger than all else in a man—than all else in the world. It has come now. Let me take you home."

"Than what else?" she said slowly, and became even paler than before.

He strove to release himself from the possession of the moment, and in his struggle answered with a sort of savagery.

"Than scruple—than power—even than a man's determination and decent pride."

"Are you proud?" she half whispered quite brokenly. "I am not—since I waited for the ringing of the church bell—since I heard it toll. After that the world was empty—and it was as empty of decent pride as of everything else. There was nothing left. I was the humblest broken thing on earth."

"You!" he gasped. "Do you know I think I shall go mad directly perhaps it is happening now. YOU were humble and broken—your world was empty! Because——?"

"Look at me, Lord Mount Dunstan," and the sweetest voice in the world was a tender, wild little cry to him. "Oh LOOK at me!"

He caught her out-thrown hands and looked down into the beautiful passionate soul of her. The moment had come, and the tidal wave rising to its height swept all the common earth away when, with a savage sob, he caught and held her close and hard against that which thudded racing in his breast.

And they stood and swayed together, folded in each other's arms, while the wind from the marshes lifted its voice like an exulting human thing as it swept about them.

CHAPTER XLIX

AT STORNHAM AND AT BROADMORLANDS

The exulting wind had swept the clouds away, and the moon rode in a dark blue sea of sky, making the night light purely clear, when they drew a little apart, that they might better see the wonderfulness in each other's faces. It was so mysteriously great a thing that they felt near to awe.

"I fought too long. I wore out my body's endurance, and now I am quaking like a boy. Red Godwyn did not begin his wooing like this. Forgive me," Mount Dunstan said at last.

"Do you know," with lovely trembling lips and voice, "that for long— long—you have been unkind to me?"

It was merely human that he should swiftly enfold her again, and answer with his lips against her cheek.

"Unkind! Unkind! Oh, the heavenly woman's sweetness of your telling me so—the heavenly sweetness of it!" he exclaimed passionately and low. "And I was one of those who are 'by the roadside everywhere,' an unkempt, raging beggar, who might not decently ask you for a crust."

"It was all wrong—wrong!" she whispered back to him, and he poured forth the tenderest, fierce words of confession and prayer, and she listened, drinking them in, with now and then a soft sob pressed against the roughness of the enrapturing tweed. For a space they had both forgotten her hurt, because there are other things than terror which hypnotise pain. Mount Dunstan was to be praised for remembering it first. He must take her back to Stornham and her sister without further delay.

"I will put your saddle on Anstruthers' horse, or mine, and lift you to your seat. There is a farmhouse about two miles away, where I will take you first for food and warmth. Perhaps it would be well for you to stay there to rest for an hour or so, and I will send a message to Lady Anstruthers."

"I will go to the place, and eat and drink what you advise," she answered. "But I beg you to take me back to Rosalie without delay. I feel that I must see her."

"I feel that I must see her, too," he said. "But for her—God bless her!" he added, after his sudden pause.

Betty knew that the exclamation meant strong feeling, and that somehow in the past hours Rosalie had awakened it. But it was only when, after their refreshment at the farm, they had taken horse again and were riding homeward together, that she heard from him what had passed between them.

"All that has led to this may seem the merest chance," he said. "But surely a strange thing has come about. I know that without understanding it." He leaned over and touched her hand. "You, who are Life—without understanding I ride here beside you, believing that you brought me back."

"I tried—I tried! With all my strength, I tried."

"After I had seen your sister to-day, I guessed—I knew. But not at first. I was not ill of the fever, as excited rumour had it; but I was ill, and the doctors and the vicar were alarmed. I had fought too long, and I was giving up, as I have seen the poor fellows in the ballroom give up. If they were not dragged back they slipped out of one's hands. If the fever had developed, all would have been over quickly. I knew the doctors feared that, and I am ashamed to say I was glad of it. But, yesterday, in the morning, when I was letting myself go with a morbid pleasure in the luxurious relief of it—something reached me—some slow rising call to effort and life."

She turned towards him in her saddle, listening, her lips parted.

"I did not even ask myself what was happening, but I began to be conscious of being drawn back, and to long intensely to see you again. I was gradually filled with a restless feeling that you were near me, and that, though I could not physically hear your voice, you were surely CALLING to me. It was the thing which could not be—but it was—and because of it I could not let myself drift."

"I did call you! I was on my knees in the church asking to be forgiven if I prayed mad prayers—but praying the same thing over and over. The villagers were kneeling there, too. They crowded in, leaving everything else. You are their hero, and they were in deep earnest."

His look was gravely pondering. His life had not made a mystic of him—it was Penzance who was the mystic—but he felt himself perplexed by mysteriously suggestive thought.

"I was brought back—I was brought back," he said. "In the afternoon I fell asleep and slept profoundly until the morning. When I awoke, I realised that I was a remade man. The doctors were almost awed when I first spoke to them. Old Dr. Fenwick died later, and, after I had heard about it, the church bell was tolled. It was heard at Weaver's farmhouse, and, as everybody had been excitedly waiting for the sound, it conveyed but one idea to them—and the boy was sent racing across the fields to Stornham village. Dearest! Dearest!" he exclaimed.

She had bowed her head and burst into passionate sobbing. Because she was not of the women who wept, her moment's passion was strong and bitter.

"It need not have been!" she shuddered. "One cannot bear it—because it need not have been!"

"Stop your horse a moment," he said, reining in his own, while, with burning eyes and swelling throat, he held and steadied her. But he did not know that neither her sister nor her father had ever seen her in such mood, and that she had never so seen herself.

"You shall not remember it," he said to her.

"I will not," she answered, recovering herself. "But for one moment all the awful hours rushed back. Tell me the rest."

"We did not know that the blunder had been made until a messenger from Dole rode over to inquire and bring messages of condolence. Then we understood what had occurred and I own a sort of frenzy seized me. I knew I must see you, and, though the doctors were horribly nervous, they dare not hold me back. The day before it would not have been believed that I could leave my room. You were crying out to me, and though I did not know, I was answering, body and soul. Penzance knew I must have my way when I spoke to him—mad as it seemed. When I rode through Stornham village, more than one woman screamed at sight of me. I shall not be able to blot out of my mind your sister's face. She will tell you what we said to each other. I rode away from the Court quite half mad——" his voice became very gentle, "because of something she had told me in the first wild moments."

Lady Anstruthers had spent the night moving restlessly from one room to another, and had not been to bed when they rode side by side up the avenue in the early morning sunlight. An under keeper, crossing the park a few hundred yards above them, after one glance, dashed across the sward to the courtyard and the servants' hall. The news flashed electrically through the house, and Rosalie, like a small ghost, came out upon the steps as they reined in. Though her lips moved, she could not speak aloud, as she watched Mount Dunstan lift her sister from her horse.

"Childe Harold stumbled and I hurt my foot," said Betty, trying to be calm.

"I knew he would find you!" Rosalie answered quite faintly. "I knew you would!" turning to Mount Dunstan, adoring him with all the meaning of her small paled face.

She would have been afraid of her memory of what she had said in the strange scene which had taken place before them a few hours ago, but almost before either of the two spoke she knew that a great gulf had been crossed in some one inevitable, though unforeseen, leap. How it had been taken, when or where, did not in the least matter, when she clung to Betty and Betty clung to her.

After a few moments of moved and reverent waiting, the admirable Jennings stepped forward and addressed her in lowered voice.

"There's been little sleep in the village this night, my lady," he murmured earnestly. "I promised they should have a sign, with your permission. If the flag was run up—they're all looking out, and they'd know."

"Run it up, Jennings," Lady Anstruthers answered, "at once."

When it ran up the staff on the tower and fluttered out in gay answering to the morning breeze, children in the village began to run about shouting, men and women appeared at cottage doors, and more than one cap was thrown up in the air. But old Doby and Mrs. Welden, who had been waiting for hours, standing by Mrs. Welden's gate, caught each other's dry, trembling old hands and began to cry.

The Broadmorlands divorce scandal, having made conversation during a season quite forty years before Miss Vanderpoel appeared at Stornham Court, had been laid upon a lower shelf and buried beneath other stories long enough to be forgotten. Only one individual had not forgotten it, and he was the Duke of Broadmorlands himself, in whose mind it remained hideously clear. He had been a young man, honestly and much in love when it first revealed itself to him, and for a few months he had even thought it might end by being his death, notwithstanding that he was strong and in first-rate physical condition. He had been a fine, hearty young man of clean and rather dignified life, though he was not understood to be brilliant of mind. Privately he had ideals connected with his rank and name which he was not fluent enough clearly to express. After he had realised that he should not die of the public humiliation and disgrace, which seemed to point him out as having been the kind of gullible fool it is scarcely possible to avoid laughing at—or, so it seemed to him in his heart-seared frenzy—he thought it not improbable that he should go mad. He was harried so by memories of lovely little soft ways of Edith's (his wife's name was Edith), of the pretty sound of her laugh, and of her innocent, girlish habit of kneeling down by her bedside every night and morning to say her prayers. This had so touched him that he had sometimes knelt down to say his, too, saying to her, with slight awkward boyishness, that a fellow who has a sort of angel for his wife ought to do his best to believe in the things she believed in.

"And all the time——!" a devil who laughed used to snigger in his ear over and over again, until it was almost like the ticking of a clock during the worst months, when it did not seem probable that a man could feel his brain whirling like a Catherine wheel night and day, and still manage to hold on and not reach the point of howling and shrieking and dashing his skull against walls and furniture.

But that passed in time, and he told himself that he passed with it. Since then he had lived chiefly at Broadmorlands Castle, and was spoken of as a man who had become religious, which was not true, but, having reached the decision that religion was good for most people, he paid a good deal of attention to his church and schools, and was rigorous in the matter of curates.

He had passed seventy now, and was somewhat despotic and haughty, because a man who is a Duke and does not go out into the world to rub against men of his own class and others, but lives altogether on a great and splendid estate, saluted by every creature he meets, and universally obeyed and counted before all else, is not unlikely to forget that he is a quite ordinary human being, and not a sort of monarch.

He had done his best to forget Edith, who had soon died of being a shady curate's wife in Australia, but he had not been able to encompass it. He used, occasionally, to dream she was kneeling by the bed in her childish nightgown saying her prayers aloud, and would waken crying—as he had cried in those awful young days. Against social immorality or village light-mindedness he was relentlessly savage. He allowed for no palliating or exonerating facts. He began to see red when he heard of or saw lightness in a married woman, and the outside world frequently said that this characteristic bordered on monomania.

Nigel Anstruthers, having met him once or twice, had at first been much amused by him, and had even, by giving him an adroitly careful lead, managed to guide him into an expression of opinion. The Duke, who had heard men of his class discussed, did not in the least like him, notwithstanding his sympathetic suavity of manner and his air of being intelligently impressed by what he heard. Not long afterwards, however, it transpired that the aged rector of Broadmorlands having died, the living had been given to Ffolliott, and, hearing it, Sir Nigel was not slow to conjecture that quite decently utilisable tools would lie ready to his hand if circumstances pressed; this point of view, it will be seen, being not illogical. A man who had not been a sort of hermit would have heard enough of him to be put on his guard, and one who was a man of the world, looking normally on existence, would have reasoned coolly, and declined to concern himself about what was not his affair. But a parallel might be drawn between Broadmorlands and some old lion wounded sorely in his youth and left to drag his unhealed torment through the years of age. On one subject he had no point of view but his own, and could be roused to fury almost senseless by wholly inadequately supported facts. He presented exactly the material required—and that in mass.

About the time the flag was run up on the tower at Stornham Court a carter, driving whistling on the road near the deserted cottage, was hailed by a man who was walking slowly a few yards ahead of him. The carter thought that he was a tramp, as his clothes were plainly in bad case, which seeing, his answer was an unceremonious grunt, and it certainly did not occur to him to touch his forehead. A minute later, however, he "got a start," as he related afterwards. The tramp was a gentleman whose riding costume was torn and muddied, and who looked "gashly," though he spoke with the manner and authority which Binns, the carter, recognised as that of one of the "gentry" addressing a day-labourer.

"How far is it from here to Medham?" he inquired.

"Medham be about four mile, sir," was the answer. "I be carryin' these 'taters there to market."

"I want to get there. I have met with an accident. My horse took fright at a pheasant starting up rocketting under his nose. He threw me into a hedge and bolted. I'm badly enough bruised to want to reach a town and see a doctor. Can you give me a lift?"

"That I will, sir, ready enough," making room on the seat beside him. "You be bruised bad, sir," he said sympathetically, as his passenger climbed to his place, with a twisted face and uttering blasphemies under his breath.

"Damned badly," he answered. "No bones broken, however."

"That cut on your cheek and neck'll need plasterin', sir."

"That's a scratch. Thorn bush," curtly.

Sympathy was plainly not welcome. In fact Binns was soon of the opinion that here was an ugly customer, gentleman or no gentleman. A jolting cart was, however, not the best place for a man who seemed sore from head to foot, and done for out and out. He sat and ground his teeth, as he clung to the rough seat in the attempt to steady himself. He became more and more "gashly," and a certain awful light in his eyes alarmed the carter by leaping up at every jolt. Binns was glad when he left him at Medham Arms, and felt he had earned the half-sovereign handed to him.

Four days Anstruthers lay in bed in a room at the Inn. No one saw him but the man who brought him food. He did not send for a doctor, because he did not wish to see one. He sent for such remedies as were needed by a man who had been bruised by a fall from his horse. He made no remark which could be considered explanatory, after he had said irritably that a man was a fool to go loitering along on a nervous brute who needed watching. Whatsoever happened was his own damned fault.

Through hours of day and night he lay staring at the whitewashed beams or the blue roses on the wall paper. They were long hours, and filled with things not pleasant enough to dwell on in detail. Physical misery which made a man writhe at times was not the worst part of them. There were a thousand things less endurable. More than once he foamed at the mouth, and recognised that he gibbered like a madman.

There was but one memory which saved him from feeling that this was the very end of things. That was the memory of Broadmorlands. While a man had a weapon left, even though it could not save him, he might pay up with it—get almost even. The whole Vanderpoel lot could be plunged neck deep in a morass which would leave mud enough sticking to them, even if their money helped them to prevent its entirely closing over their heads. He could attend to that, and, after he had set it well going, he could get out. There were India, South Africa, Australia—a dozen places that would do. And then he would remember Betty Vanderpoel, and curse horribly under the bed clothes. It was the memory of Betty which outdid all others in its power to torment.

On the morning of the fifth day the Duke of Broadmorlands received a note, which he read with somewhat annoyed curiosity. A certain Sir Nigel Anstruthers, whom it appeared he ought to be able to recall, was in the neighbourhood, and wished to see him on a parochial matter of interest. "Parochial matter" was vague, and so was the Duke's recollection of the man who addressed him. If his memory served him rightly, he had met him in a country house in Somersetshire, and had heard that he was the acquaintance of the disreputable eldest son. What could a person of that sort have to say of parochial matters? The Duke considered, and then, in obedience to a rigorous conscience, decided that one ought, perhaps, to give him half an hour.

There was that in the intruder's aspect, when he arrived in the afternoon, which produced somewhat the effect of shock. In the first place, a man in his unconcealable physical condition had no right to be out of his bed. Though he plainly refused to admit the fact, his manner of bearing himself erect, and even with a certain touch of cool swagger, was, it was evident, achieved only by determined effort. He looked like a man who had not yet recovered from some evil fever. Since the meeting in Somersetshire he had aged more than the year warranted. Despite his obstinate fight with himself it was obvious that he was horribly shaky. A disagreeable scratch or cut, running from cheek to neck, did not improve his personal appearance.

He pleased his host no more than he had pleased him at their first encounter; he, in fact, repelled him strongly, by suggesting a degree of abnormality of mood which was smoothed over by an attempt at entire normality of manner. The Duke did not present an approachable front as, after Anstruthers had taken a chair, he sat and examined him with bright blue old eyes set deep on either side of a dominant nose and framed over by white eyebrows.

No, Nigel Anstruthers summed him up, it would not be easy to open the matter with the old fool. He held himself magnificently aloof, with that lack of modernity in his sense of place which, even at this late day, sometimes expressed itself here and there in the manner of the feudal survival.

"I am afraid you have been ill," with rigid civility.

"A man feels rather an outsider in confessing he has let his horse throw him into a hedge. It was my own fault entirely. I allowed myself to forget that I was riding a dangerously nervous brute. I was thinking of a painful and absorbing subject. I was badly bruised and scratched, but that was all."

"What did your doctor say?"

"That I was in luck not to have broken my neck."

"You had better have a glass of wine," touching a bell. "You do not look equal to any exertion."

In gathering himself together, Sir Nigel felt he was forced to use enormous effort. It had cost him a gruesome physical struggle to endure the drive over to Broadmorlands, though it was only a few miles from Medham. There had been something unnatural in the exertion necessary to sit upright and keep his mind decently clear. That was the worst of it. The fever and raging hours of the past days and nights had so shaken him that he had become exhausted, and his brain was not alert. He was not thinking rapidly, and several times he had lost sight of a point it was important to remember. He grew hot and cold and knew his hands and voice shook, as he answered. But, perhaps—he felt desperately—signs of emotion were not bad.

"I am not quite equal to exertion," he began slowly. "But a man cannot lie on his bed while some things are undone—a MAN cannot."

As the old Duke sat upright, the blue eyes under his bent brows were startled, as well as curious. Was the man going out of his mind about something? He looked rather like it, with the dampness starting out on his haggard face, and the ugly look suddenly stamped there. The fact was that the insensate fury which had possessed and torn Anstruthers as he had writhed in his inn bedroom had sprung upon him again in full force, and his weakness could not control it, though it would have been wiser to hold it in check. He also felt frightfully ill, which filled him with despair, and, through this fact, he lost sight of the effect he produced, as he stood up, shaking all over.

"I come to you because you are the one man who can most easily understand the thing I have been concealing for a good many years."

The Duke was irritated. Confound the objectionable idiot, what did he mean by taking that intimate tone with a man who was not prepared to concern himself in his affairs?

"Excuse me," he said, holding up an authoritative hand, "are you going to make a confession? I don't like such things. I prefer to be excused. Personal confidences are not parochial matters."

"This one is." And Sir Nigel was sickeningly conscious that he was putting the statement rashly, while at the same time all better words escaped him. "It is as much a parochial matter," losing all hold on his wits and stammering, "as was—as was—the affair of—your wife."

It was the Duke who stood up now, scarlet with anger. He sprang from his chair as if he had been a young man in whom some insult had struck blazing fire.

"You—you dare!" he shouted. "You insolent blackguard! You force your way in here and dare—dare——!" And he clenched his fist, wildly shaking it.

Nigel Anstruthers, staggering on his uncertain feet, would have shouted also, but could not, though he tried, and he heard his own voice come forth brokenly.

"Yes, I dare! I—your—my own—my——!"

Swaying and tottering, he swung round to the chair he had left, and fell into it, even while the old Duke, who stood raging before him, started back in outraged amazement. What was the fellow doing? Was he making faces at him? The drawn malignant mouth and muscles suggested it. Was he a lunatic, indeed? But the sense of disgusted outrage changed all at once to horror, as, with a countenance still more hideously livid and twisted, his visitor slid helplessly from his seat and lay a huddling heap of clothes on the floor.

CHAPTER L

THE PRIMEVAL THING

When Mr. Vanderpoel landed in England his wife was with him. This quiet-faced woman, who was known to be on her way to join her daughter in England, was much discussed, envied, and glanced at, when she promenaded the deck with her husband, or sat in her chair softly wrapped in wonderful furs. Gradually, during the past months, she had been told certain modified truths connected with her elder daughter's marriage. They had been painful truths, but had been so softened and expurgated of their worst features that it had been possible to bear them, when one realised that they did not, at least, mean that Rosy had forgotten or ceased to love her mother and father, or wish to visit her home. The steady clearness of foresight and readiness of resource which were often spoken of as being specially characteristic of Reuben S. Vanderpoel, were all required, and employed with great tenderness, in the management of this situation. As little as it was possible that his wife should know, was the utmost she must hear and be hurt by. Unless ensuing events compelled further revelations, the rest of it should be kept from her. As further protection, her husband had frankly asked her to content herself with a degree of limited information.

"I have meant all our lives, Annie, to keep from you the unpleasant things a woman need not be troubled with," he had said. "I promised myself I would when you were a girl. I knew you would face things, if I needed your help, but you were a gentle little soul, like Rosy, and I never intended that you should bear what was useless. Anstruthers was a blackguard, and girls of all nations have married blackguards before. When you have Rosy safe at home, and know nothing can hurt her again, you both may feel you would like to talk it over. Till then we won't go into detail. You trust me, I know, when I tell you that you shall hold Rosy in your arms very soon. We may have something of a fight, but there can only be one end to it in a country as decent as England. Anstruthers isn't exactly what I should call an Englishman. Men rather like him are to be found in two or three places." His good-looking, shrewd, elderly face lighted with a fine smile. "My handsome Betty has saved us a good deal by carrying out her fifteen-year-old plan of going to find her sister," he ended.

Before they landed they had decided that Mrs. Vanderpoel should be comfortably established in a hotel in London, and that after this was arranged, her husband should go to Stornham Court alone. If Sir Nigel could be induced to listen to logic, Rosalie, her child, and Betty should come at once to town.

"And, if he won't listen to logic," added Mr. Vanderpoel, with a dry composure, "they shall come just the same, my dear." And his wife put her arms round his neck and kissed him because she knew what he said was quite true, and she admired him—as she had always done—greatly.

But when the pilot came on board and there began to stir in the ship the agreeable and exciting bustle of the delivery of letters and welcoming telegrams, among Mr. Vanderpoel's many yellow envelopes he opened one the contents of which caused him to stand still for some moments—so still, indeed, that some of the bystanders began to touch each other's elbows and whisper. He certainly read the message two or three times before he folded it up, returned it to its receptacle, and walked gravely to his wife's sitting-room.

"Reuben!" she exclaimed, after her first look at him, "have you bad news? Oh, I hope not!"

He came and sat down quietly beside her, taking her hand.

"Don't be frightened, Annie, my dear," he said. "I have just been reminded of a verse in the Bible—about vengeance not belonging to mere human beings. Nigel Anstruthers has had a stroke of paralysis, and it is not his first. Apparently, even if he lies on his back for some months thinking of harm, he won't be able to do it. He is finished."

When he was carried by the express train through the country, he saw all that Betty had seen, though the summer had passed, and there were neither green trees nor hedges. He knew all that the long letters had meant of stirred emotion and affection, and he was strongly moved, though his mind was full of many things. There were the farmhouses, the square-towered churches, the red-pointed hop oasts, and the village children. How distinctly she had made him see them! His Betty—his splendid Betty! His heart beat at the thought of seeing her high, young black head, and holding her safe in his arms again. Safe! He resented having used the word, because there was a shock in seeming to admit the possibility that anything in the universe could do wrong to her. Yet one man had been villain enough to mean her harm, and to threaten her with it. He slightly shuddered as he thought of how the man was finished—done for.

The train began to puff more loudly, as it slackened its pace. It was drawing near to a rustic little station, and, as it passed in, he saw a carriage standing outside, waiting on the road, and a footman in a long coat, glancing into each window as the train went by. Two or three country people were watching it intently. Miss Vanderpoel's father was coming up from London on it. The stationmaster rushed to open the carriage door, and the footman hastened forward, but a tall lovely thing in grey was opposite the step as Mr. Vanderpoel descended it to the platform. She did not recognise the presence of any other human being than himself. For the moment she seemed to forget even the broad-shouldered man who had plainly come with her. As Reuben S. Vanderpoel folded her in his arms, she folded him and kissed him as he was not sure she had ever kissed him before.

"My splendid Betty! My own fine girl!" he said.

And when she cried out "Father! Father!" she bent and kissed the breast of his coat.

He knew who the big young man was before she turned to present him.

"This is Lord Mount Dunstan, father," she said. "Since Nigel was brought home, he has been very good to us."

Reuben S. Vanderpoel looked well into the man's eyes, as he shook hands with him warmly, and this was what he said to himself:

"Yes, she's safe. This is quite safe. It is to be trusted with the whole thing."

Not many days after her husband's arrival at Stornham Court, Mrs. Vanderpoel travelled down from London, and, during her journey, scarcely saw the wintry hedges and bare trees, because, as she sat in her cushioned corner of the railway carriage, she was inwardly offering up gentle, pathetically ardent prayers of gratitude. She was the woman who prays, and the many sad petitions of the past years were being answered at last. She was being allowed to go to Rosy—whatsoever happened, she could never be really parted from her girl again. She asked pardon many times because she had not been able to be really sorry when she had heard of her son-in-law's desperate condition. She could feel pity for him in his awful case, she told herself, but she could not wish for the thing which perhaps she ought to wish for. She had confided this to her husband with innocent, penitent tears, and he had stroked her cheek, which had always been his comforting way since they had been young things together.

"My dear," he said, "if a tiger with hydrophobia were loose among a lot of decent people—or indecent ones, for the matter of that—you would not feel it your duty to be very sorry if, in springing on a group of them, he impaled himself on an iron fence. Don't reproach yourself too much." And, though the realism of the picture he presented was such as to make her exclaim, "No! No!" there were still occasional moments when she breathed a request for pardon if she was hard of heart—this softest of creatures human.

It was arranged by the two who best knew and loved her that her meeting with Rosalie should have no spectators, and that their first hour together should be wholly unbroken in upon.

"You have not seen each other for so long," Betty said, when, on her arrival, she led her at once to the morning-room where Rosy waited, pale with joy, but when the door was opened, though the two figures were swept into each other's arms by one wild, tremulous rush of movement, there were no sounds to be heard, only caught breaths, until the door had closed again.

The talks which took place between Mr. Vanderpoel and Lord Mount Dunstan were many and long, and were of absorbing interest to both. Each presented to the other a new world, and a type of which his previous knowledge had been but incomplete.

"I wonder," Mr. Vanderpoel said, in the course of one of them, "if my world appeals to you as yours appeals to me. Naturally, from your standpoint, it scarcely seems probable. Perhaps the up-building of large financial schemes presupposes a certain degree of imagination. I am becoming a romantic New York man of business, and I revel in it. Kedgers, for instance," with the smile which, somehow, suggested Betty, "Kedgers and the Lilium Giganteum, Mrs. Welden and old Doby threaten to develop into quite necessary factors in the scheme of happiness. What Betty has felt is even more comprehensible than it seemed at first."

They walked and rode together about the countryside; when Mount Dunstan itself was swept clean of danger, and only a few convalescents lingered to be taken care of in the huge ballroom, they spent many days in going over the estate. The desolate beauty of it appealed to and touched Mr. Vanderpoel, as it had appealed to and touched his daughter, and, also, wakened in him much new and curious delight. But Mount Dunstan, with a touch of his old obstinacy, insisted that he should ignore the beauty, and look closely at less admirable things.

"You must see the worst of this," he said. "You must understand that I can put no good face upon things, that I offer nothing, because I have nothing to offer."

If he had not been swept through and through by a powerful and rapturous passion, he would have detested and abhorred these days of deliberate proud laying bare of the nakedness of the land. But in the hours he spent with Betty Vanderpoel the passion gave him knowledge of the things which, being elemental, do not concern themselves with pride and obstinacy, and do not remember them. Too much had ended, and too much begun, to leave space or thought for poor things. In their eyes, when they were together, and even when they were apart, dwelt a glow which was deeply moving to those who, looking on, were sufficiently profound of thought to understand.

Watching the two walking slowly side by side down the leafless avenue on a crystal winter day, Mr. Vanderpoel conversed with the vicar, whom he greatly liked.

"A young man of the name of Selden," he remarked, "told me more of this than he knew."

"G. Selden," said the vicar, with affectionate smiling. "He is not aware that he was largely concerned in the matter. In fact, without G. Selden, I do not know how, exactly, we should have got on. How is he, nice fellow?"

"Extremely well, and in these days in my employ. He is of the honest, indefatigable stuff which makes its way."

His own smiles, as he watched the two tall figures in the distance, settled into an expression of speculative absorption, because he was reflecting upon profoundly interesting matters.

"There is a great primeval thing which sometimes—not often, only sometimes—occurs to two people," he went on. "When it leaps into being, it is well if it is not thwarted, or done to death. It has happened to my girl and Mount Dunstan. If they had been two young tinkers by the roadside, they would have come together, and defied their beggary. As it is, I recognise, as I sit here, that the outcome of what is to be may reach far, and open up broad new ways."

"Yes," said the vicar. "She will live here and fill a strong man's life with wonderful human happiness—her splendid children will be born here, and among them will be those who lead the van and make history."

. . . . .

For some time Nigel Anstruthers lay in his room at Stornham Court, surrounded by all of aid and luxury that wealth and exalted medical science could gather about him. Sometimes he lay a livid unconscious mask, sometimes his nurses and doctors knew that in his hollow eyes there was the light of a raging half reason, and they saw that he struggled to utter coherent sounds which they might comprehend. This he never accomplished, and one day, in the midst of such an effort, he was stricken dumb again, and soon afterwards sank into stillness and died.

And the Shuttle in the hand of Fate, through every hour of every day, and through the slow, deep breathing of all the silent nights, weaves to and fro—to and fro—drawing with it the threads of human life and thought which strengthen its web: and trace the figures of its yet vague and uncompleted design.

Echo Library

www.echo-library.com

Echo Library uses advanced digital print-on-demand technology to build and preserve an exciting world class collection of rare and out-of-print books, making them readily available for everyone to enjoy.

Situated just yards from Teddington Lock on the River Thames, Echo Library was founded in 2005 by Tom Cherrington, a specialist dealer in rare and antiquarian books with a passion for literature.

Please visit our website for a complete catalogue of our books, which includes foreign language titles.

The Right to Read

Echo Library actively supports the Royal National Institute of the Blind's Right to Read initiative by publishing a comprehensive range of large print and clear print titles.

Large Print titles are in 16 point Tiresias font as recommended by the RNIB.

Clear Print titles are in 13 point Tiresias font and designed for those who find standard print difficult to read.

Customer Service

If there is a serious error in the text or layout please send details to feedback@echo-library.com and we will supply a corrected copy. If there is a printing fault or the book is damaged please refer to your supplier.

Printed in the United States
88727LV00003B/48/A